Sister Carrie

Theodore Dreiser

THE EMC MASTERPIECE SERIES

Access Editions

SERIES EDITOR

Robert D. Shepherd

EMC/Paradigm Publishing
St. Paul, Minnesota

Staff Credits:
For **EMC/Paradigm Publishing**, St. Paul, Minnesota

Laurie Skiba
Editor

Shannon O'Donnell Taylor
Associate Editor

Eileen Slater
Editorial Consultant

Jennifer J. Anderson
Assistant Editor

For **Penobscot School Publishing, Inc.**, Danvers, Massachusetts

Editorial

Robert D. Shepherd
President, Executive Editor

Christina E. Kolb
Managing Editor

Sara Hyry
Editor

Laurie A. Faria
Associate Editor

Sharon Salinger
Copyeditor

Marilyn Murphy Shepherd
Editorial Advisor

Design and Production

Charles Q. Bent
Production Manager

Sara Day
Art Director

Diane Castro
Compositor

Janet Stebbings
Compositor

Tatiana Cicuto
Compositor

ISBN 0–8219–1647–5

Published by EMC/Paradigm Publishing
875 Montreal Way
St. Paul, Minnesota 55102

Printed in the United States of America.
10 9 8 7 6 5 4 3 2 1 xxx 02 01 00 99 98 97

Table of Contents

THE LIFE AND WORKS OF

Theodore Dreiser

Theodore Dreiser

Theodore Dreiser (1871–1945). The ninth of ten children, Theodore Dreiser was born to a strict Roman Catholic father of German descent and a benevolent Mennonite mother of Czech descent. His family was impoverished and his father unemployed for much of Dreiser's childhood, and the Dreiser family frequently moved between rural Indiana and Chicago, searching for work and affordable housing. Later in life, Dreiser would write and speak bitingly of his father, blaming the family's extreme poverty on his lassitude, but he always mentioned his mother appreciatively. Experiencing the hardship of poverty at a young age sparked a desire for wealth and success in Dreiser, and this longing became a theme in *Sister Carrie* and other works.

As a youth, Dreiser watched his older siblings break away from their strictly religious home, both to find success and to live life on their own terms. His brother Paul changed his last name to Dresser and became a renowned and prosperous songwriter. His brother Rome explored Mexico and the Southwest, eventually becoming a rather wild character. His sisters also rebelled by having affairs and accepting the gifts and money of their suitors. One sister in particular made a lasting impression on Dreiser. Emma Dreiser met a young architect and became his mistress. Not long afterward, she ran off to New York with a married man, L. A. Hopkins, who had worked for a high-class saloon. Hopkins stole money from his employers to run away with Emma. Dreiser later based three major characters in *Sister Carrie,* Carrie, Drouet, and Hurstwood, on the significant people in his sister's life.

At the age of fifteen, Dreiser too sought to escape and seek his fortune. Like the heroine of *Sister Carrie,* Dreiser chose Chicago, where he worked at odd jobs, dishwasher, busboy, and shipping clerk among them. His attempt to establish himself in Chicago was a failure, so with his mother's help he finished high school. A former teacher, Mildred Fielding, then paid for one year of Dreiser's education at Indiana University. Dreiser finally found the career he wished to pursue when he became a reporter for the *Chicago Daily Globe* in

1892. Dreiser worked for several papers in Chicago, St. Louis, and Pittsburgh before moving to New York in 1894. There, he worked for several newspapers and magazines, and eventually married Sara White in 1898. He also began reading works by such scientists as T. H. Huxley and John Tyndall as well as philosophical works by Herbert Spencer. His reading helped Dreiser to form a theory that he expressed in many of his later works—he believed human beings to be motivated by powers outside their control, that instinct and social forces determine human action. He also began to see society as an unfair struggle between the strong and wealthy and the poor and weak.

In 1899, prompted by an editor and friend named Arthur Henry, Dreiser began writing his first novel, *Sister Carrie*. Both Henry and Sara helped to edit the novel, cutting more than thirty-six thousand words. Harper and Brothers rejected the manuscript when Dreiser sent it to them because they believed the "illicit relations of the heroine" were not treated delicately enough and that the book would offend readers. When Dreiser sent the book to Doubleday, Page and Company, he found an ally in the novel's reader. Frank Norris, a novelist who had written one of America's first Naturalist novels, enthusiastically recommended that the novel be published. A contract was signed while Frank Doubleday, the head of the publishing company, and his wife were on vacation. When the Doubledays returned, Mrs. Doubleday read Dreiser's novel and was horrified by the novel's "immorality"; her husband agreed. Doubleday tried to renege on its contract with Dreiser, warning him that the public would be shocked and consider the author of the work amoral. Dreiser was surprised by this view of his work, not realizing that he had just written one of the most controversial novels of the early twentieth century, and insisted on the publication of *Sister Carrie*. Doubleday decided to meet its contractual obligation but to do no more. They published only one thousand cheap copies and did not advertise the novel. Fewer than five hundred copies sold, and most of the reviewers to whom Frank Norris sent the novel were highly critical.

Depressed by his publishing experience with *Sister Carrie* and by problems with his wife and family, Dreiser became suicidal. His brother Paul Dresser rescued him by sending him to a sanitarium and afterward secured him a job with Butterick Publications, where Dreiser soon became editor-in-chief making $25,000 a year, for the time a considerable salary. Dreiser's spirits were also buoyed by *Sister Carrie*'s reception in England, where the novel was printed, earned praise, and sold well. Encouraged, Dreiser bought back the plates for the work from Doubleday; in 1907 the novel was reissued in the United States on a much larger scale and earned Dreiser a reputation as one of the great American Naturalists. Successful in getting his novel before the American public, Dreiser again began writing. Although he experienced a setback when he lost his job in 1910 due to his infatuation with a coworker's daughter, he published *Jennie Gerhardt* in 1911, and in 1912, the same year he and his wife separated, he published *The Financier*, the first volume of a planned trilogy. The second volume, *The Titan,* followed in 1914, and his next significant novel *The "Genius"* was published in 1915.

Dreiser turned to writing autobiographical work, short stories, sketches, and dramas before publishing another novel, *An American Tragedy*, ten years after *The "Genius."* This novel was based on a well-known murder case and has been called "the worst-written great novel in the world." Most critics recognized the importance of Dreiser's works but criticized his style and grammar, often labeling his writing style "elephantine."

In 1927, Dreiser visited the Soviet Union and critiqued communism in *Dreiser Looks at Russia*. Dreiser lost most of his money in the Great Depression of the 1930s, and soon moved further to the political left, producing the anticapitalist work *Tragic America* in 1931. In 1938, Dreiser moved to Los Angeles with Helen Richardson, whom he married in 1944, two years after Sara White Dreiser died. The couple lived by selling the film rights to Dreiser's works. In 1945, Dreiser joined the American Communist Party. He died in Hollywood on December 28, 1945. His last novels, *The Bulwark* and *The Stoic,* the final novel in his trilogy, were published posthumously. Today, despite objections to his style, many of Dreiser's works are considered classics. His best works, among them *Sister Carrie,* portray American society with an uncompromising realism that established Dreiser as one of the first great modern American writers.

Time Line of Dreiser's Life and Works

1871	Theodore Dreiser is born in Terre Haute, Indiana, on August 27, 1871, the ninth of ten children. During his childhood, his family frequently moves between rural Indiana and Chicago, looking for work and affordable places to live.
1886	At fifteen, Dreiser leaves his family for Chicago, where he works as dishwasher, busboy, and shipping clerk.
1889–1890	Dreiser attends Indiana University for one year.
1892	Dreiser begins a career as a newspaper reporter in Chicago.
1894	Dreiser moves to New York City and works for several newspapers and magazines.
1898	Dreiser marries Sara White.
1899	Dreiser begins *Sister Carrie.*
1900	Doubleday publishes *Sister Carrie,* largely because of Frank Norris's enthusiasm, but because of Frank Doubleday's disapproval only about a thousand copies are printed. Of these, fewer than five hundred are sold.
1901	Dreiser becomes suicidal. His brother Paul Dresser sends him to a sanitarium. William Heinemann, an English publishing company, publishes 1,500 copies of *Sister Carrie,* which sell well in England.
1906	Dreiser buys back the plates and sheets used to print *Sister Carrie* from Doubleday.
1907	B. W. Dodge, an American publishing company, reissues *Sister Carrie*; about 4,500 copies are sold in the United States.
1908	Grosset and Dunlap contract to print 10,000 copies of *Sister Carrie.*
1910	Dreiser is forced to resign as editor-in-chief of a women's magazine because of his infatuation with the daughter of one of his coworkers.
1911	*Jennie Gerhardt* is published.
1912	*The Financier* is published. Dreiser and Sara White Dreiser separate.
1913	Dreiser records his experiences in Europe in *A Traveler at Forty.*
1914	Dreiser's *The Titan* is published. It is the second book (*The Financier* is the first) of a planned trilogy.
1915	Dreiser's semiautobiographical novel *The "Genius"* is published.
1916	Dreiser writes dramas—*Plays of the Natural and Supernatural* and an autobiographical work called *Hoosier Holiday.*
1918	Dreiser's fictional collection *Free and Other Stories* is published. Dreiser writes a drama called *The Hand of the Potter.*
1919	A book of Dreiser's sketches, *Twelve Men,* is published.
1920	Dreiser's *Hey-Rub-a-Dub-Dub,* a collection of philosophical essays, is published. Dreiser begins a relationship with Helen Richardson.
1922	Dreiser's autobiographical *A Book about Myself* is published.

Dreiser's *An American Tragedy*, his first novel since *The "Genius,"* is published.	1925
Dreiser publishes an unsuccessful book of verse called *Moods, Cadenced and Declaimed.*	1926
Dreiser visits the Soviet Union. He also publishes another collection of sketches and stories called *Chains*.	1927
Dreiser publishes *Dreiser Looks at Russia*, a work critiquing communism.	1928
Dreiser writes an anticapitalist work called *Tragic America*. He also publishes *Dawn,* an autobiography of his early life. Dreiser and other writers form the Dreiser Committee to investigate conditions among Kentucky mine workers.	1931
Dreiser and Helen Richardson move from New York to Los Angeles to market the film rights to Dreiser's works.	1938
Dreiser's estranged wife, Sara White Dreiser, dies. Dreiser begins to work again on *The Bulwark*, a novel he began writing in 1912.	1942
Dreiser finishes *The Bulwark* and marries Helen Richardson.	1944
Dreiser joins the American Communist Party. Helen helps Dreiser complete *The Stoic*, the last book in Dreiser's trilogy. Theodore Dreiser dies in Hollywood, California, on December 28, 1945.	1945
The Bulwark is published.	1946
The Stoic is published.	1947
The University of Pennsylvania publishes an unexpurgated version of *Sister Carrie*, restoring the thirty-six thousand words that Arthur Henry and Sara White cut from the 1900 edition.	1981

THE HISTORICAL CONTEXT OF

Sister Carrie

An Age of Contrasts

Sister Carrie is set during the 1890s, a time when great contrasts were apparent within American society. In cities such as New York and Chicago, where most of *Sister Carrie* takes place, the mansions of the rich and the slums of the poor were often separated only by a couple of city blocks.

This disparity ballooned with an industrial boom that began in the late 1870s. This boom was the result of the exploitation of the natural resources of the newly populated West, the construction of railroads, and innovations, such as new methods for manufacturing steel. Certain industrialists amassed previously unimagined fortunes and organized trusts to dominate entire industries and eliminate the competition, bankrupting many smaller businesses. Among the most notable figures who profited during this boom were John D. Rockefeller in the oil industry, Andrew Carnegie in the steel industry, and Cornelius Vanderbilt in railroads. The wealthy lived a lifestyle best described as aristocratic—indeed many of them were richer than Europe's aristocracy. They built palaces in New York and Newport and gave lavish balls—the cost of one particular ball given in the 1890s was more than $360,000.

While a few businessmen profited, poverty continued to exist and expand as an influx of immigrants and people from rural areas flocked to the cities. Journalists of the period like Jacob Riis, author of *How the Other Half Lives,* revealed that hundreds of thousands of the impoverished lived crammed into squalid slums that are difficult for a modern individual who lives in an age of housing laws to imagine. By 1890, the Bureau of the Census revealed that the days of Western expansion were coming to a close and that more and more people were flocking to cities. In 1880 only 28 percent of the American population was urban; by 1890, 40 percent of Americans lived in urban areas. One percent of the population controlled more than half its wealth.

During this period, labor organized to form unions to win for the average worker a living wage and improved working conditions. Union members began to demand more concessions from the large corporations which determined hours of labor and salaries, as well as where workers lived and shopped. Big business seemingly received a blow with the passage of the Sherman Antitrust Act in 1890, which offered guidelines for the punishment of "contract and combinations in restraint of commerce among the several states or with foreign nations." Nevertheless, this act did little to damage big business. Ironically, it was used instead against unions to break strikes. Many strikes of Dreiser's day, most notably the Haymarket Riot and the Homestead Strike, ended in failure and even bloodshed and death for union members who were assaulted by angry guards and police. Dreiser himself reported on many strikes similar to the streetcar workers' strike he describes in *Sister Carrie*.

The situation became even more drastic for many Americans in 1893, when a panic on the Stock Exchange occurred and the market crashed. In the resulting depression, at the time the worst in the country's history, more than 600 banks closed, 74 railroads went out of business, and more than 15,000 other businesses collapsed. In *Sister Carrie*, George Hurstwood's period of financial success, the loss of his business in the Panic of 1893, and his resulting unemployment and poverty serve to characterize American society of the time as a whole. As Hurstwood himself observes, there existed a "walled city" of the fabulously wealthy who never observed the plight of the impoverished outside. For formerly privileged men like Hurstwood, who lost businesses in the Panic of 1893 and fell outside the walled city of wealth and privilege, it was nearly impossible to work their way back.

The Emergence of Naturalism

It is not surprising, given the startling social contrasts of the late nineteenth and early twentieth centuries, that Naturalism, initially a French literary movement, would become popular in the United States. Naturalism was essentially an extension and refinement of Realism, based on the theories and writings of French novelist Émile Zola. Inspired by the scientists and philosophers of his day, Zola held that people's actions and beliefs resulted not from free will but from the arbitrary, outside forces of heredity and environment. He believed that like a naturalist studying behavior in animals, the novelist could extensively research human society and write "scientific" fiction that demonstrated the exact causes of human behavior. Naturalists like Zola often examined the economic forces that create such disparate social classes as the stunningly rich and the miserably poor. Frank Norris, an avid fan of Zola, produced

McTeague, often considered one of the first American Naturalistic novels, in 1899. Stephen Crane's works are also considered Naturalistic in their portrayal of human beings as pawns manipulated by the indifferent forces of nature and society. While Dreiser had never read Zola prior to writing *Sister Carrie,* he had read the work of one of the writers who inspired Zola—Thomas Huxley. Dreiser's background as a reporter also may have drawn him to a Naturalistic style of writing. By the early twentieth century, Naturalism became a dominant mode in American fiction.

Morals and the Role of Women in the Nineteenth Century

Modern audiences may be surprised that Dreiser's realistic portrayal of events in *Sister Carrie* was considered scandalous. In the 1890s, however, society professed a very different moral code of behavior, placing far more restrictions on women and their actions. Throughout the nineteenth century, the ideal woman was pure, angelic, frail, and submissive to her father or husband. Women were not allowed to vote or even, for much of the century, to own property. It was difficult, if not impossible, for women to obtain divorces from their husbands, and until 1891 it was legal in England for a man to hold his wife prisoner at home. Moreover, although educational opportunities for women were much more extensive than in earlier centuries, math and science were still considered "improper" fields for women to pursue. In fact, few middle- and upper-class women's educations went beyond the teaching of propriety, or a strict code of moral behavior; foreign languages; and means of entertaining men and decorating the home, through such arts as embroidery, painting, music, song, and dance. According to propriety, women could not go out alone, especially in the evening or in a city; women should not work, except to maintain the home; and women should devote themselves to cultivating a fashionable appearance and fashionable friends. Another nineteenth-century ideal was that women should not feel sexual desire, much less act upon such feelings.

In this period, society's view of women and their behavior was threatened by one result of the Industrial Revolution—more and more women were entering the workplace. In depressed communities or during periods of economic depression, women were, in fact, often the sole supporters of their families. Most of these women worked in mills or factories where the owner or manager could pay the women lower wages than male workers would require. For the most part, society viewed working-class women harshly. They were often portrayed in the writing of the period as "fallen women," or prostitutes. In England, for many years, the police could arrest any working-class woman under suspicion of prostitution. Thus, many of Carrie's actions that seem unexceptional for a modern woman—talking to a man on a train, going out for a walk alone, or even having a job—were actions that were considered disreputable by much of Dreiser's audience. Dreiser's objective description of Carrie's affairs was considered sordid and immoral.

The "Fallen Woman" in Literature

Interestingly, although most people of the nineteenth century felt contempt for "fallen women," they loved stories about them—as long as the fallen woman either suffered a series of misfortunes before finding redemption or found herself permanently condemned to the depths of vice, destitution, and misery. Literature about fallen women is one of literature's oldest conventions, ever since Eve plucked and ate the fruit of the forbidden tree. Some of the very first novels written in the English language were tales about fallen women. Samuel Richardson's *Pamela* features a naive working-class girl like Carrie who is tempted by her master, much as Carrie is tempted by Drouet. Pamela undergoes terrible trials but her virtue remains intact and, as a reward, she marries her former master! Daniel Defoe's *Moll Flanders* and his *Roxana* both seem to celebrate exuberantly the lives of fallen women, until both heroines become penitent toward the end of their lives. Before the nineteenth century, stories about fallen women were more liberal and, in certain novels, a fallen woman triumphs in the end. By the Victorian period, however, punishment and/or repentance was almost mandatory.

Thus, what shocked Dreiser's audience was not that he wrote about a woman of easy virtue; it was that nothing terrible happens to Carrie because of her fall from virtue. Dreiser wrote about her fall realistically, without sentimentality and without surprise, seeming to indicate that such events are commonplace. What may shock a reader of this novel today is Dreiser's bleak view of human society as a corrupting force that fills human beings with longing for material success and debases their higher ideals. It is a society in which vague longing for material things is possible, but actual love is impossible.

Characters in *Sister Carrie*

Major Characters

Carrie Meeber. Carrie, the title character of the novel, is a poor young woman who leaves her family to live with her sister in Chicago and look for work. Naive and tempted by the pleasures of the city, Carrie soon succumbs to the overwhelming forces that surround her. Much of the novel focuses on Carrie's rise to fame in the theater.

George Hurstwood. Hurstwood is the novel's other main character. As a prosperous manager of an exclusive saloon in Chicago, Hurstwood becomes hopelessly infatuated with Carrie, even though he is married and has children who are Carrie's age. Much of the novel focuses on Hurstwood's descent from his status as an energetic and successful businessman at society's peak to his apathy, unemployment, and poverty in the very lowest level of the social world.

Charles Drouet. Drouet is the young, clothes-conscious traveling salesman who is Carrie's first introduction to an easier way of life. He is essentially an easygoing, although self-involved, person interested primarily in enjoying life.

Minor Characters

Minnie Hanson. Minnie is Carrie's sister who lives in Chicago. She lives a life that seems bleak to Carrie—one devoted to stinginess and toil. Although the two are not close, Minnie shows some sympathy for Carrie's situation.

Hanson. Hanson is Carrie's stern, rather miserly brother-in-law. He is critical of Carrie's actions while she remains in his house.

Mrs. Hurstwood. Mrs. Hurstwood is George Hurstwood's wife. She longs to exist in a higher social sphere, resents the loss of her husband's admiration, and is suspicious of her husband's actions.

Jessica Hurstwood. Jessica is Mr. and Mrs. Hurstwood's vain, materialistic daughter. Mrs. Hurstwood hopes to raise their social standing by finding a wealthy young man of high status for Jessica to marry.

George Hurstwood, Jr. George, Jr., the son of Mr. and Mrs. Hurstwood, is as materialistic as the rest of the family. He wishes to be independent even though he still lives in his parents' home.

Mrs. Vance. Mrs. Vance is Carrie's first friend in New York. She gives Carrie a glimpse of fashionable society and encourages Carrie's passion for fine clothes.

Mr. Ames. Ames is one of Mrs. Vance's cousins from Indianapolis, and he works for an electrical company. Carrie considers his values and intellect to be superior to that of anyone she has encountered. It has been said that Dreiser modeled the character of Ames on the American inventor Thomas Alva Edison.

Lola Osborne. Lola becomes Carrie's friend when the two work together in a chorus line. She gives Carrie advice about the theater and offers to be her roommate.

In the scene above, the New York elite mingle before an opera. Opera, theater, and other live entertainments were popular in the early 1900s. The people in the picture, shown in opulent dress, might well have been part of the audience during one of Carrie's performances.

CHAPTER 1

The Magnet Attracting: A Waif Amid Forces

When Caroline Meeber boarded the afternoon train for Chicago, her total outfit consisted of a small trunk, a cheap imitation alligator-skin satchel, a small lunch in a paper box, and a yellow leather snap purse, containing her ticket, a scrap of paper with her sister's address in Van Buren Street, and four dollars in money. It was in August, 1889. She was eighteen years of age, bright, timid, and full of the illusions of ignorance and youth. Whatever touch of regret at parting characterized her thoughts, it was certainly not for advantages now being given up. A gush of tears at her mother's farewell kiss, a touch in her throat when the cars clacked by the flour mill where her father worked by the day, a pathetic sigh as the familiar green environs of the village passed in review, and the threads which bound her so lightly to girlhood and home were irretrievably broken.

◄ *Where is Caroline Meeber going? What do her belongings indicate about her financial situation?*

◄ *What characteristics does the narrator attribute to Caroline?*

To be sure there was always the next station, where one might descend and return. There was the great city, bound more closely by these very trains which came up daily. Columbia City was not so very far away, even once she was in Chicago. What, pray, is a few hours—a few hundred miles? She looked at the little slip bearing her sister's address and wondered. She gazed at the green landscape, now passing in swift review, until her swifter thoughts replaced its impression with vague conjectures of what Chicago might be.

When a girl leaves her home at eighteen, she does one of two things. Either she falls into saving hands and becomes better, or she rapidly assumes the cosmopolitan standard of virtue and becomes worse. Of an intermediate balance, under the circumstances, there is no possibility. The city has its cunning wiles, no less than the infinitely smaller and more human tempter. There are large forces which allure with all the soulfulness of expression possible in the most cultured human. The gleam of a thousand lights is often as effective as the persuasive light in a wooing and fascinating eye. Half the undoing of the unsophisticated and natural mind is

◄ *According to the narrator, what inevitably happens to a girl who leaves home at eighteen? Do you agree?*

◄ *According to the narrator, what undoes young girls like Caroline? What is the narrator implying about Caroline's future in Chicago?*

Words For Everyday Use

en • vi • rons (en vī´rənz) *n.*, districts surrounding a town or city

con • jec • ture (kən jek´chər) *n.*, theory or prediction based on guesswork

wile (wīl) *n.*, sly trick; deceitful artifice

al • lure (ə lo͞or´) *vt.*, tempt with something desirable

accomplished by forces wholly superhuman. A blare of sound, a roar of life, a vast array of human hives, appeal to the astonished senses in equivocal terms. Without a counselor at hand to whisper cautious interpretations, what falsehoods may not these things breathe into the unguarded ear! Unrecognized for what they are, their beauty, like music, too often relaxes, then weakens, then perverts the simpler human perceptions.

▶ What is Carrie's guiding characteristic?

▶ What doesn't interest Carrie? What does? In what way would you characterize her?

Caroline, or Sister Carrie, as she had been half affectionately termed by the family, was possessed of a mind rudimentary in its power of observation and analysis. Self-interest with her was high, but not strong. It was, nevertheless, her guiding characteristic. Warm with the fancies of youth, pretty with the insipid prettiness of the formative period,[1] possessed of a figure promising eventual shapeliness and an eye alight with certain native intelligence, she was a fair example of the middle American class—two generations removed from the emigrant. Books were beyond her interest—knowledge a sealed book. In the intuitive graces she was still crude. She could scarcely toss her head gracefully. Her hands were almost ineffectual. The feet, though small, were set flatly. And yet she was interested in her charms, quick to understand the keener pleasures of life, ambitious to gain in material things. A half-equipped little knight she was, venturing to reconnoiter the mysterious city and dreaming wild dreams of some vague, far-off supremacy, which should make it prey and subject—the proper penitent, groveling at a woman's slipper.

"That," said a voice in her ear, "is one of the prettiest little resorts in Wisconsin."

"Is it?" she answered nervously.

The train was just pulling out of Waukesha. For some time she had been conscious of a man behind. She felt him observing her mass of hair. He had been fidgeting, and with natural intuition she felt a certain interest growing in that quarter. Her maidenly reserve, and a certain sense of what was conventional under the circumstances, called her to forestall and deny this familiarity, but the daring and magnetism of the individual, born of past experiences and triumphs, prevailed. She answered.

1. **formative period.** Childhood and adolescence

Words For Everyday Use

e • quiv • o • cal (ē kwiv´ə kəl) *adj.,* hard to interpret as good or bad

ru • di • men • ta • ry (ro͞o´də men´tər ē) *adj.,* not fully developed

rec • on • noi • ter (rek´ə noit´ər) *vt.,* explore

pen • i • tent (pen´i tənt) *n.,* one who seeks mercy

fore • stall (fôr stôl´) *vt.,* prevent

He leaned forward to put his elbows upon the back of her seat and proceeded to make himself volubly agreeable.

"Yes, that is a great resort for Chicago people. The hotels are swell. You are not familiar with this part of the country, are you?"

"Oh, yes, I am," answered Carrie. "That is, I live at Columbia City. I have never been through here, though."

"And so this is your first visit to Chicago," he observed.

All the time she was conscious of certain features out of the side of her eye. Flush, colorful cheeks, a light moustache, a gray fedora hat.[2] She now turned and looked upon him in full, the instincts of self-protection and coquetry mingling confusedly in her brain.

"I didn't say that," she said.

"Oh," he answered, in a very pleasing way and with an assumed air of mistake, "I thought you did."

Here was a type of the traveling canvasser[3] for a manufacturing house—a class which at that time was first being dubbed by the slang of the day "drummers." He came within the meaning of a still newer term, which had sprung into general use among Americans in 1880, and which concisely expressed the thought of one whose dress or manners are calculated to elicit the admiration of susceptible young women—a "masher." His suit was of a striped and crossed pattern of brown wool, new at that time, but since become familiar as a business suit. The low crotch of the vest revealed a stiff shirt bosom of white and pink stripes. From his coat sleeves protruded a pair of linen cuffs of the same pattern, fastened with large, gold plate buttons, set with the common yellow agates known as "cat's-eyes." His fingers bore several rings—one, the ever-enduring heavy seal—and from his vest dangled a neat gold watch chain, from which was suspended the secret insignia of the Order of Elks. The whole suit was rather tight-fitting, and was finished off with heavy-soled tan shoes, highly polished, and the gray fedora hat. He was, for the order of intellect represented, attractive, and whatever he had to recommend him, you may be sure was not lost upon Carrie, in this, her first glance.

◄ *What type of young man addresses Carrie?*

2. **fedora hat.** Soft felt hat with creased crown and wide brim
3. **canvasser.** Salesperson

Words For Everyday Use

vol • u • bly (väl´yo͞o blē) *adv.,* by means of words

co • quet • ry (kō´kə trē) *n.,* flirtation

a • gate (ag´it) *n.,* hard, semiprecious stone

▶ *What makes this type of young man popular with women?*

Lest this order of individual should permanently pass, let me put down some of the most striking characteristics of his most successful manner and method. Good clothes, of course, were the first essential, the things without which he was nothing. A strong physical nature, actuated by a keen desire for the feminine, was the next. A mind free of any consideration of the problems or forces of the world and actuated not by greed, but an insatiable love of variable pleasure. His method was always simple. Its principal element was daring, backed, of course, by an intense desire and admiration for the sex. Let him meet with a young woman once and he would approach her with an air of kindly familiarity, not unmixed with pleading, which would result in most cases in a tolerant acceptance. If she showed any tendency to coquetry he would be apt to straighten her tie, or if she "took up" with him at all, to call her by her first name. If he visited a department store it was to lounge familiarly over the counter and ask some leading questions. In more exclusive circles, on the train or in waiting stations, he went slower. If some seemingly vulnerable object appeared he was all attention—to pass the compliments of the day, to lead the way to the parlor car, carrying her grip, or, failing that, to take a seat next her with the hope of being able to court her to her destination. Pillows, books, a foot-stool, the shade lowered; all these figured in the things which he could do. If, when she reached her destination, he did not alight and attend her baggage for her, it was because, in his own estimation, he had signally failed.

▶ *How does this young man behave when he meets vulnerable young women?*

A woman should some day write the complete philosophy of clothes. No matter how young, it is one of the things she wholly comprehends. There is an indescribably faint line in the matter of a man's apparel which somehow divides for her those who are worth glancing at and those who are not. Once an individual has passed this faint line on the way downward he will get no glance from her. There is another line at which the dress of a man will cause her to study her own. This line the individual at her elbow now marked for Carrie. She became conscious of an inequality. Her own plain blue dress, with its black cotton tape trimmings, now seemed to her shabby. She felt the worn state of her shoes.

▶ *Of what does the young man's appearance make Carrie aware?*

Words For Everyday Use

ac • tu • a • ted (ak´cho͞o ā təd) *adj.,* motivated

in • sa • ti • a • ble (in sā´shə bəl) *adj.,* constantly wanting more

vul • ner • a • ble (vul´nər ə bəl) *adj.,* open to attack

"Let's see," he went on, "I know quite a number of people in your town. Morgenroth the clothier[4] and Gibson the dry goods man."

"Oh, do you?" she interrupted, aroused by memories of longings their show windows had cost her.

At last he had a clue to her interest, and followed it deftly. In a few minutes he had come about into her seat. He talked of sales of clothing, his travels, Chicago, and the amusements of that city.

"If you are going there, you will enjoy it immensely. Have you relatives?"

"I am going to visit my sister," she explained.

"You want to see Lincoln Park," he said, "and Michigan Boulevard. They are putting up great buildings there. It's a second New York—great. So much to see—theaters, crowds, fine houses—oh, you'll like that."

There was a little ache in her fancy of all he described. Her insignificance in the presence of so much magnificence faintly affected her. She realized that hers was not to be a round of pleasure, and yet there was something promising in all the material prospect he set forth. There was something satisfactory in the attention of this individual with his good clothes. She could not help smiling as he told her of some popular actress of whom she reminded him. She was not silly, and yet attention of this sort had its weight.

"You will be in Chicago some little time, won't you?" he observed at one turn of the now easy conversation.

"I don't know," said Carrie vaguely—a flash vision of the possibility of her not securing employment rising in her mind.

◄ *What is Carrie going to Chicago to do? About what is she concerned?*

"Several weeks, anyhow," he said, looking steadily into her eyes.

There was much more passing now than the mere words indicated. He recognized the indescribable thing that made up for fascination and beauty in her. She realized that she was of interest to him from the one standpoint which a woman both delights in and fears. Her manner was simple, though for the very reason that she had not yet learned the many little affectations with which women conceal their true feelings. Some things she did appeared bold. A clever companion—had she ever had one—would have warned her never to look a man in the eyes so steadily.

◄ *About what would a clever companion have warned Carrie?*

"Why do you ask?" she said.

"Well, I'm going to be there several weeks. I'm going to study stock at our place and get new samples. I might show you 'round."

4. **clothier.** Maker or seller of clothes

"I don't know whether you can or not. I mean I don't know whether I can. I shall be living with my sister, and—"

"Well, if she minds, we'll fix that." He took out his pencil and a little pocket notebook as if it were all settled. "What is your address there?"

She fumbled her purse which contained the address slip.

He reached down in his hip pocket and took out a fat purse. It was filled with slips of paper, some mileage books, a roll of greenbacks.[5] It impressed her deeply. Such a purse had never been carried by any one attentive to her. Indeed, an experienced traveler, a brisk man of the world, had never come within such close range before. The purse, the shiny tan shoes, the smart new suit, and the air with which he did things, built up for her a dim world of fortune, of which he was the center. It disposed her pleasantly toward all he might do.

► *What makes the young man appealing to Carrie?*

He took out a neat business card, on which was engraved Bartlett, Caryoe & Company, and down in the lefthand corner, Chas. H. Drouet.

► *What is this young man's name?*

"That's me," he said, putting the card in her hand and touching his name. "It's pronounced Drew-eh. Our family was French, on my father's side."

She looked at it while he put up his purse. Then he got out a letter from a bunch in his coat pocket. "This is the house I travel for," he went on, pointing to a picture on it, "corner of State and Lake." There was pride in his voice. He felt that it was something to be connected with such a place, and he made her feel that way.

"What is your address?" he began again, fixing his pencil to write.

"Carrie Meeber," she said slowly. "Three hundred and fifty-four West Van Buren Street, care S. C. Hanson."

He wrote it carefully down and got out the purse again. "You'll be at home if I come around Monday night?" he said.

"I think so," she answered.

How true it is that words are but the vague shadows of the volumes we mean. Little audible links, they are, chaining together great inaudible feelings and purposes. Here were these two, bandying little phrases, drawing purses, looking at cards, and both unconscious of how inarticulate all their real

► *What does the author say about words? Why does this statement apply to the present situation?*

5. **greenbacks.** American paper money

Words For Everyday Use

dis • pose (di spōz´) *vt.,* incline

ban • dy (ban´dē) *vt.,* exchange words carelessly back and forth

feelings were. Neither was wise enough to be sure of the working of the mind of the other. He could not tell how his luring succeeded. She could not realize that she was drifting, until he secured her address. Now she felt that she had yielded something—he, that he had gained a victory. Already they felt that they were somehow associated. Already he took control in directing the conversation. His words were easy. Her manner was relaxed.

◄ How does Carrie feel once she gives Drouet her address? How does Drouet feel?

They were nearing Chicago. Signs were everywhere numerous. Trains flashed by them. Across wide stretches of flat, open prairie they could see lines of telegraph poles stalking across the fields toward the great city. Far away were indications of suburban towns, some big smokestacks towering high in the air.

Frequently there were two-story frame houses standing out in the open fields, without fence or trees, lone outposts of the approaching army of homes.

To the child, the genius with imagination, or the wholly untraveled, the approach to a great city for the first time is a wonderful thing. Particularly if it be evening—that mystic period between the glare and gloom of the world when life is changing from one sphere or condition to another. Ah, the promise of the night. What does it not hold for the weary! What old illusion of hope is not here forever repeated! Says the soul of the toiler to itself, "I shall soon be free. I shall be in the ways and the hosts of the merry. The streets, the lamps, the lighted chamber set for dining, are for me. The theater, the halls, the parties, the ways of rest and the paths of song—these are mine in the night." Though all humanity be still enclosed in the shops, the thrill runs abroad. It is in the air. The dullest feel something which they may not always express or describe. It is the lifting of the burden of toil.

◄ According to the narrator, what effect does arriving at a city at night have upon a traveler?

Sister Carrie gazed out of the window. Her companion, affected by her wonder, so contagious are all things, felt anew some interest in the city and pointed out its marvels.

"This is northwest Chicago," said Drouet. "This is the Chicago River," and he pointed to a little muddy creek, crowded with the huge masted wanderers from far-off waters nosing the black-posted banks. With a puff, a clang, and a clatter of rails it was gone. "Chicago is getting to be a great town," he went on. "It's a wonder. You'll find lots to see here."

Words For Everyday Use

lur • ing (lo͝or´iŋ) *n.,* attempt to attract
yield (yēld) *vt.,* surrender
toil • er (toil´ər) *n.,* one who works hard with tiring effort

► *What begins to trouble Carrie?*

► *Why doesn't Carrie want Drouet to carry her bag? What does he say he will do?*

► *How does Carrie feel when her sister takes her hand? What does her sister carry with her?*

She did not hear this very well. Her heart was troubled by a kind of terror. The fact that she was alone, away from home, rushing into a great sea of life and endeavor, began to tell. She could not help but feel a little choked for breath—a little sick as her heart beat so fast. She half closed her eyes and tried to think it was nothing, that Columbia City was only a little way off.

"Chicago! Chicago!" called the brakeman, slamming open the door. They were rushing into a more crowded yard, alive with the clatter and clang of life. She began to gather up her poor little grip[6] and closed her hand firmly upon her purse. Drouet arose, kicked his legs to straighten his trousers, and seized his clean yellow grip.

"I suppose your people will be here to meet you?" he said. "Let me carry your grip."

"Oh, no," she said. "I'd rather you wouldn't. I'd rather you wouldn't be with me when I meet my sister."

"All right," he said in all kindness. "I'll be near, though, in case she isn't here, and take you out there safely."

"You're so kind," said Carrie, feeling the goodness of such attention in her strange situation.

"Chicago!" called the brakeman, drawing the word out long. They were under a great shadowy train shed, where the lamps were already beginning to shine out, with passenger cars all about and the train moving at a snail's pace. The people in the car were all up and crowding about the door.

"Well, here we are," said Drouet, leading the way to the door. "Goodbye, till I see you Monday."

"Goodbye," she answered, taking his proffered hand.

"Remember, I'll be looking till you find your sister."

She smiled into his eyes.

They filed out, and he affected to take no notice of her. A lean-faced, rather commonplace woman recognized Carrie on the platform and hurried forward.

"Why, Sister Carrie!" she began, and there was a perfunctory embrace of welcome.

Carrie realized the change of affectional atmosphere at once. Amid all the maze, uproar, and novelty she felt cold reality taking her by the hand. No world of light and merriment.

6. **grip.** Small bag or satchel for holding clothes, etc. in traveling

Words For Everyday Use

prof • fered (präf´ərd) *adj.,* offered

per • func • to • ry (pər fuŋk´tə rē) *adj.,* without care or interest; superficial

No round of amusement. Her sister carried with her most of the grimness of shift and toil.

"Why, how are all the folks at home?" she began; "how is father, and mother?"

Carrie answered, but was looking away. Down the aisle, toward the gate leading into the waiting room and the street, stood Drouet. He was looking back. When he saw that she saw him and was safe with her sister he turned to go, sending back the shadow of a smile. Only Carrie saw it. She felt something lost to her when he moved away. When he disappeared she felt his absence thoroughly. With her sister she was much alone, a lone figure in a tossing, thoughtless sea.

◀ *How does Carrie feel when Drouet disappears? To what is Carrie compared?*

CHAPTER 2

What Poverty Threatened: Of Granite and Brass

Minnie's flat, as the one-floor resident apartments were then being called, was in a part of West Van Buren Street inhabited by families of laborers and clerks, men who had come, and were still coming, with the rush of population pouring in at the rate of 50,000 a year. It was on the third floor, the front windows looking down into the street, where, at night, the lights of grocery stores were shining and children were playing. To Carrie, the sound of the little bells upon the horsecars, as they tinkled in and out of hearing, was as pleasing as it was novel. She gazed into the lighted street when Minnie brought her into the front room, and wondered at the sounds, the movement, the murmur of the vast city which stretched for miles and miles in every direction.

Mrs. Hanson, after the first greetings were over, gave Carrie the baby and proceeded to get supper. Her husband asked a few questions and sat down to read the evening paper. He was a silent man, American born, of a Swede father, and now employed as a cleaner of refrigerator cars at the stockyards. To him the presence or absence of his wife's sister was a matter of indifference. Her personal appearance did not affect him one way or the other. His one observation to the point was concerning the chances of work in Chicago.

▶ What is Carrie's brother-in-law like? What does he do for a living? How does he feel about her arrival?

"It's a big place," he said. "You can get in somewhere in a few days. Everybody does."

▶ What is Mr. Hanson's one comment to Carrie? What agreement does Carrie have with the Hansons?

It had been tacitly understood beforehand that she was to get work and pay her board. He was of a clean, saving disposition, and had already paid a number of monthly installments on two lots far out on the West Side. His ambition was some day to build a house on them.

In the interval which marked the preparation of the meal Carrie found time to study the flat. She had some slight gift of observation and that sense, so rich in every woman—intuition.

▶ What does Carrie infer from observing her sister's home?

She felt the drag of a lean and narrow life. The walls of the rooms were discordantly papered. The floors were covered with matting and the hall laid with a thin rag carpet. One

Words For Everyday Use

nov • el (näv´əl) *adj.*, new and unusual

tac • it • ly (tas´it lē) *adv.*, not openly, but by implication

dis • po • si • tion (dis´pə zish´ən) *n.*, customary frame of mind, nature, or temperament

dis • cord • ant • ly (dis kôrd´'nt lē) *adv.*, not harmoniously

could see that the furniture was of that poor, hurriedly patched together quality sold by the installment houses.

She sat with Minnie, in the kitchen, holding the baby until it began to cry. Then she walked and sang to it, until Hanson, disturbed in his reading, came and took it. A pleasant side to his nature came out here. He was patient. One could see that he was very much wrapped up in his offspring.

"Now, now," he said, walking. "There, there," and there was a certain Swedish accent noticeable in his voice.

"You'll want to see the city first, won't you?" said Minnie, when they were eating. "Well, we'll go out Sunday and see Lincoln Park."

Carrie noticed that Hanson had said nothing to this. He seemed to be thinking of something else.

"Well," she said, "I think I'll look around tomorrow. I've got Friday and Saturday, and it won't be any trouble. Which way is the business part?"

Minnie began to explain, but her husband took this part of the conversation to himself.

"It's that way," he said, pointing east. "That's east." Then he went off into the longest speech he had yet indulged in, concerning the lay of Chicago. "You'd better look in those big manufacturing houses along Franklin Street and just the other side of the river," he concluded. "Lots of girls work there. You could get home easy, too. It isn't very far."

Carrie nodded and asked her sister about the neighborhood. The latter talked in a subdued tone, telling the little she knew about it, while Hanson concerned himself with the baby. Finally he jumped up and handed the child to his wife.

"I've got to get up early in the morning, so I'll go to bed," and off he went, disappearing into the dark little bedroom off the hall, for the night.

"He works way down at the stockyards," explained Minnie, "so he's got to get up at half-past five."

"What time do you get up to get breakfast?" asked Carrie.

"At about twenty minutes of five."

Together they finished the labor of the day, Carrie washing the dishes while Minnie undressed the baby and put it to bed. Minnie's manner was one of trained industry, and Carrie could see that it was a steady round of toil with her.

◄ *At what time does the day begin in the Hanson household?*

Words For Everyday Use

sub • dued (sub do͞od´) *adj.,* low, diminished

► *What does Carrie realize about her situation? about her flirtation with Drouet?*

She began to see that her relations with Drouet would have to be abandoned. He could not come here. She read from the manner of Hanson, in the subdued air of Minnie, and, indeed, the whole atmosphere of the flat, a settled opposition to anything save a conservative round of toil. If Hanson sat every evening in the front room and read his paper, if he went to bed at nine, and Minnie a little later, what would they expect of her? She saw that she would first need to get work and establish herself on a paying basis before she could think of having company of any sort. Her little flirtation with Drouet seemed now an extraordinary thing.

"No," she said to herself, "he can't come here."

She asked Minnie for ink and paper, which were upon the mantel in the dining room, and when the latter had gone to bed at ten, got out Drouet's card and wrote him.

"I cannot have you call on me here. You will have to wait until you hear from me again. My sister's place is so small."

She troubled herself over what else to put in the letter. She wanted to make some reference to their relations upon the train, but was too timid. She concluded by thanking him for his kindness in a crude way, then puzzled over the formality of signing her name, and finally decided upon the severe, winding up with a "Very truly," which she subsequently changed to "Sincerely." She sealed and addressed the letter, and going in the front room, the alcove of which contained her bed, drew the one small rocking-chair up to the open window, and sat looking out upon the night and streets in silent wonder. Finally, wearied by her own reflections, she began to grow dull in her chair, and feeling the need of sleep, arranged her clothing for the night and went to bed.

When she awoke at eight the next morning, Hanson had gone. Her sister was busy in the dining room, which was also the sitting room, sewing. She worked, after dressing, to arrange a little breakfast for herself, and then advised with Minnie as to which way to look. The latter had changed considerably since Carrie had seen her. She was now a thin, though rugged, woman of twenty-seven, with ideas of life colored by her husband's, and fast hardening into narrower conceptions of pleasure and duty than had ever been hers in a thoroughly circumscribed youth. She had invited Carrie,

Words For Everyday Use

al • cove (al´ kōv´) *n.,* recessed section of a room

cir • cum • scribed (sur´ kəm skrībd´) *adj.,* limited

not because she longed for her presence, but because the latter was dissatisfied at home, and could probably get work and pay her board here. She was pleased to see her in a way, but reflected her husband's point of view in the matter of work. Anything was good enough so long as it paid—say, five dollars a week to begin with. A shop girl was the destiny prefigured for the newcomer. She would get in one of the great shops and do well enough until—well, until something happened. Neither of them knew exactly what. They did not figure on promotion. They did not exactly count on marriage. Things would go on, though, in a dim kind of way until the better thing would eventuate, and Carrie would be rewarded for coming and toiling in the city. It was under such auspicious circumstances that she started out this morning to look for work.

◄ Why did Carrie's sister invite her to Chicago?

◄ What expectations does the family have for Carrie? Does the narrator really mean that these circumstances are auspicious? Explain.

Before following her in her round of seeking, let us look at the sphere in which her future was to lie. In 1889 Chicago had the peculiar qualifications of growth which made such adventuresome pilgrimages even on the part of young girls plausible. Its many and growing commercial opportunities gave it widespread fame, which made of it a giant magnet, drawing to itself, from all quarters, the hopeful and the hopeless—those who had their fortune yet to make and those whose fortunes and affairs had reached a disastrous climax elsewhere. It was a city of over 500,000, with the ambition, the daring, the activity of a metropolis of a million. Its streets and houses were already scattered over an area of seventy-five square miles. Its population was not so much thriving upon established commerce as upon the industries which prepared for the arrival of others. The sound of the hammer engaged upon the erection of new structures was everywhere heard. Great industries were moving in. The huge railroad corporations which had long before recognized the prospects of the place had seized upon vast tracts of land for transfer and shipping purposes. Streetcar lines had been extended far out into the open country in anticipation of rapid growth. The city had laid miles and miles of streets and sewers through regions where, perhaps, one solitary house stood out alone—a pioneer of the populous ways to be. There were regions open to the sweeping winds and rain, which were yet lighted throughout the night with long, blinking lines

◄ When does this story take place? According to the narrator, what was Chicago like at this time? Why did so many people go there? On what did the population of the city thrive?

◄ In what way is the city unusual?

Words For Everyday Use

pre • fig • ured (prē fig´yərd) *adj.*, imagined beforehand

aus • pi • cious (ôs spish´əs) *adj.*, promising

pil • grim • age (pil´grim ij) *n.*, long journey

tract (trakt) *n.*, large area

pop • u • lous (päp´yo͞o les) *adj.*, full of people

of gas lamps, fluttering in the wind. Narrow board walks extended out, passing here a house, and there a store, at far intervals, eventually ending on the open prairie.

In the central portion was the vast wholesale and shopping district, to which the uninformed seeker for work usually drifted. It was a characteristic of Chicago then, and one not generally shared by other cities, that individual firms of any pretension occupied individual buildings. The presence of ample ground made this possible. It gave an imposing appearance to most of the wholesale houses, whose offices were upon the ground floor and in plain view of the street. The large plates of window glass, now so common, were then rapidly coming into use, and gave to the ground floor offices a distinguished and prosperous look. The casual wanderer could see as he passed a polished array of office fixtures, much frosted glass, clerks hard at work, and genteel business men in "nobby" suits and clean linen lounging about or sitting in groups. Polished brass or nickel signs at the square stone entrances announced the firm and the nature of the business in rather neat and reserved terms. The entire metropolitan center possessed a high and mighty air calculated to overawe and abash the common applicant, and to make the gulf between poverty and success seem both wide and deep.

▶ *What effect does the business district of Chicago have upon a person seeking employment?*

Into this important commercial region the timid Carrie went. She walked east along Van Buren Street through a region of lessening importance, until it deteriorated into a mass of shanties and coal yards, and finally verged upon the river. She walked bravely forward, led by an honest desire to find employment and delayed at every step by the interest of the unfolding scene, and a sense of helplessness amid so much evidence of power and force which she did not understand. These vast buildings, what were they? These strange energies and huge interests, for what purposes were they there? She could have understood the meaning of a little stonecutter's yard at Columbia City, carving little pieces of marble for individual use, but when the yards of some huge stone corporation came into view, filled with spur tracks and flat cars, transpierced by docks from the river and traversed overhead by immense trundling cranes of wood and steel, it lost all significance in her little world.

▶ *How does Carrie feel once she has set out to search for work?*

Words For Everyday Use

pre • ten • sion (prē ten´shən) *n.,* claim to distinction

shan • ty (shan´tē) *n.,* small, shabby dwelling

trans • pierced (trans pirsd´) *adj.,* pierced through

trun • dling (trun´dliŋ) *adj.,* moving on wheels

It was so with the vast railroad yards, with the crowded array of vessels she saw at the river, and the huge factories over the way, lining the water's edge. Through the open windows she could see the figures of men and women in working aprons, moving busily about. The great streets were wall-lined mysteries to her; the vast offices, strange mazes which concerned far-off individuals of importance. She could only think of people connected with them as counting money, dressing magnificently, and riding in carriages. What they dealt in, how they labored, to what end it all came, she had only the vaguest conception. It was all wonderful, all vast, all far removed, and she sank in spirit inwardly and fluttered feebly at the heart as she thought of entering any one of these mighty concerns and asking for something to do—something that she could do—anything.

◄ *What conception does Carrie form of people in the "great streets" of Chicago?*

Words For Everyday Use

ves • sel (ves´əl) *n.,* ship

fee • bly (fē´blē) *adv.,* weakly

CHAPTER 3

We Question of Fortune: Four-Fifty a Week

Once across the river and into the wholesale district, she glanced about her for some likely door at which to apply. As she contemplated the wide windows and imposing signs, she became conscious of being gazed upon and understood for what she was—a wage-seeker. She had never done this thing before, and lacked courage. To avoid a certain indefinable shame she felt at being caught spying about for a position, she quickened her steps and assumed an air of indifference supposedly common to one upon an errand. In this way she passed many manufacturing and wholesale houses without once glancing in. At last, after several blocks of walking, she felt that this would not do, and began to look about again; though without relaxing her pace. A little way on she saw a great door which, for some reason, attracted her attention. It was ornamented by a small brass sign, and seemed to be the entrance to a vast hive of six or seven floors. "Perhaps," she thought, "they may want someone," and crossed over to enter. When she came within a score of feet of the desired goal, she saw through the window a young man in a gray checked suit. That he had anything to do with the concern, she could not tell, but because he happened to be looking in her direction her weakening heart misgave her and she hurried by, too overcome with shame to enter. Over the way stood a great six-story structure, labeled Storm and King, which she viewed with rising hope. It was a wholesale dry goods concern and employed women. She could see them moving about now and then upon the upper floors. This place she decided to enter, no matter what. She crossed over and walked directly toward the entrance. As she did so, two men came out and paused in the door. A telegraph messenger in blue dashed past her and up the few steps that led to the entrance and disappeared. Several pedestrians out of the hurrying throng which filled the sidewalks passed about her as she paused, hesitating. She looked helplessly around, and then, seeing herself observed, retreated. It was too difficult a task. She could not go past them.

► *What prevents Carrie from asking anyone if jobs are available?*

Words For Everyday Use

hive (hīv) *n.,* place where many are busy

throng (thrôŋ) *n.,* great crowd

So severe a defeat told sadly upon her nerves. Her feet carried her mechanically forward, every foot of her progress being a satisfactory portion of a flight which she gladly made. Block after block passed by. Upon street lamps at the various corners she read names such as Madison, Monroe, La Salle, Clark, Dearborn, State, and still she went, her feet beginning to tire upon the broad stone flagging. She was pleased in part that the streets were bright and clean. The morning sun, shining down with steadily increasing warmth, made the shady side of the streets pleasantly cool. She looked at the blue sky overhead with more realization of its charm than had ever come to her before.

Her cowardice began to trouble her in a way. She turned back, resolving to hunt up Storm and King and enter. On the way she encountered a great wholesale[1] shoe company, through the broad plate windows of which she saw an enclosed executive department, hidden by frosted glass. Without[2] this enclosure, but just within the street entrance, sat a gray-haired gentleman at a small table, with a large open ledger before him. She walked by this institution several times hesitating, but, finding herself unobserved, faltered past the screen door and stood humbly waiting.

"Well, young lady," observed the old gentleman, looking at her somewhat kindly, "what is it you wish?"

"I am, that is, do you—I mean, do you need any help?" she stammered.

"Not just at present," he answered smiling. "Not just at present. Come in sometime next week. Occasionally we need someone."

◄ *What surprises Carrie about the man's response to her inquiry?*

She received the answer in silence and backed awkwardly out. The pleasant nature of her reception rather astonished her. She had expected that it would be more difficult, that something cold and harsh would be said—she knew not what. That she had not been put to shame and made to feel her unfortunate position, seemed remarkable.

Somewhat encouraged, she ventured into another large structure. It was a clothing company, and more people were in evidence—well-dressed men of forty and more, surrounded by brass railings.

1. **wholesale.** Selling to other businesses, not directly to consumers
2. **Without.** Outside

Words For Everyday Use

me • chan • i • cal • ly (mə kan´ə klē) *adv.,* without thought; in a machinelike way

ven • ture (ven´chər) *vi.,* go at some risk

An office boy approached her.

"Who is it you wish to see?" he asked.

"I want to see the manager," she said.

He ran away and spoke to one of a group of three men who were conferring together. One of these came toward her.

► *What setback discourages Carrie?*

"Well?" he said coldly. The greeting drove all courage from her at once.

"Do you need any help?" she stammered.

"No," he replied abruptly, and turned upon his heel.

She went foolishly out, the office boy deferentially swinging the door for her, and gladly sank into the obscuring crowd. It was a severe setback to her recently pleased mental state.

Now she walked quite aimlessly for a time, turning here and there, seeing one great company after another, but finding no courage to prosecute her single inquiry. High noon came, and with it hunger. She hunted out an unassuming restaurant and entered, but was disturbed to find that the prices were exorbitant for the size of her purse. A bowl of soup was all that she could afford, and, with this quickly eaten, she went out again. It restored her strength somewhat and made her moderately bold to pursue the search.

► *What does Carrie discover when she enters the restaurant?*

In walking a few blocks to fix upon some probable place, she again encountered the firm of Storm and King, and this time managed to get in. Some gentlemen were conferring close at hand, but took no notice of her. She was left standing, gazing nervously upon the floor. When the limit of her distress had been nearly reached, she was beckoned to by a man at one of the many desks within the nearby railing.

"Who is it you wish to see?" he inquired.

"Why, anyone, if you please," she answered. "I am looking for something to do."

"Oh, you want to see Mr. McManus," he returned. "Sit down," and he pointed to a chair against the neighboring wall. He went on leisurely writing, until after a time a short, stout gentleman came in from the street.

"Mr. McManus," called the man at the desk, "this young woman wants to see you."

The short gentleman turned about toward Carrie, and she arose and came forward.

"What can I do for you, miss?" he inquired, surveying her curiously.

Words For Everyday Use

con • fer (kən fʉr´) *vi.,* meet for discussion

def • er • en • ti • al • ly (def´ər en´shē ə lē) *adv.,* respectfully

ob • scur • ing (əb skyo͞or´iŋ) *adj.,* making less visible

pros • e • cute (präs´i kyo͞ot´) *vt.,* put forward

"I want to know if I can get a position," she inquired.

"As what?" he asked.

"Not as anything in particular," she faltered.

"Have you ever had any experience in the wholesale dry goods business?" he questioned.

"No, sir," she replied.

"Are you a stenographer[3] or typewriter?"

"No, sir."

"Well, we haven't anything here," he said. "We employ only experienced help."

She began to step backward toward the door, when something about her plaintive face attracted him.

"Have you ever worked at anything before?" he inquired.

"No, sir," she said.

"Well, now, it's hardly possible that you would get anything to do in a wholesale house of this kind. Have you tried the department stores?"

She acknowledged that she had not.

"Well, if I were you," he said, looking at her rather genially, "I would try the department stores. They often need young women as clerks."

"Thank you," she said, her whole nature relieved by this spark of friendly interest.

"Yes," he said, as she moved toward the door, "you try the department stores," and off he went.

At that time the department store was in its earliest form of successful operation, and there were not many. The first three in the United States, established about 1884, were in Chicago. Carrie was familiar with the names of several through the advertisements in the *Daily News,* and now proceeded to seek them. The words of Mr. McManus had somehow managed to restore her courage, which had fallen low, and she dared to hope that this new line would offer her something. Some time she spent in wandering up and down, thinking to encounter the buildings by chance, so readily is the mind, bent upon prosecuting a hard but needful errand, eased by that self-deception which the semblance of search, without the reality, gives. At last she inquired of a police officer, and was directed to proceed "two blocks up," where she would find "The Fair."

◄ *What does Mr. McManus tell Carrie she lacks? What does he advise her to do?*

3. **stenographer.** Office worker who takes dictation

Words For Everyday Use

gen • i • al • ly (jēn´yə lē) *adv.,* in a friendly manner

sem • blance (sem´bləns) *n.,* outward form or appearance

▶ *What does the narrator find interesting about department stores? What does the narrator's descriptions of department stores tell you about the time when this novel was written?*

▶ *How does Carrie feel about the goods she sees in the store?*

▶ *According to the narrator, how should the reader not view Carrie?*

The nature of these vast retail combinations, should they ever permanently disappear, will form an interesting chapter in the commercial history of our nation. Such a flowering out of a modest trade principle the world had never witnessed up to that time. They were along the line of the most effective retail[4] organization, with hundreds of stores coordinated into one and laid out upon the most imposing and economic basis. They were handsome, bustling, successful affairs, with a host of clerks and a swarm of patrons. Carrie passed along the busy aisles, much affected by the remarkable displays of trinkets, dress goods, stationery, and jewelry. Each separate counter was a showplace of dazzling interest and attraction. She could not help feeling the claim of each trinket and valuable upon her personally, and yet she did not stop. There was nothing there which she could not have used—nothing which she did not long to own. The dainty slippers and stockings, the delicately frilled skirts and petticoats, the laces, ribbons, hair combs, purses, all touched her with individual desire, and she felt keenly the fact that not any of these things were in the range of her purchase. She was a work-seeker, an outcast without employment, one whom the average employee could tell at a glance was poor and in need of a situation.

It must not be thought that anyone could have mistaken her for a nervous, sensitive, highstrung nature, cast unduly upon a cold, calculating, and unpoetic world. Such certainly she was not. But women are peculiarly sensitive to their adornment.

Not only did Carrie feel the drag of desire for all which was new and pleasing in apparel for women, but she noticed too, with a touch at the heart, the fine ladies who elbowed and ignored her, brushing past in utter disregard of her presence, themselves eagerly enlisted in the materials which the store contained. Carrie was not familiar with the appearance of her more fortunate sisters of the city. Neither had she before known the nature and appearance of the shop-girls with whom she now compared poorly. They were pretty in the main, some even handsome, with an air of independence and indifference which added, in the case of the more favored, a certain piquancy. Their clothes were neat, in many instances fine, and wherever she encountered the eye of one it was only to recognize in it a keen analysis of her own position—her

4. **retail.** Selling directly to the consumer

Words For Everyday Use

a • dorn • ment (ə dôrn´ mənt) *n.,* dress

pi • quan • cy (pē´kən sē) *n.,* flavor

individual shortcomings of dress and that shadow of *manner* which she thought must hang about her and make clear to all who and what she was. A flame of envy lighted in her heart. She realized in a dim way how much the city held—wealth, fashion, ease—every adornment for women, and she longed for dress and beauty with a whole heart.

On the second floor were the managerial offices, to which, after some inquiry, she was now directed. There she found other girls ahead of her, applicants like herself, but with more of that self-satisfied and independent air which experience of the city lends; girls who scrutinized her in a painful manner. After a wait of perhaps three-quarters of an hour, she was called in turn.

◄ How does Carrie compare to the other applicants?

"Now," said a sharp, quick-mannered Jew, who was sitting at a roll-top desk near the window, "have you ever worked in any other store?"

◄ What does the manager want to know? What is the end result of Carrie's interview?

"No, sir," said Carrie.

"Oh, you haven't," he said, eyeing her keenly.

"No, sir," she replied.

"Well, we prefer young women just now with some experience. I guess we can't use you."

Carrie stood waiting a moment, hardly certain whether the interview had terminated.

"Don't wait!" he exclaimed. "Remember we are very busy here."

Carrie began to move quickly to the door.

"Hold on," he said, calling her back. "Give me your name and address. We want girls occasionally."

When she had gotten safely into the street, she could scarcely restrain the tears. It was not so much the particular rebuff which she had just experienced, but the whole abashing trend of the day. She was tired and nervous. She abandoned the thought of appealing to the other department stores and now wandered on, feeling a certain safety and relief in mingling with the crowd.

◄ How does Carrie react to the day's experiences? What upsets her?

In her indifferent wandering she turned into Jackson Street, not far from the river, and was keeping her way along the south side of that imposing thoroughfare, when a piece of wrapping paper, written on with marking ink and tacked up on the door, attracted her attention. It read, "Girls wanted—wrappers & stitchers." She hesitated a moment, then entered.

Words For Everyday Use

re • buff (ri buf´) *n.,* refusal; rejection

a • bash • ing (ə bash´iŋ) *adj.,* embarrassing; humbling

thor • ough • fare (thʉr´ ō fer´) *n.,* public street

► *What are the people who work in this business like?*

► *What salary is Carrie offered?*

The firm of Speigelheim & Co., makers of boys' caps, occupied one floor of the building, fifty feet in width and some eighty feet in depth. It was a place rather dingily lighted, the darkest portions having incandescent lights, filled with machines and work benches. At the latter labored quite a company of girls and some men. The former were drabby-looking creatures, stained in face with oil and dust, clad in thin, shapeless, cotton dresses and shod with more or less worn shoes. Many of them had their sleeves rolled up, revealing bare arms, and in some cases, owing to the heat, their dresses were open at the neck. They were a fair type of nearly the lowest order of shop-girls—careless, slouchy, and more or less pale from confinement. They were not timid, however; were rich in curiosity, and strong in daring and slang.

Carrie looked about her, very much disturbed and quite sure that she did not want to work here. Aside from making her uncomfortable by sidelong glances, no one paid her the least attention. She waited until the whole department was aware of her presence. Then some word was sent around, and a foreman, in an apron and shirt sleeves, the latter rolled up to his shoulders, approached.

"Do you want to see me?" he asked.

"Do you need any help?" said Carrie, already learning directness of address.

"Do you know how to stitch caps?" he returned.

"No, sir," she replied.

"Have you ever had any experience at this kind of work?" he inquired.

She answered that she had not.

"Well," said the foreman, scratching his ear meditatively, "we do need a stitcher. We like experienced help, though. We've hardly got time to break people in." He paused and looked away out of the window. "We might, though, put you at finishing," he concluded reflectively.

"How much do you pay a week?" ventured Carrie, emboldened by a certain softness in the man's manner and his simplicity of address.

"Three and a half," he answered.

"Oh," she was about to exclaim, but checked herself and allowed her thoughts to die without expression.

"We're not exactly in need of anybody," he went on

Words For Everyday Use

clad (klad) *adj.*, clothed; dressed

em • bold • ened (em bōl´dənd) *adj.*, made braver or bolder

vaguely, looking her over as one would a package. "You can come on Monday morning, though," he added, "and I'll put you to work."

"Thank you," said Carrie weakly.

"If you come, bring an apron," he added.

He walked away and left her standing by the elevator, never so much as inquiring her name.

◄ *What doesn't the foreman ask Carrie?*

While the appearance of the shop and the announcement of the price paid per week operated very much as a blow to Carrie's fancy, the fact that work of any kind was offered after so rude a round of experience was gratifying. She could not begin to believe that she would take the place, modest as her aspirations were. She had been used to better than that. Her mere experience and the free out-of-door life of the country caused her nature to revolt at such confinement. Dirt had never been her share. Her sister's flat was clean. This place was grimy and low, the girls were careless and hardened. They must be bad-minded and hearted, she imagined. Still, a place had been offered her. Surely Chicago was not so bad if she could find one place in one day. She might find another and better later.

◄ *Why doesn't Carrie want to work at this place?*

◄ *What does Carrie begin to hope?*

Her subsequent experiences were not of a reassuring nature, however. From all the more pleasing or imposing places she was turned away abruptly with the most chilling formality. In others where she applied only the experienced were required. She met with painful rebuffs, the most trying of which had been in a manufacturing cloak house, where she had gone to the fourth floor to inquire.

◄ *What happens at the other places where Carrie seeks employment?*

"No, no," said the foreman, a rough, heavily built individual, who looked after a miserably lighted workshop, "we don't want anyone. Don't come here."

With the wane of the afternoon went her hopes, her courage, and her strength. She had been astonishingly persistent. So earnest an effort was well deserving of a better reward. On every hand, to her fatigued senses, the great business portion grew larger, harder, more stolid in its indifference. It seemed as if it was all closed to her, that the struggle was too fierce for her to hope to do anything at all. Men and women hurried by in long, shifting lines. She felt the flow of the tide of effort and interest—felt her own helplessness without quite realizing the wisp on the tide that she was. She cast

◄ *How does Carrie feel about the city? Would you feel the same way if you were in her position?*

Words For Everyday Use

wane (wān) *n.,* gradual end

stol • id (stäl´id) *adj.,* having or showing little or no emotion

wisp (wisp) *n.,* something delicate or frail

about vainly for some possible place to apply, but found no door which she had the courage to enter. It would be the same thing all over. The old humiliation of her plea, rewarded by curt denial. Sick at heart and in body, she turned to the west, the direction of Minnie's flat, which she had now fixed in mind, and began that wearisome, baffled retreat which the seeker for employment at nightfall too often makes. In passing through Fifth Avenue, south toward Van Buren Street, where she intended to take a car, she passed the door of a large wholesale shoe house, through the plate glass window of which she could see a middle-aged gentleman sitting at a small desk. One of those forlorn impulses which often grow out of a fixed sense of defeat, the last sprouting of a baffled and uprooted growth of ideas, seized upon her. She walked deliberately through the door and up to the gentleman, who looked at her weary face with partially awakened interest.

"What is it?" he said.

"Can you give me something to do?" said Carrie.

"Now, I really don't know," he said kindly. "What kind of work is it you want—you're not a typewriter, are you?"

"Oh, no," answered Carrie.

"Well, we only employ bookkeepers and typewriters here. You might go around to the side and inquire upstairs. They did want some help upstairs a few days ago. Ask for Mr. Brown."

She hastened around to the side entrance and was taken up by the elevator to the fourth floor.

"Call Mr. Brown, Willie," said the elevator man to a boy nearby.

Willie went off and presently returned with the information that Mr. Brown said she should sit down and that he would be around in a little while.

It was a portion of the stock room which gave no idea of the general character of the place, and Carrie could form no opinion of the nature of the work.

► *Where will Carrie be working? What will she be paid? Why does she accept this job?*

"So you want something to do," said Mr. Brown, after he inquired concerning the nature of her errand. "Have you ever been employed in a shoe factory before?"

"No, sir," said Carrie.

"What is your name?" he inquired, and being informed, "Well, I don't know as I have anything for you. Would you work for four and a half a week?"

Words For Everyday Use

curt (kurt) *adj.,* brief to the point of rudeness
for • lorn (fôr lôrn′) *adj.,* without hope; desperate
has • ten (hās′ən) *vi.,* move swiftly; hurry

Carrie was too worn by defeat not to feel that it was considerable. She had not expected that he would offer her less than six. She acquiesced, however, and he took her name and address.

"Well," he said, finally, "you report here at eight o'clock Monday morning. I think I can find something for you to do."

He left her revived by the possibilities, sure that she had found something at last. Instantly the blood crept warmly over her body. Her nervous tension relaxed. She walked out into the busy street and discovered a new atmosphere. Behold, the throng was moving with a lightsome step. She noticed that men and women were smiling. Scraps of conversation and notes of laughter floated to her. The air was light. People were already pouring out of the buildings, their labor ended for the day. She noticed that they were pleased, and thoughts of her sister's home and the meal that would be awaiting her quickened her steps. She hurried on, tired perhaps, but no longer weary of foot. What would not Minnie say! Ah, the long winter in Chicago—the lights, the crowd, the amusement! This was a great, pleasing metropolis after all. Her new firm was a goodly institution. Its windows were of huge plate glass. She could probably do well there. Thoughts of Drouet returned—of the things he had told her. She now felt that life was better, that it was livelier, sprightlier. She boarded a car in the best of spirits, feeling her blood still flowing pleasantly. She would live in Chicago, her mind kept saying to itself. She would have a better time than she had ever had before—she would be happy.

◄ *In what way has Carrie's job offer affected her view of the city?*

Words For Everyday Use

ac • qui • esce (ak´wē es´) *vi.*, consent without protest but without enthusiasm
me • trop • o • lis (mə träp´əl is) *n.*, large city or center of population
spright • ly (sprīt´lē) *adj.*, full of energy and spirit; lively

CHAPTER 4

The Spendings of Fancy: Facts Answer with Sneers

► *What thoughts does Carrie indulge?*

For the next two days Carrie indulged in the most high-flown speculations. Her fancy plunged recklessly into privileges and amusements which would have been much more becoming had she been cradled a child of fortune. With ready will and quick mental selection she scattered her meager four-fifty per week with a swift and graceful hand. Indeed, as she sat in her rocking chair these several evenings before going to bed and looked out upon the pleasantly lighted street, this money cleared for its prospective possessor the way to every joy and every bauble which the heart of woman may desire. "I will have a fine time," she thought.

Her sister Minnie knew nothing of these rather wild cerebrations,[1] though they exhausted the markets of delight. She was too busy scrubbing the kitchen woodwork and calculating the purchasing power of eighty cents for Sunday's dinner. When Carrie had returned home, flushed with her first success and ready, for all her weariness, to discuss the now interesting events which led up to her achievement, the former had merely smiled approvingly and inquired whether she would have to spend any of it for carfare. This consideration had not entered in before, and it did not now for long affect the glow of Carrie's enthusiasm. Disposed as she then was to calculate upon that vague basis which allows the subtraction of one sum from another without any perceptible diminution, she was happy.

► *Why doesn't the thought of spending some of her wages on carfare bother Carrie?*

When Hanson came home at seven o'clock, he was inclined to be a little crusty—his usual demeanor before supper. This never showed so much in anything he said as in a certain solemnity of countenance and the silent manner in which he slopped about. He had a pair of yellow carpet slippers which he enjoyed wearing, and these he would immediately substitute for his solid pair of shoes. This, and washing his face with the aid of common washing soap until

1. **cerebrations.** Thoughts

Words For Everyday Use

bau • ble (bô´bəl´) *n.*, showy but worthless thing

dim • i • nu • tion (dim´ə no͞o´shən) *n.*, lessening

de • mean • or (di mēn´ər) *n.*, manner

coun • te • nance (koun´tə nəns) *n.*, facial expression

it glowed a shiny red, constituted his only preparation for his evening meal. He would then get his evening paper and read in silence.

For a young man, this was rather a morbid turn of character, and so affected Carrie. Indeed, it affected the entire atmosphere of the flat, as such things are inclined to do, and gave to his wife's mind its subdued and tactful turn, anxious to avoid taciturn replies. Under the influence of Carrie's announcement he brightened up somewhat.

"You didn't lose any time, did you?" he remarked, smiling a little.

◀ How does Hanson's comment make Carrie feel?

"No," returned Carrie with a touch of pride.

He asked her one or two more questions and then turned to play with the baby, leaving the subject until it was brought up again by Minnie at the table.

Carrie, however, was not to be reduced to the common level of observation which prevailed in the flat.

"It seems to be such a large company," she said at one place. "Great big plate-glass windows and lots of clerks. The man I saw said they hired ever so many people."

"It's not very hard to get work now," put in Hanson, "if you look right."

◀ What does Hanson say about the job market? Do you think this comment lessens Carrie's feeling of accomplishment?

Minnie, under the warming influence of Carrie's good spirits and her husband's somewhat conversational mood, began to tell Carrie of some of the well-known things to see—things the enjoyment of which cost nothing.

"You'd like to see Michigan Avenue. There are such fine houses. It is such a fine street."

"Where is H. R. Jacob's?" interrupted Carrie, mentioning one of the theaters devoted to melodrama[2] which went by that name at the time.

"Oh, it's not very far from here," answered Minnie. "It's in Halstead Street, right up here."

"How I'd like to go there. I crossed Halstead Street today, didn't I?"

At this there was a slight halt in the natural reply. Thoughts are a strangely permeating factor. At her suggestion of going to the theater, the unspoken shade of disapproval to the doing of those things which involved the expenditure of money—shades of feeling which arose in the mind of Hanson

◀ How do Carrie's sister and brother-in-law react when she mentions the theater? Why do they react in this way?

2. **melodrama.** Dramatic style incorporating music and sensational elements

Words For Everyday Use

con • sti • tute (kän´stə to͞ot) *vt.,* make up
tac • i • turn (tas´ə tʉrn) *adj.,* uncommunicative
per • me • at • ing (pʉr´mē āt´iŋ) *adj.,* able to spread

and then in Minnie—slightly affected the atmosphere of the table. Minnie answered "yes," but Carrie could feel that going to the theater was poorly <u>advocated</u> here. The subject was put off for a little while until Hanson, through with his meal, took his paper and went into the front room.

When they were alone, the two sisters began a somewhat freer conversation, Carrie interrupting it to hum a little, as they worked at the dishes.

"I should like to walk up and see Halstead Street, if it isn't too far," said Carrie, after a time. "Why don't we go to the theater tonight?"

"Oh, I don't think Sven would want to go tonight," returned Minnie. "He has to get up so early."

"He wouldn't mind—he'd enjoy it," said Carrie.

"No, he doesn't go very often," returned Minnie.

"Well, I'd like to go," rejoined Carrie. "Let's you and me go."

Minnie pondered a while, not upon whether she could or would go—for that point was already negatively settled with her—but upon some means of diverting the thoughts of her sister to some other topic.

"We'll go some other time," she said at last, finding no ready means of escape.

Carrie sensed the root of the opposition at once.

"I have some money," she said. "You go with me."

Minnie shook her head.

"He could go along," said Carrie.

"No," returned Minnie softly, and rattling the dishes to drown the conversation. "He wouldn't."

► *In what way has Carrie's character developed since Minnie last saw her?*

It had been several years since Minnie had seen Carrie, and in that time that latter's character had developed a few shades. Naturally timid in all things that related to her own advancement, and especially so when without power or resource, her craving for pleasure was so strong that it was the one stay of her nature. She would speak for that when silent on all else.

"Ask him," she pleaded softly.

► *In what way will Carrie's presence benefit the Hansons? What concern does Minnie have? What does the narrator say about Minnie's mind and nature?*

Minnie was thinking of the resource which Carrie's board would add. It would pay the rent and would make the subject of expenditure a little less difficult to talk about with her husband. But if Carrie was going to think of running around in the beginning there would be a hitch somewhere. Unless

Words For Everyday Use

ad • vo • cate (ad´və kāt´) *vt.,* speak or write in support of

Carrie submitted to a solemn round of industry and saw the need of hard work without longing for play, how was her coming to the city to profit them? These thoughts were not those of a cold, hard nature at all. They were the serious reflections of a mind which invariably adjusted itself, without much complaining, to such surroundings as its industry could make for it.

At last she yielded enough to ask Hanson. It was a half-hearted procedure without a shade of desire on her part.

"Carrie wants us to go to the theater," she said, looking in upon her husband. Hanson looked up from his paper, and they exchanged a mild look, which said as plainly as anything: "This isn't what we expected."

"I don't care to go," he returned. "What does she want to see?"

"H. R. Jacob's," said Minnie.

He looked down at his paper and shook his head negatively.

When Carrie saw how they looked upon her proposition, she gained a still clearer feeling of their way of life. It weighed on her, but took no definite form of opposition.

"I think I'll go down and stand at the foot of the stairs," she said, after a time.

Minnie made no objection to this, and Carrie put on her hat and went below.

"Where has Carrie gone?" asked Hanson, coming back into the dining room when he heard the door close.

"She said she was going down to the foot of the stairs," answered Minnie. "I guess she just wants to look out a while."

"She oughtn't to be thinking about spending her money on theaters already, do you think?" he said.

"She just feels a little curious, I guess," ventured Minnie. "Everything is so new."

"I don't know," said Hanson, and went over to the baby, his forehead slightly wrinkled.

◄ For what does Hanson criticize Carrie? What does Minnie say in response?

He was thinking of a full career of vanity and wastefulness which a young girl might indulge in, and wondering how Carrie could contemplate such a course when she had so little, as yet, with which to do.

On Saturday Carrie went out by herself—first toward the river, which interested her, and then back along Jackson

Words For Everyday Use

prop • o • si • tion (präp´ə zish´ən) *n.,* something set forth for consideration

▶ *About what does Carrie speculate? How does she feel about the chance of Drouet visiting on Monday?*

Street, which was then lined by the pretty houses and fine lawns which subsequently caused it to be made into a boulevard. She was struck with the evidences of wealth, although there was, perhaps, not a person on the street worth more than a hundred thousand dollars. She was glad to be out of the flat, because already she felt that it was a narrow, humdrum place, and that interest and joy lay elsewhere. Her thoughts now were of a more liberal character, and she punctuated them with speculations as to the whereabouts of Drouet. She was not sure but that he might call anyhow Monday night, and, while she felt a little disturbed at the possibility, there was, nevertheless, just the shade of a wish that he would.

On Monday she arose early and prepared to go to work. She dressed herself in a worn shirtwaist of dotted blue percale,[3] a skirt of light brown serge[4] rather faded, and a small straw hat which she had worn all summer at Columbia City. Her shoes were old, and her necktie was in that crumpled, flattened state which time and much wearing impart. She made a very average looking shop-girl with the exception of her features. These were slightly more even than common, and gave her a sweet, reserved, and pleasing appearance.

▶ *To what are Carrie's fancies about her job and her wages compared?*

It is no easy thing to get up early in the morning when one is used to sleeping until seven and eight, as Carrie had been at home. She gained some inkling of the character of Hanson's life when, half asleep, she looked out into the dining room at six o'clock and saw him silently finishing his breakfast. By the time she was dressed he was gone, and she, Minnie, and the baby ate together, the latter being just old enough to sit in a highchair and disturb the dishes with a spoon. Her spirits were greatly subdued now when the fact of entering upon strange and untried duties confronted her. Only the ashes of all her fine fancies were remaining—ashes still concealing, nevertheless, a few red embers of hope. So subdued was she by her weakening nerves, that she ate quite in silence, going over imaginary conceptions of the character of the shoe company, the nature of the work, her employer's attitude. She was vaguely feeling that she would come in contact with the great owners, that her work would be where grave, stylishly dressed men occasionally look on.

3. **percale.** Fine, closely woven cotton cloth
4. **serge.** Strong twilled fabric

Words For Everyday Use

im • part (im pärt´) *vt.,* give
ink • ling (iŋk´liŋ) *n.,* small notion
em • ber (em´bər) *n.,* smoldering remains of a fire
grave (grāv) *adj.,* serious; important

"Well, good luck," said Minnie, when she was ready to go. They had agreed it was best to walk, that morning at least, to see if she could do it every day—sixty cents a week for carfare being quite an item under the circumstances.

"I'll tell you how it goes tonight," said Carrie.

Once in the sunlit street, with laborers tramping by in either direction, the horsecars passing crowded to the rails with the small clerks and floor help in the great wholesale houses, and men and women generally coming out of doors and passing about the neighborhood, Carrie felt slightly reassured. In the sunshine of the morning, beneath the wide, blue heavens, with a fresh wind astir, what fears, except the most desperate, can find a harborage?[5] In the night, or the gloomy chambers of the day, fears and misgivings wax strong, but out in the sunlight there is, for a time, cessation even of the terror of death.

◄ *What effect does the sunshine have on Carrie's fears and worries?*

Carrie went straight forward until she crossed the river, and then turned into Fifth Avenue. The thoroughfare, in this part, was like a walled *cañon*[6] of brownstone and dark red brick. The big windows looked shiny and clean. Trucks were rumbling in increasing numbers; men and women, girls and boys were moving onward in all directions. She met girls of her own age, who looked at her as if with contempt for her diffidence. She wondered at the magnitude of this life and at the importance of knowing much in order to do anything in it at all. Dread at her own inefficiency crept upon her. She would not know how, she would not be quick enough. Had not all the other places refused her because she did not know something or other? She would be scolded, abused, ignominiously discharged.

◄ *About what does Carrie begin to worry? In what way does this conflict with her mood moments earlier?*

It was with weak knees and a slight catch in her breathing that she came up to the great shoe company at Adams and Fifth Avenue and entered the elevator. When she stepped out on the fourth floor there was no one at hand, only great aisles of boxes piled to the ceiling. She stood, very much frightened, awaiting someone.

Presently Mr. Brown came up. He did not seem to recognize her.

"What is it you want?" he inquired.

◄ *What has Mr. Brown already forgotten? How do you think his forgetfulness makes Carrie feel?*

5. **harborage.** Shelter, place to rest
6. ***cañon.*** Spanish spelling for canyon

Words For Everyday Use

wax (waks) *vi.*, grow
ces • sa • tion (se sā´shən) *n.*, stopping; end
dif • fi • dence (dif´ə dəns) *n.*, lack of confidence; shyness
ig • no • min • i • ous • ly (ig´nə min´ ē es lē) *adv.*, shamefully; dishonorably

Carrie's heart sank.

"You said I should come this morning to see about work—"

"Oh," he interrupted. "Um—yes. What is your name?"

"Carrie Meeber."

"Yes," said he. "You come with me."

He led the way through dark, box-lined aisles which had the smell of new shoes, until they came to an iron door which opened into the factory proper. There was a large, low-ceiled room, with clacking, rattling machines at which men in white shirt sleeves and blue gingham[7] aprons were working. She followed him diffidently through the clattering automatons, keeping her eyes straight before her, and flushing slightly. They crossed to a far corner and took an elevator to the sixth floor. Out of the array of machines and benches, Mr. Brown signalled a foreman.

"This is the girl," he said, and turning to Carrie, "You go with him." He then returned, and Carrie followed her new superior to a little desk in a corner, which he used as a kind of official center.

"You've never worked at anything like this before, have you?" he questioned, rather sternly.

"No, sir," she answered.

► *What is Carrie about to learn how to do?*

He seemed rather annoyed at having to bother with such help, but put down her name and then led her across to where a line of girls occupied stools in front of clacking machines. On the shoulder of one of the girls who was punching eye-holes in one piece of the upper, by the aid of the machine, he put his hand.

"You," he said, "show this girl how to do what you're doing. When you get through, come to me."

The girl so addressed rose promptly and gave Carrie her place.

"It isn't hard to do," she said, bending over. "You just take this so, fasten it with this clamp, and start the machine."

She suited action to word, fastened the piece of leather, which was eventually to form the right half of the upper of a man's shoe, by little adjustable clamps, and pushed a small steel rod at the side of the machine. The latter jumped to the task of punching, with sharp, snapping clicks, cutting circular bits of leather out of the side of the upper, leaving the

7. **gingham.** Yarn-dyed cloth, usually woven in stripes or plaids

Words For Everyday Use

au • tom • a • ton (ô täm´ə tän´) *n.,* robot

holes which were to hold the laces. After observing a few times, the girl let her work at it alone. Seeing that it was fairly well done, she went away.

The pieces of leather came from the girl at the machine to her right, and were passed on to the girl at her left. Carrie saw at once that an average speed was necessary or the work would pile up on her and all those below would be delayed. She had no time to look about, and bent anxiously to her task. The girls at her left and right realized her predicament and feelings, and, in a way, tried to aid her, as much as they dared, by working slower.

◄ *What pressure adds to Carrie's worry about her new job? What do the other girls do to help her?*

At this task she labored incessantly for some time, finding relief from her own nervous fears and imaginings in the humdrum, mechanical movement of the machine. She felt, as the minutes passed, that the room was not very light. It had a thick odor of fresh leather, but that did not worry her. She felt the eyes of the other help upon her, and troubled lest she was not working fast enough.

Once, when she was fumbling at the little clamp, having made a slight error in setting in the leather, a great hand appeared before her eyes and fastened the clamp for her. It was the foreman. Her heart thumped so that she could scarcely see to go on.

"Start your machine," he said, "start your machine. Don't keep the line waiting."

This recovered her sufficiently and she went excitedly on, hardly breathing until the shadow moved away from behind her. Then she heaved a great breath.

As the morning wore on the room became hotter. She felt the need of a breath of fresh air and a drink of water, but did not venture to stir. The stool she sat on was without a back or footrest, and she began to feel uncomfortable. She found, after a time, that her back was beginning to ache. She twisted and turned from one position to another slightly different, but it did not ease her for long. She was beginning to weary.

◄ *How does Carrie feel after only a few hours of work?*

"Stand up, why don't you?" said the girl at her right, without any form of introduction. "They won't care."

Carrie looked at her gratefully. "I guess I will," she said.

She stood up from her stool and worked that way for a while, but it was a more difficult position. Her neck and shoulders ached in bending over.

Words For Everyday Use

pre • dic • a • ment (prē dic´ə ment) *n.,* difficult situation

in • ces • sant • ly (in ses´ənt lē) *adv.,* without stopping

▶ What do the girls Carrie works with do whenever the foreman is not overseeing them?

▶ What is Carrie doing wrong?

▶ What becomes nauseating to Carrie?

The spirit of the place impressed itself on her in a rough way. She did not venture to look around, but above the clack of the machine she could hear an occasional remark. She could also note a thing or two out of the side of her eye.

"Did you see Harry last night?" said the girl at her left, addressing her neighbor.

"No."

"You ought to have seen the tie he had on. Gee, but he was a mark."

"S-s-t," said the other girl, bending over her work. The first, silenced, instantly assumed a solemn face. The foreman passed slowly along, eyeing each worker distinctly. The moment he was gone, the conversation was resumed again.

"Say," began the girl at her left, "what jeh think he said?"

"I don't know."

"He said he saw us with Eddie Harris at Martin's last night."

"No!" They both giggled.

A youth with tan-colored hair, that needed clipping very badly, came shuffling along between the machines, bearing a basket of leather findings under his left arm, and pressed against his stomach. When near Carrie, he stretched out his right hand and gripped one girl under the arm.

"Aw, let me go," she exclaimed angrily. "Duffer."

He only grinned broadly in return.

"Rubber!" he called back as she looked after him. There was nothing of the gallant in him.

Carrie at last could scarcely sit still. Her legs began to tire and she wanted to get up and stretch. Would noon never come? It seemed as if she had worked an entire day. She was not hungry at all, but weak, and her eyes were tired, straining at the one point where the eye-punch came down. The girl at the right noticed her squirmings and felt sorry for her. She was concentrating herself too thoroughly—what she did really required less mental and physical strain. There was nothing to be done, however. The halves of the uppers came piling steadily down. Her hands began to ache at the wrists and then in the fingers, and toward the last she seemed one mass of dull, complaining muscles, fixed in an eternal position and performing a single mechanical movement which became more and more distasteful, until at last it was absolutely nauseating. When she was wondering whether the strain would ever cease, a dull sounding bell clanged somewhere down an elevator shaft, and the end came. In an instant there was a buzz of action and conversation. All the girls instantly left their stools and hurried away in an adjoining room, men passed through, coming from some department which opened on the right. The whirling wheels began to sing in a steadily modifying key, until at last they died away in a low buzz. There was an audible stillness, in which the common voice sounded strange.

Carrie got up and sought her lunch box. She was stiff, a little dizzy, and very thirsty. On the way to the small space portioned off by wood, where all the wraps and lunches were kept, she encountered the foreman, who stared at her hard.

"Well," he said, "did you get along all right?"

"I think so," she replied, very respectfully.

"Um," he replied, for want of something better, and walked on.

Under better material conditions, this kind of work would not have been so bad, but the new socialism[8] which involves pleasant working conditions for employees had not then taken hold upon manufacturing companies.

◄ Why is Carrie's workplace especially unpleasant, according to the narrator? How did the employers hope to gain something?

The place smelled of the oil of the machines and the new leather—a combination which, added to the stale odors of the building, was not pleasant even in cold weather. The floor, though regularly swept every evening, presented a littered surface. Not the slightest provision had been made for the comfort of the employees, the idea being that something was gained by giving them as little and making the work as hard and unremunerative as possible. What we know of footrests, swivelback chairs, dining rooms for the girls, clean aprons and curling irons supplied free, and a decent cloak room, were unthought of. The washrooms were disagreeable, crude, if not foul places, and the whole atmosphere was sordid.

Carrie looked about her, after she had drunk a tinful of water from a bucket in one corner, for a place to sit and eat. The other girls had ranged themselves about the windows or the workbenches of those of the men who had gone out. She saw no place which did not hold a couple or a group of girls, and being too timid to think of intruding herself, she sought out her machine and, seated upon her stool, opened her lunch on her lap. There she sat listening to the chatter and comment about her. It was, for the most part, silly and graced by the current slang. Several of the men in the room exchanged compliments with the girls at long range.

8. **socialism.** System in which the state owns the means of production and distribution and provides for the needs of its citizens; here, it implies concern for workers' well-being

Words For Everyday Use

mod • i • fy • ing (mäd´ə fī´iŋ) *adj.*, changing

au • di • ble (ôd´ə bəl) *adj.*, able to be heard

un • re • mu • ner • a • tive (un ri myo͞o´ nə rāt´iv) *adj.*, giving no payment or reward

sor • did (sôr´did) *adj.*, dirty; filthy

"Say, Kitty," called one to a girl who was doing a waltz step in a few feet of space near one of the windows, "are you going to the ball with me?"

"Look out, Kitty," called another, "you'll jar your back hair."

"Go on, Rubber," was her only comment.

▶ How does Carrie feel about her coworkers?

▶ What "average feminine distinction" does Carrie make? How would you characterize the narrator's attitude toward women?

▶ Explain whether Carrie's coworkers are all low and uncouth or if she is judging them only by their outward appearances.

As Carrie listened to this and much more of similar familiar badinage among the men and girls, she instinctively withdrew into herself. She was not used to this type, and felt that there was something hard and low about it all. She feared that the young boys about would address such remarks to her—boys who, beside Drouet, seemed uncouth and ridiculous. She made the average feminine distinction between clothes, putting worth, goodness, and distinction in a dress suit, and leaving all the unlovely qualities and those beneath notice in overalls and jumper.

She was glad when the short half hour was over and the wheels began to whirr again. Though wearied, she would be inconspicuous. This illusion ended when another young man passed along the aisle and poked her indifferently in the ribs with his thumb. She turned about, indignation leaping to her eyes, but he had gone on and only once turned to grin. She found it difficult to conquer an inclination to cry.

The girl next to her noticed her state of mind. "Don't you mind," she said. "He's too fresh."

Carrie said nothing, but bent over her work. She felt as though she could hardly endure such a life. Her idea of work had been so entirely different. All during the long afternoon she thought of the city outside and its imposing show, crowds, and fine buildings. Columbia City and the better side of her home life came back. By three o'clock she was sure it must be six, and by four it seemed as if they had forgotten to note the hour and were letting all work overtime. The foreman became a true ogre, prowling constantly about, keeping her tied down to her miserable task. What she heard of the conversation about her only made her feel sure that she did not want to make friends with any of these. When six o'clock came she hurried eagerly away, her arms aching and her limbs stiff from sitting in one position.

As she passed out along the hall after getting her hat, a young machine hand, attracted by her looks, made bold to jest with her.

Words For Everyday Use

bad • i • nage (bad´'n äzh´) *n.*, playful, teasing talk

in • dig • na • tion (in´dig nā´shən) *n.*, anger in reaction to injustice

in • cli • na • tion (in klə nā´shən) *n.*, tendency; urge

o • gre (ō´gər) *n.*, hideous tyrant

jest (jest) *vt.*, joke

"Say, Maggie," he called, "if you wait, I'll walk with you."

It was thrown so straight in her direction that she knew who was meant, but never turned to look.

In the crowded elevator, another dusty, toil-stained youth tried to make an impression on her by leering in her face.

One young man, waiting on the walk outside for the appearance of another, grinned at her as she passed.

"Ain't going my way, are you?" he called jocosely.

Carrie turned her face to the west with a subdued heart. As she turned the corner, she saw through the great shiny window the small desk at which she had applied. There were the crowds, hurrying with the same buzz and energy-yielding enthusiasm. She felt a slight relief, but it was only at her escape. She felt ashamed in the face of better dressed girls who went by. She felt as though she should be better served, and her heart revolted.

Words For Everyday Use

leer (lir´) *vi.,* look at with evil appetite or malicious triumph

jo • cose • ly (jō cōs lē) *adv.,* playfully; jokingly

CHAPTER 5

A Glittering Night-Flower: The Use of a Name

► *What effect has Carrie's letter had upon Drouet?*

Drouet did not call that evening. After receiving the letter, he had laid aside all thought of Carrie for the time being and was floating around having what he considered a gay time. On this particular evening he dined at "Rector's," a restaurant of some local fame, which occupied a basement at Clark and Monroe Streets. Thereafter he visited the resort of Fitzgerald and Moy's in Adams Street, opposite the imposing Federal Building. There he leaned over the splendid bar and swallowed a glass of plain whiskey and purchased a couple of cigars, one of which he lighted. This to him represented in part high life—a fair sample of what the whole must be.

► *What type of lifestyle does Drouet admire? How does Drouet wish others to perceive him?*

Drouet was not a drinker in excess. He was not a moneyed man. He only craved the best, as his mind conceived it, and such doings seemed to him a part of the best. Rector's, with its polished marble walls and floor, its profusion of lights, its show of china and silverware, and, above all, its reputation as a resort for actors and professional men, seemed to him the proper place for a successful man to go. He loved fine clothes, good eating, and particularly the company and acquaintanceship of successful men. When dining, it was a source of keen satisfaction to him to know that Joseph Jefferson was wont[1] to come to this same place, or that Henry E. Dixie, a well-known performer of the day, was then only a few tables off. At Rector's he could always obtain this satisfaction, for there one could encounter politicians, brokers, actors, some rich young "rounders" of the town, all eating and drinking amid a buzz of popular commonplace conversation.

► *Why does Drouet enjoy dining at Rector's?*

"That's So-and-so over there," was a common remark of these gentlemen among themselves, particularly among those who had not yet reached, but hoped to do so, the dazzling height which money to dine here lavishly represented.

"You don't say so," would be the reply.

"Why, yes, didn't you know that? Why, he's manager of the Grand Opera House."

---

1. **wont.** Accustomed

Words For Everyday Use

pro • fu • sion (prō fyo͞o zhən) *n.*, rich or lavish supply

When these things would fall upon Drouet's ears, he would straighten himself a little more stiffly and eat with solid comfort. If he had any vanity, this augmented it, and if he had any ambition, this stirred it. He would be able to flash a roll of greenbacks too some day. As it was, he could eat where they did.

◄ *What ambition for the future does Drouet have?*

His preference for Fitzgerald and Moy's Adams Street place was another yard off the same cloth. This was really a gorgeous saloon from a Chicago standpoint. Like Rector's, it was also ornamented with a blaze of incandescent lights, held in handsome chandeliers. The floors were of brightly colored tiles, the walls a composition of rich, dark, polished wood, which reflected the light, and colored stucco-work, which gave the place a very sumptuous appearance. The long bar was a blaze of lights, polished woodwork, colored and cut glassware, and many fancy bottles. It was a truly swell saloon, with rich screens, fancy wines, and a line of bar goods unsurpassed in the country.

At Rector's, Drouet had met Mr. G. W. Hurstwood, manager of Fitzgerald and Moy's. He had been pointed out as a very successful and well-known man about town. Hurstwood looked the part, for, besides being slightly under forty, he had a good, stout constitution, an active manner, and a solid, substantial air, which was composed in part of his fine clothes, his clean linen, his jewels, and, above all, his own sense of his importance. Drouet immediately conceived a notion of him as being someone worth knowing, and was glad not only to meet him, but to visit the Adams Street bar thereafter whenever he wanted a drink or a cigar.

◄ *Who manages Fitzgerald and Moy's? What reputation does this person have? What composes his "solid, substantial air"?*

Hurstwood was an interesting character after his kind. He was shrewd and clever in many little things, and capable of creating a good impression. His managerial position was fairly important—a kind of stewardship which was imposing, but lacked financial control. He had risen by perseverance and industry, through long years of service, from the position of barkeeper in a commonplace saloon to his present altitude. He had a little office in the place, set off in polished cherry and grill-work, where he kept, in a roll-top desk, the rather simple accounts of the place—supplies ordered and needed. The chief executive and financial functions devolved upon the owners—Messrs. Fitzgerald and Moy—and upon a cashier who looked after the money taken in.

Words For Everyday Use

aug • ment (ôg ment´) *vt.*, add to

in • can • des • cent (in´ kən des´ ənt) *adj.*, glowing

sump • tu • ous (sump´cho͞o əs) *adj.*, richly splendid

stout (stout) *adj.*, strong, sturdy; fat

de • volve (di välv´) *vt.*, fall

▶ *What does Hurstwood's job entail?*

▶ *How does the narrator classify Hurstwood?*

▶ *Why does Hurstwood like Drouet?*

For the most part he lounged about, dressed in excellent tailored suits of imported goods, a solitaire[2] ring, a fine blue diamond in his tie, a striking vest of some new pattern, and a watch chain of solid gold, which held a charm of rich design, and a watch of the latest make and engraving. He knew by name, and could greet personally with a "Well, old fellow," hundreds of actors, merchants, politicians, and the general run of successful characters about town, and it was part of his success to do so. He had a finely graduated scale of informality and friendship, which improved from the "How do you do?" addressed to the fifteen-dollar-a-week clerks and office *attachés,*[3] who, by long frequenting of the place, became aware of his position, to the "Why, old man, how are you?" which he addressed to those noted or rich individuals who knew him and were inclined to be friendly. There was a class, however, too rich, too famous, or too successful, with whom he could not attempt any familiarity of address, and with these he was professionally tactful, assuming a grave and dignified attitude, paying them the deference which would win their good feeling without in the least compromising his own bearing and opinions. There were, in the last place, a few good followers, neither rich nor poor, famous, nor yet remarkably successful, with whom he was friendly on the score of good-fellowship. These were the kind of men with whom he would converse longest and most seriously. He loved to go out and have a good time once in a while—to go to the races, the theaters, the sporting entertainments at some of the clubs. He kept a horse and neat trap,[4] had his wife and two children, who were well established in a neat house on the North Side near Lincoln Park, and was altogether a very acceptable individual of our great American upper class—the first grade below the luxuriously rich.

Hurstwood liked Drouet. The latter's genial nature and dressy appearance pleased him. He knew that Drouet was only a traveling salesman—and not one of many years at that—but the firm of Bartlett, Caryoe & Company was a large and prosperous house, and Drouet stood well. Hurstwood knew Caryoe quite well, having drunk a glass

2. **solitaire.** Gem, such as a diamond, that is set alone
3. ***attachés.*** Staff persons holding special or important duties
4. **trap.** Carriage

Words For Everyday Use

def • er • ence (def´ər əns) *n.,* courteous respect

now and then with him, in company with several others, when the conversation was general. Drouet had what was a help in his business, a moderate sense of humor, and could tell a good story when the occasion required. He could talk races with Hurstwood, tell interesting incidents concerning himself and his experiences with women, and report the state of trade in the cities which he visited, and so managed to make himself almost invariably agreeable. Tonight he was particularly so, since his report to the company had been favorably commented upon, his new samples had been satisfactorily selected, and his trip marked out for the next six weeks.

"Why, hello, Charlie, old man," said Hurstwood, as Drouet came in that evening about eight o'clock. "How goes it?" The room was crowded.

Drouet shook hands, beaming good nature, and they strolled toward the bar.

"Oh, all right."

"I haven't seen you in six weeks. When did you get in?"

"Friday," said Drouet. "Had a fine trip."

"Glad of it," said Hurstwood, his black eyes lit with a warmth which half displaced the cold make-believe that usually dwelt in them. "What are you going to take?" he added, as the barkeeper, in snowy jacket and tie, leaned toward them from behind the bar. "Old Pepper," said Drouet.

"A little of the same for me," put in Hurstwood.

"How long are you in town this time?" inquired Hurstwood.

"Only until Wednesday. I'm going up to St. Paul."

"George Evans was in here Saturday and said he saw you in Milwaukee last week."

"Yes, I saw George," returned Drouet. "Great old boy, isn't he? We had quite a time there together."

The barkeeper was setting out the glasses and bottle before them, and they now poured out the draught as they talked, Drouet filling his to within a third of full, as was considered proper, and Hurstwood taking the barest suggestion of whiskey and modifying it with seltzer.

"What's become of Caryoe?" remarked Hurstwood. "I haven't seen him around here in two weeks."

"Laid up, they say," exclaimed Drouet. "Say, he's a gouty[5] old boy!"

"Made a lot of money in his time, though, hasn't he?"

"Yes, wads of it," returned Drouet. "He won't live much longer. Barely comes down to the office now."

"Just one boy, hasn't he?" asked Hurstwood.

5. **gouty.** Having a form of arthritis aggravated by rich food and drink

▶ *Of what is Hurstwood a picture?*

▶ *What "anomaly," or strange social institution, does the narrator believe should be explained?*

▶ *What motivation does the narrator provide for the crowd of men who gather in this particular place?*

"Yes, and a swift-pacer," laughed Drouet.

"I guess he can't hurt the business very much, though, with the other members all there."

"No, he can't injure that any, I guess."

Hurstwood was standing, his coat open, his thumbs in his pockets, the light on his jewels and rings relieving them with agreeable distinctness. He was the picture of fastidious comfort.

To one not inclined to drink, and gifted with a more serious turn of mind, such a bubbling, chattering, glittering chamber must ever seem an anomaly, a strange commentary on nature and life. Here come the moths, in endless procession, to bask in the light of the flame. Such conversation as one may hear would not warrant a commendation of the scene upon intellectual grounds. It seems plain that schemers would choose more sequestered quarters to arrange their plans, that politicians would not gather here in company to discuss anything save formalities, where the sharp-eared may hear, and it would scarcely be justified on the score of thirst, for the majority of those who frequent these more gorgeous places have no craving for liquor. Nevertheless, the fact that here men gather, here chatter, here love to pass and rub elbows, must be explained upon some grounds. It must be that a strange bundle of passions and vague desires give rise to such a curious social institution or it would not be.

Drouet, for one, was lured as much by his longing for pleasure as by his desire to shine among his betters. The many friends he met here dropped in because they craved, without, perhaps, consciously analyzing it, the company, the glow, the atmosphere which they found. One might take it, after all, as an augur of the better social order, for the things which they satisfied here, though sensory, were not evil. No evil could come out of the contemplation of an expensively decorated chamber. The worst effect of such a thing would be, perhaps, to stir up in the material-minded an ambition to arrange their lives upon a similarly splendid basis. In the last analysis, that would scarcely be called the fault of the decorations, but rather of the innate trend of the mind. That such a scene might stir the less expensively dressed to emulate the more expensively dressed could scarcely be laid at the door of anything save the false ambition of the minds of those so affected. Remove the element so thoroughly and solely

Words For Everyday Use

fas • tid • i • ous (fas tid´ē əs) *adj.*, immaculate
bask (bask) *vi.*, warm oneself pleasantly
com • men • da • tion (kam´ən dā´shən) *n.*, act of praise
se • ques • tered (si kwes´tərd) *adj.*, secluded
au • gur (ô´ gər) *n.*, omen
em • u • late (em´yo͞o lāt´) *vt.*, imitate

complained of—liquor—and there would not be one to gainsay the qualities of beauty and enthusiasm which would remain. The pleased eye with which our modern restaurants of fashion are looked upon is proof of this assertion.

Yet, here is the fact of the lighted chamber, the dressy, greedy company, the small, self-interested palaver, the disorganized, aimless, wandering mental action which it represents—the love of light and show and finery which, to one outside, under the serene light of the eternal stars, must seem a strange and shiny thing. Under the stars and sweeping night winds, what a lamp-flower it must bloom; a strange, glittering night-flower, odor-yielding, insect-drawing, insect-infested rose of pleasure.

◄ How does the narrator characterize the people who attend this bar? Does the narrator admire them?

"See that fellow coming in there?" said Hurstwood, glancing at a gentleman just entering, arrayed in a high hat and Prince Albert coat,[6] his fat cheeks puffed and red as with good eating.

"No, where?" said Drouet.

"There," said Hurstwood, indicating the direction by a cast of his eye, "the man with the silk hat."

"Oh, yes," said Drouet, now affecting not to see. "Who is he?"

"That's Jules Wallace, the spiritualist."

Drouet followed him with his eyes, much interested.

"Doesn't look much like a man who sees spirits, does he?" said Drouet.

"Oh, I don't know," returned Hurstwood. "He's got the money, all right," and a little twinkle passed over his eyes.

"I don't go much on those things, do you?" asked Drouet.

"Well, you never can tell," said Hurstwood. "There may be something to it. I wouldn't bother about it myself, though. By the way," he added, "are you going anywhere tonight?"

"'The Hole in the Ground,'" said Drouet, mentioning the popular farce[7] of the time.

"Well, you'd better be going. It's half after eight already," and he drew out his watch.

The crowd was already thinning out considerably—some bound for the theaters, some to their clubs, and some to that most fascinating of all the pleasures—for the type of man there represented, at least—the ladies.

---

6. **Prince Albert coat.** Man's long double-breasted dress coat named after Prince Albert Edward, later Edward VII of England

7. **farce.** Exaggerated comedy

Words For Everyday Use

gain • say (gān sā´) *vt.,* speak out against, contradict

pa • lav • er (pə lav´ər) *n.,* idle chatter

▶ *To whom is Drouet referring when he mentions this "little peach"?*

"Yes, I will," said Drouet.

"Come around after the show. I have something I want to show you," said Hurstwood.

"Sure," said Drouet, elated.

"You haven't anything on hand for the night, have you?" added Hurstwood.

"Not a thing."

"Well, come round, then."

"I struck a little peach coming in on the train Friday," remarked Drouet, by way of parting. "By George, that's so, I must go and call on her before I go away."

"Oh, never mind her," Hurstwood remarked.

"Say, she was a little dandy, I tell you," went on Drouet confidentially, and trying to impress his friend.

"Twelve o'clock," said Hurstwood.

"That's right," said Drouet, going out.

Thus was Carrie's name bandied about in the most frivolous and gay of places, and that also when the little toiler was bemoaning her narrow lot, which was almost inseparable from the early stages of this, her unfolding fate.

Words For Everyday Use

be • moan (bē mōn´) *vt.*, mourn, complain of

CHAPTER 6

The Machine and the Maiden: A Knight of Today

At the flat that evening Carrie felt a new phase of its atmosphere. The fact that it was unchanged, while her feelings were different, increased her knowledge of its character. Minnie, after the good spirits Carrie manifested at first, expected a fair report. Hanson supposed that Carrie would be satisfied.

◄ *What do Minnie and Hanson assume about Carrie? What does she say to contradict their expectations?*

"Well," he said, as he came in from the hall in his working clothes, and looked at Carrie through the dining room door, "how did you make out?"

"Oh," said Carrie, "it's pretty hard. I don't like it."

There was an air about her which showed plainer than any words that she was both weary and disappointed.

"What sort of work is it?" he asked, lingering a moment as he turned upon his heel to go into the bathroom.

"Running a machine," answered Carrie.

It was very evident that it did not concern him much, save from the side of the flat's success. He was irritated a shade because it could not have come about in the throw of fortune for Carrie to be pleased.

◄ *Why does Carrie's comment about her job irritate Hanson?*

Minnie worked with less elation than she had just before Carrie arrived. The sizzle of the meat frying did not sound quite so pleasing now that Carrie had reported her discontent. To Carrie, the one relief of the whole day would have been a jolly home, a sympathetic reception, a bright supper table, and someone to say: "Oh, well, stand it a little while. You will get something better," but now this was ashes. She began to see that they looked upon her complaint as unwarranted, and that she was supposed to work on and say nothing. She knew that she was to pay four dollars for her board and room, and now she felt that it would be an exceedingly gloomy round, living with these people.

◄ *What would have made Carrie's situation more tolerable?*

Minnie was no companion for her sister—she was too old. Her thoughts were staid and solemnly adapted to a condition. If Hanson had any pleasant thoughts or happy feelings he concealed them. He seemed to do all his mental operations

◄ *In what ways does Carrie differ from her sister and brother-in-law?*

Words For Everyday Use

e • la • tion (ē lā´shən) *n.,* joy or high spirits
un • war • rant • ed (un wôr´ənt əd) *adj.,* unjustified
staid (stād) *vi.,* resisting change; fixed

without the aid of physical expression. He was as still as a deserted chamber. Carrie, on the other hand, had the blood of youth and some imagination. Her day of love and the mysteries of courtship were still ahead. She could think of things she would like to do, of clothes she would like to wear, and of places she would like to visit. These were the things upon which her mind ran, and it was like meeting with opposition at every turn to find no one here to call forth or respond to her feelings.

She had forgotten, in considering and explaining the result of her day, that Drouet might come. Now, when she saw how unreceptive these two people were, she hoped he would not. She did not know exactly what she would do or how she would explain to Drouet, if he came. After supper she changed her clothes. When she was trimly dressed she was rather a sweet little being, with large eyes and a sad mouth. Her face expressed the mingled expectancy, dissatisfaction, and depression she felt. She wandered about after the dishes were put away, talked a little with Minnie, and then decided to go down and stand in the door at the foot of the stairs. If Drouet came, she could meet him there. Her face took on the semblance of a look of happiness as she put on her hat to go below.

"Carrie doesn't seem to like her place very well," said Minnie to her husband when the latter came out, paper in hand, to sit in the dining room a few minutes.

"She ought to keep it for a time, anyhow," said Hanson. "Has she gone downstairs?"

"Yes," said Minnie.

"I'd tell her to keep it if I were you. She might be here weeks without getting another one."

Minnie said she would, and Hanson read his paper.

"If I were you," he said a little later, "I wouldn't let her stand in the door down there. It don't look good."

"I'll tell her," said Minnie.

The life of the streets continued for a long time to interest Carrie. She never wearied of wondering where the people in the cars were going or what their enjoyments were. Her imagination trod a very narrow round, always winding up at points which concerned money, looks, clothes, or enjoyment. She would have a far-off thought of Columbia City

► *What does the narrator say about Carrie's powers of imagination?*

Words For Everyday Use

sem • blance (sem´ bləns) *n.,* appearance

now and then, or an irritating rush of feeling concerning her experiences of the present day, but, on the whole, the little world about her enlisted her whole attention.

The first floor of the building, of which Hanson's flat was the third, was occupied by a bakery, and to this, while she was standing there, Hanson came down to buy a loaf of bread. She was not aware of his presence until he was quite near her.

"I'm after bread," was all he said as he passed.

The contagion of thought here demonstrated itself. While Hanson really came for bread, the thought dwelt with him that now he would see what Carrie was doing. No sooner did he draw near her with that in mind than she felt it. Of course, she had no understanding of what put it into her head, but, nevertheless, it aroused in her the first shade of real antipathy to him. She knew now that she did not like him. He was suspicious.

A thought will color a world for us. The flow of Carrie's meditations had been disturbed, and Hanson had not long gone upstairs before she followed. She had realized with the lapse of the quarter hours that Drouet was not coming, and somehow she felt a little resentful, a little as if she had been forsaken—was not good enough. She went upstairs, where everything was silent. Minnie was sewing by a lamp at the table. Hanson had already turned in for the night. In her weariness and disappointment Carrie did no more than announce that she was going to bed.

◄ *How does Carrie feel when Drouet does not show up to visit?*

"Yes, you'd better," returned Minnie. "You've got to get up early, you know."

The morning was no better. Hanson was just going out the door as Carrie came from her room. Minnie tried to talk with her during breakfast, but there was not much of interest which they could mutually discuss. As on the previous morning, Carrie walked downtown, for she began to realize now that her four-fifty would not even allow her carfare after she paid her board. This seemed a miserable arrangement. But the morning light swept away the first misgivings of the day, as morning light is ever wont to do.

At the shoe factory she put in a long day, scarcely so wearisome as the preceding, but considerably less novel. The head foreman, on his round, stopped by her machine.

"Where did you come from?" he inquired.

Words For Everyday Use

en • list (fas tid´ē əs) *vt.*, engage

con • ta • gion (kən tā´jən) *n.*, spread of something from one thing to another

an • tip • a • thy (an tip´ə thē) *n.*, strong dislike

for • sak • en (fôr sāk´ən) *adj.*, abandoned

mis • giv • ing (mis´giv´iŋ) *n.*, disturbed feeling of fear, doubt, apprehension

"Mr. Brown hired me," she replied.

"Oh, he did, eh!" and then, "See that you keep things going."

The machine girls impressed her even less favorably. They seemed satisfied with their lot, and were in a sense "common." Carrie had more imagination than they. She was not used to slang. Her instinct in the matter of dress was naturally better. She disliked to listen to the girl next to her, who was rather hardened by experience.

► *In what ways does Carrie differ from the other machine girls?*

"I'm going to quit this," she heard her remark to her neighbor. "What with the stipend and being up late, it's too much for me health."

They were free with the fellows, young and old, about the place, and exchanged banter in rude phrases, which at first shocked her. She saw that she was taken to be of the same sort and addressed accordingly.

"Hello," remarked one of the stout-wristed sole-workers to her at noon. "You're a daisy." He really expected to hear the common "Aw! go chase yourself!" in return, and was sufficiently abashed, by Carrie's silently moving away, to retreat, awkwardly grinning.

That night at the flat she was even more lonely—the dull situation was becoming harder to endure. She could see that the Hansons seldom or never had any company. Standing at the street door looking out, she ventured to walk out a little way. Her easy gait and idle manner attracted attention of an offensive but common sort. She was slightly taken back at the overtures of a well-dressed man of thirty, who in passing looked at her, reduced his pace, turned back, and said:

"Out for a little stroll, are you, this evening?"

Carrie looked at him in amazement, and then summoned sufficient thought to reply: "Why, I don't know you," backing away as she did so.

"Oh, that don't matter," said the other affably.

She bandied no more words with him, but hurried away, reaching her own door quite out of breath. There was something in the man's look which frightened her.

During the remainder of the week it was very much the same. One or two nights she found herself too tired to walk home and expended carfare. She was not very strong, and sitting all day affected her back. She went to bed one night before Hanson.

Words For Everyday Use

gait (gāt) *n.,* manner of walking

af • fa • bly (af´ə blē) *adv.,* in a friendly manner

Transplantation is not always successful in the matter of flowers or maidens. It requires sometimes a richer soil, a better atmosphere to continue even a natural growth. It would have been better if her acclimatization had been more gradual—less rigid. She would have done better if she had not secured a position so quickly, and had seen more of the city which she constantly troubled to know about.

◄ *To what is Carrie's move to the city compared? What would have made the transition easier for her?*

On the first morning it rained she found that she had no umbrella. Minnie loaned her one of hers, which was worn and faded. There was the kind of vanity in Carrie that troubled at this. She went to one of the great department stores and bought herself one, using a dollar and a quarter of her small store to pay for it.

"What did you do that for, Carrie?" asked Minnie when she saw it.

"Oh, I need one," said Carrie.

"You foolish girl."

Carrie resented this, though she did not reply. She was not going to be a common shop-girl, she thought; they need not think it, either.

On the first Saturday night Carrie paid her board, four dollars. Minnie had a quaver of conscience as she took it, but did not know how to explain to Hanson if she took less. That worthy gave up just four dollars less toward the household expenses with a smile of satisfaction. He contemplated increasing his Building and Loan payments. As for Carrie, she studied over the problem of finding clothes and amusement on fifty cents a week. She brooded over this until she was in a state of mental rebellion.

◄ *How much money does Carrie have left each week after paying her board? How does she feel about this situation?*

"I'm going up the street for a walk," she said after supper.

"Not alone are you?" asked Hanson.

"Yes," returned Carrie.

"I wouldn't," said Minnie.

"I want to see *something*," said Carrie, and by the tone she put into the last word they realized for the first time she was not pleased with them.

"What's the matter with her?" asked Hanson, when she went into the front room to get her hat.

"I don't know," said Minnie.

"Well, she ought to know better than to want to go out alone."

◄ *What behavior is considered improper in a young woman?*

Words For Everyday Use

trans • plan • ta • tion (trans´plan tā´shen) *n.,* resettlement from one place to another

ac • cli • ma • ti • za • tion (ə kli´mət tə zā´shen) *n.,* process of growing used to different circumstances

qua • ver (kwā´vər) *n.,* shiver

Carrie did not go very far, after all. She returned and stood in the door. The next day they went out to Garfield Park, but it did not please her. She did not look well enough. In the shop next day she heard the highly colored reports which girls give of their trivial amusements. They had been happy. On several days it rained and she used up carfare. One night she got thoroughly soaked, going to catch the car at Van Buren Street. All that evening she sat alone in the front room looking out upon the street, where the lights were reflected on the wet pavements, thinking. She had imagination enough to be moody.

On Saturday she paid another four dollars and pocketed her fifty cents in despair. The speaking acquaintanceship which she formed with some of the girls at the shop discovered to her the fact that they had more of their earnings to use for themselves than she did. They had young men of the kind whom she, since her experience with Drouet, felt above, who took them about. She came to thoroughly dislike the lightheaded young fellows of the shop. Not one of them had a show of refinement. She saw only their workday side.

► *What new problem does winter weather create for Carrie?*

There came a day when the first premonitory blast of winter swept over the city. It scudded the fleecy clouds in the heavens, trailed long, thin streamers of smoke from the tall stacks, and raced about the streets and corners in sharp and sudden puffs. Carrie now felt the problem of winter clothes. What was she to do? She had no winter jacket, no hat, no shoes. It was difficult to speak to Minnie about this, but at last she summoned the courage.

"I don't know what I'm going to do about clothes," she said one evening when they were together. "I need a hat."

Minnie looked serious.

"Why don't you keep part of your money and buy yourself one?" she suggested, worried over the situation which the withholding of Carrie's money would create.

"I'd like to for a week or so, if you don't mind," ventured Carrie.

"Could you pay two dollars?" asked Minnie.

Carrie readily acquiesced, glad to escape the trying situation, and liberal now that she saw a way out. She was elated and began figuring at once. She needed a hat first of all. How Minnie explained to Hanson she never knew. He said nothing

Words For Everyday Use

pre • mon • i • tor • y (prē män´ i tôr´ē) *adj.*, warning
scud (skud) *vt.*, blow swiftly before the wind
fleec • y (flēs´ ē) *adj.*, soft, light, and woolly

at all, but there were thoughts in the air which left disagreeable impressions.

The new arrangement might have worked if sickness had not intervened. It blew up cold after a rain one afternoon when Carrie was still without a jacket. She came out of the warm shop at six and shivered as the wind struck her. In the morning she was sneezing, and going downtown made it worse. That day her bones ached and she felt lightheaded. Toward evening she felt very ill, and when she reached home was not hungry. Minnie noticed her drooping actions and asked her about herself.

"I don't know," said Carrie. "I feel real bad."

She hung about the stove, suffered a chattering chill, and went to bed sick. The next morning she was thoroughly feverish.

Minnie was truly distressed at this, but maintained a kindly demeanor. Hanson said perhaps she had better go back home for a while. When she got up after three days, it was taken for granted that her position was lost. The winter was near at hand, she had no clothes and now she was out of work.

◄ *What happens as a result of Carrie's illness?*

"I don't know," said Carrie; "I'll go down Monday and see if I can't get something."

If anything, her efforts were more poorly rewarded on this trial than the last. Her clothes were nothing suitable for fall wearing. Her last money she had spent for a hat. For three days she wandered about, utterly dispirited. The attitude of the flat was fast becoming unbearable. She hated to think of going back there each evening. Hanson was so cold. She knew it could not last much longer. Shortly she would have to give up and go home.

◄ *What will happen if Carrie does not soon find work?*

On the fourth day she was downtown all day, having borrowed ten cents for lunch from Minnie. She had applied in the cheapest kind of places without success. She even answered for a waitress in a small restaurant where she saw a card in the window, but they wanted an experienced girl. She moved through the thick throng of strangers, utterly subdued in spirit. Suddenly a hand pulled her arm and turned her about.

"Well, well!" said a voice. In the first glance she beheld Drouet. He was not only rosy-cheeked, but radiant. He was the essence of sunshine and good humor. "Why, how are you, Carrie?" he said. "You're a daisy. Where have you been?"

Carrie smiled under his irresistible flood of geniality.

Words For Everyday Use

ra • di • ant (rā´dē ənt) *adj.,* shining

ge • ni • al • i • ty (jē´nē al´ə tē) *n.,* kind, cheerful sympathy

► *How does Carrie feel about running into Drouet again?*

"I've been out home," she said.

"Well," he said, "I saw you across the street there. I thought it was you. I was just coming out to your place. How are you, anyhow?"

"I'm all right," said Carrie, smiling.

Drouet looked her over and saw something different.

"Well," he said, "I want to talk to you. You're not going anywhere in particular, are you?"

"Not just now," said Carrie.

"Let's go up here and have something to eat. George! but I'm glad to see you again."

She felt so relieved in his radiant presence, so much looked after and cared for, that she assented gladly, though with the slightest air of holding back.

"Well," he said as he took her arm—and there was an exuberance of good-fellowship in the word which fairly warmed the cockles of her heart.

They went through Monroe Street to the old Windsor dining room, which was then a large, comfortable place, with an excellent cuisine and substantial service. Drouet selected a table close by the window, where the busy rout of the street could be seen. He loved the changing panorama of the street—to see and be seen as he dined.

"Now," he said, getting Carrie and himself comfortably settled, "what will you have?"

Carrie looked over the large bill of fare which the waiter handed her without really considering it. She was very hungry, and the things she saw there awakened her desires, but the high prices held her attention. "Half broiled spring chicken—seventy-five. Sirloin steak with mushrooms—one twenty-five." She had dimly heard of these things, but it seemed strange to be called to order from the list.

"I'll fix this," exclaimed Drouet. "Sst! waiter."

That officer of the board, a full-chested, round-faced negro,[1] approached, and inclined his ear.

"Sirloin with mushrooms," said Drouet. "Stuffed tomatoes."

"Yassah," assented the negro, nodding his head.

"Hashed brown potatoes."

"Yassah."

---

1. **negro.** This term for a person of African descent has been replaced by *African American.*

Words For Everyday Use

as • sent (ə sent´) *vi.,* accept

rout (rout) *n.,* mob

"Asparagus."

"Yassah."

"And a pot of coffee."

Drouet turned to Carrie. "I haven't had a thing since breakfast. Just got in from Rock Island. I was going off to dine when I saw you."

Carried smiled and smiled.

"What have you been doing?" he went on. "Tell me all about yourself. How is your sister?"

"She's well," returned Carrie, answering the last query.

He looked at her hard.

"Say," he said, "you haven't been sick, have you?"

Carrie nodded.

"Well, now, that's a blooming shame, isn't it? You don't look very well. I thought you looked a little pale. What have you been doing?"

"Working," said Carrie.

"You don't say so! At what?"

She told him.

"Rhodes, Morgenthau and Scott—why, I know that house. Over here on Fifth Avenue, isn't it? They're a closefisted[2] concern. What made you go there?"

◀ *What does Drouet say about the job Carrie lost? In what way does his attitude compare with that of Minnie and Hanson?*

"I couldn't get anything else," said Carrie frankly.

"Well, that's an outrage," said Drouet. "You oughtn't to be working for those people. Have the factory right back of the store, don't they?"

"Yes," said Carrie.

"That isn't a good house," said Drouet. "You don't want to work at anything like that, anyhow."

He chattered on at a great rate, asking questions, explaining things about himself, telling her what a good restaurant it was, until the waiter returned with an immense tray, bearing the hot savory dishes which had been ordered. Drouet fairly shone in the matter of serving. He appeared to great advantage behind the white napery and silver platters of the table and displaying his arms with a knife and fork. As he cut the meat his rings almost spoke. His new suit creaked as he stretched to reach the plates, break the bread, and pour the coffee. He helped Carrie to a rousing plateful and contributed the warmth of his spirit to her body until she was a new girl. He was a splendid fellow in the true popular understanding of the term, and captivated Carrie completely.

That little soldier of fortune took her good turn in an easy way. She felt a little out of place, but the great room soothed her and the view of the well-dressed throng outside seemed a splendid thing. Ah, what was it not to have money! What

2. **closefisted.** Overly frugal; unwilling to spend money

a thing it was to be able to come in here and dine! Drouet must be fortunate. He rode on trains, dressed in such nice clothes, was so strong, and ate in these fine places. He seemed quite a figure of a man, and she wondered at his friendship and regard for her.

"So you lost your place because you got sick, eh?" he said. "What are you going to do now?"

"Look around," she said, a thought of the need that hung outside this fine restaurant like a hungry dog at her heels passing into her eyes.

"Oh, no," said Drouet, "that won't do. How long have you been looking?"

"Four days," she answered.

► *According to Drouet, why should Carrie not continue to look for work?*

"Think of that!" he said, addressing some problematical individual. "You oughtn't to be doing anything like that. These girls," and he waved an inclusion of all shop and factory girls, "don't get anything. Why, you can't live on it, can you?"

He was a brotherly sort of creature in his demeanor. When he had scouted the idea of that kind of toil, he took another tack. Carrie was really very pretty. Even then, in her commonplace garb, her figure was evidently not bad, and her eyes were large and gentle. Drouet looked at her and his thoughts reached home. She felt his admiration. It was powerfully backed by his liberality and good humor. She felt that she liked him—that she could continue to like him ever so much. There was something even richer than that, running as a hidden strain, in her mind. Every little while her eyes would meet his, and by that means the interchanging current of feeling would be fully connected.

"Why don't you stay downtown and go to the theater with me?" he said, hitching his chair closer. The table was not very wide.

"Oh, I can't," she said.

"What are you going to do tonight?"

"Nothing," she answered, a little drearily.

"You don't like out there where you are, do you?"

"Oh, I don't know."

"What are you going to do if you don't get work?"

"Go back home, I guess."

There was the least quaver in her voice as she said this. Somehow, the influence he was exerting was powerful. They

Words For Everyday Use

scout (skout) *vt.,* reject as absurd

tack (tak) *n.,* course of action

came to an understanding of each other without words—he of her situation, she of the fact that he realized it.

"No," he said, "you can't make it!" genuine sympathy filling his mind for the time. "Let me help you. You take some of my money."

◄ *What does Drouet offer Carrie?*

"Oh, no!" she said, leaning back.

"What are you going to do?" he said.

She sat meditating, merely shaking her head.

He looked at her quite tenderly for his kind. There were some loose bills in his vest pocket—greenbacks. They were soft and noiseless, and he got his fingers about them and crumpled them up in his hand.

"Come on," he said, "I'll see you through all right. Get yourself some clothes."

◄ *What "keynote" does Drouet strike?*

It was the first reference he had made to that subject, and now she realized how bad off she was. In his crude way he had struck the keynote. Her lips trembled a little.

She had her hand out on the table before her. They were quite alone in their corner, and he put his larger, warmer hand over it.

"Aw, come, Carrie," he said, "what can you do alone? Let me help you."

He pressed her hand gently and she tried to withdraw it. At this he held it fast, and she no longer protested. Then he slipped the greenbacks he had into her palm, and when she began to protest, he whispered:

"I'll loan it to you—that's all right. I'll loan it to you."

He made her take it. She felt bound to him by a strange tie of affection now. They went out, and he walked with her far out south toward Polk Street, talking.

◄ *How does Carrie feel once she takes Drouet's money?*

"You don't want to live with those people?" he said in one place, abstractedly. Carrie heard it, but it made only a slight impression.

"Come down and meet me tomorrow," he said, "and we'll go to the matinee. Will you?"

Carrie protested a while, but acquiesced.

"You're not doing anything. Get yourself a nice pair of shoes and a jacket."

She scarcely gave a thought to the complication which would trouble her when he was gone. In his presence, she was of his own hopeful, easy-way-out mood.

"Don't you bother about those people out there," he said at parting. "I'll help you."

Carrie left him, feeling as though a great arm had slipped out before her to draw off trouble. The money she had accepted was two soft, green, handsome ten-dollar bills.

Responding to the Selection

Of the major characters you have met thus far in the novel, whom do you find most admirable? least admirable? most likable? least likable? The narrator points out that Carrie lacks "clever companions." If you were with her during her first few weeks in the city, what advice about her situation and her actions would you give her?

Reviewing the Selection

Recalling and Interpreting

1. **R:** Where is Carrie traveling? Why is she going there? What two possibilities does the narrator say are open to her? Whom does she meet on the train? Describe her new home.

2. **I:** Describe Carrie's personality. Why might it be impossible for her to enjoy living with the Hansons? Why might she be drawn to Drouet? Which of the two possibilities do you believe the narrator has in mind for Carrie? Explain.

3. **R:** What effect does downtown Chicago have upon a person seeking a job? What do most people tell Carrie she lacks? Where does she eventually find a job? How does she feel about the city once she is employed?

4. **I:** Why does the city have this effect upon a person seeking work? In what ways does Carrie's job-hunting experience contradict her expectations? In what ways does this experience reveal her own insignificance? Explain whether you would define Carrie as constant and even-tempered or as capricious and unpredictable. Explain what the narrator means when he states, "It must not be thought that any one could have mistaken her for a nervous, sensitive, high-strung nature, cast unduly upon a cold, calculating, and unpoetic world. Such certainly she was not." How does the narrator intend for the reader to view Carrie?

5. **R:** What does Mr. Brown say to Carrie when she meets him on her first day of work at the shoe factory? What is her job there? What does she think about her female coworkers? about her male coworkers? What does Carrie tell her sister and brother-in-law when asked about her first day of work?

6. **I:** Why is it important that Carrie find work quickly? Given her coworkers' actions and words, do you think Carrie evaluates her coworkers fairly? In what way is she different from them? similar to them? Why do Minnie and Hanson disapprove of Carrie's negative attitude toward her work?

7. **R:** What problem does the colder weather make more pressing for Carrie? What causes Carrie to lose her job? Whom does she run into while looking for work, and what does this person tell her about her old job and her job search? What does this person give her?

8. **I:** Why is Carrie unable simply to go out and buy the things that she needs? How does Carrie feel about running into this person? What does this person represent to her? Why do his comments on her job situation please her? Why does Carrie accept this gift? What does her acceptance represent?

Synthesizing

9. Cite some instances in chapters 1–6 in which characters mistake the surfaces of things—a person's dress, a building's decor—for substance or reality. What does the author believe motivates almost everyone? What does the author seem to be indicating about American society?

10. This story is set at the end of the nineteenth century. At this time, people, especially women, were expected to follow a stricter code of behavior than exists today. Some of Carrie's actions, such as giving Drouet her address, that seem harmless today were considered shocking or scandalous in the time when this novel was written. Which of Carrie's actions do you believe violate the code of proper behavior in her time period? Why does she violate these social taboos? Is she ignorant of proper social behavior, or is she driven to ignore these rules? Explain.

Understanding Literature (QUESTIONS FOR DISCUSSION)

1. **Naturalism. Naturalism** was a literary movement of the late nineteenth and early twentieth centuries that saw actions and events as resulting inevitably from biological or natural forces or from forces in the environment. According to Naturalism, these forces are often beyond the comprehension or control of the characters subjected to them. Taken to its extreme, Naturalism views all events as mechanically determined by external forces, including the decisions people make. Explain how each of the following passages are examples of Naturalism, and explain what they reveal about the effects of the environment on human behavior and actions.

- "The city has its cunning wiles . . . There are large forces which allure with all the soulfulness possible in the most cultured human. The gleam of a thousand lights is often as effective as the persuasive light in a wooing and fascinating eye. Half the undoing of the unsophisticated and natural mind is accomplished by forces wholly superhuman."
- "To the child, the genius with imagination, or the wholly untraveled, the approach to a great city for the first time is a wonderful thing. Particularly if it be evening . . . Ah, the promise of the night. What does it not hold for the weary! What old illusion of hope is not here forever repeated! Says the soul of the toiler to itself, 'I shall soon be free. . . . The streets, the lamps, the lighted chamber set for dining, are for me. The theater, the halls, the parties, the ways of rest and the paths of song—these are mine in the night.'"
- "Minnie was thinking of the resource which Carrie's board would add. . . . Unless Carrie submitted to a solemn round of industry and saw the need of hard work without longing for play, how was her coming to the city to profit them? These thoughts were not those of a cold, hard nature at all. They were the serious reflections of a mind which invariably adjusted itself, without much complaining, to such surroundings as its industry could make for it."

2. Metaphor. A **metaphor** is a figure of speech in which something is spoken or written about as if it were another. This figure of speech invites the reader to make a comparison between the two things. When describing Fitzgerald and Moy's bar on page 43, Dreiser writes, "Yet, here is the fact of the lighted chamber, the dressy, greedy company, the small, self-interested palaver, the disorganized, aimless, wandering mental action which it represents—the love of light and show and finery which, to one outside, under the serene light of the eternal stars, must seem a strange and shiny thing. Under the stars and sweeping night winds, what a lamp-flower it must bloom; a strange, glittering night-flower, odor-yielding, insect-drawing, insect-infested rose of pleasure." What two things are being compared? What might the insects on the rose be? In what way does the light of the chamber contrast with the natural starlight?

3. Narrator. A **narrator** is one who tells a story. While in some works of fiction, the narrator is unobtrusive, rarely making his or her views of matters known to the reader, in

Sister Carrie, the voice of the narrator is quite noticeable. In addition to being omniscient, or able to know the internal workings of the minds of the characters in the story, the narrator also expresses his own opinion on the characters and events in the story. For example, in the passage quoted in question 4 on page 56, the narrator tells the reader how he or she should view Carrie. What attitude toward women does the narrator express? Point to certain passages in which the narrator displays this attitude. Reexamine the following passage: "When a girl leaves her home at eighteen, she does one of two things. Either she falls into saving hands and becomes better, or she rapidly assumes the cosmopolitan standard of virtue and becomes worse. Of an intermediate balance, under the circumstances, there is no possibility." What assumptions and attitudes about young women are revealed in this passage? Which of the two possible futures do you think the narrator intends the reader to assume will be Carrie's? How can you tell? Does the narrator ever allow the reader to assume that there is a chance that Carrie will not "assume the cosmopolitan standard of virtue and become worse"? What is your opinion of the narrator's comments, judgments, and attitudes?

CHAPTER 7

The Lure of the Material: Beauty Speaks for Itself

The true meaning of money yet remains to be popularly explained and comprehended. When each individual realizes for himself that this thing primarily stands for and should only be accepted as a moral due—that it should be paid out as honestly stored energy, and not as a usurped privilege—many of our social, religious, and political troubles will have permanently passed. As for Carrie, her understanding of the moral significance of money was the popular understanding, nothing more. The old definition: "Money: something everybody else has and I must get," would have expressed her understanding of it thoroughly. Some of it she now held in her hand—two soft, green ten-dollar bills—and she felt that she was immensely better off for the having of them. It was something that was power in itself. One of her order of mind would have been content to be cast away upon a desert island with a bundle of money, and only the long strain of starvation would have taught her that in some cases it could have no value. Even then she would have had no conception of the relative value of the thing; her one thought would, undoubtedly, have concerned the pity of having so much power and the inability to use it.

▶ *What is Carrie's attitude toward money?*

▶ *How would Carrie feel bout being sent to a desert island with a bundle of money? What wouldn't she realize?*

The poor girl thrilled as she walked away from Drouet. She felt ashamed in part because she had been weak enough to take it, but her need was so dire, she was still glad. Now she would have a nice new jacket! Now she would buy a nice pair of pretty button shoes. She would get stockings, too, and a skirt, and, and—until already, as in the matter of her prospective salary, she had got beyond, in her desires, twice the purchasing power of her bills.

She conceived a true estimate of Drouet. To her, and indeed to all the world, he was a nice, good-hearted man. There was nothing evil in the fellow. He gave her the money out of a good heart—out of a realization of her want. He would not have given the same amount to a poor young

▶ *What "true estimate" of Drouet does Carrie form?*

Words For Everyday Use

u • surped (yōō zurpd´) *adj.*, taken by force or without right
dire (dīr) *adj.*, urgent
con • ceive (kən sēv´) *vt.*, form in one's mind

man, but we must not forget that a poor young man could not, in the nature of things, have appealed to him like a poor young girl. Femininity affected his feelings. He was the creature of an inborn desire. Yet no beggar could have caught his eye and said, "My God, mister, I'm starving," but he would gladly have handed out what was considered the proper portion to give beggars and thought no more about it. There would have been no speculation, no philosophizing. He had no mental process in him worthy the dignity of either of those terms. In his good clothes and fine health, he was a merry, unthinking moth of the lamp. Deprived of his position, and struck by a few of the involved and baffling forces which sometimes play upon man he would have been as helpless as Carrie—as helpless, as nonunderstanding, as pitiable, if you will, as she.

◄ According to the narrator, what is Drouet incapable of doing?

Now, in regard to his pursuit of women, he meant them no harm, because he did not conceive of the relation which he hoped to hold with them as being harmful. He loved to make advances to women, to have them succumb to his charms, not because he was a cold-blooded, dark, scheming villain, but because his inborn desire urged him to that as a chief delight. He was vain, he was boastful, he was as deluded by fine clothes as any silly-headed girl. A truly deep-dyed villain could have hornswaggled[1] him as readily as he could have flattered a pretty shop-girl. His fine success as a salesman lay in his geniality and the thoroughly reputable standing of his house. He bobbed about among men, a veritable bundle of enthusiasm—no power worthy the name of intellect, no thoughts worthy the adjective noble, no feelings long continued in one strain. A Madame Sappho[2] would have called him a pig; a Shakespeare would have said "my merry child"; old, drinking Caryoe thought him a clever, successful business man. In short, he was as good as his intellect conceived.

◄ What are Drouet's feelings about the way he interacts with women?

◄ In what way are Carrie and Drouet similar?

The best proof that there was something open and commendable about the man was the fact that Carrie took the money. No deep, sinister soul with ulterior motives could have given her fifteen cents under the guise of friendship. The unintellectual are not so helpless. Nature has taught the

◄ To what is the narrator comparing Carrie? Why?

1. **hornswaggled.** Swindled
2. **Sappho.** Greek lyric poet (c. 610 BC–570 BC)

Words For Everyday Use

spec • u • la • tion (spek´yo͞o lā´shən) *n.,* thinking over the various aspects of a subject
suc • cumb (sə kum´) *vi.,* yield; submit
de • lud • ed (di lo͞od´ed) *adj.,* deceived
ver • i • ta • ble (ver´i tə bəl) *adj.,* real; true
guise (gīz) *n.,* deceptive appearance

beasts of the field to fly when some unheralded danger threatens. She has put into the small, unwise head of the chipmunk the untutored[3] fear of poisons. "He keepeth His creatures whole," was not written of beasts alone. Carrie was unwise, and, therefore, like the sheep in its unwisdom, strong in feeling. The instinct of self-protection, strong in all such natures, was roused but feebly, if at all, by the overtures of Drouet.

When Carrie had gone, he felicitated himself upon her good opinion. By George, it was a shame young girls had to be knocked around like that. Cold weather coming on and no clothes. Tough. He would go around to Fitzgerald and Moy's and get a cigar. It made him feel light of foot as he thought about her.

▶ *What perplexes Carrie? What does she decide?*

Carrie reached home in high good spirits, which she could scarcely conceal. The possession of the money involved a number of points which perplexed her seriously. How should she buy any clothes when Minnie knew that she had no money? She had no sooner entered the flat than this point was settled for her. It could not be done. She could think of no way of explaining.

"How did you come out?" asked Minnie, referring to the day.

Carrie had none of the small deception which could feel one thing and say something directly opposed. She would prevaricate, but it would be in the line of her feelings at least. So instead of complaining when she felt so good, she said:

"I have the promise of something."

"Where?"

"At the Boston Store."

"Is it sure promised?" questioned Minnie.

"Well, I'm to find out tomorrow," returned Carrie, disliking to draw out a lie any longer than was necessary.

Minnie felt the atmosphere of good feeling which Carrie brought with her. She felt now was the time to express to Carrie the state of Hanson's feeling about her entire Chicago venture.

"If you shouldn't get it—" she paused, troubled for an easy way.

"If I don't get something pretty soon, I think I'll go home."

3. **untutored.** Not learned; inborn

Words For Everyday Use

un • her • ald • ed (un her´əld əd) *adj.*, unannounced

o • ver • ture (ō´vər chər) *n.*, opening moves

fe • lic • i • tate (fə lis´i tāt´) *vt.*, congratulate

pre • var • i • cate (pri var´i kāt´) *vi.*, evade the truth

Minnie saw her chance.

"Sven thinks it might be best for the winter, anyhow."

The situation flashed on Carrie at once. They were unwilling to keep her any longer, out of work. She did not blame Minnie, she did not blame Hanson very much. Now, as she sat there digesting the remark, she was glad she had Drouet's money.

◄ *What does Carrie realize?*

"Yes," she said after a few moments, "I thought of doing that."

She did not explain that the thought, however, had aroused all the antagonism of her nature. Columbia City, what was there for her? She knew its dull, little round by heart. Here was the great, mysterious city which was still a magnet for her. What she had seen only suggested its possibilities. Now to turn back on it and live the little old life out there—she almost exclaimed against the thought.

◄ *Why is Carrie opposed to returning to Columbia City?*

She had reached home early and went in the front room to think. What could she do? She could not buy new shoes and wear them here. She would need to save part of the twenty to pay her fare home. She did not want to borrow of Minnie for that. And yet, how could she explain where she even got that money? If she could only get enough to let her out easy.

She went over the tangle again and again. Here, in the morning, Drouet would expect to see her in a new jacket, and that couldn't be. The Hansons expected her to go home, and she wanted to get away, and yet she did not want to go home. In the light of the way they would look on her getting money without work, the taking of it now seemed dreadful. She began to be ashamed. The whole situation depressed her. It was all so clear when she was with Drouet. Now it was all so tangled, so hopeless—much worse than it was before, because she had the semblance of aid in her hand which she could not use.

◄ *What begins to make Carrie feel shame?*

Her spirits sank so that at supper Minnie felt that she must have had another hard day. Carrie finally decided that she would give the money back. It was wrong to take it. She would go down in the morning and hunt for work. At noon she would meet Drouet as agreed and tell him. At this decision her heart sank, until she was the old Carrie of distress.

◄ *What does Carrie decide to do?*

Curiously, she could not hold the money in her hand without feeling some relief. Even after all her depressing conclusions, she could sweep away all thought about the matter and then the twenty dollars seemed a wonderful and delightful thing. Ah, money, money, money! What a thing it was to have. How plenty of it would clear away all these troubles.

In the morning she got up and started out a little early. Her decision to hunt for work was moderately strong, but the money in her pocket, after all her troubling over it, made the

► *How does Carrie feel about looking for work again?*

► *What does Carrie do instead of continuing to look for work?*

work question the least shade less terrible. She walked into the wholesale district, but as the thought of applying came with each passing concern, her heart shrank. What a coward she was, she thought to herself. Yet she had applied so often. It would be the same old story. She walked on and on, and finally did go into one place, with the old result. She came out feeling that luck was against her. It was no use.

Without much thinking, she reached Dearborn Street. Here was the great Fair store with its multitude of delivery wagons about, its long window display, its crowd of shoppers. It readily changed her thoughts, she who was so weary of them. It was here that she had intended to come and get her new things. Now for relief from distress, she thought she would go in and see. She would look at the jackets.

There is nothing in this world more delightful than that middle state in which we mentally balance at times, possessed of the means, lured by desire, and yet deterred by conscience or want of decision. When Carrie began wandering around the store amid the fine displays she was in this mood. Her original experience in this same place had given her a high opinion of its merits. Now she paused at each individual bit of finery, where before she had hurried on. Her woman's heart was warm with desire for them. How would she look in this, how charming that would make her! She came upon the corset[4] counter and paused in rich reverie as she noted the dainty concoctions of color and lace there displayed. If she would only make up her mind, she could have one of those now. She lingered in the jewelry department. She saw the earrings, the bracelets, the pins, the chains. What would she not have given if she could have had them all! She would look fine too, if only she had some of these things.

The jackets were the greatest attraction. When she entered the store, she already had her heart fixed upon the peculiar little tan jacket with large mother-of-pearl[5] buttons which was all the rage that fall. Still she delighted to convince herself that there was nothing she would like better. She went about among the glass cases and racks where these things

4. **corset.** Close-fitting woman's undergarment worn to give a desired figure to the body

5. **mother-of-pearl.** Pearly internal layer of certain shells used in art and ornaments

Words For Everyday Use

de • terred (dē turd´) *adj.,* held back

rev • er • ie (rev´ər ē) *n.,* daydream

con • coc • tion (kən käk´ shun) *n.,* combination of ingredients

were displayed, and satisfied herself that the one she thought of was the proper one. All the time she wavered in mind, now persuading herself that she could buy it right away if she chose, now recalling to herself the actual condition. At last the noon hour was dangerously near, and she had done nothing. She must go now and return the money.

Drouet was on the corner when she came up.

"Hello," he said, "where is the jacket and"—looking down—"the shoes?"

Carrie had thought to lead up to her decision in some intelligent way, but this swept the whole fore-schemed situation by the board.

◄ *What had Carrie planned to do? What happens once she actually sees Drouet?*

"I came to tell you that—that I can't take the money."

"Oh, that's it, is it?" he returned. "Well, you come on with me. Let's go over here to Partridge's."

Carrie walked with him. Behold, the whole fabric of doubt and impossibility had slipped from her mind. She could not get at the points that were so serious, the things she was going to make plain to him.

"Have you had lunch yet? Of course you haven't. Let's go in here," and Drouet turned into one of the very nicely furnished restaurants off State Street, in Monroe.

"I mustn't take the money," said Carrie, after they were settled in a cozy corner, and Drouet had ordered the lunch. "I can't wear those things out there. They—they wouldn't know where I got them."

"What do you want to do," he smiled, "go without them?"

"I think I'll go home," she said, wearily.

"Oh, come," he said, "you've been thinking it over too long. I'll tell you what you do. You say you can't wear them out there. Why don't you rent a furnished room and leave them in that for a week?"

Carrie shook her head. Like all women, she was there to object and be convinced. It was for him to brush the doubts away and clear the path if he could.

◄ *What does the narrator say about "all women"?*

"Why are you going home?" he asked.

"Oh, I can't get anything here."

"They won't keep you?" he remarked, intuitively.

"They can't," said Carrie.

"I'll tell you what you do," he said. "You come with me. I'll take care of you."

◄ *What does Drouet suggest to Carrie? How does she receive his advice?*

Words For Everyday Use

wa • ver (wā´vər) *vi.,* teeter between choices

Carrie heard this passively. The peculiar state which she was in made it sound like the welcome breath of an open door. Drouet seemed of her own spirit and pleasing. He was clean, handsome, well-dressed, and sympathetic. His voice was the voice of a friend.

"What can you do back at Columbia City?" he went on, rousing by the words in Carrie's mind a picture of the dull world she had left. "There isn't anything down there. Chicago's the place. You can get a nice room here and some clothes, and then you can do something."

Carrie looked out through the window into the busy street. There it was, the admirable, great city, so fine when you are not poor. An elegant coach, with a prancing pair of bays, passed by, carrying in its upholstered depths a young lady.

"What will you have if you go back?" asked Drouet. There was no subtle undercurrent to the question. He imagined that she would have nothing at all of the things he thought worthwhile.

Carrie sat still, looking out. She was wondering what she could do. They would be expecting her to go home this week.

Drouet turned to the subject of the clothes she was going to buy.

"Why not get yourself a nice little jacket? You've got to have it. I'll loan you the money. You needn't worry about taking it. You can get yourself a nice room by yourself. I won't hurt you."

Carrie saw the drift, but could not express her thoughts. She felt more than ever the helplessness of her case.

"If I could only get something to do," she said.

► *According to Drouet, why should Carrie follow his advice?*

"Maybe you can," went on Drouet, "if you stay here. You can't if you go away. They won't let you stay out there. Now, why not let me get you a nice room? I won't bother you—you needn't be afraid. Then, when you get fixed up, maybe you could get something."

He looked at her pretty face and it vivified his mental resources. She was a sweet little mortal to him—there was no doubt of that. She seemed to have some power back of her actions. She was not like the common run of store-girls. She wasn't silly.

► *What does the narrator say about Carrie in comparison with Drouet?*

In reality, Carrie had more imagination than he—more taste. It was a finer mental strain in her that made possible her depression and loneliness. Her poor clothes were neat, and she held her head unconsciously in a dainty way.

Words For Everyday Use

viv • i • fy (viv´ə fī´) *vt.,* give life to

"Do you think I could get something?" she asked.

"Sure," he said, reaching over and filling her cup with tea. "I'll help you."

She looked at him, and he laughed reassuringly.

"Now I'll tell you what we'll do. We'll go over here to Partridge's and you pick out what you want. Then we'll look around for a room for you. You can leave the things there. Then we'll go to the show tonight."

Carrie shook her head.

"Well, you can go out to the flat then, that's all right. You don't need to stay in the room. Just take it and leave your things there."

She hung in doubt about this until the dinner was over.

"Let's go over and look at the jackets," he said.

Together they went. In the store they found that shine and rustle of new things which immediately laid hold of Carrie's heart. Under the influence of a good dinner and Drouet's radiating presence, the scheme proposed seemed feasible. She looked about and picked a jacket like the one which she had admired at The Fair. When she got it in her hand it seemed so much nicer. The saleswoman helped her on with it, and, by accident, it fitted perfectly. Drouet's face lightened as he saw the improvement. She looked quite smart.

◄ *What makes Drouet's plan seem "feasible" to Carrie?*

"That's the thing," he said.

Carrie turned before the glass. She could not help feeling pleased as she looked at herself. A warm glow crept into her cheeks.

"That's the thing," said Drouet. "Now pay for it."

"It's nine dollars," said Carrie.

"That's all right—take it," said Drouet.

She reached in her purse and took out one of the bills. The woman asked if she would wear the coat and went off. In a few minutes she was back and the purchase was closed.

From Partridge's they went to a shoe store, where Carrie was fitted for shoes. Drouet stood by, and when he saw how nice they looked, said, "Wear them." Carrie shook her head, however. She was thinking of returning to the flat. He bought her a purse for one thing, and a pair of gloves for another, and let her buy the stockings.

"Tomorrow," he said, "you come down here and buy yourself a skirt."

In all of Carrie's actions there was a touch of misgiving. The deeper she sank into the entanglement, the more she imagined that the thing hung upon the few remaining things she had not done. Since she had not done these, there was a way out.

◄ *Why do you think Carrie feels "a touch of misgiving?" Of what does she try to assure herself?*

► *Whom does Drouet tell Carrie to say she is?*

Drouet knew a place in Wabash Avenue where there were rooms. He showed Carrie the outside of these, and said: "Now, you're my sister." He carried the arrangement off with an easy hand when it came to the selection, looking around, criticizing, opining. "Her trunk will be here in a day or so," he observed to the landlady, who was very pleased.

When they were alone, Drouet did not change in the least. He talked in the same general way as if they were out in the street. Carrie left her things.

"Now," said Drouet, "why don't you move tonight?"

"Oh, I can't," said Carrie.

"Why not?"

"I don't want to leave them so."

He took that up as they walked along the avenue. It was a warm afternoon. The sun had come out and the wind had died down. As he talked with Carrie, he secured an accurate detail of the atmosphere of the flat.

"Come out of it," he said, "they won't care. I'll help you get along."

► *What does Drouet plan to do once Carrie is set up in her new room? What does the narrator seem to imply about Drouet's plans?*

She listened until her misgivings vanished. He would show her about a little and then help her get something. He really imagined that he would. He would be out on the road and she could be working.

"Now, I'll tell you what you do," he said, "you go out there and get whatever you want and come away."

She thought a long time about this. Finally she agreed. He would come out as far as Peoria Street and wait for her. She was to meet him at half-past eight. At half-past five she reached home, and at six her determination was hardened.

"So you didn't get it?" said Minnie, referring to Carrie's story of the Boston Store.

Carrie looked at her out of the corner of her eye. "No," she answered.

"I don't think you'd better try anymore this fall," said Minnie.

Carrie said nothing.

When Hanson came home he wore the same inscrutable demeanor. He washed in silence and went off to read his paper. At dinner Carrie felt a little nervous. The strain of her own plans was considerable, and the feeling that she was not welcome here was strong.

"Didn't find anything, eh?" said Hanson.

Words For Everyday Use

o • pine (ō pīn´) *vt.,* express opinions

in • scru • ta • ble (in skro͞ot´ə bəl) *adj.,* not easily understood

"No."

He turned to his eating again, the thought that it was a burden to have her here dwelling in his mind. She would have to go home, that was all. Once she was away, there would be no more coming back in the spring.

◄ How does Hanson feel about Carrie? Does Carrie realize how he feels?

Carrie was afraid of what she was going to do, but she was relieved to know that this condition was ending. They would not care. Hanson particularly would be glad when she went. He would not care what became of her.

After dinner she went into the bathroom, where they could not disturb her, and wrote a little note.

"Goodbye, Minnie," it read. "I'm not going home. I'm going to stay in Chicago a little while and look for work. Don't worry. I'll be all right."

In the front room Hanson was reading his paper. As usual, she helped Minnie clear away the dishes and straighten up. Then she said:

"I guess I'll stand down at the door a little while." She could scarcely prevent her voice from trembling.

Minnie remembered Hanson's remonstrance.

◄ What does Minnie tell Carrie about standing at the door? In what way will Carrie's response prove true?

"Sven doesn't think it looks good to stand down there," she said.

"Doesn't he?" said Carrie. "I won't do it anymore after this."

She put on her hat and fidgeted around the table in the little bedroom, wondering where to slip the note. Finally she put it under Minnie's hairbrush.

When she had closed the hall door, she paused a moment and wondered what they would think. Some thought of the queerness of her deed affected her. She went slowly down the stairs. She looked back up the lighted step, and then affected to stroll up the street. When she reached the corner she quickened her pace.

As she was hurrying away, Hanson came back to his wife.

"Is Carrie down at the door again?" he asked.

"Yes," said Minnie; "she said she wasn't going to do it anymore."

He went over to the baby where it was playing on the floor and began to poke his finger at it.

Drouet was on the corner waiting, in good spirits.

"Hello, Carrie," he said, as a sprightly figure of a girl drew near him. "Got here safe, did you? Well, we'll take a car."

Words For Everyday Use

re • mon • strance (ri män´strəns) *n.*, protest, warning

CHAPTER 8

Intimations by Winter: An Ambassador Summoned

► *What view does the narrator have of our civilization?*

Among the forces which sweep and play throughout the universe, untutored man is but a wisp in the wind. Our civilization is still in a middle stage, scarcely beast, in that it is no longer wholly guided by instinct; scarcely human, in that it is not yet wholly guided by reason. On the tiger no responsibility rests. We see him aligned by nature with the forces of life—he is born into their keeping and without thought he is protected. We see man far removed from the lairs of the jungles, his innate instincts dulled by too near an approach to free will, his free will not sufficiently developed to replace his instincts and afford him perfect guidance. He is becoming too wise to hearken always to instincts and desires; he is still too weak to always prevail against them. As a beast, the forces of life aligned him with them; as a man, he has not yet wholly learned to align himself with the forces. In this intermediate stage he wavers—neither drawn in harmony with nature by his instincts nor yet wisely putting himself into harmony by his own free will. He is even as a wisp in the wind, moved by every breath of passion, acting now by his will and now by his instincts, erring with one, only to retrieve by the other, falling by one, only to rise by the other—a creature of incalculable variability. We have the consolation of knowing that evolution is ever in action, that the ideal is a light that cannot fail. He will not forever balance thus between good and evil. When this jangle of free will and instinct shall have been adjusted, when perfect understanding has given the former the power to replace the latter entirely, man will no longer vary. The needle of understanding will yet point steadfast and unwavering to the distant pole of truth.

► *In what way are human beings "wisp[s] in the wind," according to the narrator?*

► *In what way does the narrator envision humans after many years of evolution?*

In Carrie—as in how many of our worldlings do they not?—instinct and reason, desire and understanding, were at war for the mastery. She followed whither[1] her craving led. She was as yet more drawn than she drew.

1. **whither.** Where

Words For Everyday Use

heark • en (härk´ən) *vi.,* give careful attention to; listen carefully

err • ing (ʉr iŋ) *n.,* falling into error

con • so • la • tion (kän ´sə lā´shən) *n.,* comfort

jan • gle (jaŋ´gəl) *n.,* harsh sound; discordant

When Minnie found the note next morning, after a night of mingled wonder and anxiety, which was not exactly touched by yearning, sorrow, or love, she exclaimed: "Well, what do you think of that?"

◄ What were Minnie's feelings when Carrie did not return home? What didn't she feel "exactly"?

"What?" said Hanson.

"Sister Carrie has gone to live somewhere else."

Hanson jumped out of bed with more celerity than he usually displayed and looked at the note. The only indication of his thoughts came in the form of a little clicking sound made by his tongue; the sound some people make when they wish to urge on a horse.

"Where do you suppose she's gone to?" said Minnie, thoroughly aroused.

◄ How would you characterize the Hansons' conversation about Carrie?

"I don't know," a touch of cynicism lighting his eye. "Now she has gone and done it."

Minnie moved her head in a puzzled way.

"Oh, oh," she said, "she doesn't know what she has done."

"Well," said Hanson, after a while, sticking his hands out before him, "what can you do?"

Minnie's womanly nature was higher than this. She figured the possibilities in such cases.

◄ What "possibilities" in Carrie's future lead Minnie to say, "poor Sister Carrie"?

"Oh," she said at last, "poor Sister Carrie!"

At the time of this particular conversation, which occurred at 5 A.M., that little soldier of fortune was sleeping a rather troubled sleep in her new room, alone.

Carrie's new state was remarkable in that she saw possibilities in it. She was no sensualist, longing to drowse sleepily in the lap of luxury. She turned about, troubled by her daring, glad of her release, wondering whether she would get something to do, wondering what Drouet would do. That worthy had his future fixed for him beyond a peradventure. He could not help what he was going to do. He could not see clearly enough to wish to do differently. He was drawn by his innate desire to act the old pursuing part. He would need to delight himself with Carrie as surely as he would need to eat his heavy breakfast. He might suffer the least rudimentary twinge of conscience in whatever he did, and in just so far he was evil and sinning. But whatever twinges of conscience he might have would be rudimentary, you may be sure.

◄ What is Drouet being drawn to do? To what is Drouet's passion for Carrie compared?

◄ What does the narrator say about Drouet's conscience?

The next day he called upon Carrie, and she saw him in her chamber. He was the same jolly, enlivening soul.

Words For Everyday Use

ce • ler • i • ty (sə ler´ i tē) *n.,* swiftness

cyn • i • ci • sm (sin´ ə si´ zəm) *n.,* scornfulness toward the motives, virtues, or integrity of others

per • ad • ven • ture (pʉr´əd ven´chər) *n.,* doubt

"Aw," he said, "what are you looking so blue about? Come on out to breakfast. You want to get your other clothes today."

Carrie looked at him with the hue of shifting thought in her large eyes.

"I wish I could get something to do," she said.

"You'll get that all right," said Drouet. "What's the use worrying right now? Get yourself fixed up. See the city. I won't hurt you."

"I know you won't," she remarked, half truthfully.

"Got on the new shoes, haven't you? Stick 'em out. George, they look fine. Put on your jacket."

Carrie obeyed.

"Say, that fits like a T, don't it?" he remarked, feeling the set of it at the waist and eyeing it from a few paces with real pleasure. "What you need now is a new skirt. Let's go to breakfast."

Carrie put on her hat.

"Where are the gloves?" he inquired.

"Here," she said, taking them out of the bureau drawer.

"Now, come on," he said.

Thus the first hour of misgiving was swept away.

► What is Carrie's reaction when she looks in the mirror after she has bought new clothes and "the little necessaries of toilet"? What does she feel for the first time?

It went this way on every occasion. Drouet did not leave her much alone. She had time for some lone wanderings, but mostly he filled her hours with sightseeing. At Carson, Pirie's he bought her a nice skirt and shirtwaist.[2] With his money she purchased the little necessaries of toilet, until at last she looked quite another maiden. The mirror convinced her of a few things which she had long believed. She was pretty, yes, indeed! How nice her hat set, and weren't her eyes pretty. She caught her little red lip with her teeth and felt her first thrill of power. Drouet was so good.

► What makes Carrie think of home?

They went to see *The Mikado*[3] one evening, an opera which was hilariously popular at that time. Before going, they made off for the Windsor dining room, which was in Dearborn Street, a considerable distance from Carrie's room. It was blowing up cold, and out of her window Carrie could see the western sky, still pink with the fading light, but steely blue at the top where it met the darkness. A long, thin cloud of pink hung in midair, shaped like some island in a far-off sea. Somehow the swaying of some dead branches of trees across the way brought back the picture with which she was familiar when she looked from their front window in December days at home.

She paused and wrung her little hands.

"What's the matter?" said Drouet.

"Oh, I don't know," she said, her lip trembling.

2. **shirtwaist.** Woman's blouse styled like a tailored shirt
3. ***The Mikado.*** Comic operetta by Gilbert and Sullivan

He sensed something, and slipped his arm over her shoulder, patting her arm.

"Come on," he said gently, "you're all right."

She turned to slip on her jacket.

"Better wear that boa[4] about your throat tonight."

They walked north on Wabash to Adams Street and then west. The lights in the stores were already shining out in gushes of golden hue. The arc lights were sputtering overhead, and high up were the lighted windows of the tall office buildings. The chill wind whipped in and out in gusty breaths. Homeward bound, the six o'clock throng bumped and jostled. Light overcoats were turned up about the ears, hats were pulled down. Little shop-girls went fluttering by in pairs and fours, chattering, laughing. It was a spectacle of warm-blooded humanity.

Suddenly a pair of eyes met Carrie's in recognition. They were looking out from a group of poorly dressed girls. Their clothes were faded and loose-hanging, their jackets old, their general makeup shabby.

◄ Whom does Carrie recognize in the crowd? In what way does this person's appearance differ from Carrie's?

Carrie recognized the glance and the girl. She was one of those who worked at the machines in the shoe factory. The latter looked, not quite sure, and then turned her head and looked. Carrie felt as if some great tide had rolled between them. The old dress and the old machine came back. She actually started. Drouet didn't notice until Carrie bumped into a pedestrian.

"You must be thinking," he said.

They dined and went to the theater. That spectacle pleased Carrie immensely. The color and grace of it caught her eye. She had vain imaginings about place and power, about far-off lands and magnificent people. When it was over, the clatter of coaches and the throng of fine ladies made her stare.

◄ What pleases Carrie about the theater? What desires and imaginings does it stir in her?

"Wait a minute," said Drouet, holding her back in the showy foyer where ladies and gentlemen were moving in a social crush, skirts rustling, lace-covered heads nodding, white teeth showing through parted lips. "Let's see."

"Sixty-seven," the coach-caller was saying, his voice lifted in a sort of euphonious cry. "Sixty-seven."

4. **boa.** Long woman's scarf of fur or feathers

Words For Everyday Use

jos • tle (jäs´əl) *vi.,* bump against

vain (vān) *adj.,* proud; conceited

eu • pho • ni • ous (yo͞o fō´nē əs) *adj.,* pleasing to the ear

"Isn't it fine?" said Carrie.

"Great," said Drouet. He was as much affected by this show of finery and gaiety as she. He pressed her arm warmly. Once she looked up, her even teeth glistening through her smiling lips, her eyes alight. As they were moving out he whispered down to her, "You look lovely!" They were right where the coach-caller was swinging open a coach door and ushering in two ladies.

"You stick to me and we'll have a coach," laughed Drouet.

Carrie scarcely heard, her head was so full of the swirl of life.

They stopped in at a restaurant for a little after-theater lunch. Just a shade of a thought of the hour entered Carrie's head, but there was no household law to govern her now. If any habits ever had time to fix upon her, they would have operated here. Habits are peculiar things. They will drive the really nonreligious mind out of bed to say prayers that are only a custom and not a devotion. The victim of habit, when he has neglected the thing which it was his custom to do, feels a little scratching in the brain, a little irritating something which comes of being out of the rut, and imagines it to be the prick of conscience, the still, small voice that is urging him ever to righteousness. If the digression is unusual enough, the drag of habit will be heavy enough to cause the unreasoning victim to return and perform the perfunctory thing. "Now, bless me," says such a mind, "I have done my duty," when, as a matter of fact, it has merely done its old, unbreakable trick once again.

▶ According to the narrator, for what do people mistake their devotion to habits?

Carrie had no excellent home principles fixed upon her. If she had, she would have been more consciously distressed. Now the lunch went off with considerable warmth. Under the influence of the varied occurrences, the fine, invisible passion which was emanating from Drouet, the food, the still unusual luxury, she relaxed and heard with open ears. She was again the victim of the city's hypnotic influence.

▶ Of what is Carrie the victim?

"Well," said Drouet at last, "we had better be going."

They had been dawdling over the dishes, and their eyes had frequently met. Carrie could not help but feel the vibration of force which followed, which, indeed, was his gaze. He had a way of touching her hand in explanation, as if to impress a fact upon her. He touched it now as he spoke of going.

They arose and went out into the street. The downtown

Words For Everyday Use

right • eous • ness (rī´chəs nəs) *n.,* virtue, right action

di • gres • sion (di gresh´ən) *n.,* movement away from the true path

em • a • nate (em´ə nāt) *vi.,* come out of

section was now bare, save for a few whistling strollers, a few owl cars, a few open resorts whose windows were still bright. Out Wabash Avenue they strolled, Drouet still pouring forth his volume of small information. He had Carrie's arm in his, and held it closely as he explained. Once in a while, after some witticism, he would look down, and his eyes would meet hers. At last they came to the steps, and Carrie stood up on the first one, her head now coming even with his own. He took her hand and held it genially. He looked steadily at her as she glanced about, warmly musing.

◄ *Where do Drouet and Carrie pause? About what do you think Carrie is musing?*

At about that hour, Minnie was soundly sleeping, after a long evening of troubled thought. She had her elbow in an awkward position under her side. The muscles so held irritated a few nerves, and now a vague scene floated in on the drowsy mind. She fancied she and Carrie were somewhere beside an old coal mine. She could see the tall runway and the heap of earth and coal cast out. There was a deep pit, into which they were looking; they could see the curious wet stones far down where the wall disappeared in vague shadows. An old basket, used for descending, was hanging there, fastened by a worn rope.

◄ *What happens to Carrie in her sister's dream?*

"Let's get in," said Carrie.

"Oh, no," said Minnie.

"Yes, come on," said Carrie.

She began to pull the basket over, and now, in spite of all protest, she had swung over and was going down.

"Carrie," she called, "Carrie, come back;" but Carrie was far down now and the shadow had swallowed her completely.

She moved her arm.

Now the mystic scenery merged queerly and the place was by waters she had never seen. They were upon some board or ground or something that reached far out, and at the end of this was Carrie. They looked about, and now the thing was sinking, and Minnie heard the low sip of the encroaching water.

"Come on, Carrie," she called, but Carrie was reaching farther out. She seemed to recede, and now it was difficult to call to her.

◄ *In what way do Minnie's dreams affect her?*

"Carrie," she called, "Carrie," but her own voice sounded far away, and the strange waters were blurring everything. She came away suffering as though she had lost something. She was more inexpressibly sad than she had ever been in life.

Words For Everyday Use

muse (myōōz) *vi.,* meditate; think deeply

en • croach • ing (en´krōch´ iŋ) *adj.,* advancing beyond former limits

re • cede (ri sēd´) *vi.,* slip away

in • ex • press • i • bly (in´eks pres´ə blē) *adj.,* unable to be described

It was this way through many shifts of the tired brain, those curious phantoms of the spirit slipping in, blurring strange scenes, one with the other. The last one made her cry out, for Carrie was slipping away somewhere over a rock, and her fingers had let loose and she had seen her falling.

"Minnie! What's the matter? Here, wake up," said Hanson, disturbed, and shaking her by the shoulder.

"Wha—what's the matter?" said Minnie, drowsily.

"Wake up," he said, "and turn over. You're talking in your sleep."

▶ How far forward in time does the narrator move the story?

A week or so later Drouet strolled into Fitzgerald and Moy's, spruce in dress and manner.

"Hello, Charlie," said Hurstwood, looking out from his office door.

Drouet strolled over and looked in upon the manager at his desk.

"When do you go out on the road again?" he inquired.

"Pretty soon," said Drouet.

"Haven't seen much of you this trip," said Hurstwood.

"Well, I've been busy," said Drouet.

They talked some few minutes on general topics.

▶ Why does Drouet invite Hurstwood to his house? What does Hurstwood understand about the situation?

"Say," said Drouet, as if struck by a sudden idea, "I want you to come out some evening."

"Out where?" inquired Hurstwood.

"Out to my house, of course," said Drouet, smiling.

Hurstwood looked up quizzically, the least suggestion of a smile hovering about his lips. He studied the face of Drouet in his wise way, and then with the demeanor of a gentleman, said: "Certainly; glad to."

"We'll have a nice game of euchre."[5]

"May I bring a nice little bottle of Sec?"[6] asked Hurstwood.

"Certainly," said Drouet. "I'll introduce you."

---

5. **euchre.** Card game
6. **Sec.** Dry wine, usually champagne

CHAPTER 9

Convention's Own Tinder-Box: The Eye That Is Green

Hurstwood's residence on the North Side, near Lincoln Park, was a brick building of a very popular type then, a three-story affair with the first floor sunk a very little below the level of the street. It had a large bay window bulging out from the second floor, and was graced in front by a small grassy plot, twenty-five feet wide and ten feet deep. There was also a small rear yard, walled in by the fences of the neighbors and holding a stable where he kept his horse and trap.

The ten rooms of the house were occupied by himself, his wife Julia, and his son and daughter, George, Jr., and Jessica. There were besides these a maidservant, represented from time to time by girls of various extraction, for Mrs. Hurstwood was not always easy to please.

◄ What does Mrs. Hurstwood frequently do? What does this reveal about her character?

"George, I let Mary go yesterday," was not an unfrequent salutation at the dinner table.

"All right," was his only reply. He had long since wearied of discussing the rancorous subject.

A lovely home atmosphere is one of the flowers of the world, than which there is nothing more tender, nothing more delicate, nothing more calculated to make strong and just the natures cradled and nourished within it. Those who have never experienced such a beneficent influence will not understand wherefore the tear springs glistening to the eyelids at some strange breath in lovely music. The mystic chords which bind and thrill the heart of the nation, they will never know.

◄ What is the effect of "a lovely home atmosphere" on its residents?

Hurstwood's residence could scarcely be said to be infused with this home spirit. It lacked that toleration and regard without which the home is nothing. There was fine furniture, arranged as soothingly as the artistic perception of the occupants warranted. There were soft rugs, rich, upholstered chairs and divans,[1] a grand piano, a marble carving of some

◄ Why doesn't the Hurstwood home have such a "lovely" atmosphere?

1. **divans.** Low couches or sofas

Words For Everyday Use

ran • cor • ous (raŋ´kər us) *adj.*, characterized by continuous ill will

be • nef • i • cent (ben´ə fish´ənt) *adj.*, good, favorable

in • fused (in fyo͞ozd´) *adj.*, filled

unknown Venus by some unknown artist, and a number of small bronzes gathered from heaven knows where, but generally sold by the large furniture houses along with everything else which goes to make the "perfectly appointed house."

In the dining room stood a sideboard laden with glistening decanters[2] and other utilities and ornaments in glass, the arrangement of which could not be questioned. Here was something Hurstwood knew about. He had studied the subject for years in his business. He took no little satisfaction in telling each Mary, shortly after she arrived, something of what the art of the thing required. He was not garrulous by any means. On the contrary, there was a fine reserve in his manner toward the entire domestic economy of his life which was all that is comprehended by the popular term, gentlemanly. He would not argue, he would not talk freely. In his manner was something of the dogmatist. What he could not correct, he would ignore. There was a tendency in him to walk away from the impossible thing.

► *How did Hurstwood once feel about his daughter? What is Jessica like now?*

There was a time when he had been considerably enamored of[3] his Jessica, especially when he was younger and more confined in his success. Now, however, in her seventeenth year, Jessica had developed a certain amount of reserve and independence which was not inviting to the richest form of parental devotion. She was in the high school, and had notions of life which were decidedly those of a patrician. She liked nice clothes and urged for them constantly. Thoughts of love and elegant individual establishments were running in her head. She met girls at the high school whose parents were truly rich and whose fathers had standing locally as partners or owners of solid businesses. These girls gave themselves the airs befitting the thriving domestic establishments from whence they issued. They were the only ones of the school about whom Jessica concerned herself.

► *What is Hurstwood, Jr., like?*

Young Hurstwood, Jr., was in his twentieth year, and was already connected in a promising capacity with a large real estate firm. He contributed nothing for the domestic expenses of the family, but was thought to be saving his money to invest in real estate. He had some ability, considerable vanity,

2. **decanters.** Decorative glass bottles from which wine is poured
3. **enamored of.** Charmed with and filled with love for

Words For Everyday Use

gar • ru • lous (gar´ə ləs) *adj.,* characterized by much talk
dog • ma • tist (dôg´mə tist) *n.,* one who arrogantly asserts an opinion without evidence
pa • tri • cian (pə trish´ən) *n.,* person of high social rank
be • fit • ting (bē fit´ iŋ) *adj.,* suitable to

and a love of pleasure that had not, as yet, infringed upon his duties, whatever they were. He came in and went out, pursuing his own plans and fancies, addressing a few words to his mother occasionally, relating some little incident to his father, but for the most part confining himself to those generalities with which most conversation concerns itself. He was not laying bare his desires for anyone to see. He did not find anyone in the house who particularly cared to see.

Mrs. Hurstwood was the type of the woman who has ever endeavored to shine and has been more or less chagrined at the evidences of superior capability in this direction elsewhere. Her knowledge of life extended to that little conventional round of society of which she was not—but longed to be—a member. She was not without realization already that this thing was impossible, so far as she was concerned. For her daughter, she hoped better things. Through Jessica she might rise a little. Through George, Jr.'s, possible success she might draw to herself the privilege of pointing proudly. Even Hurstwood was doing well enough, and she was anxious that his small real estate adventures should prosper. His property holdings, as yet, were rather small, but his income was pleasing and his position with Fitzgerald and Moy was fixed. Both those gentlemen were on pleasant and rather informal terms with him.

◄ *In what way would you describe Mrs. Hurstwood's character? For what does she long?*

The atmosphere which such personalities would create must be apparent to all. It worked out in a thousand little conversations, all of which were of the same caliber.

◄ *What type of "atmosphere" do these personalities create?*

"I'm going up to Fox Lake tomorrow," announced George, Jr., at the dinner table one Friday evening.

"What's going on up there?" queried Mrs. Hurstwood.

"Eddie Fahrway's got a new steam launch, and he wants me to come up and see how it works."

"How much did it cost him?" asked his mother.

"Oh, over two thousand dollars. He says it's a dandy."

"Old Fahrway must be making money," put in Hurstwood.

"He is, I guess. Jack told me they were shipping Vegacura to Australia now—said they sent a whole box to Cape Town last week."

"Just think of that!" said Mrs. Hurstwood, "and only four years ago they had that basement in Madison Street."

Words For Everyday Use

en • deav • or (en dev´ər) *vi.*, try
cha • grined (shə grind´) *adj.*, shamed and annoyed
cal • i • ber (kal´ə bər) *n.*, degree of worth or value

"Jack told me they were going to put up a six-story building next spring in Robey Street."

"Just think of that!" said Jessica.

On this particular occasion Hurstwood wished to leave early.

"I guess I'll be going downtown," he remarked, rising.

"Are we going to McVicker's Monday?" questioned Mrs. Hurstwood, without rising.

"Yes," he said indifferently.

They went on dining, while he went upstairs for his hat and coat. Presently the door clicked.

"I guess papa's gone," said Jessica.

The latter's school news was of a particular stripe.

"They're going to give a performance in the Lyceum,[4] upstairs," she reported one day, "and I'm going to be in it."

"Are you?" said her mother.

"Yes, and I'll have to have a new dress. Some of the nicest girls in the school are going to be in it. Miss Palmer is going to take the part of Portia."[5]

"Is she?" said Mrs. Hurstwood.

► *What view do the Hurstwoods have of less fortunate families?*

"They've got that Martha Griswold in it again. She thinks she can act."

"Her family doesn't amount to anything, does it?" said Mrs. Hurstwood sympathetically. "They haven't anything, have they?"

"No," returned Jessica, "they're poor as church mice."

She distinguished very carefully between the young boys of the school, many of whom were attracted by her beauty.

"What do you think?" she remarked to her mother one evening; "that Herbert Crane tried to make friends with me."

"Who is he, my dear?" inquired Mrs. Hurstwood.

"Oh, no one," said Jessica, pursing her pretty lips. "He's just a student there. He hasn't anything."

The other half of this picture came when young Blyford, son of Blyford, the soap manufacturer, walked home with her. Mrs. Hurstwood was on the third floor, sitting in a rocking chair reading, and happened to look out at the time.

"Who was that with you, Jessica?" she inquired, as Jessica came upstairs.

"It's Mr. Blyford, mamma," she replied.

"Is it?" said Mrs. Hurstwood.

"Yes, and he wants me to stroll over into the park with him," explained Jessica, a little flushed with running up the stairs.

"All right, my dear," said Mrs. Hurstwood. "Don't be gone long."

---

4. **Lyceum.** Hall where public lectures and concerts are held
5. **Portia.** Heroine of Shakespeare's *Merchant of Venice*

As the two went down the street, she glanced interestedly out of the window. It was a most satisfactory spectacle indeed, most satisfactory.

In this atmosphere Hurstwood had moved for a number of years, not thinking deeply concerning it. His was not the order of nature to trouble for something better, unless the better was immediately and sharply contrasted. As it was, he received and gave, irritated sometimes by the little displays of selfish indifference, pleased at times by some show of finery which supposedly made for dignity and social distinction. The life of the resort which he managed was his life. There he spent most of his time. When he went home evenings the house looked nice. With rare exceptions the meals were acceptable, being the kind that an ordinary servant can arrange. In part, he was interested in the talk of his son and daughter, who always looked well. The vanity of Mrs. Hurstwood caused her to keep her person rather showily arrayed, but to Hurstwood this was much better than plainness. There was no love lost between them. There was no great feeling of dissatisfaction. Her opinion on any subject was not startling. They did not talk enough together to come to the argument of any one point. In the accepted and popular phrase, she had her ideas and he had his. Once in a while he would meet a woman whose youth, sprightliness, and humor would make his wife seem rather deficient by contrast, but the temporary dissatisfaction which such an encounter might arouse would be counterbalanced by his social position and a certain matter of policy. He could not complicate his home life, because it might affect his relations with his employers. They wanted no scandals. A man, to hold his position, must have a dignified manner, a clean record, a respectable home anchorage. Therefore he was circumspect in all he did, and whenever he appeared in the public ways in the afternoon, or on Sunday, it was with his wife, and sometimes his children. He would visit the local resorts, or those nearby in Wisconsin, and spend a few stiff, polished days strolling about conventional places doing conventional things. He knew the need of it.

When someone of the many middle-class individuals whom he knew, who had money, would get into trouble, he would shake his head. It didn't do to talk about those things.

◄ *When is the only time Hurstwood yearns for something better?*

◄ *What relationship exists between Mr. and Mrs. Hurstwood?*

◄ *When does Hurstwood become dissatisfied with his wife? Why doesn't he act upon his feelings?*

◄ *What is Hurstwood's attitude toward formerly respectable middle-class individuals who get into "trouble"? To what type of trouble do you think Hurstwood is referring?*

Words For Everyday Use

ar • rayed (ə rēd´) *adj.*, dressed

coun • ter • bal • ance (kount´ər bal´əns) *vt.*, offset

cir • cum • spect (sʉr kəm spekt´) *adj.*, careful; well-behaved and proper

If it came up for discussion among such friends as with him passed for close, he would deprecate the folly of the thing. "It was all right to do it—all men do those things—but why wasn't he careful? A man can't be too careful." He lost sympathy for the man that made a mistake and was found out.

On this account he still devoted some time to showing his wife about—time which would have been wearisome indeed if it had not been for the people he would meet and the little enjoyments which did not depend upon her presence or absence. He watched her with considerable curiosity at times, for she was still attractive in a way and men looked at her. She was affable, vain, subject to flattery, and this combination, he knew quite well, might produce a tragedy in a woman of her home position. Owing to his order of mind, his confidence in the sex was not great. His wife never possessed the virtues which would win the confidence and admiration of a man of his nature. As long as she loved him vigorously he could see how confidence could be, but when that was no longer the binding chain—well, something might happen.

▶ *What qualities does Hurstwood's wife exhibit? What "tragedy" does Hurstwood think this combination might produce?*

During the last year or two the expenses of the family seemed a large thing. Jessica wanted fine clothes, and Mrs. Hurstwood, not to be outshone by her daughter, also frequently enlivened her apparel. Hurstwood had said nothing in the past, but one day he murmured.

▶ *What is beginning to concern Hurstwood? Does his family share the same concerns? Why, or why not?*

"Jessica must have a new dress this month," said Mrs. Hurstwood one morning.

Hurstwood was arraying himself in one of his perfection vests before the glass at the time.

"I thought she just bought one," he said.

"That was just something for evening wear," returned his wife complacently.

"It seems to me," returned Hurstwood, "that she's spending a good deal for dresses of late."

"Well, she's going out more," concluded his wife, but the tone of his voice impressed her as containing something she had not heard there before.

He was not a man who traveled much, but when he did, he had been accustomed to take her along. On one occasion recently a local aldermanic junket[6] had been arranged to

▶ *What does Hurstwood usually do when he travels?*

6. **aldermanic junket.** Excursion taken by a public official and paid for by public funds

Words For Everyday Use	
	dep • re • cate (dep´rə kāt´) *vt.,* express disapproval of
	fol • ly (fäl´ē) *n.,* foolishness
	com • pla • cent • ly (kəm plā´sənt lē) *adv.,* in an unconcerned, self-satisfied manner

visit Philadelphia—a junket that was to last ten days. Hurstwood had been invited.

"Nobody knows us down there," said one, a gentleman whose face was a slight improvement over gross ignorance and sensuality. He always wore a silk hat of most imposing proportions. "We can have a good time." His left eye moved with just the semblance of a wink. "You want to come along, George."

◄ What does a gentleman suggest to Hurstwood about an upcoming trip to Philadelphia?

The next day Hurstwood announced his intention to his wife.

"I'm going away, Julia," he said, "for a few days."

◄ In what way is Hurstwood deviating from his usual routine?

"Where?" she asked, looking up.

"To Philadelphia, on business."

She looked at him consciously, expecting something else.

"I'll have to leave you behind this time."

"All right," she replied, but he could see that she was thinking that it was a curious thing. Before he went she asked him a few more questions, and that irritated him. He began to feel that she was a disagreeable attachment.

On this trip he enjoyed himself thoroughly, and when it was over he was sorry to get back. He was not willingly a prevaricator, and hated thoroughly to make explanations concerning it. The whole incident was glossed over with general remarks, but Mrs. Hurstwood gave the subject considerable thought. She drove out more, dressed better, and attended theaters freely to make up for it.

◄ What does Mrs. Hurstwood do to "make up for" her husband's behavior?

Such an atmosphere could hardly come under the category of home life. It ran along by force of habit, by force of conventional opinion. With the lapse of time it must necessarily become dryer and dryer—must eventually be tinder,[7] easily lighted and destroyed.

◄ To what does the narrator compare Hurstwood's home life?

7. **tinder.** Dry, easily lit material used to start a fire

Words For Everyday Use

con • ven • tion • al (kən ven´shə nel) *adj.,* conforming to formal or accepted standards

CHAPTER 10

The Counsel of Winter: Fortune's Ambassador Calls

► Why does Carrie's mental state deserve consideration? According to the narrator, what does society demand of women?

In the light of the world's attitude toward woman and her duties, the nature of Carrie's mental state deserves consideration. Actions such as hers are measured by an arbitrary scale. Society possesses a conventional standard whereby it judges all things. All men should be good, all women virtuous. Wherefore, villain, hast thou failed?

For all the liberal analysis of Spencer[1] and our modern naturalistic philosophers, we have but an infantile perception of morals. There is more in the subject than mere conformity to a law of evolution. It is yet deeper than conformity to things of earth alone. It is more involved than we, as yet, perceive. Answer, first, why the heart thrills; explain wherefore some plaintive note goes wandering about the world, undying; make clear the rose's subtle alchemy[2] evolving its ruddy lamp in light and rain. In the essence of these facts lie the first principles of morals.

► What different reactions do Drouet and Carrie have to the new relationship that exists between them?

"Oh," thought Drouet, "how delicious is my conquest."

"Ah," thought Carrie, with mournful misgivings, "what is it I have lost?"

Before this world-old proposition[3] we stand, serious, interested, confused; endeavoring to evolve the true theory of morals—the true answer to what is right.

► How would a certain part of society view Carrie's situation? Why?

In the view of a certain stratum of society, Carrie was comfortably established—in the eyes of the starveling, beaten by every wind and gusty sheet of rain, she was safe in a halcyon harbour. Drouet had taken three rooms, furnished, in Ogden Place, facing Union Park, on the West Side. That was a little, green-carpeted breathing spot, than which, today, there is nothing more beautiful in Chicago. It afforded a vista pleasant to contemplate. The best room looked out upon the lawn of the park, now sear and brown, where a little lake

1. **Spencer.** British philosopher (1820–1903) who applied the theory of evolution to philosophy and ethics
2. **alchemy.** Transformation, especially the miraculous change into something better
3. **proposition.** Logic

Words For Everyday Use

ar • bi • trar • y (är´bə trer´ē) *adj.,* based on whims, not rules
vir • tu • ous (vʉr´cho͞o əs) *adj.,* moral; chaste
in • fan • tile (in´fən tīl) *adj.,* childlike
rud • dy (rud´ē) *adj.,* red
stra • tum (strāt´əm) *n.,* level
hal • cy • on (hal´sē ən) *adj.,* tranquil
sear (sēr) *adj.,* withered

lay sheltered. Over the bare limbs of the trees, which now swayed in the wintry wind, rose the steeple of the Union Park Congregational Church, and far off the towers of several others.

The rooms were comfortably enough furnished. There was a good Brussels carpet on the floor, rich in dull red and lemon shades, and representing large *jardinières*[4] filled with gorgeous, impossible flowers. There was a large pier-glass mirror between the two windows. A large, soft, green, plush-covered couch occupied one corner, and several rocking chairs were set about. Some pictures, several rugs, a few small pieces of bric-a-brac,[5] and the tale of contents is told.

In the bedroom, off the front room, was Carrie's trunk, bought by Drouet, and in the wardrobe built into the wall quite an array of clothing—more than she had ever possessed before, and of very becoming designs. There was a third room for possible use as a kitchen, where Drouet had Carrie establish a little portable gas stove for the preparation of small lunches, oysters, Welsh rarebits,[6] and the like, of which he was exceedingly fond; and, lastly, a bath. The whole place was cozy, in that it was lighted by gas and heated by furnace registers, possessing also a small grate,[7] set with an asbestos[8] back, a method of cheerful warming which was then first coming into use. By her industry and natural love of order, which now developed, the place maintained an air pleasing in the extreme.

Here, then, was Carrie, established in a pleasant fashion, free of certain difficulties which most ominously confronted her, laden with many new ones which were of a mental order, and altogether so turned about in all of her earthly relationships that she might well have been a new and different individual. She looked into her glass and saw a prettier Carrie than she had seen before; she looked into her mind, a mirror prepared of her own and the world's opinions, and saw a worse. Between these two images she wavered, hesitating which to believe.

◄ *When Carrie examines both her outer and inner self, what does she find?*

4. ***jardinières.*** Ornamental stands or pots
5. **bric-a-brac.** Small objects decorating a room
6. **Welsh rarebits.** Dishes of melted cheese, often mixed with ale or beer, served on crackers or toast
7. **grate.** Fireplace
8. **asbestos.** Mineral that does not burn

Words For Everyday Use

om • i • nous • ly (äm´ə nəs lē) *adv.,* in a threatening manner
lad • en (lād´'n) *adj.,* burdened

"My, but you're a little beauty," Drouet was wont to exclaim to her.

She would look at him with large, pleased eyes.

"You know it, don't you?" he would continue.

"Oh, I don't know," she would reply, feeling delight in the fact that one should think so, hesitating to believe, though she really did, that she was vain enough to think so much of herself.

► *In what way does the narrator assess Carrie's conscience?*

Her conscience, however, was not a Drouet, interested to praise. There she heard a different voice, with which she argued, pleaded, excused. It was no just and sapient counsellor, in its last analysis. It was only an average little conscience, a thing which represented the world, her past environment, habit, convention, in a confused way. With it, the voice of the people was truly the voice of God.

"Oh, thou failure!" said the voice.

"Why?" she questioned.

► *What does Carrie's conscience tell her?*

"Look at those about," came the whispered answer. "Look at those who are good. How would they scorn to do what you have done. Look at the good girls; how will they draw away from such as you when they know you have been weak. You had not tried before you failed."

► *Does Carrie's conscience truly disturb her? What answer does she give her conscience?*

It was when Carrie was alone, looking out across the park, that she would be listening to this. It would come infrequently—when something else did not interfere, when the pleasant side was not too apparent, when Drouet was not there. It was somewhat clear in utterance at first, but never wholly convincing. There was always an answer, always the December days threatened. She was alone; she was desireful; she was fearful of the whistling wind. The voice of want made answer for her.

► *According to the narrator, what effects does the city in winter have upon all people as well as "dogs"?*

Once the bright days of summer pass by, a city takes on that somber garb of gray, wrapt in which it goes about its labors during the long winter. Its endless buildings look gray, its sky and its streets assume a somber hue; the scattered, leafless trees and windblown dust and paper but add to the general solemnity of color. There seems to be something in the chill breezes which scurry through the long, narrow thoroughfares productive of rueful thoughts. Not poets alone, nor artists, nor that superior order of mind which arrogates to itself all refinement, feel this, but dogs

Words For Everyday Use

sa • pi • ent (sā´pē ənt) *adj.,* wise
garb (gärb) *n.,* clothing
rue • ful (ro͞o´fəl) *adj.,* moved by regret
ar • ro • gate (ar´ə gāt) *vt.,* claim or seize without right

and all men. These feel as much as the poet, though they have not the same power of expression. The sparrow upon the wire, the cat in the doorway, the dray horse[9] tugging his weary load, feel the long, keen breaths of winter. It strikes to the heart of all life, animate and inanimate. If it were not for the artificial fires of merriment, the rush of profit-seeking trade, and pleasure-selling amusements; if the various merchants failed to make the customary display within and without their establishments; if our streets were not strung with signs of gorgeous hues and thronged with hurrying purchasers, we would quickly discover how firmly the chill hand of winter lays upon the heart; how dispiriting are the days during which the sun withholds a portion of our allowance of light and warmth. We are more dependent upon these things than is often thought. We are insects produced by heat, and pass without it.

In the drag of such a gray day the secret voice would reassert itself, feebly and more feebly.

Such mental conflict was not always uppermost. Carrie was not by any means a gloomy soul. More, she had not the mind to get firm hold upon a definite truth. When she could not find her way out of the labyrinth of illogic which thought upon the subject created, she would turn away entirely.

◄ *What prevents Carrie from being melancholy all the time?*

Drouet, all the time, was conducting himself in a model way for one of his sort. He took her about a great deal, spent money upon her, and when he traveled took her with him. There were times when she would be alone for two or three days, while he made the shorter circuits of his business, but, as a rule, she saw a great deal of him.

"Say, Carrie," he said one morning, shortly after they had so established themselves, "I've invited my friend Hurstwood to come out some day and spend the evening with us."

"Who is he?" asked Carrie, doubtfully.

"Oh, he's a nice man. He's manager of Fitzgerald and Moy's."

"What's that?" said Carrie.

"The finest resort in town. It's a way-up, swell place."

Carrie puzzled a moment. She was wondering what Drouet had told him, what her attitude would be.

"That's all right," said Drouet, feeling her thought. "He doesn't know anything. You're Mrs. Drouet now."

◄ *What does Drouet say to reassure Carrie about Hurstwood's impending visit? Why does Carrie feel that this remark is inconsiderate?*

9. **dray horse.** Horse that pulls a low, heavy cart without sides

Words For Everyday Use

lab • y • rinth (lab´ə rinth´) *n.,* maze

► *What does Drouet's "property" render him unable to do? Do you think he is telling the truth or just making excuses? Explain.*

► *How does Carrie feel about Drouet? According to the narrator, why is she better off for being able to find fault in him?*

► *Once Carrie meets Hurstwood, what does she discover about him in comparison with Drouet?*

There was something about this which struck Carrie as slightly inconsiderate. She could see that Drouet did not have the keenest sensibilities.

"Why don't we get married?" she inquired, thinking of the voluble promises he had made.

"Well, we will," he said, "just as soon as I get this little deal of mine closed up."

He was referring to some property which he said he had, and which required so much attention, adjustment, and what not, that somehow or other it interfered with his free moral, personal actions.

"Just as soon as I get back from my Denver trip in January we'll do it."

Carrie accepted this as basis for hope—it was a sort of salve to her conscience, a pleasant way out. Under the circumstances, things would be righted. Her actions would be justified.

She really was not enamored of Drouet. She was more clever than he. In a dim way, she was beginning to see where he lacked. If it had not been for this, if she had not been able to measure and judge him in a way, she would have been worse off than she was. She would have adored him. She would have been utterly wretched in her fear of not gaining his affection, of losing his interest, of being swept away and left without an anchorage. As it was, she wavered a little, slightly anxious, at first, to gain him completely, but later feeling at ease in waiting. She was not exactly sure what she thought of him—what she wanted to do.

When Hurstwood called, she met a man who was more clever than Drouet in a hundred ways. He paid that peculiar deference to women which every member of the sex appreciates. He was not overawed, he was not overbold. His great charm was attentiveness. Schooled in winning those birds of fine feather among his own sex, the merchants and professionals who visited his resort, he could use even greater tact when endeavoring to prove agreeable to someone who charmed him. In a pretty woman of any refinement of feeling whatsoever he found his greatest incentive. He was mild, placid, assured, giving the impression that he wished to be of service only—to do something which would make the lady more pleased.

Drouet had ability in this line himself when the game was worth the candle, but he was too much the egotist to reach

Words For Everyday Use

salve (sav) *n.,* anything that soothes or heals
plac • id (plas´id) *adj.,* calm
e • go • tist (ē´gō tist) *n.,* self-absorbed person

the polish which Hurstwood possessed. He was too buoyant, too full of ruddy life, too assured. He succeeded with many who were not quite schooled in the art of love. He failed dismally where the woman was slightly experienced and possessed innate refinement. In the case of Carrie he found a woman who was all of the latter, but none of the former. He was lucky in the fact that opportunity tumbled into his lap, as it were. A few years later, with a little more experience, the slightest tide of success, and he had not been able to approach Carrie at all.

◄ According to the narrator, why wouldn't Drouet have succeeded with Carrie were she older and more experienced?

"You ought to have a piano here, Drouet," said Hurstwood, smiling at Carrie, on the evening in question, "so that your wife could play."

Drouet had not thought of that.

"So we ought," he observed readily.

"Oh, I don't play," ventured Carrie.

"It isn't very difficult," returned Hurstwood. "You could do very well in a few weeks."

He was in the best form for entertaining this evening. His clothes were particularly new and rich in appearance. The coat lapels stood out with that medium stiffness which excellent cloth possesses. The vest was of a rich Scotch plaid, set with a double row of round mother-of-pearl buttons. His cravat[10] was a shiny combination of silken threads, not loud, not inconspicuous. What he wore did not strike the eye so forcibly as that which Drouet had on, but Carrie could see the elegance of the material. Hurstwood's shoes were of soft, black calf, polished only to a dull shine. Drouet wore patent leather, but Carrie could not help feeling that there was a distinction in favor of the soft leather, where all else was so rich. She noticed these things almost unconsciously. They were things which would naturally flow from the situation. She was used to Drouet's appearance.

◄ What does Carrie notice about Hurstwood's dress in comparison with Drouet's?

"Suppose we have a little game of euchre?" suggested Hurstwood, after a light round of conversation. He was rather dexterous in avoiding everything that would suggest that he knew anything of Carrie's past. He kept away from personalities altogether, and confined himself to those things which did not concern individuals at all. By his manner,

◄ In what way does Hurstwood try to put Carrie at ease?

10. **cravat.** Necktie

Words For Everyday Use

buoy • ant (boi´ənt) *adj.,* high-spirited

in • con • spic • u • ous (in´kən spik´ yo͞o əs) *adj.,* attracting little attention

dex • ter • ous (deks´tər əs) *adj.,* skillful

he put Carrie at her ease, and by his deference and pleasantries he amused her. He pretended to be seriously interested in all she said.

"I don't know how to play," said Carrie.

"Charlie, you are neglecting a part of your duty," he observed to Drouet most affably. "Between us, though," he went on, "we can show you."

► *What makes Drouet appreciate Carrie more?*

By his tact he made Drouet feel that he admired his choice. There was something in his manner that showed that he was pleased to be there. Drouet felt really closer to him than ever before. It gave him more respect for Carrie. Her appearance came into a new light, under Hurstwood's appreciation. The situation livened considerably.

"Now, let me see," said Hurstwood, looking over Carrie's shoulder very deferentially. "What have you?" He studied for a moment. "That's rather good," he said.

"You're lucky. Now, I'll show you how to trounce your husband. You take my advice."

"Here," said Drouet, "if you two are going to scheme together, I won't stand a ghost of a show. Hurstwood's a regular sharp."

"No, it's your wife. She brings me luck. Why shouldn't she win?"

Carrie looked gratefully at Hurstwood, and smiled at Drouet. The former took the air of a mere friend. He was simply there to enjoy himself. Anything that Carrie did was pleasing to him, nothing more.

"There," he said, holding back one of his own good cards, and giving Carrie a chance to take a trick. "I count that clever playing for a beginner."

The latter laughed gleefully as she saw the hand coming her way. It was as if she were invincible when Hurstwood helped her.

► *In what way does Hurstwood look at Carrie? What is he careful to hide?*

He did not look at her often. When he did, it was with a mild light in his eye. Not a shade was there of anything save geniality and kindness. He took back the shifty, clever gleam, and replaced it with one of innocence. Carrie could not guess but that it was pleasure with him in the immediate thing. She felt that he considered she was doing a great deal.

"It's unfair to let such playing go without earning something," he said after a time, slipping his finger into the little coin pocket of his coat. "Let's play for dimes."

Words For Everyday Use

trounce (trouns) *vt.,* defeat thoroughly

in • vin • ci • ble (in vin´sə bəl) *adj.,* unbeatable

"All right," said Drouet, fishing for bills.

Hurstwood was quicker. His fingers were full of new ten-cent pieces. "Here we are," he said, supplying each one with a little stack.

"Oh, this is gambling," smiled Carrie. "It's bad."

"No," said Drouet, "only fun. If you never play for more than that, you will go to Heaven."

"Don't you moralize," said Hurstwood to Carrie gently, "until you see what becomes of the money."

◄ How does Carrie feel about gambling? What do the two men tell her about her moral scruples?

Drouet smiled.

"If your husband gets them, he'll tell you how bad it is."

Drouet laughed loud.

There was such an ingratiating tone about Hurstwood's voice, the insinuation was so perceptible that even Carrie got the humor of it.

"When do you leave?" said Hurstwood to Drouet.

"On Wednesday," he replied.

"It's rather hard to have your husband running about like that, isn't it?" said Hurstwood, addressing Carrie.

"She's going along with me this time," said Drouet.

"You must both go with me to the theater before you go."

"Certainly," said Drouet. "Eh, Carrie?"

"I'd like it ever so much," she replied.

Hurstwood did his best to see that Carrie won the money. He rejoiced in her success, kept counting her winnings, and finally gathered and put them in her extended hand. They spread a little lunch, at which he served the wine, and afterward he used fine tact in going.

"Now," he said, addressing first Carrie and then Drouet with his eyes, "you must be ready at 7:30. I'll come and get you."

They went with him to the door and there was his cab waiting, its red lamps gleaming cheerfully in the shadow.

"Now," he observed to Drouet, with a tone of good-fellowship, "when you leave your wife alone, you must let me show her around a little. It will break up her loneliness."

◄ What suggestion does Hurstwood make to Drouet?

"Sure," said Drouet, quite pleased at the attention shown.

"You're so kind," observed Carrie.

"Not at all," said Hurstwood, "I would want your husband to do as much for me."

Words For Everyday Use

mor • al • ize (môr´əl iz´) *vi.*, state the terms of right

in • gra • ti • at • ing (in grā´shē āt´ iŋ) *adj.*, able to insert oneself into another's good graces

in • sin • u • a • tion (in sin´yo͞o ā´shən) *n.*, intent to win favor

per • cep • ti • ble (pər sep´tə bəl) *adj.*, easily noticed

He smiled and went lightly away. Carrie was thoroughly impressed. She had never come in contact with such grace. As for Drouet, he was equally pleased.

"There's a nice man," he remarked to Carrie, as they returned to their cozy chamber. "A good friend of mine, too."

"He seems to be," said Carrie.

CHAPTER 11

The Persuasion of Fashion: Feeling Guards O'er Its Own

Carrie was an apt student of fortune's ways—of fortune's superficialities. Seeing a thing, she would immediately set to inquiring how she would look, properly related to it. Be it known that this is not fine feeling, it is not wisdom. The greatest minds are not so afflicted; and, on the contrary, the lowest order of mind is not so disturbed. Fine clothes to her were a vast persuasion; they spoke tenderly and Jesuitically[1] for themselves. When she came within earshot of their pleading, desire in her bent a willing ear. The voice of the so-called inanimate![2] Who shall translate for us the language of the stones?

◄ What is Carrie's main concern in life? According to the narrator, who is not afflicted with the same mindset?

"My dear," said the lace collar she secured from Partridge's, "I fit you beautifully; don't give me up."

"Ah, such little feet," said the leather of the soft new shoes; "how effectively I cover them. What a pity they should ever want my aid."

Once these things were in her hand, on her person, she might dream of giving them up; the method by which they came might intrude itself so forcibly that she would ache to be rid of the thought of it, but she would not give them up. "Put on the old clothes—that torn pair of shoes," was called to her by her conscience in vain. She could possibly have conquered the fear of hunger and gone back; the thought of hard work and a narrow round of suffering would, under the last pressure of conscience, have yielded, but spoil her appearance?—be old-clothed and poor-appearing?—never!

◄ What could Carrie's conscience convince her to do? What couldn't it convince her to do?

Drouet heightened her opinion on this and allied subjects in such a manner as to weaken her power of resisting their influence. It is so easy to do this when the thing opined is in the line of what we desire. In his hearty way, he insisted upon her good looks. He looked at her admiringly, and she took it at its full value. Under the circumstances, she did not need to carry herself as pretty women do. She picked that

1. **Jesuitically.** Like the Society of Jesus, a monastic order of the Roman Catholic church said to practice arguments difficult to contradict
2. **inanimate.** Thing without life

Words For Everyday Use

su • per • fi • ci • al • i • ty (sōō´pər fish´ē al´ə tē) *n.,* shallow, surface thing

af • flict • ed (ə flikt´əd) *adj.,* affected, as by a disorder

► *What does Drouet point out to Carrie?*

knowledge up fast enough for herself. Drouet had a habit, characteristic of his kind, of looking after stylishly dressed or pretty women on the street and remarking upon them. He had just enough of the feminine love of dress to be a good judge—not of intellect, but of clothes. He saw how they set their little feet, how they carried their chins, with what grace and sinuosity they swung their bodies. A dainty, self-conscious swaying of the hips by a woman was to him as alluring as the glint of rare wine to a toper.[3] He would turn and follow the disappearing vision with his eyes. He would thrill as a child with the unhindered passion that was in him. He loved the thing that women love in themselves, grace. At this, their own shrine,[4] he knelt with them, an ardent devotee.[5]

"Did you see that woman who went by just now?" he said to Carrie on the first day they took a walk together. "Fine stepper, wasn't she?"

Carrie looked, and observed the grace commended.

► *How do Drouet's comments make Carrie feel? What does she resolve to learn?*

"Yes, she is," she returned, cheerfully, a little suggestion of possible defect in herself awakening in her mind. If that was so fine, she must look at it more closely. Instinctively, she felt a desire to imitate it. Surely she could do that too.

When one of her mind sees many things emphasized and reemphasized and admired, she gathers the logic of it and applies accordingly. Drouet was not shrewd enough to see that this was not tactful. He could not see that it would be better to make her feel that she was competing with herself, not others better than herself. He would not have done it with an older, wiser woman, but in Carrie he saw only the novice. Less clever than she, he was naturally unable to comprehend her sensibility. He went on educating and wounding her, a thing rather foolish in one whose admiration for his pupil and victim was apt to grow.

Carrie took the instructions affably. She saw what Drouet liked; in a vague way she saw where he was weak. It lessens a woman's opinion of a man when she learns that his admiration is so pointedly and generously distributed. She sees but one object of supreme compliment in this world, and that is herself. If a man is to succeed with many women, he must be all in all to each.

3. **toper.** Drunkard
4. **shrine.** Site or structure used in worship or devotion
5. **devotee.** Follower

Words For Everyday Use

sin • u • os • i • ty (sin´yo͞o äs´ə tē) *n.,* quality of having supple move

ar • dent (ärd´'nt) *adj.,* passionate

com • mend (kə mend´) *vt.,* praise

shrewd (shro͞od) *adj.,* having keen intelligence; cunning

In her own apartments Carrie saw things which were lessons in the same school.

In the same house with her lived an official of one of the theaters, Mr. Frank A. Hale, manager of the Standard, and his wife, a pleasing-looking brunette of thirty-five. They were people of a sort very common in America today, who live respectably from hand to mouth. Hale received a salary of forty-five dollars a week. His wife, quite attractive, affected the feeling of youth, and objected to that sort of home life which means the care of a house and the raising of a family. Like Drouet and Carrie, they also occupied three rooms on the floor above.

◄ *Who begins to influence Carrie?*

Not long after she arrived Mrs. Hale established social relations with her, and together they went about. For a long time this was her only companionship, and the gossip of the manager's wife formed the medium through which she saw the world. Such trivialities, such praises of wealth, such conventional expression of morals as sifted through this passive creature's mind, fell upon Carrie and for the while confused her.

On the other hand, her own feelings were a corrective influence. The constant drag to something better was not to be denied. By those things which address the heart was she steadily recalled. In the apartments across the hall were a young girl and her mother. They were from Evansville, Indiana, the wife and daughter of a railroad treasurer. The daughter was here to study music, the mother to keep her company.

Carrie did not make their acquaintance, but she saw the daughter coming in and going out. A few times she had seen her at the piano in the parlor, and not infrequently had heard her play. This young woman was particularly dressy for her station, and wore a jeweled ring or two which flashed upon her white fingers as she played.

Now Carrie was affected by music. Her nervous composition responded to certain strains, much as certain strings of a harp vibrate when a corresponding key of a piano is struck. She was delicately molded in sentiment, and answered with vague ruminations to certain wistful chords. They awoke longings for those things which she did not have. They

◄ *How does Carrie feel about music? What effect does it have upon her?*

Words For Everyday Use

sift (sift) *vt.*, pass through, as if through a sieve
ru • mi • na • tion (ro͞o´mə nā shen) *n.*, thoughts
wist • ful (wist´fəl) *adj.*, showing or expressing vague yearnings

caused her to cling closer to things she possessed. One short song the young lady played in a most soulful and tender mood. Carrie heard it through the open door from the parlor below. It was at that hour between afternoon and night when, for the idle, the wanderer, things are apt to take on a wistful aspect. The mind wanders forth on far journeys and returns with sheaves of withered and departed joys. Carrie sat at her window looking out. Drouet had been away since ten in the morning. She had amused herself with a walk, a book by Bertha M. Clay[6] which Drouet had left there, though she did not wholly enjoy the latter, and by changing her dress for the evening. Now she sat looking out across the park as wistful and depressed as the nature which craves variety and life can be under such circumstances. As she contemplated her new state, the strain from the parlor below stole upward. With it her thoughts became colored and enmeshed. She reverted to the things which were best and saddest within the small limit of her experience. She became for the moment a repentant.

While she was in this mood Drouet came in, bringing with him an entirely different atmosphere. It was dusk and Carrie had neglected to light the lamp. The fire in the grate, too, had burned low.

"Where are you, Cad?" he said, using a pet name he had given her.

"Here," she answered.

► *What becomes clear to Carrie when Drouet enters? Why might the narrator call this Drouet's "first great mistake"?*

There was something delicate and lonely in her voice, but he could not hear it. He had not the poetry in him that would seek a woman out under such circumstances and console her for the tragedy of life. Instead, he struck a match and lighted the gas.

"Hello," he exclaimed, "you've been crying."

Her eyes were still wet with a few vague tears.

"Pshaw,"[7] he said, "you don't want to do that."

He took her hand, feeling in his good-natured egotism that it was probably lack of his presence which had made her lonely.

"Come on, now," he went on; "it's all right. Let's waltz a little to that music."

6. **Bertha M. Clay.** Pseudonym of Charlotte M. Brame (1836–1884), who wrote sentimental romances, often centered on a fatal love between a nobleman and a lowborn girl

7. **Pshaw.** Exclamation of impatience or contempt

Words For Everyday Use

sheaf (shēf) *n.,* harvested bundle, like a bundle of hay

en • meshed (en mesh'd´) *adj.,* tangled

re • vert (ri vʉrt´) *vi.,* go back in action, thought, or speech

re • pent • ant (ri pen tənt) *n.,* one who feels sorry for having wronged

He could not have introduced a more incongruous proposition. It made clear to Carrie that he could not sympathize with her. She could not have framed thoughts which would have expressed his defect or made clear the difference between them, but she felt it. It was his first great mistake.

What Drouet said about the girl's grace, as she tripped out evenings accompanied by her mother, caused Carrie to perceive the nature and value of those little modish ways which women adopt when they would presume to be something. She looked in the mirror and pursed up her lips, accompanying it with a little toss of the head, as she had seen the railroad treasurer's daughter do. She caught up her skirts with an easy swing, for had not Drouet remarked that in her and several others, and Carrie was naturally imitative. She began to get the hang of those little things which the pretty woman who has vanity invariably adopts. In short, her knowledge of grace doubled, and with it her appearance changed. She became a girl of considerable taste.

◄ *In what way is Carrie changing?*

Drouet noticed this. He saw the new bow in her hair and the new way of arranging her locks which she affected one morning.

"You look fine that way, Cad," he said.

"Do I?" she replied, sweetly. It made her try for other effects that selfsame[8] day.

She used her feet less heavily, a thing that was brought about by her attempting to imitate the treasurer's daughter's graceful carriage. How much influence the presence of that young woman in the same house had upon her it would be difficult to say. But, because of all these things, when Hurstwood called he had found a young woman who was much more than the Carrie to whom Drouet had first spoken. The primary defects of dress and manner had passed. She was pretty, graceful, rich in the timidity born of uncertainty, and with a something childlike in her large eyes which captured the fancy of this starched and conventional poser among men. It was the ancient attraction of the fresh for the stale. If there was a touch of appreciation left in him for the bloom and unsophistication which is the charm of youth, it rekindled now. He looked into her pretty face and felt the

◄ *How does Hurstwood feel about Carrie when he sees her again? In what way does the narrator explain this "attraction"?*

8. **selfsame.** Same

Words For Everyday Use

in • con • gru • ous (in käŋ´groo əs) *adj.*, ridiculously unsuitable

mod • ish (mōd´ish) *adj.*, fashionable

re • kin • dle (rē kin´del) *vi.*, become lit again, like a candle

► For what does Hurstwood give Carrie credit at first glance?

► Who sees Drouet with his dinner companion? Why does Drouet begin to worry?

subtle waves of young life radiating therefrom. In that large clear eye he could see nothing that his *blasé*[9] nature could understand as guile. The little vanity, if he could have perceived it there, would have touched him as a pleasant thing.

"I wonder," he said, as he rode away in his cab, "how Drouet came to win her."

He gave her credit for feelings superior to Drouet at the first glance.

The cab plopped along between the far-receding lines of gas lamps on either hand. He folded his gloved hands and saw only the lighted chamber and Carrie's face. He was pondering over the delight of youthful beauty.

"I'll have a bouquet for her," he thought. "Drouet won't mind."

He never for a moment concealed the fact of her attraction for himself. He troubled himself not at all about Drouet's priority. He was merely floating those gossamer threads of thought which, like the spider's, he hoped would lay hold somewhere. He did not know, he could not guess, what the result would be.

A few weeks later Drouet, in his peregrinations, encountered one of his well-dressed lady acquaintances in Chicago on his return from a short trip to Omaha. He had intended to hurry out to Ogden Place and surprise Carrie, but now he fell into an interesting conversation and soon modified his original intention.

"Let's go to dinner," he said, little recking any chance meeting which might trouble his way.

"Certainly," said his companion.

They visited one of the better restaurants for a social chat. It was five in the afternoon when they met; it was seven-thirty before the last bone was picked.

Drouet was just finishing a little incident he was relating, and his face was expanding into a smile, when Hurstwood's eye caught his own. The latter had come in with several friends, and, seeing Drouet and some woman, not Carrie, drew his own conclusion.

"Ah, the rascal," he thought, and then, with a touch of righteous sympathy, "that's pretty hard on the little girl."

9. ***blasé.*** Having indulged in pleasure to the point where one becomes bored by it

Words For Everyday Use

guile (gīl) *n.,* slyness and cunning
gos • sa • mer (gäs´ə mər) *adj.,* light, thin, and filmy
per • e • gri • na • tion (per´ə gri nā shen) *n.,* travel
reck (rek) *vt.,* have concern for

Drouet jumped from one easy thought to another as he caught Hurstwood's eye. He felt but very little misgiving, until he saw that Hurstwood was cautiously pretending not to see. Then some of the latter's impression forced itself upon him. He thought of Carrie and their last meeting. By George, he would have to explain this to Hurstwood. Such a chance half-hour with an old friend must not have anything more attached to it than it really warranted.

For the first time he was troubled. Here was a moral complication of which he could not possibly get the ends. Hurstwood would laugh at him for being a fickle boy. He would laugh with Hurstwood. Carrie would never hear, his present companion at table would never know, and yet he could not help feeling that he was getting the worst of it—there was some faint stigma attached, and he was not guilty. He broke up the dinner by becoming dull, and saw his companion on her car. Then he went home.

"He hasn't talked to me about any of these later flames," thought Hurstwood to himself. "He thinks I think he cares for the girl out there."

◄ In what different ways do Hurstwood and Drouet interpret the situation?

"He ought not to think I'm knocking around, since I have just introduced him out there," thought Drouet.

"I saw you," Hurstwood said, genially, the next time Drouet drifted in to his polished resort, from which he could not stay away. He raised his forefinger indicatively, as parents do to children.

"An old acquaintance of mine that I ran into just as I was coming up from the station," explained Drouet. "She used to be quite a beauty."

"Still attracts a little, eh?" returned the other, affecting to jest.

"Oh, no," said Drouet, "just couldn't escape her this time."

"How long are you here?" asked Hurstwood.

"Only a few days."

"You must bring the girl down and take dinner with me," he said. "I'm afraid you keep her cooped up out there. I'll get a box for Joe Jefferson."[10]

"Not me," answered the drummer. "Sure I'll come."

This pleased Hurstwood immensely. He gave Drouet no credit for any feelings toward Carrie whatever. He envied him, and now, as he looked at the well-dressed, jolly salesman, whom he

◄ What does Hurstwood assume about Drouet's feelings? How is Hurstwood beginning to feel about Drouet?

10. **Joe Jefferson.** Joseph Jefferson (1825–1905), American actor

Words For Everyday Use	
	stig • ma (stig´mə) *n.,* something that detracts from the character or reputation of a person
	in • dic • a • tive • ly (in dik´ə tiv lē) *adv.,* with suggestion and authority

so much liked, the gleam of the rival glowed in his eye. He began to "size up" Drouet from the standpoints of wit and fascination. He began to look to see where he was weak. There was no disputing that, whatever he might think of him as a good fellow, he felt a certain amount of contempt for him as a lover. He could hoodwink[11] him all right. Why, if he would just let Carrie see one such little incident as that of Thursday, it would settle the matter. He ran on in thought, almost exulting, the while he laughed and chatted, and Drouet felt nothing. He had no power of analyzing the glance and the atmosphere of a man like Hurstwood. He stood and smiled and accepted the invitation while his friend examined him with the eye of a hawk.

The object of this peculiarly involved comedy was not thinking of either. She was busy adjusting her thoughts and feelings to newer conditions, and was not in danger of suffering disturbing pangs from either quarter.

One evening Drouet found her dressing herself before the glass.

"Cad," said he, catching her, "I believe you're getting vain."

"Nothing of the kind," she returned, smiling.

► *Why can't Carrie go out with Drouet that night?*

"Well, you're mighty pretty," he went on, slipping his arm around her. "Put on that navy blue dress of yours and I'll take you to the show."

"Oh, I've promised Mrs. Hale to go with her to the Exposition[12] tonight," she returned, apologetically.

"You did, eh?" he said, studying the situation abstractedly. "I wouldn't care to go to that myself."

"Well, I don't know," answered Carrie, puzzling, but not offering to break her promise in his favor.

Just then a knock came at their door and the maidservant handed a letter in.

"He says there's an answer expected," she explained.

► *What does Carrie quickly decide once she receives the note from Hurstwood?*

"It's from Hurstwood," said Drouet, noting the superscription[13] as he tore it open.

"You are to come down and see Joe Jefferson with me tonight," it ran in part. "It's my turn, as we agreed the other day. All other bets are off."

"Well, what do you say to this?" asked Drouet, innocently, while Carrie's mind bubbled with favorable replies.

---

11. **hoodwink.** Mislead or confuse by trickery
12. **Exposition.** Permanent fair in the Exposition Building on Michigan Avenue
13. **superscription.** Heading

Words For Everyday Use

con • tempt (kən tempt´) *n.,* scorn
ex • ult (eg sult´) *vi.,* rejoice greatly
pang (paŋ) *n.,* sudden sharp physical or emotional pain

"You had better decide, Charlie," she said, reservedly.

"I guess we had better go, if you can break that engagement upstairs," said Drouet.

"Oh, I can," returned Carrie without thinking.

Drouet selected writing paper while Carrie went to change her dress. She hardly explained to herself why this latest invitation appealed to her most.

"Shall I wear my hair as I did yesterday?" she asked, as she came out with several articles of apparel pending.

"Sure," he returned, pleasantly.

She was relieved to see that he felt nothing. She did not credit her willingness to go to any fascination Hurstwood held for her. It seemed that the combination of Hurstwood, Drouet, and herself was more agreeable than anything else that had been suggested. She arrayed herself most carefully and they started off, extending excuses upstairs.

◄ *About what is Carrie relieved? Explain whether she is truly interested in Hurstwood.*

"I say," said Hurstwood, as they came up the theater lobby, "we are exceedingly charming this evening."

Carrie fluttered under his approving glance.

"Now, then," he said, leading the way up the foyer into the theater.

If ever there was dressiness it was here. It was the personification of the old term spick and span.

"Did you ever see Jefferson?" he questioned, as he leaned toward Carrie in the box.

"I never did," she returned.

"He's delightful, delightful," he went on, giving the commonplace rendition of approval which such men know. He sent Drouet after a program, and then discoursed to Carrie concerning Jefferson as he had heard of him. The former was pleased beyond expression, and was really hypnotized by the environment, the trappings[14] of the box, the elegance of her companion. Several times their eyes accidentally met, and then there poured into hers such a flood of feeling as she had never before experienced. She could not for the moment explain it, for in the next glance or the next move of the hand there was seeming indifference, mingled only with the kindest attention.

Drouet shared in the conversation, but he was almost dull

14. **trappings.** Ornaments or adornments

Words For Everyday Use	
	pend • ing (pen´diŋ) *adj.,* awaiting decision
	ren • di • tion (ren dish´ən) *n.,* version
	dis • course (dis´kôrs´) *vi.,* give a long, formal talk

► *How does Carrie feel about Drouet by the end of the third act?*

in comparison. Hurstwood entertained them both, and now it was driven into Carrie's mind that here was the superior man. She instinctively felt that he was stronger and higher, and yet withal[15] so simple. By the end of the third act she was sure that Drouet was only a kindly soul, but otherwise defective. He sank every moment in her estimation by the strong comparison.

"I have had such a nice time," said Carrie, when it was all over and they were coming out.

► *What doesn't Drouet realize?*

"Yes, indeed," added Drouet, who was not in the least aware that a battle had been fought and his defenses weakened. He was like the Emperor of China, who sat glorying in himself, unaware that his fairest provinces were being wrested from him.

"Well, you have saved me a dreary evening," returned Hurstwood. "Goodnight."

He took Carrie's little hand, and a current of feeling swept from one to the other.

"I'm so tired," said Carrie, leaning back in the car when Drouet began to talk.

"Well, you rest a little while I smoke," he said, rising, and then he foolishly went to the forward platform of the car and left the game as it stood.

---

15. **withal.** Despite that

Words For Everyday Use

prov • ince (präv´ins) *n.,* territory

wrest (rest) *vt.,* take or extract by force

CHAPTER 12

Of the Lamps of the Mansions: The Ambassador's Plea

Mrs. Hurstwood was not aware of any of her husband's moral defections, though she might readily have suspected his tendencies, which she well understood. She was a woman upon whose action under provocation you could never count. Hurstwood, for one, had not the slightest idea of what she would do under certain circumstances. He had never seen her thoroughly aroused. In fact, she was not a woman who would fly into a passion. She had too little faith in mankind not to know that they were erring. She was too calculating to jeopardize any advantage she might gain in the way of information by fruitless clamor. Her wrath would never wreak itself in one fell blow. She would wait and brood, studying the details and adding to them until her power might be commensurate with her desire for revenge. At the same time, she would not delay to inflict any injury, big or little, which would wound the object of her revenge and still leave him uncertain as to the source of the evil. She was a cold, self-centered woman, with many a thought of her own which never found expression, not even by so much as the glint of an eye.

◄ *Why might Mrs. Hurstwood be a particularly dangerous enemy to make?*

Hurstwood felt some of this in her nature, though he did not actually perceive it. He dwelt with her in peace and some satisfaction. He did not fear her in the least—there was no cause for it. She still took a faint pride in him, which was augmented by her desire to have her social integrity maintained. She was secretly somewhat pleased by the fact that much of her husband's property was in her name, a precaution which Hurstwood had taken when his home interests were somewhat more alluring than at present. His wife had not the slightest reason to feel that anything would ever go amiss with their household, and yet the shadows which run before gave her a thought of the good of it now and then. She was in a position to become refractory with considerable advantage, and Hurstwood conducted himself circumspectly

◄ *What has Hurstwood done with much of his property? What effect does this have on his relationship with his wife?*

Words For Everyday Use

prov • o • ca • tion (präv´ə kā´shən) *n.*, irritation

clam • or (klam´ər) *n.*, loud complaint

wreak (rēk) *vt.*, give free play to

com • men • su • rate (kə men ´shoor it) *adj.*, equal to

re • frac • tory (ri frak´tər ē) *adj.*, hard to manage

because he felt that he could not be sure of anything once she became dissatisfied.

It so happened that on the night when Hurstwood, Carrie, and Drouet were in the box at McVicker's, George, Jr., was in the sixth row of the parquet[1] with the daughter of H. B. Carmichael, the third partner of a wholesale drygoods house of that city. Hurstwood did not see his son, for he sat, as was his wont, as far back as possible, leaving himself just partially visible, when he bent forward, to those within the first six rows in question. It was his wont to sit this way in every theater—to make his personality as inconspicuous as possible where it would be no advantage to him to have it otherwise.

He never moved but what, if there was any danger of his conduct being misconstrued or ill-reported, he looked carefully about him and counted the cost of every inch of conspicuity.[2]

► Who sees Hurstwood at the theater?

The next morning at breakfast his son said:

"I saw you, Governor,[3] last night."

"Were you at McVicker's?" said Hurstwood, with the best grace in the world.

"Yes," said young George.

"Who with?"

"Miss Carmichael."

Mrs. Hurstwood directed an inquiring glance at her husband, but could not judge from his appearance whether it was any more than a casual look into the theater which was referred to.

"How was the play?" she inquired.

"Very good," returned Hurstwood, "only it's the same old thing, 'Rip Van Winkle'."

"Whom did you go with?" queried his wife, with assumed indifference.

"Charlie Drouet and his wife. They are friends of Moy's, visiting here."

► Why wouldn't Hurstwood's social activities normally disturb his wife? Why is she so curious about this particular visit to the theater?

Owing to the peculiar nature of his position, such a disclosure as this would ordinarily create no difficulty. His wife took it for granted that his situation called for certain social movements in which she might not be included. But of late he had pleaded office duty on several occasions when his wife asked for his company to any evening entertainment.

1. **parquet.** Main floor of a theater
2. **conspicuity.** Openness to view
3. **Governor.** Polite form of address for a man

Words For Everyday Use

in • con • spic • u • ous (in´kən spik´ yo͞o əs) *adj.*, hard to see or perceive; attracting little attention

mis • con • strued (mis ´kən stro͞od´) *adj.*, misinterpreted

dis • clo • sure (dis klōz´zher) *n.*, revelation

He had done so in regard to the very evening in question only the morning before.

"I thought you were going to be busy," she remarked, very carefully.

"So I was," he exclaimed. "I couldn't help the interruption, but I made up for it afterward by working until two."

This settled the discussion for the time being, but there was a residue of opinion which was not satisfactory. There was no time at which the claims of his wife could have been more unsatisfactorily pushed. For years he had been steadily modifying his matrimonial devotion, and found her company dull. Now that a new light shone upon the horizon, this older luminary paled in the west. He was satisfied to turn his face away entirely, and any call to look back was irksome.

◄ In what way do Mr. and Mrs. Hurstwood's attitudes toward their marriage differ?

She, on the contrary, was not at all inclined to accept anything less than a complete fulfillment of the letter of their relationship, though the spirit might be wanting.

"We are coming downtown this afternoon," she remarked, a few days later. "I want you to come over to Kinsley's and meet Mr. Phillips and his wife. They're stopping at the Tremont, and we're going to show them around a little."

After the occurrence of Wednesday, he could not refuse, though the Phillips were about as uninteresting as vanity and ignorance could make them. He agreed, but it was with short grace. He was angry when he left the house.

"I'll put a stop to this," he thought. "I'm not going to be bothered fooling around with visitors when I have work to do."

Not long after this Mrs. Hurstwood came with a similar proposition, only it was to a matinee this time.

◄ Why do the feelings of "mutual antagonism" increase in the Hurstwood household?

"My dear," he returned, "I haven't time. I'm too busy."

"You find time to go with other people, though," she replied, with considerable irritation.

"Nothing of the kind," he answered. "I can't avoid business relations, and that's all there is to it."

"Well, never mind," she exclaimed. Her lips tightened. The feeling of mutual antagonism was increased.

On the other hand, his interest in Drouet's little shop-girl grew in an almost evenly balanced proportion. That young lady, under the stress of her situation and the tutelage of her new friend, changed effectively. She had the aptitude of the

Words For Everyday Use

mod • i • fy (mäd´ə fī) *vt.,* alter

lu • mi • nar • y (lo͞o´mə ner´ē) *n.,* body which gives off light, such as the sun or moon

irk • some (ʉrk´səm) *adj.,* tiresome or annoying

an • tag • o • nism (an tag´ə niz'əm) *n.,* hostility

► *In what way is Carrie changing under Hurstwood's influence? under Mrs. Hale's?*

► *What does Mrs. Hale like to spend her time doing?*

► *What does Carrie associate with wealth and fine things? What does she think would happen if she were to own such a fine home? Do you think she is correct? Explain.*

struggler who seeks emancipation. The glow of a more showy life was not lost upon her. She did not grow in knowledge so much as she awakened in the matter of desire. Mrs. Hale's extended harangues upon the subjects of wealth and position taught her to distinguish between degrees of wealth.

Mrs. Hale loved to drive in the afternoon in the sun when it was fine, and to satisfy her soul with a sight of those mansions and lawns which she could not afford. On the North Side had been erected a number of elegant mansions along what is now known as the North Shore Drive. The present lake wall of stone and granitoid[4] was not then in place, but the road had been well laid out, the intermediate spaces of lawn were lovely to look upon, and the houses were thoroughly new and imposing. When the winter season had passed and the first fine days of the early spring appeared, Mrs. Hale secured a buggy for an afternoon and invited Carrie. They rode first through Lincoln Park and on far out toward Evanston, turning back at four and arriving at the north end of the Shore Drive at about five o'clock. At this time of year the days are still comparatively short, and the shadows of the evening were beginning to settle down upon the great city. Lamps were beginning to burn with that mellow radiance which seems almost watery and translucent to the eye. There was a softness in the air which speaks with an infinite delicacy of feeling to the flesh as well as to the soul. Carrie felt that it was a lovely day. She was ripened by it in spirit for many suggestions. As they drove along the smooth pavement an occasional carriage passed. She saw one stop and the footman[5] dismount, opening the door for a gentleman who seemed to be leisurely returning from some afternoon pleasure. Across the broad lawns, now first freshening into green, she saw lamps faintly glowing upon rich interiors. Now it was but a chair, now a table, now an ornate corner, which met her eye, but it appealed to her as almost nothing else could. Such childish fancies as she had had of fairy palaces and kingly quarters now came back. She imagined that across these richly carved entrance ways, where the globed and crystalled lamps shone upon paneled doors set with stained and designed panes of glass, was neither

4. **granitoid.** Manufactured, granitelike substance
5. **footman.** Servant who accompanies a carriage

Words For Everyday Use

e • man • ci • pa • tion (ē man´sə pā shən) *n.,* freedom from restraint

ha • rangue (hə raŋ´) *n.,* long, noisy, or scolding speech

dis • mount (dis mount´) *vi.,* get off or down

care nor unsatisfied desire. She was perfectly certain that here was happiness. If she could but stroll up yon[6] broad walk, cross that rich entrance way, which to her was of the beauty of a jewel, and sweep in grace and luxury to possession and command—oh! how quickly would sadness flee; how, in an instant, would the heartache end. She gazed and gazed, wondering, delighting, longing, and all the while the siren voice of the unrestful was whispering in her ear.

"If we could have such a home as that," said Mrs. Hale sadly, "how delightful it would be."

"And yet they do say," said Carrie, "that no one is ever happy."

She had heard so much of the canting philosophy of the grapeless fox.

"I notice," said Mrs. Hale, "that they all try mighty hard, though, to take their misery in a mansion."

When she came to her own rooms, Carrie saw their comparative insignificance. She was not so dull but that she could perceive they were but three small rooms in a moderately well-furnished boarding house. She was not contrasting it now with what she had had, but what she had so recently seen. The glow of the palatial doors was still in her eye, the roll of cushioned carriages still in her ears. What, after all, was Drouet? What was she? At her window, she thought it over, rocking to and fro, and gazing out across the lamp-lit park toward the lamp-lit houses on Warren and Ashland avenues. She was too wrought up[7] to care to go down to eat, too pensive to do aught[8] but rock and sing. Some old tunes crept to her lips, and, as she sang them, her heart sank. She longed and longed and longed. It was now for the old cottage room in Columbia City, now the mansion upon the Shore Drive, now the fine dress of some lady, now the elegance of some scene. She was sad beyond measure, and yet uncertain, wishing, fancying. Finally, it seemed as if all her state was one of loneliness and forsakenness, and she could scarce refrain from trembling at the lip. She hummed and hummed as the moments went by, sitting in the shadow by the window, and was therein as happy, though she did not perceive it, as she ever would be.

◄ *How does Carrie feel about her place, herself, and Drouet once she returns from the mansions?*

◄ *What does Carrie spend her time doing? Do you think it is a good idea for her to spend all her time longing for things she does not have?*

◄ *What does the narrator reveal about Carrie's future?*

6. **yon.** That or those, at a distance
7. **wrought up.** Disturbed or excited
8. **aught.** Anything

Words For Everyday Use

cant • ing (kant iŋ) *adj.,* meaningless, conventional
pa • la • tial (pə lā´shəl) *adj.,* like a palace
pen • sive (pen´siv) *adj.,* deep in thought

While Carrie was still in this frame of mind, the house-servant brought up the intelligence that Mr. Hurstwood was in the parlor asking to see Mr. and Mrs. Drouet.

"I guess he doesn't know that Charlie is out of town," thought Carrie.

She had seen comparatively little of the manager during the winter, but had been kept constantly in mind of him by one thing and another, principally by the strong impression he had made. She was quite disturbed for the moment as to her appearance, but soon satisfied herself by the aid of the mirror, and went below.

Hurstwood was in his best form, as usual. He hadn't heard that Drouet was out of town. He was but slightly affected by the intelligence, and devoted himself to the more general topics which would interest Carrie. It was surprising—the ease with which he conducted a conversation. He was like every man who has had the advantage of practice and knows he has sympathy. He knew that Carrie listened to him pleasurably, and, without the least effort, he fell into a train of observation which absorbed her fancy. He drew up his chair and modulated his voice to such a degree that what he said seemed wholly confidential. He confined himself almost exclusively to his observation of men and pleasures. He had been here and there, he had seen this and that. Somehow he made Carrie wish to see similar things, and all the while kept her aware of himself. She could not shut out the consciousness of his individuality and presence for a moment. He would raise his eyes slowly in smiling emphasis of something, and she was fixed by their magnetism. He would draw out, with the easiest grace, her approval. Once he touched her hand for emphasis and she only smiled. He seemed to radiate an atmosphere which suffused her being. He was never dull for a minute, and seemed to make her clever. At least, she brightened under his influence until all her best side was exhibited. She felt that she was more clever with him than with others. At least, he seemed to find so much in her to applaud. There was not the slightest touch of patronage. Drouet was full of it.

▶ Why do you think Hurstwood discusses pleasures to amuse Carrie? Explain why this topic is likely to gain her attention.

▶ How does Carrie feel about herself in Hurstwood's presence? Why?

There had been something so personal, so subtle, in each meeting between them, both when Drouet was present and when he was absent, that Carrie could not speak of it without

Words For Everyday Use	
	mod • u • late (mäj´ə lāt´) *vt.,* regulate; adjust
	suf • fuse (sə fyo͞oz´) *vt.,* overspread and fill
	pa • tron • age (pā´trən ij) *n.,* behavior that shows awareness of another's lower standing or ability

feeling a sense of difficulty. She was no talker. She could never arrange her thoughts in fluent order. It was always a matter of feeling with her, strong and deep. Each time there had been no sentence of importance which she could relate, and as for the glances and sensations, what woman would reveal them? Such things had never been between her and Drouet. As a matter of fact, they could never be. She had been dominated by distress and the enthusiastic forces of relief which Drouet represented at an opportune moment when she yielded to him. Now she was persuaded by secret current feelings which Drouet had never understood. Hurstwood's glance was as effective as the spoken words of a lover, and more. They called for no immediate decision, and could not be answered.

◄ *In what way do the feelings that drew Carrie to Drouet differ from the feelings that are drawing her to Hurstwood?*

People in general attach too much importance to words. They are under the illusion that talking effects great results. As a matter of fact, words are, as a rule, the shallowest portion of all the argument. They but dimly represent the great surging feelings and desires which lie behind. When the distraction of the tongue is removed, the heart listens.

◄ *What does the narrator say about words?*

In this conversation she heard, instead of his words, the voices of the things which he represented. How suave was the counsel of his appearance! How feelingly did his superior state speak for itself! The growing desire he felt for her lay upon her spirit as a gentle hand. She did not need to tremble at all, because it was invisible; she did not need to worry over what other people would say—what she herself would say—because it had no tangibility. She was being pleaded with, persuaded, led into denying old rights and assuming new ones, and yet there were no words to prove it. Such conversation as was indulged in held the same relationship to the actual mental enactments of the twain[9] that the low music of the orchestra does to the dramatic incident which it is used to cover.

"Have you ever seen the houses along the Lake Shore on the North Side?" asked Hurstwood.

"Why, I was just over there this afternoon—Mrs. Hale and I. Aren't they beautiful?"

"They're very fine," he answered.

"Oh, me," said Carrie, pensively. "I wish I could live in such a place."

9. **twain.** Two

► *What does Hurstwood say to Carrie that he thinks has struck a "deep chord"?*

"You're not happy," said Hurstwood, slowly, after a slight pause.

He had raised his eyes solemnly and was looking into her own. He assumed that he had struck a deep chord. Now was a slight chance to say a word in his own behalf. He leaned over quietly and continued his steady gaze. He felt the critical character of the period. She endeavored to stir, but it was useless. The whole strength of a man's nature was working. He had good cause to urge him on. He looked and looked, and the longer the situation lasted the more difficult it became. The little shop-girl was getting into deep water. She was letting her few supports float away from her.

"Oh," she said at last, "you mustn't look at me like that."

"I can't help it," he answered.

She relaxed a little and let the situation endure, giving him strength.

"You are not satisfied with life, are you?"

"No," she answered, weakly.

He saw he was the master of the situation—he felt it. He reached over and touched her hand.

"You mustn't," she exclaimed, jumping up.

"I didn't intend to," he answered, easily.

She did not run away, as she might have done. She did not terminate the interview, but he drifted off into a pleasant field of thought with the readiest grace. Not long after he rose to go, and she felt that he was in power.

► *Of what does Hurstwood assure Carrie? Why doesn't she respond?*

"You mustn't feel bad," he said, kindly; "things will straighten out in the course of time."

She made no answer, because she could think of nothing to say.

"We are good friends, aren't we?" he said, extending his hand.

"Yes," she answered.

"Not a word, then, until I see you again."

He retained a hold on her hand.

"I can't promise," she said, doubtfully.

"You must be more generous than that," he said, in such a simple way that she was touched.

"Let's not talk about it anymore," she returned.

"All right," he said, brightening.

Words For Everyday Use

ter • mi • nate (tʉr´mə nāt) *vt.*, end

He went down the steps and into his cab. Carrie closed the door and ascended into her room. She undid her broad lace collar before the mirror and unfastened her pretty alligator belt which she had recently bought.

"I'm getting terrible," she said, honestly affected by a feeling of trouble and shame. "I don't seem to do anything right."

She unloosed her hair after a time, and let it hang in loose brown waves. Her mind was going over the events of the evening.

"I don't know," she murmured at last, "what I can do."

"Well," said Hurstwood as he rode away, "she likes me all right; that I know."

◄ How does Hurstwood feel after meeting with Carrie? To what time in his life does the meeting bring him back? How can you tell?

The aroused manager whistled merrily for a good four miles to his office an old melody that he had not recalled for fifteen years.

Words For Everyday Use

as • cend (ə send´) *vi.,* go up

Responding to the Selection

How do you feel about Carrie's situation? What do you think of the choices she has made? her value system? In chapters 7–12, Carrie's conscience proves to be ineffectual. Imagine that you are her conscience. What instructions or advice would you have to give?

Reviewing the Selection

Recalling and Interpreting

1. **R:** What does Carrie resolve to do in chapter 7 once she realizes she can't appear in the Hansons' flat with new clothes? What stops her from doing so? What do she and Drouet do instead? What instruction does Drouet give Carrie when they go to rent the room? What promise does Carrie make to Minnie before she leaves her flat for good?

2. **I:** Explain whether Carrie really wants to go through with the resolution she has made. What does Drouet's instruction reveal about the situation in which Carrie has put herself? Why do you think Carrie finds it so easy to leave her current situation? Explain whether Minnie understands the significance of Carrie's final words.

3. **R:** In chapter 8, page 74, what does the narrator say about most "consciences"? What does the narrator say Carrie lacks? What happens when Carrie and Drouet arrive at the steps to Carrie's new rooms? Of what is Carrie's sister dreaming at that exact moment? How far ahead does Dreiser move the story after relating Minnie's dreams?

4. **I:** What does the narrator want the reader to understand from the discussion of conscience, the pause at the stairs, Minnie's dreams, and the leap forward in time? What do Minnie's dreams reveal she understands about Carrie's situation? In what way do these dreams show a new side of Minnie? Why do you think Dreiser used an indirect method of relating events rather than simply revealing what occurred? What concerns about his audience might Dreiser have had?

5. **R:** In chapter 9, what does the narrator say about the spirit, or atmosphere, of the Hurstwood home? What are Jessica's primary concerns? What does Mrs. Hurstwood long to do? What types of things does the family discuss? What is Hurstwood's attitude toward respectable men who get themselves in "trouble"? Why does he himself avoid "trouble"? What does he do to deviate from his usual routine that upsets his wife?

6. **I:** Explain the significance of the title of chapter 9, "Convention's Own Tinder-Box: The Eye That Is Green." What does Hurstwood mean by "trouble"? In what way is the Hurstwood residence like a tinder-box? In what way is Hurstwood's situation similar to Carrie's at the beginning of chapter 7? What do you think is about to happen to him? Why?

7. **R:** What does Drouet say to reassure Carrie when he tells her that Hurstwood is coming to visit? What excuse does Drouet make for failing to make their relationship "legitimate"? What is Carrie's attitude toward gambling? What do Hurstwood and Drouet say about her moral scruples? How does Hurstwood begin to feel about Carrie? about Drouet?

8. **I:** Why does Carrie find Drouet's remark to be inconsiderate? Explain whether you think that Drouet intends to marry Carrie at all. In what way does the gambling incident reflect her relationship with the two men? When Drouet announces that Hurstwood is a good friend, Carrie says, "he seems to be." In what way is Hurstwood pretending to be something else in his relationship with Drouet? with Carrie?

Synthesizing

9. In chapters 7–12, Drouet and Carrie are often compared and contrasted. What are some of their similarities and differences? Why does Carrie begin to despise Drouet after meeting Hurstwood? Explain whether Carrie is really falling in love with Hurstwood. Why is Hurstwood attracted to Carrie?

10. After her own fall from virtue, Carrie's conscience tells her, "You had not tried before you failed." Explain whether this is an accurate assessment of Carrie's situation. Why doesn't Carrie put up more of a struggle to do what is considered "moral" and "right"? Explain whether the narrator serves as Carrie's conscience. Does the narrator condemn her? judge her? Why do you think the author decided to take this stance toward Carrie's fall? How do you think readers of the time reacted to Dreiser's not judging Carrie more harshly?

Understanding Literature (QUESTIONS FOR DISCUSSION)

1. **Character and Characterization.** A **character** is a person who figures in the action of a literary work. Characterization is the use of literary techniques to create a character. Writers use three major techniques to create characters: direct description, portrayal of characters' behavior, and representation of characters' internal states. For more information on characterization, see the Handbook of Literary Terms. Would you define Carrie as an active or passive character? Explain whether it seems to you that Carrie makes many active decisions or whether she seems to get swept along passively in the unfolding of events. Find examples of events or passages in chapters 7–12 to support your opinion. Explain whether Carrie experiences passionate desire for people and things or vague yearnings and longings. In what way is this related to her role as an active or passive character?

2. **Personification. Personification** is a figure of speech in which an idea, animal, or thing is described as if it were a human. What things are personified in Carrie's mind at the beginning of chapter 11? In what way are these things portrayed as human? In chapter 8, page 62, to what is Carrie compared? Why might this technique be considered the opposite of personification? What is significant about the way that Dreiser uses personification in these chapters?

3. **Foil.** A **foil** is a character whose attributes, or characteristics, contrast with, and therefore throw into relief, the attributes of another character. For example, in these chapters, Hurstwood becomes for Carrie a foil to Drouet. In chapter 8, Carrie runs into a character who serves as her own foil—one of the girls she used to work with at the factory. In what ways are these characters similar? In what ways do they differ? Why does Carrie feel as if "some great tide had rolled between them"? Why is it significant that their differences are superficial, given this story's focus?

4. **Symbol.** A **symbol** is a thing that stands for or represents both itself and something else. In chapter 8, Minnie dreams that Carrie lowers herself into a pit at a coal mine. What might this symbol represent? Explain why it is significant that Dreiser chooses a pit in a coal mine as his symbol. What is Dreiser indicating about industrial society? In chapter 12, Carrie rocks in a rocking-chair as she daydreams about the past and the future. What might this rocking represent?

CHAPTER 13

His Credentials Accepted: A Babel of Tongues

It was not quite two days after the scene between Carrie and Hurstwood in the Ogden Place parlor before he again put in his appearance. He had been thinking almost uninterruptedly of her. Her leniency had, in a way, inflamed his regard. He felt that he must succeed with her, and that speedily.

The reason for his interest, not to say fascination, was deeper than mere desire. It was a flowering out of feelings which had been withering in dry and almost barren soil for many years. It is probable that Carrie represented a better order of woman than had ever attracted him before. He had had no love affair since that which culminated in his marriage, and since then time and the world had taught him how raw and erroneous was his original judgment. Whenever he thought of it, he told himself that, if he had it to do over again, he would never marry such a woman. At the same time, his experience with women in general had lessened his respect for the sex. He maintained a cynical attitude, well grounded on numerous experiences. Such women as he had known were of nearly one type, selfish, ignorant, flashy. The wives of his friends were not inspiring to look upon. His own wife had developed a cold, commonplace nature which to him was anything but pleasing. What he knew of that underworld where grovel the beast-men of society (and he knew a great deal) had hardened his nature. He looked upon most women with suspicion—a single eye to the utility of beauty and dress. He followed them with a keen, suggestive glance. At the same time, he was not so dull but that a good woman commanded his respect. Personally, he did not attempt to analyze the marvel of a saintly woman. He would take off his hat, and would silence the light-tongued and the vicious in her presence—much as the Irish keeper of a Bowery hall[1] will humble himself before a Sister

◄ *Why is Hurstwood fascinated by Carrie?*

◄ *How does Hurstwood look upon most women?*

1. **Bowery hall.** Saloon on Bowery Street, or the district around this street, in New York City. The area is characterized by many cheap hotels and saloons.

Words For Everyday Use

le • ni • en • cy (lēn´yən sē) *n.,* easiness
bar • ren (bar´ ən) *adj.,* having little or no vegetation
cul • mi • nate (kul´mə nāt) *vi.,* result
er • ro • ne • ous (ər rō´ nē əs) *adj.,* mistaken; wrong

of Mercy, and pay toll to charity with a willing and reverent hand. But he would not think much upon the question of why he did so.

A man in his situation who comes, after a long round of worthless or hardening experiences, upon a young, unsophisticated, innocent soul, is apt either to hold aloof, out of a sense of his own remoteness, or to draw near and become fascinated and elated by his discovery. It is only by a roundabout process that such men ever do draw near such a girl. They have no method, no understanding of how to ingratiate themselves in youthful favor, save when they find virtue in the toils. If, unfortunately, the fly has got caught in the net, the spider can come forth and talk business upon its own terms. So when maidenhood has wandered into the moil of the city, when it is brought within the circle of the "rounder" and the *roué*,[2] even though it be at the outermost rim, they can come forth and use their alluring arts.

▶ *What were Hurstwood's expectations when meeting Carrie? Why does Carrie surprise him?*

Hurstwood had gone, at Drouet's invitation, to meet a new baggage of fine clothes and pretty features. He entered, expecting to indulge in an evening of lightsome frolic, and then lose track of the newcomer forever. Instead he found a woman whose youth and beauty attracted him. In the mild light of Carrie's eye was nothing of the calculation of the mistress. In the diffident manner was nothing of the art of the courtesan.[3] He saw at once that a mistake had been made, that some difficult conditions had pushed this troubled creature into his presence, and his interest was enlisted. Here sympathy sprang to the rescue, but it was not unmixed with selfishness. He wanted to win Carrie because he thought her fate mingled with his was better than if it were united with Drouet's. He envied the drummer his conquest as he had never envied any man in all the course of his experience.

▶ *What "mistake" does Hurstwood believe has been made? Why does he want to win Carrie?*

▶ *According to the narrator, in what way is Carrie better than Hurstwood?*

Carrie was certainly better than this man, as she was superior, mentally, to Drouet. She came fresh from the air of the village, the light of the country still in her eye. Here was neither guile nor rapacity. There were slight inherited traits of both in her, but they were rudimentary. She was too full of wonder and desire to be greedy. She still looked about her

2. **the "rounder" and the *roué*.** Those who overindulge in drinking and gambling
3. **courtesan.** Prostitute, especially a mistress of a king or nobleman

Words For Everyday Use

rev • er • ent (rev´ ər ənt) *adj.*, with deeply respectful feeling
a • loof (ə lo͞of´) *adj.*, emotionally distant
re • mote • ness (ri mōt nəs) *n.*, distance from another
in • gra • ti • ate (in grā´ shē āt´) *vt.*, bring oneself into another's favor or good graces
moil (moil) *n.*, confusion; turmoil
ra • pac • i • ty (rə pas´ ə tē) *n.*, greed

upon the great maze of the city without understanding. Hurstwood felt the bloom and the youth. He picked her as he would the fresh fruit of a tree. He felt as fresh in her presence as one who is taken out of the flash of summer to the first cool breath of spring.

Carrie, left alone since the scene in question, and having no one with whom to counsel, had at first wandered from one strange mental conclusion to another, until at last, tired out, she gave it up. She owed something to Drouet, she thought. It did not seem more than yesterday that he had aided her when she was worried and distressed. She had the kindliest feelings for him in every way. She gave him credit for his good looks, his generous feelings, and even, in fact, failed to recollect his egotism when he was absent; but she could not feel any binding influence keeping her for him as against all others. In fact, such a thought had never had any grounding, even in Drouet's desires.

◄ What obligations does Carrie feel to Drouet? Does she feel as though she must stay with him forever?

The truth is, that this goodly drummer carried the doom of all enduring relationships in his own lightsome manner and unstable fancy. He went merrily on, assured that he was alluring all, that affection followed tenderly in his wake, that things would endure unchangingly for his pleasure. When he missed some old face, or found some door finally shut to him, it did not grieve him deeply. He was too young, too successful. He would remain thus young in spirit until he was dead.

◄ How does Drouet feel when one of his old girlfriends no longer wishes to see him?

As for Hurstwood, he was alive with thoughts and feelings concerning Carrie. He had no definite plans regarding her, but he was determined to make her confess an affection for him. He thought he saw in her drooping eye, her unstable glance, her wavering manner, the symptoms of a budding passion. He wanted to stand near her and make her lay her hand in his—he wanted to find out what her next step would be—what the next sign of feeling for him would be. Such anxiety and enthusiasm had not affected him for years. He was a youth again in feeling—a cavalier in action.

◄ How does Hurstwood assume Carrie feels about him? Do you think he is right? Explain.

In his position opportunity for taking his evenings out was excellent. He was a most faithful worker in general, and a man who commanded the confidence of his employers in so far as the distribution of his time was concerned. He could take such hours off as he chose, for it was well known that he fulfilled his managerial duties successfully, whatever time he

Words For Everyday Use

cav • a • lier (kav´ə lir´) *n.,* gallant or courteous gentleman

might take. His grace, tact, and ornate appearance gave the place an air which was most essential, while at the same time his long experience made him a most excellent judge of its stock necessities. Bartenders and assistants might come and go, singly or in groups, but, so long as he was present, the host of old-time customers would barely notice the change. He gave the place the atmosphere to which they were used. Consequently, he arranged his hours very much to suit himself, taking now an afternoon, now an evening, but invariably returning between eleven and twelve to witness the last hour or two of the day's business and look after the closing details.

"You see that things are safe and all the employees are out when you go home, George," Moy had once remarked to him, and he never once, in all the period of his long service, neglected to do this. Neither of the owners had for years been in the resort after five in the afternoon, and yet their manager as faithfully fulfilled this request as if they had been there regularly to observe.

On this Friday afternoon, scarcely two days after his previous visit, he made up his mind to see Carrie. He could not stay away longer.

"Evans," he said, addressing the head barkeeper, "if anyone calls, I will be back between four and five."

He hurried to Madison Street and boarded a horsecar, which carried him to Ogden Place in half an hour.

Carrie had thought of going for a walk, and had put on a light gray woolen dress with a jaunty double-breasted jacket. She had out her hat and gloves, and was fastening a white lace tie about her throat when the housemaid brought up the information that Mr. Hurstwood wished to see her.

She started slightly at the announcement, but told the girl to say that she would come down in a moment, and proceeded to hasten her dressing.

▶ Explain whether Carrie has definite feelings for Hurstwood.

Carrie could not have told herself at this moment whether she was glad or sorry that the impressive manager was awaiting her presence. She was slightly flurried and tingling in the cheeks, but it was more nervousness than either fear or favor. She did not try to conjecture what the drift of the conversation would be. She only felt that she must be careful, and that Hurstwood had an indefinable fascination for her. Then she gave her tie its last touch with her fingers and went below.

Words For Everyday Use

flur • ried (flʉr´ ēd) *adj.*, agitated

con • jec • ture (kən jek´ chər) *vt.*, guess

The deep-feeling manager was himself a little strained in the nerves by the thorough consciousness of his mission. He felt that he must make a strong play on this occasion, but now that the hour was come, and he heard Carrie's feet upon the stair, his nerve failed him. He sank a little in determination, for he was not so sure, after all, what her opinion might be.

When she entered the room, however, her appearance gave him courage. She looked simple and charming enough to strengthen the daring of any lover. Her apparent nervousness dispelled his own.

◄ *What gives Hurstwood the courage to pursue his relationship with Carrie?*

"How are you?" he said, easily. "I could not resist the temptation to come out this afternoon, it was so pleasant."

"Yes," said Carrie, halting before him, "I was just preparing to go for a walk myself."

"Oh, were you?" he said. "Supposing, then, you get your hat and we both go?"

They crossed the park and went west along Washington Boulevard, beautiful with its broad macadamized road,[4] and large frame houses set back from the sidewalks. It was a street where many of the more prosperous residents of the West Side lived, and Hurstwood could not help feeling nervous over the publicity of it. They had gone but a few blocks when a livery stable[5] sign in one of the side streets solved the difficulty for him. He would take her to drive along the new Boulevard.

◄ *Why does Hurstwood decide to take Carrie for a drive instead of walking with her down Washington Boulevard?*

The Boulevard at that time was little more than a country road. The part he intended showing her was much farther out on this same West Side, where there was scarcely a house. It connected Douglas Park with Washington or South Park, and was nothing more than a neatly *made* road, running due south for some five miles over an open, grassy prairie, and then due east over the same kind of prairie for the same distance. There was not a house to be encountered anywhere along the larger part of the route, and any conversation would be pleasantly free of interruption.

At the stable he picked a gentle horse, and they were soon out of range of either public observation or hearing.

"Can you drive?" he said, after a time.

"I never tried," said Carrie.

4. **macadamized road.** Street created by a process of rolling successive layers of small broken stones on a dry earth roadbed

5. **livery stable.** Stable where horses and carriages are kept for hire

Words For Everyday Use

pros • per • ous (präs´ pər əs) *adj.*, well-to-do

He put the reins in her hand, and folded his arms.

"You see there's nothing to it much," he said, smilingly.

"Not when you have a gentle horse," said Carrie.

"You can handle a horse as well as anyone, after a little practice," he added, encouragingly.

He had been looking for some time for a break in the conversation when he could give it a serious turn. Once or twice he had held his peace, hoping that in silence her thoughts would take the color of his own, but she had lightly continued the subject. Presently, however, his silence controlled the situation. The drift of his thoughts began to tell. He gazed fixedly at nothing in particular, as if he were thinking of something which concerned her not at all. His thoughts, however, spoke for themselves. She was very much aware that a climax was pending.

"Do you know," he said, "I have spent the happiest evenings in years since I have known you?"

"Have you?" she said, with assumed airiness, but still excited by the conviction which the tone of his voice carried.

"I was going to tell you the other evening," he added, "but somehow the opportunity slipped away."

► In what way do Carrie's and Hurstwood's approaches to communication differ?

Carrie was listening without attempting to reply. She could think of nothing worthwhile to say. Despite all the ideas concerning right which had troubled her vaguely since she had last seen him, she was now influenced again strongly in his favor.

"I came out here today," he went on, solemnly, "to tell you just how I feel—to see if you wouldn't listen to me."

Hurstwood was something of a romanticist after his kind. He was capable of strong feelings—often poetic ones—and under a stress of desire, such as the present, he waxed eloquent. That is, his feelings and his voice were colored with that seeming repression and pathos which is the essence of eloquence.

► How does Carrie respond when Hurstwood proclaims his love?

"You know," he said, putting his hand on her arm, and keeping a strange silence while he formulated words, "that I love you?"

Carrie did not stir at the words. She was bound up completely in the man's atmosphere. He would have church-like silence in order to express his feelings, and she kept it. She did not move her eyes from the flat, open scene before her. Hurstwood waited for a few moments, and then repeated the words.

Words For Everyday Use

pa • thos (pā´thäs´) *n.*, feelings of sorrow, pity, or compassion

"You must not say that," she said, weakly.

Her words were not convincing at all. They were the result of a feeble thought that something ought to be said. He paid no attention to them whatever.

"Carrie," he said, using her first name with sympathetic familiarity, "I want you to love me. You don't know how much I need someone to waste a little affection on me. I am practically alone. There is nothing in my life that is pleasant or delightful. It's all work and worry with people who are nothing to me."

◄ Do you think that Hurstwood's state is as pitiable as he claims? Why, or why not?

As he said this, Hurstwood really imagined that his state was pitiful. He had the ability to get off at a distance and view himself objectively—of seeing what he wanted to see in the things which made up his existence. Now, as he spoke, his voice trembled with that peculiar vibration which is the result of tensity. It went ringing home to his companion's heart.

"Why, I should think," she said, turning upon him large eyes which were full of sympathy and feeling, "that you would be very happy. You know so much of the world."

◄ In what ways do Carrie's and Hurstwood's estimations of happiness differ?

"That is it," he said, his voice dropping to a soft minor, "I know too much of the world."

It was an important thing to her to hear one so well-positioned and powerful speaking in this manner. She could not help feeling the strangeness of her situation. How was it that, in so little a while, the narrow life of the country had fallen from her as a garment, and the city, with all its mystery, taken its place? Here was this greatest mystery, the man of money and affairs sitting beside her, appealing to her. Behold, he had ease and comfort, his strength was great, his position high, his clothing rich, and yet he was appealing to her. She could formulate no thought which would be just and right. She troubled herself no more upon the matter. She only basked in the warmth of his feeling, which was as a grateful blaze to one who is cold. Hurstwood glowed with his own intensity, and the heat of his passion was already melting the wax of his companion's scruples.

◄ What effect are Hurstwood's words having upon Carrie?

"You think," he said, "I am happy; that I ought not to complain? If you were to meet all day with people who care absolutely nothing about you, if you went day after day to a place where there was nothing but show and indifference, if there was not one person in all those you knew to whom you

Words For Everyday Use

scru • ple (skrōō´ pəl) *n.,* consideration based on ethical or moral principles

could appeal for sympathy or talk to with pleasure, perhaps you would be unhappy too."

He was striking a chord now which found sympathetic response in her own situation. She knew what it was to meet with people who were indifferent, to walk alone amid so many who cared absolutely nothing about you. Had not she? Was not she at this very moment quite alone? Who was there among all whom she knew to whom she could appeal for sympathy? Not one. She was left to herself to brood and wonder.

"I could be content," went on Hurstwood, "if I had you to love me. If I had you to go to; you for a companion. As it is, I simply move about from place to place without any satisfaction. Time hangs heavily on my hands. Before you came I did nothing but idle and drift into anything that offered itself. Since you came—well, I've had you to think about."

The old illusion that here was someone who needed her aid began to grow in Carrie's mind. She truly pitied this sad, lonely figure. To think that all his fine state should be so barren for want of her; that he needed to make such an appeal when she herself was lonely and without anchor. Surely, this was too bad.

"I am not very bad," he said, apologetically, as if he owed it to her to explain on this score. "You think, probably, that I roam around, and get into all sorts of evil? I have been rather reckless, but I could easily come out of that. I need you to draw me back, if my life ever amounts to anything."

Carrie looked at him with the tenderness which virtue ever feels in its hope of reclaiming vice. How could such a man need reclaiming? His errors, what were they, that she could correct? Small they must be, where all was so fine. At worst, they were gilded affairs, and with what leniency are gilded errors viewed.

He put himself in such a lonely light that she was deeply moved.

"Is it that way?" she mused.

He slipped his arm about her waist, and she could not find the heart to draw away. With his free hand he seized upon her fingers. A breath of soft spring wind went bounding over the road, rolling some brown twigs of the previous autumn before it. The horse paced leisurely on, unguided.

Words For Everyday Use

gild • ed (gild´əd) *adj.*, coated with gold

"Tell me," he said, softly, "that you love me."

Her eyes fell consciously.

"Own to it, dear," he said, feelingly; "you do, don't you?"

She made no answer, but he felt his victory.

"Tell me," he said, richly, drawing her so close that their lips were near together. He pressed her hand warmly, and then released it to touch her cheek.

"You do?" he said, pressing his lips to her own.

For answer, her lips replied.

"Now," he said, joyously, his fine eyes ablaze, "you're my own girl, aren't you?"

By way of further conclusion, her head lay softly upon his shoulder.

◄ *What does Hurstwood want Carrie to do? What does she do instead? Do you think Hurstwood interprets this gesture as the words he longs to hear?*

◄ *What is the outcome of this meeting between Carrie and Hurstwood?*

CHAPTER 14

With Eyes and Not Seeing: One Influence Wanes

Carrie in her rooms that evening was in a fine glow, physically and mentally. She was deeply rejoicing in her affection for Hurstwood and his love, and looked forward with fine fancy to their next meeting Sunday night. They had agreed, without any feeling of enforced secrecy, that she should come downtown and meet him, though, after all, the need of it was the cause.

Mrs. Hale, from her upper window, saw her come in.

► Who looks critically at Carrie's actions? Predict what might result from her indiscreet meetings with Hurstwood.

"Um," she thought to herself, "she goes riding with another man when her husband is out of the city. He had better keep an eye on her."

The truth is that Mrs. Hale was not the only one who had a thought on this score. The housemaid who had welcomed Hurstwood had her opinion also. She had no particular regard for Carrie, whom she took to be cold and disagreeable. At the same time, she had a fancy for the merry and easy-mannered Drouet, who threw her a pleasant remark now and then, and in other ways extended her the evidence of that regard which he had for all members of the sex. Hurstwood was more reserved and critical in his manner. He did not appeal to this bodiced functionary in the same pleasant way. She wondered that he came so frequently, that Mrs. Drouet should go out with him this afternoon when Mr. Drouet was absent. She gave vent to her opinions in the kitchen where the cook was. As a result, a hum of gossip was set going which moved about the house in that secret manner common to gossip.

Carrie, now that she had yielded sufficiently to Hurstwood to confess her affection, no longer troubled about her attitude toward him. Temporarily she gave little thought to Drouet, thinking only of the dignity and grace of her lover and of his consuming affection for her. On the first evening, she did little but go over the details of the afternoon. It was the first time her sympathies had ever been thoroughly aroused, and they threw a new light on her character. She had some power of initiative, latent before, which

► In what way is Carrie changing?

Words For Everyday Use	**la • tent** (lāt´ 'nt) *adj.,* present but inactive

now began to exert itself. She looked more practically upon her state and began to see glimmerings of a way out. Hurstwood seemed a drag in the direction of honor. Her feelings were exceedingly creditable, in that they constructed out of these recent developments something which conquered freedom from dishonor. She had no idea what Hurstwood's next word would be. She only took his affection to be a fine thing, and appended better, more generous results accordingly.

◄ *How does Carrie view Hurstwood? Does Hurstwood plan to behave as Carrie expects him to?*

As yet, Hurstwood had only a thought of pleasure without responsibility. He did not feel that he was doing anything to complicate his life. His position was secure, his home-life, if not satisfactory, was at least undisturbed, his personal liberty rather untrammeled. Carrie's love represented only so much added pleasure. He would enjoy this new gift over and above his ordinary allowance of pleasure. He would be happy with her and his own affairs would go on as they had, undisturbed.

◄ *In what way does Hurstwood view Carrie's love? Does he expect it to change his life in any way? Explain whether he believes that love involves responsibility.*

On Sunday evening Carrie dined with him at a place he had selected in East Adams Street, and thereafter they took a cab to what was then a pleasant evening resort out on Cottage Grove Avenue near Thirty-ninth Street. In the process of his declaration he soon realized that Carrie took his love upon a higher basis than he had anticipated. She kept him at a distance in a rather earnest way, and submitted only to those tender tokens of affection which better become the inexperienced lover. Hurstwood saw that she was not to be possessed for the asking, and deferred pressing his suit too warmly.

◄ *What does Hurstwood realize once he meets Carrie again?*

Since he feigned to believe in her married state he found that he had to carry out the part. His triumph, he saw, was still at a little distance. How far he could not guess.

They were returning to Ogden Place in the cab, when he asked:

"When will I see you again?"

"I don't know," she answered, wondering herself.

"Why not come down to The Fair," he suggested, "next Tuesday?"

She shook her head.

"Not so soon," she answered.

"I'll tell you what I'll do," he added. "I'll write you, care of this West Side post office. Could you call next Tuesday?"

Carrie assented.

Words For Everyday Use

un • tram • meled (un tram´ əld) *adj.*, unconfined
de • fer (dē fʉr´) *vt.*, postpone
feign (fān) *vt.*, pretend

The cab stopped one door out of the way according to his call.

"Goodnight," he whispered, as the cab rolled away.

Unfortunately for the smooth progression of this affair, Drouet returned. Hurstwood was sitting in his imposing little office the next afternoon when he saw Drouet enter.

"Why, hello, Charles," he called affably; "back again?"

"Yes," smiled Drouet, approaching and looking in at the door.

Hurstwood arose.

"Well," he said, looking the drummer[1] over, "rosy as ever, eh?"

They began talking of the people they knew and things that had happened.

"Been home yet?" finally asked Hurstwood.

"No, I am going, though," said Drouet.

► *In what way is Hurstwood careful not to arouse Drouet's suspicions?*

"I remembered the little girl out there," said Hurstwood, "and called once. Thought you wouldn't want her left quite alone."

"Right you are," agreed Drouet. "How is she?"

"Very well," said Hurstwood. "Rather anxious about you, though. You'd better go out now and cheer her up."

"I will," said Drouet, smilingly.

"Like to have you both come down and go to the show with me Wednesday," concluded Hurstwood at parting.

"Thanks, old man," said his friend, "I'll see what the girl says and let you know."

They separated in the most cordial manner.

► *Does Drouet seem to recognize Hurstwood's true motivations? Explain.*

"There's a nice fellow," Drouet thought to himself as he turned the corner toward Madison.

"Drouet is a good fellow," Hurstwood thought to himself as he went back into his office, "but he's no man for Carrie."

The thought of the latter turned his mind into a most pleasant vein, and he wondered how he would get ahead of the drummer.

When Drouet entered Carrie's presence, he caught her in his arms as usual, but she responded to his kiss with a tremor of opposition.

"Well," he said, "I had a great trip."

"Did you? How did you come out with that La Crosse[2] man you were telling me about?"

"Oh, fine; sold him a complete line. There was another fellow there, representing Burnstein, a regular hook-nosed sheeny, but he wasn't in it. I made him look like nothing at all."

1. **drummer.** Salesperson
2. **La Crosse.** City in western Wisconsin on the Mississippi River

As he undid his collar and unfastened his studs, preparatory to washing his face and changing his clothes, he dilated upon his trip. Carrie could not help listening with amusement to his animated descriptions.

"I tell you," he said, "I surprised the people at the office. I've sold more goods this last quarter than any other man of our house on the road. I sold three thousand dollars' worth in La Crosse."

He plunged his face in a basin of water, and puffed and blew as he rubbed his neck and ears with his hands, while Carrie gazed upon him with mingled thoughts of recollection and present judgment. He was still wiping his face, when he continued:

"I'm going to strike for a raise in June. They can afford to pay it, as much business as I turn in. I'll get it too, don't you forget."

"I hope you do," said Carrie.

"And then if that little real estate deal I've got on goes through, we'll get married," he said with a great show of earnestness, the while he took his place before the mirror and began brushing his hair.

"I don't believe you ever intend to marry me, Charlie," Carrie said ruefully. The recent protestations of Hurstwood had given her courage to say this.

◄ *What does Carrie realize?*

"Oh, yes I do—course I do—what put that into your head?"

He had stopped his trifling before the mirror now and crossed over to her. For the first time Carrie felt as if she must move away from him.

"But you've been saying that so long," she said, looking with her pretty face upturned into his.

"Well, and I mean it too, but it takes money to live as I want to. Now, when I get this increase, I can come pretty near fixing things all right, and I'll do it. Now, don't you worry, girlie."

He patted her reassuringly upon the shoulder, but Carrie felt how really futile had been her hopes. She could clearly see that this easy-going soul intended no move in her behalf. He was simply letting things drift because he preferred the free round of his present state to any legal trammelings.

In contrast, Hurstwood appeared strong and sincere. He had no easy manner of putting her off. He sympathized with her and showed her what her true value was. He needed her, while Drouet did not care.

Words For Everyday Use

di • late (dī´ lāt) *vt.,* speak or write in detail

ear • nest • ness (ʉr´ nist nes) *n.,* sincerity; seriousness

prot • es • ta • tion (prōt´es tā´shən) *n.,* strong declaration

fu • tile (fyo͞o t´'l) *adj.,* worthless

"Oh, no," she said remorsefully, her tone reflecting some of her own success and more of her helplessness, "you never will."

"Well, you wait a little while and see," he concluded. "I'll marry you all right."

► To what purpose does Carrie put Drouet's false promise to marry her?

Carrie looked at him and felt justified. She was looking for something which would calm her conscience, and here it was, a light, airy disregard of her claims upon his justice. He had faithfully promised to marry her, and this was the way he fulfilled his promise.

"Say," he said, after he had, as he thought, pleasantly disposed of the marriage question, "I saw Hurstwood today, and he wants us to go to the theater with him."

Carrie started at the name, but recovered quickly enough to avoid notice.

"When?" she asked, with assumed indifference.

"Wednesday. We'll go, won't we?"

"If you think so," she answered, her manner being so enforcedly reserved as to almost excite suspicion. Drouet noticed something, but he thought it was due to her feelings concerning their talk about marriage.

"He called once, he said."

"Yes," said Carrie, "he was out here Sunday evening."

"Was he?" said Drouet. "I thought from what he said that he had called a week or so ago."

"So he did," answered Carrie, who was wholly unaware of what conversation her lovers might have held. She was all at sea mentally, and fearful of some entanglement which might ensue from what she would answer.

► Would you be suspicious if you were Drouet? What do Drouet's responses reveal about his character?

"Oh, then he called twice?" said Drouet, the first shade of misunderstanding showing in his face.

"Yes," said Carrie innocently, feeling now that Hurstwood must have mentioned but one call.

Drouet imagined that he must have misunderstood his friend. He did not attach particular importance to the information, after all.

"What did he have to say?" he queried, with slightly increased curiosity.

"He said he came because he thought I might be lonely. You hadn't been in there so long he wondered what had become of you."

Words For Everyday Use

en • sue (en so͞o´) *vi.,* happen as a result

que • ry (kwir´ē) *vt.,* ask about

"George is a fine fellow," said Drouet, rather gratified by his conception of the manager's interest. "Come on and we'll go out to dinner."

When Hurstwood saw that Drouet was back he wrote at once to Carrie, saying:

"I told him I called on you, dearest, when he was away. I did not say how often, but he probably thought once. Let me know of anything you may have said. Answer by special messenger when you get this, and, darling, I must see you. Let me know if you can't meet me at Jackson and Throop Streets Wednesday afternoon at two o'clock. I want to speak with you before we meet at the theater."

Carrie received this Tuesday morning when she called at the West Side branch of the post office, and answered at once.

"I said you called twice," she wrote. "He didn't seem to mind. I will try and be at Throop Street if nothing interferes. I seem to be getting very bad. It's wrong to act as I do, I know."

Hurstwood, when he met her as agreed, reassured her on this score.

"You mustn't worry, sweetheart," he said. "Just as soon as he goes on the road again we will arrange something. We'll fix it so that you won't have to deceive anyone."

Carrie imagined that he would marry her at once, though he had not directly said so, and her spirits rose. She proposed to make the best of the situation until Drouet left again.

◄ In what way does Carrie interpret Hurstwood's promise that she will no longer have to deceive anyone?

"Don't show any more interest in me than you ever have," Hurstwood counseled concerning the evening at the theater.

"You mustn't look at me steadily then," she answered, mindful of the power of his eyes.

"I won't," he said, squeezing her hand at parting and giving the glance she had just cautioned against.

"There," she said playfully, pointing a finger at him.

"The show hasn't begun yet," he returned.

He watched her walk from him with tender solicitation. Such youth and prettiness reacted upon him more subtly than wine.

At the theater things passed as they had in Hurstwood's favor. If he had been pleasing to Carrie before, how much more so was he now. His grace was more permeating because it found a readier medium. Carrie watched his every movement with pleasure. She almost forgot poor Drouet, who babbled on as if he were the host.

Words For Everyday Use

grat • i • fied (grat´ i fīd) *adj.*, pleased
con • cep • tion (kən sep´ shən) *n.*, idea; understanding
so • lic • i • ta • tion (sə lis´ i tā shən) *n.*, care

► *In what way does Hurstwood's treatment of Drouet reveal him to be more noble than most men in his position?*

► *How does Drouet feel about the husband in the play? Why does Hurstwood respond "gently" on the subject?*

Hurstwood was too clever to give the slightest indication of a change. He paid, if anything, more attention to his old friend than usual, and yet in no way held him up to that subtle ridicule which a lover in favor may so secretly practice before the mistress of his heart. If anything, he felt the injustice of the game as it stood, and was not cheap enough to add to it the slightest mental taunt.

Only the play produced an ironical situation, and this was due to Drouet alone.

The scene was one in *The Covenant,* in which the wife listened to the seductive voice of a lover in the absence of her husband.

"Served him right," said Drouet afterward, even in view of her keen expiation of her error. "I haven't any pity for a man who would be such a chump as that."

"Well, you never can tell," returned Hurstwood gently. "He probably thought he was right."

"Well, a man ought to be more attentive than that to his wife if he wants to keep her."

They had come out of the lobby and made their way through the showy crush about the entranceway.

"Say, mister," said a voice at Hurstwood's side, "would you mind giving me the price of a bed?"

Hurstwood was interestedly remarking to Carrie.

"Honest to God, mister, I'm without a place to sleep."

The plea was that of a gaunt-faced man of about thirty, who looked the picture of privation and wretchedness. Drouet was the first to see. He handed over a dime with an upwelling feeling of pity in his heart. Hurstwood scarcely noticed the incident. Carrie quickly forgot.

Words For Everyday Use

- **ex • pi • a • tion** (eks´ pē ā shən) *n.,* atonement for wrongdoing
- **gaunt** (gônt) *adj.,* thin and bony
- **pri • va • tion** (pri vā shən) *n.,* lack of the necessities of life
- **up • well • ing** (up´ wel´ iŋ) *n.,* rising flow

CHAPTER 15

The Irk of the Old Ties: The Magic of Youth

The complete ignoring by Hurstwood of his own home came with the growth of his affection for Carrie. His actions, in all that related to his family, were of the most perfunctory kind. He sat at breakfast with his wife and children, absorbed in his own fancies, which reached far without the realm of their interests. He read his paper, which was heightened in interest by the shallowness of the themes discussed by his son and daughter. Between himself and his wife ran a river of indifference.

◄ *What effect does Hurstwood's interest in Carrie have on his family life?*

Now that Carrie had come, he was in a fair way to be blissful again. There was delight in going downtown evenings. When he walked forth in the short days, the street lamps had a merry twinkle. He began to experience the almost forgotten feeling which hastens the lover's feet. When he looked at his fine clothes, he saw them with her eyes—and her eyes were young.

◄ *How does Hurstwood see himself now?*

When in the flush of such feelings he heard his wife's voice, when the insistent demands of matrimony recalled him from dreams to a stale practice, how it grated. He then knew that this was a chain which bound his feet.

"George," said Mrs. Hurstwood, in that tone of voice which had long since come to be associated in his mind with demands, "we want you to get us a season ticket to the races."

"Do you want to go to all of them?" he said with a rising inflection.

"Yes," she answered.

The races in question were soon to open at Washington Park, on the South Side, and were considered quite society affairs among those who did not affect religious rectitude and conservatism. Mrs. Hurstwood had never asked for a whole season ticket before, but this year certain considerations decided her to get a box. For one thing, one of her neighbors, a certain Mr. and Mrs. Ramsey, who were possessors of money, made out of the coal business, had done so. In the next place, her favorite physician, Dr. Beale, a gentleman inclined to horses and betting, had talked with her concerning his

Words For Everyday Use

grate (grāt) *vt.,* irritate
in • flec • tion (in flek´ shən) *n.,* change in tone or pitch
rec • ti • tude (rek´ tə to͞od´) *n.,* conduct based on high moral principles
con • ser • va • tism (kən sʉr´ və tiz´əm) *n.,* traditional principles and practices

intention to enter a two-year-old in the Derby. In the third place, she wished to exhibit Jessica, who was gaining in maturity and beauty, and whom she hoped to marry to a man of means. Her own desire to be about in such things and parade among her acquaintances and the common throng was as much an incentive as anything.

Hurstwood thought over the proposition a few moments without answering. They were in the sitting room on the second floor, waiting for supper. It was the evening of his engagement with Carrie and Drouet to see *The Covenant*, which had brought him home to make some alterations in his dress.

"You're sure separate tickets wouldn't do as well?" he asked, hesitating to say anything more rugged.

"No," she replied impatiently.

"Well," he said, taking offense at her manner, "you needn't get mad about it. I'm just asking you."

"I'm not mad," she snapped. "I'm merely asking you for a season ticket."

"And I'm telling you," he returned, fixing a clear, steady eye on her, "that it's no easy thing to get. I'm not sure whether the manager will give it to me."

He had been thinking all the time of his "pull" with the racetrack magnates.

"We can buy it then," she exclaimed sharply.

"You talk easy," he said. "A season family ticket costs one hundred and fifty dollars."

"I'll not argue with you," she replied with determination. "I want the ticket and that's all there is to it."

She had risen, and now walked angrily out of the room.

"Well, you get it then," he said grimly, though in a modified tone of voice.

As usual, the table was one short that evening.

The next morning he had cooled down considerably, and later the ticket was duly secured, though it did not heal matters. He did not mind giving his family a fair share of all that he earned, but he did not like to be forced to provide against his will.

"Did you know, mother," said Jessica another day, "the Spencers are getting ready to go away?"

"No. Where, I wonder?"

Words For Everyday Use

rug • ged (rug´id) *adj.,* harsh

mag • nate (mag´nāt) *n.,* important, influential person

du • ly (do͞o´lē) *adv.,* in the right time and manner

"Europe," said Jessica. "I met Georgine yesterday and she told me. She just put on more airs[1] about it."

"Did she say when?"

"Monday, I think. They'll get a notice in the papers again—they always do."

"Never mind," said Mrs. Hurstwood consolingly, "we'll go one of these days."

Hurstwood moved his eyes over the paper slowly, but said nothing.

"'We sail for Liverpool from New York,'" Jessica exclaimed, mocking her acquaintance. "'Expect to spend most of the "summah" in France,'—vain thing. As if it was anything to go to Europe."

"It must be if you envy her so much," put in Hurstwood.

It grated upon him to see the feeling his daughter displayed.

"Don't worry over them, my dear," said Mrs. Hurstwood.

"Did George get off?" asked Jessica of her mother another day, thus revealing something that Hurstwood had heard nothing about.

"Where has he gone?" he asked, looking up. He had never before been kept in ignorance concerning departures.

"He was going to Wheaton,"[2] said Jessica, not noticing the slight put upon her father.

"What's out there?" he asked, secretly irritated and chagrined to think that he should be made to pump for information in this manner.

"A tennis match," said Jessica.

"He didn't say anything to me," Hurstwood concluded, finding it difficult to refrain from a bitter tone.

"I guess he must have forgotten," exclaimed his wife blandly.

In the past he had always commanded a certain amount of respect, which was a compound of appreciation and awe. The familiarity which in part still existed between himself and his daughter he had courted. As it was, it did not go beyond the light assumption of words. The *tone* was always modest. Whatever had been, however, had lacked affection, and now he saw that he was losing track of their doings. His knowledge was no longer intimate. He sometimes saw them

◄ Why do you think Mrs. Hurstwood and Jessica have this conversation in front of Mr. Hurstwood?

◄ What change does Hurstwood see in his relationship with his family?

1. **put on more airs.** Boasted; acted superior
2. **Wheaton.** Town approximately 10 miles west of downtown Chicago

Words For Everyday Use

bland • ly (bland´ lē) *adv.,* smoothly

at table, and sometimes did not. He heard of their doings occasionally, more often not. Some days he found that he was all at sea as to what they were talking about—things they had arranged to do or that they had done in his absence. More affecting was the feeling that there were little things going on of which he no longer heard. Jessica was beginning to feel that her affairs were her own. George, Jr., flourished about as if he were a man entirely and must needs have private matters. All this Hurstwood could see, and it left a trace of feeling, for he was used to being considered—in his official position, at least—and felt that his importance should not begin to wane here. To darken it all, he saw the same indifference and independence growing in his wife, while he looked on and paid the bills.

► How does Hurstwood feel about his changing role in his family?

He consoled himself with the thought, however, that, after all, he was not without affection. Things might go as they would at his house, but he had Carrie outside of it. With his mind's eye[3] he looked into her comfortable room in Ogden Place, where he had spent several such delightful evenings, and thought how charming it would be when Drouet was disposed of entirely and she was waiting evenings in cozy little quarters for him. That no cause would come up whereby Drouet would be led to inform Carrie concerning his married state, he felt hopeful. Things were going so smoothly that he believed they would not change. Shortly now he would persuade Carrie and all would be satisfactory.

► What does Hurstwood imagine his relationship with Carrie will be like?

The day after their theater visit he began writing her regularly—a letter every morning, and begging her to do as much for him. He was not literary by any means, but experience of the world and his growing affection gave him somewhat of a style. This he exercised at his office desk with perfect deliberation. He purchased a box of delicately colored and scented writing paper in monogram, which he kept locked in one of the drawers. His friends now wondered at the cleric and very official-looking nature of his position. The five bartenders viewed with respect the duties which could call a man to do so much desk-work and penmanship.

Hurstwood surprised himself with his fluency. By the natural law which governs all effort, what he wrote reacted upon him. He began to feel those subtleties which he could

3. **mind's eye.** Imagination

Words For Everyday Use

wane (wān) *vi.,* lessen

de • lib • er • a • tion (di lib´ər ā´shən) *n.,* design, forethought

cler • ic (kler´ ik) *adj.,* having to do with business writing

find words to express. With every expression came increased conception. Those inmost breathings which there found words took bold upon him. He thought Carrie worthy of all the affection he could there express.

Carrie was indeed worth loving if ever youth and grace are to command that token of acknowledgment from life in their bloom. Experience had not yet taken away that freshness of the spirit which is the charm of the body. Her soft eyes contained in their liquid luster no suggestion of the knowledge of disappointment. She had been troubled in a way by doubt and longing, but these had made no deeper impression than could be traced in a certain open wistfulness of glance and speech. The mouth had the expression at times, in talking and in repose, of one who might be upon the verge of tears. It was not that grief was thus ever present. The pronunciation of certain syllables gave to her lips this peculiarity of formation—a formation as suggestive and moving as pathos itself.

◄ *By what has Carrie been troubled?*

There was nothing bold in her manner. Life had not taught her domination—superciliousness of grace, which is the lordly power of some women. Her longing for consideration was not sufficiently powerful to move her to demand it. Even now she lacked self-assurance, but there was that in what she had already experienced which left her a little less than timid. She wanted pleasure, she wanted position, and yet she was confused as to what these things might be. Every hour the kaleidoscope of human affairs threw a new luster upon something, and therewith it became for her the desired—the all. Another shift of the box, and some other had become the beautiful, the perfect.

On her spiritual side, also, she was rich in feeling, as such a nature well might be. Sorrow in her was aroused by many a spectacle—an uncritical upwelling of grief for the weak and the helpless. She was constantly pained by the sight of the white-faced, ragged men who slopped desperately by her in a sort of wretched mental stupor. The poorly clad girls who went blowing by her window evenings, hurrying home from some of the shops of the West Side, she pitied from the depths of her heart. She would stand and bite her lips as they passed, shaking her little head and wondering. They had so little, she thought. It was so sad to be ragged and poor. The hang of faded clothes pained her eyes.

◄ *What are Carrie's "spiritual" feelings?*

◄ *What pains Carrie most about the poor? Why is this typical, given her character?*

Words For Everyday Use

re • pose (ri pōz´) *n.*, rest

su • per • cil • i • ous • ness (so͞o´pər sil´ ē əs nəs) *n.*, prideful manner

"And they have to work so hard!" was her only comment.

On the street sometimes she would see men working—Irishmen with picks, coal-heavers with great loads to shovel, Americans busy about some work which was a mere matter of strength—and they touched her fancy. Toil, now that she was free of it, seemed even a more desolate thing than when she was part of it. She saw it through a mist of fancy—a pale, somber half-light, which was the essence of poetic feeling. Her old father, in his flour-dusted miller's[4] suit, sometimes returned to her in memory, revived by a face in a window. A shoemaker pegging at his last, a blastman seen through a narrow window in some basement where iron was being melted, a bench-worker seen high aloft in some window, his coat off, his sleeves rolled up; these took her back in fancy to the details of the mill. She felt, though she seldom expressed them, sad thoughts upon this score. Her sympathies were ever with that underworld of toil from which she had so recently sprung, and which she best understood.

► *Why is Carrie so sympathetic toward laborers?*

Though Hurstwood did not know it, he was dealing with one whose feelings were as tender and as delicate as this. He did not know, but it was this in her, after all, which attracted him. He never attempted to analyze the nature of his affection. It was sufficient that there was tenderness in her eye, weakness in her manner, good nature and hope, in her thoughts. He drew near this lily, which had sucked its waxen beauty and perfume from below a depth of waters which he had never penetrated, and out of ooze and mold[5] which he could not understand. He drew near because it was waxen and fresh. It lightened his feelings for him. It made the morning worthwhile.

In a material way, she was considerably improved. Her awkwardness had all but passed, leaving, if anything, a quaint residue which was as pleasing as perfect grace. Her little shoes now fitted her smartly and had high heels. She had learned much about laces and those little neckpieces which add so much to a woman's appearance. Her form had filled out until it was admirably plump and well-rounded.

---

4. **miller's.** Belonging to one who operates a mill, a mechanism that grinds grain into flour

5. **ooze and mold.** Mud and decayed plant life; here it refers to Carrie's background.

Words For Everyday Use

wax • en (wak´ sən) *adj.,* waxlike

Hurstwood wrote her one morning, asking her to meet him in Jefferson Park, Monroe Street. He did not consider it policy to call anymore, even when Drouet was at home.

The next afternoon he was in the pretty little park by one, and had found a rustic bench beneath the green leaves of a lilac bush which bordered one of the paths. It was at that season of the year when the fulness of spring had not yet worn quite away. At a little pond nearby some cleanly dressed children were sailing white canvas boats. In the shade of a green pagoda[6] a bebuttoned officer of the law was resting, his arms folded, his club at rest in his belt. An old gardener was upon the lawn, with a pair of pruning shears, looking after some bushes. High overhead was the clear blue sky of the new summer, and in the thickness of the shiny green leaves of the trees hopped and twittered the busy sparrows.

Hurstwood had come out of his own home that morning feeling much of the same old annoyance. At his store he had idled, there being no need to write. He had come away to this place with the lightness of heart which characterizes those who put weariness behind. Now, in the shade of this cool, green bush, he looked about him with the fancy of the lover. He heard the carts go lumbering by upon the neighboring streets, but they were far off, and only buzzed upon his ear. The hum of the surrounding city was faint, the clang of an occasional bell was as music. He looked and dreamed a new dream of pleasure which concerned his present fixed condition not at all. He got back in fancy to the old Hurstwood, who was neither married nor fixed in a solid position for life. He remembered the light spirit in which he once looked after the girls—how he had danced, escorted them home, hung over their gates. He almost wished he was back there again—here in this pleasant scene he felt as if he were wholly free.

◄ *For what time in his life does Hurstwood long? What did he enjoy about this time in his life?*

At two Carrie came tripping along the walk toward him, rosy and clean. She had just recently donned[7] a sailor hat for the season with a hand of pretty white-dotted blue silk. Her skirt was of a rich blue material, and her shirtwaist matched it, with a thin stripe of blue upon a snow-white ground—stripes that were as fine as hairs. Her brown shoes peeped occasionally from beneath her skirt. She carried her gloves in her hand.

Hurstwood looked up at her with delight.

"You came, dearest," he said eagerly, standing to meet her and taking her hand.

6. **pagoda.** Small ornamental building of Asian design
7. **donned.** Put on

"Of course," she said, smiling; "did you think I wouldn't?"

"I didn't know," he replied.

He looked at her forehead, which was moist from her brisk walk. Then he took out one of his own soft, scented silk handkerchiefs and touched her face here and there.

"Now," he said affectionately, "you're all right."

They were happy in being near one another—in looking into each other's eyes. Finally, when the long flush of delight had subsided, he said:

"When is Charlie going away again?"

"I don't know," she answered. "He says he has some things to do for the house here now."

Hurstwood grew serious, and he lapsed into quiet thought. He looked up after a time to say:

▶ *What is unusual about Hurstwood and Carrie's manner of discussing this topic?*

"Come away and leave him."

He turned his eyes to the boys with the boats, as if the request were of little importance.

"Where would we go?" she asked in much the same manner, rolling her gloves, and looking into a neighboring tree.

"Where do you want to go?" he inquired.

There was something in the tone in which he said this which made her feel as if she must record her feelings against any local habitation.

"We can't stay in Chicago," she replied.

He had no thought that this was in her mind—that any removal would be suggested.

"Why not?" he asked softly.

"Oh, because," she said, "I wouldn't want to."

▶ *Why doesn't Hurstwood take Carrie's desire to move away from Chicago seriously?*

He listened to this, with but dull perception of what it meant. It had no serious ring to it. The question was not up for immediate decision.

"I would have to give up my position," he said.

The tone he used made it seem as if the matter deserved only slight consideration. Carrie thought a little, the while enjoying the pretty scene.

"I wouldn't like to live in Chicago and him here," she said, thinking of Drouet.

▶ *What does Hurstwood point out about Chicago?*

"It's a big town, dearest," Hurstwood answered. "It would be as good as moving to another part of the country to move to the South Side."

He had fixed upon that region as an objective point.

▶ *What subject does Carrie bring up for the first time?*

"Anyhow," said Carrie, "I shouldn't want to get married as long as he is here. I wouldn't want to run away."

The suggestion of marriage struck Hurstwood forcibly. He saw clearly that this was her idea—he felt that it was not to be gotten over easily. Bigamy lightened the horizon of his shadowy thoughts for a moment. He wondered for the life of him how it would all come out. He could not see that he was making any progress save in her regard. When he looked at her now, he thought her beautiful. What a thing it was to have her love him, even if it be entangling! She increased in value in his eyes because of her objection. She was something to struggle for, and that was everything. How different from the women who yielded willingly! He swept the thought of them from his mind.

◄ *What idea does Hurstwood entertain?*

"And you don't know when he'll go away?" asked Hurstwood, quietly.

She shook her head.

He sighed.

"You're a determined little miss, aren't you?" he said, after a few moments, looking up into her eyes.

She felt a wave of feeling sweep over her at this. It was pride at what seemed his admiration—affection for the man who could feel this concerning her.

"No," she said coyly, "but what can I do?"

Again he folded his hands and looked away over the lawn into the street.

"I wish," he said pathetically, "you would come to me. I don't like to be away from you this way. What good is there in waiting? You're not any happier, are you?"

"Happier!" she exclaimed softly, "you know better than that."

"Here we are then," he went on in the same tone, "wasting our days. If you are not happy, do you think I am? I sit and write to you the biggest part of the time. I'll tell you what, Carrie," he exclaimed, throwing sudden force of expression into his voice and fixing her with his eyes, "I can't live without you, and that's all there is to it. Now," he concluded, showing the palm of one of his white hands in a sort of at-an-end, helpless expression, "what shall I do?"

This shifting of the burden to her appealed to Carrie. The semblance of the load without the weight touched the woman's heart.

"Can't you wait a little while yet?" she said tenderly. "I'll try and find out when he's going."

Words For Everyday Use

big • a • my (big´ ə mē) *n.,* criminal practice of marrying while a previous marriage is still in effect

"What good will it do?" he asked, holding the same strain of feeling.

"Well, perhaps we can arrange to go somewhere."

She really did not see anything clearer than before, but she was getting into that frame of mind where, out of sympathy, a woman yields.

Hurstwood did not understand. He was wondering how she was to be persuaded—what appeal would move her to forsake Drouet. He began to wonder how far her affection for him would carry her. He was thinking of some question which would make her tell.

► *What question does Hurstwood ask Carrie? Why does he ask this?*

Finally he hit upon one of those problematical propositions which often disguise our own desires while leading us to an understanding of the difficulties which others make for us, and so discover for us a way. It had not the slightest connection with anything intended on his part, and was spoken at random before he had given it a moment's serious thought.

"Carrie," he said, looking into her face and assuming a serious look which he did not feel, "suppose I were to come to you next week, or this week for that matter—tonight say—and tell you I had to go away—that I couldn't stay another minute and wasn't coming back anymore—would you come with me?"

His sweetheart viewed him with the most affectionate glance, her answer ready before the words were out of his mouth.

"Yes," she said.

"You wouldn't stop to argue or arrange?"

"Not if you couldn't wait."

He smiled when he saw that she took him seriously, and he thought what a chance it would afford for a possible junket of a week or two. He had a notion to tell her that he was joking and so brush away her sweet seriousness, but the effect of it was too delightful. He let it stand.

"Suppose we didn't have time to get married here?" he added, an afterthought striking him.

"If we got married as soon as we got to the other end of the journey it would be all right."

"I meant that," he said.

"Yes."

The morning seemed peculiarly bright to him now. He

Words For Everyday Use

prop • o • si • tion (präp´ ə zish´ ən) *n.,* proposal

wondered whatever could have put such a thought into his head. Impossible as it was, he could not help smiling at its cleverness. It showed how she loved him. There was no doubt in his mind now, and he would find a way to win her.

"Well," he said, jokingly, "I'll come and get you one of these evenings," and then he laughed.

"I wouldn't stay with you, though, if you didn't marry me," Carrie added reflectively.

"I don't want you to," he said tenderly, taking her hand.

She was extremely happy now that she understood. She loved him the more for thinking that he would rescue her so. As for him, the marriage clause did not dwell in his mind. He was thinking that with such affection there could be no bar to his eventual happiness.

"Let's stroll about," he said gaily, rising and surveying all the lovely park.

"All right," said Carrie.

They passed the young Irishman, who looked after them with envious eyes.

"'Tis a foine couple," he observed to himself. "They must be rich."

◀ *What does Hurstwood say he will do? Explain whether you think he is really joking. What warning does Carrie give Hurstwood?*

CHAPTER 16

A Witless Aladdin: The Gate to the World

In the course of his present stay in Chicago, Drouet paid some slight attention to the secret order to which he belonged. During his last trip he had received a new light on its importance.

"I tell you," said another drummer to him, "it's a great thing. Look at Hazenstab. He isn't so deuced[1] clever. Of course he's got a good house behind him, but that won't do alone. I tell you it's his degree. He's a way-up Mason, and that goes a long way. He's got a secret sign that stands for something."

Drouet resolved then and there that he would take more interest in such matters. So when he got back to Chicago he repaired to his local lodge headquarters.

"I say, Drouet," said Mr. Harry Quincel, an individual who was very prominent in this local branch of the Elks, "you're the man that can help us out."

It was after the business meeting and things were going socially with a hum. Drouet was bobbing around chatting and joking with a score of individuals whom he knew.

"What are you up to?" he inquired genially, turning a smiling face upon his secret brother.

► *What does Harry Quincel ask of Drouet? Why does Drouet say he can do this when he doesn't have anyone in mind?*

"We're trying to get up some theatricals for two weeks from today, and we want to know if you don't know some young lady who could take a part—it's an easy part."

"Sure," said Drouet, "what is it?" He did not trouble to remember that he knew no one to whom he could appeal on this score. His innate good nature, however, dictated a favorable reply.

"Well, now, I'll tell you what we are trying to do," went on Mr. Quincel. "We are trying to get a new set of furniture for the lodge. There isn't enough money in the treasury at the present time, and we thought we would raise it by a little entertainment."

"Sure," interrupted Drouet, "that's a good idea."

1. **deuced.** Euphemism for "damned," meaning darned, confounded

Words For Everyday Use

in • nate (in´ nāt´) *adj.,* inborn

"Several of the boys around here have got talent. There's Harry Burbeck, he does a fine black-face[2] turn. Mac Lewis is all right at heavy dramatics. Did you ever hear him recite 'Over the Hills'?"

"Never did."

"Well, I tell you, he does it fine."

"And you want me to get some woman to take a part?" questioned Drouet, anxious to terminate the subject and get on to something else. "What are you going to play?"

"*Under the Gaslight,*" said Mr. Quincel, mentioning Augustin Daly's famous production, which had worn from a great public success down to an amateur theatrical favorite, with many of the troublesome accessories cut out and the *dramatis personae*[3] reduced to the smallest possible number.

Drouet had seen this play some time in the past.

"That's it," he said; "that's a fine play. It will go all right. You ought to make a lot of money out of that."

"We think we'll do very well," Mr. Quincel replied. "Don't you forget now," he concluded, Drouet showing signs of restlessness; "some young woman to take the part of Laura."

◀ *What character traits does Drouet's behavior reveal?*

"Sure, I'll attend to it."

He moved away, forgetting almost all about it the moment Mr. Quincel had ceased talking. He had not even thought to ask the time or place.

Drouet was reminded of his promise a day or two later by the receipt of a letter announcing that the first rehearsal was set for the following Friday evening, and urging him to kindly forward the young lady's address at once, in order that the part might be delivered to her.

"Now, who the deuce do I know?" asked the drummer reflectively, scratching his rosy ear. "I don't know anyone that knows anything about amateur theatricals."

He went over in memory the names of a number of women he knew, and finally fixed on one, largely because of the convenient location of her home on the West Side, and promised himself that as he came out that evening he would see her. When, however, he started west on the car he forgot, and was only reminded of his delinquency by an item in the *Evening News*—a small three-line affair under the head of Secret Society Notes—which stated the Custer Lodge of the Order of Elks would give a theatrical performance in Avery Hall on the 16th, when *Under the Gaslight* would be produced.

"George!" exclaimed Drouet, "I forgot that."

"What?" inquired Carrie.

2. **black-face.** Make-up used by actors portraying African Americans
3. ***dramatis personae.*** Characters in a play

They were at their little table in the room which might have been used for a kitchen, where Carrie occasionally served a meal. Tonight the fancy had caught her, and the little table was spread with a pleasing repast.

"Why, my lodge entertainment. They're going to give a play, and they wanted me to get them some young lady to take a part."

"What is it they're going to play?"

"*Under the Gaslight.*"

"When?"

"On the 16th."

"Well, why don't you?" asked Carrie.

"I don't know anyone," he replied.

Suddenly he looked up.

► *How does Carrie feel when Drouet suggests that she take the role?*

"Say," he said, "how would you like to take the part?"

"Me?" said Carrie. "I can't act."

"How do you know?" questioned Drouet reflectively.

"Because," answered Carrie, "I never did."

Nevertheless, she was pleased to think he would ask. Her eyes brightened, for if there was anything that enlisted her sympathies it was the art of the stage.

True to his nature, Drouet clung to this idea as an easy way out.

"That's nothing. You can act all you have to down there."

"No, I can't," said Carrie weakly, very much drawn toward the proposition and yet fearful.

"Yes, you can. Now, why don't you do it? They need someone, and it will be lots of fun for you."

"Oh, no, it won't," said Carrie seriously.

"You'd like that. I know you would. I've seen you dancing around here and giving imitations and that's why I asked you. You're clever enough, all right."

"No, I'm not," said Carrie shyly.

"Now, I'll tell you what you do. You go down and see about it. It'll be fun for you. The rest of the company isn't going to be any good. They haven't any experience. What do they know about theatricals?"

He frowned as he thought of their ignorance.

"Hand me the coffee," he added.

"I don't believe I could act, Charlie," Carrie went on pettishly. "You don't think I could, do you?"

Words For Everyday Use

re • past (ri past´) *n.,* meal

pet • tish • ly (pet´ ish lē) *adv.,* in a sulky manner

"Sure. Out o' sight. I bet you make a hit. Now you want to go, I know you do. I knew it when I came home. That's why I asked you."

"What is the play, did you say?"

"*Under the Gaslight.*"

"What part would they want me to take?"

"Oh, one of the heroines—I don't know."

"What sort of a play is it?"

"Well," said Drouet, whose memory for such things was not the best, "it's about a girl who gets kidnapped by a couple of crooks—a man and a woman that live in the slums. She had some money or something and they wanted to get it. I don't know now how it did go exactly."

"Don't you know what part I would have to take?"

"No, I don't, to tell the truth." He thought a moment. "Yes, I do, too. Laura, that's the thing—you're to be Laura."

"And you can't remember what the part is like?"

"To save me, Cad, I can't," he answered. "I ought to, too; I've seen the play enough. There's a girl in it that was stolen when she was an infant—was picked off the street or something—and she's the one that's hounded by the two old criminals I was telling you about." He stopped with a mouthful of pie poised on a fork before his face. "She comes very near getting drowned—no, that's not it. I'll tell you what I'll do," he concluded hopelessly, "I'll get you the book. I can't remember now for the life of me."

"Well, I don't know," said Carrie, when he had concluded, her interest and desire to shine dramatically struggling with her timidity for the mastery. "I might go if you thought I'd do all right."

◄ *What feelings struggle within Carrie?*

"Of course, you'll do," said Drouet, who, in his efforts to enthuse Carrie, had interested himself. "Do you think I'd come home here and urge you to do something that I didn't think you would make a success of? You can act all right. It'll be good for you."

"When must I go?" said Carrie, reflectively.

"The first rehearsal is Friday night. I'll get the part for you tonight."

"All right," said Carrie resignedly, "I'll do it, but if I make a failure now it's your fault."

"You won't fail," assured Drouet. "Just act as you do around here. Be natural. You're all right. I've often thought you'd make a corking[4] good actress."

"Did you really?" asked Carrie.

---

4. **corking.** Slang term meaning "terrific"

▶ *What has Drouet unknowingly done?*

▶ *What qualities within Carrie make her fit for the stage? What does the narrator note about Carrie's soul?*

▶ *What does the narrator see as the basis of dramatic art?*

▶ *What has Carrie often thought while attending the theater?*

"That's right," said the drummer.

He little knew as he went out of the door that night what a secret flame he had kindled in the bosom of the girl he left behind. Carrie was possessed of that sympathetic, impressionable nature which, ever in the most developed form, has been the glory of the drama. She was created with that passivity of soul which is always the mirror of the active world. She possessed an innate taste for imitation and no small ability. Even without practice, she could sometimes restore dramatic situations she had witnessed by recreating, before her mirror, the expressions of the various faces taking part in the scene. She loved to modulate her voice after the conventional manner of the distressed heroine, and repeat such pathetic fragments as appealed most to her sympathies. Of late, seeing the airy grace of the ingenue[5] in several well-constructed plays, she had been moved to secretly imitate it, and many were the little movements and expressions of the body in which she indulged from time to time in the privacy of her chamber. On several occasions, when Drouet had caught her admiring herself, as he imagined, in the mirror, she was doing nothing more than recalling some little grace of the mouth or the eyes which she had witnessed in another. Under his airy accusation she mistook this for vanity and accepted the blame with a faint sense of error, though, as a matter of fact, it was nothing more than the first subtle outcroppings of an artistic nature, endeavoring to recreate the perfect likeness of some phase of beauty which appealed to her. In such feeble tendencies, be it known, such outworking of desire to reproduce life, lies the basis of all dramatic art.

Now, when Carrie heard Drouet's laudatory opinion of her dramatic ability, her body tingled with satisfaction. Like the flame which welds the loosened particles into a solid mass, his words united those floating wisps of feeling which she had felt, but never believed, concerning her possible ability, and made them into a gaudy shred of hope. Like all human beings, she had a touch of vanity. She felt that she could do things if she only had a chance. How often had she looked at the well-dressed actresses on the stage and wondered how she would look, how delightful she would feel if only she were in

5. **ingenue.** Young female character

Words For Everyday Use

out • crop • ping (out´ kräp´iŋ) *n.,* something that protrudes
laud • a • to • ry (lôd´ ə tôr´ ē) *adj.,* expressing praise
gaud • y (gôd´ ē) *adj.,* bright and showy

their place. The glamour, the tense situation, the fine clothes, the applause, these had lured her until she felt that she, too, could act—that she, too, could compel acknowledgment of power. Now she was told that she really could—that little things she had done about the house had made even him feel her power. It was a delightful sensation while it lasted.

When Drouet was gone, she sat down in her rocking-chair by the window to think about it. As usual, imagination exaggerated the possibilities for her. It was as if he had put fifty cents in her hand and she had exercised the thoughts of a thousand dollars. She saw herself in a score of pathetic situations in which she assumed a tremulous voice and suffering manner. Her mind delighted itself with scenes of luxury and refinement, situations in which she was the cynosure[6] of all eyes, the arbiter[7] of all fates. As she rocked to and fro she felt the tensity of woe in abandonment, the magnificence of wrath after deception, the languor of sorrow after defeat. Thoughts of all the charming women she had seen in plays—every fancy, every illusion which she had concerning the stage—now came back as a returning tide after the ebb.[8] She built up feelings and a determination which the occasion did not warrant.

◄ In what way is Carrie letting her imagination run away with her? Is her role in this amateur performance likely to lead to what she imagines?

Drouet dropped in at the lodge when he went downtown, and swashed around with a great air, as Quincel met him.

"Where is that young lady you were going to get for us?" asked the latter.

"I've got her," said Drouet.

"Have you?" said Quincel, rather surprised by his promptness; "that's good. What's her address?" and he pulled out his notebook in order to be able to send her part to her.

"You want to send her her part?" asked the drummer.

"Yes."

"Well, I'll take it. I'm going right by her house in the morning."

"What did you say her address was? We only want it in case we have any information to send her."

"Twenty-nine Ogden Place."

"And her name?"

---

6. **cynosure.** Person or thing that is the center of attention
7. **arbiter.** Judge
8. **ebb.** Ebb tide, when water flows back to the sea

Words For Everyday Use

trem • u • lous (trem´yo͞o ləs) *adj.*, trembling
lan • guor (laŋ´gər) *n.*, pleasant stillness
swash (swäsh) *vi.*, swagger

▶ *What does Drouet give as Carrie's name? Why does he do this?*

"Carrie Madenda," said the drummer, firing at random. The lodge members knew him to be single.

"That sounds like somebody that can act, doesn't it?" said Quincel.

"Yes, it does."

He took the part home to Carrie and handed it to her with the manner of one who does a favor.

"He says that's the best part. Do you think you can do it?"

"I don't know until I look it over. You know I'm afraid, now that I've said I would."

"Oh, go on. What have you got to be afraid of? It's a cheap company. The rest of them aren't as good as you are."

"Well, I'll see," said Carrie, pleased to have the part, for all her misgivings.

He sidled around, dressing and fidgeting before he arranged to make his next remark.

▶ *What reasons does Drouet give Carrie for giving her an assumed name?*

"They were getting ready to print the programs," he said, "and I gave them the name of Carrie Madenda. Was that all right?"

"Yes, I guess so," said his companion, looking up at him. She was thinking it was slightly strange.

"If you didn't make a hit, you know," he went on.

"Oh, yes," she answered, rather pleased now with his caution. It was clever for Drouet.

"I didn't want to introduce you as my wife, because you'd feel worse then if you didn't *go*. They all know me so well. But you'll *go* all right. Anyhow, you'll probably never meet any of them again."

"Oh, I don't care," said Carrie desperately. She was determined now to have a try at the fascinating game.

Drouet breathed a sigh of relief. He had been afraid that he was about to precipitate another conversation upon the marriage question.

▶ *What type of role is Carrie to play?*

The part of Laura, as Carrie found out when she began to examine it, was one of suffering and tears. As delineated by Mr. Daly, it was true to the most sacred traditions of melodrama as he found it when he began his career. The sorrowful demeanor, the tremolo music,[9] the long, explanatory, cumulative addresses, all were there.

9. **tremolo music.** Trembling effect produced by the rapid reiteration of the same tone

Words For Everyday Use

si • dle (sid´'l) *vi.,* move sideways in a shy or stealthy manner

pre • cip • i • tate (prē sip´ ə tāt´) *vt.,* cause to happen before needed or desired

cu • mu • la • tive (kyo͞o´ myo͞o lāt´ iv) *adj.,* growing as time progresses

"Poor fellow," read Carrie, consulting the text and drawing her voice out pathetically. "Martin, be sure and give him a glass of wine before he goes."

She was surprised at the briefness of the entire part, not knowing that she must be on the stage while others were talking, and not only be there, but also keep herself in harmony with the dramatic movement of the scenes.

"I think I can do that, though," she concluded.

When Drouet came the next night, she was very much satisfied with her day's study.

"Well, how goes it, Caddie?" he said.

"All right," she laughed. "I think I have it memorized nearly."

"That's good," he said. "Let's hear some of it."

"Oh, I don't know whether I can get up and say it off here," she said bashfully.

"Well, I don't know why you shouldn't. It'll be easier here than it will there."

"I don't know about that," she answered.

Eventually she took off the ballroom episode with considerable feeling, forgetting, as she got deeper in the scene, all about Drouet, and letting herself rise to a fine state of feeling.

"Good," said Drouet; "fine; out o' sight! You're all right, Caddie, I tell you."

He was really moved by her excellent representation and the general appearance of the pathetic little figure as it swayed and finally fainted to the floor. He had bounded up to catch her, and now held her laughing in his arms.

"Ain't you afraid you'll hurt yourself?" he asked.

"Not a bit."

"Well, you're a wonder. Say, I never knew you could do anything like that."

"I never did, either," said Carrie merrily, her face flushed with delight.

"Well, you can bet that you're all right," said Drouet. "You can take my word for that. You won't fail."

◄ *What assurance does Drouet give Carrie about her upcoming performance?*

CHAPTER 17

A Glimpse Through the Gateway: Hope Lightens the Eye

The, to Carrie, very important theatrical performance was to take place at the Avery on conditions which were to make it more noteworthy than was at first anticipated. The little dramatic student had written to Hurstwood the very morning her part was brought her that she was going to take part in a play.

"I really am," she wrote, feeling that he might take it as a jest; "I have my part now, honest, truly."

Hurstwood smiled in an indulgent way as he read this.

"I wonder what it is going to be? I must see that."

He answered at once, making a pleasant reference to her ability. "I haven't the slightest doubt you will make a success. You must come to the park tomorrow morning and tell me all about it."

Carrie gladly complied, and revealed all the details of the undertaking as she understood it.

"Well," he said, "that's fine. I'm glad to hear it. Of course, you will do well, you're so clever."

► In what way has being in a play changed Carrie?

He had truly never seen so much spirit in the girl before. Her tendency to discover a touch of sadness had for the nonce[1] disappeared. As she spoke her eyes were bright, her cheeks red. She radiated much of the pleasure which her undertakings gave her. For all her misgivings—and they were as plentiful as the moments of the day—she was still happy. She could not repress her delight in doing this little thing which, to an ordinary observer, had no importance at all.

Hurstwood was charmed by the development of the fact that the girl had capabilities. There is nothing so inspiring in life as the sight of a legitimate ambition, no matter how incipient. It gives color, force, and beauty to the possessor.

► According to the narrator, are Drouet and Hurstwood estimating Carrie's abilities accurately?

Carrie was now lightened by a touch of this divine afflatus.[2] She drew to herself commendation from her two admirers which she had not earned. Their affection for her naturally

1. **nonce.** Present
2. **afflatus.** Inspiration

Words For Everyday Use	
	re • press (ri pres´) *vt.,* restrain; hold back
	in • cip • i • ent (in sip´ē ənt) *adj.,* beginning to emerge

heightened their perception of what she was trying to do and their approval of what she did. Her inexperience conserved her own exuberant fancy, which ran riot with every straw of opportunity, making of it a golden divining rod whereby the treasure of life was to be discovered.

"Let's see," said Hurstwood, "I ought to know some of the boys in the lodge. I'm an Elk myself."

"Oh, you mustn't let him know I told you."

"That's so," said the manager.

"I'd like for you to be there, if you want to come, but I don't see how you can unless he asks you."

"I'll be there," said Hurstwood affectionately. "I can fix it so he won't know you told me. You leave it to me."

This interest of the manager was a large thing in itself for the performance, for his standing among the Elks was something worth talking about. Already he was thinking of a box with some friends, and flowers for Carrie. He would make it a dress-suit affair and give the little girl a chance.

Within a day or two, Drouet dropped into the Adams Street resort, and he was at once spied by Hurstwood. It was at five in the afternoon and the place was crowded with merchants, actors, managers, politicians, a goodly company of rotund, rosy figures, silk-hatted, starchy-bosomed, beringed and bescarfpinned to the queen's taste. John L. Sullivan, the pugilist,[3] was at one end of the glittering bar, surrounded by a company of loudly dressed sports, who were holding a most animated conversation. Drouet came across the floor with a festive stride, a new pair of tan shoes squeaking audibly at his progress.

"Well, sir," said Hurstwood, "I was wondering what had become of you. I thought you had gone out of town again."

Drouet laughed.

"If you don't report more regularly we'll have to cut you off the list."

"Couldn't help it," said the drummer, "I've been busy."

They strolled over toward the bar amid the noisy, shifting company of notables. The dressy manager was shaken by the hand three times in as many minutes.

"I hear your lodge is going to give a performance," observed Hurstwood, in the most offhand manner.

3. **pugilist.** Boxer

Words For Everyday Use

ex • u • ber • ant (eg zo͞o´ bər ənt) *adj.,* full of life; uninhibited

► *What does Hurstwood do to make sure he can attend the performance?*

"Yes, who told you?"

"No one," said Hurstwood. "They just sent me a couple of tickets, which I can have for two dollars. Is it going to be any good?"

"I don't know," replied the drummer. "They've been trying to get me to get some woman to take a part."

"I wasn't intending to go," said the manager easily. "I'll subscribe, of course. How are things over there?"

"All right. They're going to fit things up out of the proceeds."

"Well," said the manager, "I hope they make a success of it. Have another?"

He did not intend to say any more. Now, if he should appear on the scene with a few friends, he could say that he had been urged to come along. Drouet had a desire to wipe out the possibility of confusion.

"I think the girl is going to take a part in it," he said abruptly, after thinking it over.

"You don't say so! How did that happen?"

"Well, they were short and wanted me to find them someone. I told Carrie, and she seems to want to try."

"Good for her," said the manager. "It'll be a real nice affair. Do her good, too. Has she ever had any experience?"

"Not a bit."

"Oh, well, it isn't anything very serious."

"She's clever, though," said Drouet, casting off any imputation against Carrie's ability. "She picks up her part quick enough."

"You don't say so!" said the manager.

"Yes, sir; she surprised me the other night. By George, if she didn't."

"We must give her a nice little send-off," said the manager. "I'll look after the flowers."

Drouet smiled at his good nature.

"After the show you must come with me and we'll have a little supper."

"I think she'll do all right," said Drouet.

"I want to see her. She's got to do all right. We'll make her," and the manager gave one of his quick, steely half-smiles, which was a compound of good nature and shrewdness.

Carrie, meanwhile, attended the first rehearsal. At this performance Mr. Quincel presided, aided by Mr. Millice, a

Words For Everyday Use

im • pu • ta • tion (im pyo͞o tā´ shən) *n.,* charge

young man who had some qualifications of past experience, which were not exactly understood by anyone. He was so experienced and so business-like, however, that he came very near being rude—failing to remember, as he did, that the individuals he was trying to instruct were volunteer players and not salaried underlings.

◄ *In what way is Mr. Millice rude?*

"Now, Miss Madenda," he said, addressing Carrie, who stood in one part uncertain as to what move to make, "you don't want to stand like that. Put expression in your face. Remember, you are troubled over the intrusion of the stranger. Walk so," and he struck out across the Avery stage in a most drooping manner.

Carrie did not exactly fancy the suggestion, but the novelty of the situation, the presence of strangers, all more or less nervous, and the desire to do anything rather than make a failure, made her timid. She walked in imitation of her mentor as requested, inwardly feeling that there was something strangely lacking.

◄ *What does Carrie think of Millice's suggestion for her role?*

"Now, Mrs. Morgan," said the director to one young married woman who was to take the part of Pearl, "you sit here. Now, Mr. Bamberger, you stand here, so. Now, what is it you say?"

"Explain," said Mr. Bamberger feebly. He had the part of Ray, Laura's lover, the society individual who was to waver in his thoughts of marrying her, upon finding that she was a waif[4] and a nobody by birth.

"How is that—what does your text say?"

"Explain," repeated Mr. Bamberger, looking intently at his part.

"Yes, but it also says," the director remarked, "that you are to look shocked. Now, say it again, and see if you can't look shocked."

"Explain!" demanded Mr. Bamberger vigorously.

"No, no, that won't do! Say it this way—*explain.*"

"Explain," said Mr. Bamberger, giving a modified imitation.

"That's better. Now go on."

"One night," resumed Mrs. Morgan, whose lines came next, "father and mother were going to the opera. When they were crossing Broadway, the usual crowd of children accosted them for alms[5]—"

4. **waif.** Person without home or friends, especially a homeless child
5. **alms.** Money given to beggars

Words For Everyday Use

ac • cost (ə kôst´) *vt.,* approach in an intrusive way

"Hold on," said the director, rushing forward, his arm extended. "Put more feeling into what you are saying."

Mrs. Morgan looked at him as if she feared a personal assault. Her eye lightened with resentment.

"Remember, Mrs. Morgan," he added, ignoring the gleam, but modifying his manner, "that you're detailing a pathetic story. You are now supposed to be telling something that is a grief to you. It requires feeling, repression, thus: 'The usual crowd of children accosted them for alms.'"

"All right," said Mrs. Morgan.

"Now, go on."

"As mother felt in her pocket for some change, her fingers touched a cold and trembling hand which had clutched her purse."

"Very good," interrupted the director, nodding his head significantly.

"A pickpocket! Well!" exclaimed Mr. Bamberger, speaking the lines that here fell to him.

"No, no, Mr. Bamberger," said the director, approaching, "not that way. 'A pickpocket—well?' so. That's the idea."

► What suggestion does Carrie make? Is her idea sensible?

"Don't you think," said Carrie weakly, noticing that it had not been proved yet whether the members of the company knew their lines, let alone the details of expression, "that it would be better if we just went through our lines once to see if we know them? We might pick up some points."

"A very good idea, Miss Madenda," said Mr. Quincel, who sat at the side of the stage, looking serenely on and volunteering opinions which the director did not heed.

"All right," said the latter, somewhat abashed, "it might be well to do it." Then brightening, with a show of authority, "Suppose we run right through, putting in as much expression as we can."

"Good," said Mr. Quincel.

"This hand," resumed Mrs. Morgan, glancing up at Mr. Bamberger and down at her book, as the lines proceeded, "my mother grasped in her own, and so tight that a small, feeble voice uttered an exclamation of pain. Mother looked down, and there beside her was a little ragged girl."

"Very good," observed the director, now hopelessly idle.

"The thief!" exclaimed Mr. Bamberger.

"Louder," put in the director, finding it almost impossible to keep his hands off.

"The thief!" roared poor Bamberger.

"Yes, but a thief hardly six years old, with a face like an angel's. 'Stop,' said my mother. 'What are you doing?'

"'Trying to steal,' said the child.

"'Don't you know that it is wicked to do so?' asked my father.

"'No,' said the girl, 'but it is dreadful to be hungry.'

"'Who told you to steal?' asked my mother.

"'She—there,' said the child, pointing to a squalid woman in a doorway opposite, who fled suddenly down the street. 'That is old Judas,' said the girl."

Mrs. Morgan read this rather flatly, and the director was in despair. He fidgeted around, and then went over to Mr. Quincel.

"What do you think of them?" he asked.

"Oh, I guess we'll be able to whip them into shape," said the latter, with an air of strength under difficulties.

"I don't know," said the director. "That fellow Bamberger strikes me as being a pretty poor shift for a lover."

"He's all we've got," said Quincel, rolling up his eyes. "Harrison went back on me at the last minute. Who else can we get?"

"I don't know," said the director. "I'm afraid he'll never pick up."

At this moment Bamberger was exclaiming, "Pearl, you are joking with me."

"Look at that now," said the director, whispering behind his hand. "My Lord! what can you do with a man who drawls out a sentence like that?"

"Do the best you can," said Quincel consolingly.

The rendition ran on in this wise[6] until it came to where Carrie, as Laura, comes into the room to explain to Ray, who, after hearing Pearl's statement about her birth, had written the letter repudiating her, which, however, he did not deliver. Bamberger was just concluding the words of Ray, "I must go before she returns. Her step! Too late," and was cramming the letter in his pocket, when she began sweetly with:

"Ray!"

"Miss—Miss Courtland," Bamberger faltered weakly.

Carrie looked at him a moment and forgot all about the company present. She began to feel the part, and summoned an indifferent smile to her lips, turning as the lines directed and going to a window, as if he were not present. She did it with a grace which was fascinating to look upon.

◄ *Why is the little girl in the play stealing?*

◄ *In what way do the director's thoughts on Carrie's acting abilities differ from his thoughts on the other players?*

6. **wise.** Manner

Words For Everyday Use

drawl (drôl) *vt.,* speak slowly, prolonging the vowels
ren • di • tion (ren dish´ən) *n.,* performance
re • pu • di • ate (ri pyo͞o´dē āt) *vt.,* disown

"Who is that woman?" asked the director, watching Carrie in her little scene with Bamberger.

"Miss Madenda," said Quincel.

"I know her name," said the director, "but what does she do?"

"I don't know," said Quincel. "She's a friend of one of our members."

"Well, she's got more gumption than anyone I've seen here so far—seems to take an interest in what she's doing."

"Pretty, too, isn't she?" said Quincel.

The director strolled away without answering.

In the second scene, where she was supposed to face the company in the ballroom, she did even better, winning the smile of the director, who volunteered, because of her fascination for him, to come over and speak with her.

"Were you ever on the stage?" he asked insinuatingly.

"No," said Carrie.

"You do so well, I thought you might have had some experience."

Carrie only smiled consciously.

He walked away to listen to Bamberger, who was feebly spouting some ardent line.

Mrs. Morgan saw the drift of things and gleamed at Carrie with envious and snapping black eyes.

"She's some cheap professional," she gave herself the satisfaction of thinking, and scorned and hated her accordingly.

► What does Drouet do to hurt Carrie's feelings? In what way does his insensitivity affect their relationship?

The rehearsal ended for one day, and Carrie went home feeling that she had acquitted herself satisfactorily. The words of the director were ringing in her ears, and she longed for an opportunity to tell Hurstwood. She wanted him to know just how well she was doing. Drouet, too, was an object for her confidences. She could hardly wait until he should ask her, and yet she did not have the vanity to bring it up. The drummer, however, had another line of thought tonight, and her little experience did not appeal to him as important. He let the conversation drop, save for what she chose to recite without solicitation, and Carrie was not good at that. He took it for granted that she was doing very well and he was relieved of further worry. Consequently he threw Carrie into repression, which was irritating. She felt his indifference keenly and longed to see Hurstwood. It was as if he

Words For Everyday Use

gump • tion (gump´shən) *n.,* courage and initiative

re • pres • sion (ri presh´ ən) *n.,* state of being subdued or restrained

were now the only friend she had on earth. The next morning Drouet was interested again, but the damage had been done.

She got a pretty letter from the manager, saying that by the time she got it he would be waiting for her in the park. When she came, he shone upon her as the morning sun.

"Well, my dear," he asked, "how did you come out?"

"Well enough," she said, still somewhat reduced after Drouet.

"Now, tell me just what you did. Was it pleasant?"

Carrie related the incidents of the rehearsal, warming up as she proceeded.

"Well, that's delightful," said Hurstwood. "I'm so glad. I must get over there to see you. When is the next rehearsal?"

"Tuesday," said Carrie, "but they don't allow visitors."

"I imagine I could get in," said Hurstwood significantly.

She was completely restored and delighted by his consideration, but she made him promise not to come around.

"Now you must do your best to please me," he said encouragingly. "Just remember that I want you to succeed. We will make the performance worthwhile. You do that now."

"I'll try," said Carrie, brimming with affection and enthusiasm.

"That's the girl," said Hurstwood fondly. "Now, remember," shaking an affectionate finger at her, "your best."

"I will," she answered, looking back.

The whole earth was brimming sunshine that morning. She tripped along, the clear sky pouring liquid blue into her soul. Oh, blessed are the children of endeavor in this, that they try and are hopeful. And blessed also are they who, knowing, smile and approve.

◄ *In what way does Hurstwood's attitude toward Carrie differ from Drouet's?*

◄ *According to the narrator, who is blessed?*

CHAPTER 18

Just Over the Border: A Hail and Farewell

► *What has Hurstwood done to try to ensure the performance's success?*

By the evening of the 16th the subtle hand of Hurstwood had made itself apparent. He had given the word among his friends—and they were many and influential—that here was something which they ought to attend, and, as a consequence, the sale of tickets by Mr. Quincel, acting for the lodge, had been large. Small four-line notes had appeared in all of the daily newspapers. These he had arranged for by the aid of one of his newspaper friends on the "Times," Mr. Harry McGarren, the managing editor.

"Say, Harry," Hurstwood said to him one evening, as the latter stood at the bar drinking before wending his belated way homeward, "you can help the boys out, I guess."

"What is it?" said McGarren, pleased to be consulted by the opulent manager.

"The Custer Lodge is getting up a little entertainment for their own good, and they'd like a little newspaper notice. You know what I mean—a squib[1] or two saying that it's going to take place."

"Certainly," said McGarren, "I can fix that for you, George."

► *Does Hurstwood make his efforts on behalf of the performance known?*

At the same time Hurstwood kept himself wholly in the background. The members of Custer Lodge could scarcely understand why their little affair was taking so well. Mr. Harry Quincel was looked upon as quite a star for this sort of work.

By the time the 16th had arrived Hurstwood's friends had rallied like Romans to a senator's call. A well-dressed, good-natured, flatteringly-inclined audience was assured from the moment he thought of assisting Carrie.

► *How does Carrie feel before the performance?*

That little student had mastered her part to her own satisfaction, much as she trembled for her fate when she should once face the gathered throng, behind the glare of the footlights. She tried to console herself with the thought that a score of other persons, men and women, were equally tremulous concerning the outcome of their efforts, but she could

1. **squib.** Short news item

Words For Everyday Use

wend (wend) *vt.,* proceed

op • u • lent (äp´ yo͞o lənt) *adj.,* very wealthy

not disassociate the general danger from her own individual liability. She feared that she would forget her lines, that she might be unable to master the feeling which she now felt concerning her own movements in the play. At times she wished that she had never gone into the affair; at others, she trembled lest she should be paralyzed with fear and stand white and gasping, not knowing what to say and spoiling the entire performance.

In the matter of the company, Mr. Bamberger had disappeared. That hopeless example had fallen under the lance[2] of the director's criticism. Mrs. Morgan was still present, but envious and determined, if for nothing more than spite, to do as well as Carrie at least. A loafing professional had been called in to assume the role of Ray, and, while he was a poor stick of his kind, he was not troubled by any of those qualms which attack the spirit of those who have never faced an audience. He swashed about (cautioned though he was to maintain silence concerning his past theatrical relationships) in such a self-confident manner that he was like to convince everyone of his identity by mere matter of circumstantial evidence.

"It is so easy," he said to Mrs. Morgan, in the usual affected stage voice. "An audience would be the last thing to trouble me. It's the spirit of the part, you know, that is difficult."

Carrie disliked his appearance, but she was too much the actress not to swallow his qualities with complaisance, seeing that she must suffer his fictitious love for the evening.

At six she was ready to go. Theatrical paraphernalia had been provided over and above her care. She had practiced her make-up in the morning, had rehearsed and arranged her material for the evening by one o'clock, and had gone home to have a final look at her part, waiting for the evening to come.

On this occasion the lodge sent a carriage. Drouet rode with her as far as the door, and then went about the neighboring stores, looking for some good cigars. The little actress marched nervously into her dressing room and began that painfully anticipated matter of make-up which was to transform her, a simple maiden, to Laura, The Belle of Society.

---

2. **lance.** Weapon with a long wooden shaft tipped by a metal spearhead; here, a verbal attack

Words For Everyday Use	
	loaf • ing (lōf iŋ) *adj.,* idling, dawdling
	com • plai • sance (kəm plā´zəns) *n.,* willingness to please
	par • a • pher • na • li • a (par´ə fər nāl´ yə) *n.pl.,* collection of articles, belongings, or tools

► *In what way do Carrie's feelings backstage differ from the longing she felt when seeing mansions?*

The flare of the gas jets, the open trunks, suggestive of travel and display, the scattered contents of the make-up box—rouge, pearl powder, whiting, burnt cork, India ink, pencils for the eyelids, wigs, scissors, looking-glasses, drapery—in short, all the nameless paraphernalia of disguise, have a remarkable atmosphere of their own. Since her arrival in the city many things had influenced her, but always in a far-removed manner. This new atmosphere was more friendly. It was wholly unlike the great brilliant mansions which waved her coldly away, permitting her only awe and distant wonder. This took her by the hand kindly, as one who says, "My dear, come in." It opened for her as if for its own. She had wondered at the greatness of the names upon the billboards, the marvel of the long notices in the papers, the beauty of the dresses upon the stage, the atmosphere of carriages, flowers, refinement. Here was no illusion. Here was an open door to see all of that. She had come upon it as one who stumbles upon a secret passage, and, behold, she was in the chamber of diamonds and delight!

As she dressed with a flutter, in her little stage room, hearing the voices outside, seeing Mr. Quincel hurrying here and there, noting Mrs. Morgan and Mrs. Hoagland at their nervous work of preparation, seeing all the twenty members of the cast moving about and worrying over what the result would be, she could not help thinking what a delight this would be if it would endure; how perfect a state, if she could only do well now, and then sometime get a place as a real actress. The thought had taken a mighty hold upon her. It hummed in her ears as the melody of an old song.

► *What does Carrie hope to do? Why?*

Outside in the little lobby another scene was being enacted. Without the interest of Hurstwood, the little hall would probably have been comfortably filled, for the members of the lodge were moderately interested in its welfare. Hurstwood's word, however, had gone the rounds. It was to be a full-dress affair. The four boxes had been taken. Dr. Norman McNeill Hale and his wife were to occupy one. This was quite a card. C. R. Walker, drygoods merchant and possessor of at least two hundred thousand dollars, had taken another; a well-known coal merchant had been induced to take the third, and Hurstwood and his friends the fourth. Among the latter was Drouet. The people who were now pouring here

Words For Everyday Use	**en • act** (en akt´) *vt.,* perform

were not celebrities, nor even local notabilities, in a general sense. They were the lights of a certain circle—the circle of small fortunes and secret order distinctions. These gentlemen Elks knew the standing of one another. They had regard for the ability which could amass a small fortune, own a nice home, keep a *barouche*[3] or carriage, perhaps, wear fine clothes, and maintain a good mercantile position. Naturally, Hurstwood, who was a little above the order of mind which accepted this standard as perfect, who had shrewdness and much assumption of dignity, who held an imposing and authoritative position, and commanded friendship by intuitive tact in handling people, was quite a figure. He was more generally known than most others in the same circle, and was looked upon as someone whose reserve covered a mine of influence and solid financial prosperity.

◄ *What type of people are attending the performance? What do these people value?*

◄ *Why is Hurstwood highly respected among this crowd?*

Tonight he was in his element. He came with several friends directly from Rector's in a carriage. In the lobby he met Drouet, who was just returning from a trip for more cigars. All five now joined in an animated conversation concerning the company present and the general drift of lodge affairs.

"Who's here?" said Hurstwood, passing into the theater proper, where the lights were turned up and a company of gentlemen were laughing and talking in the open space back of the seats.

"Why, how do you do, Mr. Hurstwood?" came from the first individual recognized.

"Glad to see you," said the latter, grasping his hand lightly.

"Looks quite an affair, doesn't it?"

"Yes, indeed," said the manager.

"Custer seems to have the backing of its members," observed the friend.

"So it should," said the knowing manager. "I'm glad to see it."

"Well, George," said another rotund citizen, whose *avoirdupois*[4] made necessary an almost alarming display of starched shirt bosom, "how goes it with you?"

"Excellent," said the manager.

---

3. ***barouche.*** Four-wheeled carriage with a collapsible hood and a box seat in front for the driver

4. ***avoirdupois.*** Weight or heaviness (from a system of measuring weight)

Words For Everyday Use	**a • mass** (ə mas´) *vt.,* pile up; accumulate **mer • can • tile** (mʉr´ kən tīl) *adj.,* commercial; characteristic of a trader **ro • tund** (rō tund´) *adj.,* round and plump

► *Do you believe Hurstwood's claim that his wife is ill? Explain.*

► *How do Hurstwood's friends feel about themselves? How can you tell?*

"What brings you over here? You're not a member of Custer."

"Good nature," returned the manager. "Like to see the boys, you know."

"Wife here?"

"She couldn't come tonight. She's not well."

"Sorry to hear it—nothing serious, I hope."

"No, just feeling a little ill."

"I remember Mrs. Hurstwood when she was traveling once with you over to St. Joe—" and here the newcomer launched off in a trivial recollection, which was terminated by the arrival of more friends.

"Why, George, how are you?" said another genial West Side politician and lodge member. "My, but I'm glad to see you again; how are things, anyhow?"

"Very well; I see you got that nomination for alderman."[5]

"Yes, we whipped them out over there without much trouble."

"What do you suppose Hennessy will do now?"

"Oh, he'll go back to his brick business. He has a brick-yard, you know."

"I didn't know that," said the manager. "Felt pretty sore, I suppose, over his defeat."

"Perhaps," said the other, winking shrewdly.

Some of the more favored of his friends whom he had invited began to roll up in carriages now. They came shuffling in with a great show of finery and much evident feeling of content and importance.

"Here we are," said Hurstwood, turning to one from a group with whom he was talking.

"That's right," returned the newcomer, a gentleman of about forty-five.

"And say," he whispered, jovially, pulling Hurstwood over by the shoulder so that he might whisper in his ear, "if this isn't a good show, I'll punch your head."

"You ought to pay for seeing your old friends. Bother the show!"

To another who inquired, "Is it something really good?" the manager replied:

---

5. **alderman.** Representative in city government

Words For Everyday Use

jo • vi • al • ly (jō´vē ə lē) *adv.,* with good humor

"I don't know. I don't suppose so." Then, lifting his hand graciously, "For the lodge."

"Lots of boys out, eh?"

"Yes, look up Shanahan. He was just asking for you a moment ago."

It was thus that the little theater resounded to a babble of successful voices, the creak of fine clothes, the commonplace of good nature, and all largely because of this man's bidding. Look at him anytime within the half hour before the curtain was up, he was a member of an eminent group—a rounded company of five or more whose stout figures, large white bosoms, and shining pins bespoke[6] the character of their success. The gentlemen who brought their wives called him out to shake hands. Seats clicked, ushers bowed while he looked blandly on. He was evidently a light among them, reflecting in his personality the ambitions of those who greeted him. He was acknowledged, fawned upon, in a way lionized. Through it all one could see the standing of the man. It was greatness in a way, small as it was.

◄ *What does Hurstwood say about the performance in which Carrie is about to take part?*

◄ *In what way would you characterize Hurstwood's social position at this moment?*

6. **bespoke.** Past tense of *bespeak,* meaning "to make evident"

Words For Everyday Use

re • sound (ri zound´) *vi.,* echo, reverberate

em • i • nent (em´ ə nənt) *adj.,* high in rank or achievement

li • on • ize (lī´ən īz´) *vt.,* treat as a celebrity

Responding to the Selection

Imagine that you are in Carrie's position—backstage waiting for the curtains to rise. What would your thoughts and concerns be? If you were to peek into the theater to see the arrival of the crowd described in chapter 18, how would this affect your mood?

Reviewing the Selection

Recalling and Interpreting

1. **R:** In chapter 13, Carrie and Hurstwood meet alone again. What motivates Hurstwood's interest in Carrie? Why does he want to "win" her? At the chapter's end, what two things does he ask of her? What does she do in response? After her meeting with Hurstwood, about what does Carrie confront Drouet?

2. **I:** What is Hurstwood assuming about Carrie? about himself? What do his assumptions reveal about his character? Hurstwood also assumes that Carrie's responses signify what he wishes to hear. In what way is he right? In what way is he misinterpreting her responses? Why does Drouet's response to Carrie's accusation convince her that she is justified in her relationship with Hurstwood?

3. **R:** In what way is Hurstwood's relationship with his family changing? In Chapter 15, when Carrie and Hurstwood meet again, what does Hurstwood do to determine the true nature of Carrie's feelings toward him? What demands does Carrie make of Hurstwood?

4. **I:** How does Hurstwood feel about these changes in his family? Explain whether these changes are the result of his newfound infatuation with Carrie or whether they are a result of the years passing and his children growing up. Why might someone in Hurstwood's position be attracted to the "magic of youth"? Explain whether you think Hurstwood will act on the scheme he has devised.

5. **R:** Why does Drouet offer Carrie a part in a play? What "secret flame" has he kindled in Carrie? What hopes does Carrie entertain after she accepts the part? What do Drouet, Hurstwood, the director, and the other actors think of Carrie's theatrical ability?

6. **I:** How does Carrie feel about her part in the play? When Carrie enacts her part for Drouet, he says, "Well, you're a wonder. Say, I never knew you could do anything like that," and Carrie's response is "I never did, either." Why might finding a skill and a project she enjoys be especially important to someone in Carrie's position?

7. **R:** What does Drouet discuss with Carrie after her first rehearsal? What does Hurstwood discuss with Carrie? What does Hurstwood do to ensure the play's success?

8. **I:** In what way do Drouet's and Hurstwood's reactions to Carrie's newfound interest emphasize the difference between the two men? Why is Carrie drawn more strongly to Hurstwood, even though Drouet got her the part? Hurstwood chooses to allow his support of the play to remain unknown to Carrie. Why? What would Drouet do if he had accomplished what Hurstwood has?

Synthesizing

9. Unlike other characters in this novel, Carrie is not clever with words. Often, when she is unsure what she should say, she either says nothing at all or she responds weakly. Find some examples from chapters 13–18 where Carrie reveals her inability to speak. What does Carrie's communication style reveal about her as a character? In what way does her inability to speak affect the characters with whom she interacts? What is significant about the fact that she has chosen to express her feelings through acting in a drama?

10. When Carrie first began her relationship with Drouet, she made no demands of him. She makes it very clear to Hurstwood that in order for their relationship to continue, he must marry her. As the chapters progress, she becomes more outspoken on this one issue. What do Carrie's demands reveal about the way she is changing as a character? Why is Carrie becoming outspoken on the issue of her marital status? In what way is her part in the play also changing her as a character?

Understanding Literature (QUESTIONS FOR DISCUSSION)

1. Allusion. An **allusion** is a rhetorical technique in which reference is made to a person, event, object, or work from history or literature. Dreiser alludes to the Bible in chapter 13. For example, the title of chapter 13, "His Credentials Accepted: A Babel of Tongues," is an allusion to the story of the tower of Babel in Genesis. In this story the people of earth all speak one language and try to build a tower that will reach the heavens, so God confuses their language so they won't understand each other and will have to halt construction on the tower. Why do you think Dreiser chose to include this allusion as part of the title of chapter 13? What does it reveal about the events that occur in this chapter? Another allusion occurs when Hurstwood is described as picking Carrie "as he would the fresh fruit of a tree." This passage is an allusion to the story of Adam and Eve in Genesis. God had commanded that Adam and Eve never eat of the fruit of the tree of knowledge of good and evil, but Eve is tempted by the serpent to do so, and she, in turn, tempts Adam to eat of the fruit with her. Adam and Eve are cast out of the Garden of Eden as punishment for their sin. What is significant about Hurstwood's love for Carrie being described in this way? What does this allusion indicate about Hurstwood's probable future?

2. Theme. A **theme** is a central idea in a literary work. One of the themes that runs throughout this novel is superficiality—how the majority of people delude themselves by focusing on surfaces, rather than substance, or by mistaking external qualities for more meaningful internal qualities. This theme emerges a number of times in chapters 13–18 and is explored in more detail below.

- Hurstwood's job as manager is described in detail on pages 117–118. Explain whether Hurstwood's function as manager is to perform specific duties or primarily to appear as an ornament of respectability to give the bar "atmosphere." What does Hurstwood need his customers to feel in order for him to be a success at his job? What does Hurstwood's job reveal about his character?
- On page 119, Carrie's appearance strengthens Hurstwood's resolve to express his feelings for her. What does this reveal about the way Hurstwood views Carrie? Do her inner qualities and feelings matter to him as much as her outward appearance?

- On page 146 the narrator says, "She was created with that passivity of soul which is always the mirror of the active world." What is the narrator indicating about Carrie's inner and outer qualities? In what way is Carrie's interest in the theater and acting an example of importance placed on outer surfaces rather than on substance?

3. Irony. Irony is a difference between appearance and reality. Types of irony include the following: dramatic irony, in which something is known by a reader or audience but unknown to the characters; verbal irony, in which a statement is made that implies its opposite; and irony of situation, in which an event occurs that violates the expectations of the characters, the reader, or the audience. At the theater, Drouet, Hurstwood, and Carrie attend a play in which a wife listens to a lover while her husband is absent, and Drouet says, "Served him right . . . I haven't any pity for a man who would be such a chump as that. . . . a man ought to be more attentive than that to his wife if he wants to keep her." What type of irony is involved in this scene? What makes the situation ironic? Hurstwood, who is aware of the irony, responds "gently" to Drouet. What does this reveal about his character? Backstage at the theater, Carrie compares the theater favorably to great mansions by noting that, "here [the theater] was no illusion." What makes this observation ironic?

Chapter 19

An Hour in Elf Land: A Clamor Half Heard

At last the curtain was ready to go up. All the details of the make-up had been completed, and the company settled down as the leader of the small, hired orchestra tapped significantly upon his music rack with his baton and began the soft curtain-raising strain. Hurstwood ceased talking, and went with Drouet and his friend Sagar Morrison around to the box.

"Now, we'll see how the little girl does," he said to Drouet, in a tone which no one else could hear.

▶ *What goes wrong at the beginning of the play?*

On the stage, six of the characters had already appeared in the opening parlor scene. Drouet and Hurstwood saw at a glance that Carrie was not among them, and went on talking in a whisper. Mrs. Morgan, Mrs. Hoagland, and the actor who had taken Bamberger's part were representing the principal roles in this scene. The professional, whose name was Patton, had little to recommend him outside of his assurance, but this at the present moment was most palpably needed. Mrs. Morgan, as Pearl, was stiff with fright. Mrs. Hoagland was husky in the throat. The whole company was so weak-kneed that the lines were merely spoken, and nothing more. It took all the hope and uncritical good nature of the audience to keep from manifesting pity by that unrest which is the agony of failure.

▶ *What is Hurstwood's attitude toward the play? What are his expectations of Carrie's performance?*

Hurstwood was perfectly indifferent. He took it for granted that it would be worthless. All he cared for was to have it endurable enough to allow for pretension[1] and congratulation afterward.

After the first rush of fright, however, the players got over the danger of collapse. They rambled weakly forward, losing nearly all the expression which was intended, and making the thing dull in the extreme, when Carrie came in.

▶ *What goes wrong with Carrie's performance?*

One glance at her, and both Hurstwood and Drouet saw plainly that she also was weak-kneed. She came faintly across the stage, saying:

1. **pretension.** pretense

Words For Everyday Use

pal • pa • bly (pal´ pə blē) *adv.*, evidently

man • i • fest (man´ ə fest´) *vi.*, reveal; show plainly

"And you, sir; we have been looking for you since eight o'clock," but with so little color and in such a feeble voice that it was positively painful.

"She's frightened," whispered Drouet to Hurstwood.

The manager made no answer.

She had a line presently which was supposed to be funny.

"Well, that's as much as to say that I'm a sort of life pill."

It came out so flat, however, that it was a deathly thing. Drouet fidgeted. Hurstwood moved his toe the least bit.

There was another place in which Laura was to rise and, with a sense of impending disaster, say, sadly:

"I wish you hadn't said that, Pearl. You know the old proverb, 'Call a maid by a married name.'"

The lack of feeling in the thing was ridiculous. Carrie did not get it at all. She seemed to be talking in her sleep. It looked as if she were certain to be a wretched failure. She was more hopeless than Mrs. Morgan, who had recovered somewhat, and was now saying her lines clearly at least. Drouet looked away from the stage at the audience. The latter held out silently, hoping for a general change, of course. Hurstwood fixed his eye on Carrie, as if to hypnotize her into doing better. He was pouring determination of his own in her direction. He felt sorry for her.

◄ How does it seem that the audience will remember Carrie's performance?

In a few more minutes it fell to her to read the letter sent in by the strange villain. The audience had been slightly diverted by a conversation between the professional actor and a character called Snorky, impersonated by a short little American, who really developed some humor as a half-crazed, one-armed soldier, turned messenger for a living. He bawled his lines out with such defiance that, while they really did not partake of the humor intended, they were funny. Now he was off, however, and it was back to pathos, with Carrie as the chief figure. She did not recover. She wandered through the whole scene between herself and the intruding villain, straining the patience of the audience, and finally exiting, much to their relief.

◄ How does the audience feel when Carrie leaves the stage?

"She's too nervous," said Drouet, feeling in the mildness of the remark that he was lying for once.

"Better go back and say a word to her."

Drouet was glad to do anything for relief. He fairly hustled around to the side entrance, and was let in by the friendly

Words For Everyday Use

im • pend • ing (im pend´ iŋ) *adj.*, threatening to come

prov • erb (präv´ ʉrb´) *n.*, traditional saying that expresses some obvious truth

di • vert (dəvʉrt´) *vt.*, distract attention

bawl (bôl) *vi.*, shout out noisily

doorkeeper. Carrie was standing in the wings, weakly waiting her next cue, all the snap and nerve gone out of her.

"Say, Cad," he said, looking at her, "you mustn't be nervous. Wake up. Those guys out there don't amount to anything. What are you afraid of?"

"I don't know," said Carrie. "I just don't seem to be able to do it."

She was grateful for the drummer's presence, though. She had found the company so nervous that her own strength had gone.

"Come on," said Drouet. "Brace up. What are you afraid of? Go on out there now, and do the trick. What do you care?"

Carrie revived a little under the drummer's electrical, nervous condition.

► *What does Drouet say instead of admitting that Carrie's performance is bad?*

"Did I do so very bad?"

"Not a bit. All you need is a little more ginger. Do it as you showed me. Get that toss of your head you had the other night."

Carrie remembered her triumph in the room. She tried to think she could do it.

"What's next?" he said, looking at her part, which she had been studying.

"Why, the scene between Ray and me when I refuse him."

"Well, now you do that lively," said the drummer. "Put in snap, that's the thing. Act as if you didn't care."

"Your turn next, Miss Madenda," said the prompter.

"Oh, dear," said Carrie.

"Well, you're a chump for being afraid," said Drouet. "Come on now, brace up. I'll watch you from right here."

"Will you?" said Carrie.

"Yes, now go on. Don't be afraid."

The prompter signaled her.

She started out, weak as ever, but suddenly her nerve partially returned. She thought of Drouet looking.

"Ray," she said, gently, using a tone of voice much more calm than when she had last appeared. It was the scene which had pleased the director at the rehearsal.

"She's easier," thought Hurstwood to himself.

She did not do the part as she had at rehearsal, but she was better. The audience was at least not irritated. The improvement of the work of the entire company took away direct observation from her. They were making very fair progress, and now it looked as if the play would be passable, in the less trying parts at least.

Carrie came off warm and nervous.

"Well," she said, looking at him, "was it any better?"

"Well, I should say so. That's the way. Put life into it. You did that about a thousand percent better than you did the other scene. Now go on and fire up. You can do it. Knock 'em."

"Was it really better?"

"Better, I should say so. What comes next?"

"That ballroom scene."

"Well, you can do that all right," he said.

"I don't know," answered Carrie.

"Why, woman," he exclaimed, "you did it for me! Now you go out there and do it. It'll be fun for you. Just do as you did in the room. If you'll reel it off[2] that way, I'll bet you make a hit. Now, what'll you bet? You do it."

The drummer usually allowed his ardent good nature to get the better of his speech. He really did think that Carrie had acted this particular scene very well, and he wanted her to repeat it in public. His enthusiasm was due to the mere spirit of the occasion.

When the time came, he buoyed Carrie up most effectually. He began to make her feel as if she had done very well. The old melancholy of desire began to come back as he talked at her, and by the time the situation rolled around she was running high in feeling.

"I think I can do this."

"Sure you can. Now you go ahead and see."

On the stage, Mrs. Van Dam was making her cruel insinuation against Laura.

Carrie listened, and caught the infection of something—she did not know what. Her nostrils sniffed thinly.

"It means," the professional actor began, speaking as Ray, "that society is a terrible avenger of insult. Have you ever heard of the Siberian wolves? When one of the pack falls through weakness, the others devour him. It is not an elegant comparison, but there is something wolfish in society. Laura has mocked it with a pretense, and society, which is made up of pretense, will bitterly resent the mockery."

◄ To what is society compared in the play? Of what crime is Carrie's character guilty in society's eyes?

At the sound of her stage name Carrie started. She began to feel the bitterness of the situation. The feelings of the outcast descended upon her. She hung at the wing's edge, wrapt in her own mounting thoughts. She hardly heard anything more, save her own rumbling blood.

◄ What feelings fill Carrie when she considers Laura's plight?

2. **reel it off.** Produce easily and without hesitation

Words For Everyday Use

buoy (bo͞o´ ē) *vt.,* lift up in spirits

mel • an • chol • y (mel´ən käl´ē) *n.,* sadness and depression of spirits

a • veng • er (ə venj´ ər) *n.,* one who returns injury for injury

"Come, girls," said Mrs. Van Dam, solemnly, "let us look after our things. They are no longer safe when such an accomplished thief enters."

► *In what way is Carrie's acting in this scene already superior to her acting in her previous scenes?*

"Cue," said the prompter, close to her side, but she did not hear. Already she was moving forward with a steady grace, born of inspiration. She dawned upon the audience, handsome and proud, shifting, with the necessity of the situation, to a cold, white, helpless object, as the social pack moved away from her scornfully.

Hurstwood blinked his eyes and caught the infection. The radiating waves of feeling and sincerity were already breaking against the farthest walls of the chamber. The magic of passion, which will yet dissolve the world, was here at work.

There was a drawing, too, of attention, a riveting of feeling, heretofore wandering.

"Ray! Ray! Why do you not come back to her?" was the cry of Pearl.

Every eye was fixed on Carrie, still proud and scornful. They moved as she moved. Their eyes were with her eyes.

Mrs. Morgan, as Pearl, approached her.

"Let us go home," she said.

"No," answered Carrie, her voice assuming for the first time a penetrating quality which it had never known. "Stay with him!"

She pointed an almost accusing hand toward her lover. Then, with a pathos which struck home because of its utter simplicity, "He shall not suffer long."

Hurstwood realized that he was seeing something extraordinarily good. It was heightened for him by the applause of the audience as the curtain descended and the fact that it was Carrie. He thought now that she was beautiful. She had done something which was above his sphere. He felt a keen delight in realizing that she was his.

"Fine," he said, and then, seized by a sudden impulse, arose and went about to the stage door.

► *What does Hurstwood want to do? Why can't he do this?*

When he came in upon Carrie she was still with Drouet. His feelings for her were most exuberant. He was almost swept away by the strength and feeling she exhibited. His desire was to pour forth his praise with the unbounded feelings of a lover, but here was Drouet, whose affection was also rapidly reviving. The latter was more fascinated, if anything, than Hurstwood.

Words For Everyday Use

scorn • ful • ly (skôrn´ fəl lē) *adv.,* filled with or showing contempt

un • bound • ed (un bound ´əd) *adj.,* unconfined

At least, in the nature of things, it took a more ruddy form.

"Well, well," said Drouet, "you did out of sight. That was simply great. I knew you could do it. Oh, but you're a little daisy!"

Carrie's eyes flamed with the light of achievement.

"Did I do all right?"

"Did you? Well, I guess. Didn't you hear the applause?"

There was some faint sound of clapping yet.

"I thought I got it something like—I felt it."

Just then Hurstwood came in. Instinctively he felt the change in Drouet. He saw that the drummer was near to Carrie, and jealousy leaped alight in his bosom. In a flash of thought, he reproached himself for having sent him back. Also, he hated him as an intruder. He could scarcely pull himself down to the level where he would have to congratulate Carrie as a friend. Nevertheless, the man mastered himself, and it was a triumph. He almost jerked the old subtle light to his eyes.

◄ *In what way is Hurstwood also acting tonight?*

"I thought," he said, looking at Carrie, "I would come around and tell you how well you did, Mrs. Drouet. It was delightful."

Carrie took the cue, and replied:

"Oh, thank you."

"I was just telling her," put in Drouet, now delighted with his possession, "that I thought she did fine."

"Indeed you did," said Hurstwood, turning upon Carrie eyes in which she read more than the words.

Carrie laughed luxuriantly.

"If you do as well in the rest of the play, you will make us all think you are a born actress."

Carrie smiled again. She felt the acuteness of Hurstwood's position, and wished deeply that she could be alone with him, but she did not understand the change in Drouet. Hurstwood found that he could not talk, repressed as he was, and grudging Drouet every moment of his presence, he bowed himself out with the elegance of a Faust.[3] Outside he set his teeth with envy.

"Damn it!" he said, "is he always going to be in the way?" He was moody when he got back to the box, and could not talk for thinking of his wretched situation.

---

3. **Faust.** In medieval legends and later literary and operatic works, Faust is a philosopher who sells his soul to the devil in exchange for knowledge and power.

Words For Everyday Use

rud • dy (rud´ ē) *adj.*, healthy

lux • u • ri • ant • ly (lug zhoor´ ē ənt lē) *adv.*, characterized by richness and extravagance

a • cute • ness (ə kyo͞ot´ nes) *adj.*, extreme sensitivity

grudge (gruj) *vt.*, envy and resent

As the curtain for the next act arose, Drouet came back. He was very much enlivened in temper and inclined to whisper, but Hurstwood pretended interest. He fixed his eyes on the stage, although Carrie was not there, a short bit of melodramatic comedy preceding her entrance. He did not see what was going on, however. He was thinking his own thoughts, and they were wretched.

The progress of the play did not improve matters for him. Carrie, from now on, was easily the center of interest. The audience, which had been inclined to feel that nothing could be good after the first gloomy impression, now went to the other extreme and saw power where it was not. The general feeling reacted on Carrie. She presented her part with some felicity, though nothing like the intensity which had aroused the feeling at the end of the long first act.

▶ *What heightens Carrie's charm for both Hurstwood and Drouet?*

Both Hurstwood and Drouet viewed her pretty figure with rising feelings. The fact that such ability should reveal itself in her, that they should see it set forth under such effective circumstances, framed almost in massy[4] gold and shone upon by the appropriate lights of sentiment and personality, heightened her charm for them. She was more than the old Carrie to Drouet. He longed to be at home with her until he could tell her. He awaited impatiently the end, when they should go home alone.

Hurstwood, on the contrary, saw in the strength of her new attractiveness his miserable predicament. He could have cursed the man beside him. By the Lord, he could not even applaud feelingly as he would. For once he must simulate when it left a taste in his mouth.

It was in the last act that Carrie's fascination for her lovers assumed its most effective character.

Hurstwood listened to its progress, wondering when Carrie would come on. He had not long to wait. The author had used the artifice of sending all the merry company for a drive, and now Carrie came in alone. It was the first time that Hurstwood had had a chance to see her facing the audience quite alone, for nowhere else had she been without a foil of some sort. He suddenly felt, as she entered, that her old strength—the power that had grasped him at the end of

4. **massy.** Heavy

Words For Everyday Use

mel • o • dra • mat • ic (mel´ ō drə mat´ ik) *adj.*, having sensational conflicts and exaggerated emotion

fe • lic • i • ty (fə lis´ i tē) *n.*, pleasing manner

sim • u • late (sim´yo͞o lāt´) *vt.*, pretend

the first act—had come back. She seemed to be gaining feeling, now that the play was drawing to a close and the opportunity for great action was passing.

"Poor Pearl," she said, speaking with natural pathos. "It is a sad thing to want for happiness, but it is a terrible thing to see another groping about blindly for it, when it is almost within the grasp."

She was gazing now sadly out upon the open sea, her arm resting listlessly upon the polished doorpost.

Hurstwood began to feel a deep sympathy for her and for himself. He could almost feel that she was talking to him. He was, by a combination of feelings and entanglements, almost deluded by that quality of voice and manner which, like a pathetic strain of music, seems ever a personal and intimate thing. Pathos has this quality, that it seems ever addressed to one alone.

"And yet, she can be very happy with him," went on the little actress. "Her sunny temper, her joyous face will brighten any home."

She turned slowly toward the audience without seeing. There was so much simplicity in her movements that she seemed wholly alone. Then she found a seat by a table, and turned over some books, devoting a thought to them.

"With no longings for what I may not have," she breathed in conclusion—and it was almost a sigh—"my existence hidden from all save two in the wide world, and making my joy out of the joy of that innocent girl who will soon be his wife."

Hurstwood was sorry when a character, known as Peach Blossom, interrupted her. He stirred irritably, for he wished her to go on. He was charmed by the pale face, the lissome figure, draped in pearl gray, with a coiled string of pearls at the throat. Carrie had the air of one who was weary and in need of protection, and, under the fascinating make-believe of the moment, he rose in feeling until he was ready in spirit to go to her and ease her out of her misery by adding to his own delight.

◄ What "air" in Carrie stirs Hurstwood's feelings? What does he long to do?

In a moment Carrie was alone again, and was saying, with animation:

"I must return to the city, no matter what dangers may lurk here. I must go, secretly if I can; openly, if I must."

Words For Everyday Use

grope (grōp) *vi.,* search uncertainly
list • less • ly (list´ lis lē) *adv.,* without spirit or vitality
lis • some (lis´əm) *adj.,* graceful, easy, and light

There was a sound of horses' hoofs outside, and then Ray's voice saying:

"No, I shall not ride again. Put him up."

He entered, and then began a scene which had as much to do with the creation of the tragedy of affection in Hurstwood as anything in his peculiar and involved career. For Carrie had resolved to make something of this scene, and, now that the cue had come, it began to take a feeling hold upon her. Both Hurstwood and Drouet noted the rising sentiment as she proceeded.

"I thought you had gone with Pearl," she said to her lover.

"I did go part of the way, but I left the party a mile down the road."

"You and Pearl had no disagreement?"

"No—yes; that is, we always have. Our social barometers always stand at 'cloudy' and 'overcast.'"

"And whose fault is that?" she said, easily.

"Not mine," he answered, pettishly. "I know I do all I can—I say all I can—but she—"

This was rather awkwardly put by Patton, but Carrie redeemed it with a grace which was inspiring.

"But she is your wife," she said, fixing her whole attention upon the stilled actor, and softening the quality of her voice until it was again low and musical. "Ray, my friend, courtship is the text from which the whole sermon of married life takes its theme. Do not let yours be discontented and unhappy."

► *What theme of interest to Carrie is addressed in this play?*

She put her two little hands together and pressed them appealingly.

Hurstwood gazed with slightly parted lips. Drouet was fidgeting with satisfaction.

"To be my wife, yes," went on the actor in a manner which was weak by comparison, but which could not now spoil the tender atmosphere which Carrie had created and maintained. She did not seem to feel that he was wretched. She would have done nearly as well with a block of wood. The accessories she needed were within her own imagination. The acting of others could not affect them.

"And you repent already?" she said, slowly.

"I lost you," he said, seizing her little hand, "and I was at the mercy of any flirt who chose to give me an inviting look. It was your fault—you know it was—why did you leave me?"

Carrie turned slowly away, and seemed to be mastering some impulse in silence. Then she turned back.

"Ray," she said, "the greatest happiness I have ever felt has been the thought that all your affection was forever bestowed upon a virtuous woman, your equal in family, fortune, and accomplishments. What a revelation do you make to me now! What is it makes you continually war with your happiness?"

The last question was asked so simply that it came to the audience and the lover as a personal thing.

At last it came to the part where the lover exclaimed, "Be to me as you used to be."

Carrie answered, with affecting sweetness, "I cannot be that to you, but I can speak in the spirit of the Laura who is dead to you forever."

"Be it as you will," said Patton.

Hurstwood leaned forward. The whole audience was silent and intent.

"Let the woman you look upon be wise or vain," said Carrie, her eyes bent sadly upon the lover, who had sunk into a seat, "beautiful or homely, rich or poor, she has but one thing she can really give or refuse—her heart."

Drouet felt a scratch in his throat.

"Her beauty, her wit, her accomplishments, she may sell to you; but her love is the treasure without money and without price."

The manager suffered this as a personal appeal. It came to him as if they were alone, and he could hardly restrain the tears for sorrow over the hopeless, pathetic, and yet dainty and appealing woman whom he loved. Drouet also was beside himself. He was resolving that he would be to Carrie what he had never been before. He would marry her, by George! She was worth it.

◄ *What resolution does the play cause Drouet to make?*

"She asks only in return," said Carrie, scarcely hearing the small, scheduled reply of her lover, and putting herself even more in harmony with the plaintive melody now issuing from the orchestra, "that when you look upon her your eyes shall speak devotion; that when you address her your voice shall be gentle, loving, and kind; that you shall not despise her because she cannot understand all at once your vigorous thoughts and ambitious designs; for, when misfortune and evil have defeated your greatest purposes, her love remains to console you. You

◄ *What view of women did the author of this play seem to have?*

Words For Everyday Use

be • stow (be stō´) *vt.,* give, grant
plain • tive (plān´ tiv) *adj.,* mournful
des • ign (dez īn) *n.,* plan

look to the trees," she continued, while Hurstwood restrained his feelings only by the grimmest repression, "for strength and grandeur; do not despise the flowers because their fragrance is all they have to give. Remember," she concluded, tenderly, "love is all a woman has to give," and she laid a strange, sweet accent on the all, "but it is the only thing which God permits us to carry beyond the grave."

The two men were in the most harrowed state of affection. They scarcely heard the few remaining words with which the scene concluded. They only saw their idol, moving about with appealing grace, continuing a power which to them was a revelation.

Hurstwood resolved a thousand things, Drouet as well. They joined equally in the burst of applause which called Carrie out. Drouet pounded his hands until they ached. Then he jumped up again and started out. As he went, Carrie came out, and, seeing an immense basket of flowers being hurried down the aisle toward her, she waited. They were Hurstwood's. She looked toward the manager's box for a moment, caught his eye, and smiled. He could have leaped out of the box to enfold her. He forgot the need of circumspectness which his married state enforced. He almost forgot that he had with him in the box those who knew him. By the Lord, he would have that lovely girl if it took his all. He would act at once. This should be the end of Drouet, and don't you forget it. He would not wait another day. The drummer should not have her.

► *What resolution does Hurstwood make?*

He was so excited that he could not stay in the box. He went into the lobby, and then into the street, thinking. Drouet did not return. In a few minutes the last act was over, and he was crazy to have Carrie alone. He cursed the luck that could keep him smiling, bowing, shamming, when he wanted to tell her that he loved her, when he wanted to whisper to her alone. He groaned as he saw that his hopes were futile. He must even take her to supper, shamming. He finally went about and asked how she was getting along. The actors were all dressing, talking, hurrying about. Drouet was palavering himself with the looseness of excitement and passion. The manager mastered himself only by a great effort.

"We are going to supper, of course," he said, with a voice that was a mockery of his heart.

Words For Everyday Use

gran • deur (gran jər´) *adj.,* greatness
har • rowed (har´ōd) *adj.,* distressed
en • fold (en fōld´) *vt.,* embrace
cir • cum • spect • ness (sʉr´ kəm spekt´ nəs) *n.,* prudency; awareness of consequences
fu • tile (fyo͞o´'l) *adj.,* useless
pa • lav • er (pə lav´ ər) *vt.,* flatter or cajole; chat idly

"Oh, yes," said Carrie, smiling.

The little actress was in fine feather.[5] She was realizing now what it was to be petted. For once she was the admired, the sought-for. The independence of success now made its first faint showing. With the tables turned, she was looking down, rather than up, to her lover. She did not fully realize that this was so, but there was something in condescension coming from her which was infinitely sweet. When she was ready they climbed into the waiting coach and drove downtown; once, only, did she find an opportunity to express her feeling, and that was when the manager preceded Drouet in the coach and sat beside her. Before Drouet was fully in she had squeezed Hurstwood's hand in a gentle, impulsive manner. The manager was beside himself with affection. He could have sold his soul to be with her alone. "Ah," he thought, "the agony of it."

◄ In what way does success change Carrie's attitude toward Hurstwood?

Drouet hung on, thinking he was all in all. The dinner was spoiled by his enthusiasm. Hurstwood went home feeling as if he should die if he did not find affectionate relief. He whispered "tomorrow" passionately to Carrie, and she understood. He walked away from the drummer and his prize at parting feeling as if he could slay him and not regret. Carrie also felt the misery of it.

"Goodnight," he said, simulating an easy friendliness.

"Goodnight," said the little actress, tenderly.

"The fool!" he said, now hating Drouet. "The idiot! I'll do him yet, and that quick! We'll see tomorrow."

"Well, if you aren't a wonder," Drouet was saying, complacently, squeezing Carrie's arm. "You are the dandiest little girl on earth."

5. **fine feather.** Good spirits

Words For Everyday Use

pet (pet) *vt.,* pamper

con • de • scen • sion (kän´di sen´shən) *n.,* manner of a superior to an inferior

slay (slā) *vt.,* kill

CHAPTER 20

The Lure of the Spirit: The Flesh in Pursuit

Passion in a man of Hurstwood's nature takes a vigorous form. It is no musing, dreamy thing. There is none of the tendency to sing outside of my lady's window—to languish and repine in the face of difficulties. In the night he was long getting to sleep because of too much thinking, and in the morning he was early awake, seizing with alacrity upon the same dear subject and pursuing it with vigor. He was out of sorts physically, as well as disordered mentally, for did he not delight in a new manner in his Carrie, and was not Drouet in the way? Never was man more harassed than he by the thoughts of his love being held by the elated, flush-mannered drummer. He would have given anything, it seemed to him, to have the complication ended—to have Carrie acquiesce to an arrangement which would dispose of Drouet effectually and forever.

► *Why is Hurstwood out of sorts?*

What to do. He dressed thinking. He moved about in the same chamber with his wife, unmindful of her presence.

At breakfast he found himself without an appetite. The meat to which he helped himself remained on his plate untouched. His coffee grew cold, while he scanned the paper indifferently. Here and there he read a little thing, but remembered nothing. Jessica had not yet come down. His wife sat at one end of the table revolving thoughts of her own in silence. A new servant had been recently installed and had forgot the napkins. On this account the silence was irritably broken by a reproof.

"I've told you about this before, Maggie," said Mrs. Hurstwood. "I'm not going to tell you again."

Hurstwood took a glance at his wife. She was frowning. Just now her manner irritated him excessively. Her next remark was addressed to him.

"Have you made up your mind, George, when you will take your vacation?"

It was customary for them to discuss the regular summer outing at this season of the year.

"Not yet," he said, "I'm very busy just now."

Words For Everyday Use

vig • or • ous (vig´ ə rəs) *adj.,* strong and active

re • pine (rē pīn´) *vi.,* express unhappiness

a • lac • ri • ty (ə lak´ rə tē) *n.,* speed and eagerness

e • la • ted (ē lāt´ ed) *adj.,* happy or joyful

re • proof (ri pro͞of´) *n.,* correction, scolding

"Well, you'll want to make up your mind pretty soon, won't you, if we're going?" she returned.

"I guess we have a few days yet," he said.

"Hmff," she returned. "Don't wait until the season's over."

She stirred in aggravation as she said this.

"There you go again," he observed. "One would think I never did anything, the way you begin."

"Well, I want to know about it," she reiterated.

"You've got a few days yet," he insisted. "You'll not want to start before the races are over."

He was irritated to think that this should come up when he wished to have his thoughts for other purposes.

"Well, we may. Jessica doesn't want to stay until the end of the races."

"What did you want with a season ticket, then?"

"Uh!" she said, using the sound as an exclamation of disgust, "I'll not argue with you," and therewith arose to leave the table.

"Say," he said, rising, putting a note of determination in his voice which caused her to delay her departure, "what's the matter with you of late? Can't I talk with you anymore?"

"Certainly, you can *talk* with me," she replied, laying emphasis on the word.

"Well, you wouldn't think so by the way you act. Now, you want to know when I'll be ready—not for a month yet. Maybe not then."

◄ *In what way does Hurstwood respond when his wife threatens to go on vacation without him?*

"We'll go without you."

"You will, eh?" he sneered.

"Yes, we will."

He was astonished at the woman's determination, but it only irritated him the more.

"Well, we'll see about that. It seems to me you're trying to run things with a pretty high hand of late. You talk as though you settled my affairs for me. Well, you don't. You don't regulate anything that's connected with me. If you want to go, go, but you won't hurry me by any such talk as that."

He was thoroughly aroused now. His dark eyes snapped, and he crunched his paper as he laid it down. Mrs. Hurstwood said nothing more. He was just finishing when she turned on her heel and went out into the hall and upstairs. He paused for a moment, as if hesitating, then sat

Words For Everyday Use

re • it • er • ate (rē it´ə rāt´) *vt.,* repeat

down and drank a little coffee, and thereafter arose and went for his hat and gloves upon the main floor.

▶ *Why don't Jessica and her mother want to go to the races every day anymore?*

His wife had really not anticipated a row[1] of this character. She had come down to the breakfast table feeling a little out of sorts with herself and revolving a scheme which she had in her mind. Jessica had called her attention to the fact that the races were not what they were supposed to be. The social opportunities were not what they had thought they would be this year. The beautiful girl found going every day a dull thing. There was an earlier exodus[2] this year of people who were anybody to the watering places and Europe. In her own circle of acquaintances several young men in whom she was interested had gone to Waukesha.[3] She began to feel that she would like to go too, and her mother agreed with her.

▶ *How does Mrs. Hurstwood feel about her husband after her conversation with him?*

Accordingly, Mrs. Hurstwood decided to broach the subject. She was thinking this over when she came down to the table, but for some reason the atmosphere was wrong. She was not sure, after it was all over, just how the trouble had begun. She was determined now, however, that her husband was a brute, and that, under no circumstances, would she let this go by unsettled. She would have more lady-like treatment or she would know why.

For his part, the manager was loaded with the care of this new argument until he reached his office and started from there to meet Carrie. Then the other complications of love, desire, and opposition possessed him. His thoughts fled on before him upon eagles' wings. He could hardly wait until he should meet Carrie face to face. What was the night, after all, without her—what the day? She must and should be his.

▶ *What change does Carrie experience in her feelings toward Hurstwood?*

For her part, Carrie had experienced a world of fancy and feeling since she had left him, the night before. She had listened to Drouet's enthusiastic maunderings with much regard for that part which concerned herself, with very little for that which affected his own gain. She kept him at such lengths as she could, because her thoughts were with her own triumph. She felt Hurstwood's passion as a delightful background to her own achievement, and she wondered what he would have to say. She was sorry for him, too, with that

1. **row.** Argument or disagreement
2. **exodus.** Departure of a large group
3. **Waukesha.** Suburb of Milwaukee in southeastern Wisconsin

Words For Everyday Use

broach (brōch) *vt.,* bring up an issue for discussion

maun • der • ing (môn′ dər iŋ) *n.,* rambling

peculiar sorrow which finds something complimentary to itself in the misery of another. She was now experiencing the first shades of feeling of that subtle change which removes one out of the ranks of the suppliants into the lines of the dispensers of charity. She was, all in all, exceedingly happy.

On the morrow,[4] however, there was nothing in the papers concerning the event, and, in view of the flow of common, everyday things about, it now lost a shade of the glow of the previous evening. Drouet himself was not talking so much *of* as *for* her. He felt instinctively that, for some reason or other, he needed reconstruction in her regard.

"I think," he said, as he spruced around their chambers the next morning, preparatory to going downtown, "that I'll straighten out that little deal of mine this month and then we'll get married. I was talking with Mosher about that yesterday."

◄ Why does Carrie's response to Drouet's assurance that he will soon marry her alarm him? In what way is Carrie's relationship with Drouet changing?

"No, you won't," said Carrie, who was coming to feel a certain faint power to jest with the drummer.

"Yes, I will," he exclaimed, more feelingly than usual, adding, with the tone of one who pleads, "Don't you believe what I've told you?"

Carrie laughed a little.

"Of course I do," she answered.

Drouet's assurance now misgave him. Shallow as was his mental observation, there was that in the things which had happened which made his little power of analysis useless. Carrie was still with him, but not helpless and pleading. There was a lilt in her voice which was new. She did not study him with eyes expressive of dependence. The drummer was feeling the shadow of something which was coming. It colored his feelings and made him develop those little attentions and say those little words which were mere forefendations against danger.

Shortly afterward he departed, and Carrie prepared for her meeting with Hurstwood. She hurried at her toilet, which was soon made, and hastened down the stairs. At the corner she passed Drouet, but they did not see each other.

The drummer had forgotten some bills which he wished to turn into his house. He hastened up the stairs and burst

4. **morrow.** Next morning

Words For Everyday Use	**sup • pli • ant** (sup´lē ənt) *n.,* one who asks humbly or petitions earnestly **fore • fen • da • tion** (fôr´ fen dā´ shən) *n.,* warning

into the room, but found only the chambermaid, who was cleaning up.

"Hello," he exclaimed, half to himself, "has Carrie gone?"

"Your wife? Yes, she went out just a few minutes ago."

"That's strange," thought Drouet. "She didn't say a word to me. I wonder where she went?"

He hastened about, rummaging in his valise[5] for what he wanted, and finally pocketing it. Then he turned his attention to his fair neighbor, who was good-looking and kindly disposed toward him.

"What are you up to?" he said, smiling.

"Just cleaning," she replied, stopping and winding a dusting towel about her hand.

"Tired of it?"

"Not so very."

"Let me show you something," he said, affably, coming over and taking out of his pocket a little lithographed[6] card which had been issued by a wholesale tobacco company. On this was printed a picture of a pretty girl, holding a striped parasol, the colors of which could be changed by means of a revolving disk in the back, which showed red, yellow, green, and blue through little interstices[7] made in the ground occupied by the umbrella top.

"Isn't that clever?" he said, handing it to her and showing her how it worked. "You never saw anything like that before."

"Isn't it nice?" she answered.

"You can have it if you want it," he remarked.

"That's a pretty ring you have," he said, touching a commonplace setting which adorned the hand holding the card he had given her.

"Do you think so?"

"That's right," he answered, making use of a pretense at examination to secure her finger. "That's fine."

The ice being thus broken, he launched into further observation, pretending to forget that her fingers were still retained by his. She soon withdrew them, however, and retreated a few feet to rest against the windowsill.

---

5. **valise.** Suitcase

6. **lithographed.** That which is printed with a greasy material which repels water and soaks in ink

7. **interstices.** Narrow openings

Words For Everyday Use

a • dorn (ə dôrn´) *vt.,* ornament

"I didn't see you for a long time," she said, coquettishly, repulsing one of his exuberant approaches. "You must have been away."

"I was," said Drouet.

"Do you travel far?"

"Pretty far—yes."

"Do you like it?"

"Oh, not very well. You get tired of it after a while."

"I wish I could travel," said the girl, gazing idly out of the window.

"What has become of your friend, Hurstwood?" she suddenly asked, bethinking herself of the manager, who, from her own observation, seemed to contain promising material.

◄ *What does the chambermaid reveal to Drouet?*

"He's here in town. What makes you ask about him?"

"Oh, nothing, only he hasn't been here since you got back."

"How did you come to know him?"

"Didn't I take up his name a dozen times in the last month?"

"Get out," said the drummer, lightly. "He hasn't called more than half a dozen times since we've been here."

"He hasn't, eh?" said the girl, smiling. "That's all you know about it."

Drouet took on a slightly more serious tone. He was uncertain as to whether she was joking or not.

"Tease," he said, "what makes you smile that way?"

"Oh, nothing."

"Have you seen him recently?"

"Not since you came back," she laughed.

"Before?"

"Certainly."

"How often?"

"Why, nearly every day."

She was a mischievous newsmonger,[8] and was keenly wondering what the effect of her words would be.

"Who did he come to see?" asked the drummer, incredulously.

"Mrs. Drouet."

He looked rather foolish at this answer, and then attempted to correct himself so as not to appear a dupe.[9]

"Well," he said, "what of it?"

---

8. **newsmonger.** One who spreads news, especially gossip
9. **dupe.** Person easily tricked or fooled

Words For Everyday Use

co • quet • tish • ly (kō ket´ tish lē) *adv.,* flirtatiously

re • pulse (rē puls´) *vt.,* rebuff; reject

"Nothing," replied the girl, her head cocked coquettishly on one side.

"He's an old friend," he went on, getting deeper into the mire.[10]

He would have gone on further with his little flirtation, but the taste for it was temporarily removed. He was quite relieved when the girl's name was called from below.

"I've got to go," she said, moving away from him airily.

"I'll see you later," he said, with a pretense of disturbance at being interrupted.

When she was gone, he gave freer play to his feelings. His face, never easily controlled by him, expressed all the perplexity and disturbance which he felt. Could it be that Carrie had received so many visits and yet said nothing about them? Was Hurstwood lying? What did the chambermaid mean by it, anyway? He had thought there was something odd about Carrie's manner at the time. Why did she look so disturbed when he had asked her how many times Hurstwood had called? By George! he remembered now. There was something strange about the whole thing.

► *What is Drouet beginning to realize?*

He sat down in a rocking-chair to think the better, drawing up one leg on his knee and frowning mightily. His mind ran on at a great rate.

And yet Carrie hadn't acted out of the ordinary. It couldn't be, by George, that she was deceiving him. She hadn't acted that way. Why, even last night she had been as friendly toward him as could be, and Hurstwood too. Look how they acted! He could hardly believe they would try to deceive him.

His thoughts burst into words.

"She did act sort of funny at times. Here she had dressed and gone out this morning and never said a word."

He scratched his head and prepared to go downtown. He was still frowning. As he came into the hall he encountered the girl, who was now looking after another chamber. She had on a white dusting cap, beneath which her chubby face shone good-naturedly. Drouet almost forgot his worry in the fact that she was smiling on him. He put his hand familiarly on her shoulder, as if only to greet her in passing.

10. **mire.** Deep mud

Words For Everyday Use

air • i • ly (er´ ə lē) *adv.,* in an airy or light manner

"Got over being mad?" she said, still mischievously inclined.

"I'm not mad," he answered.

"I thought you were," she said, smiling.

"Quit your fooling about that," he said, in an offhand way. "Were you serious?"

"Certainly," she answered. Then, with an air of one who did not intentionally mean to create trouble, "He came lots of times. I thought you knew."

The game of deception was up with Drouet. He did not try to simulate indifference further.

"Did he spend the evenings here?" he asked.

"Sometimes. Sometimes they went out."

"In the evening?"

"Yes. You mustn't look so mad, though."

"I'm not," he said. "Did anyone else see him?"

"Of course," said the girl, as if, after all, it were nothing in particular.

"How long ago was this?"

"Just before you came back."

The drummer pinched his lip nervously.

"Don't say anything, will you?" he asked, giving the girl's arm a gentle squeeze.

"Certainly not," she returned. "I wouldn't worry over it."

"All right," he said, passing on, seriously brooding for once, and yet not wholly unconscious of the fact that he was making a most excellent impression upon the chambermaid.

◄ *Do you think Drouet is truly upset by Carrie's apparent betrayal? Why, or why not?*

"I'll see her about that," he said to himself, passionately, feeling that he had been unduly wronged. "I'll find out, b'George, whether she'll act that way or not."

Words For Everyday Use

un • du • ly (un do͞o´ lē) *adv.,* unjustly

CHAPTER 21

The Lure of the Spirit: The Flesh in Pursuit

When Carrie came Hurstwood had been waiting many minutes. His blood was warm; his nerves wrought up. He was anxious to see the woman who had stirred him so profoundly the night before.

"Here you are," he said, repressedly, feeling a spring in his limbs and an elation which was tragic in itself.

"Yes," said Carrie.

They walked on as if bound for some objective point, while Hurstwood drank in the radiance of her presence. The rustle of her pretty skirt was like music to him.

"Are you satisfied?" he asked, thinking of how well she did the night before.

"Are you?"

He tightened his fingers as he saw the smile she gave him.

"It was wonderful."

► *What does Hurstwood tell Carrie about the play?*

Carrie laughed ecstatically.

"That was one of the best things I've seen in a long time," he added.

He was dwelling on her attractiveness as he had felt it the evening before, and mingling it with the feeling her presence inspired now.

Carrie was dwelling in the atmosphere which this man created for her. Already she was enlivened and suffused with a glow. She felt his drawing toward her in every sound of his voice.

"Those were such nice flowers you sent me," she said, after a moment or two. "They were beautiful."

"Glad you liked them," he answered, simply.

He was thinking all the time that the subject of his desire was being delayed. He was anxious to turn the talk to his own feelings. All was ripe for it. His Carrie was beside him. He wanted to plunge in and expostulate with her, and yet he found himself fishing for words and feeling for a way.

"You got home all right," he said, gloomily, of a sudden, his tone modifying itself to one of self-commiseration.

"Yes," said Carrie, easily.

Words For Everyday Use

ex • pos • tu • late (eks päs´ chə lāt´) *vi.*, reason with and object to another

self-com • mis • er • a • tion (self´kə miz´ ər ā shən) *adj.*, self-pity

He looked at her steadily for a moment, slowing his pace and fixing her with his eye.

She felt the flood of feeling.

"How about me?" he asked.

This confused Carrie considerably, for she realized the floodgates were open. She didn't know exactly what to answer.

"I don't know," she answered.

He took his lower lip between his teeth for a moment, and then let it go. He stopped by the walk side and kicked the grass with his toe. He searched her face with a tender, appealing glance.

"Won't you come away from him?" he asked, intensely.

"I don't know," returned Carrie, still illogically drifting and finding nothing at which to catch.

As a matter of fact, she was in a most hopeless quandary. Here was a man whom she thoroughly liked, who exercised an influence over her, sufficient almost to delude her into the belief that she was possessed of a lively passion for him. She was still the victim of his keen eyes, his suave manners, his fine clothes. She looked and saw before her a man who was most gracious and sympathetic, who leaned toward her with a feeling that was a delight to observe. She could not resist the glow of his temperament, the light of his eye. She could hardly keep from feeling what he felt.

And yet she was not without thoughts which were disturbing. What did he know? What had Drouet told him? Was she a wife in his eyes, or what? Would he marry her? Even while he talked, and she softened, and her eyes were lighted with a tender glow, she was asking herself if Drouet had told him they were not married. There was never anything at all convincing about what Drouet said.

And yet she was not grieved at Hurstwood's love. No strain of bitterness was in it for her, whatever he knew. He was evidently sincere. His passion was real and warm. There was power in what he said. What should she do? She went on thinking this, answering vaguely, languishing affectionately, and altogether drifting, until she was on a borderless sea of speculation.

"Why don't you come away?" he said, tenderly. "I will arrange for you whatever—"

"Oh, don't," said Carrie.

◄ *What is Carrie's response now when Hurstwood asks her to leave Drouet for him?*

◄ *What concerns does Carrie have about her relationship with Hurstwood?*

◄ *What doesn't Carrie wish for Hurstwood to discuss?*

Words For Everyday Use

quan • da • ry (kwän´ də rē) *n.*, state of uncertainty

suave (swäv) *adj.*, smooth

"Don't what?" he asked. "What do you mean?"

There was a look of confusion and pain in her face. She was wondering why that miserable thought must be brought in. She was struck as by a blade with the miserable provision which was outside the pale[1] of marriage.

He himself realized that it was a wretched thing to have dragged in. He wanted to weigh the effects of it, and yet he could not see. He went beating on, flushed by her presence, clearly awakened, intensely enlisted in his plan.

"Won't you come?" he said, beginning over and with a more reverent feeling. "You know I can't do without you—you know it—it can't go on this way—can it?"

"I know," said Carrie.

"I wouldn't ask if I—I wouldn't argue with you if I could help it. Look at me, Carrie. Put yourself in my place. You don't want to stay away from me, do you?"

She shook her head as if in deep thought.

"Then why not settle the whole thing, once and for all?"

"I don't know," said Carrie.

"Don't know! Ah, Carrie, what makes you say that? Don't torment me. Be serious."

"I am," said Carrie, softly.

"You can't be, dearest, and say that. Not when you know how I love you. Look at last night."

His manner as he said this was the most quiet imaginable. His face and body retained utter composure. Only his eyes moved, and they flashed a subtle, dissolving fire. In them the whole intensity of the man's nature was distilling itself.

Carrie made no answer.

"How can you act this way, dearest?" he inquired, after a time. "You love me, don't you?"

He turned on her such a storm of feeling that she was overwhelmed. For the moment all doubts were cleared away.

"Yes," she answered, frankly and tenderly.

"Well, then you'll come, won't you—come tonight?"

Carrie shook her head in spite of her distress.

"I can't wait any longer," urged Hurstwood. "If that is too soon, come Saturday."

---

1. **outside the pale.** Beyond the enclosure, outside the area

Words For Everyday Use

pro • vi • sion (prō vizh´ ən) *n.*, condition

wretch • ed (rech´ id) *adj.*, miserable; despicable

"When will we be married?" she asked, diffidently, forgetting in her difficult situation that she had hoped he took her to be Drouet's wife.

◄ *What does Hurstwood promise to do? Is it really possible for him to keep his promise?*

The manager started, hit as he was by a problem which was more difficult than hers. He gave no sign of the thoughts that flashed like messages to his mind.

"Any time you say," he said, with ease, refusing to discolor his present delight with this miserable problem.

"Saturday?" asked Carrie.

He nodded his head.

"Well, if you will marry me then," she said, "I'll go."

The manager looked at his lovely prize, so beautiful, so winsome, so difficult to be won, and made strange resolutions. His passion had gotten to that stage now where it was no longer colored with reason. He did not trouble over little barriers of this sort in the face of so much loveliness. He would accept the situation with all its difficulties; he would not try to answer the objections which cold truth thrust upon him. He would promise anything, everything, and trust to fortune to disentangle him. He would make a try for Paradise, whatever might be the result. He would be happy, by the Lord, if it cost all honesty of statement, all abandonment of truth.

◄ *What personal resolution does Hurstwood make? Explain whether you agree with his decision?*

Carrie looked at him tenderly. She could have laid her head upon his shoulder, so delightful did it all seem.

"Well," she said, "I'll try and get ready then."

Hurstwood looked into her pretty face, crossed with little shadows of wonder and misgiving, and thought he had never seen anything more lovely.

"I'll see you again tomorrow," he said, joyously, "and we'll talk over the plans."

He walked on with her, elated beyond words, so delightful had been the result. He impressed a long story of joy and affection upon her, though there was but here and there a word. After a half-hour he began to realize that the meeting must come to an end, so exacting is the world.

"Tomorrow," he said at parting, a gaiety of manner adding wonderfully to his brave demeanor.

"Yes," said Carrie, tripping elatedly away.

There had been so much enthusiasm engendered that she was believing herself deeply in love. She sighed as she thought of her handsome adorer. Yes, she would get ready by Saturday. She would go, and they would be happy.

◄ *What feeling does Carrie mistake for love?*

Words For Everyday Use

win • some (win´ səm) *adj.*, delightful

dis • en • tan • gle (dis´ in taŋ gəl) *vt.*, free from bonds

de • mean • or (di mēn´ ər) *n.*, outward behavior; conduct

CHAPTER 22

The Blaze of the Tinder: Flesh Wars with the Flesh

► *Although Mrs. Hurstwood no longer feels love for her husband, what feelings does she retain?*

► *According to the narrator, what do women consider to be greater than a crime?*

► *How can Mrs. Hurstwood tell that her husband's "interest in life" has not lessened?*

► *To what does the narrator compare the atmosphere in the Hurstwood household?*

The misfortune of the Hurstwood household was due to the fact that jealousy, having been born of love, did not perish with it. Mrs. Hurstwood retained this in such form that subsequent influences could transform it into hate. Hurstwood was still worthy, in a physical sense, of the affection his wife had once bestowed upon him, but in a social sense he fell short. With his regard died his power to be attentive to her, and this, to a woman, is much greater than outright crime toward another. Our self-love dictates our appreciation of the good or evil in another. In Mrs. Hurstwood it discolored the very hue of her husband's indifferent nature. She saw design in deeds and phrases which sprung only from a faded appreciation of her presence.

As a consequence, she was resentful and suspicious. The jealousy that prompted her to observe every falling away from the little amenities of the married relation on his part served to give her notice of the airy grace with which he still took the world. She could see from the scrupulous care which he exercised in the matter of his personal appearance that his interest in life had abated not a jot. Every motion, every glance had something in it of the pleasure he felt in Carrie, of the zest this new pursuit of pleasure lent to his days. Mrs. Hurstwood felt something, sniffing change, as animals do danger, afar off.

This feeling was strengthened by actions of a direct and more potent nature on the part of Hurstwood. We have seen with what irritation he shirked those little duties which no longer contained any amusement or satisfaction for him, and the open snarls with which, more recently, he resented her irritating goads. These little rows were really precipitated by an atmosphere which was surcharged with dissension. That it would shower, with a sky so full of blackening thunderclouds, would scarcely be thought worthy of comment. Thus, after leaving the breakfast table this morning, raging inwardly

Words For Everyday Use

sub • se • quent (sub´si kwənt) *adj.,* following
hue (hyo͞o) *n.,* general appearance
scru • pu • lous (skro͞o pyə ləs) *adj.,* extremely careful
a • bate (ə bāt´) *vi.,* lessen
jot (jät) *n.,* smallest bit
shirk (shʉrk) *vt.,* neglect
goad (gōd) *n.,* sharp prodding
dis • sen • sion (di sen´shən) *n.,* conflict

at his blank declaration of indifference at her plans, Mrs. Hurstwood encountered Jessica in her dressing room, very leisurely arranging her hair. Hurstwood had already left the house.

"I wish you wouldn't be so late coming down to breakfast," she said, addressing Jessica, while making for her crochet basket. "Now here the things are quite cold, and you haven't eaten."

Her natural composure was sadly ruffled, and Jessica was doomed to feel the fag end[1] of the storm.

"I'm not hungry," she answered.

"Then why don't you say so, and let the girl put away the things, instead of keeping her waiting all morning?"

"She doesn't mind," answered Jessica, coolly.

"Well, I do, if she doesn't," returned the mother, "and, anyhow, I don't like you to talk that way to me. You're too young to put on such an air with your mother."

"Oh, mamma, don't row," answered Jessica. "What's the matter this morning, anyway?"

"Nothing's the matter, and I'm not rowing. You mustn't think because I indulge you in some things that you can keep everybody waiting. I won't have it."

"I'm not keeping anybody waiting," returned Jessica, sharply, stirred out of a cynical indifference to a sharp defense. "I said I wasn't hungry. I don't want any breakfast."

"Mind how you address me, missy. I'll not have it. Hear me now; I'll not have it!"

Jessica heard this last while walking out of the room, with a toss of her head and a flick of her pretty skirts indicative of the independence and indifference she felt. She did not propose to be quarreled with.

Such little arguments were all too frequent, the result of a growth of natures which were largely independent and selfish. George, Jr., manifested even greater touchiness and exaggeration in the matter of his individual rights, and attempted to make all feel that he was a man with a man's privileges—an assumption which, of all things, is most groundless and pointless in a youth of nineteen.

◄ *Why are Mrs. Hurstwood's arguments with her son and daughter growing more frequent? What thoughts does the narrator express on George, Jr.'s, attitude?*

Hurstwood was a man of authority and some fine feeling, and it irritated him excessively to find himself surrounded more and more by a world upon which he had no hold, and of which he had a lessening understanding.

Now, when such little things, such as the proposed earlier start to Waukesha, came up, they made clear to him his

1. **fag end.** Last part of anything

position. He was being made to follow, was not leading. When, in addition, a sharp temper was manifested, and to the process of shouldering him out of his authority was added a rousing intellectual kick, such as a sneer or a cynical laugh, he was unable to keep his temper. He flew into hardly repressed passion, and wished himself clear of the whole household. It seemed a most irritating drag upon all his desires and opportunities.

► *What is the one thing Mrs. Hurstwood needs before she can give in to a "rain of wrath"?*

For all this, he still retained the semblance of leadership and control, even though his wife was straining to revolt. Her display of temper and open assertion of opposition were based upon nothing more than the feeling that she could do it. She had no special evidence wherewith to justify herself—the knowledge of something which would give her both authority and excuse. The latter was all that was lacking, however, to give a solid foundation to what, in a way, seemed groundless discontent. The clear proof of one overt deed was the cold breath needed to convert the lowering clouds of suspicion into a rain of wrath.

► *What happens to arouse Mrs. Hurstwood's suspicions?*

An inkling of untoward deeds on the part of Hurstwood had come. Doctor Beale, the handsome resident physician of the neighborhood, met Mrs. Hurstwood at her own doorstep some days after Hurstwood and Carrie had taken the drive west on Washington Boulevard. Dr. Beale, coming east on the same drive, had recognized Hurstwood, but not before he was quite past him. He was not so sure of Carrie—did not know whether it was Hurstwood's wife or daughter.

"You don't speak to your friends when you meet them out driving, do you?" he said, jocosely, to Mrs. Hurstwood.

"If I see them, I do. Where was I?"

"On Washington Boulevard," he answered, expecting her eye to light with immediate remembrance.

She shook her head.

"Yes, out near Hoyne Avenue. You were with your husband."

"I guess you're mistaken," she answered. Then, remembering her husband's part in the affair, she immediately fell a prey to a host of young suspicions, of which, however, she gave no sign.

"I know I saw your husband," he went on. "I wasn't so sure about you. Perhaps it was your daughter."

"Perhaps it was," said Mrs. Hurstwood, knowing full well that such was not the case, as Jessica had been her companion

Words For Everyday Use

shoul • der • ing (shōl´ dər iŋ) *n.*, nudging

rous • ing (rou´ ziŋ) *adj.*, provocative

o • vert (ō vʉrt´) *adj.*, open, apparent

un • to • ward (un tō´ ərd) *adj.*, inappropriate

for weeks. She had recovered herself sufficiently to wish to know more of the details.

"Was it in the afternoon?" she asked, artfully, assuming an air of acquaintanceship with the matter.

"Yes, about two or three."

"It must have been Jessica," said Mrs. Hurstwood, not wishing to seem to attach any importance to the incident.

The physician had a thought or two of his own, but dismissed the matter as worthy of no further discussion on his part at least.

Mrs. Hurstwood gave this bit of information considerable thought during the next few hours, and even days. She took it for granted that the doctor had really seen her husband, and that he had been riding, most likely, with some other woman, after announcing himself as *busy* to her. As a consequence, she recalled, with rising feeling, how often he had refused to go to places with her, to share in little visits, or, indeed, take part in any of the social amenities which furnished the diversion of her existence. He had been seen at the theater with people whom he called Moy's friends; now he was seen driving, and, most likely, would have an excuse for that. Perhaps there were others of whom she did not hear, or why should he be so busy, so indifferent, of late? In the last six weeks he had become strangely irritable—strangely satisfied to pick up and go out, whether things were right or wrong in the house. Why?

She recalled, with more subtle emotions, that he did not look at her now with any of the old light of satisfaction or approval in his eye. Evidently, along with other things, he was taking her to be getting old and uninteresting. He saw her wrinkles, perhaps. She was fading, while he was still preening himself in his elegance and youth. He was still an interested factor in the merrymakings of the world, while she—but she did not pursue the thought. She only found the whole situation bitter, and hated him for it thoroughly.

◄ *What does Mrs. Hurstwood find hateful and bitter?*

Nothing came of this incident at the time, for the truth is it did not seem conclusive enough to warrant any discussion. Only the atmosphere of distrust and ill-feeling was strengthened, precipitating every now and then little sprinklings of irritable conversation, enlivened by flashes of wrath. The matter of the Waukesha outing was merely a continuation of other things of the same nature.

Words For Everyday Use

preen (prēn) *vt.,* show satisfaction or vanity in oneself

The day after Carrie's appearance on the Avery stage, Mrs. Hurstwood visited the races with Jessica and a youth of her acquaintance, Mr. Bart Taylor, the son of the owner of a local house-furnishing establishment. They had driven out early, and, as it chanced, encountered several friends of Hurstwood, all Elks, and two of whom had attended the performance the evening before. A thousand chances the subject of the performance had never been brought up had Jessica not been so engaged by the attentions of her young companion, who usurped as much time as possible. This left Mrs. Hurstwood in the mood to extend the perfunctory greetings of some who knew her into short conversations, and the short conversations of friends into long ones. It was from one who meant but to greet her perfunctorily that this interesting intelligence came.

► *What else does Mrs. Hurstwood discover?*

"I see," said this individual, who wore sporting clothes of the most attractive pattern, and had a field glass strung over his shoulder, "that you did not get over to our little entertainment last evening."

"No?" said Mrs. Hurstwood, inquiringly, and wondering why he should be using the tone he did in noting the fact that she had not been to something she knew nothing about. It was on her lips to say, "What was it?" when he added, "I saw your husband."

Her wonder was at once replaced by the more subtle quality of suspicion.

"Yes," she said, cautiously, "was it pleasant? He did not tell me much about it."

"Very. Really one of the best private theatricals I ever attended. There was one actress who surprised us all."

"Indeed," said Mrs. Hurstwood.

"It's too bad you couldn't have been there, really. I was sorry to hear you weren't feeling well."

Feeling well! Mrs. Hurstwood could have echoed the words after him open-mouthed. As it was, she extricated herself from her mingled impulse to deny and question, and said, almost raspingly:

"Yes, it is too bad."

"Looks like there will be quite a crowd here today, doesn't it?" the acquaintance observed, drifting off upon another topic.

Words For Everyday Use

u • surp (yo͞o zʉrp´) *vt.,* take without right
ex • tri • cate (eks´tri kāt) *vt.,* disentangle
rasp • ing • ly (rasp´iŋ lē) *adv.,* harshly

The manager's wife would have questioned farther, but she saw no opportunity. She was for the moment wholly at sea, anxious to think for herself, and wondering what new deception was this which caused him to give out that she was ill when she was not. Another case of her company not wanted, and excuses being made. She resolved to find out more.

"Were you at the performance last evening?" she asked of the next of Hurstwood's friends who greeted her, as she sat in her box.

"Yes. You didn't get around."

"No," she answered, "I was not feeling very well."

"So your husband told me," he answered. "Well, it was really very enjoyable. Turned out much better than I expected."

"Were there many there?"

"The house was full. It was quite an Elk night. I saw quite a number of your friends—Mrs. Harrison, Mrs. Barnes, Mrs. Collins."

"Quite a social gathering."

"Indeed it was. My wife enjoyed it very much."

Mrs. Hurstwood bit her lip.

"So," she thought, "that's the way he does. Tells my friends I am sick and cannot come."

She wondered what could induce him to go alone. There was something back of this. She rummaged her brain for a reason.

By evening, when Hurstwood reached home, she had brooded herself into a state of sullen desire for explanation and revenge. She wanted to know what this peculiar action of his imported. She was certain there was more behind it all than what she had heard, and evil curiosity mingled well with distrust and the remnants of her wrath of the morning. She, impending disaster itself, walked about with gathered shadow at the eyes and the rudimentary muscles of savagery fixing the hard lines of her mouth.

◄ In what way do Mrs. and Mr. Hurstwood's moods differ?

On the other hand, as we may well believe, the manager came home in the sunniest mood. His conversation and agreement with Carrie had raised his spirits until he was in the frame of mind of one who sings joyously. He was proud of himself, proud of his success, proud of Carrie. He could have been genial to all the world, and he bore no grudge

Words For Everyday Use

in • duce (in do͞os´) *vt.*, cause
sul • len (sul´ ən) *adj.*, resentful; sulky
im • port (im´ pôrt) *vi.*, mean, signify
rem • nant (rem´ nənt) *n.*, remainder

against his wife. He meant to be pleasant, to forget her presence, to live in the atmosphere of youth and pleasure which had been restored to him.

So now, the house, to his mind, had a most pleasing and comfortable appearance. In the hall he found an evening paper, laid there by the maid and forgotten by Mrs. Hurstwood. In the dining room the table was clean laid with linen and napery and shiny with glasses and decorated china. Through an open door he saw into the kitchen, where the fire was crackling in the stove and the evening meal already well under way. Out in the small backyard was George, Jr., frolicking with a young dog he had recently purchased, and in the parlor Jessica was playing at the piano, the sound of a merry waltz filling every nook and corner of the comfortable home. Everyone, like himself, seemed to have regained his good spirits, to be in sympathy with youth and beauty, to be inclined to joy and merrymaking. He felt as if he could say a good word all around himself, and took a most genial glance at the spread table and polished sideboard before going upstairs to read his paper in the comfortable armchair of the sitting room which looked through the open windows into the street. When he entered there, however, he found his wife brushing her hair and musing to herself the while.

▶ *What does Hurstwood assume about his family?*

He came lightly in, thinking to smooth over any feeling that might still exist by a kindly word and a ready promise, but Mrs. Hurstwood said nothing. He seated himself in the large chair, stirred lightly in making himself comfortable, opened his paper, and began to read. In a few moments he was smiling merrily over a very comical account of a baseball game which had taken place between the Chicago and Detroit teams.

The while he was doing this Mrs. Hurstwood was observing him casually though the medium of the mirror which was before her. She noticed his pleasant and contented manner, his airy grace and smiling humor, and it merely aggravated her the more. She wondered how he could think to carry himself so in her presence after the cynicism, indifference, and neglect he had heretofore manifested and would continue to manifest so long as she would endure it. She thought how she should like to tell him—what stress and emphasis she would lend her assertions, how she could

▶ *What aggravates Mrs. Hurstwood even more?*

Words For Everyday Use

frolic (fräl´ ik) *vi.*, play

drive over this whole affair until satisfaction should be rendered her. Indeed, the shining sword of her wrath was but weakly suspended by a thread of thought.

In the meanwhile Hurstwood encountered a humorous item concerning a stranger who had arrived in the city and became entangled with a bunco-steerer.[2] It amused him immensely, and at last he stirred and chuckled to himself. He wished that he might enlist his wife's attention and read it to her.

"Ha, ha," he exclaimed softly, as if to himself, "that's funny."

Mrs. Hurstwood kept on arranging her hair, not so much as deigning a glance.

He stirred again and went on to another subject. At last he felt as if his good humor must find some outlet. Julia was probably still out of humor over that affair of this morning, but that could easily be straightened. As a matter of fact, she was in the wrong, but he didn't care. She could go to Waukesha right away if she wanted to. The sooner the better. He would tell her that as soon as he got a chance, and the whole thing would blow over.

"Did you notice," he said, at last, breaking forth concerning another item which he had found, "that they have entered suit to compel the Illinois Central to get off the lake front, Julia?" he asked.

She could scarcely force herself to answer, but managed to say "No," sharply.

Hurstwood pricked up his ears. There was a note in her voice which vibrated keenly.

"It would be a good thing if they did," he went on, half to himself, half to her, though he felt that something was amiss in that quarter. He withdrew his attention to his paper very circumspectly, listening mentally for the little sounds which should show him what was on foot.

As a matter of fact, no man as clever as Hurstwood—as observant and sensitive to atmospheres of many sorts, particularly upon his own plane of thought—would have made the mistake which he did in regard to his wife, wrought up as she was, had he not been occupied mentally with a very different train of thought. Had not the influence of Carrie's regard for him, the elation which her promise aroused in

◄ *Why is Hurstwood unable to notice his wife's mood?*

2. **bunco-steerer.** Person who leads unwary country visitors into areas where they are then robbed

Words For Everyday Use

wrath (rath) *n.,* intense anger, fury

deign (dān) *vt.,* condescend to something beneath one's dignity

him, lasted over, he would not have seen the house in so pleasant a mood. It was not extraordinarily bright and merry this evening. He was merely very much mistaken, and would have been much more fitted to cope with it had he come home in his normal state.

After he had studied his paper a few moments longer, he felt that he ought to modify matters in some way or other. Evidently his wife was not going to patch up peace at a word. So he said:

"Where did George get the dog he has there in the yard?"

"I don't know," she snapped.

He put his paper down on his knees and gazed idly out of the window. He did not propose to lose his temper, but merely to be persistent and agreeable, and by a few questions bring around a mild understanding of some sort.

► *Of what does Mrs. Hurstwood accuse her husband? What is his reaction?*

"Why do you feel so bad about that affair of this morning?" he said, at last. "We needn't quarrel about that. You know you can go to Waukesha if you want to."

"So you can stay here and trifle around with someone else?" she exclaimed, turning to him a determined countenance upon which was drawn a sharp and wrathful sneer.

He stopped as if slapped in the face. In an instant his persuasive, conciliatory manner fled. He was on the defensive at a wink and puzzled for a word to reply.

"What do you mean?" he said at last, straightening himself and gazing at the cold, determined figure before him, who paid no attention, but went on arranging herself before the mirror.

"You know what I mean," she said, finally, as if there were a world of information which she held in reserve—which she did not need to tell.

"Well, I don't," he said, stubbornly, yet nervous and alert for what should come next. The finality of the woman's manner took away his feeling of superiority in battle.

She made no answer.

► *How does Mrs. Hurstwood react to this sign of weakness in her husband?*

"Hmph!" he murmured, with a movement of his head to one side. It was the weakest thing he had ever done. It was totally unassured.

Mrs. Hurstwood noticed the lack of color in it. She turned upon him, animal-like, able to strike an effectual second blow.

"I want the Waukesha money tomorrow morning," she said.

Words For Everyday Use

con • cil • i • a • to • ry (kən sil´ ē ə tôr´ ē) *adj.,* intended to make up with another

He looked at her in amazement. Never before had he seen such a cold, steely determination in her eye—such a cruel look of indifference. She seemed a thorough master of her mood—thoroughly confident and determined to wrest all control from him. He felt that all his resources could not defend him. He must attack.

"What do you mean?" he said, jumping up. "You want! I'd like to know what's got into you tonight."

"Nothing's *got* into me," she said, flaming. "I want that money. You can do your swaggering afterward."

"Swaggering, eh! What! You'll get nothing from me. What do you mean by your insinuations, anyhow?"

"Where were you last night?" she answered. The words were hot as they came. "Who were you driving with on Washington Boulevard? Who were you with at the theater when George saw you? Do you think I'm a fool to be duped by you? Do you think I'll sit at home here and take your 'too busy' and 'can't come,' while you parade around and make out that I'm unable to come? I want you to know that lordly airs[3] have come to an end so far as I am concerned. You can't dictate to me nor my children. I'm through with you entirely."

According to Mrs. Hurstwood, in what way is the house going to change?

"It's a lie," he said, driven to a corner and knowing no other excuse.

"Lie, eh!" she said, fiercely, but with returning reserve; "you may call it a lie if you want to, but I know."

"It's a lie, I tell you," he said, in a low, sharp voice. "You've been searching around for some cheap accusation for months, and now you think you have it. You think you'll spring something and get the upper hand. Well, I tell you, you can't. As long as I'm in this house I'm master of it, and you or any one else won't dictate to me—do you hear?"

He crept toward her with a light in his eye that was ominous. Something in the woman's cool, cynical, upper-handish manner, as if she were already master, caused him to feel for the moment as if he could strangle her.

She gazed at him—a pythoness[4] in humor.

"I'm not dictating to you," she returned; "I'm telling you what I want."

3. **lordly airs.** Acting as the master
4. **pythoness.** Female of a deadly snake

Words For Everyday Use	**wrest** (rest) *vt.*, take by force

▶ *What does Hurstwood realize?*

▶ *What is Mrs. Hurstwood threatening to do?*

The answer was so cool, so rich in bravado, that somehow it took the wind out of his sails. He could not attack her, he could not ask her for proofs. Somehow he felt evidence, law, the remembrance of all his property which she held in her name, to be shining in her glance. He was like a vessel, powerful and dangerous, but rolling and floundering without sail.

"And I'm telling you," he said in the end, slightly recovering himself, "what you'll not get."

"We'll see about it," she said. "I'll find out what my rights are. Perhaps you'll talk to a lawyer, if you won't to me."

It was a magnificent play, and had its effect. Hurstwood fell back beaten. He knew now that he had more than mere bluff to contend with. He felt that he was face to face with a dull proposition. What to say he hardly knew. All the merriment had gone out of the day. He was disturbed, wretched, resentful. What should he do?

"Do as you please," he said, at last. "I'll have nothing more to do with you," and out he strode.

Words For Everyday Use

floun • der • ing (floun´dər iŋ) *adj.*, moving in a lost and awkward way

CHAPTER 23

A Spirit in Travail: One Rung Put Behind

When Carrie reached her own room she had already fallen a prey to those doubts and misgivings which are ever the result of a lack of decision. She could not persuade herself as to the advisability of her promise, or that now, having given her word, she ought to keep it. She went over the whole ground in Hurstwood's absence, and discovered little objections that had not occurred to her in the warmth of the manager's argument. She saw where she had put herself in a peculiar light, namely, that of agreeing to marry when she was already supposedly married. She remembered a few things Drouet had done, and now that it came to walking away from him without a word, she felt as if she were doing wrong. Now, she was comfortably situated, and to one who is more or less afraid of the world, this is an urgent matter, and one which puts up strange, uncanny arguments. "You do not know what will come. There are miserable things outside. People go a-begging. Women are wretched. You never can tell what will happen. Remember the time you were hungry. Stick to what you have."

◄ In what "peculiar light" has Carrie put herself?

◄ What fears does Carrie have about leaving her comfortable situation?

Curiously, for all her leaning toward Hurstwood, he had not taken a firm hold on her understanding. She was listening, smiling, approving, and yet not finally agreeing. This was due to a lack of power on his part, a lack of that majesty of passion that sweeps the mind from its seat, fuses and melts all arguments and theories into a tangled mass, and destroys for the time being the reasoning power. This majesty of passion is possessed by nearly every man once in his life, but it is usually an attribute of youth and conduces to the first successful mating.

◄ According to the narrator, why doesn't Carrie completely agree with Hurstwood's plan?

Hurstwood, being an older man, could scarcely be said to retain the fire of youth, though he did possess a passion warm and unreasoning. It was strong enough to induce the leaning toward him which, on Carrie's part, we have seen. She might have been said to be imagining herself in love, when she was not. Women frequently do this. It flows from the fact that in each exists a bias toward affection, a craving for the pleasure of being loved. The longing to be shielded, bettered, sympathized with, is one of the attributes of the sex. This, coupled

◄ According to the narrator, why do women often imagine themselves to be in love?

Words For Everyday Use

ma • jes • ty (maj´ is tē) *n.,* grandeur or stateliness
fuse (fyo͞oz) *vt.,* unite or blend

with sentiment and a natural tendency to emotion, often makes refusing difficult. It persuades them that they are in love.

► *About what does Drouet wish to confront Carrie? Does Drouet perceive Hurstwood as a serious threat to his relationship with Carrie? Why, or why not?*

Once at home, she changed her clothes and straightened the rooms for herself. In the matter of the arrangement of the furniture she never took the housemaid's opinion. That young woman invariably put one of the rocking-chairs in the corner, and Carrie as regularly moved it out. Today she hardly noticed that it was in the wrong place, so absorbed was she in her own thoughts. She worked about the room until Drouet put in appearance at five o'clock. The drummer was flushed and excited and full of determination to know all about her relations with Hurstwood. Nevertheless, after going over the subject in his mind the livelong day, he was rather weary of it and wished it over with. He did not foresee serious consequences of any sort, and yet he rather hesitated to begin. Carrie was sitting by the window when he came in, rocking and looking out.

"Well," she said innocently, weary of her own mental discussion and wondering at his haste and ill-concealed excitement, "what makes you hurry so?"

Drouet hesitated, now that he was in her presence, uncertain as to what course to pursue. He was no diplomat. He could neither read nor see.

"When did you get home?" he asked foolishly.

"Oh, an hour or so ago. What makes you ask that?"

"You weren't here," he said, "when I came back this morning, and I thought you had gone out."

"So I did," said Carrie simply. "I went for a walk."

Drouet looked at her wonderingly. For all his lack of dignity in such matters he did not know how to begin. He stared at her in the most flagrant manner until at last she said:

"What makes you stare at me so? What's the matter?"

"Nothing," he answered. "I was just thinking."

"Just thinking what?" she returned smilingly, puzzled by his attitude.

"Oh, nothing—nothing much."

"Well, then, what makes you look so?"

Drouet was standing by the dresser, gazing at her in a comic manner. He had laid off his hat and gloves and was now fidgeting with the little toilet pieces which were nearest him. He hesitated to believe that the pretty woman before him was involved in anything so unsatisfactory to himself.

Words For Everyday Use

flushed (flushd') *adj.,* pink in the cheeks

dip • lo • mat (dip´ lə mat´) *n.,* person skilled in dealing with others

fla • grant (flā´ grənt) *adj.,* glaring; brazen

He was very much inclined to feel that it was all right, after all. Yet the knowledge imparted to him by the chambermaid was rankling in his mind. He wanted to plunge in with a straight remark of some sort, but he knew not what.

"Where did you go this morning?" he finally asked weakly.

"Why, I went for a walk," said Carrie.

"Sure you did?" he asked.

"Yes, what makes you ask?"

She was beginning to see now that he knew something. Instantly she drew herself into a more reserved position. Her cheeks blanched slightly.

"I thought maybe you didn't," he said, beating about the bush in the most useless manner.

Carrie gazed at him, and as she did so her ebbing courage halted. She saw that he himself was hesitating, and with a woman's intuition realized that there was no occasion for great alarm.

◄ *What does Carrie realize when she notes how Drouet approaches the subject?*

"What makes you talk like that?" she asked, wrinkling her pretty forehead. "You act so funny tonight."

"I feel funny," he answered.

They looked at one another for a moment, and then Drouet plunged desperately into his subject.

"What's this about you and Hurstwood?" he asked.

"Me and Hurstwood—what do you mean?"

"Didn't he come here a dozen times while I was away?"

"A dozen times," repeated Carrie, guiltily. "No, but what do you mean?"

"Somebody said that you went out riding with him and that he came here every night."

"No such thing," answered Carrie. "It isn't true. Who told you that?"

She was flushing scarlet to the roots of her hair, but Drouet did not catch the full hue of her face, owing to the modified light of the room. He was regaining much confidence as Carrie defended herself with denials.

◄ *What doesn't Drouet notice?*

"Well, someone," he said. "You're sure you didn't?"

"Certainly," said Carrie. "You know how often he came."

Drouet paused for a moment and thought.

"I know what you told me," he said finally.

He moved nervously about, while Carrie looked at him confusedly.

Words For Everyday Use	
	ran • kle (raŋ´ kəl) *vt.,* cause lingering irritation
	blanch (blanch) *vt.,* whiten
	ebb • ing (eb´ iŋ) *adj.,* weakening

► *What does Drouet reveal about Hurstwood that shocks Carrie? Why might this shock her?*

► *Why does Carrie blame Drouet for the situation?*

"Well, I know that I didn't tell you any such thing as that," said Carrie, recovering herself.

"If I were you," went on Drouet, ignoring her last remark, "I wouldn't have anything to do with him. He's a married man, you know."

"Who—who is?" said Carrie, stumbling at the word.

"Why, Hurstwood," said Drouet, noting the effect and feeling that he was delivering a telling blow.

"Hurstwood!" exclaimed Carrie, rising. Her face had changed several shades since this announcement was made. She looked within and without herself in a half-dazed way.

"Who told you this?" she asked, forgetting that her interest was out of order and exceedingly incriminating.

"Why, I know it. I've always known it," said Drouet.

Carrie was feeling about for a right thought. She was making a most miserable showing, and yet feelings were generating within her which were anything but crumbling cowardice.

"I thought I told you," he added.

"No, you didn't," she contradicted, suddenly recovering her voice. "You didn't do anything of the kind."

Drouet listened to her in astonishment. This was something new.

"I thought I did," he said.

Carrie looked around her very solemnly and then went over to the window.

"You oughtn't to have had anything to do with him," said Drouet in an injured tone, "after all I've done for you."

"You," said Carrie, "you! What have you done for me?"

Her little brain had been surging with contradictory feelings—shame at exposure, shame at Hurstwood's perfidy, anger at Drouet's deception, the mockery he had made of her. Now one clear idea came into her head. He was at fault. There was no doubt about it. Why did he bring Hurstwood out—Hurstwood, a married man, and never say a word to her? Never mind now about Hurstwood's perfidy—why had he done this? Why hadn't he warned her? There he stood now, guilty of this miserable breach of confidence and talking about what he had done for her!

"Well, I like that," exclaimed Drouet, little realizing the fire his remark had generated. "I think I've done a good deal."

"You have, eh?" she answered. "You've deceived me—that's what you've done. You've brought your friends out

Words For Everyday Use

surge (sʉrj) *vt.*, heave
con • tra • dic • to • ry (kän´ trə dik´ tə rē) *adj.*, opposing
per • fi • dy (pʉr´ fə dē) *n.*, betrayal of faith
mock • er • y (mäk´ ər ē) *n.*, ridicule

here under false pretenses. You've made me out to be—Oh," and with this her voice broke and she pressed her two little hands together tragically.

"I don't see what that's got to do with it," said the drummer quaintly.

"No," she answered, recovering herself and shutting her teeth. "No, of course you don't see. There isn't anything you see. You couldn't have told me in the first place, could you? You had to make me out wrong until it was too late. Now you come sneaking around with your information and your talk about what you have done."

◄ *What side of Carrie is Drouet seeing for the first time?*

Drouet had never suspected this side of Carrie's nature. She was alive with feeling, her eyes snapping, her lips quivering, her whole body sensible of the injury she felt, and partaking of her wrath.

"Who's sneaking?" he asked, mildly conscious of error on his part, but certain that he was wronged.

"You are," stamped Carrie. "You're a horrid, conceited coward, that's what you are. If you had any sense of manhood in you, you wouldn't have thought of doing any such thing."

The drummer stared.

"I'm not a coward," he said. "What do you mean by going with other men, anyway?"

"Other men!" exclaimed Carrie. "Other men—you know better than that. I did go with Mr. Hurstwood, but whose fault was it? Didn't you bring him here? You told him yourself that he should come out here and take me out. Now, after it's all over, you come and tell me that I oughtn't to go with him and that he's a married man."

She paused at the sound of the last two words and wrung her hands. The knowledge of Hurstwood's perfidy wounded her like a knife.

"Oh," she sobbed, repressing herself wonderfully and keeping her eyes dry. "Oh, oh!"

"Well, I didn't think you'd be running around with him when I was away," insisted Drouet.

"Didn't think!" said Carrie, now angered to the core by the man's peculiar attitude. "Of course not. You thought only of what would be to your satisfaction. You thought you'd make a toy of me—a plaything. Well, I'll show you that you won't. I'll have nothing more to do with you at all. You can take your old things and keep them," and unfastening a little pin he had

◄ *Of what does Carrie accuse Drouet? What does she vow?*

Words For Everyday Use

par • take (pär tāk) *vt.*, participate; take part

given her, she flung it vigorously upon the floor and began to move about as if to gather up the things which belonged to her.

By this Drouet was not only irritated but fascinated the more. He looked at her in amazement, and finally said:

"I don't see where your wrath comes in. I've got the right of this thing. You oughtn't to have done anything that wasn't right after all I did for you."

"What have you done for me?" asked Carrie blazing, her head thrown back and her lips parted.

"I think I've done a good deal," said the drummer, looking around. "I've given you all the clothes you wanted, haven't I? I've taken you everywhere you wanted to go. You've had as much as I've had, and more too."

Carrie was not ungrateful, whatever else might be said of her. In so far as her mind could construe, she acknowledged benefits received. She hardly knew how to answer this, and yet her wrath was not placated. She felt that the drummer had injured her irreparably.

"Did I ask you to?" she returned.

"Well, I did it," said Drouet, "and you took it."

"You talk as though I had persuaded you," answered Carrie. "You stand there and throw up what you've done. I don't want your old things. I'll not have them. You take them tonight and do what you please with them. I'll not stay here another minute."

"That's nice!" he answered, becoming angered now at the sense of his own approaching loss. "Use everything and abuse me and then walk off. That's just like a woman. I take you when you haven't got anything, and then when someone else comes along, why I'm no good. I always thought it'd come out that way."

He felt really hurt as he thought of his treatment, and looked as if he saw no way of obtaining justice.

"It's not so," said Carrie, "and I'm not going with anybody else. You have been as miserable and inconsiderate as you can be. I hate you, I tell you, and I wouldn't live with you another minute. You're a big, insulting"—here she hesitated and used no word at all—"or you wouldn't talk that way."

She had secured her hat and jacket and slipped the latter on over her little evening dress. Some wisps of wavy hair had loosened from the bands at the side of her head and were

Words For Everyday Use

pla • cat • ed (plā´ kā təd) *adj.*, appeased

ir • rep • a • ra • bly (ir rep´ ə rə blē) *adv.*, beyond repair

straggling over her hot, red cheeks. She was angry, mortified, grief-stricken. Her large eyes were full of the anguish of tears, but her lids were not yet wet. She was distracted and uncertain, deciding and doing things without an aim or conclusion, and she had not the slightest conception of how the whole difficulty would end.

"Well, that's a fine finish," said Drouet. "Pack up and pull out, eh? You take the cake. I bet you were knocking around with Hurstwood or you wouldn't act like that. I don't want the old rooms. You needn't pull out for me. You can have them for all I care, but b'George, you haven't done me right."

◀ *Do you think Drouet is justified in resenting the way Carrie has treated him?*

"I'll not live with you," said Carrie. "I don't want to live with you. You've done nothing but brag around ever since you've been here."

"Aw, I haven't anything of the kind," he answered.

Carrie walked over to the door.

"Where are you going?" he said, stepping over and heading her off.

"Let me out," she said.

"Where are you going?" he repeated.

He was, above all, sympathetic, and the sight of Carrie wandering out, he knew not where, affected him, despite his grievance.

◀ *Despite his anger, how does Drouet still feel about Carrie?*

Carrie merely pulled at the door.

The strain of the situation was too much for her, however. She made one more vain effort and then burst into tears.

"Now, be reasonable, Cad," said Drouet gently. "What do you want to rush out for this way? You haven't any place to go. Why not stay here now and be quiet? I'll not bother you. I don't want to stay here any longer."

Carrie had gone sobbing from the door to the window. She was so overcome she could not speak.

"Be reasonable now," he said. "I don't want to hold you. You can go if you want to, but why don't you think it over? Lord knows, I don't want to stop you."

◀ *What does Drouet advise Carrie to do?*

He received no answer. Carrie was quieting, however, under the influence of his plea.

"You stay here now, and I'll go," he added at last.

Carrie listened to this with mingled feelings. Her mind was shaken loose from the little mooring of logic that it had. She was stirred by this thought, angered by that—her own

Words For Everyday Use

moor • ing (moor iŋ) *n.,* beliefs, habits, or ties that make one feel secure

injustice, Hurstwood's, Drouet's, their respective qualities of kindness and favor, the threat of the world outside, in which she had failed once before, the impossibility of this state inside, where the chambers were no longer justly hers, the effect of the argument upon her nerves, all combined to make her a mass of jangling fibers—an anchorless, storm-beaten little craft which could do absolutely nothing but drift.

"Say," said Drouet, coming over to her after a few moments, with a new idea, and putting his hand upon her.

"Don't!" said Carrie, drawing away, but not removing her handkerchief from her eyes.

"Never mind about this quarrel now. Let it go. You stay here until the month's out, anyhow, and then you can tell better what you want to do. Eh?"

Carrie made no answer.

"You'd better do that," he said. "There's no use your packing up now. You can't go anywhere."

Still he got nothing for his words.

"If you'll do that, we'll call it off for the present and I'll get out."

Carrie lowered her handkerchief slightly and looked out of the window.

► *Why might Drouet's behavior make Carrie feel regret?*

"Will you do that?" he asked.

Still no answer.

"Will you?" he repeated.

She only looked vaguely into the street.

"Aw! come on," he said, "tell me. Will you?"

"I don't know," said Carrie softly, forced to answer.

"Promise me you'll do that," he said, "and we'll quit talking about it. It'll be the best thing for you."

Carrie heard him, but she could not bring herself to answer reasonably. She felt that the man was gentle, and that his interest in her had not abated, and it made her suffer a pang of regret. She was in a most helpless plight.

As for Drouet, his attitude had been that of the jealous lover. Now his feelings were a mixture of anger at deception, sorrow at losing Carrie, misery at being defeated. He wanted his rights in some way or other, and yet his rights included the retaining of Carrie, the making her feel her error.

"Will you?" he urged.

"Well, I'll see," said Carrie.

This left the matter as open as before, but it was something. It looked as if the quarrel would blow over, if they could only get some way of talking to one another. Carrie was ashamed, and Drouet aggrieved. He pretended to take up the task of packing some things in a valise.

Now, as Carrie watched him out of the corner of her eye, certain sound thoughts came into her head. He had erred, true, but what had she done? He was kindly and good-natured for all his egotism. Throughout this argument he had said nothing very harsh. On the other hand there was Hurstwood—a greater deceiver than he. He had pretended all this affection, all this passion, and he was lying to her all the while. Oh, the perfidy of men! And she had loved him. There could be nothing more in that quarter. She would see Hurstwood no more. She would write him and let him know what she thought. Thereupon what would she do? Here were these rooms. Here was Drouet, pleading for her to remain. Evidently things could go on here somewhat as before, if all were arranged. It would be better than the street, without a place to lay her head.

◄ *In what way does Carrie compare Hurstwood and Drouet now? What does she resolve to do?*

All this she thought of as Drouet rummaged the drawers for collars and labored long and painstakingly at finding a shirt-stud. He was in no hurry to rush this matter. He felt an attraction to Carrie which would not down. He could not think that the thing would end by his walking out of the room. There must be some way round, some way to make her own up that he was right and she was wrong—to patch up a peace and shut out Hurstwood forever. Mercy, how he turned at the man's shameless duplicity.

"Do you think," he said, after a few moments' silence, "that you'll try and get on the stage?"

He was wondering what she was intending.

"I don't know what I'll do yet," said Carrie.

"If you do, maybe I can help you. I've got a lot of friends in that line."

She made no answer to this.

"Don't go and try to knock around now without any money. Let me help you," he said. "It's no easy thing to go on your own hook here."

Carrie only rocked back and forth in her chair.

"I don't want you to go up against a hard game that way."

He bestirred himself about some other details and Carrie rocked on.

"Why don't you tell me all about this thing," he said, after a time, "and let's call it off? You don't really care for Hurstwood, do you?"

Words For Everyday Use

be • stir (bē stʉr) *vt.*, busy

"Why do you want to start on that again?" said Carrie. "You were to blame."

"No, I wasn't," he answered.

"Yes, you were, too," said Carrie. "You shouldn't have ever told me such a story as that."

"But you didn't have much to do with him, did you?" went on Drouet, anxious for his own peace of mind to get some direct denial from her.

"I won't talk about it," said Carrie, pained at the quizzical turn the peace arrangement had taken.

"What's the use of acting like that now, Cad?" insisted the drummer, stopping in his work and putting up a hand expressively. "You might let me know where I stand, at least."

"I won't," said Carrie, feeling no refuge but in anger. "Whatever has happened is your own fault."

► *What thought makes Drouet feel a new rush of anger and resentment?*

"Then you do care for him?" said Drouet, stopping completely and experiencing a rush of feeling.

"Oh, stop!" said Carrie.

"Well, I'll not be made a fool of," exclaimed Drouet. "You may trifle around with him if you want to, but you can't lead me. You can tell me or not, just as you want to, but I won't fool any longer!"

He shoved the last few remaining things he had laid out into his valise and snapped it with a vengeance. Then he grabbed his coat, which he had laid off to work, picked up his gloves, and started out.

"You can go to the deuce as far as I am concerned," he said, as he reached the door. "I'm no sucker," and with that he opened it with a jerk and closed it equally vigorously.

► *To what does the narrator compare love?*

Carrie listened at her window view, more astonished than anything else at this sudden rise of passion in the drummer. She could hardly believe her senses—so good-natured and tractable had he invariably been. It was not for her to see the wellspring of human passion. A real flame of love is a subtle thing. It burns as a will-o'-the-wisp,[1] dancing onward to fairy lands of delight. It roars as a furnace. Too often jealousy is the quality upon which it feeds.

---

1. **will-o'-the-wisp.** Phosphorescence in the woods caused by decaying plant matter

Words For Everyday Use

ref • uge (ref´ yōōj) *n.,* shelter
tri • fle (tri´ fəl) *vt.,* dally
trac • ta • ble (trak´ tə b'l) *adj.,* easily managed

CHAPTER 24

Ashes of Tinder: A Face at the Window

That night Hurstwood remained downtown entirely, going to the Palmer House for a bed after his work was through. He was in a fevered state of mind, owing to the blight his wife's action threatened to cast upon his entire future. While he was not sure how much significance might be attached to the threat she had made, he was sure that her attitude, if long continued, would cause him no end of trouble. She was determined, and had worsted him in a very important contest. How would it be from now on? He walked the floor of his little office, and later that of his room, putting one thing and another together to no avail.

Mrs. Hurstwood, on the contrary, had decided not to lose her advantage by inaction. Now that she had practically cowed him, she would follow up her work with demands, the acknowledgment of which would make her word *law* in the future. He would have to pay her the money which she would now regularly demand or there would be trouble. It did not matter what he did. She really did not care whether he came home anymore or not. The household would move along much more pleasantly without him, and she could do as she wished without consulting anyone. Now she proposed to consult a lawyer and hire a detective. She would find out at once just what advantages she could gain.

◄ *What has Mrs. Hurstwood decided while her husband is still pondering his next move?*

Hurstwood walked the floor, mentally arranging the chief points of his situation. "She has that property in her name," he kept saying to himself. "What a fool trick that was. Curse it! What a fool move that was."

◄ *What does Hurstwood regret?*

He also thought of his managerial position. "If she raises a row now I'll lose this thing. They won't have me around if my name gets in the papers. My friends, too!" He grew more angry as he thought of the talk any action on her part would create. How would the papers talk about it? Every man he knew would be wondering. He would have to explain and deny and make a general mark of himself. Then Moy would come and confer with him and there would be the devil to pay.

◄ *What will happen to Hurstwood if his wife "raises a row"?*

Many little wrinkles gathered between his eyes as he contemplated this, and his brow moistened. He saw no solution of anything—not a loophole left.

Words For Everyday Use

blight (blīt) *n.,* thing that destroys or devastates

cow (kou) *vt.,* make timid or submissive by filling with fear; intimidate

► *About what doesn't Hurstwood worry? Should he?*

Through all this thoughts of Carrie flashed upon him, and the approaching affair of Saturday. Tangled as all his matters were, he did not worry over that. It was the one pleasing thing in this whole rout of trouble. He could arrange that satisfactorily, for Carrie would be glad to wait, if necessary. He would see how things turned out tomorrow, and then he would talk to her. They were going to meet as usual. He saw only her pretty face and neat figure and wondered why life was not arranged so that such joy as he found with her could be steadily maintained. How much more pleasant it would be. Then he would take up his wife's threat again, and the wrinkles and moisture would return.

In the morning he came over from the hotel and opened his mail, but there was nothing in it outside the ordinary run. For some reason he felt as if something might come that way, and was relieved when all the envelopes had been scanned and nothing suspicious noticed. He began to feel the appetite that had been wanting before he had reached the office, and decided before going out to the park to meet Carrie to drop in at the Grand Pacific and have a pot of coffee and some rolls. While the danger had not lessened, it had not as yet materialized, and with him no news was good news. If he could only get plenty of time to think, perhaps something would turn up. Surely, surely, this thing would not drift along to catastrophe and he not find a way out.

► *When Carrie doesn't keep her appointment with Hurstwood, who doesn't he think might be the cause?*

His spirits fell, however, when, upon reaching the park, he waited and waited and Carrie did not come. He held his favorite post for an hour or more, then arose and began to walk about restlessly. Could something have happened out there to keep her away? Could she have been reached by his wife? Surely not. So little did he consider Drouet that it never once occurred to him to worry about his finding out. He grew restless as he ruminated, and then decided that perhaps it was nothing. She had not been able to get away this morning. That was why no letter notifying him had come. He would get one today. It would probably be on his desk when he got back. He would look for it at once.

After a time he gave up waiting and drearily headed for the Madison car. To add to his distress, the bright blue sky became overcast with little fleecy clouds which shut out the sun. The wind veered to the east, and by the time he reached his office it was threatening to drizzle all afternoon.

Words For Everyday Use

rout (rout) *n.,* disastrous defeat

He went in and examined his letters, but there was nothing from Carrie. Fortunately, there was nothing from his wife either. He thanked his stars that he did not have to confront that proposition just now when he needed to think so much. He walked the floor again, pretending to be in an ordinary mood, but secretly troubled beyond the expression of words.

At one-thirty he went to Rector's for lunch, and when he returned a messenger was waiting for him. He looked at the little chap with a feeling of doubt.

"I'm to bring an answer," said the boy.

Hurstwood recognized his wife's writing. He tore it open and read without a show of feeling. It began in the most formal manner and was sharply and coldly worded throughout.

"I want you to send the money I asked for at once. I need it to carry out my plans. You can stay away if you want to. It doesn't matter in the least. I must have some money. So don't delay, but send it by the boy."

◄ *What does Hurstwood's wife demand of him?*

When he had finished it, he stood holding it in his hands. The audacity of the thing took his breath. It roused his ire also—the deepest element of revolt in him. His first impulse was to write but four words in reply—"Go to the devil!"—but he compromised by telling the boy that there would be no reply. Then he sat down in his chair and gazed without seeing, contemplating the result of his work. What would she do about that? The confounded wretch! Was she going to try to bulldoze him into submission? He would go up there and have it out with her, that's what he would do. She was carrying things with too high a hand. These were his first thoughts.

Later, however, his old discretion asserted itself. Something had to be done. A climax was near and she would not sit idle. He knew her well enough to know that when she had decided upon a plan she would follow it up. Possibly matters would go into a lawyer's hands at once.

"Damn her!" he said softly, with his teeth firmly set, "I'll make it hot for her if she causes me trouble. I'll make her change her tone if I have to use force to do it!"

He arose from his chair and went and looked out into the street. The long drizzle had begun. Pedestrians had turned up collars, and trousers at the bottom. Hands were hidden in the pockets of the umbrellaless; umbrellas were up. The street looked like a sea of round black cloth roofs, twisting,

Words For Everyday Use

au • dac • i • ty (ô das´ ə tē) *n.*, shamelessness; boldness
ire (īr) *n.*, anger; wrath

bobbing, moving. Trucks and vans were rattling in a noisy line and everywhere men were shielding themselves as best they could. He scarcely noticed the picture. He was forever confronting his wife, demanding of her to change her attitude toward him before he worked her bodily harm.

► *When Mrs. Hurstwood doesn't receive the money she wants, what does she threaten to do?*

At four o'clock another note came, which simply said that if the money was not forthcoming that evening the matter would be laid before Fitzgerald and Moy on the morrow, and other steps would be taken to get it.

Hurstwood almost exclaimed out loud at the insistency of this thing. Yes, he would send her the money. He'd take it to her—he would go up there and have a talk with her, and that at once.

He put on his hat and looked around for his umbrella. He would have some arrangement of this thing.

He called a cab and was driven through the dreary rain to the North Side. On the way his temper cooled as he thought of the details of the case. What did she know? What had she done? Maybe she'd got hold of Carrie, who knows—or Drouet. Perhaps she really had evidence, and was prepared to fell him as a man does another from secret ambush. She was shrewd. Why should she taunt him this way unless she had good grounds?

He began to wish that he had compromised in some way or other—that he had sent the money. Perhaps he could do it up here. He would go in and see, anyhow. He would have no row.

► *What happens when Hurstwood tries to get into his own house?*

By the time he reached his own street he was keenly alive to the difficulties of his situation and wished over and over that some solution would offer itself, that he could see his way out. He alighted and went up the steps to the front door, but it was with a nervous palpitation of the heart. He pulled out his key and tried to insert it, but another key was on the inside. He shook at the knob, but the door was locked. Then he rang the bell. No answer. He rang again—this time harder. Still no answer. He jangled it fiercely several times in succession, but without avail. Then he went below.

There was a door which opened under the steps into the kitchen, protected by an iron grating, intended as a safeguard against burglars. When he reached this he noticed that it also was bolted and that the kitchen windows were down. What could it mean? He rang the bell and then waited.

Words For Everyday Use

a • light (ə līt´) *vi.,* get down from

pal • pi • ta • tion (pal´ pə tā´shən) *n.,* fluttering or trembling

Finally, seeing that no one was coming, he turned and went back to his cab.

"I guess they've gone out," he said apologetically to the individual who was hiding his red face in a loose tarpaulin[1] raincoat.

"I saw a young girl up in that winder," returned the cabby.

Hurstwood looked, but there was no face there now. He climbed moodily into the cab, relieved and distressed.

So this was the game, was it? Shut him out and make him pay. Well, by the Lord, that did beat all!

---

1. **tarpaulin.** Waterproof material

Responding to the Selection

With which character at this point in the story do you have the most sympathy—Carrie, Drouet, Mr. Hurstwood, or Mrs. Hurstwood? If you were in this character's position, what decisions would you make or what actions would you take at the end of chapter 24?

Reviewing the Selection

Recalling and Interpreting

1. **R**: On the night of the play, what goes wrong with Carrie's performance at first? What does she do to improve her performance? What frustrates Hurstwood at the theater? What does he resolve to do as soon as possible?

2. **I**: In what way does Carrie's performance change both Drouet's and Hurstwood's feelings for her? Explain whether they are judging her performance and the play accurately or whether they are swayed by the sentimentality of the play and their feelings for her. In what way does her success in the play change Carrie's attitude toward Drouet and Hurstwood? What is the significance of the title of chapter 19, "An Hour in Elfland: A Clamor Half Heard"? What does it indicate about Carrie's performance and its lasting effects?

3. **R**: In chapter 20, what goes wrong in the Hurstwood household? What does Drouet discover? What does Hurstwood promise Carrie they will do on Saturday?

4. **I**: Why are both the difficulties in the Hurstwood home and Drouet's discovery both inevitable given Hurstwood's and Carrie's behavior? Is it possible for Hurstwood to actually keep his promise to Carrie? Explain what you think of his decision that "He would promise anything, everything, and trust to fortune to disentangle him. He would make a try for Paradise, whatever might be the result. He would be happy, by the Lord, if it cost all honesty of statement, all abandonment of truth." What seems to be happening to Hurstwood as a character?

5. **R**: What happens that makes Mrs. Hurstwood suspect her husband? What accusations, demands, and threats does she make? How does he respond?

6. **I**: Why does Hurstwood make the mistake of assuming his household is in a merry mood? What does this reveal about his character? Why is Hurstwood unable to stand up to his wife?

7. **R:** About what issue does Drouet confront Carrie? Of what does he inform her? What does Carrie say Drouet tried to do to her? What offer does Drouet make to Carrie?

8. **I:** Why does Carrie blame Drouet when he imparts his bad news? If Carrie isn't in love with Hurstwood, why is she so upset to learn this news? Explain whether Carrie is justified when she says that Drouet tried to do this thing to her. Explain whether Drouet is justified in his anger. Why is Drouet concerned with Carrie's fate even though she has hurt him? What does this reveal about his character?

Synthesizing

9. Compare and contrast Hurstwood's position at the end of chapter 18 with his position at the end of chapter 24. In what way has Hurstwood experienced a "fall"? Why do you think the author chose to show Hurstwood at his pinnacle of success and importance before undermining his status in chapters 19–24?

10. In times of difficulty and in times of success, characters can reveal very different aspects of their personalities. What different sides of Hurstwood, Drouet, and Carrie are revealed in chapters 19–24? Explain whether the qualities that have emerged in these characters change your feelings toward them in any way.

Understanding Literature (QUESTIONS FOR DISCUSSION)

1. **Conflict and Rising Action.** A **conflict** is a struggle between two forces in a literary work. A plot involves the introduction, development, and eventual resolution of a conflict. One side of the central conflict is usually taken by the main character. That character may struggle against another character, against the forces of nature, against society or social norms, against fate, or against some element within himself or herself. A struggle that takes place between a character and some outside force is called an **external conflict**. A struggle that takes place within a character is called an **internal conflict**. The **rising action**, or complication, develops the conflict to a high point of intensity, moving toward the climax, crisis, or turning point. Based on what you know of the story at this point, what is the central conflict? What external and internal conflicts does Hurstwood face in chapters 19–24? What external and internal conflicts does Carrie face? Explain why the action in chapters 19–24 can be considered the rising action leading toward some turning point or climax.

2. **Sentimentality and Melodrama. Sentimentality** is an excessive expression of emotion. Much popular literature and drama of the nineteenth and twentieth centuries is characterized by sentimentality. **Melodramas** are plays with unrealistic, or exaggerated, characters and plots. The characters are mostly one-dimensional stock characters—completely good heroes and heroines and entirely wicked villains. Melodramas were extremely popular, dominating the stage in the late nineteenth and early twentieth centuries. Based on what Dreiser reveals of the play in which Carrie takes part, explain why this drama might be classified as sentimental melodrama. What events in the play seem overly emotional and unrealistic? In what way is the character that Carrie plays unrealistic? In what way does the sentimentality of the play compare and contrast with the events of chapters 19–24 in Dreiser's work? Would you classify these chapters as sentimental or melodramatic? Explain.

CHAPTER 25

Ashes of Tinder: The Loosing of Stays

When Hurstwood got back to his office again he was in a greater quandary than ever. Lord, Lord, he thought, what had he got into? How could things have taken such a violent turn, and so quickly? He could hardly realize how it had all come about. It seemed a monstrous, unnatural, unwarranted condition which had suddenly descended upon him without his let[1] or hindrance.

Meanwhile he gave a thought now and then to Carrie. What could be the trouble in that quarter? No letter had come, no word of any kind, and yet here it was late in the evening and she had agreed to meet him that morning. Tomorrow they were to have met and gone off—where? He saw that in the excitement of recent events he had not formulated a plan upon that score. He was desperately in love, and would have taken great chances to win her under ordinary circumstances, but now—now what? Supposing she had found out something? Supposing she, too, wrote him and told him that she knew all—that she would have nothing more to do with him? It would be just like this to happen as things were going now. Meanwhile he had not sent the money.

◄ What does Hurstwood suppose might have happened? What does he suppose Carrie might do?

He strolled up and down the polished floor of the resort, his hands in his pockets, his brow wrinkled, his mouth set. He was getting some vague comfort out of a good cigar, but it was no panacea[2] for the ill which affected him. Every once in a while he would clinch his fingers and tap his foot—signs of the stirring mental process he was undergoing. His whole nature was vigorously and powerfully shaken up, and he was finding what limits the mind has to endurance. He drank more brandy and soda than he had any evening in months. He was altogether a fine example of great mental perturbation.

For all his study nothing came of the evening except this—he sent the money. It was with great opposition, after two or three hours of the most urgent mental affirmation

◄ What does Hurstwood finally do? How does he feel about doing this?

1. **let.** Permission
2. **panacea.** Cure

Words For Everyday Use	
	quan • da • ry (kwän´də rē) *n.,* state of uncertainty; dilemma
	per • tur • ba • tion (pʉr´tər bā´shən) *n.,* disturbance; agitation

and denial, that at last he got an envelope, placed in it the requested amount, and slowly sealed it up.

Then he called Harry, the boy of all work around the place.

"You take this to this address," he said, handing him the envelope, "and give it to Mrs. Hurstwood."

"Yes, sir," said the boy.

"If she isn't there bring it back."

"Yes, sir."

"You've seen my wife?" he asked as a precautionary measure as the boy turned to go.

"Oh, yes, sir. I know her."

"All right, now. Hurry right back."

"Any answer?"

"I guess not."

The boy hastened away and the manager fell to his musings. Now he had done it. There was no use speculating over that. He was beaten for tonight and he might just as well make the best of it. But, oh, the wretchedness of being forced this way! He could see her meeting the boy at the door and smiling sardonically. She would take the envelope and know that she had triumphed. If he only had that letter back he wouldn't send it. He breathed heavily and wiped the moisture from his face.

For relief, he arose and joined in conversation with a few friends who were drinking. He tried to get the interest of things about him, but it was not to be. All the time his thoughts would run out to his home and see the scene being therein enacted. All the time he was wondering what she would say when the boy handed her the envelope.

In about an hour and three-quarters the boy returned. He had evidently delivered the package, for, as he came up, he made no sign of taking anything out of his pocket.

"Well?" said Hurstwood.

"I gave it to her."

"My wife?"

"Yes, sir."

"Any answer?"

"She said it was high time."

Hurstwood scowled fiercely.

There was no more to be done upon that score that night. He went on brooding over his situation until midnight, when he repaired again to the Palmer House. He wondered

► *What is Mrs. Hurstwood's only response when she receives the money?*

Words For Everyday Use

mus • ing (myo͞o´ziŋ) *n.,* meditation; reflection

sar • don • i • cal • ly (sär dän´ik lē) *adv.,* bitterly; sarcastically

what the morning would bring forth, and slept anything but soundly upon it.

Next day he went again to the office and opened his mail, suspicious and hopeful of its contents. No word from Carrie. Nothing from his wife, which was pleasant.

The fact that he had sent the money and that she had received it worked to the ease of his mind, for, as the thought that he had done it receded, his chagrin at it grew less and his hope of peace more. He fancied, as he sat at his desk, that nothing would be done for a week or two. Meanwhile, he would have time to think.

This process of *thinking* began by a reversion to Carrie and the arrangement by which he was to get her away from Drouet. How about that now? His pain at her failure to meet or write him rapidly increased as he devoted himself to this subject. He decided to write her care of the West Side post office and ask for an explanation, as well as to have her meet him. The thought that this letter would probably not reach her until Monday chafed him exceedingly. He must get some speedier method—but how?

He thought upon it for a half-hour, not contemplating a messenger or a cab direct to the house, owing to the exposure of it, but finding that time was slipping away to no purpose, he wrote the letter and then began to think again.

The hours slipped by, and with them the possibility of the union he had contemplated. He had thought to be joyously aiding Carrie by now in the task of joining her interests to his, and here it was afternoon and nothing done. Three o'clock came, four, five, six, and no letter. The helpless manager paced the floor and grimly endured the gloom of defeat. He saw a busy Saturday ushered out, the Sabbath[3] in, and nothing done. All day, the bar being closed, he brooded alone, shut out from home, from the excitement of his resort, from Carrie, and without the ability to alter his condition one iota.[4] It was the worst Sunday he had spent in his life.

◄ *What had Hurstwood hoped to accomplish by this time?*

In Monday's second mail he encountered a very legal-looking letter which held his interest for some time. It bore the imprint of the law offices of McGregor, James and Hay, and with a very formal "Dear Sir," and "We beg to state,"

3. **Sabbath.** Sunday
4. **iota.** Bit

Words For Everyday Use

re • ver • sion (ri vʉr´zhən) *n.*, return
chafe (chāf) *vt.*, annoy; irritate

► *Why have lawyers contacted Hurstwood?*

went on to inform him briefly that they had been retained by Mrs. Julia Hurstwood to adjust certain matters which related to her sustenance and property rights, and would he kindly call and see them about the matter at once.

He read it through carefully several times, and then merely shook his head. It seemed as if his family troubles were just beginning.

"Well!" he said after a time, quite audibly, "I don't know."

Then he folded it up and put it in his pocket.

► *What makes Carrie more attractive to Hurstwood?*

To add to his misery there was no word from Carrie. He was quite certain now that she knew he was married and was angered at his perfidy. His loss seemed all the more bitter now that he needed her most. He thought he would go out and insist on seeing her if she did not send him word of some sort soon. He was really affected most miserably of all by this desertion. He had loved her earnestly enough, but now that the possibility of losing her stared him in the face she seemed much more attractive. He really pined for a word, and looked out upon her with his mind's eye in the most wistful manner. He did not propose to lose her, whatever she might think. Come what might, he would adjust this matter, and soon. He would go to her and tell her all his family complications. He would explain to her just where he stood and how much he needed her. Surely she couldn't go back on him now? It wasn't possible. He would plead until her anger would melt—until she would forgive him.

Suddenly he thought: "Supposing she isn't out there—suppose she has gone?"

He was forced to take his feet. It was too much to think of and sit still.

Nevertheless, his rousing availed him nothing.

On Tuesday it was the same way. He did manage to bring himself into the mood to go out to Carrie, but when he got in Ogden Place he thought he saw a man watching him and went away. He did not go within a block of the house.

► *What hurts Hurstwood? Do you think his hurt is justified? Why, or why not?*

One of the galling incidents of this visit was that he came back on a Randolph Street car, and without noticing arrived almost opposite the building of the concern with which his son was connected. This sent a pang through his heart. He had called on his boy there several times. Now the lad had not sent him a word. His absence did not seem to be noticed

Words For Everyday Use

sus • te • nance (sus´ tə nəns) *n.,* means of support

rous • ing (rou´ziŋ) *n.,* violent stir

gall • ing (gôl´iŋ) *adj.,* bitterly irritating

by either of his children. Well, well, fortune plays a man queer tricks. He got back to his office and joined in a conversation with friends. It was as if idle chatter deadened the sense of misery.

That night he dined at Rector's and returned at once to his office. In the bustle and show of the latter was his only relief. He troubled over many little details and talked perfunctorily to everybody. He stayed at his desk long after all others had gone, and only quitted it when the night watchman on his round pulled at the front door to see if it was safely locked.

On Wednesday, he received another polite note from McGregor, James and Hay. It read:

Dear Sir:

We beg to inform you that we are instructed to wait until tomorrow (Thursday) at one o'clock, before filing suit against you, on behalf of Mrs. Julia Hurstwood, for divorce and alimony. If we do not hear from you before that time we shall consider that you do not wish to compromise the matter in any way and act accordingly.

Very truly yours, etc.

◄ What does the second letter from the lawyers say?

"Compromise!" exclaimed Hurstwood bitterly. "Compromise!" Again he shook his head.

So here it was spread out clear before him, and now he knew what to expect. If he didn't go and see them they would sue him promptly. If he did, he would be offered terms that would make his blood boil. He folded the letter and put it with the other one. Then he put on his hat and went for a turn about the block.

CHAPTER 26

The Ambassador Fallen: A Search for the Gate

Carrie, left alone by Drouet, listened to his retreating steps, scarcely realizing what had happened. She knew that he had stormed out. It was some moments before she questioned whether he would return, not now exactly, but ever. She looked around her upon the rooms, out of which the evening light was dying, and wondered why she did not feel quite the same toward them. She went over to the dresser and struck a match, lighting the gas. Then she went back to the rocker to think.

It was some time before she could collect her thoughts, but when she did, this truth began to take on importance. She was quite alone. Suppose Drouet did not come back? Suppose she should never hear anything more of him? This fine arrangement of chambers would not last long. She would have to quit them.

► *What concern does Carrie have?*

To her credit, be it said, she never once counted on Hurstwood. She could only approach that subject with a pang of sorrow and regret. For a truth, she was rather shocked and frightened by this evidence of human depravity. He would have tricked her without turning an eyelash. She would have been led into a newer and worse situation. And yet she could not keep out the pictures of his looks and manners. Only this one deed seemed strange and miserable. It contrasted sharply with all she felt and knew concerning the man.

► *What does the narrator say is to Carrie's credit?*

But she was alone. That was the greater thought just at present. How about that? Would she go out to work again? Would she begin to look around in the business district? The stage! Oh, yes. Drouet had spoken about that. Was there any hope there? She moved to and fro, in deep and varied thoughts, while the minutes slipped away and night fell completely. She had had nothing to eat, and yet there she sat, thinking it over.

She remembered that she was hungry and went to the little cupboard in the rear room where were the remains of one of their breakfasts. She looked at these things with certain misgivings. The contemplation of food had more significance than usual.

► *Why does food have more significance than usual to Carrie?*

While she was eating she began to wonder how much money she had. It struck her as exceedingly important, and without ado she went to look for her purse. It was on the dresser, and in it were seven dollars in bills and some change.

She quailed as she thought of the insignificance of the amount and rejoiced because the rent was paid until the end of the month. She began also to think what she would have done if she had gone out into the street when she first started. By the side of that situation, as she looked at it now, the present seemed agreeable. She had a little time at least, and then, perhaps, everything would come out all right, after all.

Drouet had gone, but what of it? He did not seem seriously angry. He only acted as if he were huffy. He would come back—of course he would. There was his cane in the corner. Here was one of his collars. He had left his light overcoat in the wardrobe. She looked about and tried to assure herself with the sight of a dozen such details, but, alas, the secondary thought arrived. Supposing he did come back. Then what?

Here was another proposition nearly, if not quite, as disturbing. She would have to talk with and explain to him. He would want her to admit that he was right. It would be impossible for her to live with him.

◄ *What does Carrie feel would make it impossible to live with Drouet?*

On Friday Carrie remembered her appointment with Hurstwood, and the passing of the hour when she should, by all right of promise, have been in his company served to keep the calamity which had befallen her exceedingly fresh and clear. In her nervousness and stress of mind she felt it necessary to act, and consequently put on a brown street dress, and at eleven o'clock started to visit the business portion once again. She must look for work.

The rain, which threatened at twelve and began at one, served equally well to cause her to retrace her steps and remain within doors as it did to reduce Hurstwood's spirits and give him a wretched day.

The morrow was Saturday, a half-holiday in many business quarters, and besides it was a balmy, radiant day, with the trees and grass shining exceedingly green after the rain of the night before. When she went out the sparrows were twittering merrily in joyous choruses. She could not help feeling, as she looked across the lovely park, that life was a joyous thing for those who did not need to worry, and she wished over and over that something might interfere now to preserve for her the comfortable state which she had occupied. She did not want Drouet or his money when she thought of it, nor

Words For Everyday Use

balm • y (bäm´ē) *adj.*, warm, mild, pleasant

anything more to do with Hurstwood, but only the content and ease of mind she had experienced, for, after all, she had been happy—happier, at least, than she was now when confronted by the necessity of making her way alone.

When she arrived in the business part it was quite eleven o'clock, and the business had little longer to run. She did not realize this at first, being affected by some of the old distress which was a result of her earlier adventure into this strenuous and exacting quarter. She wandered about, assuring herself that she was making up her mind to look for something, and at the same time feeling that perhaps it was not necessary to be in such haste about it. The thing was difficult to encounter, and she had a few days. Besides, she was not sure that she was really face to face again with the bitter problem of self-sustenance. Anyhow, there was one change for the better. She knew that she had improved in appearance. Her manner had vastly changed. Her clothes were becoming, and men—well-dressed men, some of the kind who before had gazed at her indifferently from behind their polished railings and imposing office partitions—now gazed into her face with a soft light in their eyes. In a way, she felt the power and satisfaction of the thing, but it did not wholly reassure her. She looked for nothing save what might come legitimately and without the appearance of special favor. She wanted something, but no man should buy her by false protestations or favor. She proposed to earn her living honestly.

► *What one advantage does Carrie see in looking for work now?*

► *What is Carrie determined to do?*

► *Explain whether Carrie seems serious about looking for work.*

"This store closes at one on Saturdays," was a pleasing and satisfactory legend to see upon doors which she felt she ought to enter and inquire for work. It gave her an excuse, and after encountering quite a number of them, and noting that the clock registered 12:15, she decided that it would be no use to seek further today, so she got on a car and went to Lincoln Park. There was always something to see there—the flowers, the animals, the lake—and she flattered herself that on Monday she would be up betimes[1] and searching. Besides, many things might happen between now and Monday.

Sunday passed with equal doubts, worries, assurances, and heaven knows what vagaries of mind and spirit. Every half-hour in the day the thought would come to her most

1. **betimes.** Early

Words For Everyday Use

par • ti • tion (pär tish´ən) *n.,* wall

va • gar • y (və ger´ē) *n.,* unpredictable shift

sharply, like the tail of a swishing whip, that action—immediate action—was imperative. At other times she would look about her and assure herself that things were not so bad—that certainly she would come out safe and sound. At such times she would think of Drouet's advice about going on the stage, and saw some chance for herself in that quarter. She decided to take up that opportunity on the morrow.

◄ *In what profession does Carrie hope to find employment?*

Accordingly, she arose early Monday morning and dressed herself carefully. She did not know just how such applications were made, but she took it to be a matter which related more directly to the theater buildings. All you had to do was to inquire of some one about the theater for the manager and ask for a position. If there was anything, you might get it, or, at least, he could tell you how.

She had had no experience with this class of individuals whatsoever, and did not know the salacity and humor of the theatrical tribe. She only knew of the position which Mr. Hale occupied, but, of all things, she did not wish to encounter that personage, on account of her intimacy with his wife.

There was, however, at this time, one theater, the Chicago Opera House, which was considerably in the public eye, and its manager, David A. Henderson, had a fair local reputation. Carrie had seen one or two elaborate performances there and had heard of several others. She knew nothing of Henderson nor of the methods of applying, but she instinctively felt that this would be a likely place, and accordingly strolled about in that neighborhood. She came bravely enough to the showy entranceway, with the polished and begilded lobby, set with framed pictures out of the current attraction, leading up to the quiet box office, but she could get no further. A noted comic opera comedian was holding forth that week, and the air of distinction and prosperity overawed her. She could not imagine that there would be anything in such a lofty sphere for her. She almost trembled at the audacity which might have carried her on to a terrible rebuff. She could find heart only to look at the pictures which were showy and then walk out. It seemed to her as if she had made a splendid escape and that it would be foolhardy to think of applying in that quarter again.

◄ *Why doesn't Carrie ask for work?*

This little experience settled her hunting for one day. She looked around elsewhere, but it was from the outside. She

Words For Everyday Use		
	im • per • a • tive (im per´ə tiv) *adj.*, absolutely necessary	**o • ver • awe** (ō´vər ô´) *vt.*, overcome or subdue by inspiring awe
	sa • lac • i • ty (sə las´ə tē) *n.*, lecherousness	**loft • y** (lôf´tē) *adj.*, high in status
		re • buff (ri buf´) *n.*, rejection

got the location of several playhouses fixed in her mind—notably the Grand Opera House and McVicker's, both of which were leading in attractions—and then came away. Her spirits were materially reduced, owing to the newly restored sense of magnitude of the great interests and the insignificance of her claims upon society, such as she understood them to be.

That night she was visited by Mrs. Hale, whose chatter and protracted stay made it impossible to dwell upon her predicament or the fortune of the day. Before retiring, however, she sat down to think, and gave herself up to the most gloomy forebodings. Drouet had not put in an appearance. She had had no word from any quarter, she had spent a dollar of her precious sum in procuring food and paying carfare. It was evident that she would not endure long. Besides, she had discovered no resource.

► *Why doesn't Carrie seriously consider returning to her sister?*

In this situation her thoughts went out to her sister in Van Buren Street, whom she had not seen since the night of her flight, and to her home at Columbia City, which seemed now a part of something that could not be again. She looked for no refuge in that direction. Nothing but sorrow was brought her by thoughts of Hurstwood, which would return. That he could have chosen to dupe her in so ready a manner seemed a cruel thing.

Tuesday came, and with it appropriate indecision and speculation. She was in no mood, after her failure of the day before, to hasten forth upon her work-seeking errand, and yet she rebuked herself for what she considered her weakness the day before. Accordingly she started out to revisit the Chicago Opera House, but possessed scarcely enough courage to approach.

She did manage to inquire at the box office, however.

"Manager of the company or the house?" asked the smartly dressed individual who took care of the tickets. He was favorably impressed by Carrie's looks.

"I don't know," said Carrie, taken back by the question.

"You couldn't see the manager of the house today, anyhow," volunteered the young man. "He's out of town."

He noted her puzzled look, and then added: "What is it you wish to see about?"

"I want to see about getting a position," she answered.

Words For Everyday Use

pro • tract • ed (prō trakt´'d) *adj.,* prolonged; drawn out
fore • bod • ing (fôr bōd´ iŋ) *n.,* prediction
pro • cure (prō kyoor´) *vt.,* obtain
re • buke (ri byo͞ok´) *vt.,* scold; blame

"You'd better see the manager of the company," he returned, "but he isn't here now."

"When will he be in?" asked Carrie, somewhat relieved by this information.

"Well, you might find him in between eleven and twelve. He's here after two o'clock."

Carrie thanked him and walked briskly out, while the young man gazed after her through one of the side windows of his gilded coop.

◄ *What does the young man think of Carrie?*

"Good-looking," he said to himself, and proceeded to visions of condescensions on her part which were exceedingly flattering to himself.

One of the principal comedy companies of the day was playing an engagement at the Grand Opera House. Here Carrie asked to see the manager of the company. She little knew the trivial authority of this individual, or that had there been a vacancy an actor would have been sent on from New York to fill it.

◄ *Of what aspects of the business she is looking to enter is Carrie unaware?*

"His office is upstairs," said a man in the box office.

Several persons were in the manager's office, two lounging near a window, another talking to an individual sitting at a roll-top desk—the manager. Carrie glanced nervously about, and began to fear that she should have to make her appeal before the assembled company, two of whom—the occupants of the window—were already observing her carefully.

"I can't do it," the manager was saying; "it's a rule of Mr. Frohman's never to allow visitors back of the stage. No, no!"

Carrie timidly waited, standing. There were chairs, but no one motioned her to be seated. The individual to whom the manager had been talking went away quite crestfallen. That luminary gazed earnestly at some papers before him, as if they were of the greatest concern.

"Did you see that in the *Herald* this morning about Nat Goodwin, Harris?"

"No," said the person addressed. "What was it?"

"Made quite a curtain address at Hooley's last night. Better look it up."

Harris reached over to a table and began to look for the "Herald."

"What is it?" said the manager to Carrie, apparently noticing her for the first time. He thought he was going to be held up for free tickets.

Words For Everyday Use

crest • fall • en (krest´ fôl´ən) *adj.,* disheartened

▶ *Why does Carrie pretend she is only seeking advice?*

▶ *How is Carrie's request received?*

Carrie summoned up all her courage, which was little at best. She realized that she was a novice, and felt as if a rebuff were certain. Of this she was so sure that she only wished now to pretend she had called for advice.

"Can you tell me how to go about getting on the stage?"

It was the best way after all to have gone about the matter. She was interesting, in a manner, to the occupant of the chair, and the simplicity of her request and attitude took his fancy. He smiled, as did the others in the room, who, however, made some slight effort to conceal their humor.

"I don't know," he answered, looking her brazenly over. "Have you ever had any experience upon the stage?"

"A little," answered Carrie. "I have taken part in amateur performances."

She thought she had to make some sort of showing in order to retain his interest.

"Never studied for the stage?" he said, putting on an air intended as much to impress his friends with his discretion as Carrie.

"No, sir."

"Well, I don't know," he answered, tipping lazily back in his chair while she stood before him. "What makes you want to get on the stage?"

She felt abashed at the man's daring, but could only smile in answer to his engaging smirk, and say:

"I need to make a living."

▶ *Where does the manager say Carrie should go to pursue acting?*

"Oh," he answered, rather taken by her trim appearance, and feeling as if he might scrape up an acquaintance with her. "That's a good reason, isn't it? Well, Chicago is not a good place for what you want to do. You ought to be in New York. There's more chance there. You could hardly expect to get started out here."

▶ *In what way does the manager interpret Carrie's smile?*

Carrie smiled genially, grateful that he should condescend to advise her even so much. He noticed the smile, and put a slightly different construction on it. He thought he saw an easy chance for a little flirtation.

"Sit down," he said, pulling a chair forward from the side of his desk and dropping his voice so that the two men in the room should not hear. Those two gave each other the suggestion of a wink.

Words For Everyday Use

bra • zen • ly (brā´zən lē) *adv.,* boldly

dis • cre • tion (di skresh´ən) *n.,* authority to make decisions

"Well, I'll be going, Barney," said one, breaking away and so addressing the manager. "See you this afternoon."

"All right," said the manager.

The remaining individual took up a paper as if to read.

"Did you have any idea what sort of part you would like to get?" asked the manager softly.

"Oh, no," said Carrie. "I would take anything to begin with."

"I see," he said. "Do you live here in the city?"

"Yes, sir."

The manager smiled most blandly.

"Have you ever tried to get in as a chorus girl?" he asked, assuming a more confidential air.

Carrie began to feel that there was something exuberant and unnatural in his manner.

"No," she said.

"That's the way most girls begin," he went on, "who go on the stage. It's a good way to get experience."

He was turning on her a glance of the companionable and persuasive manner.

"I didn't know that," said Carrie.

"It's a difficult thing," he went on, "but there's always a chance, you know." Then, as if he suddenly remembered, he pulled out his watch and consulted it. "I've an appointment at two," he said, "and I've got to go to lunch now. Would you care to come and dine with me? We can talk it over there."

◄ *What does Carrie realize?*

"Oh, no," said Carrie, the whole motive of the man flashing on her at once. "I have an engagement myself."

"That's too bad," he said, realizing that he had been a little beforehand[2] in his offer and that Carrie was about to go away. "Come in later. I may know of something."

"Thank you," she answered, with some trepidation, and went out.

"She was good-looking, wasn't she?" said the manager's companion, who had not caught all the details of the game he had played.

"Yes, in a way," said the other, sore to think the game had been lost. "She'd never make an actress, though. Just another chorus girl—that's all."

◄ *What does the manager say about Carrie's chances in the theater?*

This little experience nearly destroyed her ambition to call upon the manager at the Chicago Opera House, but she

2. **beforehand.** Premature

Words For Everyday Use

trep • i • da • tion (trep´ə dā´shən) *n.*, fear

decided to do so after a time. He was of a more sedate turn of mind. He said at once that there was no opening of any sort, and seemed to consider her search foolish.

"Chicago is no place to get a start," he said. "You ought to be in New York."

Still she persisted, and went to McVicker's, where she could not find anyone. *The Old Homestead* was running there, but the person to whom she was referred was not to be found.

These little expeditions took up her time until quite four o'clock, when she was weary enough to go home. She felt as if she ought to continue and inquire elsewhere, but the results so far were too dispiriting. She took the car and arrived at Ogden Place in three-quarters of an hour, but decided to ride on to the West Side branch of the post office, where she was accustomed to receive Hurstwood's letters. There was one there now, written Saturday, which she tore open and read with mingled feelings. There was so much warmth in it and such tense complaint at her having failed to meet him, and her subsequent silence, that she rather pitied the man. That he loved her was evident enough. That he had wished and dared to do so, married as he was, was the evil. She felt as if the thing deserved an answer, and consequently decided that she would write and let him know that she knew of his married state and was justly incensed at his deception. She would tell him that it was all over between them.

► *What feelings does Carrie have about Hurstwood when reading his letter?*

At her room, the wording of this missive[3] occupied her for some time, for she fell to the task at once. It was most difficult.

"You do not need to have me explain why I did not meet you," she wrote in part. "How could you deceive me so? You cannot expect me to have anything more to do with you. I wouldn't under any circumstances. Oh, how could you act so?" she added in a burst of feeling. "You have caused me more misery than you can think. I hope you will get over your infatuation for me. We must not meet anymore. Goodbye."

She took the letter the next morning, and at the corner dropped it reluctantly into the letterbox, still uncertain as to whether she should do so or not. Then she took the car and went downtown.

3. **missive.** Letter

Words For Everyday Use

se • date (si dāt´) *adj.*, calm, composed, serious

in • censed (in sensd´) *adj.*, enraged

in • fat • u • a • tion (in fach´ o͞o ā´ shən) *n.*, foolish or shallow love or affection

This was the dull season with the department stores, but she was listened to with more consideration than was usually accorded to young women applicants, owing to her neat and attractive appearance. She was asked the same old questions with which she was already familiar.

◀ *Why is Carrie given special attention when applying for jobs at the department stores?*

"What can you do? Have you ever worked in a retail store before? Are you experienced?"

At The Fair, See and Company's, and all the great stores it was much the same. It was the dull season, she might come in a little later, possibly they would like to have her.

When she arrived at the house at the end of the day, weary and disheartened, she discovered that Drouet had been there. His umbrella and light overcoat were gone. She thought she missed other things, but could not be sure. Everything had not been taken.

So his going was crystallizing into staying. What was she to do now? Evidently she would be facing the world in the same old way within a day or two. Her clothes would get poor. She put her two hands together in her customary expressive way and pressed her fingers. Large tears gathered in her eyes and broke hot across her cheeks. She was alone, very much alone.

Drouet really had called, but it was with a very different mind from that which Carrie had imagined. He expected to find her, to justify his return by claiming that he came to get the remaining portion of his wardrobe, and before he got away again to patch up a peace.

◀ *With what intention had Drouet come to the house?*

Accordingly, when he arrived, he was disappointed to find Carrie out. He trifled about, hoping that she was somewhere in the neighborhood and would soon return. He constantly listened, expecting to hear her foot on the stair.

When he did so, it was his intention to make believe that he had just come in and was disturbed at being caught. Then he would explain his need of his clothes and find out how things stood.

Wait as he did, however, Carrie did not come. From pottering around among the drawers, in momentary expectation of her arrival, he changed to looking out of the window, and from that to resting himself in the rocking-chair. Still no Carrie. He began to grow restless and lit a cigar. After that he walked the floor. Then he looked out of the window and saw

Words For Everyday Use

ac • cord (ə kôrd´) *vt.*, grant

crys • tal • lize (kris´təl īz´) *vt.*, take on a definite form

clouds gathering. He remembered an appointment at three. He began to think that it would be useless to wait, and got hold of his umbrella and light coat, intending to take these things, anyway. It would scare her, he hoped. Tomorrow he would come back for the others. He would find out how things stood.

As he started to go he felt truly sorry that he had missed her. There was a little picture of her on the wall, showing her arrayed in the little jacket he had first bought her—her face a little more wistful than he had seen it lately. He was really touched by it, and looked into the eyes of it with a rather rare feeling for him.

"You didn't do me right, Cad," he said, as if he were addressing her in the flesh.

Then he went to the door, took a good look around, and went out.

CHAPTER 27

When Waters Engulf Us We Reach for a Star

It was when he returned from his disturbed stroll about the streets, after receiving the decisive note from McGregor, James and Hay, that Hurstwood found the letter Carrie had written him that morning. He thrilled intensely as he noted the handwriting, and rapidly tore it open.

"Then," he thought, "she loves me or she would not have written to me at all."

He was slightly depressed at the tenor of the note for the first few minutes, but soon recovered. "She wouldn't write at all if she didn't care for me."

◄ Why isn't Hurstwood depressed by the content of Carrie's letter?

This was his one resource against the depression which held him. He could extract little from the wording of the letter, but the spirit he thought he knew.

There was really something exceedingly human—if not pathetic—in his being thus relieved by a clearly worded reproof. He who had for so long remained satisfied with himself now looked outside of himself for comfort—and to such a source. The mystic cords of affection! How they bind us all.

The color came to his cheeks. For the moment he forgot the letter from McGregor, James and Hay. If he could only have Carrie, perhaps he could get out of the whole entanglement—perhaps it would not matter. He wouldn't care what his wife did with herself if only he might not lose Carrie. He stood up and walked about, dreaming his delightful dream of a life continued with this lovely possessor of his heart.

It was not long, however, before the old worry was back for consideration, and with it what weariness! He thought of the morrow and the suit. He had done nothing, and here was the afternoon slipping away. It was now a quarter of four. At five the attorneys would have gone home. He still had the morrow until noon. Even as he thought, the last fifteen minutes passed away and it was five. Then he abandoned the thought of seeing them anymore that day and turned to Carrie.

◄ Explain whether it seems as if Hurstwood intends to speak to the lawyers and work out a compromise with his wife.

It is to be observed that the man did not justify himself to himself. He was not troubling about that. His whole thought was the possibility of persuading Carrie. Nothing was wrong in

Words For Everyday Use

de • ci • sive (dē sī´siv) *adj.*, firm; resolute

ten • or (ten´ər) *n.*, tone

re • proof (ri pro͞of´) *n.*, something said or done to express disapproval

that. He loved her dearly. Their mutual happiness depended upon it. Would that Drouet were only away!

While he was thinking thus elatedly, he remembered that he wanted some clean linen in the morning.

This he purchased, together with a half-dozen ties, and went to the Palmer House. As he entered he thought he saw Drouet ascending the stairs with a key. Surely not Drouet! Then he thought, perhaps they had changed their abode temporarily. He went straight up to the desk.

► *What gives Hurstwood renewed hope?*

"Is Mr. Drouet stopping here?" he asked of the clerk.

"I think he is," said the latter, consulting his private registry list. "Yes."

"Is that so?" exclaimed Hurstwood, otherwise concealing his astonishment. "Alone?" he added.

"Yes," said the clerk.

Hurstwood turned away and set his lips so as best to express and conceal his feelings.

"How's that?" he thought. "They've had a row."

He hastened to his room with rising spirits and changed his linen. As he did so, he made up his mind that if Carrie was alone, or if she had gone to another place, it behooved[1] him to find out. He decided to call at once.

"I know what I'll do," he thought. "I'll go to the door and ask if Mr. Drouet is at home. That will bring out whether he is there or not and where Carrie is."

He was almost moved to some muscular display as he thought of it. He decided to go immediately after supper.

On coming down from his room at six, he looked carefully about to see if Drouet was present and then went out to lunch. He could scarcely eat, however, he was so anxious to be about his errand. Before starting he thought it well to discover where Drouet would be, and returned to his hotel.

"Has Mr. Drouet gone out?" he asked of the clerk.

"No," answered the latter, "he's in his room. Do you wish to send up a card?"

"No, I'll call around later," answered Hurstwood, and strolled out.

He took a Madison car and went direct to Ogden Place, this time walking boldly up to the door. The chambermaid answered his knock.

1. **behooved.** Was necessary to

Words For Everyday Use

a • bode (ə bōd´) *n.,* residence

"Is Mr. Drouet in?" said Hurstwood blandly.

"He is out of the city," said the girl, who had heard Carrie tell this to Mrs. Hale.

"Is Mrs. Drouet in?"

"No, she has gone to the theater."

"Is that so?" said Hurstwood, considerably taken back; then, as if burdened with something important, "You don't know to which theater?"

The girl really had no idea where she had gone, but not liking Hurstwood, and wishing to cause him trouble, answered: "Yes, Hooley's."

"Thank you," returned the manager, and tipping his hat slightly, went away.

"I'll look in at Hooley's," thought he, but as a matter of fact he did not. Before he had reached the central portion of the city he thought the whole matter over and decided it would be useless. As much as he longed to see Carrie, he knew she would be with someone and did not wish to intrude with his plea there. A little later he might do so—in the morning. Only in the morning he had the lawyer question before him.

◄ What does Hurstwood plan to do? Why doesn't he follow through with this plan?

This little pilgrimage threw quite a wet blanket upon his rising spirits. He was soon down again to his old worry, and reached the resort anxious to find relief. Quite a company of gentlemen were making the place lively with their conversation. A group of Cook County politicians were conferring about a round cherry-wood table in the rear portion of the room. Several young merrymakers were chattering at the bar before making a belated visit to the theater. A shabbily genteel individual, with a red nose and an old high hat, was sipping a quiet glass of ale alone at one end of the bar. Hurstwood nodded to the politicians and went into his office.

About ten o'clock a friend of his, Mr. Frank L. Taintor, a local sport and racing man, dropped in, and seeing Hurstwood alone in his office came to the door.

"Hello, George!" he exclaimed.

"How are you, Frank?" said Hurstwood, somewhat relieved by the sight of him. "Sit down," and he motioned him to one of the chairs in the little room.

"What's the matter, George?" asked Taintor. "You look a little glum. Haven't lost at the track, have you?"

"I'm not feeling very well tonight. I had a slight cold the other day."

"Take whiskey, George," said Taintor. "You ought to know that."

Hurstwood smiled.

▶ *Among which social sphere does Hurstwood believe he belongs?*

While they were still conferring there, several other of Hurstwood's friends entered, and not long after eleven, the theaters being out, some actors began to drop in—among them some notabilities.[2]

Then began one of those pointless social conversations so common in American resorts where the would-be *gilded* attempt to rub off gilt from those who have it in abundance. If Hurstwood had one leaning, it was toward notabilities. He considered that, if anywhere, he belonged among them. He was too proud to toady,[3] too keen not to strictly observe the plane he occupied when there were those present who did not appreciate him, but, in situations like the present, where he could shine as a gentleman and be received without equivocation as a friend and equal among men of known ability, he was most delighted. It was on such occasions, if ever, that he would "take something." When the social flavor was strong enough he would even unbend to the extent of drinking glass for glass with his associates, punctiliously observing his turn to pay as if he were an outsider like the others. If he ever approached intoxication—or rather that ruddy warmth and comfortableness which precedes the more sloven state—it was when individuals such as these were gathered about him, when he was one of a circle of chatting celebrities. Tonight, disturbed as was his state, he was rather relieved to find company, and now that notabilities were gathered, he laid aside his troubles for the nonce, and joined in right heartily.

It was not long before the imbibing began to tell. Stories began to crop up—those ever-enduring, droll stories which form the major portion of the conversation among American men under such circumstances.

Twelve o'clock arrived, the hour for closing, and with it the company took leave. Hurstwood shook hands with them most cordially. He was very roseate physically. He had arrived at that state where his mind, though clear, was, nevertheless, warm in its fancies. He felt as if his troubles were not very serious. Going into his office, he began to turn over certain accounts, awaiting the departure of the bartenders and the cashier, who soon left.

2. **notabilities.** People of distinction
3. **toady.** Flatter or grovel

Words For Everyday Use

e • quiv • o • ca • tion (ē kwiv´ə kā shən) *n.*, doubt; ambiguity

punc • til • i • ous • ly (puŋk til´ē əs lē) *adv.*, very carefully

slov • en (sluv´ən) *adj.*, sloppy

im • bib • ing (im bīb´iŋ) *n.*, drinking, especially of alcohol

ro • se • ate (rō´zē it) *adj.*, rosy

It was the manager's duty, as well as his custom, after all were gone to see that everything was safely closed up for the night. As a rule, no money except the cash taken in after banking hours was kept about the place, and that was locked in the safe by the cashier, who, with the owners, was joint keeper of the secret combination, but, nevertheless, Hurstwood nightly took the precaution to try the cash drawers and the safe in order to see that they were tightly closed. Then he would lock his own little office and set the proper light burning near the safe, after which he would take his departure.

◀ *What is one of Hurstwood's duties?*

Never in his experience had he found anything out of order, but tonight, after shutting down his desk, he came out and tried the safe. His way was to give a sharp pull. This time the door responded. He was slightly surprised at that, and looking in found the money cases as left for the day, apparently unprotected. His first thought was, of course, to inspect the drawers and shut the door.

◀ *What unusual thing does Hurstwood discover when closing up for the night?*

"I'll speak to Mayhew about this tomorrow," he thought.

The latter had certainly imagined upon going out a half-hour before that he had turned the knob on the door so as to spring the lock. He had never failed to do so before. But tonight Mayhew had other thoughts. He had been revolving the problem of a business of his own.

"I'll look in here," thought the manager, pulling out the money drawers. He did not know why he wished to look in there. It was quite a superfluous action, which another time might not have happened at all.

As he did so, a layer of bills, in parcels of a thousand, such as banks issue, caught his eye. He could not tell how much they represented, but paused to view them. Then he pulled out the second of the cash drawers. In that were the receipts of the day.

◀ *What catches Hurstwood's eye?*

"I didn't know Fitzgerald and Moy ever left any money this way," his mind said to itself. "They must have forgotten it."

He looked at the other drawer and paused again.

"Count them," said a voice in his ear.

He put his hand into the first of the boxes and lifted the stack, letting the separate parcels fall. They were bills of fifty and one hundred dollars done in packages of a thousand. He thought he counted ten such.

◀ *What does an internal voice advise Hurstwood to do? How much money is in the safe? What does the voice ask him?*

Words For Everyday Use

su • per • flu • ous (sə pʉr´flo͞o əs) *adj.,* unnecessary

▶ *How much is Hurstwood worth? What will become of his money?*

▶ *What does Hurstwood see as the solution to his problems?*

"Why don't I shut the safe?" his mind said to itself, lingering. "What makes me pause here?"

For answer there came the strangest words:

"Did you ever have ten thousand dollars in ready money?"

Lo, the manager remembered that he had never had so much. All his property had been slowly accumulated, and now his wife owned that. He was worth more than forty thousand, all told—but she would get that.

He puzzled as he thought of these things, then pushed in the drawers and closed the door, pausing with his hand upon the knob, which might so easily lock it all beyond temptation. Still he paused. Finally he went to the windows and pulled down the curtains. Then he tried the door, which he had previously locked. What was this thing, making him suspicious? Why did he wish to move about so quietly? He came back to the end of the counter as if to rest his arm and think. Then he went and unlocked his little office door and turned on the light. He also opened his desk, sitting down before it, only to think strange thoughts.

"The safe is open," said a voice. "There is just the least little crack in it. The lock has not been sprung."

The manager floundered among a jumble of thoughts. Now all the entanglement of the day came back. Also the thought that here was a solution. That money would do it. If he had that and Carrie. He rose up and stood stock-still, looking at the floor.

"What about it?" his mind asked, and for answer he put his hand slowly up and scratched his head.

The manager was no fool to be led blindly away by such an errant proposition as this, but his situation was peculiar. Wine was in his veins. It had crept up into his head and given him a warm view of the situation. It also colored the possibilities of ten thousand for him. He could see great opportunities with that. He could get Carrie. Oh, yes, he could! He could get rid of his wife. That letter, too, was waiting discussion tomorrow morning. He would not need to answer that. He went back to the safe and put his hand on the knob. Then he pulled the door open and took the drawer with the money quite out.

With it once out and before him, it seemed a foolish thing to think about leaving it. Certainly it would. Why, he could live quietly with Carrie for years.

Words For Everyday Use

er • rant (er´ənt) *adj.,* straying from the right course

Lord! what was that? For the first time he was tense, as if a stern hand had been laid upon his shoulder. He looked fearfully around. Not a soul was present. Not a sound. Someone was shuffling by on the sidewalk. He took the box and the money and put it back in the safe. Then he partly closed the door again.

To those who have never wavered in conscience, the predicament of the individual whose mind is less strongly constituted and who trembles in the balance between duty and desire is scarcely appreciable, unless graphically portrayed. Those who have never heard that solemn voice of the ghostly clock which ticks with awful distinctness, "thou shalt," "thou shalt not," "thou shalt," "thou shalt not," are in no position to judge. Not alone in sensitive, highly organized natures is such a mental conflict possible. The dullest specimen of humanity, when drawn by desire toward evil, is recalled by a sense of right, which is proportionate in power and strength to his evil tendency. We must remember that it may not be a knowledge of right, for no knowledge of right is predicated of the animal's instinctive recoil at evil. Men are still led by instinct before they are regulated by knowledge. It is instinct which recalls the criminal—it is instinct (where highly organized reasoning is absent) which gives the criminal his feeling of danger, his fear of wrong.

◄ According to the narrator, who is in no position to judge Hurstwood's thoughts and actions?

◄ According to the narrator, what regulates behavior in humans?

At every first adventure, then, into some untried evil, the mind wavers. The clock of thought ticks out its wish and its denial. To those who have never experienced such a mental dilemma, the following will appeal on the simple ground of revelation.

When Hurstwood put the money back, his nature again resumed its ease and daring. No one had observed him. He was quite alone. No one could tell what he wished to do. He could work this thing out for himself.

The imbibation of the evening had not yet worn off. Moist as was his brow, tremble as did his hand once after the nameless fright, he was still flushed with the fumes of liquor. He scarcely noticed that the time was passing. He went over his situation once again, his eye always seeing the money in a lump, his mind always seeing what it would do. He strolled into his little room, then to the door, then to the safe again. He put his hand on the knob and opened it. There was the money! Surely no harm could come from looking at it!

Words For Everyday Use

pred • i • cate (pred´ i kāt´) *vt.*, state; assert

re • coil (ri koil´) *n.*, drawing back

► *What words are used to describe the bills? What does Hurstwood decide to do?*

He took out the drawer again and lifted the bills. They were so smooth, so compact, so portable. How little they made, after all. He decided he would take them. Yes, he would. He would put them in his pocket. Then he looked at that and saw they would not go there. His hand satchel! To be sure, his hand satchel. They would go in that—all of it would. No one would think anything of it either. He went into the little office and took it from the shelf in the corner. Now he set it upon his desk and went out toward the safe. For some reason he did not want to fill it out in the big room.

First he brought the bills and then the loose receipts of the day. He would take it all. He put the empty drawers back and pushed the iron door almost to, then stood beside it meditating.

The wavering of a mind under such circumstances is an almost inexplicable thing, and yet it is absolutely true. Hurstwood could not bring himself to act definitely. He wanted to think about it—to ponder over it, to decide whether it were best. He was drawn by such a keen desire for Carrie, driven by such a state of turmoil in his own affairs that he thought constantly it would be best, and yet he wavered. He did not know what evil might result from it to him—how soon he might come to grief. The true ethics of the situation never once occurred to him, and never would have, under any circumstances.

► *What never occurs to Hurstwood?*

After he had all the money in the handbag, a revulsion of feeling seized him. He would not do it—no! Think of what a scandal it would make. The police! They would be after him. He would have to fly, and where? Oh, the terror of being a fugitive from justice! He took out the two boxes and put all the money back. In his excitement he forgot what he was doing, and put the sums in the wrong boxes. As he pushed the door to, he thought he remembered doing it wrong and opened the door again. There were the two boxes mixed.

He took them out and straightened the matter, but now the terror had gone. Why be afraid?

► *What happens to determine Hurstwood's course of action? Do you think this was an accident? Why, or why not?*

While the money was in his hand the lock clicked. It had sprung! Did he do it? He grabbed at the knob and pulled vigorously. It had closed. Heavens! he was in for it now, sure enough.

The moment he realized that the safe was locked for a surety, the sweat burst out upon his brow and he trembled

Words For Everyday Use

re • vul • sion (ri vul´shən) *n.,* drawing back in disgust

violently. He looked about him and decided instantly. There was no delaying now.

"Supposing I do lay it on the top," he said, "and go away, they'll know who took it. I'm the last to close up. Besides, other things will happen."

At once he became the man of action.

"I must get out of this," he thought.

He hurried into his little room, took down his light overcoat and hat, locked his desk, and grabbed the satchel. Then he turned out all but one light and opened the door. He tried to put on his old assured air, but it was almost gone. He was repenting rapidly.

"I wish I hadn't done that," he said. "That was a mistake."

He walked steadily down the street, greeting a night watchman whom he knew who was trying doors. He must get out of the city, and that quickly.

◄ *What must Hurstwood do?*

"I wonder how the trains run?" he thought.

Instantly he pulled out his watch and looked. It was nearly half-past one.

At the first drug store he stopped, seeing a long-distance telephone booth inside. It was a famous drug store, and contained one of the first private telephone booths ever erected.

"I want to use your 'phone a minute," he said to the night clerk.

The latter nodded.

"Give me 1643," he called to Central, after looking up the Michigan Central depot number. Soon he got the ticket agent.

"How do the trains leave here for Detroit?" he asked.

The man explained the hours.

"No more tonight?"

"Nothing with a sleeper. Yes, there is, too," he added. "There is a mail train out of here at three o'clock."

"All right," said Hurstwood. "What time does that get to Detroit?"

He was thinking if he could only get there and cross the river into Canada, he could take his time about getting to Montreal. He was relieved to learn that it would reach there by noon.

"Mayhew won't open the safe till nine," he thought. "They can't get on my track before noon."

Then he thought of Carrie. With what speed must he get her, if he got her at all. She would have to come along. He jumped into the nearest cab standing by.

◄ *What does Hurstwood hurry to do before the train leaves?*

"To Ogden Place," he said sharply. "I'll give you a dollar more if you make good time."

► *What does Hurstwood do to get Carrie to come with him?*

The cabby beat his horse into a sort of imitation gallop, which was fairly fast, however. On the way Hurstwood thought what to do. Reaching the number, he hurried up the steps and did not spare the bell in waking the servant.

"Is Mrs. Drouet in?" he asked.

"Yes," said the astonished girl.

"Tell her to dress and come to the door at once. Her husband is in the hospital, injured, and wants to see her."

The servant girl hurried upstairs, convinced by the man's strained and emphatic manner.

"What!" said Carrie, lighting the gas and searching for her clothes.

"Mr. Drouet is hurt and in the hospital. He wants to see you. The cab's downstairs."

Carrie dressed very rapidly, and soon appeared below, forgetting everything save the necessities.

"Drouet is hurt," said Hurstwood quickly. "He wants to see you. Come quickly."

Carrie was so bewildered that she swallowed the whole story.

"Get in," said Hurstwood, helping her and jumping after.

The cabby began to turn the horse around.

"Michigan Central depot," he said, standing up and speaking so low that Carrie could not hear, "as fast as you can go."

Words For Everyday Use

em • phat • ic (em fat´ik) *adj.,* strong and definite

CHAPTER 28

A Pilgrim, an Outlaw: The Spirit Detained

The cab had not traveled a short block before Carrie, settling herself and thoroughly waking in the night atmosphere, asked:

"What's the matter with him? Is he hurt badly?"

"It isn't anything very serious," Hurstwood said solemnly. He was very much disturbed over his own situation, and now that he had Carrie with him, he only wanted to get safely out of reach of the law. Therefore he was in no mood for anything save such words as would further his plans distinctly.

Carrie did not forget that there was something to be settled between her and Hurstwood, but the thought was ignored in her agitation. The one thing was to finish this strange pilgrimage.

"Where is he?"

"Way out on the South Side," said Hurstwood. "We'll have to take the train. It's the quickest way."

Carrie said nothing, and the horse gamboled on. The weirdness of the city by night held her attention. She looked at the long receding rows of lamps and studied the dark, silent houses.

"How did he hurt himself?" she asked—meaning what was the nature of his injuries. Hurstwood understood. He hated to lie any more than necessary, and yet he wanted no protests until he was out of danger.

"I don't know exactly," he said. "They just called me up to go and get you and bring you out. They said there wasn't any need for alarm, but that I shouldn't fail to bring you."

The man's serious manner convinced Carrie, and she became silent, wondering.

◄ *What convinces Carrie that Hurstwood's words are true? What is the real reason for Hurstwood's manner?*

Hurstwood examined his watch and urged the man to hurry. For one in so delicate a position he was exceedingly cool. He could only think of how needful it was to make the train and get quietly away. Carrie seemed quite tractable, and he congratulated himself.

In due time they reached the depot, and after helping her out he handed the man a five-dollar bill and hurried on.

Words For Everyday Use

gam • bol (gam´bəl) *vi.*, move playfully

"You wait here," he said to Carrie, when they reached the waiting room, "while I get the tickets."

"Have I much time to catch the train for Detroit?" he asked of the agent.

"Four minutes," said the latter.

He paid for two tickets as circumspectly as possible.

"Is it far?" said Carrie, as he hurried back.

"Not very," he said. "We must get right in."

He pushed her before him at the gate, stood between her and the ticket man while the latter punched their tickets, so that she could not see, and then hurried after.

There was a long line of express and passenger cars and one or two common day coaches. As the train had only recently been made up and few passengers were expected, there were only one or two brakemen waiting. They entered the rear day coach and sat down. Almost immediately, "All aboard," resounded faintly from the outside, and the train started.

Carrie began to think it was a little bit curious—this going to a depot—but said nothing. The whole incident was so out of the natural that she did not attach too much weight to anything she imagined.

"How have you been?" asked Hurstwood gently, for he now breathed easier.

► What pleases Hurstwood about Carrie? What do you think of his failure to relieve her anxiety?

"Very well," said Carrie, who was so disturbed that she could not bring a proper attitude to bear in the matter. She was still nervous to reach Drouet and see what could be the matter. Hurstwood contemplated her and felt this. He was not disturbed that it should be so. He did not trouble because she was moved sympathetically in the matter. It was one of the qualities in her which pleased him exceedingly. He was only thinking how he should explain. Even this was not the most serious thing in his mind, however. His own deed and present flight were the great shadows which weighed upon him.

"What a fool I was to do that," he said over and over. "What a mistake!"

In his sober senses, he could scarcely realize that the thing had been done. He could not begin to feel that he was a fugitive from justice. He had often read of such things, and had thought they must be terrible, but now that the thing was upon him, he only sat and looked into the past. The future was a thing which concerned the Canadian line. He wanted to reach that. As for the rest, he surveyed his actions for the evening, and counted them parts of a great mistake.

"Still," he said, "what could I have done?"

Then he would decide to make the best of it, and would begin to do so by starting the whole inquiry over again. It was a fruitless, harassing round, and left him in a queer mood to deal with the proposition he had in the presence of Carrie.

The train clacked through the yards along the lake front, and ran rather slowly to Twenty-fourth Street. Brakes and signals were visible without. The engine gave short calls with its whistle, and frequently the bell rang. Several brakemen came through, bearing lanterns. They were locking the vestibules[1] and putting the cars in order for a long run.

Presently it began to gain speed, and Carrie saw the silent streets flashing by in rapid succession. The engine also began its whistle-calls of four parts, with which it signaled danger to important crossings.

"Is it very far?" asked Carrie.

"Not so very," said Hurstwood. He could hardly repress a smile at her simplicity. He wanted to explain and conciliate her, but he also wanted to be well out of Chicago.

◄ *What amuses Hurstwood?*

In the lapse of another half-hour it became apparent to Carrie that it was quite a run to wherever he was taking her, anyhow.

"Is it in Chicago?" she asked nervously. They were now far beyond the city limits, and the train was scudding across the Indiana line at a great rate.

"No," he said, "not where we are going."

There was something in the way he said this which aroused her in an instant.

Her pretty brow began to contract.

"We are going to see Charlie, aren't we?" she asked.

He felt that the time was up. An explanation might as well come now as later. Therefore, he shook his head in the most gentle negative.

"What?" said Carrie. She was nonplussed at the possibility of the errand being different from what she had thought.

He only looked at her in the most kindly and mollifying way.

"Well, where are you taking me, then?" she asked, her voice showing the quality of fright.

◄ *How does Carrie feel when Hurstwood reveals his intentions?*

"I'll tell you, Carrie, if you'll be quiet. I want you to come along with me to another city."

"Oh," said Carrie, her voice rising into a weak cry. "Let me off. I don't want to go with you."

1. **vestibules.** Passageways between the cars of a train

Words For Everyday Use	
	con • cil • i • ate (kän sil´ē āt) *vt.*, soothe; placate
	non • plussed (nän´plüs'd) *adj.*, perplexed; bewildered
	mol • li • fy • ing (mäl´ə fī iŋ) *adj.*, soothing; calming

She was quite appalled at the man's audacity. This was something which had never for a moment entered her head. Her one thought now was to get off and away. If only the flying train could be stopped, the terrible trick would be amended.

She arose and tried to push out into the aisle—anywhere. She knew she had to do something. Hurstwood laid a gentle hand on her.

"Sit still, Carrie," he said. "Sit still. It won't do you any good to get up here. Listen to me and I'll tell you what I'll do. Wait a moment."

She was pushing at his knees, but he only pulled her back. No one saw this little altercation, for very few persons were in the car, and they were attempting to doze.

"I won't," said Carrie, who was, nevertheless, complying against her will. "Let me go," she said. "How dare you?" and large tears began to gather in her eyes.

Hurstwood was now fully aroused to the immediate difficulty, and ceased to think of his own situation. He must do something with this girl, or she would cause him trouble. He tried the art of persuasion with all his powers aroused.

"Look here now, Carrie," he said, "you mustn't act this way. I didn't mean to hurt your feelings. I don't want to do anything to make you feel bad."

"Oh," sobbed Carrie, "oh, oh—oo—o!"

"There, there," he said, "you mustn't cry. Won't you listen to me? Listen to me a minute, and I'll tell you why I came to do this thing. I couldn't help it. I assure you I couldn't. Won't you listen?"

Her sobs disturbed him so that he was quite sure she did not hear a word he said.

"Won't you listen?" he asked.

"No, I won't," said Carrie, flashing up. "I want you to take me out of this, or I'll tell the conductor. I won't go with you. It's a shame," and again sobs of fright cut off her desire for expression.

► *Why does Hurstwood want to straighten out the situation immediately?*

Hurstwood listened with some astonishment. He felt that she had just cause for feeling as she did, and yet he wished that he could straighten this thing out quickly. Shortly the conductor would come through for the tickets. He wanted no noise, no trouble of any kind. Before everything he must make her quiet.

Words For Everyday Use

a • mend • ed (ə mend´'d) *adj.,* corrected

al • ter • ca • tion (ôl´tər kā´shən) *n.,* heated argument

com • ply (kəm plī´) *vi.,* act in accordance with

"You couldn't get out until the train stops again," said Hurstwood. "It won't be very long until we reach another station. You can get out then if you want to. I won't stop you. All I want you to do is to listen a moment. You'll let me tell you, won't you?"

Carrie seemed not to listen. She only turned her head toward the window, where outside all was black. The train was speeding with steady grace across the fields and through patches of wood. The long whistles came with sad, musical effect as the lonely woodland crossings were approached.

Now the conductor entered the car and took up the one or two fares that had been added at Chicago. He approached Hurstwood, who handed out the tickets. Poised as she was to act, Carrie made no move. She did not look about.

◄ *What opportunity to act does Carrie lose?*

When the conductor had gone again Hurstwood felt relieved.

"You're angry at me because I deceived you," he said. "I didn't mean to, Carrie. As I live I didn't. I couldn't help it. I couldn't stay away from you after the first time I saw you."

He was ignoring the last deception as something that might go by the board. He wanted to convince her that his wife could no longer be a factor in their relationship. The money he had stolen he tried to shut out of his mind.

"Don't talk to me," said Carrie, "I hate you. I want you to go away from me. I am going to get out at the very next station."

She was in a tremble of excitement and opposition as she spoke.

"All right," he said, "but you'll hear me out, won't you? After all you have said about loving me, you might hear me. I don't want to do you any harm. I'll give you the money to go back with when you go. I merely want to tell you, Carrie. You can't stop me from loving you, whatever you may think."

He looked at her tenderly, but received no reply.

"You think I have deceived you badly, but I haven't. I didn't do it willingly. I'm through with my wife. She hasn't any claims on me. I'll never see her anymore. That's why I'm here tonight. That's why I came and got you."

◄ *Explain who is right—Hurstwood or Carrie. Has Hurstwood deceived her?*

"You said Charlie was hurt," said Carrie, savagely. "You deceived me. You've been deceiving me all the time, and now you want to force me to run away with you."

Words For Everyday Use

sav • age • ly (sav´ij lē) *adv.,* fiercely

She was so excited that she got up and tried to get by him again. He let her, and she took another seat. Then he followed.

"Don't run away from me, Carrie," he said gently. "Let me explain. If you will only hear me out you will see where I stand. I tell you my wife is nothing to me. She hasn't been anything for years or I wouldn't have ever come near you. I'm going to get a divorce just as soon as I can. I'll never see her again. I'm done with all that. You're the only person I want. If I can have you I won't ever think of another woman again."

► *What mixed feelings does Carrie have about Hurstwood's actions?*

Carrie heard all this in a very ruffled state. It sounded sincere enough, however, despite all he had done. There was a tenseness in Hurstwood's voice and manner which could but have some effect. She did not want anything to do with him. He was married, he had deceived her once, and now again, and she thought him terrible. Still there is something in such daring and power which is fascinating to a woman, especially if she can be made to feel that it is all prompted by love of her.

The progress of the train was having a great deal to do with the solution of this difficult situation. The speeding wheels and disappearing country put Chicago farther and farther behind. Carrie could feel that she was being borne a long distance off—that the engine was making an almost through run to some distant city. She felt at times as if she could cry out and make such a row that someone would come to her aid; at other times it seemed an almost useless thing—so far was she from any aid, no matter what she did. All the while Hurstwood was endeavoring to formulate his plea in such a way that it would strike home and bring her into sympathy with him.

"I was simply put where I didn't know what else to do."

Carrie deigned no suggestion of hearing this.

"When I saw you wouldn't come unless I could marry you, I decided to put everything else behind me and get you to come away with me. I'm going off now to another city. I want to go to Montreal for a while, and then anywhere you want to. We'll go and live in New York, if you say."

"I'll not have anything to do with you," said Carrie. "I want to get off this train. Where are we going?"

"To Detroit," said Hurstwood.

"Oh!" said Carrie, in a burst of anguish. So distant and definite a point seemed to increase the difficulty.

Words For Everyday Use

ruf • fled (ruf´əld) *adj.,* disturbed

deign (dān) *vi.,* condescend to do something beneath one's dignity

an • guish (aŋ´gwish) *n.,* great suffering

"Won't you come along with me?" he said, as if there was great danger that she would not. "You won't need to do anything but travel with me. I'll not trouble you in any way. You can see Montreal and New York, and then if you don't want to stay you can go back. It will be better than trying to go back tonight."

◀ *What proposition begins to sway Carrie's mind?*

The first gleam of fairness shone in this proposition for Carrie. It seemed a plausible thing to do, much as she feared his opposition if she tried to carry it out. Montreal and New York! Even now she was speeding toward those great, strange lands, and could see them if she liked. She thought, but made no sign.

Hurstwood thought he saw a shade of compliance in this. He redoubled his ardor.

"Think," he said, "what I've given up. I can't go back to Chicago anymore. I've got to stay away and live alone now, if you don't come with me. You won't go back on me entirely, will you, Carrie?"

"I don't want you to talk to me," she answered forcibly.

Hurstwood kept silent for a while.

Carrie felt the train to be slowing down. It was the moment to act if she was to act at all. She stirred uneasily.

"Don't think of going, Carrie," he said. "If you ever cared for me at all, come along and let's start right. I'll do whatever you say. I'll marry you, or I'll let you go back. Give yourself time to think it over. I wouldn't have wanted you to come if I hadn't loved you. I tell you, Carrie, before God, I can't live without you. I won't!"

There was the tensity of fierceness in the man's plea which appealed deeply to her sympathies. It was a dissolving fire which was actuating him now. He was loving her too intensely to think of giving her up in this, his hour of distress. He clutched her hand nervously and pressed it with all the force of an appeal.

The train was now all but stopped. It was running by some cars on a side track. Everything outside was dark and dreary. A few sprinkles on the window began to indicate that it was raining. Carrie hung in a quandary, balancing between decision and helplessness. Now the train stopped, and she was listening to his plea. The engine backed a few feet and all was still.

Words For Everyday Use

com • pli • ance (kəm plī´əns) *n.,* submission

► *How is Carrie beginning to feel about the situation? How would you feel if you were in her position?*

She wavered, totally unable to make a move. Minute after minute slipped by and still she hesitated, he pleading.

"Will you let me come back if I want to?" she asked, as if she now had the upper hand and her companion was utterly subdued.

"Of course," he answered, "you know I will."

Carrie only listened as one who has granted a temporary amnesty. She began to feel as if the matter were in her hands entirely.

The train was again in rapid motion. Hurstwood changed the subject.

"Aren't you very tired?" he said.

"No," she answered.

"Won't you let me get you a berth in the sleeper?"[2]

She shook her head, though for all her distress and his trickery she was beginning to notice what she had always felt—his thoughtfulness.

"Oh, yes," he said, "you will feel so much better."

She shook her head.

"Let me fix my coat for you, anyway," and he arose and arranged his light coat in a comfortable position to receive her head.

"There," he said tenderly, "now see if you can't rest a little." He could have kissed her for her compliance. He took his seat beside her and thought a moment.

"I believe we're in for a heavy rain," he said.

"So it looks," said Carrie, whose nerves were quieting under the sound of the raindrops, driven by a gusty wind, as the train swept on frantically through the shadow to a newer world.

The fact that he had in a measure mollified Carrie was a source of satisfaction to Hurstwood, but it furnished only the most temporary relief. Now that her opposition was out of the way, he had all of his time to devote to the consideration of his own error.

► *How does Hurstwood feel about his theft now? What does he realize he has lost through his actions?*

His condition was bitter in the extreme, for he did not want the miserable sum he had stolen. He did not want to be a thief. That sum or any other could never compensate for the state which he had thus foolishly doffed. It could not give him back his host of friends, his name, his house and

2. **berth in the sleeper.** Built-in bed or bunk in a sleeping car on a train

Words For Everyday Use

am • nes • ty (am´nəs tē) *n.*, pardon
doff (däf) *vt.*, put aside or discard

family, nor Carrie, as he had meant to have her. He was shut out from Chicago—from his easy, comfortable state. He had robbed himself of his dignity, his merry meetings, his pleasant evenings. And for what? The more he thought of it the more unbearable it became. He began to think that he would try and restore himself to his old state. He would return the miserable thievings of the night and explain. Perhaps Moy would understand. Perhaps they would forgive him and let him come back.

◄ *What does Hurstwood consider doing? What do you think of this plan?*

By noontime the train rolled into Detroit and he began to feel exceedingly nervous. The police must be on his track by now. They had probably notified all the police of the big cities, and detectives would be watching for him. He remembered instances in which defaulters had been captured. Consequently, he breathed heavily and paled somewhat. His hands felt as if they must have something to do. He simulated interest in several scenes without which he did not feel. He repeatedly beat his foot upon the floor.

◄ *What does Hurstwood think is probably happening by this time?*

Carrie noticed his agitation, but said nothing. She had no idea what it meant or that it was important.

He wondered now why he had not asked whether this train went on through to Montreal or some Canadian point. Perhaps he could have saved time. He jumped up and sought the conductor.

"Does any part of this train go to Montreal?" he asked.

"Yes, the next sleeper back does."

He would have asked more, but it did not seem wise, so he decided to inquire at the depot.

The train rolled into the yards, clanging and puffing.

"I think we had better go right on through to Montreal," he said to Carrie. "I'll see what the connections are when we get off."

He was exceedingly nervous, but did his best to put on a calm exterior. Carrie only looked at him with large, troubled eyes. She was drifting mentally, unable to say to herself what to do.

The train stopped and Hurstwood led the way out. He looked warily around him, pretending to look after Carrie. Seeing nothing that indicated studied observation, he made his way to the ticket office.

"The next train for Montreal leaves when?" he asked.

"In twenty minutes," said the man.

Words For Everyday Use

de • fault • er (dē fôlt´ ər) *n.,* one who fails to pay money where due

He bought two tickets and Pullman berths. Then he hastened back to Carrie.

"We go right out again," he said, scarcely noticing that Carrie looked tired and weary.

"I wish I was out of all this," she exclaimed gloomily.

"You'll feel better when we reach Montreal," he said.

"I haven't an earthly thing with me," said Carrie; "not even a handkerchief."

"You can buy all you want as soon as you get there, dearest," he explained. "You can call in a dressmaker."

Now the crier[3] called the train ready and they got on. Hurstwood breathed a sigh of relief as it started. There was a short run to the river, and there they were ferried over. They had barely pulled the train off the ferryboat when he settled back with a sigh.

"It won't be so very long now," he said, remembering her in his relief. "We get there the first thing in the morning."

Carrie scarcely deigned to reply.

"I'll see if there is a dining car," he added. "I'm hungry."

3. **crier.** Official who calls out announcements

CHAPTER 29

The Solace of Travel: The Boats of the Sea

To the untraveled, territory other than their own familiar hearth[1] is invariably fascinating. Next to love, it is the one thing which solaces and delights. Things new are too important to be neglected, and mind, which is a mere reflection of sensory impressions, succumbs to the flood of objects. Thus lovers are forgotten, sorrows laid aside, death hidden from view. There is a world of accumulated feeling back of the trite dramatic expression—"I am going away."

◀ *According to the narrator, what effect does seeing new places for the first time have upon people? To what other experience does the narrator compare it?*

As Carrie looked out upon the flying scenery she almost forgot that she had been tricked into this long journey against her will and that she was without the necessary apparel for traveling. She quite forgot Hurstwood's presence at times, and looked away to homely farmhouses and cozy cottages in villages with wondering eyes. It was an interesting world to her. Her life had just begun. She did not feel herself defeated at all. Neither was she blasted in hope. The great city held much. Possibly she would come out of bondage into freedom—who knows? Perhaps she would be happy. These thoughts raised her above the level of erring. She was saved in that she was hopeful.

◀ *What thoughts entertain Carrie as she gazes upon the passing landscape?*

The following morning the train pulled safely into Montreal and they stepped down, Hurstwood glad to be out of danger, Carrie wondering at the novel atmosphere of the northern city. Long before, Hurstwood had been here, and now he remembered the name of the hotel at which he had stopped. As they came out of the main entrance of the depot he heard it called anew by a busman.

"We'll go right up and get rooms," he said.

At the clerk's office Hurstwood swung the register about while the clerk came forward. He was thinking what name he would put down. With the latter before him he found no time for hesitation. A name he had seen out of the car window came swiftly to him. It was pleasing enough. With an easy hand he wrote, "G. W. Murdock and wife." It was the

◀ *What alias does Hurstwood assume?*

1. **hearth.** Fireside, therefore, home

Words For Everyday Use

suc • cumb (sə kum´) *vt.,* yield; submit
trite (trīt) *adj.,* stale through overuse

largest concession to necessity he felt like making. His initials he could not spare.

When they were shown their room Carrie saw at once that he had secured her a lovely chamber.

"You have a bath there," said he. "Now you can clean up when you are ready."

Carrie went over and looked out the window, while Hurstwood looked at himself in the glass. He felt dusty and unclean. He had no trunk, no change of linen, not even a hairbrush.

"I'll ring for soap and towels," he said, "and send you up a hairbrush. Then you can bathe and get ready for breakfast. I'll go for a shave and come back and get you, and then we'll go out and look for some clothes for you."

He smiled good-naturedly as he said this.

"All right," said Carrie.

She sat down in one of the rocking-chairs, while Hurstwood waited for the boy, who soon knocked.

"Soap, towels, and a pitcher of ice water."

"Yes, sir."

"I'll go now," he said to Carrie, coming toward her and holding out his hands, but she did not move to take them.

"You're not mad at me, are you?" he asked softly.

"Oh, no!" she answered, rather indifferently.

"Don't you care for me at all?"

She made no answer, but looked steadily toward the window.

► What does Carrie say when Hurstwood asks her if she can try to love him? What reasons does she have for her response?

"Don't you think you could love me a little?" he pleaded, taking one of her hands, which she endeavored to draw away. "You once said you did."

"What made you deceive me so?" asked Carrie.

"I couldn't help it," he said, "I wanted you too much."

"You didn't have any right to want me," she answered, striking cleanly home.

"Oh, well, Carrie," he answered, "here I am. It's too late now. Won't you try and care for me a little?"

He looked rather worsted[2] in thought as he stood before her.

She shook her head negatively.

"Let me start all over again. Be my wife from today on."

Carrie rose up as if to step away, he holding her hand. Now he slipped his arm about her and she struggled, but in

2. **worsted.** Defeated

Words For Everyday Use

con • ces • sion (kən sesh´ ən) *n.*, act of yielding or granting

vain. He held her quite close. Instantly there flamed up in his body the all-compelling desire. His affection took an ardent form.

"Let me go," said Carrie, who was folded close to him.

"Won't you love me?" he said. "Won't you be mine from now on?"

Carrie had never been ill-disposed toward him. Only a moment before she had been listening with some complacency, remembering her old affection for him. He was so handsome, so daring!

Now, however, this feeling had changed to one of opposition, which rose feebly. It mastered her for a moment, and then, held close as she was, began to wane. Something else in her spoke. This man, to whose bosom she was being pressed, was strong; he was passionate, he loved her, and she was alone. If she did not turn to him—accept of his love—where else might she go? Her resistance half dissolved in the flood of his strong feeling.

◀ *What thoughts make Carrie's resistance dissolve?*

She found him lifting her head and looking into her eyes. What magnetism there was she could never know. His many sins, however, were for the moment all forgotten.

He pressed her closer and kissed her, and she felt that further opposition was useless.

"Will you marry me?" she asked, forgetting *how*.

"This very day," he said, with all delight.

Now the hall-boy pounded on the door and he released his hold upon her regretfully.

"You get ready now, will you," he said, "at once?"

"Yes," she answered.

"I'll be back in three-quarters of an hour."

Carrie, flushed and excited, moved away as he admitted the boy.

Below stairs, he halted in the lobby to look for a barber shop. For the moment, he was in fine feather. His recent victory over Carrie seemed to atone for much he had endured during the last few days. Life seemed worth fighting for. This eastward flight from all things customary and attached seemed as if it might have happiness in store. The storm showed a rainbow at the end of which might be a pot of gold.

He was about to cross to a little red-and-white striped bar which was fastened up beside a door when a voice greeted him familiarly. Instantly his heart sank.

◀ *What makes Hurstwood's heart sink? Why?*

Words For Everyday Use

com • pla • cen • cy (kəm plā´sən sē) *n.*, quiet satisfaction; contentment

a • tone (ə tōn´) *vt.*, make amends for

"Why, hello, George, old man!" said the voice. "What are you doing down here?"

Hurstwood was already confronted, and recognized his friend Kenny, the stockbroker.

"Just attending to a little private matter," he answered, his mind working like a keyboard of a telephone station. This man evidently did not know—he had not read the papers.

"Well, it seems strange to see you way up here," said Mr. Kenny genially. "Stopping here?"

"Yes," said Hurstwood uneasily, thinking of his handwriting on the register.

"Going to be in town long?"

"No, only a day or so."

"Is that so? Had your breakfast?"

"Yes," said Hurstwood, lying blandly. "I'm just going for a shave."

"Won't you come have a drink?"

"Not until afterward," said the ex-manager. "I'll see you later. Are you stopping here?"

"Yes," said Mr. Kenny, and then, turning the word again, added: "How are things out in Chicago?"

"About the same as usual," said Hurstwood, smiling genially.

"Wife with you?"

"No."

"Well, I must see more of you today. I'm just going in here for breakfast. Come in when you're through."

"I will," said Hurstwood, moving away. The whole conversation was a trial to him. It seemed to add complications with every word. This man called up a thousand memories. He represented everything he had left. Chicago, his wife, the elegant resort—all these were in his greeting and inquiries. And here he was in this same hotel expecting to confer with him, unquestionably waiting to have a good time with him. All at once the Chicago papers would arrive. The local papers would have accounts in them this very day. He forgot his triumph with Carrie in the possibility of soon being known for what he was, in this man's eyes, a safe-breaker. He could have groaned as he went into the barber shop. He decided to escape and seek a more secluded hotel.

► *Why does Hurstwood decide to seek a more secluded hotel?*

Accordingly, when he came out he was glad to see the lobby clear, and hastened toward the stairs. He would get Carrie and go out by the ladies' entrance. They would have breakfast in some more inconspicuous place.

Across the lobby, however, another individual was surveying him. He was of a commonplace Irish type, small of stature, cheaply dressed, and with a head that seemed a smaller edition of some huge ward politician's. This individual had been evidently talking with the clerk, but now he surveyed the ex-manager keenly.

◄ What does Hurstwood think when he notices this individual?

Hurstwood felt the long-range examination and recognized the type. Instinctively he felt that the man was a detective—that he was being watched. He hurried across, pretending not to notice, but in his mind was a world of thoughts. What would happen now? What could these people do? He began to trouble concerning the extradition[3] laws. He did not understand them absolutely. Perhaps he could be arrested. Oh, if Carrie should find out! Montreal was too warm for him. He began to long to be out of it.

Carrie had bathed and was waiting when he arrived. She looked refreshed—more delightful than ever, but reserved. Since he had gone she had resumed somewhat of her cold attitude toward him. Love was not blazing in her heart. He felt it, and his troubles seemed increased. He could not take her in his arms; he did not even try. Something about her forbade it. In part his opinion was the result of his own experiences and reflections below stairs.

◄ In what way has Carrie's attitude changed when Hurstwood returns? How have Hurstwood's "experiences and reflections below stairs" affected his perception?

"You're ready, are you?" he said kindly.

"Yes," she answered.

"We'll go out for breakfast. This place down here doesn't appeal to me very much."

"All right," said Carrie.

They went out, and at the corner the commonplace Irish individual was standing, eyeing him. Hurstwood could scarcely refrain from showing that he knew of this chap's presence. The insolence in the fellow's eye was galling. Still they passed, and he explained to Carrie concerning the city. Another restaurant was not long in showing itself, and here they entered.

"What a queer town this is," said Carrie, who marveled at it solely because it was not like Chicago.

"It isn't as lively as Chicago," said Hurstwood. "Don't you like it?"

3. **extradition.** Transfer of a criminal for prosecution from place of capture to place where the crime was committed

Words For Everyday Use

stat • ure (stach´ər) *n.,* height of a person

in • so • lence (in´sə ləns) *n.,* disrespect

"No," said Carrie, whose feelings were already localized in the great Western city.

"Well, it isn't as interesting," said Hurstwood.

"What's here?" asked Carrie, wondering at his choosing to visit this town.

"Nothing much," returned Hurstwood. "It's quite a resort. There's some pretty scenery about here."

Carrie listened, but with a feeling of unrest. There was much about her situation which destroyed the possibility of appreciation.

"We won't stay here long," said Hurstwood, who was now really glad to note her dissatisfaction. "You pick out your clothes as soon as breakfast is over and we'll run down to New York soon. You'll like that. It's a lot more like a city than any place outside Chicago."

► Why does Hurstwood wish to go to New York?

He was really planning to slip out and away. He would see what these detectives would do—what move his employers at Chicago would make—then he would slip away—down to New York, where it was easy to hide. He knew enough about that city to know that its mysteries and possibilities of mystification were infinite.

The more he thought, however, the more wretched his situation became. He saw that getting here did not exactly clear up the ground. The firm would probably employ detectives to watch him—Pinkerton men or agents of Mooney and Boland. They might arrest him the moment he tried to leave Canada. So he might be compelled to remain here months, and in what a state!

Back at the hotel Hurstwood was anxious and yet fearful to see the morning papers. He wanted to know how far the news of his criminal deed had spread. So he told Carrie he would be up in a few moments, and went to secure and scan the dailies. No familiar or suspicious faces were about, and yet he did not like reading in the lobby, so he sought the main parlor on the floor above and, seated by a window there, looked them over. Very little was given to his crime, but it was there, several "sticks" in all, among all the riffraff of telegraphed murders, accidents, marriages, and other news. He wished, half sadly, that he could undo it all. Every moment of his time in this far-off abode of safety but added to his feeling that he had made a great mistake. There could have been an easier way out if he had only known.

Words For Everyday Use

riff • raff (rif´ raf) *n.,* rubbish; trash

a • bode (ə bōd´) *n.,* residence; home

He left the papers before going to the room, thinking thus to keep them out of the hands of Carrie.

"Well, how are you feeling?" he asked of her. She was engaged in looking out of the window.

"Oh, all right," she answered.

He came over, and was about to begin a conversation with her, when a knock came at their door.

"Maybe it's one of my parcels," said Carrie.

Hurstwood opened the door, outside of which stood the individual whom he had so thoroughly suspected.

"You're Mr. Hurstwood, are you?" said the latter, with a volume of affected shrewdness and assurance.

"Yes," said Hurstwood calmly. He knew the type so thoroughly that some of his old familiar indifference to it returned. Such men as these were of the lowest stratum welcomed at the resort. He stepped out and closed the door.

"Well, you know what I am here for, don't you?" said the man confidentially.

"I can guess," said Hurstwood softly.

◄ *What does the detective wish to know? What threats does the detective make?*

"Well, do you intend to try and keep the money?"

"That's my affair," said Hurstwood grimly.

"You can't do it, you know," said the detective, eyeing him coolly.

"Look here, my man," said Hurstwood authoritatively, "you don't understand anything about this case, and I can't explain to you. Whatever I intend to do I'll do without advice from the outside. You'll have to excuse me."

"Well, now, there's no use of your talking that way," said the man, "when you're in the hands of the police. We can make a lot of trouble for you if we want to. You're not registered right in this house, you haven't got your wife with you, and the newspapers don't know you're here yet. You might as well be reasonable."

"What do you want to know?" asked Hurstwood.

"Whether you're going to send back that money or not."

Hurstwood paused and studied the floor.

"There's no use explaining to you about this," he said at last. "There's no use of your asking me. I'm no fool, you know. I know just what you can do and what you can't. You can create a lot of trouble if you want to. I know that all right, but it won't help you to get the money. Now, I've made

Words For Everyday Use

stra • tum (strāt´əm) *n.,* level

up my mind what to do. I've already written Fitzgerald and Moy, so there's nothing I can say. You wait until you hear more from them."

All the time he had been talking he had been moving away from the door, down the corridor, out of the hearing of Carrie. They were now near the end where the corridor opened into the large general parlor.

"You won't give it up?" said the man.

The words irritated Hurstwood greatly. Hot blood poured into his brain. Many thoughts formulated themselves. He was no thief. He didn't want the money. If he could only explain to Fitzgerald and Moy, maybe it would be all right again.

"See here," he said, "there's no use my talking about this at all. I respect your power all right, but I'll have to deal with the people who know."

"Well, you can't get out of Canada with it," said the man.

"I don't want to get out," said Hurstwood. "When I get ready there'll be nothing to stop me for."

He turned back, and the detective watched him closely. It seemed an intolerable thing. Still he went on and into the room.

"Who was it?" asked Carrie.

"A friend of mine from Chicago."

The whole of this conversation was such a shock that, coming as it did after all the other worry of the past week, it sufficed to induce a deep gloom and moral revulsion in Hurstwood. What hurt him most was the fact that he was being pursued as a thief. He began to see the nature of that social injustice which sees but one side—often but a single point in a long tragedy. All the newspapers noted but one thing, his taking the money. How and wherefore were but indifferently dealt with. All the complications which led up to it were unknown. He was accused without being understood.

► *What upsets Hurstwood about his situation? Explain whether his feelings are justifiable.*

Sitting in his room with Carrie the same day, he decided to send the money back. He would write Fitzgerald and Moy, explain all, and then send it by express. Maybe they would forgive him. Perhaps they would ask him back. He would make good the false statement he had made about writing them. Then he would leave this peculiar town.

► *What does Hurstwood decide to do?*

For an hour he thought over this plausible statement of the tangle. He wanted to tell them about his wife, but couldn't. He finally narrowed it down to an assertion that he was light-headed from entertaining friends, had found the safe open, and having gone so far as to take the money out, had accidentally closed it. This act he regretted very much. He was sorry he had put them to so much trouble. He would undo

► *What does Hurstwood admit in the letter?*

what he could by sending the money back—the major portion of it. The remainder he would pay up as soon as he could. Was there any possibility of his being restored? This he only hinted at.

The troubled state of the man's mind may be judged by the very construction of this letter. For the nonce he forgot what a painful thing it would be to resume his old place, even if it were given him. He forgot that he had severed himself from the past as by a sword, and that if he did manage to in some way reunite himself with it, the jagged line of separation and reunion would always show. He was always forgetting something—his wife, Carrie, his need of money, present situation, or something—and so did not reason clearly. Nevertheless, he sent the letter, waiting a reply before sending the money.

◄ What important fact has Hurstwood forgotten in writing the letter?

Meanwhile, he accepted his present situation with Carrie, getting what joy out of it he could.

Out came the sun by noon, and poured a golden flood through their open windows. Sparrows were twittering. There were laughter and song in the air. Hurstwood could not keep his eyes from Carrie. She seemed the one ray of sunshine in all his trouble. Oh, if she would only love him wholly—only throw her arms around him in the blissful spirit in which he had seen her in the little park in Chicago—how happy he would be! It would repay him; it would show him that he had not lost all. He would not care.

"Carrie," he said, getting up once and coming over to her, "are you going to stay with me from now on?"

She looked at him quizzically, but melted with sympathy as the value of the look upon his face forced itself upon her. It was love now, keen and strong—love enhanced by difficulty and worry. She could not help smiling.

"Let me be everything to you from now on," he said. "Don't make me worry anymore. I'll be true to you. We'll go to New York and get a nice flat. I'll go into business again, and we'll be happy. Won't you be mine?"

Carrie listened quite solemnly. There was no great passion in her, but the drift of things and this man's proximity created a semblance of affection. She felt rather sorry for him—a sorrow born of what had only recently been a great admiration. True love she had never felt for him. She would have known as much if she could have analyzed her feelings, but

◄ What does Carrie feel for Hurstwood rather than love?

Words For Everyday Use

sev • er (sev´ər) *vt.,* separate

prox • i • mi • ty (präks im´ə tē) *n.,* nearness

this thing which she now felt aroused by his great feeling broke down the barriers between them.

"You'll stay with me, won't you?" he asked.

"Yes," she said, nodding her head.

He gathered her to himself, imprinting kisses upon her lips and cheeks.

▶ *How does Hurstwood marry Carrie?*

"You must marry me, though," she said.

"I'll get a license today," he answered.

"How?" she asked.

"Under a new name," he answered. "I'll take a new name and live a new life. From now on I'm Murdock."

"Oh, don't take that name," said Carrie.

"Why not?" he said.

"I don't like it."

"Well, what shall I take?" he asked.

"Oh, anything, only don't take that."

He thought a while, still keeping his arms about her, and then said:

"How would Wheeler do?"

"That's all right," said Carrie.

"Well, then, Wheeler," he said. "I'll get the license this afternoon."

They were married by a Baptist minister, the first divine they found convenient.

▶ *What does Hurstwood's firm want from him? Do they have any plans of giving him back his old job? How much of the money does Hurstwood keep?*

At last the Chicago firm answered. It was by Mr. Moy's dictation. He was astonished that Hurstwood had done this; very sorry that it had come about as it had. If the money were returned, they would not trouble to prosecute him, as they really bore him no ill will. As for his returning, or their restoring him to his former position, they had not quite decided what the effect of it would be. They would think it over and correspond with him later, possibly, after a little time, and so on.

The sum and substance of it was that there was no hope, and they wanted the money with the least trouble possible. Hurstwood read his doom. He decided to pay $9,500 to the agent whom they said they would send, keeping $1,300 for his own use. He telegraphed his acquiescence, explained to the representative who called at the hotel the same day, took a certificate of payment, and told Carrie to pack her trunk. He was slightly depressed over this newest move at the time he began to make it, but eventually restored himself. He feared that even yet he might be seized and taken back, so he tried to conceal his movements, but it was scarcely possible. He ordered Carrie's trunk sent to the depot, where he had it sent by express to New York. No one seemed to be observing him, but he left at night. He was greatly agitated lest at the first station across the border or at the depot in New York there should be waiting for him an officer of the law.

Carrie, ignorant of his theft and his fears, enjoyed the entry into the latter city in the morning. The round green hills sentineling the broad, expansive bosom of the Hudson held her attention by their beauty as the train followed the line of the stream. She had heard of the Hudson River, the great city of New York, and now she looked out, filling her mind with the wonder of it.

◄ What mental state is Hurstwood in as they enter New York? How does Carrie feel as they enter the city?

As the train turned east at Spuyten Duyvil[4] and followed the east bank of the Harlem River, Hurstwood nervously called her attention to the fact that they were on the edge of the city. After her experience with Chicago, she expected long lines of cars—a great highway of tracks—and noted the difference. The sight of a few boats in the Harlem and more in the East River tickled her young heart. It was the first sign of the great sea. Next came a plain street with five-story brick flats, and then the train plunged into the tunnel.

"Grand Central Station!" called the trainman, as, after a few minutes of darkness and smoke, daylight reappeared. Hurstwood arose and gathered up his small grip. He was screwed up to the highest tension. With Carrie he waited at the door and then dismounted. No one approached him, but he glanced furtively to and fro as he made for the street entrance. So excited was he that he forgot all about Carrie, who fell behind, wondering at his self-absorption. As he passed through the depot proper the strain reached its climax and began to wane. All at once he was on the sidewalk, and none but cabmen hailed him. He heaved a great breath and turned, remembering Carrie.

"I thought you were going to run off and leave me," she said.

"I was trying to remember which car takes us to the Gilsey," he answered.

Carrie hardly heard him, so interested was she in the busy scene.

"How large is New York?" she asked.

"Oh, a million or more,"[5] said Hurstwood.

---

4. **Spuyten Duyvil.** Canal connecting the Hudson and Harlem rivers
5. **a million or more.** The official census of 1890 for New York City was a million and a half.

Words For Everyday Use

sen • ti • nel (sen´ti nəl) *vt.,* guard

self- • ab • sorp • tion (self-ab sôrp´shən) *n.,* preoccupation with one's own affairs or interests

► *What disagreeable thought enters Hurstwood's mind?*

He looked around and hailed a cab, but he did so in a changed way.

For the first time in years the thought that he must count these little expenses flashed through his mind. It was a disagreeable thing.

He decided he would lose no time living in hotels but would rent a flat. Accordingly he told Carrie, and she agreed.

"We'll look today, if you want to," she said.

Suddenly he thought of his experience in Montreal. At the more important hotels he would be certain to meet Chicagoans whom he knew. He stood up and spoke to the driver.

"Take me to the Belford," he said, knowing it to be less frequented by those whom he knew. Then he sat down.

"Where is the residence part?" asked Carrie, who did not take the tall five-story walls on either hand to be the abodes of families.

"Everywhere," said Hurstwood, who knew the city fairly well. "There are no lawns in New York. All these are houses."

► *What is Carrie's opinion of the residences in New York? In what way is she changing?*

"Well, then, I don't like it," said Carrie, who was coming to have a few opinions of her own.

CHAPTER 30

The Kingdom of Greatness: The Pilgrim Adream

Whatever a man like Hurstwood could be in Chicago, it is very evident that he would be but an inconspicuous drop in an ocean like New York. In Chicago, whose population still ranged about 500,000, millionaires were not numerous. The rich had not become so conspicuously rich as to drown all moderate incomes in obscurity. The attention of the inhabitants was not so distracted by local celebrities in the dramatic, artistic, social, and religious fields as to shut the well-positioned man from view. In Chicago the two roads to distinction were politics and trade. In New York the roads were any one of a half-hundred, and each had been diligently pursued by hundreds, so that celebrities were numerous. The sea was already full of whales. A common fish must needs disappear wholly from view—remain unseen. In other words, Hurstwood was nothing.

◄ *Explain why Hurstwood's position in New York is much different from his position in Chicago.*

There is a more subtle result of such a situation as this, which, though not always taken into account, produces the tragedies of the world. The great create an atmosphere which reacts badly upon the small. This atmosphere is easily and quickly felt. Walk among the magnificent residences, the splendid equipages,[1] the gilded shops, restaurants, resorts of all kinds; scent the flowers, the silks, the wines; drink of the laughter springing from the soul of luxurious content, of the glances which gleam like light from defiant spears; feel the quality of the smiles which cut like glistening swords and of strides born of place, and you shall know of what is the atmosphere of the high and mighty. Little use to argue that of such is not the kingdom of greatness, but so long as the world is attracted by this and the human heart views this as the one desirable realm which it must attain, so long, to that heart, will this remain the realm of greatness. So long, also, will the atmosphere of this realm work its desperate results in the soul of man. It is like a chemical reagent.[2] One day of it, like one drop of the other, will so affect and discolor the views, the aims, the desire of the mind, that it will thereafter remain forever dyed. A day of it

◄ *According to the narrator, what does the atmosphere of the great produce?*

1. **equipages.** Horse-drawn carriages with uniformed servants
2. **reagent.** Chemical substance that causes change in another substance

Words For Everyday Use

realm (relm) *n.,* region; kingdom

▶ *In what way does the atmosphere of the great lead to ruin?*

▶ *What strength in such an atmosphere does Hurstwood lack? Why does he lack this quality?*

to the untried mind is like opium[3] to the untried body. A craving is set up which, if gratified, shall eternally result in dreams and death. Aye! dreams unfulfilled—gnawing, luring, idle phantoms which beckon and lead, beckon and lead, until death and dissolution dissolve their power and restore us blind to nature's heart.

A man of Hurstwood's age and temperament is not subject to the illusions and burning desires of youth, but neither has he the strength of hope which gushes as a fountain in the heart of youth. Such an atmosphere could not incite in him the cravings of a boy of eighteen, but in so far as they were excited, the lack of hope made them proportionately bitter. He could not fail to notice the signs of affluence and luxury on every hand. He had been to New York before and knew the resources of its folly. In part it was an awesome place to him, for here gathered all that he most respected on this earth—wealth, place, and fame. The majority of the celebrities with whom he had tipped glasses in his day as manager hailed from this self-centered and populous spot. The most inviting stories of pleasure and luxury had been told of places and individuals here. He knew it to be true that unconsciously he was brushing elbows with fortune the livelong day; that a hundred or five hundred thousand gave no one the privilege of living more than comfortably in so wealthy a place. Fashion and pomp[4] required more ample sums, so that the poor man was nowhere. All this he realized, now quite sharply, as he faced the city, cut off from his friends, despoiled of his modest fortune, and even his name, and forced to begin the battle for place and comfort all over again. He was not old, but he was not so dull but that he could feel he soon would be. Of a sudden, then, this show of fine clothes, place, and power took on peculiar significance. It was emphasized by contrast with his own distressing state.

And it was distressing. He soon found that freedom from fear of arrest was not the *sine qua non*[5] of his existence. That danger dissolved, the next necessity became the grievous thing. The paltry sum of thirteen hundred and some odd

3. **opium.** Addictive narcotic drug extracted from the juice of the opium poppy
4. **pomp.** Showy display
5. ***sine qua non.*** "Without which, nothing"; Latin phrase indicating an essential element or condition

Words For Everyday Use

de • spoil (dē spoil´) *vt.,* rob; deprive
pal • try (pôl´trē) *adj.,* practically worthless

dollars set against the need of rent, clothing, food, and pleasure for years to come was a spectacle little calculated to induce peace of mind in one who had been accustomed to spend five times that sum in the course of a year. He thought upon the subject rather actively the first few days he was in New York, and decided that he must act quickly. As a consequence, he consulted the business opportunities advertised in the morning papers and began investigations on his own account.

◄ *Why does the amount of money Hurstwood has strike him as pitifully small?*

That was not before he had become settled, however. Carrie and he went looking for a flat, as arranged, and found one in Seventy-eighth Street near Amsterdam Avenue. It was a five-story building, and their flat was on the third floor. Owing to the fact that the street was not yet built up solidly, it was possible to see east to the green tops of the trees in Central Park and west to the broad waters of the Hudson, a glimpse of which was to be had out of the west windows. For the privilege of six rooms and a bath, running in a straight line, they were compelled to pay thirty-five dollars a month—an average, and yet exorbitant, rent for a home at the time. Carrie noticed the difference between the size of the rooms here and in Chicago and mentioned it.

◄ *How much is an "exorbitant" rent in this period?*

"You'll not find anything better, dear," said Hurstwood, "unless you go into one of the old-fashioned houses, and then you won't have any of these conveniences."

Carrie picked out the new abode because of its newness and bright woodwork. It was one of the very new ones supplied with steam heat, which was a great advantage. The stationary range, hot and cold water, dumbwaiter, speaking tubes,[6] and call-bell for the janitor pleased her very much. She had enough of the instincts of a housewife to take great satisfaction in these things.

◄ *What "modern" advantages does this apartment offer?*

Hurstwood made arrangement with one of the installment houses whereby they furnished the flat complete and accepted fifty dollars down and ten dollars a month. He then had a little plate, bearing the name G. W. Wheeler, made, which he placed on his letter box in the hall. It sounded exceedingly odd to Carrie to be called Mrs. Wheeler by the

6. **stationary range . . . speaking tubes.** Among the amenities of Carrie's new home were a stove fixed in one place, hot and cold running water, a small elevator for moving food from floor to floor, and a tube that allowed her to speak to people in other rooms in the building.

Words For Everyday Use

ex • or • bi • tant (eg zor´bi tənt) *adj.*, exceedingly expensive

janitor, but in time she became used to it and looked upon the name as her own.

These house details settled, Hurstwood visited some of the advertised opportunities to purchase an interest in some flourishing downtown bar. After the palatial resort in Adams Street, he could not stomach the commonplace saloons which he found advertised. He lost a number of days looking up these and finding them disagreeable. He did, however, gain considerable knowledge by talking, for he discovered the influence of Tammany Hall[7] and the value of standing in with the police. The most profitable and flourishing places he found to be those which conducted anything but a legitimate business, such as that controlled by Fitzgerald and Moy. Elegant back rooms and private drinking booths on the second floor were usually adjuncts of very profitable places. He saw by portly keepers, whose shirt fronts shone with large diamonds, and whose clothes were properly cut, that the liquor business here, as elsewhere, yielded the same golden profit.

► *In New York, which are the most prosperous resorts?*

At last he found an individual who had a resort in Warren Street, which seemed an excellent venture. It was fairly well-appearing and susceptible of improvement. The owner claimed the business to be excellent, and it certainly looked so.

"We deal with a very good class of people," he told Hurstwood. "Merchants, salesmen, and professionals. It's a well-dressed class. No bums. We don't allow 'em in the place."

Hurstwood listened to the cash register ring, and watched the trade for a while.

"It's profitable enough for two, is it?" he asked.

"You can see for yourself if you're any judge of the liquor trade," said the owner. "This is only one of the two places I have. The other is down in Nassau Street. I can't tend to them both alone. If I had someone who knew the business thoroughly I wouldn't mind sharing with him in this one and letting him manage it."

"I've had experience enough," said Hurstwood blandly, but he felt a little diffident about referring to Fitzgerald and Moy.

"Well, you can suit yourself, Mr. Wheeler," said the proprietor.

7. **Tammany Hall.** Powerful Democratic political organization of New York City

Words For Everyday Use

pa • la • tial (pə lā´shəl) *adj.*, large and magnificent
flour • ish • ing (flʉr´ish iŋ) *adj.*, thriving; succeeding
ad • junct (a´ juŋkt´) *n.*, addition
pro • pri • e • tor (prō prī´ə tər) *n.*, owner

He only offered a third interest in the stock, fixtures, and goodwill, and this in return for a thousand dollars and managerial ability on the part of the one who should come in. There was no property involved, because the owner of the saloon merely rented from an estate.

The offer was genuine enough, but it was a question with Hurstwood whether a third interest in that locality could be made to yield one hundred and fifty dollars a month, which he figured he must have in order to meet the ordinary family expenses and be comfortable. It was not the time, however, after many failures to find what he wanted, to hesitate. It looked as though a third would pay a hundred a month now. By judicious management and improvement, it might be made to pay more. Accordingly he agreed to enter into partnership, and made over his thousand dollars, preparing to enter the next day.

◄ *What concern does Hurstwood have about this business opportunity?*

His first inclination was to be elated, and he confided to Carrie that he thought he had made an excellent arrangement. Time, however, introduced food for reflection. He found his partner to be very disagreeable. Frequently he was the worse for liquor, which made him surly. This was the last thing which Hurstwood was used to in business. Besides, the business varied. It was nothing like the class of patronage which he had enjoyed in Chicago. He found that it would take a long time to make friends. These people hurried in and out without seeking the pleasures of friendship. It was no gathering or lounging place. Whole days and weeks passed, without one such hearty greeting as he had been wont to enjoy every day in Chicago.

◄ *In what way does this resort differ from Fitzgerald and Moy's?*

For another thing, Hurstwood missed the celebrities—those well-dressed, *élite*[8] individuals who lend grace to the average bars and bring news from far-off and exclusive circles. He did not see one such in a month. Evenings, when still at his post, he would occasionally read in the evening papers incidents concerning celebrities whom he knew—whom he had drunk a glass with many a time. They would visit a bar like Fitzgerald and Moy's in Chicago, or the Hoffman House, uptown, but he knew that he would never see them down here.

◄ *What does Hurstwood miss?*

8. ***élite.*** Most distinguished; finest

Words For Everyday Use

ju • di • cious (jo͞o dish´əs) *adj.*, wise and careful

in • cli • na • tion (in´klə nā´shən) *n.*, tendency

e • la • ted (ē lā´təd) *adj.*, joyful

sur • ly (sʉr´lē) *adj.*, bad-tempered

pa • tron • age (pā´trən ij) *n.*, clientele

► *What humiliation does Hurstwood experience?*

Again, the business did not pay as well as he thought. It increased a little, but he found he would have to watch his household expenses, which was humiliating.

► *How does Hurstwood feel about his home situation at first? What soon begins to happen?*

In the very beginning it was a delight to go home late at night, as he did, and find Carrie. He managed to run up and take dinner with her between six and seven, and to remain home until nine o'clock in the morning, but the novelty of this waned after a time, and he began to feel the drag of his duties.

The first month had scarcely passed before Carrie said in a very natural way: "I think I'll go down this week and buy a dress."

"What kind?" said Hurstwood.

"Oh, something for street wear."

"All right," he answered, smiling, although he noted mentally that it would be more agreeable to his finances if she didn't. Nothing was said about it the next day, but the following morning he asked:

"Have you done anything about your dress?"

"Not yet," said Carrie.

He paused a few moments, as if in thought, and then said:

► *What does Hurstwood ask Carrie to do? Of what does this remind her? In what way does it change her opinion of Hurstwood?*

"Would you mind putting it off a few days?"

"No," replied Carrie, who did not catch the drift of his remarks. She had never thought of him in connection with money troubles before. "Why?"

"Well, I'll tell you," said Hurstwood. "This investment of mine is taking a lot of money just now. I expect to get it all back shortly, but just at present I am running close."

"Oh!" answered Carrie. "Why, certainly, dear. Why didn't you tell me before?"

"It wasn't necessary," said Hurstwood.

For all her acquiescence, there was something about the way Hurstwood spoke which reminded Carrie of Drouet and his little deal which he was always about to put through. It was only the thought of a second, but it was a beginning. It was something new in her thinking of Hurstwood.

► *What troubling signs does Carrie notice?*

Other things followed from time to time, little things of the same sort, which in their cumulative effect were eventually equal to a full revelation. Carrie was not dull by any means. Two persons cannot long dwell together without coming to an understanding of one another. The mental difficulties of an individual reveal themselves whether he voluntarily confesses them or not. Trouble gets in the air and contributes gloom, which speaks for itself. Hurstwood dressed as nicely as usual, but they were the same clothes he had in Canada. Carrie noticed that he did not install a large wardrobe, though his own was anything but large. She noticed, also, that he did not suggest many amusements, said nothing about the food, seemed concerned about his business. This was not the easy Hurstwood of Chicago—not the liberal, opulent Hurstwood she had known. The change was too obvious to escape detection.

In time she began to feel that a change had come about, and that she was not in his confidence. He was evidently secretive and kept his own counsel. She found herself asking him questions about little things. This is a disagreeable state to a woman. Great love makes it seem reasonable, sometimes plausible, but never satisfactory. Where great love is not, a more definite and less satisfactory conclusion is reached.

As for Hurstwood, he was making a great fight against the difficulties of a changed condition. He was too shrewd not to realize the tremendous mistake he had made, and appreciate that he had done well in getting where he was, and yet he could not help contrasting his present state with his former, hour after hour, and day after day.

Besides, he had the disagreeable fear of meeting old-time friends, ever since one such encounter which he made shortly after his arrival in the city. It was in Broadway[9] that he saw a man approaching him whom he knew. There was no time for simulating nonrecognition. The exchange of glances had been too sharp, the knowledge of each other too apparent. So the friend, a buyer for one of the Chicago wholesale houses, felt, perforce, the necessity of stopping.

"How are you?" he said, extending his hand with an evident mixture of feeling and a lack of plausible interest.

"Very well," said Hurstwood, equally embarrassed. "How is it with you?"

"All right; I'm down here doing a little buying. Are you located here now?"

"Yes," said Hurstwood, "I have a place down in Warren Street."

"Is that so?" said the friend. "Glad to hear it. I'll come down and see you."

"Do," said Hurstwood.

"So long," said the other, smiling affably and going on.

"He never asked for my number," thought Hurstwood; "he wouldn't think of coming." He wiped his forehead,

◄ *How can Hurstwood tell that his former friend isn't planning to visit him? Why won't his former friend even "think of coming"?*

9. **Broadway.** Important street in New York City; center of the city's theater district

Words For Everyday Use

plau • si • ble (plô´zə bəl) *adj.*, acceptable

per • force (pər fôrs´) *adv.*, by or through necessity

which had grown damp, and hoped sincerely he would meet no one else.

► *What assumption is Hurstwood making about his and Carrie's relationship? What does he fail to "take account of"?*

These things told upon his good nature, such as it was. His one hope was that things would change for the better in a money way. He had Carrie. His furniture was being paid for. He was maintaining his position. As for Carrie, the amusements he could give her would have to do for the present. He could probably keep up his pretensions sufficiently long without exposure to make good, and then all would be well. He failed therein to take account of the frailties of human nature—the difficulties of matrimonial life. Carrie was young. With him and with her varying mental states were common. At any moment the extremes of feeling might be antipolarized[10] at the dinner table. This often happens in the best regulated families. Little things brought out on such occasions need great love to obliterate them afterward. Where that is not, both parties count two and two and make a problem after a while.

10. **antipolarized.** Present in direct opposition

Words For Everyday Use

frail • ty (frāl´tē) *n.*, weakness

ob • lit • er • ate (ə blit´ər āt´) *vt.*, do away with

Responding to the Selection

Imagine either that you are Hurstwood after he locks the money out of the safe or that you are Carrie when she learns that Hurstwood is taking her away from Chicago. Explain how you would handle the situation if you were in one of these positions. What would you do similarly? differently?

Reviewing the Selection

Recalling and Interpreting

1. **R:** In chapter 25, from whom does Hurstwood receive two letters? What do these letters say? What does Hurstwood begin to wonder about Carrie?

2. **I:** What thoughts keep intruding whenever Hurstwood dwells on his family situation? Although days pass in chapter 25, Hurstwood can barely make up his mind to send his wife the money she requested and can make no decision on what he should do about the letters. Why does he avoid rather than deal with his difficulties? In what way do difficulties and stress seem to affect Hurstwood as a character?

3. **R:** What concerns does Carrie have once Drouet leaves? To whom doesn't she plan to turn for help? What becomes most significant to Carrie? What happens when she goes to look for work at the department stores? at the theaters?

4. **I:** Explain whether Drouet has given up Carrie altogether. Explain whether Carrie seems serious about looking for work. Is she serious about pursuing the theater? Evaluate how independent Carrie is. What factors contributed to her lack of development in this way?

5. **R:** In chapter 27, what crime does Hurstwood commit? Where does he decide to go? What lie does he tell Carrie to convince her to go with him? How does Carrie feel when she first learns of Hurstwood's deception? In chapter 29, with what mixed feelings does Carrie regard Hurstwood in Montreal? What does Hurstwood eventually do with the money? Under what name do Hurstwood and Carrie marry? What is Carrie's initial opinion of New York?

6. **I:** Why does Hurstwood commit this crime? Why doesn't Carrie act on her feelings and leave Hurstwood? Explain whether, given Carrie's feelings, her marriage to Hurstwood is a good decision. Explain whether you think their marriage is legitimate.

7. **R:** In what way is Hurstwood's social position in New York different from the one he held in Chicago? In what way is his new place of employment different from his former

one? How does he feel about his relationship with Carrie at first? What threatens to become an issue in their relationship?

8. **I:** In what way might the atmosphere of New York, as described by the narrator, affect Hurstwood adversely? What quality necessary for success in this city does he lack? Explain the way Hurstwood's values and his view of love are changing. What does he think of his crime now? What does he realize should have been, perhaps, more important to him than love?

Synthesizing

9. Are the decisions that the characters make in chapters 25–30 the result of carefully thought out plans or are they whims? Find some examples to support your opinion. What do you think Dreiser may be indicating about humans in general? about chance?

10. As you may have gathered from many of the events that occur in this chapter, the United States was very different one hundred years ago. For example, divorces were very rare and considered scandalous. Apartments could be rented for thirty-five dollars a month. People carried fewer forms of identification, and without fingerprints and other identifying information on computer, it was much easier for a person simply to assume a new name and disappear into society. If you wanted to "translate" Dreiser's tale for a contemporary audience, what details in chapters 25–30 would you alter? For example, what would you do to make the situation between Mr. and Mrs. Hurstwood and Carrie seem more scandalous to a contemporary audience? What modern difficulties might Hurstwood experience once he commits his crime? What would a modern woman do if she found herself in a position similar to Carrie's?

Understanding Literature (QUESTIONS FOR DISCUSSION)

1. Foreshadowing. Foreshadowing is the act of presenting materials that hint at events to occur later in a story. In what way was Hurstwood's flight with Carrie foreshadowed in an earlier chapter? What events in these chapters may foreshadow what will happen to the relationship between Hurstwood and Carrie? What passages foreshadow potential financial difficulties for Hurstwood?

2. Crisis. In the plot of a story or drama, the **crisis** is that point in the development of the conflict at which a decisive event occurs, causing the main character's situation to become better or worse. What event in chapters 25–30 do you consider to be the crisis of this literary work? In what way is this decisive event likely to change the situations of the characters involved?

CHAPTER 31

A Pet of Good Fortune: Broadway Flaunts Its Joys

The effect of the city and his own situation on Hurstwood was paralleled in the case of Carrie, who accepted the things fortune provided with the most genial good nature. New York, despite her first expression of disapproval, soon interested her exceedingly. Its clear atmosphere, more populous thoroughfares, and peculiar indifference struck her forcibly. She had never seen such a little flat as hers, and yet it soon enlisted her affection. The new furniture made an excellent showing, the sideboard which Hurstwood himself arranged gleamed brightly. The furniture for each room was appropriate, and in the so-called parlor, or front room, was installed a piano, because Carrie said she would like to learn to play. She kept a servant and developed rapidly in household tactics and information. For the first time in her life she felt settled, and somewhat justified in the eyes of society as she conceived of it. Her thoughts were merry and innocent enough. For a long while she concerned herself over the arrangement of New York flats, and wondered at ten families living in one building and all remaining strange and indifferent to each other. She also marveled at the whistles of the hundreds of vessels in the harbor—the long, low cries of the Sound steamers and ferryboats when fog was on. The mere fact that these things spoke from the sea made them wonderful. She looked much at what she could see of the Hudson from her west windows and of the great city building up rapidly on either hand. It was much to ponder over, and sufficed to entertain her for more than a year without becoming stale.

◄ *What is the effect of the city on Carrie?*

◄ *How does Carrie feel for the first time in her life?*

For another thing, Hurstwood was exceedingly interesting in his affection for her. Troubled as he was, he never exposed his difficulties to her. He carried himself with the same self-important air, took his new state with easy familiarity, and rejoiced in Carrie's proclivities and successes. Each evening he arrived promptly to dinner, and found the little dining room a most inviting spectacle. In a way, the smallness of the room added to its luxury. It looked full and replete. The white-covered table was arrayed with pretty dishes and lighted with

◄ *What pleases Carrie about Hurstwood's behavior?*

Words For Everyday Use

pro • cliv • i • ty (prō kliv´ə tē) *n.,* taste

re • plete (rē plēt´) *adj.,* well-supplied

a four-armed candelabra, each light of which was topped with a red shade. Between Carrie and the girl the steaks and chops came out all right, and canned goods did the rest for a while. Carrie studied the art of making biscuit, and soon reached the stage where she could show a plate of light, palatable morsels for her labor.

In this manner the second, third, and fourth months passed. Winter came, and with it a feeling that indoors was best, so that the attending of theaters was not much talked of. Hurstwood made great efforts to meet all expenditures without a show of feeling one way or the other. He pretended that he was reinvesting his money in strengthening the business for greater ends in the future. He contented himself with a very moderate allowance of personal apparel, and rarely suggested anything for Carrie. Thus the first winter passed.

► *What image is Hurstwood trying hard to preserve?*

In the second year, the business which Hurstwood managed did increase somewhat. He got out of it regularly the $150 per month which he had anticipated. Unfortunately, by this time Carrie had reached certain conclusions, and he had scraped up a few acquaintances.

Being of a passive and receptive rather than an active and aggressive nature, Carrie accepted the situation. Her state seemed satisfactory enough. Once in a while they would go to a theater together, occasionally in season to the beaches and different points about the city, but they picked up no acquaintances. Hurstwood naturally abandoned his show of fine manners with her and modified his attitude to one of easy familiarity. There were no misunderstandings, no apparent differences of opinion. In fact, without money or visiting friends, he led a life which could neither arouse jealousy nor comment. Carrie rather sympathized with his efforts and thought nothing upon her lack of entertainment such as she had enjoyed in Chicago. New York as a corporate entity and her flat temporarily seemed sufficient.

► *In what way is life with Hurstwood different than Carrie expected? Why doesn't she complain?*

However, as Hurstwood's business increased, he, as stated, began to pick up acquaintances. He also began to allow himself more clothes. He convinced himself that his home life was very precious to him, but allowed that he could occasionally stay away from dinner. The first time he did this he sent a message saying that he would be detained. Carrie ate alone, and wished that it might not happen again. The second

► *What does Hurstwood begin to do?*

Words For Everyday Use

pal • at • a • ble (pal´ə tə bəl) *adj.*, fit to be eaten

de • tain (dē tān´) *vt.*, keep late

time, also, he sent word, but at the last moment. The third time he forgot entirely and explained afterward. These events were months apart, each.

"Where were you, George?" asked Carrie, after the first absence.

"Tied up at the office," he said genially. "There were some accounts I had to straighten."

"I'm sorry you couldn't get home," she said kindly. "I was fixing to have such a nice dinner."

The second time he gave a similar excuse, but the third time the feeling about it in Carrie's mind was a little bit out of the ordinary.

"I couldn't get home," he said, when he came in later in the evening, "I was so busy."

"Couldn't you have sent me word?" asked Carrie.

"I meant to," he said, "but you know I forgot it until it was too late to do any good."

"And I had such a good dinner!" said Carrie.

Now, it so happened that from his observations of Carrie he began to imagine that she was of the thoroughly domestic type of mind. He really thought, after a year, that her chief expression in life was finding its natural channel in household duties. Notwithstanding the fact that he had observed her act in Chicago, and that during the past year he had only seen her limited in her relations to her flat and him by conditions which he made, and that she had not gained any friends or associates, he drew this peculiar conclusion. With it came a feeling of satisfaction in having a wife who could thus be content, and this satisfaction worked its natural result. That is, since he imagined he saw her satisfied, he felt called upon to give only that which contributed to such satisfaction. He supplied the furniture, the decorations, the food, and the necessary clothing. Thoughts of entertaining her, leading her out into the shine and show of life, grew less and less. He felt attracted to the outer world, but did not think she would care to go along. Once he went to the theater alone. Another time he joined a couple of his new friends at an evening game of poker. Since his money-feathers were beginning to grow again he felt like sprucing about.[1] All this,

◄ *In what way does Hurstwood misread Carrie? With what does he imagine she is content?*

◄ *What activity does Hurstwood no longer consider? What does he himself do?*

1. **sprucing about.** Socializing

Words For Everyday Use

chan • nel (chan´əl) *n.,* course; route

however, in a much less imposing way than had been his wont in Chicago. He avoided the gay places where he would be apt to meet those who had known him.

► *Why should Hurstwood have "duly considered" Carrie's "placid" manner?*

Now, Carrie began to feel this in various sensory ways. She was not the kind to be seriously disturbed by his actions. Not loving him greatly, she could not be jealous in a disturbing way. In fact, she was not jealous at all. Hurstwood was pleased with her placid manner, when he should have duly considered it. When he did not come home it did not seem anything like a terrible thing to her. She gave him credit for having the usual allurements of men—people to talk to, places to stop, friends to consult with. She was perfectly willing that he should enjoy himself in his way, but she did not care to be neglected herself. Her state still seemed fairly reasonable, however. All she did observe was that Hurstwood was somewhat different.

► *What is the only reason Carrie meets her new neighbors?*

Sometime in the second year of their residence in Seventy-eighth Street the flat across the hall from Carrie became vacant, and into it moved a very handsome young woman and her husband, with both of whom Carrie afterward became acquainted. This was brought about solely by the arrangement of the flats, which were united in one place, as it were, by the dumbwaiter. This useful elevator, by which fuel, groceries, and the like were sent up from the basement, and garbage and waste sent down, was used by both residents on one floor; that is, a small door opened into it from each flat.

If the occupants of both flats answered to the whistle of the janitor at the same time, they would stand face to face when they opened the dumbwaiter doors. One morning, when Carrie went to remove her paper, the newcomer, a handsome brunette of perhaps twenty-three years of age, was there for a like purpose. She was in a nightrobe and dressing gown, with her hair very much tousled, but she looked so pretty and good-natured that Carrie instantly conceived a liking for her. The newcomer did no more than smile shamefacedly, but it was sufficient. Carrie felt that she would like to know her, and a similar feeling stirred in the mind of the other, who admired Carrie's innocent face.

"That's a real pretty woman who has moved in nextdoor," said Carrie to Hurstwood at the breakfast table.

Words For Everyday Use

suf • fi • cient (sə fish´ənt) *adj.,* enough

"Who are they?" asked Hurstwood.

"I don't know," said Carrie. "The name on the bell is Vance. Someone over there plays beautifully. I guess it must be she."

"Well, you never can tell what sort of people you're living next to in this town, can you?" said Hurstwood, expressing the customary New York opinion about neighbors.

"Just think," said Carrie, "I have been in this house with nine other families for over a year and I don't know a soul. These people have been here over a month, and I haven't seen anyone before this morning."

◄ About what does Carrie complain to Hurstwood? Explain whether his response is constructive or helpful in any way.

"It's just as well," said Hurstwood. "You never know who you're going to get in with. Some of these people are pretty bad company."

"I expect so," said Carrie, agreeably.

The conversation turned to other things, and Carrie thought no more upon the subject until a day or two later, when, going out to market, she encountered Mrs. Vance coming in. The latter recognized her and nodded, for which Carrie returned a smile. This settled the probability of acquaintanceship. If there had been no faint recognition on this occasion, there would have been no future association.

Carrie saw no more of Mrs. Vance for several weeks, but she heard her play through the thin walls which divided the front rooms of the flats, and was pleased by the merry selection of pieces and the brilliance of their rendition. She could play only moderately herself, and such variety as Mrs. Vance exercised bordered, for Carrie, upon the verge of great art. Everything she had seen and heard thus far—the merest scraps and shadows—indicated that these people were, in a measure, refined and in comfortable circumstances. So Carrie was ready for any extension of the friendship which might follow.

◄ What do the "scraps and shadows" Carrie sees and hears indicate about the Vances?

One day Carrie's bell rang and the servant, who was in the kitchen, pressed the button which caused the front door of the general entrance on the ground floor to be electrically unlatched. When Carrie waited at her own door on the third floor to see who it might be coming up to call on her, Mrs. Vance appeared.

"I hope you'll excuse me," she said. "I went out a while ago and forgot my outside key, so I thought I'd ring your bell."

This was a common trick of other residents of the building,

Words For Everyday Use

re • fined (ri fīnd´) *adj.*, elegant; cultivated

whenever they had forgotten their outside keys. They did not apologize for it, however.

"Certainly," said Carrie. "I'm glad you did. I do the same thing sometimes."

"Isn't it just delightful weather?" said Mrs. Vance, pausing for a moment.

Thus, after a few more preliminaries, this visiting acquaintance was well launched, and in the young Mrs. Vance Carrie found an agreeable companion.

On several occasions Carrie visited her and was visited. Both flats were good to look upon, though that of the Vances tended somewhat more to the luxurious.

"I want you to come over this evening and meet my husband," said Mrs. Vance, not long after their intimacy began. "He wants to meet you. You play cards, don't you?"

"A little," said Carrie.

"Well, we'll have a game of cards. If your husband comes home bring him over."

"He's not coming to dinner tonight," said Carrie.

"Well, when he does come we'll call him in."

Carrie acquiesced, and that evening met the portly Vance, an individual a few years younger than Hurstwood, and who owed his seemingly comfortable matrimonial state much more to his money than to his good looks. He thought well of Carrie upon the first glance and laid himself out to be genial, teaching her a new game of cards and talking to her about New York and its pleasures. Mrs. Vance played some upon the piano, and at last Hurstwood came.

"I am very glad to meet you," he said to Mrs. Vance when Carrie introduced him, showing much of the old grace which had captivated Carrie.

"Did you think your wife had run away?" said Mr. Vance, extending his hand upon introduction.

"I didn't know but what she might have found a better husband," said Hurstwood.

► *What realizations suddenly fill Carrie with gloom?*

He now turned his attention to Mrs. Vance, and in a flash Carrie saw again what she for some time had subconsciously missed in Hurstwood—the adroitness and flattery of which he was capable. She also saw that she was not well-dressed—not nearly as well-dressed—as Mrs. Vance. These were not vague ideas any longer. Her situation was cleared up for her.

Words For Everyday Use

a • droit • ness (ə droit´nəs) *n.*, cleverness

She felt that her life was becoming stale, and therein she felt cause for gloom. The old helpful, urging melancholy was restored. The desirous Carrie was whispered to concerning her possibilities.

There were no immediate results to this awakening, for Carrie had little power of initiative; but, nevertheless, she seemed ever capable of getting herself into the tide of change where she would be easily borne along. Hurstwood noticed nothing. He had been unconscious of the marked contrasts which Carrie had observed. He did not even detect the shade of melancholy which settled in her eyes. Worst of all, she now began to feel the loneliness of the flat and seek the company of Mrs. Vance, who liked her exceedingly.

◄ *What does Carrie's character prevent her from doing? What does Carrie always seem able to do, according to the narrator?*

"Let's go to the matinee this afternoon," said Mrs. Vance, who had stepped across into Carrie's flat one morning, still arrayed in a soft pink dressing gown, which she had donned upon rising. Hurstwood and Vance had gone their separate ways nearly an hour before.

"All right," said Carrie, noticing the air of the petted and well-groomed woman in Mrs. Vance's general appearance. She looked as though she was dearly loved and her every wish gratified. "What shall we see?"

◄ *What does Carrie believe Mrs. Vance's appearance demonstrates? In what way might Carrie contrast her situation with Mrs. Vance's?*

"Oh, I do want to see Nat Goodwin," said Mrs. Vance. "I do think he is the jolliest actor. The papers say this is such a good play."

"What time will we have to start?" asked Carrie.

"Let's go at one and walk down Broadway from Thirty-fourth Street," said Mrs. Vance. "It's such an interesting walk. He's at the Madison Square."

"I'll be glad to go," said Carrie. "How much will we have to pay for seats?"

"Not more than a dollar," said Mrs. Vance.

The latter departed, and at one o'clock reappeared, stunningly arrayed in a dark-blue walking dress, with a nobby[2] hat to match. Carrie had gotten herself up charmingly enough, but this woman pained her by contrast. She seemed to have so many dainty little things which Carrie had not. There were trinkets of gold, an elegant green leather purse set with her initials, a fancy handkerchief, exceedingly rich in design, and the like. Carrie felt that she needed more and better clothes to compare with this woman, and that anyone looking at the two would pick Mrs. Vance for her raiment[3] alone. It was a trying, though rather unjust thought, for Carrie had now developed an equally pleasing figure, and had grown in comeliness until she was a thoroughly attractive type of her

◄ *How does Mrs. Vance's appearance make Carrie feel?*

2. **nobby.** Fashionable; stylish
3. **raiment.** Clothing

color of beauty. There was some difference in the clothing of the two, both of quality and age, but this difference was not especially noticeable. It served, however, to augment Carrie's dissatisfaction with her state.

The walk down Broadway, then as now, was one of the remarkable features of the city. There gathered, before the matinee and afterward, not only all the pretty women who love a showy parade, but the men who love to gaze upon and admire them. It was a very imposing procession of pretty faces and fine clothes. Women appeared in their very best hats, shoes, and gloves, and walked arm in arm on their way to the fine shops or theaters strung along from Fourteenth to Thirty-fourth streets. Equally the men paraded with the very latest they could afford. A tailor might have secured hints on suit measurements, a shoemaker on proper lasts[4] and colors, a hatter on hats. It was literally true that if a lover of fine clothes secured a new suit, it was sure to have its first airing on Broadway. So true and well understood was this fact, that several years later a popular song, detailing this and other facts concerning the afternoon parade on matinee days, and entitled "What Right Has He on Broadway?" was published, and had quite a vogue[5] about the music halls of the city.

In all her stay in the city, Carrie had never heard of this showy parade; had never even been on Broadway when it was taking place. On the other hand, it was a familiar thing to Mrs. Vance, who not only knew of it as an entity, but had often been in it, going purposely to see and be seen, to create a stir with her beauty and dispel any tendency to fall short in dressiness by contrasting herself with the beauty and fashion of the town.

► *What do "fashionable" people do on the street?*

Carrie stepped along easily enough after they got out of the car at Thirty-fourth Street, but soon fixed her eyes upon the lovely company which swarmed by and with them as they proceeded. She noticed suddenly that Mrs. Vance's manner had rather stiffened under the gaze of handsome men and elegantly dressed ladies, whose glances were not modified by any rules of propriety. To stare seemed the proper and natural thing. Carrie found herself stared at and ogled. Men in flawless topcoats, high hats, and silver-headed walking

4. **lasts.** Form shaped like a person's foot on which shoes are made
5. **vogue.** Fashion

Words For Everyday Use

en • ti • ty (en´tə tē) *n.,* anything which exists
o • gle (ō´gəl) *vt.,* look over boldly

sticks elbowed near and looked too often into conscious eyes. Ladies rustled by in dresses of stiff cloth, shedding affected smiles and perfume. Carrie noticed among them the sprinkling of goodness and the heavy percentage of vice. The rouged and powdered cheeks and lips, the scented hair, the large, misty, and languorous eye, were common enough. With a start she awoke to find that she was in fashion's crowd, on parade in a showplace—and such a showplace! Jewellers' windows gleamed along the path with remarkable frequency. Florist shops, furriers, haberdashers, confectioners[6]—all followed in rapid succession. The street was full of coaches. Pompous doormen in immense coats, shiny brass belts and buttons, waited in front of expensive salesrooms. Coachmen in tan boots, white tights, and blue jackets waited obsequiously for the mistresses of carriages who were shopping inside. The whole street bore the flavor of riches and show, and Carrie felt that she was not of it. She could not, for the life of her, assume the attitude and smartness of Mrs. Vance, who, in her beauty, was all assurance. She could only imagine that it must be evident to many that she was the less handsomely dressed of the two. It cut her to the quick, and she resolved that she would not come here again until she looked better. At the same time she longed to feel the delight of parading here as an equal. Ah, then she would be happy!

◄ *What does Carrie resolve? What does she believe will make her happy?*

6. **furriers, haberdashers, confectioners.** Makers of furs, men's accessories, and candy

Words For Everyday Use

vice (vīs) *n.,* evil or wicked conduct or behavior

ob • se • qui • ous • ly (ob sē´ kwē əs´ lē) *adv.,* compliantly; in a manner attempting to please

CHAPTER 32

The Feast of Belshazzar: A Seer to Translate

Such feelings as were generated in Carrie by this walk put her in an exceedingly receptive mood for the pathos which followed in the play. The actor whom they had gone to see had achieved his popularity by presenting a mellow type of comedy, in which sufficient sorrow was introduced to lend contrast and relief to humor. For Carrie, as we well know, the stage had a great attraction. She had never forgotten her one histrionic achievement in Chicago. It dwelt in her mind and occupied her consciousness during many long afternoons in which her rocking-chair and her latest novel contributed the only pleasures of her state. Never could she witness a play without having her own ability vividly brought to consciousness. Some scenes made her long to be a part of them—to give expression to the feelings which she, in the place of the character represented, would feel. Almost invariably she would carry the vivid imaginations away with her and brood over them the next day alone. She lived as much in these things as in the realities which made up her daily life.

► *What thoughts spring to Carrie's mind every time she sees a play?*

It was not often that she came to the play stirred to her heart's core by actualities. Today a low song of longing had been set singing in her heart by the finery, the merriment, the beauty she had seen. Oh, these women who had passed her by, hundreds and hundreds strong, who were they? Whence[1] came the rich, elegant dresses, the astonishingly colored buttons, the knick-knacks of silver and gold? Where were these lovely creatures housed? Amid what elegancies of carved furniture, decorated walls, elaborate tapestries did they move? Where were their rich apartments, loaded with all that money could provide? In what stables champed these sleek, nervous horses and rested the gorgeous carriages? Where lounged the richly groomed footmen? Oh, the mansions, the lights, the perfume, the loaded boudoirs[2] and tables! New York must be filled with such bowers,[3] or the

► *What does Carrie imagine the lives of these women are like?*

1. **Whence.** From what place; from where
2. **boudoirs.** Women's bedrooms, sitting rooms, or dressing rooms
3. **bowers.** Women's private rooms; boudoirs

Words For Everyday Use

his • tri • on • ic (his trē än´ik) *adj.,* theatrical

tap • es • try (tap´əs trē) *n.,* heavy woven cloth decorated with pictures and used as a wall hanging

beautiful, insolent, supercilious creatures could not be. Some hothouses[4] held them. It ached her to know that she was not one of them—that, alas, she had dreamed a dream and it had not come true. She wondered at her own solitude these two years past—her indifference to the fact that she had never achieved what she had expected.

◄ What pains Carrie?

The play was one of those drawing room concoctions in which charmingly overdressed ladies and gentlemen suffer the pangs of love and jealousy amid gilded surroundings. Such bon-mots[5] are ever enticing to those who have all their days longed for such material surroundings and have never had them gratified. They have the charm of showing suffering under ideal conditions. Who would not grieve upon a gilded chair? Who would not suffer amid perfumed tapestries, cushioned furniture, and liveried[6] servants? Grief under such circumstances becomes an enticing thing. Carrie longed to be of it. She wanted to take her sufferings, whatever they were, in such a world, or failing that, at least to simulate them under such charming conditions upon the stage. So affected was her mind by what she had seen, that the play now seemed an extraordinarily beautiful thing. She was soon lost in the world it represented, and wished that she might never return. Between the acts she studied the galaxy of matinee attendants in front rows and boxes, and conceived a new idea of the possibilities of New York. She was sure she had not seen it all—that the city was one whirl of pleasure and delight.

◄ What "charm" do such plays have? What emotions does Carrie long to experience? In what surroundings does she long to experience these feelings?

Going out, the same Broadway taught her a sharper lesson. The scene she had witnessed coming down was now augmented and at its height. Such a crush of finery and folly she had never seen. It clinched her convictions concerning her state. She had not lived, could not lay claim to having lived, until something of this had come into her own life. Women were spending money like water; she could see that in every elegant shop she passed. Flowers, candy, jewelry, seemed the principal things in which the elegant dames were interested. And she had scarcely enough pin money to indulge in such outings as this a few times a month.

That night the pretty little flat seemed a commonplace thing. It was not what the rest of the world was enjoying. She saw the servant working at dinner with an indifferent eye. In her mind were running scenes of the play. Particularly she remembered one beautiful actress—the sweetheart who had been wooed and won. The grace of this

◄ In what way has going to a theater on Broadway changed the way Carrie feels about her home?

4. **hothouses.** Glass structures in which delicate or exotic plants grow
5. **bon-mots.** Clever or witty remarks
6. **liveried.** In uniform

woman had won Carrie's heart. Her dresses had been all that art could suggest, her sufferings had been so real. The anguish which she had portrayed Carrie could feel. It was done as she was sure she could do it. There were places in which she could even do better. Hence she repeated the lines to herself. Oh, if she could only have such a part, how broad would be her life! She, too, could act appealingly.

► *What does Carrie do frequently when she is moody or needs to think?*

When Hurstwood came, Carrie was moody. She was sitting, rocking and thinking, and did not care to have her enticing imaginations broken in upon; so she said little or nothing.

"What's the matter, Carrie?" said Hurstwood after a time, noticing her quiet, almost moody state.

"Nothing," said Carrie. "I don't feel very well tonight."

"Not sick, are you?" he asked, approaching very close.

"Oh, no," she said, almost pettishly, "I just don't feel very good."

"That's too bad," he said, stepping away and adjusting his vest after his slight bending over. "I was thinking we might go to a show tonight."

"I don't want to go," said Carrie, annoyed that her fine visions should have thus been broken into and driven out of her mind. "I've been to the matinee this afternoon."

"Oh, you have?" said Hurstwood. "What was it?"

"A Gold Mine."

"How was it?"

"Pretty good," said Carrie.

"And you don't want to go again tonight?"

"I don't think I do," she said.

Nevertheless, wakened out of her melancholia and called to the dinner table, she changed her mind. A little food in the stomach does wonders. She went again, and in so doing temporarily recovered her equanimity. The great awakening blow had, however, been delivered. As often as she might recover from these discontented thoughts now, they would occur again. Time and repetition—ah, the wonder of it! The dropping water and the solid stone—how utterly it yields at last!

Not long after this matinee experience—perhaps a month—Mrs. Vance invited Carrie to an evening at the theater with them. She heard Carrie say that Hurstwood was not coming home to dinner.

Words For Everyday Use

mel • an • cho • li • a (mel´ən kō´ lē ə) *n.,* extreme depression of spirits

e • qua • nim • i • ty (ek´ wə nim´ə tē) *n.,* evenness of temper

"Why don't you come with us? Don't get dinner for yourself. We're going down to Sherry's for dinner and then over to the Lyceum. Come along with us."

"I think I will," answered Carrie.

She began to dress at three o'clock for her departure at half-past five for the noted dining room which was then crowding Delmonico's for position in society. In this dressing Carrie showed the influence of her association with the dashing Mrs. Vance. She had constantly had her attention called by the latter to novelties in everything which pertains to a woman's apparel.

◄ *In what is Mrs. Vance instructing Carrie?*

"Are you going to get such and such a hat?" or, "Have you seen the new gloves with the oval pearl buttons?" were but sample phrases out of a large selection.

"The next time you get a pair of shoes, dearie," said Mrs. Vance, "get button, with thick soles and patent-leather tips. They're all the rage this fall."

"I will," said Carrie.

"Oh, dear, have you seen the new shirtwaists at Altman's? They have some of the loveliest patterns. I saw one there that I know would look stunning on you. I said so when I saw it."

Carrie listened to these things with considerable interest, for they were suggested with more of friendliness than is usually common between pretty women. Mrs. Vance liked Carrie's stable good nature so well that she really took pleasure in suggesting to her the latest things.

"Why don't you get yourself one of those nice serge skirts they're selling at Lord & Taylor's?" she said one day. "They're the circular style, and they're going to be worn from now on. A dark blue one would look so nice on you."

Carrie listened with eager ears. These things never came up between her and Hurstwood. Nevertheless, she began to suggest one thing and another, which Hurstwood agreed to without any expression of opinion. He noticed the new tendency on Carrie's part, and finally, hearing much of Mrs. Vance and her delightful ways, suspected whence the change came. He was not inclined to offer the slightest objection so soon, but he felt that Carrie's wants were expanding. This did not appeal to him exactly, but he cared for her in his own way, and so the thing stood. Still, there was something in the details of the transactions which caused Carrie to feel that her requests were not a delight to him. He did not enthuse over the purchases. This led her to believe that neglect was creeping in, and so another small wedge was entered.

◄ *What does Hurstwood notice about Carrie? To whom does he attribute this change?*

◄ *What does Carrie realize? What "small wedge" threatens Carrie's and Hurstwood's relationship?*

Nevertheless, one of the results of Mrs. Vance's suggestions was the fact that on this occasion Carrie was dressed somewhat to her own satisfaction. She had on her best, but there was comfort in the thought that if she must confine herself to a *best,* it was neat and fitting. She looked the well-groomed woman of twenty-one, and Mrs. Vance praised her, which brought color to her plump cheeks and a noticeable brightness into her large eyes. It was threatening rain, and Mr. Vance, at his wife's request, had called a coach.

"Your husband isn't coming?" suggested Mr. Vance, as he met Carrie in his little parlor.

"No, he said he wouldn't be home for dinner."

"Better leave a little note for him, telling him where we are. He might turn up."

"I will," said Carrie, who had not thought of it before.

"Tell him we'll be at Sherry's until eight o'clock. He knows, though, I guess."

Carrie crossed the hall with rustling skirts, and scrawled the note, gloves on. When she returned a newcomer was in the Vance flat.

► *To whom does Mrs. Vance introduce Carrie?*

"Mrs. Wheeler, let me introduce Mr. Ames, a cousin of mine," said Mrs. Vance. "He's going along with us, aren't you, Bob?"

"I'm very glad to meet you," said Ames, bowing politely to Carrie.

The latter caught in a glance the dimensions of a very stalwart figure. She also noticed that he was smooth-shaven, good looking, and young, but nothing more.

"Mr. Ames is just down in New York for a few days," put in Vance, "and we're trying to show him around a little."

"Oh, are you?" said Carrie, taking another glance at the newcomer.

"Yes; I am just on here from Indianapolis for a week or so," said young Ames, seating himself on the edge of a chair to wait while Mrs. Vance completed the last touches of her toilet.

"I guess you find New York quite a thing to see, don't you?" said Carrie, venturing something to avoid a possible deadly silence.

"It is rather large to get around in a week," answered Ames, pleasantly.

He was an exceedingly genial soul, this young man, and

Words For Everyday Use

stal • wart (stôl´wərt) *adj.,* strong and well-built

wholly free of affectation. It seemed to Carrie he was as yet only overcoming the last traces of the bashfulness of youth. He did not seem apt at conversation, but he had the merit of being well-dressed and wholly courageous. Carrie felt as if it were not going to be hard to talk to him.

"Well, I guess we're ready now. The coach is outside."

"Come on, people," said Mrs. Vance, coming in smiling. "Bob, you'll have to look after Mrs. Wheeler."

"I'll try to," said Bob smiling, and edging closer to Carrie. "You won't need much watching, will you?" he volunteered, in a sort of ingratiating and help-me-out kind of way.

"Not very, I hope," said Carrie.

They descended the stairs, Mrs. Vance offering suggestions, and climbed into the open coach.

"All right," said Vance, slamming the coach door, and the conveyance[7] rolled away.

"What is it we're going to see?" asked Ames.

"Sothern," said Vance, "in *Lord Chumley.*"

"Oh, he is so good!" said Mrs. Vance. "He's just the funniest man."

"I notice the papers praise it," said Ames.

"I haven't any doubt," put in Vance, "but we'll all enjoy it very much."

Ames had taken a seat beside Carrie, and accordingly he felt it his bounden duty to pay her some attention. He was interested to find her so young a wife, and so pretty, though it was only a respectful interest. There was nothing of the dashing lady's man about him. He had respect for the married state, and thought only of some pretty marriageable girls in Indianapolis.

◄ *In what way does Ames's attitude toward Carrie differ from the attitude of most men she has encountered?*

"Are you a born New Yorker?" asked Ames of Carrie.

"Oh, no; I've only been here for two years."

"Oh, well, you've had time to see a great deal of it, anyhow."

"I don't seem to have," answered Carrie. "It's about as strange to me as when I first came here."

"You're not from the West, are you?"

"Yes. I'm from Wisconsin," she answered.

"Well, it does seem as if most people in this town haven't been here so very long. I hear of lots of Indiana people in my line who are here."

7. **conveyance.** That which transports, in this case, the coach

Words For Everyday Use

af • fec • ta • tion (af´ek tā´shən) *n.,* artificial behavior meant to impress others

bound • en (boun´dən) *adj.,* necessary

"What is your line?" asked Carrie.

"I'm connected with an electrical company," said the youth.

Carrie followed up this desultory conversation with occasional interruptions from the Vances. Several times it became general and partially humorous, and in that manner the restaurant was reached.

Carrie had noticed the appearance of gaiety and pleasure-seeking in the streets which they were following. Coaches were numerous, pedestrians many, and in Fifty-ninth Street the street cars were crowded. At Fifty-ninth Street and Fifth Avenue a blaze of lights from several new hotels which bordered the Plaza Square gave a suggestion of sumptuous hotel life. Fifth Avenue, the home of the wealthy, was noticeably crowded with carriages, and gentlemen in evening dress. At Sherry's an imposing doorman opened the coach door and helped them out. Young Ames held Carrie's elbow as he helped her up the steps. They entered the lobby already swarming with patrons, and then, after divesting themselves of their wraps, went into a sumptuous dining room.

▶ How does Carrie feel about Sherry's?

In all Carrie's experience she had never seen anything like this. In the whole time she had been in New York Hurstwood's modified state had not permitted his bringing her to such a place. There was an almost indescribable atmosphere about it which convinced the newcomer that this was the proper thing. Here was the place where the matter of expense limited the patrons to the moneyed or pleasure-loving class. Carrie had read of it often in the "Morning" and "Evening World." She had seen notices of dances, parties, balls, and suppers at Sherry's. The Misses So-and-so would give a party on Wednesday evening at Sherry's. Young Mr. So-and-so would entertain a party of friends at a private luncheon on the sixteenth, at Sherry's. The common run of conventional, perfunctory notices of the doings of society, which she could scarcely refrain from scanning each day, had given her a distinct idea of the gorgeousness and luxury of this wonderful temple of gastronomy. Now, at last, she was really in it. She had come up the imposing steps, guarded by the large and portly doorman. She had seen the lobby, guarded by another large and portly gentleman, and been waited upon by uniformed youths who took care of canes, overcoats, and the like. Here was the splendid dining chamber, all decorated

Words For Everyday Use

des • ul • to • ry (des´əl tôr´ē) *adj.,* disconnected; not methodical; haphazard

di • vest (də vest´) *vt.,* strip of clothing or equipment

gas • tron • o • my (gas trän´ə mē) *n.,* art of fine dining

and aglow, where the wealthy ate. Ah, how fortunate was Mrs. Vance; young, beautiful, and well-off—at least, sufficiently so to come here in a coach. What a wonderful thing it was to be rich.

Vance led the way through lanes of shining tables, at which were seated parties of two, three, four, five, or six. The air of assurance and dignity about it all was exceedingly noticeable to the novitiate. Incandescent lights, the reflection of their glow in polished glasses, and the shine of gilt[8] upon the walls, combined into one tone of light which it requires minutes of complacent observation to separate and take particular note of. The white shirt fronts of the gentlemen, the bright costumes of the ladies, diamonds, jewels, fine feathers—all were exceedingly noticeable.

Carrie walked with an air equal to that of Mrs. Vance, and accepted the seat which the head waiter provided for her. She was keenly aware of all the little things that were done—the little genuflections and attentions of the waiters and head waiter which Americans pay for. The air with which the latter pulled out each chair, and the wave of the hand with which he motioned them to be seated, were worth several dollars in themselves.

◄ What, to Carrie's mind, makes this restaurant worth the money it costs to dine there?

Once seated, there began that exhibition of showy, wasteful, and unwholesome gastronomy as practiced by wealthy Americans, which is the wonder and astonishment of true culture and dignity the world over. The large bill of fare held an array of dishes sufficient to feed an army, sidelined with prices which made reasonable expenditure a ridiculous impossibility—an order of soup at fifty cents or a dollar, with a dozen kinds to choose from; oysters in forty styles and at sixty cents the half-dozen; entrees, fish, and meats at prices which would house one overnight in an average hotel. One dollar fifty and two dollars seemed to be the most common figures upon this most tastefully printed bill of fare.

Carrie noticed this, and in scanning it the price of spring chicken carried her back to that other bill of fare and far different occasion when, for the first time, she sat with Drouet in a good restaurant in Chicago. It was only momentary—a sad note as out of an old song—and then it was gone. But in

◄ What memory does this restaurant recall for Carrie?

8. **gilt.** Gold overlay

Words For Everyday Use

no • vi • ti • ate (nō vish´ē it) *n.,* one new to something

gen • u • flec • tion (jen´yo͞o flekt´shən) *n.,* servile action or courtesy

that flash was seen the other Carrie—poor, hungry, drifting at her wits' ends,[9] and all Chicago a cold and closed world, from which she only wandered because she could not find work.

On the walls were designs in color, square spots of robin's-egg blue, set in ornate frames of gilt, whose corners were elaborate moldings of fruit and flowers, with fat cupids hovering in angelic comfort. On the ceilings were colored traceries with more gilt, leading to a center where spread a cluster of lights—incandescent globes mingled with glittering prisms and stucco tendrils[10] of gilt. The floor was of a reddish hue, waxed and polished, and in every direction were mirrors—tall, brilliant, bevel-edged mirrors—reflecting and re-reflecting forms, faces, and candelabra[11] a score and a hundred[12] times.

The tables were not so remarkable in themselves, and yet the imprint of Sherry upon the napery, the name of Tiffany upon the silverware, the name of Haviland upon the china, and over all the glow of the small, red-shaded candelabra and the reflected tints of the walls on garments and faces, made them seem remarkable. Each waiter added an air of exclusiveness and elegance by the manner in which he bowed, scraped, touched, and trifled with things. The exclusively personal attention which he devoted to each one, standing half bent, ear to one side, elbows akimbo,[13] saying: "Soup—green turtle, yes. One portion, yes. Oysters—certainly—half-dozen—yes. Asparagus. Olives—yes."

► What does Carrie's "poor little mind" do?

It would be the same with each one, only Vance essayed to order for all, inviting counsel and suggestions. Carrie studied the company with open eyes. So this was high life in New York. It was so that the rich spent their days and evenings. Her poor little mind could not rise above applying each scene to all society. Every fine lady must be in the crowd on Broadway in the afternoon, in the theater at the matinee, in the coaches and dining halls at night. It must be glow and shine everywhere, with coaches waiting, and footmen attending, and she was out of it all. In two long years she had never even been in such a place as this.

---

9. **wits' ends.** Limit of one's ability to cope
10. **incandescent . . . tendrils.** Shining globes mixed with shining shapes and vines
11. **candelabra.** Large branched candlestick
12. **a score and a hundred.** One hundred and twenty
13. **elbows akimbo.** Hands on hips, elbows bent

Words For Everyday Use

tri • fle (trī´fəl) *vi.*, fuss

Vance was in his element here, as Hurstwood would have been in former days. He ordered freely of soup, oysters, roast meats, and side dishes, and had several bottles of wine brought, which were set down beside the table in a wicker basket.

Ames was looking away rather abstractedly at the crowd and showed an interesting profile to Carrie. His forehead was high, his nose rather large and strong, his chin moderately pleasing. He had a good, wide, well-shaped mouth, and his dark brown hair was parted slightly on one side. He seemed to have the least touch of boyishness to Carrie, and yet he was a man full grown.

"Do you know," he said, turning back to Carrie, after his reflection, "I sometimes think it is a shame for people to spend so much money this way."

◄ *What observation does Ames make?*

Carrie looked at him a moment with the faintest touch of surprise at his seriousness. He seemed to be thinking about something over which she had never pondered.

"Do you?" she answered, interestedly.

"Yes," he said, "they pay so much more than these things are worth. They put on so much show."

"I don't know why people shouldn't spend when they have it," said Mrs. Vance.

"It doesn't do any harm," said Vance, who was still studying the bill of fare, though he had ordered.

Ames was looking away again, and Carrie was again looking at his forehead. To her he seemed to be thinking about strange things. As he studied the crowd his eye was mild.

"Look at that woman's dress over there," he said, again turning to Carrie, and nodding in a direction.

"Where?" said Carrie, following his eyes.

"Over there in the corner—way over. Do you see that brooch?"

"Isn't it large?" said Carrie.

"One of the largest clusters of jewels I have ever seen," said Ames.

"It is, isn't it?" said Carrie. She felt as if she would like to be agreeable to this young man, and also there came with it, or perhaps preceded it, the slightest shade of a feeling that he was better educated than she was—that his mind was better. He seemed to look it, and the saving grace in Carrie was that she could understand that people could be wiser. She had seen a number of people in her life who reminded her of what she had vaguely come to think of as scholars. This strong young man beside her, with his clear, natural look, seemed to get a hold of things which she did not quite understand, but approved of. It was fine to be so, as a man, she thought.

◄ *What does Carrie realize about Ames? How does she feel about "scholars"?*

The conversation changed to a book that was having its vogue at the time—*Moulding a Maiden,* by Albert Ross. Mrs. Vance had read it. Vance had seen it discussed in some of the papers.

"A man can make quite a strike writing a book," said Vance. "I notice this fellow Ross is very much talked about." He was looking at Carrie as he spoke.

"I hadn't heard of him," said Carrie, honestly.

"Oh, I have," said Mrs. Vance. "He's written lots of things. This last story is pretty good."

"He doesn't amount to much," said Ames.

Carrie turned her eyes toward him as to an oracle.[14]

► *How does Carrie feel when Ames criticizes a book she has enjoyed? Why doesn't Carrie defend her opinion?*

"His stuff is nearly as bad as *Dora Thorne,*" concluded Ames.

Carrie felt this as a personal reproof. She read *Dora Thorne,* or had a great deal in the past. It seemed only fair to her, but she supposed that people thought it very fine. Now this clear-eyed, fine-headed youth, who looked something like a student to her, made fun of it. It was poor to him, not worth reading. She looked down, and for the first time felt the pain of not understanding.

Yet there was nothing sarcastic or supercilious in the way Ames spoke. He had very little of that in him. Carrie felt that it was just kindly thought of a high order—the right thing to think, and wondered what else was right, according to him. He seemed to notice that she listened and rather sympathized with him, and from now on he talked mostly to her.

As the waiter bowed and scraped about, felt the dishes to see if they were hot enough, brought spoons and forks, and did all those little attentive things calculated to impress the luxury of the situation upon the diner, Ames also leaned slightly to one side and told her of Indianapolis in an intelligent way. He really had a very bright mind, which was finding its chief development in electrical knowledge. His sympathies for other forms of information, however, and for types of people, were quick and warm. The red glow on his head gave it a sandy tinge and put a bright glint in his eye. Carrie noticed all these things as he leaned toward her and felt exceedingly young. This man was far ahead of her. He seemed wiser than Hurstwood, saner and brighter than Drouet. He seemed innocent and clean, and she thought that he was exceedingly pleasant. She noticed, also, that his interest in her was a far-off one. She was not in his life, nor any of the things that touched his life, and yet now, as he spoke of these things, they appealed to her.

---

14. **oracle.** Prophet of great knowledge or wisdom

"I shouldn't care to be rich," he told her, as the dinner proceeded and the supply of food warmed up his sympathies; "not rich enough to spend my money this way."

"Oh, wouldn't you?" said Carrie, the, to her, new attitude forcing itself distinctly upon her for the first time.

"No," he said. "What good would it do? A man doesn't need this sort of thing to be happy."

Carrie thought of this doubtfully; but, coming from him, it had weight with her.

"He probably could be happy," she thought to herself, "all alone. He's so strong."

Mr. and Mrs. Vance kept up a running fire of interruptions, and these impressive things by Ames came at odd moments. They were sufficient, however, for the atmosphere that went with this youth impressed itself upon Carrie without words. There was something in him, or the world he moved in, which appealed to her. He reminded her of scenes she had seen on the stage—the sorrows and sacrifices that always went with she knew not what. He had taken away some of the bitterness of the contrast between this life and her life, and all by a certain calm indifference which concerned only him.

As they went out, he took her arm and helped her into the coach, and then they were off again, and so to the show.

During the acts Carrie found herself listening to him very attentively. He mentioned things in the play which she most approved of—things which swayed her deeply.

"Don't you think it rather fine to be an actor?" she asked once.

"Yes, I do," he said, "to be a good one. I think the theater a great thing."

Just this little approval set Carrie's heart bounding. Ah, if she could only be an actress—a good one! This man was wise—he knew—and he approved of it. If she were a fine actress, such men as he would approve of her. She felt that he was good to speak as he had, although it did not concern her at all. She did not know why she felt this way.

At the close of the show it suddenly developed that he was not going back with them.

"Oh, aren't you?" said Carrie, with an unwarrantable feeling.

"Oh, no," he said; "I'm stopping right around here in Thirty-third Street."

◄ *What attitude toward wealth does Ames express? Why is Carrie surprised? Why does she give his opinion some weight?*

◄ *How does Ames's approval of acting as a profession make Carrie feel?*

Words For Everyday Use

un • war • rant • a • ble (un wôr´ənt ə bəl) *adj.,* unreasonable

Carrie could not say anything else, but somehow this development shocked her. She had been regretting the wane of a pleasant evening, but she had thought there was a half-hour more. Oh, the half-hours, the minutes of the world; what miseries and griefs are crowded into them!

She said goodbye with feigned indifference. What matter could it make? Still, the coach seemed lorn.

When she went into her own flat she had this to think about. She did not know whether she would ever see this man anymore. What difference could it make—what difference could it make?

► *What does Carrie do instead of going to bed?*

Hurstwood had returned, and was already in bed. His clothes were scattered loosely about. Carrie came to the door and saw him, then retreated. She did not want to go in yet a while. She wanted to think. It was disagreeable to her.

Back in the dining room she sat in her chair and rocked. Her little hands were folded tightly as she thought. Through a fog of longing and conflicting desires she was beginning to see. Oh, ye legions of hope and pity—of sorrow and pain! She was rocking, and beginning to see.

Words For Everyday Use

lorn (lôrn) *adj.*, empty, abandoned

CHAPTER 33

Without the Walled City: The Slope of the Years

The immediate result of this was nothing. Results from such things are usually long in growing. Morning brings a change of feeling. The existent condition invariably pleads for itself. It is only at odd moments that we get glimpses of the misery of things. The heart understands when it is confronted with contrasts. Take them away and the ache subsides.

Carrie went on, leading much this same life for six months thereafter or more. She did not see Ames anymore. He called once upon the Vances, but she only heard about it through the young wife. Then he went West, and there was a gradual subsidence of whatever personal attraction had existed. The mental effect of the thing had not gone, however, and never would entirely. She had an ideal to contrast men by—particularly men close to her.

◄ *What is the lasting effect of Ames upon Carrie? To whom might she contrast Ames?*

During all this time—a period rapidly approaching three years—Hurstwood had been moving along in an even path. There was no apparent slope downward, and distinctly none upward, so far as the casual observer might have seen. But psychologically there was a change, which was marked enough to suggest the future very distinctly indeed. This was in the mere matter of the halt his career had received when he departed from Chicago. A man's fortune or material progress is very much the same as his bodily growth. Either he is growing stronger, healthier, wiser, as the youth approaching manhood, or he is growing weaker, older, less incisive mentally, as the man approaching old age. There are no other states. Frequently there is a period between the cessation of youthful accretion and the setting in, in the case of the middle-aged man, of the tendency toward decay when the two processes are almost perfectly balanced and there is little doing in either direction. Given time enough, however, the balance becomes a sagging to the grave side. Slowly at first, then with a modest momentum, and at last the graveward process is in the full swing. So it is frequently with man's fortune. If its process of accretion is never halted, if the balancing stage is never reached, there will be no toppling. Rich

◄ *According to the narrator, in what way are men's fortunes and their bodily growth alike? What does the narrator seem to be indicating about what might happen to Hurstwood?*

Words For Everyday Use	
	sub • sid • ence (sub sī´ dəns) *n.,* lessening
	in • ci • sive (in si´siv) *adj.,* keen; sharp
	ces • sa • tion (se sā´ shən) *n.,* end
	ac • cre • tion (ə krē´ shən) *n.,* accumulation

► *What is the only thing that can save the fortune of an older man, according to the narrator?*

men are, frequently, in these days, saved from this dissolution of their fortune by their ability to hire younger brains. These younger brains look upon the interests of the fortune as their own, and so steady and direct its progress. If each individual were left absolutely to the care of his own interests, and were given time enough in which to grow exceedingly old, his fortune would pass as his strength and will. He and his would be utterly dissolved and scattered unto the four winds of the heavens.

But now see wherein the parallel changes. A fortune, like a man, is an organism which draws to itself other minds and other strength than that inherent in the founder. Beside the young minds drawn to it by salaries, it becomes allied with young forces, which make for its existence even when the strength and wisdom of the founder are fading. It may be conserved by the growth of a community or of a state. It may be involved in providing something for which there is a growing demand. This removes it at once beyond the special care of the founder. It needs not so much foresight now as direction. The man wanes, the need continues or grows, and the fortune, fallen into whose hands it may, continues. Hence, some men never recognize the turning in the tide of their abilities. It is only in chance cases, where a fortune or a state of success is wrested from them, that the lack of ability to do as they did formerly becomes apparent. Hurstwood, set down under new conditions, was in a position to see that he was no longer young. If he did not, it was due wholly to the fact that his state was so well-balanced that an absolute change for the worse did not show.

► *According to the narrator, what produces "marked physical deterioration"?*

Not trained to reason or introspect himself, he could not analyze the change that was taking place in his mind, and hence his body, but he felt the depression of it. Constant comparison between his old state and his new showed a balance for the worse, which produced a constant state of gloom or, at least, depression. Now, it has been shown experimentally that a constantly subdued frame of mind produces certain poisons in the blood, called katastates, just as virtuous feelings of pleasure and delight produce helpful chemicals called anastates. The poisons generated by remorse inveigh against the system, and eventually produce marked physical deterioration. To these Hurstwood was subject.

Words For Everyday Use

dis • so • lu • tion (dis´ə lo͞o´ shən) *n.*, disintegration
al • lied (a līd´) *adj.*, united
in • tro • spect (in´trō spekt´) *vt.*, look into one's own feelings or mind
in • veigh (in vā´) *vi.*, make a violent attack

In the course of time it told upon his temper. His eye no longer possessed that buoyant, searching shrewdness which had characterized it in Adams Street. His step was not as sharp and firm. He was given to thinking, thinking, thinking. The new friends he made were not celebrities. They were of a cheaper, a slightly more sensual and cruder, grade. He could not possibly take the pleasure in this company that he had in that of those fine frequenters of the Chicago resort. He was left to brood.

Slowly, exceedingly slowly, his desire to greet, conciliate, and make at home these people who visited the Warren Street place passed from him. More and more slowly the significance of the realm he had left began to be clear. It did not seem so wonderful to be in it when he was in it. It had seemed very easy for anyone to get up there and have ample raiment and money to spend, but now that he was out of it, how far off it became. He began to see as one sees a city with a wall about it. Men were posted at the gates. You could not get in. Those inside did not care to come out to see who you were. They were so merry inside there that all those outside were forgotten, and he was on the outside.

◀ *In what perspective is Hurstwood beginning to see his old and his new positions? To what does he compare the difference between his old and his new social spheres?*

Each day he could read in the evening papers of the doings within this walled city. In the notices of passengers for Europe he read the names of eminent frequenters of his old resort. In the theatrical column appeared, from time to time, announcements of the latest successes of men he had known. He knew that they were at their old gaieties. Pullmans were hauling them to and fro about the land, papers were greeting them with interesting mentions, the elegant lobbies of hotels and the glow of polished dining rooms were keeping them close within the walled city. Men whom he had known, men whom he had tipped glasses with—rich men, and he was forgotten! Who was Mr. Wheeler? What was the Warren Street resort? Bah!

If one thinks that such thoughts do not come to so common a type of mind—that such feelings require a higher mental development—I would urge for their consideration the fact that it is the higher mental development that does away with such thoughts. It is the higher mental development which induces philosophy and that fortitude which refuses to dwell upon such things—refuses to be made to suffer by their consideration. The

◀ *According to the narrator, what would someone with "higher mental development" do in Hurstwood's position rather than suffer?*

Words For Everyday Use

con • cil • i • ate (kən sil´ē āt´) *vt.,* make happy

for • ti • tude (fôrt´ə to͞od´) *n.,* strength to bear misfortune

common type of mind is exceedingly keen on all matters which relate to its physical welfare—exceedingly keen. It is the unintellectual miser who sweats blood at the loss of a hundred dollars. It is the Epictetus[1] who smiles when the last vestige of physical welfare is removed.

▶ *What is the effect on his job of Hurstwood's regret?*

The time came, in the third year, when this thinking began to produce results in the Warren Street place. The tide of patronage dropped a little below what it had been at its best since he had been there. This irritated and worried him.

▶ *What makes Carrie thoughts turn "rebellious"?*

There came a night when he confessed to Carrie that the business was not doing as well this month as it had the month before. This was in lieu of certain suggestions she had made concerning little things she wanted to buy. She had not failed to notice that he did not seem to consult her about buying clothes for himself. For the first time, it struck her as a ruse, or that he said it so that she would not think of asking for things. Her reply was mild enough, but her thoughts were rebellious. He was not looking after her at all. She was depending for her enjoyment upon the Vances.

And now the latter announced that they were going away. It was approaching spring, and they were going North.

▶ *What causes Carrie sorrow?*

"Oh, yes," said Mrs. Vance to Carrie, "we think we might as well give up the flat and store our things. We'll be gone for the summer, and it would be a useless expense. I think we'll settle a little farther downtown when we come back."

Carrie heard this with genuine sorrow. She had enjoyed Mrs. Vance's companionship so much. There was no one else in the house whom she knew. Again she would be all alone.

Hurstwood's gloom over the slight decrease in profits and the departure of the Vances came together. So Carrie had loneliness and this mood of her husband to enjoy at the same time. It was a grievous thing. She became restless and dissatisfied, not exactly, as she thought, with Hurstwood, but with life. What was it? A very dull round indeed. What did she have? Nothing but this narrow, little flat. The Vances could travel, they could do the things worth doing, and here she was. For what was she made, anyhow? More thought followed, and then tears—tears seemed justified, and the only relief in the world.

1. **Epictetus.** Great philosopher of ancient Rome who professed Stoicism, which taught indifference to emotion and the external world

Words For Everyday Use

ves • tige (ves´ tij) *n.,* trace of something that once existed

ruse (ro͞oz) *n.,* trick; deception

For another period this state continued, the twain leading a rather monotonous life, and then there was a slight change for the worse. One evening, Hurstwood, after thinking about a way to modify Carrie's desire for clothes and the general strain upon his ability to provide, said:

"I don't think I'll ever be able to do much with Shaughnessy."

"What's the matter?" said Carrie.

"Oh, he's a slow, greedy 'mick'! He won't agree to anything to improve the place, and it won't ever pay without it."

"Can't you make him?" said Carrie.

"No; I've tried. The only thing I can see, if I want to improve, is to get hold of a place of my own."

"Why don't you?" said Carrie.

"Well, all I have is tied up in there just now. If I had a chance to save a while I think I could open a place that would give us plenty of money."

"Can't we save?" said Carrie.

"We might try it," he suggested. "I've been thinking that if we'd take a smaller flat downtown and live economically for a year, I would have enough, with what I have invested, to open a good place. Then we could arrange to live as you want to."

"It would suit me all right," said Carrie, who, nevertheless, felt badly to think it had come to this. Talk of a smaller flat sounded like poverty.

"There are lots of nice little flats down around Sixth Avenue, below Fourteenth Street. We might get one down there."

"I'll look at them if you say so," said Carrie.

"I think I could break away from this fellow inside of a year," said Hurstwood. "Nothing will ever come of this arrangement as it's going on now."

"I'll look around," said Carrie, observing that the proposed change seemed to be a serious thing with him.

The upshot of this was that the change was eventually effected; not without great gloom on the part of Carrie. It really affected her more seriously than anything that had yet happened. She began to look upon Hurstwood wholly as a man, and not as a lover or husband. She felt thoroughly bound to him as a wife, and that her lot was cast with his, whatever it might be; but she began to see that he was gloomy and taciturn, not a young, strong, and buoyant man.

◄ *What does Hurstwood plan to do? What does he want to do to save money for this venture?*

◄ *How are Carrie's feelings for Hurstwood changing? In what way is she beginning to view him? What does she remember?*

Words For Everyday Use

tac • i • turn (tas´ə tərn) *adj.*, uncommunicative

He looked a little bit old to her about the eyes and mouth now, and there were other things which placed him in his true rank, so far as her estimation was concerned. She began to feel that she had made a mistake. Incidentally, she also began to recall the fact that he had practically forced her to flee with him.

▶ *How does Carrie feel about their new place?*

The new flat was located in Thirteenth Street, a half block west of Sixth Avenue, and contained only four rooms. The new neighborhood did not appeal to Carrie as much. There were no trees here, no west view of the river. The street was solidly built up. There were twelve families here, respectable enough, but nothing like the Vances. Richer people required more space.

Being left alone in this little place, Carrie did without a girl. She made it charming enough, but could not make it delight her. Hurstwood was not inwardly pleased to think that they should have to modify their state, but he argued that he could do nothing. He must put the best face on it, and let it go at that.

▶ *What "disease" is beginning to claim Hurstwood? What does he spend his time doing? What has slipped away?*

▶ *For what does Hurstwood's partner begin to hope?*

He tried to show Carrie that there was no cause for financial alarm, but only congratulation over the chance he would have at the end of the year by taking her rather more frequently to the theater and by providing a liberal table. This was for the time only. He was getting in the frame of mind where he wanted principally to be alone and to be allowed to think. The disease of brooding was beginning to claim him as a victim. Only the newspapers and his own thoughts were worthwhile. The delight of love had again slipped away. It was a case of live, now, making the best you can out of a very commonplace station in life.

The road downward has but few landings and level places. The very state of his mind, superinduced by his condition, caused the breach to widen between him and his partner. At last that individual began to wish that Hurstwood was out of it. It so happened, however, that a real estate deal on the part of the owner of the land arranged things even more effectually than ill will could have schemed.

"Did you see that?" said Shaughnessy one morning to Hurstwood, pointing to the real estate column in a copy of the *Herald,* which he held.

Words For Everyday Use

su • per • in • duced (so͞o´pər in do͞osd´) *adj.,* added as a complicating condition

"No, what is it?" said Hurstwood, looking down the items of news.

"The man who owns this ground has sold it."

"You don't say so?" said Hurstwood.

He looked, and there was the notice. Mr. August Viele had yesterday registered the transfer of the lot, 25 x 75 feet, at the corner of Warren and Hudson streets, to J. F. Slawson for the sum of $57,000.

"Our lease expires when?" asked Hurstwood, thinking. "Next February, isn't it?"

"That's right," said Shaughnessy.

"It doesn't say what the new man's going to do with it," remarked Hurstwood, looking back to the paper.

"We'll hear, I guess, soon enough," said Shaughnessy.

Sure enough, it did develop. Mr. Slawson owned the property adjoining, and was going to put up a modern office building. The present one was to be torn down. It would take probably a year and a half to complete the other one.

◄ *What happens to fulfill Shaughnessy's hope to get rid of Hurstwood?*

All these things developed by degrees, and Hurstwood began to ponder over what would become of the saloon. One day he spoke about it to his partner.

"Do you think it would be worthwhile to open up somewhere else in the neighborhood?"

"What would be the use?" said Shaughnessy. "We couldn't get another corner around here."

"It wouldn't pay anywhere else, do you think?"

"I wouldn't try it," said the other.

The approaching change now took on a most serious aspect to Hurstwood. Dissolution meant the loss of his thousand dollars, and he could not save another thousand in the time. He understood that Shaughnessy was merely tired of the arrangement, and would probably lease the new corner, when completed, alone. He began to worry about the necessity of a new connection and to see impending serious financial straits unless something turned up. This left him in no mood to enjoy his flat or Carrie, and consequently the depression invaded that quarter.

◄ *Why is this situation so serious?*

Meanwhile, he took such time as he could to look about, but opportunities were not numerous. More, he had not the same impressive personality which he had when he first came to New York. Bad thoughts had put a shade into his eyes which did not impress others favorably. Neither had he thirteen hundred dollars in hand to talk with. About a month later, finding that he had not made any progress, Shaughnessy reported definitely that Slawson would not extend the lease.

◄ *Why is it difficult for Hurstwood to find another business opportunity?*

"I guess this thing's got to come to an end," he said, affecting an air of concern.

"Well, if it has, it has," answered Hurstwood, grimly. He would not give the other a key to his opinions, whatever they were. He should not have the satisfaction.

A day or two later he saw that he must say something to Carrie.

"You know," he said, "I think I'm going to get the worst of my deal down there."

"How is that?" asked Carrie in astonishment.

"Well, the man who owns the ground has sold it, and the new owner won't release it to us. The business may come to an end."

"Can't you start somewhere else?"

"There doesn't seem to be anyplace. Shaughnessy doesn't want to."

▶ *What does Carrie suddenly realize about their situation?*

"Do you lose what you put in?"

"Yes," said Hurstwood, whose face was a study.

"Oh, isn't that too bad?" said Carrie.

"It's a trick," said Hurstwood. "That's all. They'll start another place there all right."

Carrie looked at him, and gathered from his whole demeanor what it meant. It was serious, very serious.

"Do you think you can get something else?" she ventured, timidly.

Hurstwood thought a while. It was all up with the bluff about money and investment. She could see now that he was "broke."

"I don't know," he said solemnly; "I can try."

CHAPTER 34

The Grind of the Millstones: A Sample of Chaff

Carrie pondered over this situation as consistently as Hurstwood, once she got the facts adjusted in her mind. It took several days for her to fully realize that the approach of the dissolution of her husband's business meant commonplace struggle and privation. Her mind went back to her early venture in Chicago, the Hansons and their flat, and her heart revolted. That was terrible! Everything about poverty was terrible. She wished she knew a way out. Her recent experiences with the Vances had wholly unfitted her to view her own state with complacence. The glamour of the high life of the city had, in the few experiences afforded her by the former, seized her completely. She had been taught how to dress and where to go without having ample means to do either. Now, these things—ever-present realities as they were—filled her eyes and mind. The more circumscribed became her state, the more entrancing seemed this other. And now poverty threatened to seize her entirely and to remove this other world far upward like a heaven to which any Lazarus[1] might extend, appealingly, his hands.

◄ *What does it take some time for Carrie to understand about the situation? Of what does this realization remind her?*

So, too, the ideal brought into her life by Ames remained. He had gone, but here was his word that riches were not everything; that there was a great deal more in the world than she knew; that the stage was good, and the literature she read poor. He was a strong man and clean—how much stronger and better than Hurstwood and Drouet she only half formulated to herself, but the difference was painful. It was something to which she voluntarily closed her eyes.

◄ *What ideas inspired by Ames remain in Carrie's mind?*

During the last three months of the Warren Street connection, Hurstwood took parts of days off and hunted, tracking the business advertisements. It was a more or less depressing business, wholly because of the thought that he must soon get something or he would begin to live on the few hundred dollars he was saving, and then he would have nothing to invest—he would have to hire out as a clerk.

1. **Lazarus.** Diseased beggar in Jesus' parable of the rich man and the beggar: Luke 16:19–31

Words For Everyday Use

am • ple (amp´əl) *adj.*, abundant; adequate

► *What does Hurstwood think of the business opportunities he finds?*

► *What seems to be the economic situation in general in this part of the country?*

Everything he discovered in his line advertised as an opportunity, was either too expensive or too wretched for him. Besides, winter was coming, the papers were announcing hardships, and there was a general feeling of hard times in the air, or, at least, he thought so. In his worry, other people's worries became apparent. No item about a firm failing, a family starving, or a man dying upon the streets, supposedly of starvation, but arrested his eye as he scanned the morning papers. Once the *World* came out with a flaring announcement about "80,000 people out of employment in New York this winter," which struck as a knife at his heart.

"Eighty thousand!" he thought. "What an awful thing that is."

This was new reasoning for Hurstwood. In the old days the world had seemed to be getting along well enough. He had been wont to see similar things in the *Daily News,* in Chicago, but they did not hold his attention. Now, these things were like gray clouds hovering along the horizon of a clear day. They threatened to cover and obscure his life with chilly grayness. He tried to shake them off, to forget and brace up. Sometimes he said to himself, mentally:

"What's the use worrying? I'm not out yet. I've got six weeks more. Even if worst comes to worst, I've got enough to live on for six months."

► *How long have Carrie and Hurstwood been together? To whom are Hurstwood's thoughts turning? Why?*

Curiously, as he troubled over his future, his thoughts occasionally reverted to his wife and family. He had avoided such thoughts for the first three years as much as possible. He hated her, and he could get along without her. Let her go. He would do well enough. Now, however, when he was not doing well enough, he began to wonder what she was doing, how his children were getting along. He could see them living as nicely as ever, occupying the comfortable house and using his property.

► *What is Hurstwood trying to justify? Why?*

"By George! it's a shame they should have it all," he vaguely thought to himself on several occasions. "I didn't do anything."

As he looked back now and analyzed the situation which led up to his taking the money, he began mildly to justify himself. What had he done—what in the world—that should bar him out this way and heap such difficulties upon him? It seemed only yesterday to him since he was comfortable and well-to-do. But now it was all wrested from him.

Words For Everyday Use

ob • scure (əb skyo͞or´) *vt.,* cover with darkness

"She didn't deserve what she got out of me, that is sure. I didn't do so much, if everybody could just know."

There was no thought that the facts ought to be advertised. It was only a mental justification he was seeking from himself—something that would enable him to bear his state as a righteous man.

One afternoon, five weeks before the Warren Street place closed up, he left the saloon to visit three or four places he saw advertised in the *Herald.* One was down in Gold Street, and he visited that, but did not enter. It was such a cheap looking place he felt that he could not abide it. Another was on the Bowery, which he knew contained many showy resorts. It was near Grand Street, and turned out to be very handsomely fitted up. He talked around about investments for fully three-quarters of an hour with the proprietor, who maintained that his health was poor, and that was the reason he wished a partner.

◀ How much would Hurstwood need to buy a half interest in the place near Grand Street? By how much is he short?

"Well, now, just how much money would it take to buy a half interest here?" said Hurstwood, who saw seven hundred dollars as his limit.

"Three thousand," said the man.

Hurstwood's jaw fell.

"Cash?" he said.

"Cash."

He tried to put on an air of deliberation, as one who might really buy; but his eyes showed gloom. He wound up by saying he would think it over, and came away. The man he had been talking to sensed his condition in a vague way.

"I don't think he wants to buy," he said to himself. "He doesn't talk right."

The afternoon was as gray as lead and cold. It was blowing up a disagreeable winter wind. He visited a place far up on the east side, near Sixty-ninth Street, and it was five o'clock, and growing dim, when he reached there. A portly German kept this place.

"How about this ad of yours?" asked Hurstwood, who rather objected to the looks of the place.

"Oh, dat iss all over," said the German. "I vill not sell now."

"Oh, is that so?"

"Yes; dere is nothing to dat. It iss all over."

"Very well," said Hurstwood, turning around.

The German paid no more attention to him, and it made him angry.

"The crazy ass!" he said to himself. "What does he want to advertise for?"

► *How does Hurstwood appear to Carrie now?*

► *What angers Carrie?*

Wholly depressed, he started for Thirteenth Street. The flat had only a light in the kitchen, where Carrie was working. He struck a match and, lighting the gas, sat down in the dining room without even greeting her. She came to the door and looked in.

"It's you, is it?" she said, and went back.

"Yes," he said, without even looking up from the evening paper he had bought.

Carrie saw things were wrong with him. He was not so handsome when gloomy. The lines at the sides of the eyes were deepened. Naturally dark of skin, gloom made him look slightly sinister. He was quite a disagreeable figure.

Carrie set the table and brought in the meal.

"Dinner's ready," she said, passing him for something.

He did not answer, reading on.

She came in and sat down at her place, feeling exceedingly wretched.

"Won't you eat now?" she asked.

He folded his paper and drew near, silence holding for a time, except for the "Pass me's."

"It's been gloomy today, hasn't it?" ventured Carrie, after a time.

"Yes," he said.

He only picked at his food.

"Are you still sure to close up?" said Carrie, venturing to take up the subject which they had discussed often enough.

"Of course we are," he said, with the slightest modification of sharpness.

This retort angered Carrie. She had had a dreary day of it herself.

"You needn't talk like that," she said.

"Oh!" he exclaimed, pushing back from the table, as if to say more, but letting it go at that. Then he picked up his paper. Carrie left her seat, containing herself with difficulty. He saw she was hurt.

"Don't go 'way," he said, as she started back into the kitchen. "Eat your dinner."

She passed, not answering.

He looked at the paper a few moments, and then rose up and put on his coat.

"I'm going downtown, Carrie," he said, coming out. "I'm out of sorts tonight."

Words For Everyday Use

re • tort (ri tôrt´) *n.,* sharp reply

She did not answer.

"Don't be angry," he said. "It will be all right tomorrow."

He looked at her, but she paid no attention to him, working at her dishes.

"Goodbye!" he said finally, and went out.

This was the first strong result of the situation between them, but with the nearing of the last day of business the gloom became almost a permanent thing. Hurstwood could not conceal his feelings about the matter. Carrie could not help wondering where she was drifting. It got so that they talked even less than usual, and yet it was not Hurstwood who felt any objection to Carrie. It was Carrie who shied away from him. This he noticed. It aroused an objection to her becoming indifferent to him. He made the possibility of friendly intercourse almost a giant task, and then noticed with discontent that Carrie added to it by her manner and made it more impossible.

◄ *What does Hurstwood notice?*

At last the final day came. When it actually arrived, Hurstwood, who had got his mind into such a state where a thunderclap and raging storm would have seemed highly appropriate, was rather relieved to find that it was a plain, ordinary day. The sun shone, the temperature was pleasant. He felt, as he came to the breakfast table, that it wasn't so terrible, after all.

"Well," he said to Carrie, "today's my last day on earth."

Carrie smiled in answer to his humor.

Hurstwood glanced over his paper rather gaily. He seemed to have lost a load.

"I'll go down for a little while," he said after breakfast, "and then I'll look around. Tomorrow I'll spend the whole day looking about. I think I can get something, now this thing's off my hands."

He went out smiling and visited the place. Shaughnessy was there. They had made all arrangements to share according to their interests. When, however, he had been there several hours, gone out three more, and returned, his elation had departed. As much as he had objected to the place, now that it was no longer to exist, he felt sorry. He wished that things were different.

Shaughnessy was coolly business-like.

"Well," he said at five o'clock, "we might as well count the change and divide."

They did so. The fixtures had already been sold and the sum divided.

"Goodnight," said Hurstwood at the final moment, in a last effort to be genial.

"So long," said Shaughnessy, scarcely deigning a notice.

Thus the Warren Street arrangement was permanently concluded.

Carrie had prepared a good dinner at the flat, but after his ride up, Hurstwood was in a solemn and reflective mood.

"Well?" said Carrie, inquisitively.

"I'm out of that," he answered, taking off his coat.

As she looked at him, she wondered what his financial state was now. They ate and talked a little.

"Will you have enough to buy in anywhere else?" asked Carrie.

"No," he said. "I'll have to get something else and save up."

"It would be nice if you could get some place," said Carrie, prompted by anxiety and hope.

"I guess I will," he said reflectively.

For some days thereafter he put on his overcoat regularly in the morning and sallied forth. On these ventures he first consoled himself with the thought that with the seven hundred dollars he had he could still make some advantageous arrangement. He thought about going to some brewery, which, as he knew, frequently controlled saloons which they leased, and get them to help him. Then he remembered that he would have to pay out several hundred anyway for fixtures and that he would have nothing left for his monthly expenses. It was costing him nearly eighty dollars a month to live.

"No," he said, in his sanest moments, "I can't do it. I'll get something else and save up."

► What makes getting a position complicated for Hurstwood?

This getting-something proposition complicated itself the moment he began to think of what it was he wanted to do. Manage a place? Where should he get such a position? The papers contained no requests for managers. Such positions, he knew well enough, were either secured by long years of service or were bought with a half or third interest. Into a place important enough to need such a manager he had not money enough to buy.

► Why does Hurstwood's appearance make his job search difficult?

Nevertheless, he started out. His clothes were very good and his appearance still excellent, but it involved the trouble of deluding. People, looking at him, imagined instantly that a man of his age, stout and well-dressed, must be well off. He appeared a comfortable owner of something, a man from whom the common run of mortals could well expect gratuities.

Words For Everyday Use

sal • ly forth (sal´ē fôrth) *vi.*, go out, as to battle

de • lude (di lo͞od´) *vt.*, fool, as by false promises

Being now forty-three years of age, and comfortably built, walking was not easy. He had not been used to exercise for many years. His legs tired, his shoulders ached, and his feet pained him at the close of the day, even when he took street cars in almost every direction. The mere getting up and down, if long continued, produced this result.

The fact that people took him to be better off than he was, he well understood. It was so painfully clear to him that it retarded his search. Not that he wished to be less well-appearing, but that he was ashamed to belie his appearance by incongruous appeals. So he hesitated, wondering what to do.

He thought of the hotels, but instantly he remembered that he had had no experience as a clerk, and, what was more important, no acquaintances or friends in that line to whom he could go. He did know some hotel owners in several cities, including New York, but they knew of his dealings with Fitzgerald and Moy. He could not apply to them. He thought of other lines suggested by large buildings or businesses which he knew of—wholesale groceries, hardware, insurance concerns, and the like—but he had had no experience.

How to go about getting anything was a bitter thought. Would he have to go personally and ask; wait outside an office door, and, then, distinguished and affluent looking, announce that he was looking for something to do? He strained painfully at the thought. No, he could not do that.

◄ What is Hurstwood too proud to do?

He really strolled about, thinking, and then, the weather being cold, stepped into a hotel. He knew hotels well enough to know that any decent looking individual was welcome to a chair in the lobby. This was in the Broadway Central, which was then one of the most important hotels in the city. Taking a chair here was a painful thing to him. To think he should come to this! He had heard loungers about hotels called chair-warmers. He had called them that himself in his day. But here he was, despite the possibility of meeting someone who knew him, shielding himself from cold and the weariness of the streets in a hotel lobby.

◄ Where does Hurstwood go to get warm? What did Hurstwood himself formerly call people who habitually did this?

"I can't do this way," he said to himself. "There's no use of my starting out mornings without first thinking up some place to go. I'll think of some places and then look them up."

It occurred to him that the positions of bartenders were sometimes open, but he put this out of his mind. Bartender—he, the ex-manager!

◄ For what job is Hurstwood unwilling to look? Why?

Words For Everyday Use

be • lie (bē lī´) *vt.,* disguise or misrepresent

in • con • gru • ous (in käŋ´gro͞o əs) *adj.,* unsuitable; inappropriate

af • flu • ent (af´lo͞o ənt) *adj.,* wealthy

► *Where does Hurstwood gladly sit?*

► *In what way does Hurstwood look at the last of his money?*

It grew awfully dull sitting in the hotel lobby, and so at four he went home. He tried to put on a business air as he went in, but it was a feeble imitation. The rocking-chair in the dining room was comfortable. He sank into it gladly, with several papers he had bought, and began to read.

As she was going through the room to begin preparing dinner, Carrie said:

"The man was here for the rent today."

"Oh, was he?" said Hurstwood.

The least wrinkle crept into his brow as he remembered that this was February 2d, the time the man always called. He fished down in his pocket for his purse, getting the first taste of paying out when nothing is coming in. He looked at the fat, green roll as a sick man looks at the one possible saving cure. Then he counted off twenty-eight dollars.

"Here you are," he said to Carrie, when she came through again.

He buried himself in his papers and read. Oh, the rest of it—the relief from walking and thinking! What Lethean waters[2] were these floods of telegraphed intelligence! He forgot his troubles, in part. Here was a young, handsome woman, if you might believe the newspaper drawing, suing a rich, fat, candy-making husband in Brooklyn for divorce. Here was another item detailing the wrecking of a vessel in ice and snow off Prince's Bay[3] on Staten Island. A long, bright column told of the doings in the theatrical world—the plays produced, the actors appearing, the managers making announcements. Fannie Davenport was just opening at the Fifth Avenue. Daly was producing *King Lear.* He read of the early departure for the season of a party composed of the Vanderbilts and their friends for Florida. An interesting shooting affray was on in the mountains of Kentucky. So he read, read, read, rocking in the warm room near the radiator and waiting for dinner to be served.

2. **Lethean waters.** Water of the River Lethe; according to Greek and Roman mythology, drinking of this water causes forgetfulness and memory loss

3. **Prince's Bay.** Error for Princess Bay

Words For Everyday Use

af • fray (ə frā´) *n.*, noisy brawl

CHAPTER 35

The Passing of Effort: The Visage of Care

The next morning he looked over the papers and waded through a long list of advertisements, making a few notes. Then he turned to the male-help-wanted column, but with disagreeable feelings. The day was before him—a long day in which to discover something—and this was how he must begin to discover. He scanned the long column, which mostly concerned bakers, bushel-men, cooks, compositors,[1] drivers, and the like, finding two things only which arrested his eye. One was a cashier wanted in a wholesale furniture house, and the other a salesman for a whiskey house. He had never thought of the latter. At once he decided to look that up.

The firm in question was Alsbery & Co., whiskey brokers.

He was admitted almost at once to the manager on his appearance.

"Good morning, sir," said the latter, thinking at first that he was encountering one of his out-of-town customers.

"Good morning," said Hurstwood. "You advertised, I believe, for a salesman?"

"Oh," said the man, showing plainly the enlightenment which had come to him. "Yes. Yes, I did."

"I thought I'd drop in," said Hurstwood, with dignity. "I've had some experience in that line myself."

"Oh, have you?" said the man. "What experience have you had?"

"Well, I've managed several liquor houses in my time. Recently I owned a third-interest in a saloon at Warren and Hudson streets."

"I see," said the man.

Hurstwood ceased, waiting for some suggestion.

"We did want a salesman," said the man. "I don't know as it's anything you'd care to take hold of, though."

◄ *Why doesn't Hurstwood please his potential employer?*

"I see," said Hurstwood. "Well, I'm in no position to choose, at present. If it were open, I should be glad to get it."

1. **bushel-men . . . compositors.** Handymen . . . typesetters

Words For Everyday Use

wade (wād) *vi.,* go forward with effort or difficulty

en • light • en • ment (en līt´'n mənt) *n.,* understanding; clarification

The man did not take kindly at all to his "no position to choose." He wanted someone who wasn't thinking of a choice or something better. Especially not an old man. He wanted someone young, active, and glad to work actively for a moderate sum. Hurstwood did not please him at all. He had more of an air than his employers.

"Well," he said in answer, "we'd be glad to consider your application. We shan't decide for a few days yet. Suppose you send us your references."

"I will," said Hurstwood.

► *Why doesn't Hurstwood go into the furniture company to see about the job advertised?*

He nodded good morning and came away. At the corner he looked at the furniture company's address, and saw that it was in West Twenty-third Street. Accordingly, he went up there. The place was not large enough, however. It looked moderate, the men in it idle and small salaried. He walked by, glancing in, and then decided not to go in there.

"They want a girl, probably, at ten a week," he said.

► *Where does Hurstwood go once again?*

At one o'clock he thought of eating, and went to a restaurant in Madison Square. There he pondered over places which he might look up. He was tired. It was blowing up gray again. Across the way, through Madison Square Park, stood the great hotels, looking down upon a busy scene. He decided to go over to the lobby of one and sit a while. It was warm in there and bright. He had seen no one he knew at the Broadway Central. In all likelihood he would encounter no one here. Finding a seat on one of the red plush divans close to the great windows which look out on Broadway's busy rout, he sat musing. His state did not seem so bad in here. Sitting still and looking out, he could take some slight consolation in the few hundred dollars he had in his purse. He could forget, in a measure, the weariness of the street and his tiresome searches. Still, it was only escape from a severe to a less severe state. He was still gloomy and disheartened. There, minutes seemed to go very slowly. An hour was a long, long time in passing. It was filled for him with observations and mental comments concerning the actual guests of the hotel, who passed in and out, and those more prosperous pedestrians whose good fortune showed in their clothes and spirits as they passed along Broadway, outside. It was nearly the first time since he had arrived in the city that his leisure afforded him ample opportunity to contemplate

Words For Everyday Use

pon • der (pän´dər) *vt.,* think deeply about

this spectacle. Now, being, perforce, idle himself, he wondered at the activity of others. How gay were the youths he saw, how pretty the women. Such fine clothes they all wore. They were so intent upon getting somewhere. He saw coquettish glances cast by magnificent girls. Ah, the money it required to train with such—how well he knew! How long it had been since he had had the opportunity to do so!

The clock outside registered four. It was a little early, but he thought he would go back to the flat.

This going back to the flat was coupled with the thought that Carrie would think he was sitting around too much if he came home early. He hoped he wouldn't have to, but the day hung heavily on his hands. Over there he was on his own ground. He could sit in his rocking-chair and read. This busy, distracting, suggestive scene was shut out. He could read his papers. Accordingly, he went home. Carrie was reading, quite alone. It was rather dark in the flat, shut in as it was.

◄ *Why does Hurstwood want to sit in his rocking-chair and read?*

"You'll hurt your eyes," he said when he saw her.

After taking off his coat, he felt it incumbent upon[2] him to make some little report of his day.

"I've been talking with a wholesale liquor company," he said. "I may go out on the road."

"Wouldn't that be nice!" said Carrie.

"It wouldn't be such a bad thing," he answered.

Always from the man at the corner now he bought two papers—the *Evening World* and *Evening Sun*. So now he merely picked his papers up, as he came by, without stopping.

He drew up his chair near the radiator and lighted the gas. Then it was as the evening before. His difficulties vanished in the items he so well loved to read.

The next day was even worse than the one before, because now he could not think of where to go. Nothing he saw in the papers he studied—till ten o'clock—appealed to him. He felt that he ought to go out, and yet he sickened at the thought. Where to, where to?

"You mustn't forget to leave me my money for this week," said Carrie, quietly.

They had an arrangement by which he placed twelve dollars a week in her hands, out of which to pay current expenses. He heaved a little sigh as she said this, and drew out his purse. Again he felt the dread of the thing. Here he was taking off, taking off, and nothing coming in.

"Lord!" he said, in his own thoughts, "this can't go on."

To Carrie he said nothing whatsoever. She could feel that her request disturbed him. To pay her would soon become a distressing thing.

◄ *What does Carrie resent?*

2. **incumbent upon.** Resting upon as a duty or obligation

"Yet, what have I got to do with it?" she thought. "Oh, why should I be made to worry?"

Hurstwood went out and made for Broadway. He wanted to think up some place. Before long, though, he reached the Grand Hotel at Thirty-first Street. He knew of its comfortable lobby. He was cold after his twenty blocks' walk.

"I'll go in their barber shop and get a shave," he thought.

Thus he justified himself in sitting down in here after his tonsorial[3] treatment.

Again, time hanging heavily on his hands, he went home early, and this continued for several days, each day the need to hunt paining him, and each day disgust, depression, shamefacedness driving him into lobby idleness.

At last three days came in which a storm prevailed, and he did not go out at all. The snow began to fall late one afternoon. It was a regular flurry of large, soft, white flakes. In the morning it was still coming down with a high wind, and the papers announced a blizzard. From out the front windows one could see a deep, soft bedding.

"I guess I'll not try to go out today," he said to Carrie at breakfast. "It's going to be awful bad, so the papers say."

"The man hasn't brought my coal, either," said Carrie, who ordered by the bushel.[4]

"I'll go over and see about it," said Hurstwood. This was the first time he had ever suggested doing an errand, but, somehow, the wish to sit about the house prompted it as a sort of compensation for the privilege.

All day and all night it snowed, and the city began to suffer from a general blockade of traffic. Great attention was given to the details of the storm by the newspapers, which played up the distress of the poor in large type.

► *What does Hurstwood do during the storm?*

Hurstwood sat and read by his radiator in the corner. He did not try to think about his need of work. This storm being so terrific, and tying up all things, robbed him of the need. He made himself wholly comfortable and toasted his feet.

Carrie observed his ease with some misgiving. For all the fury of the storm she doubted his comfort. He took his situation too philosophically.

Hurstwood, however, read on and on. He did not pay much attention to Carrie. She fulfilled her household duties and said little to disturb him.

The next day it was still snowing, and the next, bitter cold. Hurstwood took the alarm of the paper and sat still. Now he volunteered to do a few other little things. One was

3. **tonsorial.** Having to do with barbers
4. **bushel.** Unit of measurement, very small in regards to coal

to go to the butcher, another to the grocery. He really thought nothing of these little services in connection with their true significance. He felt as if he were not wholly useless—indeed, in such a stress of weather, quite worthwhile about the house.

◄ What else does Hurstwood volunteer to do to make himself feel useful?

On the fourth day, however, it cleared, and he read that the storm was over. Now, however, he idled, thinking how sloppy the streets would be.

It was noon before he finally abandoned his papers and got underway. Owing to the slightly warmer temperature the streets were bad. He went across Fourteenth Street on the car and got a transfer south on Broadway. One little advertisement he had, relating to a saloon down in Pearl Street. When he reached the Broadway Central, however, he changed his mind.

◄ Why doesn't Hurstwood even bother looking at the saloon on Pearl Street?

"What's the use?" he thought, looking out upon the slop and snow. "I couldn't buy into it. It's a thousand to one nothing comes of it. I guess I'll get off," and off he got. In the lobby he took a seat and waited again, wondering what he could do.

While he was idly pondering, satisfied to be inside, a well-dressed man passed up the lobby, stopped, looked sharply, as if not sure of his memory, and then approached. Hurstwood recognized Cargill, the owner of the large stables in Chicago of the same name, whom he had last seen at Avery Hall, the night Carrie appeared there. The remembrance of how this individual brought up his wife to shake hands on that occasion was also on the instant clear.

Hurstwood was greatly abashed. His eyes expressed the difficulty he felt.

◄ How do both men feel about meeting each other? Why?

"Why, it's Hurstwood!" said Cargill, remembering now, and sorry that he had not recognized him quickly enough in the beginning to have avoided this meeting.

"Yes," said Hurstwood. "How are you?"

"Very well," said Cargill, troubled for something to talk about. "Stopping here?"

"No," said Hurstwood, "just keeping an appointment."

"I knew you had left Chicago. I was wondering what had become of you."

"Oh, I'm here now," answered Hurstwood, anxious to get away.

"Doing well, I suppose?"

"Excellent."

"Glad to hear it."

They looked at one another, rather embarrassed.

"Well, I have an engagement with a friend upstairs. I'll leave you. So long."

Hurstwood nodded his head.

"Damn it all," he murmured, turning toward the door. "I knew that would happen."

He walked several blocks up the street. His watch only registered 1:30. He tried to think of some place to go or something to do. The day was so bad he wanted only to be inside. Finally his feet began to feel wet and cold, and he boarded a car. This took him to Fifty-ninth Street, which was as good as anywhere else. Landed here, he turned to walk back along Seventh Avenue, but the slush was too much. The misery of lounging about with nowhere to go became intolerable. He felt as if he were catching cold.

Stopping at a corner, he waited for a car southbound. This was no day to be out; he would go home.

Carrie was surprised to see him at a quarter of three.

"It's a miserable day out," was all he said. Then he took off his coat and changed his shoes.

► What happens to Hurstwood? What does Carrie think about the way this affects his appearance?

That night he felt a cold coming on and took quinine.[5] He was feverish until morning, and sat about the next day while Carrie waited on him. He was a helpless creature in sickness, not very handsome in a dull-colored bath gown and his hair uncombed. He looked haggard about the eyes and quite old. Carrie noticed this, and it did not appeal to her. She wanted to be good-natured and sympathetic, but something about the man held her aloof.

Toward evening he looked so badly in the weak light that she suggested he go to bed.

"You'd better sleep alone," she said, "you'll feel better. I'll open your bed for you now."

"All right," he said.

As she did all these things, she was in a most despondent state.

"What a life! What a life!" was her one thought.

► Why does Carrie cry?

Once during the day, when he sat near the radiator, hunched up and reading, she passed through, and seeing him, wrinkled her brows. In the front room, where it was not so warm, she sat by the window and cried. This was the life cut out for her, was it? To live cooped up in a small flat with someone who was out of work, idle, and indifferent to her. She was merely a servant to him now, nothing more.

5. **quinine.** Medicine made from cinchona bark

Words For Everyday Use

hag • gard (hag´ərd) *adj.,* having a wild, worn look

de • spond • ent (di spän´dənt) *adj.,* dejected; discouraged

This crying made her eyes red, and when, in preparing his bed, she lighted the gas, and, having prepared it, called him in, he noticed the fact.

"What's the matter with you?" he asked, looking into her face. His voice was hoarse and his unkempt head only added to its gruesome quality.

"Nothing," said Carrie, weakly.

"You've been crying," he said.

"I haven't either," she answered.

It was not for love of him, that he knew.

"You needn't cry," he said, getting into bed. "Things will come out all right."

In a day or two he was up again, but rough weather holding, he stayed in. The Italian newsdealer now delivered the morning papers, and these he read assiduously. A few times after that he ventured out, but meeting another of his old-time friends, he began to feel uneasy sitting about hotel corridors.

Every day he came home early, and at last made no pretence of going anywhere. Winter was no time to look for anything.

Naturally, being about the house, he noticed the way Carrie did things. She was far from perfect in household methods and economy, and her little deviations on this score first caught his eye. Not, however, before her regular demand for her allowance became a grievous thing. Sitting around as he did, the weeks seemed to pass very quickly. Every Tuesday Carrie asked for her money.

"Do you think we live as cheaply as we might?" he asked one Tuesday morning.

"I do the best I can," said Carrie.

Nothing was added to this at the moment, but the next day he said:

"Do you ever go to the Gansevoort Market over here?"

"I didn't know there was such a market," said Carrie.

"They say you can get things lots cheaper there."

Carrie was very indifferent to the suggestion. These were things which she did not like at all.

"How much do you pay for a pound of meat?" he asked one day.

◄ *What does Hurstwood know about Carrie's tears?*

◄ *What does Hurstwood finally give up doing?*

◄ *What becomes a grievance to Hurstwood? What becomes a "mania" with him? What does he do more and more often?*

Words For Everyday Use

as • sid • u • ous • ly (ə sij´o͞o əs lē) *adv.,* diligently

"Oh, there are different prices," said Carrie. "Sirloin steak is twenty-two cents."

"That's steep, isn't it?" he answered.

So he asked about other things, until finally, with the passing days, it seemed to become a mania with him. He learned the prices and remembered them.

His errand-running capacity also improved. It began in a small way, of course. Carrie, going to get her hat one morning, was stopped by him.

"Where are you going, Carrie?" he asked.

"Over to the baker's," she answered.

"I'd just as leave[6] go for you," he said.

She acquiesced, and he went. Each afternoon he would go to the corner for the papers.

"Is there anything you want?" he would say.

By degrees she began to use him. Doing this, however, she lost the weekly payment of twelve dollars.

"You want to pay me today," she said one Tuesday, about this time.

"How much?" he asked.

She understood well enough what it meant.

"Well, about five dollars," she answered. "I owe the coal man."

The same day he said:

"I think this Italian up here on the corner sells coal at twenty-five cents a bushel. I'll trade with him."

Carrie heard this with indifference.

"All right," she said.

Then it came to be:

► *What does Carrie do now whenever she needs something for the household? What is the drawback of Hurstwood's new interest?*

► *What grieves Carrie? How does she view Hurstwood?*

"George, I must have some coal today," or, "You must get some meat of some kind for dinner."

He would find out what she needed and order.

Accompanying this plan came skimpiness.

"I only got a half-pound of steak," he said, coming in one afternoon with his papers. "We never seem to eat very much."

These miserable details ate the heart out of Carrie. They blackened her days and grieved her soul. Oh, how this man had changed! All day and all day, here he sat, reading his papers. The world seemed to have no attraction. Once in a while he would go out, in fine weather, it might be four or five hours, between eleven and four. She could do nothing but view him with gnawing contempt.

It was apathy with Hurstwood, resulting from his inability to see his way out. Each month drew from his small store.

---

6. **just as leave.** Just as soon

Now, he had only five hundred dollars left, and this he hugged, half feeling as if he could stave off[7] absolute necessity for an indefinite period. Sitting around the house, he decided to wear some old clothes he had. This came first with the bad days. Only once he apologized in the very beginning:

◄ In what way does Hurstwood's appearance begin to suffer?

"It's so bad today, I'll just wear these around."

Eventually these became the permanent thing.

Also, he had been wont to pay fifteen cents for a shave, and a tip of ten cents. In his first distress, he cut down the tip to five, then to nothing. Later, he tried a ten-cent barber shop, and, finding that the shave was satisfactory, patronized regularly. Later still, he put off shaving to every other day, then to every third, and so on, until once a week became the rule. On Saturday he was a sight to see.

Of course, as his own self-respect vanished, it perished for him in Carrie. She could not understand what had gotten into the man. He had some money, he had a decent suit remaining, he was not bad looking when dressed up. She did not forget her own difficult struggle in Chicago, but she did not forget either that she had never ceased trying. He never tried. He did not even consult the ads in the papers anymore.

◄ In what way does Carrie compare her former searches for work with Hurstwood's? Is it true that Carrie "never ceased trying"? Explain.

Finally, a distinct impression escaped from her.

"What makes you put so much butter on the steak?" he asked her one evening, standing around in the kitchen.

◄ About what does Hurstwood complain? What is the effect of Carrie's cutting remark? Why does she reply as she does?

"To make it good, of course," she answered.

"Butter is awful dear[8] these days," he suggested.

"You wouldn't mind it if you were working," she answered.

He shut up after this, and went in to his paper, but the retort rankled in his mind. It was the first cutting remark that had come from her.

That same evening, Carrie, after reading, went off to the front room to bed. This was unusual. When Hurstwood decided to go, he retired, as usual, without a light. It was then that he discovered Carrie's absence.

"That's funny," he said; "maybe she's sitting up."

He gave the matter no more thought, but slept. In the morning she was not beside him. Strange to say, this passed without comment.

Night approaching, and a slightly more conversational feeling prevailing, Carrie said:

"I think I'll sleep alone tonight. I have a headache."

"All right," said Hurstwood.

---

7. **stave off.** Keep off
8. **dear.** Expensive

► *What has Carrie started to do?*

The third night she went to her front bed without apologies.

This was a grim blow to Hurstwood, but he never mentioned it.

"All right," he said to himself, with an irrepressible frown, "let her sleep alone."

Words For Everyday Use

ir • re • press • i • ble (ir´ri pres´ ə bəl) *adj.,* impossible to restrain or control

CHAPTER 36

A Grim Retrogression: The Phantom of Chance

The Vances, who had been back in the city ever since Christmas, had not forgotten Carrie; but they, or rather Mrs. Vance, had never called on her, for the very simple reason that Carrie had never sent her address. True to her nature, she corresponded with Mrs. Vance as long as she still lived in Seventy-eighth Street, but when she was compelled to move into Thirteenth, her fear that the latter would take it as an indication of reduced circumstances caused her to study some way of avoiding the necessity of giving her address. Not finding any convenient method, she sorrowfully resigned the privilege of writing to her friend entirely. The latter wondered at this strange silence, thought Carrie must have left the city, and in the end gave her up as lost. So she was thoroughly surprised to encounter her in Fourteenth Street, where she had gone shopping. Carrie was there for the same purpose.

◀ *Why has Carrie stopped writing to her friend, Mrs. Vance?*

"Why, Mrs. Wheeler," said Mrs. Vance, looking Carrie over in a glance, "where have you been? Why haven't you been to see me? I've been wondering all this time what had become of you. Really, I—"

"I'm so glad to see you," said Carrie, pleased and yet nonplussed. Of all times, this was the worst to encounter Mrs. Vance. "Why, I'm living downtown here. I've been intending to come and see you. Where are you living now?"

"In Fifty-eighth Street," said Mrs. Vance, "just off Seventh Avenue—218. Why don't you come and see me?"

"I will," said Carrie. "Really, I've been wanting to come. I know I ought to. It's a shame. But you know—"

"What's your number?" said Mrs. Vance.

"Thirteenth Street," said Carrie, reluctantly. "112 West."

"Oh," said Mrs. Vance, "that's right near here, isn't it?"

"Yes," said Carrie. "You must come down and see me some time."

"Well, you're a fine one," said Mrs. Vance, laughing, the while noting that Carrie's appearance had modified somewhat. "The address, too," she added to herself. "They must be hard up."

◀ *What can Mrs. Vance tell from Carrie's appearance and address?*

Still she liked Carrie well enough to take her in tow.

"Come with me in here a minute," she exclaimed, turning into a store.

When Carrie returned home, there was Hurstwood, reading as usual. He seemed to take his condition with the utmost nonchalance. His beard was at least four days old.

"Oh," thought Carrie, "if she were to come here and see him?"

She shook her head in absolute misery. It looked as if her situation was becoming unbearable.

Driven to desperation, she asked at dinner:

"Did you ever hear any more from that wholesale house?"

"No," he said. "They don't want an inexperienced man."

Carrie dropped the subject, feeling unable to say more.

"I met Mrs. Vance this afternoon," she said, after a time.

"Did, eh?" he answered.

"They're back in New York now," Carrie went on. "She did look so nice."

"Well, she can afford it as long as he puts up for it," returned Hurstwood. "He's got a soft job."

Hurstwood was looking into the paper. He could not see the look of infinite weariness and discontent Carrie gave him.

"She said she thought she'd call here some day."

► *What doesn't Hurstwood like about Mrs. Vance?*

"She's been long getting round to it, hasn't she?" said Hurstwood, with a kind of sarcasm.

The woman didn't appeal to him from her spending side.

"Oh, I don't know," said Carrie, angered by the man's attitude. "Perhaps I didn't want her to come."

"She's too gay," said Hurstwood, significantly. "No one can keep up with her pace unless they've got a lot of money."

"Mr. Vance doesn't seem to find it very hard."

► *What thoughts please Hurstwood?*

"He may not now," answered Hurstwood, doggedly, well understanding the inference; "but his life isn't done yet. You can't tell what'll happen. He may get down like anybody else."

There was something quite knavish in the man's attitude. His eye seemed to be cocked with a twinkle upon the fortunate, expecting their defeat. His own state seemed a thing apart—not considered.

This thing was the remains of his old-time cocksureness and independence. Sitting in his flat, and reading of the doings of other people, sometimes this independent, undefeated mood came upon him. Forgetting the weariness of the streets and the degradation of search, he would sometimes prick up his ears. It was as if he said:

Words For Everyday Use

dog • ged • ly (dôg´id lē) *adv.,* stubbornly

in • fer • ence (in´fər əns) *n.,* implication

knav • ish (nāv´ ish) *adj.,* mischievous

cock • sure • ness (käk´shoor´nəs) *n.,* overconfidence

deg • ra • da • tion (deg´rə dā´ shən) *n.,* that which brings one to a lower position

"I can do something. I'm not down yet. There's a lot of things coming to me if I want to go after them."

It was in this mood that he would occasionally dress up, go for a shave, and, putting on his gloves, sally forth quite actively. Not with any definite aim. It was more a barometric condition.[1] He felt just right for being outside and doing something.

On such occasions, his money went also. He knew of several poker rooms downtown. A few acquaintances he had in downtown resorts and about the City Hall. It was a change to see them and exchange a few friendly commonplaces.

He had once been accustomed to hold a pretty fair hand at poker. Many a friendly game had netted him a hundred dollars or more at the time when that sum was merely sauce to the dish of the game—not the all in all. Now, he thought of playing.

◄ *What has Hurstwood decided to do to get money? Explain whether this is a wise decision.*

"I might win a couple of hundred. I'm not out of practice."

It is but fair to say that this thought had occurred to him several times before he acted upon it.

The poker room which he first invaded was over a saloon in West Street, near one of the ferries. He had been there before. Several games were going. These he watched for a time and noticed that the pots were quite large for the ante[2] involved.

"Deal me a hand," he said at the beginning of a new shuffle. He pulled up a chair and studied his cards. Those playing made that quiet study of him which is so unapparent, and yet invariably so searching.

Poor fortune was with him at first. He received a mixed collection without progression or pairs. The pot was opened.

"I pass," he said.

On the strength of this, he was content to lose his ante. The deals did fairly by him in the long run, causing him to come away with a few dollars to the good.

The next afternoon he was back again, seeking amusement and profit. This time he followed up three of a kind to his doom. There was a better hand across the table, held by a pugnacious Irish youth, who was a political hanger-on[3] of

1. **barometric condition.** Change in the atmosphere
2. **ante.** Stake that each person must put into the pot before receiving cards
3. **hanger-on.** Unnecessary member of a group who looks for personal gain

Words For Everyday Use

pug • na • cious (pug nā´shəs) *adj.*, eager and ready to fight

the Tammany district in which they were located. Hurstwood was surprised at the persistence of this individual, whose bets came with a *sang-froid*[4] which, if a bluff, was excellent art. Hurstwood began to doubt, but kept, or thought to keep, at least, the cool demeanor with which, in olden times, he deceived those psychic students of the gaming table, who seem to read thoughts and moods, rather than exterior evidences, however subtle. He could not down the cowardly thought that this man had something better and would stay to the end, drawing his last dollar into the pot, should he choose to go so far. Still, he hoped to win much—his hand was excellent. Why not raise it five more?

"I raise you three," said the youth.

"Make it five," said Hurstwood, pushing out his chips.

"Come again," said the youth, pushing out a small pile of reds.

"Let me have some more chips," said Hurstwood to the keeper in charge, taking out a bill.

A cynical grin lit up the face of his youthful opponent. When the chips were laid out, Hurstwood met the raise.

"Five again," said the youth.

► *How much money has Hurstwood lost? How much does he have left?*

Hurstwood's brow was wet. He was deep in now—very deep for him. Sixty dollars of his good money was up. He was ordinarily no coward, but the thought of losing so much weakened him. Finally he gave way. He would not trust to this fine hand any longer.

"I call," he said.

"A full house!" said the youth, spreading out his cards.

Hurstwood's hand dropped.

"I thought I had you," he said, weakly.

The youth raked in his chips, and Hurstwood came away, not without first stopping to count his remaining cash on the stair.

"Three hundred and forty dollars," he said.

With this loss and ordinary expenses, so much had already gone.

Back in the flat, he decided he would play no more.

Remembering Mrs. Vance's promise to call, Carrie made one other mild protest. It was concerning Hurstwood's appearance. This very day, coming home, he changed his clothes to the old togs[5] he sat around in.

► *Why does Hurstwood's behavior almost make Carrie hate him?*

"What makes you always put on those old clothes?" asked Carrie.

"What's the use wearing my good ones around here?" he asked.

4. ***sang-froid.*** "Cold blood"; French expression meaning "coolly, without emotion"
5. **togs.** Clothes; outfit

"Well, I should think you'd feel better." Then she added: "Someone might call."

"Who?" he said.

"Well, Mrs. Vance," said Carrie.

"She needn't see me," he answered, sullenly.

This lack of pride and interest made Carrie almost hate him.

"Oh," she thought, "there he sits. 'She needn't see me.' I should think he would be ashamed of himself."

The real bitterness of this thing was added when Mrs. Vance did call. It was on one of her shopping rounds. Making her way up the commonplace hall, she knocked at Carrie's door. To her subsequent and agonizing distress, Carrie was out. Hurstwood opened the door, half-thinking that the knock was Carrie's. For once, he was taken honestly aback. The lost voice of youth and pride spoke in him.

"Why," he said, actually stammering, "how do you do?"

"How do you do?" said Mrs. Vance, who could scarcely believe her eyes. His great confusion she instantly perceived. He did not know whether to invite her in or not.

"Is your wife at home?" she inquired.

"No," he said, "Carrie's out; but won't you step in? She'll be back shortly."

"No-o," said Mrs. Vance, realizing the change of it all. "I'm really very much in a hurry. I thought I'd just run up and look in, but I couldn't stay. Just tell your wife she must come and see me."

"I will," said Hurstwood, standing back, and feeling intense relief at her going. He was so ashamed that he folded his hands weakly, as he sat in the chair afterward, and thought.

Carrie, coming in from another direction, thought she saw Mrs. Vance going away. She strained her eyes, but could not make sure.

"Was anybody here just now?" she asked of Hurstwood.

"Yes," he said guiltily; "Mrs. Vance."

"Did she see you?" she asked, expressing her full despair.

This cut Hurstwood like a whip, and made him sullen.

"If she had eyes, she did. I opened the door."

"Oh," said Carrie, closing one hand tightly out of sheer nervousness. "What did she have to say?"

"Nothing," he answered. "She couldn't stay."

"And you looking like that!" said Carrie, throwing aside a long reserve.

"What of it?" he said, angering. "I didn't know she was coming, did I?"

◄ *What does Carrie say that hurts Hurstwood? How does Hurstwood feel about what has occurred?*

"You knew she might," said Carrie. "I told you she said she was coming. I've asked you a dozen times to wear your other clothes. Oh, I think this is just terrible."

"Oh, let up," he answered. "What difference does it make? You couldn't associate with her, anyway. They've got too much money."

"Who said I wanted to?" said Carrie, fiercely.

"Well, you act like it, rowing around over my looks. You'd think I'd committed—"

Carrie interrupted:

"It's true," she said. "I couldn't if I wanted to, but whose fault is it? You're very free to sit and talk about who I could associate with. Why don't you get out and look for work?"

► *What does Carrie tell Hurstwood to do?*

This was a thunderbolt in camp.

"What's it to you?" he said, rising, almost fiercely. "I pay the rent, don't I? I furnish the—"

"Yes, you pay the rent," said Carrie. "You talk as if there was nothing else in the world but a flat to sit around in. You haven't done a thing for three months except sit around and interfere here. I'd like to know what you married me for?"

► *What does Hurstwood reveal to Carrie? Explain whether Carrie had even remotely suspected this news.*

"I didn't marry you," he said, in a snarling tone.

"I'd like to know what you did, then, in Montreal?" she answered.

"Well, I didn't marry you," he answered. "You can get that out of your head. You talk as though you didn't know."

Carrie looked at him a moment, her eyes distending. She had believed it was all legal and binding enough.

► *What does Hurstwood say that makes Carrie "break . . . under the strain"?*

"What did you lie to me for, then?" she asked, fiercely. "What did you force me to run away with you for?"

Her voice became almost a sob.

"Force!" he said, with curled lip. "A lot of forcing I did."

"Oh!" said Carrie, breaking under the strain, and turning. "Oh, oh!" and she hurried into the front room.

Hurstwood was now hot and waked up. It was a great shaking up for him, both mental and moral. He wiped his brow as he looked around, and then went for his clothes and dressed. Not a sound came from Carrie; she ceased sobbing when she heard him dressing. She thought, at first, with the faintest alarm, of being left without money—not of losing him, though he might be going away permanently. She heard him open the top of the wardrobe and take out his hat. Then the dining room door closed, and she knew he had gone.

► *What thought alarms Carrie? What thought does not?*

Words For Everyday Use

dis • tend (di stend´) *vi.*, stand out

After a few moments of silence, she stood up, dry-eyed, and looked out the window. Hurstwood was just strolling up the street, from the flat, toward Sixth Avenue.

The latter made progress along Thirteenth and across Fourteenth Street to Union Square.

"Look for work!" he said to himself. "Look for work! She tells me to get out and look for work."

He tried to shield himself from his own mental accusation, which told him that she was right.

"What a cursed thing that Mrs. Vance's call was, anyhow," he thought. "Stood right there, and looked me over. I know what she was thinking."

He remembered the few times he had seen her in Seventy-eighth Street. She was always a swell-looker, and he had tried to put on the air of being worthy of such as she, in front of her. Now, to think she had caught him looking this way. He wrinkled his forehead in his distress.

"The devil!" he said a dozen times in an hour.

It was a quarter after four when he left the house. Carrie was in tears. There would be no dinner that night.

"What the deuce," he said, swaggering mentally to hide his own shame from himself. "I'm not so bad. I'm not down yet."

He looked around the square, and seeing the several large hotels, decided to go to one for dinner. He would get his papers and make himself comfortable there.

◄ *To what is Hurstwood becoming addicted?*

He ascended into the fine parlor of the Morton House, then one of the best New York hotels, and, finding a cushioned seat, read. It did not trouble him much that his decreasing sum of money did not allow of such extravagance. Like the morphine[6] fiend, he was becoming addicted to his ease. Anything to relieve his mental distress, to satisfy his craving for comfort. He must do it. No thoughts for the morrow—he could not stand to think of it anymore than he could of any other calamity. Like the certainty of death, he tried to shut the certainty of soon being without a dollar completely out of his mind, and he came very near doing it.

Well-dressed guests moving to and fro over the thick carpets carried him back to the old days. A young lady, a guest

6. **morphine.** Pain-killing medicine derived from opium

Words For Everyday Use

swag • ger (swaˊ gər) *vi.*, move with exaggerated arrogance

ca • la • mi • ty (kə lamˊ ə tē) *n.*, disaster

of the house, playing a piano in an alcove pleased him. He sat there reading.

His dinner cost him $1.50. By eight o'clock he was through, and then, seeing guests leaving and the crowd of pleasure-seekers thickening outside, wondered where he should go. Not home. Carrie would be up. No, he would not go back there this evening. He would stay out and knock around as a man who was independent—not broke—well might. He bought a cigar, and went outside on the corner where other individuals were lounging—brokers, racing people, thespians[7]—his own flesh and blood. As he stood there, he thought of the old evenings in Chicago, and how he used to dispose of them. Many's the game he had had. This took him to poker.

► *What does Hurstwood decide to try once more?*

"I didn't do that thing right the other day," he thought, referring to his loss of sixty dollars. "I shouldn't have weakened. I could have bluffed that fellow down. I wasn't in form, that's what ailed me."

Then he studied the possibilities of the game as it had been played, and began to figure how he might have won, in several instances, by bluffing a little harder.

"I'm old enough to play poker and do something with it. I'll try my hand tonight."

Visions of a big stake floated before him. Supposing he did win a couple of hundred, wouldn't he be in it? Lots of sports[8] he knew made their living at this game, and a good living, too.

"They always had as much as I had," he thought.

So off he went to a poker room in the neighborhood, feeling much as he had in the old days. In this period of self-forgetfulness, aroused first by the shock of argument and perfected by a dinner in the hotel, with cocktails and cigars, he was as nearly like the old Hurstwood as he would ever be again. It was not the old Hurstwood—only a man arguing with a divided conscience and lured by a phantom.

This poker room was much like the other one, only it was a back room in a better drinking resort. Hurstwood watched a while, and then, seeing an interesting game, joined in. As before, it went easy for a while, he winning a few times and

7. **thespians.** Actors
8. **sports.** Gamblers

Words For Everyday Use

ail (āl) *vt.,* trouble

cheering up, losing a few pots[9] and growing more interested and determined on that account. At last the fascinating game took a strong hold on him. He enjoyed its risks and ventured, on a trifling hand, to bluff the company and secure a fair stake. To his self-satisfaction intense and strong, he did it.

In the height of this feeling he began to think his luck was with him. No one else had done so well. Now came another moderate hand, and again he tried to open the jackpot on it. There were others there who were almost reading his heart, so close was their observation.

◄ What does one poker player resolve to do after having been bluffed by Hurstwood?

"I have three of a kind," said one of the players to himself. "I'll just stay with the fellow to the finish."

The result was that bidding began.

"I raise you ten."

"Good."

"Ten more."

"Good."

"Ten again."

"Right you are."

It got to where Hurstwood had seventy-five dollars up. The other man really became serious. Perhaps this individual (Hurstwood) really did have a stiff hand.

◄ How much money has Hurstwood lost playing poker?

"I call," he said.

Hurstwood showed his hand. He was done. The bitter fact that he had lost seventy-five dollars made him desperate.

"Let's have another pot," he said, grimly.

"All right," said the man.

Some of the other players quit, but observant loungers took their places. Time passed, and it came to twelve o'clock. Hurstwood held on, neither winning nor losing much. Then he grew weary, and on a last hand lost twenty more. He was sick at heart.

At a quarter after one in the morning he came out of the place. The chill, bare streets seemed a mockery of his state. He walked slowly west, little thinking of his row with Carrie. He ascended the stairs and went into his room as if there had been no trouble. It was his loss that occupied his mind. Sitting down on the bedside he counted his money. There was now but a hundred and ninety dollars and some change. He put it up and began to undress.

"I wonder what's getting into me, anyhow?" he said.

In the morning Carrie scarcely spoke, and he felt as if he must go out again. He had treated her badly, but he could

9. **pots.** Amount to be won in a card game

not afford to make up. Now desperation seized him, and for a day or two, going out thus, he lived like a gentleman—or what he conceived to be a gentleman—which took money. For his escapades he was soon poorer in mind and body, to say nothing of his purse, which had lost thirty by the process. Then he came down to cold, bitter sense again.

"The rent man comes today," said Carrie, greeting him thus indifferently three mornings later.

"He does?"

"Yes; this is the second," answered Carrie.

Hurstwood frowned. Then in despair he got out his purse.

"It seems an awful lot to pay for rent," he said.

He was nearing his last hundred dollars.

► *How much money does Hurstwood have left?*

Words For Everyday Use

es • ca • pade (es´ kə pād) *n.,* reckless adventure

Responding to the Selection

By the end of chapter 36, both Hurstwood and Carrie are in difficult positions. Do you feel more sympathy for Hurstwood or for Carrie? Explain. What would you have done to prevent the situation from becoming so dire if you were in either one of these characters' positions?

Reviewing the Selection

Recalling and Interpreting

1. **R:** In chapter 31, what is Hurstwood careful to conceal from Carrie? What does he pretend? What does Hurstwood start to do in his free time? What assumptions does Hurstwood make about Carrie? Who befriends Carrie in Hurstwood's absence and to what world does this person introduce Carrie? What feelings do the presence of well-dressed women spark in Carrie?

2. **I:** In what way does Hurstwood's handling of his finances contribute to the theme of superficiality in the novel? What does it indicate about the way his state has altered? Why might Hurstwood deliberately misread Carrie?

3. **R:** In chapter 32, in what way does the narrator describe the matinee Carrie attends with Mrs. Vance? What does Carrie long to do? Who goes to dinner with Carrie and the Vances one night? What are this person's opinions of the restaurant, the literature Carrie enjoys, riches, and acting? What is Carrie's opinion of this person?

4. **I:** Why, given the narrator's description of the play, is Carrie's desire wryly humorous? Why doesn't Hurstwood approve of Carrie's friendship with Mrs. Vance? Why might Carrie value Mrs. Vance's friendship so highly? Why does Carrie find this person's opinions surprising? Explain whether you think this person's ideas and opinions are closer to the author's own than those of many of the other characters. At the end of chapter 32, the narrator says that Carrie "was rocking, and beginning to see." What is Carrie beginning to see? What is the lasting effect of this person upon Carrie?

5. **R:** In chapter 33, what happens to the Vances? What does Hurstwood finally admit to Carrie? What does he decide to do? What happens to Hurstwood's business? What is happening in New York in general? In chapter 34, what

difficulties does Hurstwood experience in his job search? What does Hurstwood do for relief from his troubles?

6. **I:** How does Carrie feel about these two occurrences in chapter 33? Explain whether Hurstwood seems very serious about getting another job. In what way has the loss of his business changed him as a character? Before, Carrie was always described as idling away her time by daydreaming and sitting in a rocking-chair. What is significant about the fact that Hurstwood now does the same?

7. **R:** What further setbacks in his job search does Hurstwood experience in chapter 35? In what way does Hurstwood's role in the house change as he is about the house more? In what way does Hurstwood's appearance change? In chapter 36, what occurrence finally prompts Carrie to reproach Hurstwood? What does Hurstwood say to revenge himself upon Carrie? In what way does Hurstwood lose even more money? How much money does he have left at the end of chapter 36?

8. **I:** In what way does Hurstwood's unemployment change his relationship with Carrie? How does Carrie feel about him now? In what way does Hurstwood's outward decline reflect his mental state? Why is this occurrence in chapter 36 the one that finally evokes a strong response from Carrie? Now that Carrie knows the truth, predict what effect this news will have on her relationship with Hurstwood. Throughout chapters 31–36, Dreiser keeps careful track of each dollar Hurstwood spends. Why?

Synthesizing

9. At the end of chapter 31, Carrie resolves that if she were better dressed, "ah, then she would be happy!" Almost all the characters in this novel feel at different points that if some particular desire is granted, they will achieve happiness. Explain whether, given the unfolding of events in this novel, this thought process is valid, or whether, when a character's desires are granted, the character simply longs for something else. What does Dreiser seem to be indicating about human nature?

10. In chapter 33, Dreiser reveals what he perceives to be a law that governs human "fortunes" in industrial society. Briefly explain this "law" in your own words. What does this reveal about what the author intends for Hurstwood's "fortune"? for Carrie's? What is your opinion of this "law"?

Fortune has a variety of meanings. In the context of Dreiser's "law," it can mean both "the turns and courses of luck accompanying one's progress through life" and "wealth." Which do you believe the author intends? In what way is a person's "wealth" his or her "destiny" in this novel?

Understanding Literature (QUESTIONS FOR DISCUSSION)

1. **Foil.** A **foil** is a character whose attributes, or characteristics, contrast with, and therefore throw into relief, the attributes of another character. Explain whether Mr. Ames serves as a foil to the rest of the characters in the novel. What do his attributes reveal about these characters?

2. **Allusion.** An **allusion** is a rhetorical technique in which reference is made to a person, event, object, or work from history or literature. The title of chapter 32, "The Feast of Belshazzar: A Seer to Translate," is an allusion to a story from chapter 5 of the Book of Daniel in the Bible. Daniel was a Jewish prophet who had been educated in Babylon under the rule of Nebuchadnezzar, a Babylonian king who conquered Judah, sacked Jerusalem, and brought many Israelites into captivity in Babylon. In this chapter, a later king called Belshazzar is holding a great feast and commands that the gold and silver vessels stolen from Jerusalem be brought in so that the king, the lords, and the ladies might drink from them. Immediately fingers appear and write a message on the wall of the feasting chamber. Daniel is called in to interpret the writing. He chastises Belshazzar for failing to humble his heart and for dishonoring the Lord by using the vessels from the Temple in Jerusalem. Daniel then interprets the words to mean "God has numbered the days of your kingdom and brought it to an end . . . you have been weighed on the scales and found wanting . . . your kingdom is divided and given to the Medes and the Persians," predicting the fall of Babylon.

In general, Babylon is associated in the Bible with lavish wealth, lascivious behavior, and sinfulness. Explain why Dreiser chose to refer to this story in the title of chapter 32. In what way are characters in this chapter like the Babylonians at the feast of Belshazzar? Who is the seer or prophet in chapter 32? In what way does this seer translate or interpret events? What does the implicit comparison of the fashionable world of New York City to Babylon reveal about Dreiser's view of society?

3. **Feminist Criticism. Feminist criticism** evaluates and interprets works of art with regard to their portrayal of or influence upon gender roles. Some feminist critics point out gender bias in literary works by analyzing differences in literary depictions of males and females. Review Dreiser's depiction of Carrie and Mr. Ames's interaction in chapter 32. What evidence of gender bias might a feminist critic find? What view of gender roles does Dreiser take?

4. **Metaphor.** A **metaphor** is a figure of speech in which one thing is spoken or written about as if it were another. This figure of speech invites the reader to make a comparison between the two things. Examine the "walled city" metaphor on page 303. In what way is life inside and outside this city different? What two things is the reader invited to compare? In what way are these two things alike?

CHAPTER 37

The Spirit Awakens: New Search for the Gate

It would be useless to explain how in due time the last fifty dollars was in sight. The seven hundred, by his process of handling, had only carried them into June. Before the final hundred mark was reached he began to indicate that a calamity was approaching.

"I don't know," he said one day, taking a trivial expenditure for meat as a text, "it seems to take an awful lot for us to live."

"It doesn't seem to me," said Carrie, "that we spend very much."

"My money is nearly gone," he said, "and I hardly know where it's gone to."

"All that seven hundred dollars?" asked Carrie.

"All but a hundred."

He looked so disconsolate that it scared her. She began to see that she herself had been drifting. She had felt it all the time.

"Well, George," she exclaimed, "why don't you get out and look for something? You could find something."

◄ *Does Hurstwood see any way out of this difficult situation?*

"I have looked," he said. "You can't make people give you a place."

She gazed weakly at him and said: "Well, what do you think you will do? A hundred dollars won't last long."

"I don't know," he said. "I can't do any more than look."

Carrie became frightened over this announcement. She thought desperately upon the subject. Frequently she had considered the stage as a door through which she might enter that gilded state which she had so much craved. Now, as in Chicago, it came as a last resource in distress. Something must be done if he did not get work soon. Perhaps she would have to go out and battle again alone.

◄ *What does Carrie think about doing if Hurstwood doesn't find work?*

She began to wonder how one would go about getting a place. Her experience in Chicago proved that she had not tried the right way. There must be people who would listen to and try you—men who would give you an opportunity.

They were talking at the breakfast table, a morning or two later, when she brought up the dramatic subject by saying

Words For Everyday Use

dis • con • so • late (dis kän′sə lit) *adj.*, unhappy

that she saw that Sarah Bernhardt[1] was coming to this country. Hurstwood had seen it, too.

"How do people get on the stage, George?" she finally asked, innocently.

"I don't know," he said. "There must be dramatic agents."

Carrie was sipping coffee, and did not look up.

"Regular people who get you a place?"

"Yes, I think so," he answered.

Suddenly the air with which she asked attracted his attention.

"You're not still thinking about being an actress, are you?" he asked.

"No," she answered, "I was just wondering."

► Why does Hurstwood object to the idea of Carrie becoming an actress?

Without being clear, there was something in the thought which he objected to. He did not believe any more, after three years of observation, that Carrie would ever do anything great in that line. She seemed too simple, too yielding. His idea of the art was that it involved something more pompous. If she tried to get on the stage she would fall into the hands of some cheap manager and become like the rest of them. He had a good idea of what he meant by them. Carrie was pretty. She would get along all right, but where would he be?

"I'd get that idea out of my head, if I were you. It's a lot more difficult than you think."

Carrie felt this to contain, in some way, an aspersion upon her ability.

"You said I did real well in Chicago," she rejoined.

"You did," he answered, seeing that he was arousing opposition, "but Chicago isn't New York, by a big jump."

Carrie did not answer this at all. It hurt her.

"The stage," he went on, "is all right if you can be one of the big guns, but there's nothing to the rest of it. It takes a long while to get up."

"Oh, I don't know," said Carrie, slightly aroused.

► What does Hurstwood fear?

► What quality in Carrie has Hurstwood overlooked? Why?

In a flash, he thought he foresaw the result of this thing. Now, when the worst of his situation was approaching, she would get on the stage in some cheap way and forsake him. Strangely, he had not conceived well of her mental ability. That was because he did not understand the nature of

1. **Sarah Bernhardt.** Famous French actress (1844–1923)

Words For Everyday Use

as • per • sion (ə spur´zhən) *n.,* damaging or disparaging remark

emotional greatness. He had never learned that a person might be emotionally—instead of intellectually—great. Avery Hall was too far away for him to look back and sharply remember. He had lived with this woman too long.

"Well, I do," he answered. "If I were you I wouldn't think of it. It's not much of a profession for a woman."

"It's better than going hungry," said Carrie. "If you don't want me to do that, why don't you get work yourself?"

There was no answer ready for this. He had got used to the suggestion.

"Oh, let up," he answered.

The result of this was that she secretly resolved to try. It didn't matter about him. She was not going to be dragged into poverty and something worse to suit him. She could act. She could get something and then work up. What would he say then? She pictured herself already appearing in some fine performance on Broadway; of going every evening to her dressing room and making up. Then she would come out at eleven o'clock and see the carriages ranged about, waiting for the people. It did not matter whether she was the star or not. If she were only once in, getting a decent salary, wearing the kind of clothes she liked, having the money to do with, going here and there as she pleased, how delightful it would all be. Her mind ran over this picture all the day long. Hurstwood's dreary state made its beauty become more and more vivid.

◄ *What is Carrie's secret resolution?*

Curiously this idea soon took hold of Hurstwood. His vanishing sum suggested that he would need sustenance. Why could not Carrie assist him a little until he could get something?

◄ *Why does Hurstwood change his mind about Carrie's trying to work as an actress?*

He came in one day with something of this idea in his mind.

"I met John B. Drake today," he said. "He's going to open a hotel here in the fall. He says that he can make a place for me then."

◄ *Explain whether you think the story Hurstwood tells Carrie is true.*

"Who is he?" asked Carrie.

"He's the man that runs the Grand Pacific in Chicago."

"Oh," said Carrie.

"I'd get about fourteen hundred a year out of that."

"That would be good, wouldn't it?" she said, sympathetically.

"If I can only get over this summer," he added, "I think I'll be all right. I'm hearing from some of my friends again."

Words For Everyday Use

sus • te • nance (sus´tə nəns) *n.,* support

Carrie swallowed this story in all its pristine beauty. She sincerely wished he could get through the summer. He looked so hopeless.

"How much money have you left?"

"Only fifty dollars."

"Oh, mercy," she exclaimed, "what will we do? It's only twenty days until the rent will be due again."

Hurstwood rested his head on his hands and looked blankly at the floor.

"Maybe you could get something in the stage line?" he blandly suggested.

"Maybe I could," said Carrie, glad that someone approved of the idea.

"I'll lay my hand to whatever I can get," he said, now that he saw her brighten up. "I can get something."

She cleaned up the things one morning after he had gone, dressed as neatly as her wardrobe permitted, and set out for Broadway. She did not know that thoroughfare very well. To her it was a wonderful conglomeration of everything great and mighty. The theaters were there—these agencies must be somewhere about.

She decided to stop in at the Madison Square Theater and ask how to find the theatrical agents. This seemed the sensible way. Accordingly, when she reached that theater she applied to the clerk at the box office.

► *What surprises the clerk?*

"Eh?" he said, looking out. "Dramatic agents? I don't know. You'll find them in the *Clipper*,[2] though. They all advertise in that."

"Is that a paper?" said Carrie.

"Yes," said the clerk, marveling at such ignorance of a common fact. "You can get it at the news stands," he added politely, seeing how pretty the inquirer was.

Carrie proceeded to get the *Clipper*, and tried to find the agents by looking over it as she stood beside the stand. This could not be done so easily. Thirteenth Street was a number of blocks off, but she went back, carrying the precious paper and regretting the waste of time.

Hurstwood was already there, sitting in his place.

"Where were you?" he asked.

"I've been trying to find some dramatic agents."

---

2. ***Clipper.*** The *New York Clipper* was a professional theater newspaper published in New York during the 1890s.

Words For Everyday Use

pris • tine (pris´ tēn´) *adj.*, characteristic of an earlier period or condition; innocent

con • glom • er • a • tion (kən gläm´ər ā´shən) *n.*, mixture or collection of miscellaneous things

He felt a little diffident about asking concerning her success. The paper she began to scan attracted his attention.

"What have you got there?" he asked.

"The *Clipper*. The man said I'd find their addresses in here."

"Have you been all the way over to Broadway to find that out? I could have told you."

"Why didn't you?" she asked, without looking up.

"You never asked me," he returned.

She went hunting aimlessly through the crowded columns. Her mind was distracted by this man's indifference. The difficulty of the situation she was facing was only added to by all he did. Self-commiseration brewed in her heart. Tears trembled along her eyelids but did not fall. Hurstwood noticed something.

"Let me look."

To recover herself she went into the front room while he searched. Presently she returned. He had a pencil, and was writing upon an envelope.

"Here're three," he said.

Carrie took it and found that one was Mrs. Bermudez, another Marcus Jenks, a third Percy Weil. She paused only a moment, and then moved toward the door.

"I might as well go right away," she said, without looking back.

Hurstwood saw her depart with some faint stirrings of shame, which were the expression of a manhood rapidly becoming stultified. He sat a while, and then it became too much. He got up and put on his hat.

◄ *How does Hurstwood feel when Carrie goes out to look for work? Why?*

"I guess I'll go out," he said to himself, and went, strolling nowhere in particular, but feeling somehow that he must go.

Carrie's first call was upon Mrs. Bermudez, whose address was quite the nearest. It was an old-fashioned residence turned into offices. Mrs. Bermudez's offices consisted of what formerly had been a back chamber and a hall bedroom, marked "Private."

As Carrie entered she noticed several persons lounging about—men, who said nothing and did nothing.

While she was waiting to be noticed, the door of the hall bedroom opened and from it issued two very mannish-looking women, very tightly dressed, and wearing white collars and cuffs. After them came a portly lady of about forty-five, light-

Words For Everyday Use

stul • ti • fied (stul´tə fīd) *adj.,* worthless

haired, sharp-eyed, and evidently good-natured. At least she was smiling.

"Now, don't forget about that," said one of the mannish women.

"I won't," said the portly woman. "Let's see," she added, "where are you the first week in February?"

"Pittsburg," said the woman.

"I'll write you there."

"All right," said the other, and the two passed out.

Instantly the portly lady's face became exceedingly sober and shrewd. She turned about and fixed on Carrie a very searching eye.

"Well," she said, "young woman, what can I do for you?"

"Are you Mrs. Bermudez?"

"Yes."

"Well," said Carrie, hesitating how to begin, "do you get places for persons upon the stage?"

"Yes."

"Could you get me one?"

"Have you ever had any experience?"

"A very little," said Carrie.

"Whom did you play with?"

"Oh, with no one," said Carrie. "It was just a show gotten—"

"Oh, I see," said the woman, interrupting her. "No, I don't know of anything now."

Carrie's countenance fell.

► *What does Mrs. Bermudez say Carrie needs to do to get on stage in New York?*

"You want to get some New York experience," concluded the affable Mrs. Bermudez. "We'll take your name, though."

Carrie stood looking while the lady retired to her office.

"What is your address?" inquired a young lady behind the counter, taking up the curtailed conversation.

"Mrs. George Wheeler," said Carrie, moving over to where she was writing. The woman wrote her address in full and then allowed her to depart at her leisure.

She encountered a very similar experience in the office of Mr. Jenks, only he varied it by saying at the close: "If you could play at some local house, or had a program with your name on it, I might do something."

In the third place the individual asked:

"What sort of work do you want to do?"

Words For Everyday Use

cur • tailed (kər tāld´) *adj.*, cut unnaturally short

"What do you mean?" said Carrie.

"Well, do you want to get in a comedy or on the vaudeville stage or in the chorus?"

"Oh, I'd like to get a part in a play," said Carrie.

"Well," said the man, "it'll cost you something to do that."

"How much?" said Carrie, who, ridiculous as it may seem, had not thought of this before.

"Well, that's for you to say," he answered shrewdly.

Carrie looked at him curiously. She hardly knew how to continue the inquiry.

"Could you get me a part if I paid?"

"If we didn't you'd get your money back."

"Oh," she said.

The agent saw he was dealing with an inexperienced soul, and continued accordingly.

"You'd want to deposit fifty dollars, anyway. No agent would trouble about you for less than that."

Carrie saw a light.

"Thank you," she said. "I'll think about it."

She started to go, and then bethought[3] herself.

"How soon would I get a place?" she asked.

"Well, that's hard to say," said the man. "You might get one in a week, or it might be a month. You'd get the first thing that we thought you could do."

"I see," said Carrie, and then, half-smiling to be agreeable, she walked out.

The agent studied a moment, and then said to himself:

"It's funny how anxious these women are to get on the stage."

Carrie found ample food for reflection in the fifty-dollar proposition. "Maybe they'd take my money and not give me anything," she thought. She had some jewelry—a diamond ring and pin and several other pieces. She could get fifty dollars for those if she went to a pawnbroker.[4]

Hurstwood was home before her. He had not thought she would be so long seeking.

"Well?" he said, not venturing to ask what news.

"I didn't find out anything today," said Carrie, taking off her gloves. "They all want money to get you a place."

"How much?" asked Hurstwood.

"Fifty dollars."

"They don't want anything, do they?"

"Oh, they're like everybody else. You can't tell whether they'd ever get you anything after you did pay them."

◄ *What does the third agent say Carrie must do to get on stage?*

3. **bethought.** Reconsidered

4. **pawnbroker.** One who loans money on the security of personal property pledged in his or her keeping

"Well, I wouldn't put up fifty on that basis," said Hurstwood, as if he were deciding, money in hand.

"I don't know," said Carrie. "I think I'll try some of the managers."

Hurstwood heard this, dead to the horror of it. He rocked a little to and fro, and chewed at his finger. It seemed all very natural in such extreme states. He would do better later on.

CHAPTER 38

In Elf Land Disporting: The Grim World Without

When Carrie renewed her search, as she did the next day, going to the Casino, she found that in the opera chorus, as in other fields, employment is difficult to secure. Girls who can stand in a line and look pretty are as numerous as laborers who can swing a pick. She found there was no discrimination between one and the other of applicants, save as regards a conventional standard of prettiness and form. Their own opinion or knowledge of their ability went for nothing.

◄ *What does Carrie discover about choruses?*

"Where shall I find Mr. Gray?" she asked of a sulky doorman at the stage entrance of the Casino.

"You can't see him now; he's busy."

"Do you know when I can see him?"

"Got an appointment with him?"

"No."

"Well, you'll have to call at his office."

"Oh, dear!" exclaimed Carrie. "Where is his office?"

He gave her the number.

She knew there was no need of calling there now. He would not be in. Nothing remained but to employ the intermediate hours in search.

The dismal story of ventures in other places is quickly told. Mr. Daly saw no one save by appointment. Carrie waited an hour in a dingy office, quite in spite of obstacles, to learn this fact of the placid, indifferent Mr. Dorney.

"You will have to write and ask him to see you."

So she went away.

At the Empire Theater she found a hive of peculiarly listless and indifferent individuals. Everything ornately upholstered, everything carefully finished, everything remarkably reserved.

At the Lyceum she entered one of those secluded, understairway closets, berugged and bepanneled, which causes one to feel the greatness of all positions of authority. Here was reserve itself done into a box office clerk, a doorman, and an assistant, glorying in their fine positions.

Words For Everyday Use

up • hol • stered (up hōl´stərd) *adj.,* fitted and covered with material

► *What attitude does Carrie encounter in her search?*

"Ah, be very humble now—very humble indeed. Tell us what it is you require. Tell it quickly, nervously, and without a vestige of self-respect. If no trouble to us in any way, we may see what we can do."

This was the atmosphere of the Lyceum—the attitude, for that matter, of every managerial office in the city. These little proprietors of businesses are lords indeed on their own ground.

Carrie came away wearily, somewhat more abashed for her pains.

Hurstwood heard the details of the weary and unavailing search that evening.

"I didn't get to see anyone," said Carrie. "I just walked, and walked, and waited around."

Hurstwood only looked at her.

"I suppose you have to have some friends before you can get in," she added, disconsolately.

► *Why isn't Hurstwood more sympathetic to Carrie's difficulties?*

Hurstwood saw the difficulty of this thing, and yet it did not seem so terrible. Carrie was tired and dispirited, but now she could rest. Viewing the world from his rocking-chair, its bitterness did not seem to approach so rapidly. Tomorrow was another day.

Tomorrow came, and the next, and the next.

Carrie saw the manager at the Casino once.

"Come around," he said, "the first of next week. I may make some changes then."

► *Why might Carrie get a part in the chorus at the Casino?*

He was a large and corpulent individual, surfeited with good clothes and good eating, who judged women as another would horseflesh. Carrie was pretty and graceful. She might be put in even if she did not have any experience. One of the proprietors had suggested that the chorus was a little weak on looks.

The first of next week was some days off yet. The first of the month was drawing near. Carrie began to worry as she had never worried before.

► *What does Carrie begin to suspect?*

"Do you really look for anything when you go out?" she asked Hurstwood one morning as a climax to some painful thoughts of her own.

"Of course I do," he said pettishly, troubling only a little over the disgrace of the insinuation.

Words For Everyday Use

un • a • vail • ing (un´ə vāl´iŋ) *adj.,* producing nothing

cor • pu • lent (kôr´pyo͞o lənt) *adj.,* overweight

sur • feit • ed (sʉr´fit əd) *adj.,* more than satisfied

"I'd take anything," she said, "for the present. It will soon be the first of the month again."

She looked the picture of despair.

Hurstwood quit reading his paper and changed his clothes.

"He would look for something," he thought. "He would go and see if some brewery couldn't get him in somewhere. Yes, he would take a position as bartender, if he could get it."

It was the same sort of pilgrimage he had made before. One or two slight rebuffs, and the bravado disappeared.

◀ *In what way does the narrator characterize Hurstwood's expeditions to look for work?*

"No use," he thought. "I might as well go on back home."

Now that his money was so low, he began to observe his clothes and feel that even his best ones were beginning to look commonplace. This was a bitter thought.

Carrie came in after he did.

"I went to see some of the variety managers," she said, aimlessly. "You have to have an act. They don't want anybody that hasn't."

"I saw some of the brewery people today," said Hurstwood. "One man told me he'd try to make a place for me in two or three weeks."

In the face of so much distress on Carrie's part, he had to make some showing, and it was thus he did so. It was lassitude's apology to energy.

Monday Carrie went again to the Casino.

"Did I tell you to come around today?" said the manager, looking her over as she stood before him.

"You said the first of the week," said Carrie, greatly abashed.

"Ever had any experience?" he asked again, almost severely.

Carrie owned to ignorance.

He looked her over again as he stirred among some papers. He was secretly pleased with this pretty, disturbed-looking young woman. "Come around to the theater tomorrow morning."

Carrie's heart bounded to her throat.

"I will," she said with difficulty. She could see he wanted her, and turned to go.

"Would he really put her to work? Oh, blessed fortune, could it be?"

Already the hard rumble of the city through the open windows became pleasant.

Words For Everyday Use

las • si • tude (las´i to͞od) *n.,* lack of energy

► *What thought disturbs Carrie's excitement to share the news with Hurstwood?*

► *What does Carrie forget when comparing her and Hurstwood's situations?*

A sharp voice answered her mental interrogation, driving away all immediate fears on that score.

"Be sure you're there promptly," the manager said roughly. "You'll be dropped if you're not."

Carrie hastened away. She did not quarrel now with Hurstwood's idleness. She had a place—she had a place! This sang in her ears.

In her delight she was almost anxious to tell Hurstwood. But, as she walked homeward, and her survey of the facts of the case became larger, she began to think of the anomaly of her finding work in several weeks and his lounging in idleness for a number of months.

"Why don't he get something?" she openly said to herself. "If I can he surely ought to. It wasn't very hard for me."

She forgot her youth and her beauty. The handicap of age she did not, in her enthusiasm, perceive.

Thus, ever, the voice of success.

Still, she could not keep her secret. She tried to be calm and indifferent, but it was a palpable sham.

"Well?" he said, seeing her relieved face.

"I have a place."

"You have?" he said, breathing a better breath.

"Yes."

"What sort of a place is it?" he asked, feeling in his veins as if now he might get something good also.

"In the chorus," she answered.

"Is it the Casino show you told me about?"

"Yes," she answered. "I begin rehearsing tomorrow."

There was more explanation volunteered by Carrie, because she was happy. At last Hurstwood said:

"Do you know how much you'll get?"

"No, I didn't want to ask," said Carrie. "I guess they pay twelve or fourteen dollars a week."

"About that, I guess," said Hurstwood.

There was a good dinner in the flat that evening, owing to the mere lifting of the terrible strain. Hurstwood went out for a shave, and returned with a fair-sized sirloin steak.

"Now, tomorrow," he thought, "I'll look around myself," and with renewed hope he lifted his eyes from the ground.

On the morrow Carrie reported promptly and was given a place in the line. She saw a large, empty, shadowy playhouse,

Words For Everyday Use

in • ter • ro • ga • tion (in ter´ə gā´shən) *n.,* question

a • nom • a • ly (ə näm´ə lē) *n.,* oddity; peculiarity

pal • pa • ble (pal´pə bəl) *adj.,* obvious

still redolent of the perfumes and blazonry[1] of the night, and notable for its rich, oriental appearance. The wonder of it awed and delighted her. Blessed be its wondrous reality. How hard she would try to be worthy of it. It was above the common mass, above idleness, above want, above insignificance. People came to it in finery and carriages to see. It was ever a center of light and mirth.[2] And here she was of it. Oh, if she could only remain, how happy would be her days!

◄ *How does Carrie feel about her position?*

"What is your name?" said the manager, who was conducting the drill.

"Madenda," she replied, instantly mindful of the name Drouet had selected in Chicago. "Carrie Madenda."

◄ *What names does Carrie choose to give?*

"Well, now, Miss Madenda," he said, very affably, as Carrie thought, "you go over there."

Then he called to a young woman who was already of the company:

"Miss Clark, you pair with Miss Madenda."

This young lady stepped forward, so that Carrie saw where to go, and the rehearsal began.

Carrie soon found that while this drilling had some slight resemblance to the rehearsals as conducted at Avery Hall, the attitude of the manager was much more pronounced. She had marveled at the insistence and superior airs of Mr. Millice, but the individual conducting here had the same insistence, coupled with almost brutal roughness. As the drilling proceeded, he seemed to wax exceedingly wroth[3] over trifles, and to increase his lung power in proportion. It was very evident that he had a great contempt for any assumption of dignity or innocence on the part of these young women.

◄ *What is evident from the manager's manner?*

"Clark," he would call—meaning, of course, Miss Clark—"why don't you catch step there?"

"By fours, right! Right, I said, right! For heaven's sake, get on to yourself! Right!" and in saying this he would lift the last sounds into a vehement roar.

"Maitland! Maitland!" he called once.

A nervous, comely-dressed little girl stepped out. Carrie trembled for her out of the fullness of her own sympathies and fear.

1. **blazonry.** Bright lights
2. **mirth.** Merriment
3. **wroth.** Angry

Words For Everyday Use

red • o • lent (red´'l ənt) *adj.,* smelling of; fragrant

ve • he • ment (vē´ə mənt) *adj.,* forceful

"Yes, sir," said Miss Maitland.

"Is there anything the matter with your ears?"

"No, sir."

"Do you know what 'column left' means?"

"Yes, sir."

"Well, what are you stumbling around the right for? Want to break up the line?"

"I was just—"

"Never mind what you were just. Keep your ears open."

Carrie pitied, and trembled for her turn.

Yet another suffered the pain of personal rebuke.

"Hold on a minute," cried the manager, throwing up his hands, as if in despair. His demeanor was fierce.

"Elvers," he shouted, "what have you got in your mouth?"

"Nothing," said Miss Elvers, while some smiled and stood nervously by.

"Well, are you talking?"

"No, sir."

"Well, keep your mouth still then. Now, all together again."

► What brings on Carrie's "trouble" with the manager?

At last Carrie's turn came. It was because of her extreme anxiety to do all that was required that brought on trouble.

She heard someone called.

"Mason," said the voice. "Miss Mason."

She looked around to see who it could be. A girl behind shoved her a little, but she did not understand.

"You, you!" said the manager. "Can't you hear?"

"Oh," said Carrie, collapsing, and blushing fiercely.

"Isn't your name Mason?" asked the manager.

"No, sir," said Carrie, "it's Madenda."

"Well, what's the matter with your feet? Can't you dance?"

"Yes, sir," said Carrie, who had long since learned this art.

"Why don't you do it then? Don't go shuffling along as if you were dead. I've got to have people with life in them."

Carrie's cheek burned with a crimson heat. Her lips trembled a little.

"Yes, sir," she said.

It was this constant urging, coupled with irascibility and energy, for three long hours. Carrie came away worn enough in body, but too excited in mind to notice it. She meant to go home and practice her evolutions as prescribed. She would not err in any way, if she could help it.

Words For Everyday Use

i • ras • ci • bil • i • ty (i ras´ə bil´ə tē) *n.,* irritability

When she reached the flat Hurstwood was not there. For a wonder he was out looking for work, as she supposed. She took only a mouthful to eat and then practiced on, sustained by visions of freedom from financial distress—"The sound of glory ringing in her ears."[4]

When Hurstwood returned he was not so elated as when he went away, and now she was obliged to drop practice and get dinner. Here was an early irritation. She would have her work and this. Was she going to act and keep house?

◄ What irritations and disappointments spoil Carrie's joy?

"I'll not do it," she said, "after I get started. He can take his meals out."

Each day thereafter brought its cares. She found it was not such a wonderful thing to be in the chorus, and she also learned that her salary would be twelve dollars a week. After a few days she had her first sight of those high and mighties—the leading ladies and gentlemen. She saw that they were privileged and deferred to. She was nothing—absolutely nothing at all.

At home was Hurstwood, daily giving her cause for thought. He seemed to get nothing to do, and yet he made bold to inquire how she was getting along. The regularity with which he did this smacked of[5] someone who was waiting to live upon her labor. Now that she had a visible means of support, this irritated her. He seemed to be depending upon her little twelve dollars.

◄ What can Carrie tell from Hurstwood's manner?

"How are you getting along?" he would blandly inquire.

"Oh, all right," she would reply.

"Find it easy?"

"It will be all right when I get used to it."

His paper would then engross his thoughts.

"I got some lard," he would add, as an afterthought. "I thought maybe you might want to make some biscuit."

The calm suggestion of the man astonished her a little, especially in the light of recent developments. Her dawning independence gave her more courage to observe, and she felt as if she wanted to say things. Still she could not talk to him as she had to Drouet. There was something in the man's manner of which she had always stood in awe. He seemed to have some invisible strength in reserve.

◄ What astonishes Carrie about Hurstwood?

4. **"The sound . . . ears."** Probably a quotation from a poem or song
5. **smacked of.** Had a flavor or taste of

Words For Everyday Use

en • gross (en grōs´) *vt.,* occupy

One day, after her first week's rehearsal, what she expected came openly to the surface.

"We'll have to be rather saving," he said, laying down some meat he had purchased. "You won't get any money for a week or so yet."

"No," said Carrie, who was stirring a pan at the stove.

"I've only got the rent and thirteen dollars more," he added.

"That's it," she said to herself. "I'm to use my money now."

Instantly she remembered that she had hoped to buy a few things for herself. She needed clothes. Her hat was not nice.

"What will twelve dollars do toward keeping up this flat?" she thought. "I can't do it. Why doesn't he get something to do?"

The important night of the first real performance came. She did not suggest to Hurstwood that he come and see. He did not think of going. It would only be money wasted. She had such a small part.

The advertisements were already in the papers; the posters upon the billboards. The leading lady and many members were cited. Carrie was nothing.

As in Chicago, she was seized with stage fright as the very first entrance of the ballet approached, but later she recovered. The apparent and painful insignificance of the part took fear away from her. She felt that she was so obscure it did not matter. Fortunately, she did not have to wear tights.[6] A group of twelve were assigned pretty golden-hued skirts which came only to a line about an inch above the knee. Carrie happened to be one of the twelve.

In standing about the stage, marching, and occasionally lifting up her voice in the general chorus, she had a chance to observe the audience and to see the inauguration of a great hit. There was plenty of applause, but she could not help noting how poorly some of the women of alleged ability did.

► *What does Carrie think of some of the actresses?*

"I could do better than that," Carrie ventured to herself, in several instances. To do her justice, she was right.

After it was over she dressed quickly, and as the manager had scolded some others and passed her, she imagined she must have proved satisfactory. She wanted to get out quickly, because she knew but few, and the stars were gossiping. Outside were carriages and some correct youths in attractive

6. **Fortunately . . . tights.** In the period when this story takes place, it was considered scandalous for a woman to reveal her legs.

Words For Everyday Use

in • au • gu • ra • tion (in ô´gyo͞o rā´shən) *n.,* formal beginning

clothing, waiting. Carrie saw that she was scanned closely. The flutter of an eyelash would have brought her a companion. That she did not give.

One experienced youth volunteered, anyhow.

"Not going home alone, are you?" he said.

Carrie merely hastened her steps and took the Sixth Avenue car. Her head was so full of the wonder of it that she had time for nothing else.

"Did you hear any more from the brewery?" she asked at the end of the week, hoping by the question to stir him on to action.

"No," he answered, "they're not quite ready yet. I think something will come of that, though."

She said nothing more then, objecting to giving up her own money, and yet feeling that such would have to be the case. Hurstwood felt the crisis, and artfully decided to appeal to Carrie. He had long since realized how good-natured she was, how much she would stand. There was some little shame in him at the thought of doing so, but he justified himself with the thought that he really would get something. Rent day gave him his opportunity.

◄ *What does Hurstwood decide to do?*

"Well," he said, as he counted it out, "that's about the last of my money. I'll have to get something pretty soon."

Carrie looked at him askance, half-suspicious of an appeal.

"If I could only hold out a little longer I think I could get something. Drake is sure to open a hotel here in September."

"Is he?" said Carrie, thinking of the short month that still remained until that time.

"Would you mind helping me out until then?" he said appealingly. "I think I'll be all right after that time."

"No," said Carrie, feeling sadly handicapped by fate.

"We can get along if we economize. I'll pay you back all right."

"Oh, I'll help you," said Carrie, feeling quite hard-hearted at thus forcing him to humbly appeal, and yet her desire for the benefit of her earnings wrung a faint protest from her.

"Why don't you take anything, George, temporarily?" she said. "What difference does it make? Maybe, after a while, you'll get something better."

"I will take anything," he said, relieved, and wincing under reproof. "I'd just as leave dig on the streets. Nobody knows me here."

Words For Everyday Use

a • skance (ə skans´) *adv.*, with a sideways glance

winc • ing (wins iŋ) *adj.*, grimacing

"Oh, you needn't do that," said Carrie, hurt by the pity of it. "But there must be other things."

"I'll get something!" he said, assuming determination.

Then he went back to his paper.

CHAPTER 39

Of Lights and of Shadows: The Parting of Worlds

What Hurstwood got as the result of the determination was more self-assurance that each particular day was not the day. At the same time, Carrie passed through thirty days of mental distress.

Her need of clothes—to say nothing of her desire for ornaments—grew rapidly as the fact developed that for all her work she was not to have them. The sympathy she felt for Hurstwood, at the time he asked her to tide him over, vanished with these newer urgings of decency. He was not always renewing his request, but this love of good appearance was. It insisted, and Carrie wished to satisfy it, wished more and more that Hurstwood was not in the way.

◄ *What makes Carrie's sympathy for Hurstwood vanish?*

Hurstwood reasoned, when he neared the last ten dollars, that he had better keep a little pocket change and not become wholly dependent for carfare, shaves, and the like; so when this sum was still in his hand he announced himself as penniless.

◄ *What does Hurstwood lie about to Carrie?*

"I'm clear out," he said to Carrie one afternoon. "I paid for some coal this morning, and that took all but ten or fifteen cents."

"I've got some money there in my purse."

Hurstwood went to get it, starting for a can of tomatoes. Carrie scarcely noticed that this was the beginning of the new order. He took out fifteen cents and bought the can with it. Thereafter it was dribs and drabs of this sort, until one morning Carrie suddenly remembered that she would not be back until close to dinner time.

"We're all out of flour," she said; "you'd better get some this afternoon. We haven't any meat, either. How would it do if we had liver and bacon?"

"Suits me," said Hurstwood.

"Better get a half or three-quarters of a pound of that."

"Half'll be enough," volunteered Hurstwood.

She opened her purse and laid down a half dollar. He pretended not to notice it.

Hurstwood bought the flour—which all grocers sold in 3 1/2 pound packages—for thirteen cents and paid fifteen cents for a half-pound of liver and bacon. He left the packages, together with the balance of twenty-two cents, upon the kitchen table, where Carrie found it. It did not escape her that the change was accurate. There was something sad in

◄ *What saddens Carrie?*

realizing that, after all, all that he wanted of her was something to eat. She felt as if hard thoughts were unjust. Maybe he would get something yet. He had no vices.

That very evening, however, on going into the theater, one of the chorus girls passed her all newly arrayed in a pretty mottled tweed suit, which took Carrie's eye. The young woman wore a fine bunch of violets and seemed in high spirits. She smiled at Carrie good-naturedly as she passed, showing pretty, even teeth, and Carrie smiled back.

"She can afford to dress well," thought Carrie, "and so could I, if I could only keep my money. I haven't a decent tie of any kind to wear."

She put out her foot and looked at her shoe reflectively.

"I'll get a pair of shoes Saturday, anyhow; I don't care what happens."

One of the sweetest and most sympathetic little chorus girls in the company made friends with her because in Carrie she found nothing to frighten her away. She was a gay little Manon,[1] unwitting of society's fierce conception of morality, but, nevertheless, good to her neighbor and charitable. Little license was allowed the chorus in the matter of conversation, but, nevertheless, some was indulged in.

"It's warm tonight, isn't it?" said this girl, arrayed in pink fleshings and an imitation golden helmet. She also carried a shining shield.

"Yes; it is," said Carrie, pleased that someone should talk to her.

"I'm almost roasting," said the girl.

Carrie looked into her pretty face, with its large blue eyes, and saw little beads of moisture.

"There's more marching in this opera than ever I did before," added the girl.

"Have you been in others?" asked Carrie, surprised at her experience.

"Lots of them," said the girl; "haven't you?"

"This is my first experience."

"Oh, is it? I thought I saw you the time they ran *The Queen's Mate* here."

"No," said Carrie, shaking her head; "not me."

---

1. **Manon.** Fictional character; here, meaning an actress of easy virtue

Words For Everyday Use

mot • tled (mät´'l'd) *adj.,* of different colors

con • cep • tion (kən sep´shən) *n.,* notion

This conversation was interrupted by the blare of the orchestra and the sputtering of the calcium lights[2] in the wings as the line was called to form for a new entrance. No further opportunity for conversation occurred, but the next evening, when they were getting ready for the stage, this girl appeared anew at her side.

"They say this show is going on the road next month."

◄ *What advice about the theater does this young woman give Carrie?*

"Is it?" said Carrie.

"Yes; do you think you'll go?"

"I don't know; I guess so, if they'll take me."

"Oh, they'll take you. I wouldn't go. They won't give you any more, and it will cost you everything you make to live. I never leave New York. There are too many shows going on here."

"Can you always get in another show?"

"I always have. There's one going on up at the Broadway this month. I'm going to try and get in that if this one really goes."

Carrie heard this with aroused intelligence. Evidently it wasn't so very difficult to get on. Maybe she also could get a place if this show went away.

"Do they all pay about the same?" she asked.

"Yes. Sometimes you get a little more. This show doesn't pay very much."

"I get twelve," said Carrie.

"Do you?" said the girl. "They pay me fifteen, and you do more work than I do. I wouldn't stand it if I were you. They're just giving you less because they think you don't know. You ought to be making fifteen."

◄ *What does the woman tell Carrie about her salary?*

"Well, I'm not," said Carrie.

"Well, you'll get more at the next place if you want it," went on the girl, who admired Carrie very much. "You do fine, and the manager knows it."

To say the truth, Carrie did unconsciously move about with an air pleasing and somewhat distinctive. It was due wholly to her natural manner and total lack of self-consciousness.

"Do you suppose I could get more up at the Broadway?"

"Of course you can," answered the girl. "You come with me when I go. I'll do the talking."

Carrie heard this, flushing with thankfulness. She liked this little gaslight soldier.[3] She seemed so experienced and self-reliant in her tinsel helmet and military accoutrements.[4]

"My future must be assured if I can always get work this way," thought Carrie.

---

2. **calcium lights.** Brilliant lights created by the incandescence of lime, formerly used in theaters

3. **gaslight soldier.** One who fights for survival in the spotlights, i.e., an actor; also refers to her military-style costume

4. **accoutrements.** Accessories

Still, in the morning, when her household duties would infringe upon her and Hurstwood sat there, a perfect load to contemplate, her fate seemed dismal and unrelieved. It did not take so very much to feed them under Hurstwood's close-measured buying, and there would possibly be enough for rent, but it left nothing else. Carrie bought the shoes and some other things, which complicated the rent problem very seriously. Suddenly, a week from the fatal day, Carrie realized that they were going to run short.

"I don't believe," she exclaimed, looking into her purse at breakfast, "that I'll have enough to pay the rent."

"How much have you?" inquired Hurstwood.

"Well, I've got twenty-two dollars, but there's everything to be paid for this week yet, and if I use all I get Saturday to pay this, there won't be any left for next week. Do you think your hotel man will open his hotel this month?"

"I think so," returned Hurstwood. "He said he would."

After a while, Hurstwood said:

"Don't worry about it. Maybe the grocer will wait. He can do that. We've traded there long enough to make him trust us for a week or two."

"Do you think he will?" she asked.

"I think so."

On this account, Hurstwood, this very day, looked grocer Oeslogge clearly in the eye as he ordered a pound of coffee, and said:

"Do you mind carrying my account until the end of every week?"

"No, no, Mr. Wheeler," said Mr. Oeslogge. "Dat iss all right."

Hurstwood, still tactful in distress, added nothing to this. It seemed an easy thing. He looked out of the door, and then gathered up his coffee when ready and came away. The game of a desperate man had begun.

Rent was paid, and now came the grocer. Hurstwood managed by paving out of his own ten and collecting from Carrie at the end of the week. Then he delayed a day next time settling with the grocer, and so soon had his ten back, with Oeslogge getting his pay on this Thursday or Friday for last Saturday's bill.

This entanglement made Carrie anxious for a change of some sort. Hurstwood did not seem to realize that she had a right to anything. He schemed to make what she earned cover all expenses, but seemed not to trouble over adding anything himself.

▶ What does Carrie notice about Hurstwood's behavior? For how long has Hurstwood been unemployed?

"He talks about worrying," thought Carrie. "If he worried enough he couldn't sit there and wait for me. He'd get something to do. No man could go seven months without finding something if he tried."

The sight of him always around in his untidy clothes and gloomy appearance drove Carrie to seek relief in other places. Twice a week there were matinees, and then Hurstwood ate a cold snack, which he prepared himself. Two other days there were rehearsals beginning at ten in the morning and lasting usually until one. Now, to this Carrie added a few visits to one or two chorus girls, including the blue-eyed soldier of the golden helmet. She did it because it was pleasant and a relief from dullness of the home over which her husband brooded.

The blue-eyed soldier's name was Osborne—Lola Osborne. Her room was in Nineteenth Street near Fourth Avenue, a block now given up wholly to office buildings. Here she had a comfortable back room, looking over a collection of back yards in which grew a number of shade trees pleasant to see.

"Isn't your home in New York?" she asked of Lola one day.

"Yes; but I can't get along with my people. They always want me to do what they want. Do you live here?"

"Yes," said Carrie.

"With your family?"

Carrie was ashamed to say that she was married. She had talked so much about getting more salary and confessed to so much anxiety about her future, that now, when the direct question of fact was waiting, she could not tell this girl.

◀ What is Carrie ashamed to admit? Why?

"With some relatives," she answered.

Miss Osborne took it for granted that, like herself, Carrie's time was her own. She invariably asked her to stay, proposing little outings and other things of that sort until Carrie began neglecting her dinner hours. Hurstwood noticed it, but felt in no position to quarrel with her. Several times she came so late as scarcely to have an hour in which to patch up a meal and start for the theater.

"Do you rehearse in the afternoons?" Hurstwood once asked, concealing almost completely the cynical protest and regret which prompted it.

"No; I was looking around for another place," said Carrie.

As a matter of fact she was, but only in such a way as furnished the least straw of an excuse. Miss Osborne and she had gone to the office of the manager who was to produce

Words For Everyday Use

cyn • i • cal (sin´i kəl) *adj.,* believing that people are motivated only by selfishness

the new opera at the Broadway and returned straight to the former's room, where they had been since three o'clock.

Carrie felt this question to be an infringement on her liberty. She did not take into account how much liberty she was securing. Only the last step, the newest freedom, must not be questioned.

Hurstwood saw it all clearly enough. He was shrewd after his kind, and yet there was enough decency in the man to stop him from making an effectual protest. In his almost inexplicable apathy he was content to droop supinely while Carrie drifted out of his life, just as he was willing supinely to see opportunity pass beyond his control. He could not help clinging and protesting in a mild, irritating, and ineffectual way, however—a way that simply widened the breach by slow degrees.

► *What does Hurstwood's "inexplicable apathy" make him content to do?*

A further enlargement of this chasm between them came when the manager, looking between the wings upon the brightly lighted stage where the chorus was going through some of its glittering evolutions, said to the master of the ballet:

► *What "promotion" does Carrie receive?*

"Who is that fourth girl there on the right—the one coming round at the end now?"

"Oh," said the ballet-master, "that's Miss Madenda."

"She's good-looking. Why don't you let her head that line?"

"I will," said the man.

"Just do that. She'll look better there than the woman you've got."

"All right. I will do that," said the master.

The next evening Carrie was called out, much as if for an error.

"You lead your company tonight," said the master.

"Yes, sir," said Carrie.

"Put snap into it," he added. "We must have snap."

"Yes, sir," replied Carrie.

Astonished at this change, she thought that the heretofore leader must be ill; but when she saw her in the line, with a distinct expression of something unfavorable in her eye, she began to think that perhaps it was merit.

She had a chic[5] way of tossing her head to one side, and holding her arms as if for action—not listlessly. In front of the line this showed up even more effectually.

5. **chic.** Cleverly stylish

Words For Everyday Use

in • fringe • ment (in frinj´mənt) *n.,* violation

su • pine • ly (so͞o´pin´lē) *adj.,* inactively; passively; listlessly

chasm (kaz'əm) *n.,* deep crack in the earth's surface

"That girl knows how to carry herself," said the manager, another evening. He began to think that he should like to talk with her. If he hadn't made it a rule to have nothing to do with the members of the chorus, he would have approached her most unbendingly.

"Put that girl at the head of the white column," he suggested to the man in charge of the ballet.

This white column consisted of some twenty girls, all in snow-white flannel trimmed with silver and blue. Its leader was most stunningly arrayed in the same colors, elaborated, however, with epaulets[6] and a belt of silver, with a short sword dangling at one side. Carrie was fitted for this costume, and a few days later appeared, proud of her new laurels.[7] She was especially gratified to find that her salary was now eighteen instead of twelve.

◄ How much of a raise does Carrie receive? Whom doesn't she inform?

Hurstwood heard nothing about this.

"I'll not give him the rest of my money," said Carrie. "I do enough. I am going to get me something to wear."

As a matter of fact, during this second month she had been buying for herself as recklessly as she dared, regardless of the consequences. There were impending more complications rent day, and more extension of the credit system in the neighborhood. Now, however, she proposed to do better by herself.

Her first move was to buy a shirtwaist, and in studying these she found how little her money would buy—how much, if she could only use all. She forgot that if she were alone she would have to pay for a room and board, and imagined that every cent of her eighteen could be spent for clothes and things that she liked.

◄ What does Carrie forget would happen even if she did not have to support Hurstwood?

At last she picked upon something, which not only used up all her surplus above twelve, but invaded that sum. She knew she was going too far, but her feminine love of finery prevailed. The next day Hurstwood said:

"We owe the grocer five dollars and forty cents this week."

"Do we?" said Carrie, frowning a little.

She looked in her purse to leave it.

"I've only got eight dollars and twenty cents altogether."

"We owe the milkman sixty cents," added Hurstwood.

"Yes, and there's the coal man," said Carrie.

Hurstwood said nothing. He had seen the new things she was buying; the way she was neglecting household duties; the readiness with which she was slipping out afternoons and staying. He felt that something was going to happen. All at once she spoke:

---

6. **epaulets.** Shoulder ornaments on a uniform

7. **laurels.** Wreaths of laurel leaves were bestowed on winners of contests in ancient Greece; therefore, signs of fame and honor

► *In what way does Hurstwood try to justify his position to Carrie?*

"I don't know," she said; "I can't do it all. I don't earn enough."

This was a direct challenge. Hurstwood had to take it up. He tried to be calm.

"I don't want you to do it all," he said. "I only want a little help until I can get something to do."

"Oh, yes," answered Carrie. "That's always the way. It takes more than I can earn to pay for things. I don't see what I'm going to do."

"Well, I've tried to get something," he exclaimed. "What do you want me to do?"

"You couldn't have tried so very hard," said Carrie. "I got something."

"Well, I did," he said, angered almost to harsh words. "You needn't throw up your success to me. All I asked was a little help until I could get something. I'm not down yet. I'll come up all right."

He tried to speak steadily, but his voice trembled a little.

Carrie's anger melted on the instant. She felt ashamed.

"Well," she said, "here's the money," and emptied it out on the table. "I haven't got quite enough to pay it all. If they can wait until Saturday, though, I'll have some more."

"You keep it," said Hurstwood, sadly. "I only want enough to pay the grocer."

She put it back, and proceeded to get dinner early and in good time. Her little bravado made her feel as if she ought to make amends.

In a little while their old thoughts returned to both.

"She's making more than she says," thought Hurstwood. "She says she's making twelve, but that wouldn't buy all those things. I don't care. Let her keep her money. I'll get something again one of these days. Then she can go to the deuce."

He only said this in his anger, but it prefigured a possible course of action and attitude well enough.

"I don't care," thought Carrie. "He ought to be told to get out and do something. It isn't right that I should support him."

In these days Carrie was introduced to several youths, friends of Miss Osborne, who were of the kind most aptly described as gay and festive. They called once to get Miss Osborne for an afternoon drive. Carrie was with her at the time.

"Come and go along," said Lola.

"No, I can't," said Carrie.

"Oh, yes, come and go. What have you got to do?"

"I have to be home by five," said Carrie.

"What for?"

"Oh, dinner."

"They'll take us to dinner," said Lola.

"Oh, no," said Carrie. "I won't go. I can't."

"Oh, do come. They're awful nice boys. We'll get you back in time. We're only going for a drive in Central Park."

Carrie thought a while, and at last yielded.

"Now, I must be back by half-past four," she said.

The information went in one ear of Lola and out the other.

After Drouet and Hurstwood, there was the least touch of cynicism in her attitude toward young men—especially of the gay and frivolous sort. She felt a little older than they. Some of their pretty compliments seemed silly. Still, she was young in heart and body and youth appealed to her.

◄ What mixed feelings does Carrie have toward the young men?

"Oh, we'll be right back, Miss Madenda," said one of the chaps, bowing. "You wouldn't think we'd keep you overtime, now, would you?"

"Well, I don't know," said Carrie, smiling.

They were off for a drive—she, looking about and noticing fine clothing, the young men voicing those silly pleasantries and weak quips which pass for humor in coy circles. Carrie saw the great park parade of carriages, beginning at the Fifty-ninth Street entrance and winding past the Museum of Art to the exit at 110th Street and Seventh Avenue. Her eye was once more taken by the show of wealth—the elaborate costumes, elegant harnesses, spirited horses, and, above all, the beauty. Once more the plague of poverty galled her, but now she forgot in a measure her own troubles so far as to forget Hurstwood. He waited until four, five, and even six. It was getting dark when he got up out of his chair.

"I guess she isn't coming home," he said, grimly.

"That's the way," he thought. "She's getting a start now. I'm out of it."

Carrie had really discovered her neglect, but only at a quarter after five, and the open carriage was now far up Seventh Avenue, near the Harlem River.

"What time is it?" she inquired. "I must be getting back."

"A quarter after five," said her companion, consulting an elegant, open-faced watch.

"Oh, dear me!" exclaimed Carrie. Then she settled back with a sigh. "There's no use crying over spilt milk," she said. "It's too late."

Words For Everyday Use

quip (kwip) *n.,* joking remark

coy (koi) *adj.,* not serious

"Of course it is," said the youth, who saw visions of a fine dinner now, and such invigorating talk as would result in a reunion after the show. He was greatly taken with Carrie. "We'll drive down to Delmonico's now and have something there, won't we, Orrin?"

"To be sure," replied Orrin, gaily.

Carrie thought of Hurstwood. Never before had she neglected dinner without an excuse.

▶ *Of what time does this dinner remind Carrie?*

They drove back, and at 6:15 sat down to dine. It was the Sherry incident over again, the remembrance of which came painfully back to Carrie. She remembered Mrs. Vance, who had never called again after Hurstwood's reception, and Ames.

At this figure her mind halted. It was a strong, clean vision. He liked better books than she read, better people than she associated with. His ideals burned in her heart.

▶ *What does Carrie wonder?*

"It's fine to be a good actress," came distinctly back.

What sort of an actress was she?

"What are you thinking about, Miss Madenda?" inquired her merry companion. "Come, now, let's see if I can guess."

"Oh, no," said Carrie. "Don't try."

She shook it off and ate. She forgot, in part, and was merry. When it came to the after-theater proposition, however, she shook her head.

"No," she said, "I can't. I have a previous engagement."

"Oh, now, Miss Madenda," pleaded the youth.

"No," said Carrie, "I can't. You've been so kind, but you'll have to excuse me."

The youth looked exceedingly crestfallen.

"Cheer up, old man," whispered his companion. "We'll go around, anyhow. She may change her mind."

Words For Everyday Use

in • vig • or • at • ing (in vig´ər āt iŋ) *adj.*, lively; energetic

crest • fal • len (krest´fôl ən) *adj.*, disheartened

CHAPTER 40

A Public Dissension: A Final Appeal

There was no after-theater lark,[1] however, so far as Carrie was concerned. She made her way homeward, thinking about her absence. Hurstwood was asleep, but roused up to look as she passed through to her own bed.

"Is that you?" he said.

"Yes," she answered.

The next morning at breakfast she felt like apologizing.

"I couldn't get home last evening," she said.

"Ah, Carrie," he answered, "what's the use saying that? I don't care. You needn't tell me that, though."

"I couldn't," said Carrie, her color rising. Then, seeing that he looked as if he said "I know," she exclaimed: "Oh, all right. I don't care."

From now on, her indifference to the flat was even greater. There seemed no common ground on which they could talk to one another. She let herself be asked for expenses. It became so with him that he hated to do it. He preferred standing off the butcher and baker. He ran up a grocery bill of sixteen dollars with Oeslogge, laying in a supply of staple articles, so that they would not have to buy any of those things for some time to come. Then he changed his grocery. It was the same with the butcher and several others. Carrie never heard anything of this directly from him. He asked for such as he could expect, drifting farther and farther into a situation which could have but one ending.

In this fashion, September went by.

"Isn't Mr. Drake going to open his hotel?" Carrie asked several times.

"Yes. He won't do it before October, though, now."

Carrie became disgusted. "Such a man," she said to herself frequently. More and more she visited. She put most of her spare money in clothes, which, after all, was not an astonishing amount. At last the opera she was with announced its departure within four weeks. "Last two weeks of the Great Comic Opera success—The——," etc., was upon all billboards and in the newspapers, before she acted.

"I'm not going out on the road," said Miss Osborne.

Carrie went with her to apply to another manager.

"Ever had any experience?" was one of his questions.

"I'm with the company at the Casino now."

◄ *What does Carrie say when she tries to apologize and offer an excuse? How does Hurstwood respond?*

◄ *What does Hurstwood do instead of asking Carrie for money?*

◄ *What excuse does Hurstwood offer when asked about his continued state of unemployment?*

1. **lark.** Frolic, merriment

"Oh, you are?" he said.

The end of this was another engagement at twenty per week.

Carrie was delighted. She began to feel that she had a place in the world. People recognized ability.

▶ *What does Hurstwood spend his time doing?*

So changed was her state that the home atmosphere became intolerable. It was all poverty and trouble there, or seemed to be, because it was a load to bear. It became a place to keep away from. Still she slept there, and did a fair amount of work, keeping it in order. It was a sitting place for Hurstwood. He sat and rocked, rocked and read, enveloped in the gloom of his own fate. October went by, and November. It was the dead of winter almost before he knew it, and there he sat.

▶ *About what has Hurstwood stopped talking?*

Carrie was doing better, that he knew. Her clothes were improved now, even fine. He saw her coming and going, sometimes picturing to himself her rise. Little eating had thinned him somewhat. He had no appetite. His clothes, too, were a poor man's clothes. Talk about getting something had become even too threadbare and ridiculous for him. So he folded his hands and waited—for what, he could not anticipate.

At last, however, troubles became too thick. The hounding of creditors, the indifference of Carrie, the silence of the flat, and presence of winter, all joined to produce a climax. It was effected by the arrival of Oeslogge, personally, when Carrie was there.

"I call about my bill," said Mr. Oeslogge.

Carrie was only faintly surprised.

"How much is it?" she asked.

"Sixteen dollars," he replied.

"Oh, that much?" said Carrie. "Is this right?" she asked, turning to Hurstwood.

"Yes," he said.

"Well, I never heard anything about it."

She looked as if she thought he had been contracting some needless expense.

"Well, we had it all right," he answered. Then he went to the door. "I can't pay you anything on that today," he said, mildly.

"Well, when can you?" said the grocer.

"Not before Saturday, anyhow," said Hurstwood.

"Huh!" returned the grocer. "This is fine. I must have that. I need the money."

Carrie was standing farther back in the room, hearing it all. She was greatly distressed. It was so bad and commonplace. Hurstwood was annoyed also.

"Well," he said, "there's no use talking about it now. If you'll come in Saturday, I'll pay you something on it."

The grocery man went away.

"How are we going to pay it?" asked Carrie, astonished by the bill. "I can't do it."

"Well, you don't have to," he said. "He can't get what he can't get. He'll have to wait."

"I don't see how we ran up such a bill as that," said Carrie.

"Well, we ate it," said Hurstwood.

"It's funny," she replied, still doubting.

"What's the use of your standing there and talking like that, now?" he asked. "Do you think I've had it alone? You talk as if I'd taken something."

"Well, it's too much, anyhow," said Carrie. "I oughtn't to be made to pay for it. I've got more than I can pay for now."

"All right," replied Hurstwood, sitting down in silence. He was sick of the grind of this thing.

Carrie went out, and there he sat, determining to do something.

There had been appearing in the papers about this time rumors and notices of an approaching strike on the trolley lines in Brooklyn. There was general dissatisfaction as to the hours of labor required and the wages paid. As usual—and for some inexplicable reason—the men chose the winter for the forcing of the hand of their employers and the settlement of their difficulties.

Hurstwood had been reading of this thing, and wondering concerning the huge tie-up which would follow. A day or two before this trouble with Carrie, it came. On a cold afternoon, when everything was gray and it threatened to snow, the papers announced that the men had been called out on all the lines.

Being so utterly idle, and his mind filled with the numerous predictions which had been made concerning the scarcity of labor this winter and the panicky state of the financial market, Hurstwood read this with interest. He noted the claims of the striking motormen and conductors, who said that they had been wont to receive two dollars a day in times past, but that for a year or more "trippers" had been introduced, which cut down their chance of livelihood one-half, and increased their hours of servitude from ten to twelve, and even fourteen. These "trippers" were men put on during the busy and rush hours, to take a car out for one trip. The compensation paid for such a trip was only twenty-five cents. When the rush or busy hours were over, they were laid off. Worst of all, no man might know when he was going to get a car. He must come to the barns in the morning and wait around in fair and foul weather until such time as he was

◄ *What complaint do the workers on the trolley lines have?*

needed. Two trips were an average reward for so much waiting—a little over three hours' work for fifty cents. The work of waiting was not counted.

The men complained that this system was extending, and that the time was not far off when but a few out of 7,000 employees would have regular two-dollar-a-day work at all. They demanded that the system be abolished, and that ten hours be considered a day's work, barring unavoidable delays, with $2.25 pay. They demanded immediate acceptance of these terms, which the various trolley companies refused.

Hurstwood at first sympathized with the demands of these men—indeed, it is a question whether he did not always sympathize with them to the end, belie him as his actions might. Reading nearly all the news, he was attracted first by the scareheads[2] with which the trouble was noted in the *World*. He read it fully—the names of the seven companies involved, the number of men.

"They're foolish to strike in this sort of weather," he thought to himself. "Let 'em win if they can, though."

The next day there was even a larger notice of it. "Brooklynites Walk," said the *World*. "Knights of Labor Tie up the Trolley Lines Across the Bridge." "About Seven Thousand Men Out."

Hurstwood read this, formulating to himself his own idea of what would be the outcome. He was a great believer in the strength of corporations.

► *Even though Hurstwood sympathizes with the workers, what is his opinion of the situation?*

"They can't win," he said, concerning the men. "They haven't any money. The police will protect the companies. They've got to. The public has to have its cars."

He didn't sympathize with the corporations, but strength was with them. So was property and public utility.

"Those fellows can't win," he thought.

Among other things, he noticed a circular[3] issued by one of the companies, which read:

ATLANTIC AVENUE RAILROAD

SPECIAL NOTICE

The motormen and conductors and other employees of this company having abruptly left its service, an opportunity is now given to all loyal men who have struck against their will to be reinstated, providing they will make their applications by twelve o'clock noon on Wednesday, January

2. **scareheads.** Sensational or alarming newspaper headlines
3. **circular.** Paper or leaflet intended for wide distribution

16th. Such men will be given employment (with guaranteed protection) in the order in which such applications are received, and runs and positions assigned them accordingly. Otherwise, they will be considered discharged, and every vacancy will be filled by a new man as soon as his services can be secured.

(Signed)
Benjamin Norton,
PRESIDENT

He also noted among the want ads one which read:

WANTED—50 skilled motormen, accustomed to Westinghouse system, to run U.S. mail cars only, in the City of Brooklyn; protection guaranteed.

◄ *What positions does Hurstwood note advertised in the paper?*

He noted particularly in each the "protection guaranteed." It signified to him the unassailable power of the companies.

"They've got the militia[4] on their side," he thought. "There isn't anything those men can do."

While this was still in his mind, the incident with Oeslogge and Carrie occurred. There had been a good deal to irritate him, but this seemed much the worst. Never before had she accused him of stealing—or very near that. She doubted the naturalness of so large a bill. And he had worked so hard to make expenses seem light. He had been "doing" butcher and baker in order not to call on her. He had eaten very little—almost nothing.

◄ *Of what does Hurstwood feel that Carrie has accused him?*

"Damn it all!" he said. "I can get something. I'm not down yet."

He thought that he really must do something now. It was too cheap to sit around after such an insinuation as this. Why, after a little, he would be standing anything.

◄ *What does Hurstwood decide to do?*

He got up and looked out the window into the chilly street. It came gradually into his mind, as he stood there, to go to Brooklyn.

"Why not?" his mind said. "Anyone can get work over there. You'll get two a day."

"How about accidents?" said a voice. "You might get hurt."

"Oh, there won't be much of that," he answered. "They've called out the police. Anyone who wants to run a car will be protected all right."

"You don't know how to run a car," rejoined the voice.

"I won't apply as a motorman," he answered. "I can ring up fares all right."

"They'll want motormen mostly."

"They'll take anybody; that I know."

4. **militia.** Soldiers

For several hours he argued pro and con with this mental counselor, feeling no need to act at once in a matter so sure of profit.

In the morning he put on his best clothes, which were poor enough, and began stirring about, putting some bread and meat into a page of a newspaper. Carrie watched him, interested in this new move.

"Where are you going?" she asked.

"Over to Brooklyn," he answered. Then, seeing her still inquisitive, he added: "I think I can get on over there."

"On the trolley lines?" said Carrie, astonished.

"Yes," he rejoined.

"Aren't you afraid?" she asked.

"What of?" he answered. "The police are protecting them."

"The paper said four men were hurt yesterday."

"Yes," he returned; "but you can't go by what the papers say. They'll run the cars all right."

► *What makes Carrie feel sorry?*

He looked rather determined now, in a desolate sort of way, and Carrie felt very sorry. Something of the old Hurstwood was here—the least shadow of what was once shrewd and pleasant strength. Outside, it was cloudy and blowing a few flakes of snow.

"What a day to go over there," thought Carrie.

Now he left before she did, which was a remarkable thing, and tramped eastward to Fourteenth Street and Sixth Avenue, where he took the car. He had read that scores of applicants were applying at the office of the Brooklyn City Railroad building and were being received. He made his way there by horsecar and ferry—a dark, silent man—to the offices in question. It was a long way, for no cars were running, and the day was cold; but he trudged along grimly. Once in Brooklyn, he could clearly see and feel that a strike was on. People showed it in their manner. Along the routes of certain tracks not a car was running. About certain corners and nearby saloons small groups of men were lounging. Several spring wagons passed him, equipped with plain wooden chairs, and labeled "Flatbush" or "Prospect Park. Fare, Ten Cents." He noticed cold and even gloomy faces. Labor was having its little war.

When he came near the office in question, he saw a few men standing about, and some policemen. On the far corners

Words For Everyday Use

des • o • late (des´ ə lit) *adj.*, lonely; solitary

trudge (truj) *vi.*, walk wearily or laboriously

were other men—whom he took to be strikers—watching. All the houses were small and wooden, the streets poorly paved. After New York, Brooklyn looked actually poor and hard-up.

He made his way into the heart of the small group, eyed by policemen and the men already there. One of the officers addressed him.

"What are you looking for?"

"I want to see if I can get a place."

"The offices are up those steps," said the bluecoat. His face was a very neutral thing to contemplate. In his heart of hearts, he sympathized with the strikers and hated this "scab."[5] In his heart of hearts, also, he felt the dignity and use of the police force, which commanded order. Of its true social significance, he never once dreamed. His was not the mind for that. The two feelings blended in him—neutralized one another and him. He would have fought for this man as determinedly as for himself, and yet only so far as commanded. Strip him of his uniform, and he would have soon picked his side.

◀ *What is the police officer's opinion of Hurstwood? of the strike?*

Hurstwood ascended a dusty flight of steps and entered a small, dust-colored office, in which were a railing, a long desk, and several clerks.

"Well, sir?" said a middle-aged man, looking up at him from the long desk.

"Do you want to hire any men?" inquired Hurstwood.

"What are you—a motorman?"

"No; I'm not anything," said Hurstwood.

He was not at all abashed by his position. He knew these people needed men. If one didn't take him, another would. This man could take him or leave him, just as he chose.

"Well, we prefer experienced men, of course," said the man. He paused, while Hurstwood smiled indifferently. Then he added: "Still, I guess you can learn. What is your name?"

"Wheeler," said Hurstwood.

The man wrote an order on a small card. "Take that to our barns," he said, "and give it to the foreman.[6] He'll show you what to do."

Hurstwood went down and out. He walked straight away in the direction indicated, while the policemen looked after.

◀ *What do the officers know about the situation?*

"There's another wants to try it," said Officer Kiely to Officer Macey.

"I have my mind he'll get his fill," returned the latter, quietly.

They had been in strikes before.

5. **"scab."** Worker who replaces a union worker during a strike
6. **foreman.** Person in charge of a group of workers

CHAPTER 41

The Strike

The barn at which Hurstwood applied was exceedingly short-handed, and was being operated practically by three men as directors. There were a lot of green hands around—queer, hungry-looking men, who looked as if want had driven them to desperate means. They tried to be lively and willing, but there was an air of hang-dog[1] diffidence about the place.

Hurstwood went back through the barns and out into a large, enclosed lot, where were a series of tracks and loops. A half-dozen cars were there, manned by instructors, each with a pupil at the lever. More pupils were waiting at one of the rear doors of the barn.

In silence Hurstwood viewed this scene, and waited. His companions took his eye for a while, though they did not interest him much more than the cars. They were an uncomfortable-looking gang, however. One or two were very thin and lean. Several were quite stout. Several others were raw-boned and sallow, as if they had been beaten upon by all sorts of rough weather.

"Did you see by the paper they are going to call out the militia?" Hurstwood heard one of them remark.

"Oh, they'll do that," returned the other. "They always do."

"Think we're liable to have much trouble?" said another, whom Hurstwood did not see.

"Not very."

► What has been happening to the "scabs" who take over work during the strike?

"That Scotchman that went out on the last car," put in a voice, "told me that they hit him in the car with a cinder."[2]

A small, nervous laugh accompanied this.

"One of those fellows on the Fifth Avenue line must have had a hell of a time, according to the papers," drawled another. "They broke his car windows and pulled him off into the street 'fore the police could stop 'em."

"Yes; but there are more police around today," was added by another.

1. **hang-dog.** Ashamed and cringing
2. **cinder.** Any matter, such as coal or wood, partly burned, but not reduced to ashes

Words For Everyday Use

sal • low (sal´ō) *adj.,* sickly in complexion

Hurstwood hearkened without much mental comment. These talkers seemed scared to him. Their gabbling was feverish—things said to quiet their own minds. He looked out into the yard and waited.

Two of the men got around quite near him, but behind his back. They were rather social, and he listened to what they said.

"Are you a railroad man?" said one.

"Me? No. I've always worked in a paper factory."

"I had a job in Newark until last October," returned the other, with reciprocal feeling.

There were some words which passed too low to hear. Then the conversation became strong again.

"I don't blame these fellers for striking," said one. "They've got the right of it, all right, but I had to get something to do."

"Same here," said the other. "If I had any job in Newark I wouldn't be over here takin' chances like these."

"It's hell these days, ain't it?" said the man. "A poor man ain't nowhere. You could starve, by God, right in the streets, and there ain't most no one would help you."

◄ *What does the man say about being poor?*

"Right you are," said the other. "The job I had I lost 'cause they shut down. They run all summer and lay up a big stock, and then shut down."

Hurstwood paid some little attention to this. Somehow, he felt a little superior to these two—a little better off. To him these were ignorant and commonplace, poor sheep in a driver's hand.

◄ *How does Hurstwood feel about these men? Is he really in any better position than they are?*

"Poor devils," he thought, speaking out of the thoughts and feelings of a bygone period of success.

"Next," said one of the instructors.

"You're next," said a neighbor, touching him.

He went out and climbed on the platform. The instructor took it for granted that no preliminaries were needed.

"You see this handle," he said, reaching up to an electric cut-off, which was fastened to the roof. "This throws the current off or on. If you want to reverse the car you turn it over here. If you want to send it forward, you put it over here. If you want to cut off the power, you keep it in the middle."

Hurstwood smiled at the simple information.

"Now, this handle here regulates your speed. To here," he said, pointing with his finger, "gives you about four miles an

Words For Everyday Use

gab • bling (gab´bliŋ) *n.,* chatter

re • cip • ro • cal (ri sip´rə kəl) *adj.,* shared; equal

► *Of what is Hurstwood confident?*

► *What does Hurstwood soon discover?*

hour. This is eight. When it's full on, you make about fourteen miles an hour."

Hurstwood watched him calmly. He had seen motormen work before. He knew just about how they did it, and was sure he could do as well, with a very little practice.

The instructor explained a few more details, and then said:

"Now, we'll back her up."

Hurstwood stood placidly by, while the car rolled back into the yard.

"One thing you want to be careful about, and that is to start easy. Give one degree time to act before you start another. The one fault of most men is that they always want to throw her wide open. That's bad. It's dangerous, too. Wears out the motor. You don't want to do that."

"I see," said Hurstwood.

He waited and waited, while the man talked on.

"Now you take it," he said, finally.

The ex-manager laid hand to the lever and pushed it gently, as he thought. It worked much easier than he imagined, however, with the result that the car jerked quickly forward, throwing him back against the door. He straightened up sheepishly, while the instructor stopped the car with the brake.

"You want to be careful about that," was all he said.

Hurstwood found, however, that handling a brake and regulating speed were not so instantly mastered as he had imagined. Once or twice he would have plowed through the rear fence if it had not been for the hand and word of his companion. The latter was rather patient with him, but he never smiled.

"You've got to get the knack of working both arms at once," he said. "It takes a little practice."

One o'clock came while he was still on the car practicing, and he began to feel hungry. The day set in snowing, and he was cold. He grew weary of running to and fro on the short track.

They ran the car to the end and both got off. Hurstwood went into the barn and sought a car step, pulling out his paper-wrapped lunch from his pocket. There was no water and the bread was dry, but he enjoyed it. There was no ceremony about dining. He swallowed and looked about, contemplating the dull, homely labor of the thing. It was disagreeable—miserably disagreeable—in all its phases. Not because it was bitter, but because it was hard. It would be hard to anyone, he thought.

After eating, he stood about as before, waiting until his turn came.

The intention was to give him an afternoon of practice, but the greater part of the time was spent in waiting about.

At last evening came, and with it hunger and a debate with himself as to how he should spend the night. It was half-past five. He must soon eat. If he tried to go home, it would take him two hours and a half of cold walking and riding. Besides, he had orders to report at seven the next morning, and going home would necessitate his rising at an unholy and disagreeable hour. He had only something like a dollar and fifteen cents of Carrie's money, with which he had intended to pay the two weeks' coal bill before the present idea struck him.

"They must have some place around here," he thought. "Where does that fellow from Newark stay?"

Finally he decided to ask. There was a young fellow standing near one of the doors in the cold, waiting a last turn. He was a mere boy in years—twenty-one about—but with a body lank and long, because of privation. A little good living would have made this youth plump and swaggering.

"How do they arrange this, if a man hasn't any money?" inquired Hurstwood, discreetly.

The fellow turned a keen, watchful face on the inquirer.

"You mean eat?" he replied.

"Yes, and sleep. I can't go back to New York tonight."

"The foreman'll fix that if you ask him, I guess. He did me."

◄ *What arrangements are made for poor men like Hurstwood?*

"That so?"

"Yes. I just told him I didn't have anything. Gee, I couldn't go home. I live way over in Hoboken."[3]

Hurstwood only cleared his throat by way of acknowledgment.

"They've got a place upstairs here, I understand. I don't know what sort of a thing it is. Purty tough, I guess. He gave me a meal ticket this noon. I know that wasn't much."

Hurstwood smiled grimly, and the boy laughed.

"It ain't no fun, is it?" he inquired, wishing vainly for a cheery reply.

"Not much," answered Hurstwood.

"I'd tackle him now," volunteered the youth. "He may go 'way."

Hurstwood did so.

"Isn't there someplace I can stay around here tonight?" he inquired. "If I have to go back to New York, I'm afraid I won't—"

"There're some cots upstairs," interrupted the man, "if you want one of them."

3. **Hoboken.** City in New Jersey, across the Hudson River from New York City

"That'll do," he assented.

He meant to ask for a meal ticket, but the seemingly proper moment never came, and he decided to pay himself that night.

"I'll ask him in the morning."

He ate in a cheap restaurant in the vicinity, and, being cold and lonely, went straight off to seek the loft in question. The company was not attempting to run cars after nightfall. It was so advised by the police.

The room seemed to have been a lounging place for night workers. There were some nine cots in the place, two or three wooden chairs, a soap box, and a small, round-bellied stove, in which a fire was blazing. Early as he was, another man was there before him. The latter was sitting beside the stove warming his hands.

Hurstwood approached and held out his own toward the fire. He was sick of the bareness and privation of all things connected with his venture, but was steeling himself to hold out. He fancied he could for a while.

"Cold, isn't it?" said the early guest.

"Rather."

A long silence.

"Not much of a place to sleep in, is it?" said the man.

"Better than nothing," replied Hurstwood.

Another silence.

"I believe I'll turn in," said the man.

► *What disgusts Hurstwood?*

Rising, he went to one of the cots and stretched himself, removing only his shoes, and pulling the one blanket and dirty old comforter over him in a sort of bundle. The sight disgusted Hurstwood, but he did not dwell on it, choosing to gaze into the stove and think of something else. Presently he decided to retire, and picked a cot, also removing his shoes.

While he was doing so, the youth who had advised him to come here entered, and, seeing Hurstwood, tried to be genial.

"Better'n nothin'," he observed, looking around.

Hurstwood did not take this to himself. He thought it to be an expression of individual satisfaction, and so did not answer. The youth imagined he was out of sorts, and set to whistling softly. Seeing another man asleep, he quit that and lapsed into silence.

Hurstwood made the best of a bad lot by keeping on his clothes and pushing away the dirty covering from his head, but at last he dozed in sheer weariness. The covering became more and more comfortable, its character was forgotten, and he pulled it about his neck and slept.

► *About what does Hurstwood dream? In what way does his dream contrast with reality?*

In the morning he was aroused out of a pleasant dream by several men stirring about in the cold, cheerless room. He had been back in Chicago in fancy, in his own comfortable home. Jessica had been arranging to go somewhere, and he had been talking with her about it. This was so clear in his mind, that he was startled now by the contrast of this room. He raised his head, and the cold, bitter reality jarred him into wakefulness.

"Guess I'd better get up," he said.

There was no water on this floor. He put on his shoes in the cold and stood up, shaking himself in his stiffness. His clothes felt disagreeable, his hair bad.

"Hell!" he muttered, as he put on his hat.

Downstairs things were stirring again.

He found a hydrant, with a trough[4] which had once been used for horses, but there was no towel here, and his handkerchief was soiled from yesterday. He contented himself with wetting his eyes with the ice-cold water. Then he sought the foreman, who was already on the ground.

"Had your breakfast yet?" inquired that worthy.[5]

"No," said Hurstwood.

"Better get it, then; your car won't be ready for a little while."

Hurstwood hesitated.

"Could you let me have a meal ticket?" he asked, with an effort.

"Here you are," said the man, handing him one.

He breakfasted as poorly as the night before on some fried steak and bad coffee. Then he went back.

"Here," said the foreman, motioning him, when he came in. "You take this car out in a few minutes."

Hurstwood climbed up on the platform in the gloomy barn and waited for a signal. He was nervous, and yet the thing was a relief. Anything was better than the barn.

On this the fourth day of the strike, the situation had taken a turn for the worse. The strikers, following the counsel of their leaders and the newspapers, had struggled peaceably enough. There had been no great violence done. Cars had been stopped, it is true, and the men argued with. Some crews had been won over and led away, some windows broken, some jeering and yelling done; but in no more than five or six instances had men been seriously injured. These by crowds whose acts the leaders disclaimed.

Idleness, however, and the sight of the company, backed by the police, triumphing, angered the men. They saw that each day more cars were going on, each day more declarations were being made by the company officials that the effective opposition of the strikers was broken. This put desperate thoughts

◄ *Of what change in the strikers' mood is Hurstwood unaware?*

4. **trough.** Open box that holds water or food for animals
5. **worthy.** Prominent or important person

in the minds of the men. Peaceful methods meant, they saw, that the companies would soon run all their cars and those who had complained would be forgotten. There was nothing so helpful to the companies as peaceful methods.

All at once they blazed forth, and for a week there was storm and stress. Cars were assailed, men attacked, policemen struggled with, tracks torn up, and shots fired, until at last street fights and mob movements became frequent, and the city was invested with militia.

Hurstwood knew nothing of the change of temper.

"Run your car out," called the foreman, waving a vigorous hand at him. A green conductor jumped up behind and rang the bell twice as a signal to start. Hurstwood turned the lever and ran the car out through the door into the street in front of the barn. Here two brawny policemen got up beside him on the platform—one on either hand.

At the sound of a gong near the barn door, two bells were given by the conductor and Hurstwood opened his lever.

The two policemen looked about them calmly.

"'Tis cold, all right, this morning," said the one on the left, who possessed a rich brogue.[6]

"I had enough of it yesterday," said the other. "I wouldn't want a steady job of this."

"Nor I."

Neither paid the slightest attention to Hurstwood, who stood facing the cold wind, which was chilling him completely, and thinking of his orders.

► *What instructions did the foreman give Hurstwood?*

"Keep a steady gait," the foreman had said. "Don't stop for anyone who doesn't look like a real passenger. Whatever you do, don't stop for a crowd."

The two officers kept silent for a few moments.

"The last man must have gone through all right," said the officer on the left. "I don't see his car anywhere."

"Who's on there?" asked the second officer, referring, of course, to its complement of policemen.

"Schaeffer and Ryan."

There was another silence, in which the car ran smoothly along. There were not so many houses along this part of the way. Hurstwood did not see many people either. The situation was not wholly disagreeable to him. He would do well enough.

6. **brogue.** English as spoken by Irish immigrants

Words For Everyday Use

brawn • y (brôn´ ē) *adj.,* strong and muscular

He was brought out of this feeling by the sudden appearance of a curve ahead, which he had not expected. He shut off the current and did an energetic turn at the brake, but not in time to avoid an unnaturally quick turn. It shook him up and made him feel like making apologetic remarks, but he refrained.

"You want to look out for them things," said the officer on the left, condescendingly.

"That's right," agreed Hurstwood, shamefacedly.

"There's lots of them on this line," said the officer on the right.

Around the corner a more populated way appeared. One or two pedestrians were in view ahead. A boy coming out of a gate with a tin milk bucket gave Hurstwood his first objectionable greeting.

"Scab!" he yelled. "Scab!"

Hurstwood heard it, but tried to make no comment, even to himself. He knew he would get that, and much more of the same sort, probably.

At a corner farther up a man stood by the track and signaled the car to stop.

"Never mind him," said one of the officers. "He's up to some game."

Hurstwood obeyed. At the corner he saw the wisdom of it. No sooner did the man perceive the intention to ignore him, than he shook his fist.

"Ah, you bloody coward!" he yelled.

Some half dozen men, standing on the corner, flung taunts and jeers[7] after the speeding car.

Hurstwood winced the least bit. The real thing was slightly worse than the thoughts of it had been.

Now came in sight, three or four blocks farther on, a heap of something on the track.

◄ *What have the workers done to stop the trolley?*

"They've been at work, here, all right," said one of the policemen.

"We'll have an argument, maybe," said the other.

Hurstwood ran the car close and stopped. He had not done so wholly, however, before a crowd gathered about. It was composed of ex-motormen and conductors in part, with a sprinkling of friends and sympathizers.

◄ *Who confronts Hurstwood? What do they ask him to do?*

"Come off the car, pardner," said one of the men in a voice meant to be conciliatory. "You don't want to take the bread out of another man's mouth, do you?"

Hurstwood held to his brake and lever, pale and very uncertain what to do.

7. **flung taunts and jeers.** Mocked

"Stand back," yelled one of the officers, leaning over the platform railing. "Clear out of this, now. Give the man a chance to do his work."

"Listen, pardner," said the leader, ignoring the policeman and addressing Hurstwood. "We're all working men, like yourself. If you were a regular motorman, and had been treated as we've been, you wouldn't want anyone to come in and take your place, would you? You wouldn't want anyone to do you out of your chance to get your rights, would you?"

"Shut her off! shut her off!" urged the other of the policemen, roughly. "Get out of this, now," and he jumped the railing and landed before the crowd and began shoving. Instantly the other officer was down beside him.

"Stand back, now," they yelled. "Get out of this. What the hell do you mean? Out, now."

It was like a small swarm of bees.

"Don't shove me," said one of the strikers, determinedly. "I'm not doing anything."

"Get out of this!" cried the officer, swinging his club. "I'll give ye a bat on the sconce.[8] Back, now."

"What the hell!" cried another of the strikers, pushing the other way, adding at the same time some lusty oaths.[9]

Crack came an officer's club on his forehead. He blinked his eyes blindly a few times, wabbled on his legs, threw up his hands, and staggered back. In return, a swift fist landed on the officer's neck.

Infuriated by this, the latter plunged left and right, laying about madly with his club. He was ably assisted by his brother of the blue, who poured ponderous oaths upon the troubled waters. No severe damage was done, owing to the agility of the strikers in keeping out of reach. They stood about the sidewalk now and jeered.

► *What do the officers order Hurstwood and the conductor to do?*

"Where is the conductor?" yelled one of the officers, getting his eye on that individual, who had come nervously forward to stand by Hurstwood. The latter had stood gazing upon the scene with more astonishment than fear.

"Why don't you come down here and get these stones off the track?" inquired the officer. "What you standing there for? Do you want to stay here all day? Get down."

8. **sconce.** Head
9. **lusty oaths.** Crude, profane curses

Words For Everyday Use

in • fu • ri • at • ed (in fyo͞or´ē āt´əd) *adj.,* enraged
pon • der • ous (pän´dər əs) *adj.,* heavy
a • gil • i • ty (ə jil´ə tē) *n.,* quick and easy movement

Hurstwood breathed heavily in excitement and jumped down with the nervous conductor as if he had been called.

"Hurry up, now," said the other policeman.

Cold as it was, these officers were hot and mad. Hurstwood worked with the conductor, lifting stone after stone and warming himself by the work.

"Ah, you scab, you!" yelled the crowd. "You coward! Steal a man's job, will you? Rob the poor, will you, you thief? We'll get you yet, now. Wait."

Not all of this was delivered by one man. It came from here and there, incorporated with much more of the same sort and curses.

"Work, you blackguards,"[10] yelled a voice. "Do the dirty work. You're the suckers that keep the poor people down!"

"May God starve ye yet," yelled an old Irish woman, who now threw open a nearby window and stuck out her head.

"Yes, and you," she added, catching the eye of one of the policemen. "You bloody, murtherin' thafe! Crack my son over the head, will you, you hard-hearted, murtherin' divil? Ah, ye—"

But the officer turned a deaf ear.

"Go to the devil, you old hag," he half-muttered as he stared round upon the scattered company.

Now the stones were off, and Hurstwood took his place again amid a continued chorus of epithets. Both officers got up beside him and the conductor rang the bell, when, bang! bang! through window and door came rocks and stones. One narrowly grazed Hurstwood's head. Another shattered the window behind.

◄ What does the crowd begin doing once the track is free?

"Throw open your lever," yelled one of the officers, grabbing at the handle himself.

Hurstwood complied and the car shot away, followed by a rattle of stones and a rain of curses.

"That —— hit me in the neck," said one of the officers. "I gave him a good crack for it, though."

"I think I must have left spots on some of them," said the other.

"I know that big guy that called us a ——," said the first. "I'll get him yet for that."

10. **blackguards.** Low and vulgar wrongdoers

Words For Everyday Use

ep • i • thet (ep´ə thet´) *n.*, adjective, noun, or phrase used to characterize a person or thing, often disparaging

"I thought we were in for it sure, once there," said the second.

Hurstwood, warmed and excited, gazed steadily ahead. It was an astonishing experience for him. He had read of these things, but the reality seemed something altogether new. He was no coward in spirit. The fact that he had suffered this much now rather operated to arouse a stolid determination to stick it out. He did not recur in thought to New York or the flat. This one trip seemed a consuming thing.

They now ran into the business heart of Brooklyn uninterrupted. People gazed at the broken windows of the car and at Hurstwood in his plain clothes. Voices called "scab" now and then, as well as other epithets, but no crowd attacked the car. At the downtown end of the line, one of the officers went to call up his station and report the trouble.

"There's a gang out there," he said, "laying for us yet. Better send someone over there and clean them out."

The car ran back more quietly—hooted, watched, flung at, but not attacked. Hurstwood breathed freely when he saw the barns.

"Well," he observed to himself, "I came out of that all right."

The car was turned in and he was allowed to loaf a while, but later he was again called. This time a new team of officers was aboard. Slightly more confident, he sped the car along the commonplace streets and felt somewhat less fearful. On one side, however, he suffered intensely. The day was raw, with a sprinkling of snow and a gusty wind, made all the more intolerable by the speed of the car. His clothing was not intended for this sort of work. He shivered, stamped his feet, and beat his arms as he had seen other motormen do in the past, but said nothing. The novelty and danger of the situation modified in a way his disgust and distress at being compelled to be here, but not enough to prevent him from feeling grim and sour. This was a dog's life, he thought. It was a tough thing to have to come to.

► *What makes Hurstwood's job more difficult?*

The one thought that strengthened him was the insult offered by Carrie. He was not down so low as to take all that, he thought. He could do something—this, even—for a while. It would get better. He would save a little.

A boy threw a clod of mud while he was thus reflecting and hit him upon the arm. It hurt sharply and angered him more than he had been any time since morning.

Words For Everyday Use

sto • lid (stäl´id) *adj.,* unemotional; impassive

clod (kläd) *n.,* lump

"The little cur!"[11] he muttered.

"Hurt you?" asked one of the policemen.

"No," he answered.

At one of the corners, where the car slowed up because of a turn, an ex-motorman, standing on the sidewalk, called to him:

"Won't you come out, pardner, and be a man? Remember we're fighting for decent day's wages, that's all. We've got families to support." The man seemed most peaceably inclined.

Hurstwood pretended not to see him. He kept his eyes straight on before and opened the lever wide. The voice had something appealing in it.

All morning this went on and long into the afternoon. He made three such trips. The dinner he had was no stay for such work and the cold was telling on him. At each end of the line he stopped to thaw out, but he could have groaned at the anguish of it. One of the barnmen, out of pity, loaned him a heavy cap and a pair of sheepskin gloves, and for once he was extremely thankful.

On the second trip of the afternoon he ran into a crowd about half way along the line, that had blocked the car's progress with an old telegraph pole.

"Get that thing off the track," shouted the two policemen.

"Yah, yah, yah!" yelled the crowd. "Get it off yourself."

The two policemen got down and Hurstwood started to follow.

"You stay there," one called. "Someone will run away with your car."

Amid the babel[12] of voices, Hurstwood heard one close beside him.

◄ What does the man once again urge Hurstwood to do?

"Come down, pardner, and be a man. Don't fight the poor. Leave that to the corporations."

He saw the same fellow who had called to him from the corner. Now, as before, he pretended not to hear him.

"Come down," the man repeated gently. "You don't want to fight poor men. Don't fight at all." It was a most philosophic and jesuitical motorman.

A third policeman joined the other two from somewhere and someone ran to telephone for more officers. Hurstwood gazed about, determined but fearful.

A man grabbed him by the coat.

"Come off of that," he exclaimed, jerking at him and trying to pull him over the railing.

"Let go," said Hurstwood, savagely.

---

11. **cur.** Mongrel dog; mean, cowardly person

12. **babel.** Confusion of voices and sounds, from the Biblical tower of Babel, the completion of which God prevented by confusing its builders' language: Genesis 11:1–10

"I'll show you—you scab!" cried a young Irishman, jumping up on the car and aiming a blow at Hurstwood. The latter ducked and caught it on the shoulder instead of the jaw.

"Away from here," shouted an officer, hastening to the rescue, and adding, of course, the usual oaths.

Hurstwood recovered himself, pale and trembling. It was becoming serious with him now. People were looking up and jeering at him. One girl was making faces.

He began to waver in his resolution, when a patrol wagon rolled up and more officers dismounted. Now the track was quickly cleared and the release effected.

"Let her go now, quick," said the officer, and again he was off.

The end came with a real mob, which met the car on its return trip a mile or two from the barns. It was an exceedingly poor-looking neighborhood. He wanted to run fast through it, but again the track was blocked. He saw men carrying something out to it when he was yet a half-dozen blocks away.

"There they are again!" exclaimed one policeman.

"I'll give them something this time," said the second officer, whose patience was becoming worn. Hurstwood suffered a qualm of body as the car rolled up. As before, the crowd began hooting, but now, rather than come near, they threw things. One or two windows were smashed and Hurstwood dodged a stone.

► *What does the crowd do this time?*

Both policemen ran out toward the crowd, but the latter replied by running toward the car. A woman—a mere girl in appearance—was among these, bearing a rough stick. She was exceedingly wrathful and struck at Hurstwood, who dodged. Thereupon, her companions, duly encouraged, jumped on the car and pulled Hurstwood over. He had hardly time to speak or shout before he fell.

"Let go of me," he said, falling on his side.

"Ah, you sucker," he heard someone say. Kicks and blows rained on him. He seemed to be suffocating. Then two men seemed to be dragging him off and he wrestled for freedom.

"Let up," said a voice, "you're all right. Stand up."

He was let loose and recovered himself. Now he recognized two officers. He felt as if he would faint from exhaustion. Something was wet on his chin. He put up his hand and felt, then looked. It was red.

"They cut me," he said, foolishly, fishing for his handkerchief.

"Now, now," said one of the officers. "It's only a scratch."

His senses became cleared now and he looked around. He was standing in a little store, where they left him for the moment. Outside, he could see, as he stood wiping his chin, the car and the excited crowd. A patrol wagon was there, and another.

He walked over and looked out. It was an ambulance, backing in.

He saw some energetic charging by the police and arrests being made.

"Come on, now, if you want to take your car," said an officer, opening the door and looking in.

He walked out, feeling rather uncertain of himself. He was very cold and frightened.

"Where's the conductor?" he asked.

"Oh, he's not here now," said the policeman.

Hurstwood went toward the car and stepped nervously on. As he did so there was a pistol shot. Something stung his shoulder.

◄ *What makes Hurstwood determined to leave?*

"Who fired that?" he heard an officer exclaim. "By God! who did that?" Both left him, running toward a certain building. He paused a moment and then got down.

"George!" exclaimed Hurstwood, weakly, "this is too much for me."

He walked nervously to the corner and hurried down a side street.

"Whew!" he said, drawing in his breath.

A half block away, a small girl gazed at him.

"You'd better sneak," she called.

He walked homeward in a blinding snowstorm, reaching the ferry by dusk. The cabins were filled with comfortable souls, who studied him curiously. His head was still in such a whirl that he felt confused. All the wonder of the twinkling lights of the river in a white storm passed for nothing. He trudged doggedly on until he reached the flat. There he entered and found the room warm. Carrie was gone. A couple of evening papers were lying on the table where she left them. He lit the gas and sat down. Then he got up and stripped to examine his shoulder. It was a mere scratch. He washed his hands and face, still in a brown study,[13] apparently, and combed his hair. Then he looked for something to eat, and finally, his hunger gone, sat down in his comfortable rocking-chair. It was a wonderful relief.

13. **brown study.** Condition of being deep in thought

Words For Everyday Use

dog • ged • ly (dôg´id lē) *adv.*, persistently; stubbornly

He put his hand to his chin, forgetting, for the moment, the papers.

"Well," he said, after a time, his nature recovering itself, "That's a pretty tough game over there."

Then he turned and saw the papers. With half a sigh he picked up the *World*.

"Strike Spreading in Brooklyn," he read. "Rioting Breaks Out in all Parts of the City."

He adjusted his paper very comfortably and continued. It was the one thing he read with absorbing interest.

CHAPTER 42

A Touch of Spring: The Empty Shell

Those who look upon Hurstwood's Brooklyn venture as an error of judgment will none the less realize the negative influence on him of the fact that he had tried and failed. Carrie got a wrong idea of it. He said so little that she imagined he had encountered nothing worse than the ordinary roughness—quitting so soon in the face of this seemed trifling. He did not want to work.

What is the negative effect of this experience on Hurstwood? What does Carrie assume about the situation? Why?

She was now one of a group of oriental beauties who, in the second act of the comic opera, were paraded by the vizier[1] before the new potentate[2] as the treasures of his harem. There was no word assigned to any of them, but on the evening when Hurstwood was housing himself in the loft of the street-car barn, the leading comedian and star, feeling exceedingly facetious, said in a profound voice, which created a ripple of laughter:

What happens one night to make Carrie momentarily the center of attention? How is she received by the audience?

"Well, who are you?"

It merely happened to be Carrie who was curtsying before him. It might as well have been any of the others, so far as he was concerned. He expected no answer and a dull one would have been reproved. But Carrie, whose experience and belief in herself gave her daring, curtsied sweetly again and answered:

"I am yours truly."

It was a trivial thing to say, and yet something in the way she did it caught the audience, which laughed heartily at the mock-fierce potentate towering before the young woman. The comedian also liked it, hearing the laughter.

"I thought your name was Smith," he returned, endeavoring to get the last laugh.

Carrie almost trembled for her daring after she had said this. All members of the company had been warned that to interpolate lines or "business" meant a fine or worse. She did not know what to think.

1. **vizier.** Counselor to an Arabian or Turkish ruler
2. **potentate.** Ruler

Words For Everyday Use

fa • ce • tious (fə sē´shəs) *adj.,* inappropriately humorous

in • ter • po • late (in tʉr´pə lāt´) *vt.,* insert an interruption

► *What does the "great comedian" tell Carrie to do?*

As she was standing in her proper position in the wings, awaiting another entry, the great comedian made his exit past her and paused in recognition.

"You can just leave that in hereafter," he remarked, seeing how intelligent she appeared. "Don't add any more, though."

"Thank you," said Carrie, humbly. When he went on she found herself trembling violently.

"Well, you're in luck," remarked another member of the chorus. "There isn't another one of us has got a line."

There was no gainsaying the value of this. Everybody in the company realized that she had got a start. Carrie hugged herself when next evening the lines got the same applause. She went home rejoicing, knowing that soon something must come of it. It was Hurstwood who, by his presence, caused her merry thoughts to flee and replaced them with sharp longings for an end of distress.

The next day she asked him about his venture.

"They're not trying to run any cars except with police. They don't want anybody just now—not before next week."

► *What is beginning to happen to Hurstwood?*

Next week came, but Carrie saw no change. Hurstwood seemed more apathetic than ever. He saw her off mornings to rehearsals and the like with the utmost calm. He read and read. Several times he found himself staring at an item, but thinking of something else. The first of these lapses that he sharply noticed concerned a hilarious party he had once attended at a driving club, of which he had been a member. He sat, gazing downward, and gradually thought he heard the old voices and the clink of glasses.

"You're a dandy, Hurstwood," his friend Walker said. He was standing again well-dressed, smiling, good-natured, the recipient of encores for a good story.

All at once he looked up. The room was so still it seemed ghostlike. He heard the clock ticking audibly and half-suspected that he had been dozing. The paper was so straight in his hands, however, and the items he had been reading so directly before him, that he rid himself of the doze idea. Still, it seemed peculiar. When it occurred a second time, however, it did not seem quite so strange.

Butcher and grocery man, baker and coal man—not the group with whom he was then dealing, but those who had trusted him to the limit—called. He met them all blandly,

Words For Everyday Use

gain • say (gān´sā´) *vt.*, deny; oppose

becoming deft in excuse. At last he became bold, pretended to be out, or waved them off.

"They can't get blood out of a turnip," he said. "If I had it I'd pay them."

Carrie's little soldier friend, Miss Osborne, seeing her succeeding, had become a sort of satellite. Little Osborne could never of herself amount to anything. She seemed to realize it in a sort of pussy-like way and instinctively concluded to cling with her soft little claws to Carrie.

"Oh, you'll get up," she kept telling Carrie with admiration. "You're so good."

Timid as Carrie was, she was strong in capability. The reliance of others made her feel as if she must, and when she must she dared. Experience of the world and of necessity was in her favor. No longer the lightest word of a man made her head dizzy. She had learned that men could change and fail. Flattery in its most palpable form had lost its force with her. It required superiority—kindly superiority—to move her—the superiority of a genius like Ames.

◄ *What factors are now in Carrie's favor? What has she learned?*

"I don't like the actors in our company," she told Lola one day. "They're all so stuck on themselves."

"Don't you think Mr. Barclay's pretty nice?" inquired Lola, who had received a condescending smile or two from that quarter.

"Oh, he's nice enough," answered Carrie; "but he isn't sincere. He assumes such an air."

Lola felt for her first hold upon Carrie in the following manner:

"Are you paying room-rent where you are?"

◄ *What tempting offer does Lola make?*

"Certainly," answered Carrie. "Why?"

"I know where I could get the loveliest room and bath, cheap. It's too big for me, but it would be just right for two, and the rent is only six dollars a week for both."

"Where?" said Carrie.

"In Seventeenth Street."

"Well, I don't know as I'd care to change," said Carrie, who was already turning over the three-dollar rate in her mind. She was thinking if she had only herself to support this would leave her seventeen for herself.

Nothing came of this until after the Brooklyn adventure of Hurstwood's and her success with the speaking part. Then

Words For Everyday Use

deft (deft) *adj.,* skillful

► *What does Carrie believe her leaving would accomplish? What are her concerns?*

she began to feel as if she must be free. She thought of leaving Hurstwood and thus making him act for himself, but he had developed such peculiar traits she feared he might resist any effort to throw him off. He might hunt her out at the show and hound her in that way. She did not wholly believe that he would, but he might. This, she knew, would be an embarrassing thing if he made himself conspicuous in any way. It troubled her greatly.

Things were precipitated by the offer of a better part. One of the actresses playing the part of a modest sweetheart gave notice of leaving and Carrie was selected.

"How much are you going to get?" asked Miss Osborne, on hearing the good news.

"I didn't ask him," said Carrie.

"Well, find out. Goodness, you'll never get anything if you don't ask. Tell them you must have forty dollars, anyhow."

"Oh, no," said Carrie.

"Certainly!" exclaimed Lola. "Ask 'em, anyway."

Carrie succumbed to this prompting, waiting, however, until the manager gave her notice of what clothing she must have to fit the part.

"How much do I get?" she inquired.

► *How much money will Carrie be paid a week for her new role?*

► *What makes her decide to consider seriously leaving Hurstwood?*

"Thirty-five dollars," he replied.

Carrie was too much astonished and delighted to think of mentioning forty. She was nearly beside herself, and almost hugged Lola, who clung to her at the news.

"It isn't as much as you ought to get," said the latter, "especially when you've got to buy clothes."

Carrie remembered this with a start. Where to get the money? She had none laid up for such an emergency. Rent day was drawing near.

"I'll not do it," she said, remembering her necessity. "I don't use the flat. I'm not going to give up my money this time. I'll move."

Fitting into this came another appeal from Miss Osborne, more urgent than ever.

"Come live with me, won't you?" she pleaded. "We can have the loveliest room. It won't cost you hardly anything that way."

"I'd like to," said Carrie, frankly.

"Oh, do," said Lola. "We'll have such a good time."

Carrie thought a while.

"I believe I will," she said, and then added: "I'll have to see first, though."

With the idea thus grounded, rent day approaching, and clothes calling for instant purchase, she soon found excuse in Hurstwood's lassitude. He said less and drooped more than ever.

As rent day approached, an idea grew in him. It was fostered by the demands of creditors and the impossibility of holding up many more. Twenty-eight dollars was too much for rent. "It's hard on her," he thought. "We could get a cheaper place."

Stirred with this idea, he spoke at the breakfast table.

"Don't you think we pay too much rent here?" he asked.

"Indeed I do," said Carrie, not catching his drift.

"I should think we could get a smaller place," he suggested. "We don't need four rooms."

Her countenance, had he been scrutinizing her, would have exhibited the disturbance she felt at this evidence of his determination to stay by her. He saw nothing remarkable in asking her to come down lower.

"Oh, I don't know," she answered, growing wary.

"There must be places around here where we could get a couple of rooms, which would do just as well."

Her heart revolted. "Never!" she thought. Who would furnish the money to move? To think of being in two rooms with him! She resolved to spend her money for clothes quickly, before something terrible happened. That very day she did it. Having done so, there was but one other thing to do.

"Lola," she said, visiting her friend, "I think I'll come."

"Oh, jolly!" cried the latter.

"Can we get it right away?" she asked, meaning the room.

"Certainly," cried Lola.

They went to look at it. Carrie had saved ten dollars from her expenditures—enough for this and her board beside. Her enlarged salary would not begin for ten days yet—would not reach her for seventeen. She paid half of the six dollars with her friend.

"Now, I've just enough to get on to the end of the week," she confided.

"Oh, I've got some," said Lola. "I've got twenty-five dollars, if you need it."

"No," said Carrie. "I guess I'll get along."

They decided to move Friday, which was two days away. Now that the thing was settled, Carrie's heart misgave her.

◄ *What idea makes Carrie's heart revolt and cause her to decide to leave Hurstwood?*

Words For Everyday Use

fur • nish (furʹ nish) *vt.,* supply; provide

► *How does Hurstwood appear to her now?*

► *Of what is Hurstwood unaware?*

She felt very much like a criminal in the matter. Each day looking at Hurstwood, she had realized that, along with the disagreeableness of his attitude, there was something pathetic.

She looked at him the same evening she had made up her mind to go, and now he seemed not so shiftless and worthless, but run down and beaten upon by chance. His eyes were not keen, his face marked, his hands flabby. She thought his hair had a touch of gray. All unconscious of his doom, he rocked and read his paper, while she glanced at him.

Knowing that the end was so near, she became rather solicitous.

"Will you go over and get some canned peaches?" she asked Hurstwood, laying down a two-dollar bill.

"Certainly," he said, looking in wonder at the money.

"See if you can get some nice asparagus," she added. "I'll cook it for dinner."

Hurstwood rose and took the money, slipping on his overcoat and getting his hat. Carrie noticed that both of these articles of apparel were old and poor-looking in appearance. It was plain enough before, but now it came home with peculiar force. Perhaps he couldn't help it, after all. He had done well in Chicago. She remembered his fine appearance the days he had met her in the park. Then he was so sprightly, so clean. Had it been all his fault?

He came back and laid the change down with the food.

"You'd better keep it," she observed. "We'll need other things."

"No," he said, with a sort of pride; "you keep it."

"Oh, go on and keep it," she replied, rather unnerved. "There'll be other things."

He wondered at this, not knowing the pathetic figure he had become in her eyes. She restrained herself with difficulty from showing a quaver in her voice.

To say truly, this would have been Carrie's attitude in any case. She had looked back at times upon her parting from Drouet and had regretted that she had served him so badly. She hoped she would never meet him again, but she was ashamed of her conduct. Not that she had any choice in the final separation. She had gone willingly to seek him, with sympathy in her heart, when Hurstwood had reported him ill. There was something cruel somewhere, and not being

Words For Everyday Use

shift • less (shift´lis) *adj.*, lazy

so • lic • i • tous (sə lis´ə təs) *adj.*, attentive; affectionate

able to track it mentally to its logical lair,[3] she concluded with feeling that he would never understand what Hurstwood had done and would see hard-hearted decision in her deed; hence her shame. Not that she cared for him. She did not want to make anyone who had been good to her feel badly.

She did not realize what she was doing by allowing these feelings to possess her. Hurstwood, noticing the kindness, conceived better of her. "Carrie's good-natured, anyhow," he thought.

Going to Miss Osborne's that afternoon, she found that little lady packing and singing.

"Why don't you come over with me today?" she asked.

"Oh, I can't," said Carrie. "I'll be there Friday. Would you mind lending me the twenty-five dollars you spoke of?"

◄ *What does Carrie ask Lola to do?*

"Why, no," said Lola, going for her purse.

"I want to get some other things," said Carrie.

"Oh, that's all right," answered the little girl, good-naturedly, glad to be of service.

It had been days since Hurstwood had done more than go to the grocery or to the newsstand. Now the weariness of indoors was upon him—had been for two days—but chill, gray weather had held him back. Friday broke fair and warm. It was one of those lovely harbingers[4] of spring, given as a sign in dreary winter that earth is not forsaken of warmth and beauty. The blue heaven, holding its one golden orb, poured down a crystal wash of warm light. It was plain, from the voice of the sparrows, that all was halcyon outside. Carrie raised the front windows, and felt the south wind blowing.

"It's lovely out today," she remarked.

"Is it?" said Hurstwood.

After breakfast, he immediately got his other clothes.

"Will you be back for lunch?" asked Carrie, nervously.

"No," he said.

He went out into the streets and tramped north, along Seventh Avenue, idly fixing upon the Harlem River as an objective point. He had seen some ships up there, the time he had called upon the brewers. He wondered how the territory thereabouts was growing.

Passing Fifty-ninth Street, he took the west side of Central Park, which he followed to Seventy-eighth Street. Then he remembered the neighborhood and turned over to look at

---

3. **lair.** Place of refuge or hiding

4. **harbingers.** Things that come before to announce or give an indication of what follows

the mass of buildings erected. It was very much improved. The great open spaces were filling up. Coming back, he kept to the Park until 110th Street, and then turned into Seventh Avenue again, reaching the pretty river by one o'clock.

There it ran winding before his gaze, shining brightly in the clear light, between the undulating banks on the right and the tall, tree-covered heights on the left. The spring-like atmosphere woke him to a sense of its loveliness, and for a few moments he stood looking at it, folding his hands behind his back. Then he turned and followed it toward the east side, idly seeking the ships he had seen. It was four o'clock before the waning day, with its suggestion of a cooler evening, caused him to return. He was hungry and would enjoy eating in the warm room.

When he reached the flat by half-past five, it was still dark. He knew that Carrie was not there, not only because there was no light showing through the transom,[5] but because the evening papers were stuck between the outside knob and the door. He opened with his key and went in. Everything was still dark. Lighting the gas, he sat down, preparing to wait a little while. Even if Carrie did come now, dinner would be late. He read until six, then got up to fix something for himself.

► *What does Hurstwood finally notice? In what way does this object "speak for itself"?*

As he did so, he noticed that the room seemed a little queer. What was it? He looked around, as if he missed something, and then saw an envelope near where he had been sitting. It spoke for itself, almost without further action on his part.

Reaching over, he took it, a sort of chill settling upon him even while he reached. The crackle of the envelope in his hands was loud. Green paper money lay soft within the note.

► *What reason does Carrie give for leaving? How much money does she leave for Hurstwood?*

"Dear George," he read, crunching the money in one hand. "I'm going away. I'm not coming back anymore. It's no use trying to keep up the flat; I can't do it. I wouldn't mind helping you, if I could, but I can't support us both, and pay the rent. I need what little I make to pay for my clothes. I'm leaving twenty dollars. It's all I have just now. You can do whatever you like with the furniture. I won't want it.—Carrie."

He dropped the note and looked quietly round. Now he knew what he missed. It was the little ornamental clock, which was hers. It had gone from the mantelpiece. He went

5. **transom.** Small window or shutterlike panel directly over a door or window

Words For Everyday Use

un • du • lat • ing (un´dyo͞o lāt iŋ) *adj.,* wavy

into the front room, his bedroom, the parlor, lighting the gas as he went. From the chiffonier[6] had gone the knick-knacks of silver and plate. From the table-top, the lace coverings. He opened the wardrobe—no clothes of hers. He opened the drawers—nothing of hers. Her trunk was gone from its accustomed place. Back in his own room hung his old clothes, just as he had left them. Nothing else was gone.

He stepped into the parlor and stood for a few moments looking vacantly at the floor. The silence grew oppressive. The little flat seemed wonderfully deserted. He wholly forgot that he was hungry, that it was only dinnertime. It seemed later in the night.

Suddenly, he found that the money was still in his hands. There were twenty dollars in all, as she had said. Now he walked back, leaving the lights ablaze, and feeling as if the flat were empty.

"I'll get out of this," he said to himself.

Then the sheer loneliness of his situation rushed upon him in full.

"Left me!" he muttered, and repeated, "left me!"

The place that had been so comfortable, where he had spent so many days of warmth, was now a memory. Something colder and chillier confronted him. He sank down in his chair, resting his chin in his hand—mere sensation, without thought, holding him.

Then something like a bereaved affection and self-pity swept over him.

"She needn't have gone away," he said. "I'd have got something."

◄ *What does Hurstwood tell himself?*

He sat a long while without rocking, and added quite clearly, out loud:

"I tried, didn't I?"

At midnight he was still rocking, staring at the floor.

6. **chiffonier.** Narrow chest of drawers, often with a mirror

Words For Everyday Use

be • reaved (bē rēvd´) *adj.*, grieving

Responding to the Selection

Explain whether Carrie is justified in leaving Hurstwood. Would you do the same if you were in her position? Why, or why not?

Reviewing the Selection

Recalling and Interpreting

1. **R:** In chapter 37, what announcement of Hurstwood's alarms Carrie? What does Carrie think of doing to solve this problem? In chapter 38, what job does Carrie get? What does she soon realize about her job? What does Hurstwood still expect Carrie to do around the house? What does Hurstwood ask Carrie to do at the end of chapter 38?

2. **I:** How does Hurstwood feel about Carrie's suggestion at first? Why does he soon change his mind? In what way does Carrie's approach to her job search differ from Hurstwood's approach? In what way does finding her own job change Carrie's feelings toward Hurstwood? Hurstwood keeps saying that he will "get something," but then returns to reading his papers. In your opinion, why can't Hurstwood find a job? What do you think the author's explanation would have been?

3. **R:** In chapter 39, who befriends Carrie and what advice does this person give Carrie about her line of work? What does Carrie begin doing more and more often rather than returning home? What lie does Carrie tell her new friend? What promotion does Carrie receive? What doesn't she tell Hurstwood? In chapters 39 and 40, what does Hurstwood begin to do instead of asking Carrie for money to pay for necessities? How does Carrie find out about Hurstwood's financial scheme? What does she refuse to do?

4. **I:** Why does Carrie lie to her friend? Why does Carrie deceive Hurstwood? Carrie has been supported by Hurstwood for years. Why does she resent supporting him so much? What does this reveal about the time period in which they live? Why doesn't Hurstwood simply ask Carrie for the money for household expenses? How does Carrie's refusal make Hurstwood feel?

5. **R:** What strike has Hurstwood read about in the papers? Why are these workers striking? What are the companies doing about the strike? What are conditions like at Hurstwood's job? What do the strikers keep doing to interrupt Hurstwood's work? Why does Hurstwood leave this job?

6. **I:** Explain why Hurstwood finally resolves to look for work. Why does he decide to work for this company even though it is against his moral convictions? What does this reveal about the way he is changing as a character? Why did Hurstwood assume that working as a motorman would be easy? How does Carrie feel about Hurstwood leaving this job? Why doesn't he reveal the truth? What do you think the effect of trying and failing will be on Hurstwood's character?

7. **R:** What happens to draw attention to Carrie one night in the theater? What does Hurstwood note beginning to happen to his mind? What further promotion does Carrie receive? What offer does Lola make? What does Hurstwood suggest to Carrie to save money? What does Carrie do as a result of this suggestion? What does she leave for Hurstwood?

8. **I:** Why does this event mark a turning point in Carrie's fortunes in the theater? Why don't Hurstwood's mental lapses alarm him more? Why doesn't Hurstwood's suggestion that Carrie "come down lower" not strike him as "remarkable"? Why does Hurstwood's suggestion prove the proverbial "straw that breaks the camel's back"? In other words, why is this suggestion all the excuse Carrie needs to determine her course of action? What does Carrie's leaving this behind reveal about her character? about the way her relationship with Hurstwood has been drastically altered? Carrie hopes that Hurstwood will be forced to become self-sufficient without her. Explain whether you think, based on Hurstwood's reaction to her departure, whether this hope is likely to prove true.

Synthesizing

9. Throughout chapters 37–42, Carrie and Hurstwood's interactions with each other are marked by deception. Find some examples of the way in which they lie to each other. Explain whether in most cases the deception is eventually revealed and whether lying is a new habit with either character. Why have they started lying to each other more frequently? In what way does this deceit mark the unraveling of their ties to each other? Would you say that their whole relationship has been a lie? Why, or why not? In chapter 21, Hurstwood resolved, "he would be happy . . . if it cost him all honesty of statement, all abandonment of truth." In what way has this resolution proved true? untrue? To what extent can most of Hurstwood's problems be attributed to his tendency to deceive?

10. Carrie's big break in the theater is prompted when an actor on a whim asks her, "Well, who are you?" Why is this question significant given Carrie's role in the play and her position of relative unimportance in the theater? Why is it an appropriate question given the way Carrie is growing and changing as a character? Explore Carrie's response to this significant question: "I am yours truly." What does it indicate about her as a character?

Understanding Literature (QUESTIONS FOR DISCUSSION)

1. **Characterization and Static and Dynamic Characters. Characterization** is the use of literary techniques to create a character. A **character** is a person who figures in the action of a literary work. A **static character** is one who does not change during the course of the action. A **dynamic character** is one who does change. On pages 342–343 the narrator directly reveals the way in which Carrie is "great" as a character. What great quality does she possess? Explain whether you agree with this assessment of her character. The narrator describes one of Hurstwood's lies as "lassitude's apology to energy." Of what is the narrator making Carrie and Hurstwood examples? What are the dominant characteristics the narrator wishes the reader to see in these characters? Explain whether you would define Hurstwood as a static or a dynamic character. In what way would you define Carrie?

2. Archetype. An **archetype** is an inherited, often unconscious, ancestral memory or motif that recurs throughout history and literature. The theme of the fall from innocence into experience is one of the most ancient archetypes in world literature, appearing in the Biblical story of Adam and Eve and countless myths, as well as contemporary fiction. While some writers have seen the loss of innocence as a negative experience, others have seen it as a necessary part of growing up. What view does Dreiser take of Carrie's loss of innocence and her gain of experience in society?

3. Naturalism, Realism, and Sentimentality. Naturalism was a literary movement of the late nineteenth and early twentieth centuries that saw actions and events as resulting inevitably from biological or natural forces in the environment. Naturalist writers extensively researched their subjects to portray them as realistically as possible. Many Naturalistic writers, including Naturalism's founder Émile Zola, focused their writing on the way biological or environmental forces contributed to the disparity of conditions between the working class and the wealthy owners of corporations. **Realism** is the attempt to render in art an accurate portrayal of reality. **Sentimentality** is an excessive expression of emotion. In what way is Dreiser's depiction of the trolley workers' strike a good example of Naturalism? Dreiser had worked as a reporter and had covered events such as the trolley workers' strike because labor's struggle against large corporations was becoming increasingly common in the early twentieth century. In what way does Dreiser portray the strike and Hurstwood's job as a motorman with the Naturalist's eye for Realism and the reporter's eye for detail? With whom do you think Dreiser's own sympathies lay—labor or the corporations? Explain whether Dreiser's depiction of the strike is strictly Realistic or if it is touched by sentimentality in some way.

CHAPTER 43

The World Turns Flatterer: An Eye in the Dark

Installed in her comfortable room, Carrie wondered how Hurstwood had taken her departure. She arranged a few things hastily and then left for the theater, half expecting to encounter him at the door. Not finding him, her dread lifted, and she felt more kindly toward him. She quite forgot him until about to come out, after the show, when the chance of his being there frightened her. As day after day passed and she heard nothing at all, the thought of being bothered by him passed. In a little while she was, except for occasional thoughts, wholly free of the gloom with which her life had been weighed in the flat.

► *What is the effect of Carrie's leaving Hurstwood on her mood?*

It is curious to note how quickly a profession absorbs one. Carrie became wise in theatrical lore, hearing the gossip of little Lola. She learned what the theatrical papers were, which ones published items about actresses and the like. She began to read the newspaper notices, not only of the opera in which she had so small a part, but of others. Gradually the desire for notice took hold of her. She longed to be renowned like others, and read with avidity all the complimentary or critical comments made concerning others high in her profession. The showy world in which her interest lay completely absorbed her.

► *What completely absorbs Carrie? For what does she long?*

It was about this time that the newspapers and magazines were beginning to pay that illustrative attention to the beauties of the stage which has since become fervid. The newspapers, and particularly the Sunday newspapers, indulged in large decorative theatrical pages, in which the faces and forms of well-known theatrical celebrities appeared, enclosed with artistic scrolls. The magazines also—or at least one or two of the newer ones—published occasional portraits of pretty stars, and now and again photos of scenes from various plays. Carrie watched these with growing interest. When would a scene from her opera appear? When would some paper think her photo worthwhile?

The Sunday before taking her new part she scanned the theatrical pages for some little notice. It would have accorded

Words For Everyday Use

lore (lôr) *n.,* specialized knowledge

fer • vid (fur´vid) *adj.,* impassioned; fervent; intense devoted

with her expectations if nothing had been said, but there in the squibs, tailing off several more substantial items, was a wee notice. Carrie read it with a tingling body:

"The part of Katisha, the country maid, in *The Wives of Abdul* at the Broadway, heretofore played by Inez Carew, will be hereafter filled by Carrie Madenda, one of the cleverest members of the chorus."

◄ *What notice in one of the theatrical papers delights Carrie?*

Carrie hugged herself with delight. Oh, wasn't it just fine! At last! The first, the long-hoped for, the delightful notice! And they called her clever. She could hardly restrain herself from laughing loudly. Had Lola seen it?

"They've got a notice here of the part I'm going to play tomorrow night," said Carrie to her friend.

"Oh, jolly! Have they?" cried Lola, running to her. "That's all right," she said, looking. "You'll get more now, if you do well. I had my picture in the *World* once."

"Did you?" asked Carrie.

"Did I? Well, I should say," returned the little girl. "They had a frame around it."

Carrie laughed.

"They've never published my picture."

"But they will," said Lola. "You'll see. You do better than most that get theirs in now."

Carrie felt deeply grateful for this. She almost loved Lola for the sympathy and praise she extended. It was so helpful to her—so almost necessary.

Fulfilling her part capably brought another notice in the papers that she was doing her work acceptably. This pleased her immensely. She began to think the world was taking note of her.

The first week she got her thirty-five dollars, it seemed an enormous sum. Paying only three dollars for room rent seemed ridiculous. After giving Lola her twenty-five, she still had seven dollars left. With four left over from previous earnings, she had eleven. Five of this went to pay the regular installment on the clothes she had to buy. The next week she was even in greater feather.[1] Now, only three dollars need be paid for room rent and five on her clothes. The rest she had for food and her own whims.

"You'd better save a little for summer," cautioned Lola. "We'll probably close in May."

"I intend to," said Carrie.

The regular entrance of thirty-five dollars a week to one who has endured scant allowances for several years is a demoralizing thing. Carrie found her purse bursting with

◄ *In what way does more money affect Carrie's life?*

1. **greater feather.** Better humor or condition

good green bills of comfortable denominations.[2] Having no one dependent upon her, she began to buy pretty clothes and pleasing trinkets, to eat well, and to ornament her room. Friends were not long in gathering about. She met a few young men who belonged to Lola's staff. The members of the opera company made her acquaintance without the formality of introduction. One of these discovered a fancy for her. On several occasions he strolled home with her.

"Let's stop in and have a rarebit," he suggested one midnight.

"Very well," said Carrie.

► *What criticisms does Carrie have of her dinner partner?*

In the rosy restaurant, filled with the merry lovers of late hours, she found herself criticizing this man. He was too stilted, too self-opinionated. He did not talk of anything that lifted her above the common run of clothes and material success. When it was all over, he smiled most graciously.

"Got to go straight home, have you?" he said.

"Yes," she answered, with an air of quiet understanding.

"She's not so inexperienced as she looks," he thought, and thereafter his respect and ardor were increased.

She could not help sharing in Lola's love for a good time. There were days when they went carriage riding, nights when after the show they dined, afternoons when they strolled along Broadway, tastefully dressed. She was getting in the metropolitan whirl of pleasure.

At last her picture appeared in one of the weeklies. She had not known of it, and it took her breath. "Miss Carrie Madenda," it was labeled. "One of the favorites of *The Wives of Abdul* company." At Lola's advice she had had some pictures taken by Sarony.[3] They had got one there. She thought of going down and buying a few copies of the paper, but remembered that there was no one she knew well enough to send them to. Only Lola, apparently, in all the world was interested.

► *Why doesn't Carrie buy more copies of the paper in which her likeness appeared?*

► *What has Carrie learned about the world? What does she lack?*

The metropolis is a cold place socially, and Carrie soon found that a little money brought her nothing. The world of wealth and distinction was quite as far away as ever. She could feel that there was no warm, sympathetic friendship back of the easy merriment with which many approached

2. **Carrie found . . . denominations.** Carrie has many bills of high value.
3. **Sarony.** Napoleon Sarony was the leading theatrical photographer of the day.

Words For Everyday Use

stilt • ed (stil´tid) *adj.*, stiff, not natural
ar • dor (är´dər) *n.*, emotional warmth

her. All seemed to be seeking their own amusement, regardless of the possible sad consequence to others. So much for the lessons of Hurstwood and Drouet.

In April she learned that the opera would probably last until the middle or the end of May, according to the size of the audiences. Next season it would go on the road. She wondered if she would be with it. As usual, Miss Osborne, owing to her moderate salary, was for securing a home engagement.

"They're putting on a summer play at the Casino," she announced, after figuratively putting her ear to the ground. "Let's try and get in that."

"I'm willing," said Carrie.

They tried in time and were apprised of the proper date to apply again. That was May 16th. Meanwhile their own show closed May 5th.

"Those that want to go with the show next season," said the manager, "will have to sign this week."

"Don't you sign," advised Lola. "I wouldn't go."

"I know," said Carrie, "but maybe I can't get anything else."

"Well, I won't," said the little girl, who had a resource in her admirers. "I went once and I didn't have anything at the end of the season."

Carrie thought this over. She had never been on the road.

"We can get along," added Lola. "I always have."

Carrie did not sign.

The manager who was putting on the summer skit at the Casino had never heard of Carrie, but the several notices she had received, her published picture, and the program bearing her name had some little weight with him. He gave her a silent part at thirty dollars a week.

◄ *What has weight with theater managers?*

"Didn't I tell you?" said Lola. "It doesn't do you any good to go away from New York. They forget all about you if you do."

Now, because Carrie was pretty, the gentlemen who made up the advance illustrations of shows about to appear for the Sunday papers selected Carrie's photo along with others to illustrate the announcement. Because she was very pretty, they gave it excellent space and drew scrolls about it. Carrie was delighted. Still, the management did not seem to have seen anything of it. At least, no more attention was paid to her than before. At the same time there seemed very little in

Words For Everyday Use

ap • prise (ə prīz´) *vt.*, inform

▶ *What type of part is Carrie's? What did the author intend for the part? What do the author and manager intend to do if Carrie does not work out?*

▶ *In what way does Carrie's unhappiness with her part secure her job?*

her part. It consisted of standing around in all sorts of scenes, a silent little Quakeress. The author of the skit had fancied that a great deal could be made of such a part, given to the right actress, but now, since it had been doled out to Carrie, he would as leave have had it cut out.

"Don't kick, old man," remarked the manager. "If it don't go the first week we will cut it out."

Carrie had no warning of this halcyon intention. She practiced her part ruefully, feeling that she was effectually shelved. At the dress rehearsal she was disconsolate.

"That isn't so bad," said the author, the manager noting the curious effect which Carrie's blues had upon the part. "Tell her to frown a little more when Sparks dances."

Carrie did not know it, but there was the least show of wrinkles between her eyes and her mouth was puckered quaintly.

"Frown a little more, Miss Madenda," said the stage manager.

Carrie instantly brightened up, thinking he had meant it as a rebuke.

"No; frown," he said. "Frown as you did before."

Carrie looked at him in astonishment.

"I mean it," he said. "Frown hard when Mr. Sparks dances. I want to see how it looks."

It was easy enough to do. Carrie scowled. The effect was something so quaint and droll it caught even the manager.

"That is good," he said. "If she'll do that all through, I think it will take."

Going over to Carrie, he said:

"Suppose you try frowning all through. Do it hard. Look mad. It'll make the part really funny."

On the opening night it looked to Carrie as if there were nothing to her part, after all. The happy, sweltering audience did not seem to see her in the first act. She frowned and frowned, but to no effect. Eyes were riveted upon the more elaborate efforts of the stars.

In the second act, the crowd, wearied by a dull conversation, roved with its eyes about the stage and sighted her. There she was, gray-suited, sweet-faced, demure, but scowling. At first the general idea was that she was temporarily irritated, that the look was genuine and not fun at all. As she

Words For Everyday Use

dole (dōl) *vt.,* give
rue • ful • ly (ro͞o´fəl lē) *adv.,* regretfully
quaint • ly (kwānt´lē) *adv.,* in an unusual and pleasing manner
droll (drōl) *adj.,* humorous
rove (rōv) *vi.,* wander

went on frowning, looking now at one principal and now at the other, the audience began to smile. The portly gentlemen in the front rows began to feel that she was a delicious little morsel. It was the kind of frown they would have loved to force away with kisses. All the gentlemen yearned toward her. She was capital.[4]

◄ Why is Carrie's frown a success with the audience?

At last, the chief comedian, singing in the center of the stage, noticed a giggle where it was not expected. Then another and another. When the place came for loud applause it was only moderate. What could be the trouble? He realized that something was up.

All at once, after an exit, he caught sight of Carrie. She was frowning alone on the stage and the audience was giggling and laughing.

"By George, I won't stand that!" thought the thespian. "I'm not going to have my work cut up by someone else. Either she quits that when I do my turn or I quit."

◄ What is the star's opinion of Carrie's frown?

"Why, that's all right," said the manager, when the kick came. "That's what she's supposed to do. You needn't pay any attention to that."

"But she ruins my work."

"No, she don't," returned the former, soothingly. "It's only a little fun on the side."

"It is, eh?" exclaimed the big comedian. "She killed my hand all right. I'm not going to stand that."

"Well, wait until after the show. Wait until tomorrow. We'll see what we can do."

The next act, however, settled what was to be done. Carrie was the chief feature of the play. The audience, the more it studied her, the more it indicated its delight. Every other feature paled beside the quaint, teasing, delightful atmosphere which Carrie contributed while on the stage. Manager and company realized she had made a hit.

◄ What success has come to Carrie because of her frown?

The critics of the daily papers completed her triumph. There were long notices in praise of the quality of the burlesque,[5] touched with recurrent references to Carrie. The contagious mirth of the thing was repeatedly emphasized.

"Miss Madenda presents one of the most delightful bits of character work ever seen on the Casino stage," observed the

4. **capital.** First-rate, smashing
5. **burlesque.** Comedy

Words For Everyday Use

port • ly (pôrt´ lē) *adj.*, fat
mor • sel (môr´səl) *n.*, dainty tidbit

sage critic of the *Sun*. "It is a bit of quiet, unassuming drollery which warms like good wine. Evidently the part was not intended to take precedence, as Miss Madenda is not often on the stage, but the audience, with the characteristic perversity of such bodies, selected for itself. The little Quakeress was marked for a favorite the moment she appeared, and thereafter easily held attention and applause. The vagaries of fortune are indeed curious."

The critic of the *Evening World*, seeking as usual to establish a catch phrase which should "go" with the town, wound up by advising: "If you wish to be merry, see Carrie frown."

► *In what way is the play now advertised?*

The result was miraculous so far as Carrie's fortune was concerned. Even during the morning she received a congratulatory message from the manager.

"You seem to have taken the town by storm," he wrote. "This is delightful. I am as glad for your sake as for my own."

The author also sent word.

That evening when she entered the theater the manager had a most pleasant greeting for her.

"Mr. Stevens," he said, referring to the author, "is preparing a little song, which he would like you to sing next week."

"Oh, I can't sing," returned Carrie.

"It isn't anything difficult. 'It's something that is very simple,' he says, 'and would suit you exactly.'"

"Of course, I wouldn't mind trying," said Carrie, archly.

"Would you mind coming to the box office a few moments before you dress?" observed the manager, in addition. "There's a little matter I want to speak to you about."

"Certainly," replied Carrie.

In that latter place the manager produced a paper.

► *To what figure is Carrie's weekly salary raised?*

"Now, of course," he said, "we want to be fair with you in the matter of salary. Your contract here only calls for thirty dollars a week for the next three months. How would it do to make it, say, one hundred and fifty a week and extend it for twelve months?"

"Oh, very well," said Carrie, scarcely believing her ears.

"Supposing, then, you just sign this."

Carrie looked and beheld a new contract made out like the other one, with the exception of the new figures of salary and time. With a hand trembling from excitement she affixed her name.

Words For Everyday Use

prec • e • dence (pres´ə dəns) *n.*, priority

per • ver • si • ty (pər vʉr´sə tē) *n.*, deviation from the norm

va • ga • ry (vā gər´ē) *n.*, unpredictable or odd action or event

arch • ly (ärch´lē) *adv.*, mischievously

"One hundred and fifty a week!" she murmured, when she was again alone. She found, after all—as what millionaire has not?—that there was no realizing, in consciousness, the meaning of large sums. It was only a shimmering, glittering phrase in which lay a world of possibilities.

◄ How does Carrie feel about her new salary?

Down in a third-rate Bleecker Street hotel, the brooding Hurstwood read the dramatic item covering Carrie's success, without at first realizing who was meant. Then suddenly it came to him and he read the whole thing over again.

◄ Where is Hurstwood when he learns of Carrie's success?

"That's her, all right, I guess," he said.

Then he looked about upon a dingy, moth-eaten hotel lobby.

"I guess she's struck it," he thought, a picture of the old shiny, plush-covered world coming back, with its lights, its ornaments, its carriages, and flowers. Ah, she was in the walled city now! Its splendid gates had opened, admitting her from a cold, dreary outside. She seemed a creature afar off—like every other celebrity he had known.

◄ According to Hurstwood, to what world has Carrie been admitted?

"Well, let her have it," he said. "I won't bother her."

It was the grim resolution of a bent, bedraggled, but unbroken pride.

◄ What does Hurstwood resolve? Why?

Words For Everyday Use

be • drag • gled (bē drag´əl'd) *adj.,* wet, limp, and muddied

CHAPTER 44

And This Is Not Elf Land: What Gold Will Not Buy

When Carrie got back on the stage, she found that over night her dressing room had been changed.

"You are to use this room, Miss Madenda," said one of the stage lackeys.[1]

No longer any need of climbing several flights of steps to a small coop shared with another. Instead, a comparatively large and commodious chamber with conveniences not enjoyed by the small fry overhead. She breathed deeply and with delight. Her sensations were more physical than mental. In fact, she was scarcely thinking at all. Heart and body were having their say.

▶ *In what way has Carrie's success changed the way she is treated by others in the theater?*

Gradually the deference and congratulation gave her a mental appreciation of her state. She was no longer ordered, but requested, and that politely. The other members of the cast looked at her enviously as she came out arrayed in her simple habit, which she wore all through the play. All those who had supposedly been her equals and superiors now smiled the smile of sociability, as much as to say: "How friendly we have always been." Only the star comedian whose part had been so deeply injured stalked by himself. Figuratively, he could not kiss the hand that smote[2] him.

▶ *Has Carrie's success changed her?*

Doing her simple part, Carrie gradually realized the meaning of the applause which was for her, and it was sweet. She felt mildly guilty of something—perhaps unworthiness. When her associates addressed her in the wings she only smiled weakly. The pride and daring of place were not for her. It never once crossed her mind to be reserved or haughty—to be other than she had been. After the performances she rode to her room with Lola, in a carriage provided.

Then came a week in which the first fruits of success were offered to her lips—bowl after bowl. It did not matter that her splendid salary had not begun. The world seemed

1. **lackeys.** Male servants of low rank
2. **smote.** Struck

Words For Everyday Use

com • mo • di • ous (kə mō´dē əs) *adj.*, spacious

satisfied with the promise. She began to get letters and cards. A Mr. Withers—whom she did not know from Adam[3]—having learned by some hook or crook where she resided, bowed himself politely in.

"You will excuse me for intruding," he said; "but have you been thinking of changing your apartments?"

"I hadn't thought of it," returned Carrie.

"Well, I am connected with the Wellington—the new hotel on Broadway. You have probably seen notices of it in the papers."

Carrie recognized the name as standing for one of the newest and most imposing hostelries. She had heard it spoken of as having a splendid restaurant.

"Just so," went on Mr. Withers, accepting her acknowledgment of familiarity. "We have some very elegant rooms at present which we would like to have you look at, if you have not made up your mind where you intend to reside for the summer. Our apartments are perfect in every detail—hot and cold water, private baths, special hall service for every floor, elevators and all that. You know what our restaurant is."

◄ *Why has Mr. Withers come to visit Carrie?*

Carrie looked at him quietly. She was wondering whether he took her to be a millionaire.

"What are your rates?" she inquired.

"Well, now, that is what I came to talk with you privately about. Our regular rates are anywhere from three to fifty dollars a day."

◄ *What special offer does Mr. Withers make Carrie? Why does he make this offer?*

"Mercy!" interrupted Carrie. "I couldn't pay any such rate as that."

"I know how you feel about it," exclaimed Mr. Withers, halting. "But just let me explain. I said those are our regular rates. Like every other hotel we make special ones, however. Possibly you have not thought about it, but your name is worth something to us."

"Oh!" ejaculated Carrie, seeing at a glance.

"Of course. Every hotel depends upon the repute of its patrons. A well-known actress like yourself," and he bowed politely, while Carrie flushed, "draws attention to the hotel, and—although you may not believe it—patrons."

"Oh, yes," returned Carrie, vacantly, trying to arrange this curious proposition in her mind.

3. **did not know from Adam.** Did not know at all

Words For Everyday Use

re • pute (ri pyo͞ot´) *n.,* reputation

"Now," continued Mr. Withers, swaying his derby hat[4] softly and beating one of his polished shoes upon the floor, "I want to arrange, if possible, to have you come and stop at the Wellington. You need not trouble about terms. In fact, we need hardly discuss them. Anything will do for the summer—a mere figure—anything that you think you could afford to pay."

Carrie was about to interrupt, but he gave her no chance.

"You can come today or tomorrow—the earlier the better—and we will give you your choice of nice, light, outside rooms—the very best we have."

"You're very kind," said Carrie, touched by the agent's extreme affability. "I should like to come very much. I would want to pay what is right, however. I shouldn't want to—"

"You need not trouble about that at all," interrupted Mr. Withers. "We can arrange that to your entire satisfaction at any time. If three dollars a day is satisfactory to you, it will be so to us. All you have to do is to pay that sum to the clerk at the end of the week or month, just as you wish, and he will give you a receipt for what the rooms would cost if charged for at our regular rates."

The speaker paused.

"Suppose you come and look at the rooms," he added.

"I'd be glad to," said Carrie, "but I have a rehearsal this morning."

"I did not mean at once," he returned. "Any time will do. Would this afternoon be inconvenient?"

"Not at all," said Carrie.

► *Whom does Carrie insist on bringing with her?*

Suddenly she remembered Lola, who was out at the time.

"I have a roommate," she added, "who will have to go wherever I do. I forgot about that."

"Oh, very well," said Mr. Withers, blandly. "It is for you to say whom you want with you. As I say, all that can be arranged to suit yourself."

He bowed and backed toward the door.

"At four, then, we may expect you?"

"Yes," said Carrie.

"I will be there to show you," and so Mr. Withers withdrew.

After rehearsal Carrie informed Lola.

"Did they really?" exclaimed the latter, thinking of the Wellington as a group of managers. "Isn't that fine? Oh, jolly! It's so swell. That's where we dined that night we went with those two Cushing boys. Don't you know?"

"I remember," said Carrie.

"Oh, it's as fine as it can be."

4. **derby hat.** Stiff felt hat with a round crown and curved brim

"We'd better be going up there," observed Carrie, later in the afternoon.

The rooms which Mr. Withers displayed to Carrie and Lola were three and bath—a suite on the parlor floor. They were done in chocolate and dark red, with rugs and hangings to match. Three windows looked down into busy Broadway on the east, three into a side street which crossed there. There were two lovely bedrooms, set with brass and white enamel beds, white, ribbon-trimmed chairs and chiffoniers to match. In the third room, or parlor, was a piano, a heavy piano lamp, with a shade of gorgeous pattern, a library table, several huge easy rockers, some dado[5] book shelves, and a gilt curio[6] case, filled with oddities. Pictures were upon the walls, soft Turkish pillows upon the divan, footstools of brown plush upon the floor. Such accommodations would ordinarily cost a hundred dollars a week.

◄ What would Carrie's accommodations normally cost?

"Oh, lovely!" exclaimed Lola, walking about.

"It is comfortable," said Carrie, who was lifting a lace curtain and looking down into crowded Broadway.

The bath was a handsome affair, done in white enamel, with a large, blue-bordered stone tub and nickel trimmings. It was bright and commodious, with a beveled mirror set in the wall at one end and incandescent lights arranged in three places.

"Do you find these satisfactory?" observed Mr. Withers.

"Oh, very," answered Carrie.

"Well, then, any time you find it convenient to move in, they are ready. The boy will bring you the keys at the door."

Carrie noted the elegantly carpeted and decorated hall, the marbled lobby, and showy waiting room. It was such a place as she had often dreamed of occupying.

"I guess we'd better move right away, don't you think so?" she observed to Lola, thinking of the commonplace chamber in Seventeenth Street.

"Oh, by all means," said the latter.

The next day her trunks left for the new abode.

Dressing, the matinee on Wednesday, a knock came at her dressing room door.

Carrie looked at the card handed by the boy and suffered a shock of surprise.

"Tell her I'll be right out," she said softly. Then, looking at the card, added: "Mrs. Vance."

◄ Who calls upon Carrie? What doesn't this person reveal in her manner?

"Why, you little sinner," the latter exclaimed, as she saw Carrie coming toward her across the now vacant stage. "How in the world did this happen?"

5. **dado.** Lower part of the wall
6. **curio.** Unusual or rare article

Carrie laughed merrily. There was no trace of embarrassment in her friend's manner. You would have thought that the long separation had come about accidentally.

"I don't know," returned Carrie, warming, in spite of her first troubled feelings, toward this handsome, good-natured young matron.[7]

"Well, you know, I saw your picture in the Sunday paper, but your name threw me off. I thought it must be you or somebody that looked just like you, and I said: 'Well, now, I will go right down there and see.' I was never more surprised in my life. How are you, anyway?"

"Oh, very well," returned Carrie. "How have you been?"

"Fine. But aren't you a success! Dear, oh! All the papers talking about you. I should think you would be just too proud to breathe. I was almost afraid to come back here this afternoon."

"Oh, nonsense," said Carrie, blushing. "You know I'd be glad to see you."

"Well, anyhow, here you are. Can't you come up and take dinner with me now? Where are you stopping?"

"At the Wellington," said Carrie, who permitted herself a touch of pride in the acknowledgment.

"Oh, are you?" exclaimed the other, upon whom the name was not without its proper effect.

► *What subject does Mrs. Vance avoid? What does she assume?*

Tactfully, Mrs. Vance avoided the subject of Hurstwood, of whom she could not help thinking. No doubt Carrie had left him. That much she surmised.

"Oh, I don't think I can," said Carrie, "tonight. I have so little time. I must be back here by 7:30. Won't you come and dine with me?"

"I'd be delighted, but I can't tonight," said Mrs. Vance, studying Carrie's fine appearance. The latter's good fortune made her seem more than ever worthy and delightful in the other's eyes. "I promised faithfully to be home at six." Glancing at the small gold watch pinned to her bosom, she added: "I must be going, too. Tell me when you're coming up, if at all."

"Why, any time you like," said Carrie.

"Well, tomorrow then. I'm living at the Chelsea now."

7. **matron.** Married woman

Words For Everyday Use

sur • mise (sər mīz´) *vt.,* guess or figure

"Moved again?" exclaimed Carrie, laughing.

"Yes. You know I can't stay six months in one place. I just have to move. Remember now—half-past five."

"I won't forget," said Carrie, casting a glance at her as she went away. Then it came to her that she was as good as this woman now—perhaps better. Something in the other's solicitude and interest made her feel as if she were the one to condescend.

◄ *What does Carrie realize about Mrs. Vance's manner?*

Now, as on each preceding day, letters were handed her by the doorman at the Casino. This was a feature which had rapidly developed since Monday. What they contained she well knew. *Mash notes*[8] were old affairs in their mildest form. She remembered having received her first one far back in Columbia City. Since then, as a chorus girl, she had received others—gentlemen who prayed for an engagement. They were common sport between her and Lola, who received some also. They both frequently made light of them.

Now, however, they came thick and fast. Gentlemen with fortunes did not hesitate to note, as an addition to their own amiable collection of virtues, that they had their horses and carriages. Thus one:

◄ *What type of letter does Carrie receive in abundance each day?*

"I have a million in my own right. I could give you every luxury. There isn't anything you could ask for that you couldn't have. I say this, not because I want to speak of my money, but because I love you and wish to gratify your every desire. It is love that prompts me to write. Will you not give me one half-hour in which to plead my cause?"

Such of these letters as came while Carrie was still in the Seventeenth Street place were read with more interest—though never delight—than those which arrived after she was installed in her luxurious quarters at the Wellington. Even there her vanity—or that self-appreciation which, in its more rabid form, is called vanity—was not sufficiently cloyed to make these things wearisome. Adulation, being new in any form, pleased her. Only she was sufficiently wise to distinguish between her old condition and her new one. She had not had fame or money before. Now they had come. She had not had adulation and affectionate propositions before. Now they had come. Wherefore? She smiled to think that men

◄ *What does Carrie realize is the cause of this sudden outpouring of affection?*

8. ***Mash notes.*** Love letters

Words For Everyday Use

rab • id (rab´id) *adj.*, violent; uncontrollable

ad • u • la • tion (ad´jo͞o lā´shən) *n.*, intense admiration

should suddenly find her so much more attractive. In the least way it incited her to coolness and indifference.

"Do look here," she remarked to Lola. "See what this man says: 'If you will only deign to grant me one half-hour,'" she repeated, with an imitation of languor. "The idea. Aren't men silly?"

"He must have lots of money, the way he talks," observed Lola.

► *What does Lola find odd?*

"That's what they all say," said Carrie, innocently.

"Why don't you see him," suggested Lola, "and hear what he has to say?"

"Indeed I won't," said Carrie. "I know what he'd say. I don't want to meet anybody that way."

Lola looked at her with big, merry eyes.

"He couldn't hurt you," she returned. "You might have some fun with him."

Carrie shook her head.

"You're awfully queer," returned the little, blue-eyed soldier.

Thus crowded fortune. For this whole week, though her large salary had not yet arrived, it was as if the world understood and trusted her. Without money—or the requisite sum, at least—she enjoyed the luxuries which money could buy. For her the doors of fine places seemed to open quite without the asking. These palatial chambers, how marvelously they came to her. The elegant apartments of Mrs. Vance in the Chelsea—these were hers. Men sent flowers, love notes, offers of fortune. And still her dreams ran riot. The one hundred and fifty! the one hundred and fifty! What a door to an Aladdin's cave it seemed to be. Each day, her head almost turned by developments, her fancies of what her fortune must be, with ample money, grew and multiplied. She conceived of delights which were not—saw lights of joy that never were on land or sea. Then, at last, after a world of anticipation, came her first installment of one hundred and fifty dollars.

It was paid to her in greenbacks—three twenties, six tens, and six fives. Thus collected it made a very convenient roll. It was accompanied by a smile and a salutation from the cashier who paid it.

"Ah, yes," said the latter, when she applied; "Miss Madenda—one hundred and fifty dollars. Quite a success the show seems to have made."

Words For Everyday Use

in • cite (in sīt´) *vt.,* rouse

req • ui • site (rek´wə zit) *adj.,* required

"Yes, indeed," returned Carrie.

Right after came one of the insignificant members of the company, and she heard the changed tone of address.

"How much?" said the same cashier, sharply. One, such as she had only recently been, was waiting for her modest salary. It took her back to the few weeks in which she had collected—or rather had received—almost with the air of a domestic, four-fifty per week from a lordly foreman in a shoe factory—a man who, in distributing the envelopes, had the manner of a prince doling out favors to a servile group of petitioners. She knew that out in Chicago this very day the same factory chamber was full of poor homely-clad girls working in long lines at clattering machines; that at noon they would eat a miserable lunch in a half-hour; that Saturday they would gather, as they had when she was one of them, and accept the small pay for work a hundred times harder than she was now doing. Oh, it was so easy now! The world was so rosy and bright. She felt so thrilled that she must needs walk back to the hotel to think, wondering what she should do.

◀ *Of what does Carrie's success remind her? Is she aware of her good fortune?*

It does not take money long to make plain its impotence, providing the desires are in the realm of affection. With her one hundred and fifty in hand, Carrie could think of nothing particularly to do. In itself, as a tangible, apparent thing which she could touch and look upon, it was a diverting thing for a few days, but this soon passed. Her hotel bill did not require its use. Her clothes had for some time been wholly satisfactory. Another day or two and she would receive another hundred and fifty. It began to appear as if this were not so startlingly necessary to maintain her present state. If she wanted to do anything better or move higher she must have more—a great deal more.

Now a critic called to get up one of those tinsel interviews which shine with clever observations, show up the wit of critics, display the folly of celebrities, and divert the public. He liked Carrie, and said so, publicly—adding, however, that she was merely pretty, good-natured, and lucky. This cut like a knife. The *Herald*, getting up an entertainment for the benefit of its free ice fund, did her the honor to beg her to appear along with celebrities for nothing. She was visited by a young author, who had a play which he thought she

◀ *What assessment of her abilities cuts Carrie "like a knife"?*

◀ *What is Carrie unable to do, much to her embarrassment?*

Words For Everyday Use

ser • vile (sʉr´vəl) *adj.*, humble; servantlike

could produce. Alas, she could not judge. It hurt her to think it. Then she found she must put her money in the bank for safety, and so moving, finally reached the place where it struck her that the door to life's perfect enjoyment was not open.

Gradually she began to think it was because it was summer. Nothing was going on much save such entertainments as the one in which she was star. Fifth Avenue was boarded up where the rich had deserted their mansions. Madison Avenue was little better. Broadway was full of loafing thespians in search of next season engagements. The whole city was quiet and her nights were taken up with her work. Hence the feeling that there was little to do.

► *How is Carrie beginning to feel about her situation?*

"I don't know," she said to Lola one day, sitting at one of the windows which looked down into Broadway, "I get lonely; don't you?"

"No," said Lola, "not very often. You won't go anywhere. That's what's the matter with you."

"Where can I go?"

► *Why won't Carrie date her admirers as Lola does?*

"Why, there're lots of places," returned Lola, who was thinking of her own lightsome tourneys[9] with the gay youths. "You won't go with anybody."

"I don't want to go with these people who write to me. I know what kind they are."

"You oughtn't to be lonely," said Lola, thinking of Carrie's success. "There're lots would give their ears to be in your shoes."

Carrie looked out again at the passing crowd.

"I don't know," she said.

Unconsciously her idle hands were beginning to weary.

9. **tourneys.** Games

CHAPTER 45

Curious Shifts of the Poor

The gloomy Hurstwood, sitting in his cheap hotel, where he had taken refuge with seventy dollars—the price of his furniture—between him and nothing, saw a hot summer out and a cool fall in, reading. He was not wholly indifferent to the fact that his money was slipping away. As fifty cents after fifty cents were paid out for a day's lodging he became uneasy, and finally took a cheaper room—thirty-five cents a day—to make his money last longer. Frequently he saw notices of Carrie. Her picture was in the *World* once or twice, and an old *Herald* he found in a chair informed him that she had recently appeared with some others at a benefit for something or other. He read these things with mingled feelings. Each one seemed to put her farther and farther away into a realm which became more imposing as it receded from him. On the billboards, too, he saw a pretty poster, showing her as the Quaker Maid, demure and dainty. More than once he stopped and looked at these, gazing at the pretty face in a sullen sort of way. His clothes were shabby, and he presented a marked contrast to all that she now seemed to be.

◄ *How much money does Hurstwood have? How did he get this money?*

◄ *How does Hurstwood feel when he reads about Carrie's success?*

Somehow, so long as he knew she was at the Casino, though he had never any intention of going near her, there was a subconscious comfort for him—he was not quite alone. The show seemed such a fixture that, after a month or two, he began to take it for granted that it was still running. In September it went on the road and he did not notice it. When all but twenty dollars of his money was gone, he moved to a fifteen-cent lodging-house in the Bowery, where there was a bare lounging room filled with tables and benches as well as some chairs. Here his preference was to close his eyes and dream of other days, a habit which grew upon him. It was not sleep at first, but a mental hearkening back to scenes and incidents in his Chicago life. As the present became darker, the past grew brighter, and all that concerned it stood in relief.

◄ *How does Hurstwood spend his time in the shabby hotel?*

He was unconscious of just how much this habit had hold of him until one day he found his lips repeating an old answer he had made to one of his friends. They were in

◄ *What does Hurstwood find himself doing?*

Words For Everyday Use

de • mure (də myo͝or´) *adj.*, affectedly modest or shy

Fitzgerald and Moy's. It was as if he stood in the door of his elegant little office, comfortably dressed, talking to Sagar Morrison about the value of South Chicago real estate in which the latter was about to invest.

"How would you like to come in on that with me?" he heard Morrison say.

"Not me," he answered, just as he had years before. "I have my hands full now."

The movement of his lips aroused him. He wondered whether he had really spoken. The next time he noticed anything of the sort he did talk.

"Why don't you jump, you bloody fool?" he was saying. "Jump!"

It was a funny English story he was telling to a company of actors. Even as his voice recalled him, he was smiling. A crusty old codger,[1] sitting nearby seemed disturbed; at least, he stared in a most pointed way. Hurstwood straightened up. The humor of the memory fled in an instant and he felt ashamed. For relief, he left his chair and strolled out into the streets.

► *What upsets Hurstwood? Why?*

One day, looking down the ad columns of the *Evening World*, he saw where a new play was at the Casino. Instantly, he came to a mental halt. Carrie had gone! He remembered seeing a poster of her only yesterday, but no doubt it was one left uncovered by the new signs. Curiously, this fact shook him up. He had almost to admit that somehow he was depending upon her being in the city. Now she was gone. He wondered how this important fact had skipped him. Goodness knows when she would be back now. Impelled by a nervous fear, he rose and went into the dingy hall, where he counted his remaining money, unseen. There were but ten dollars in all.

► *What does Hurstwood consider doing now that he has only ten dollars left? Why does this thought horrify him?*

He wondered how all these other lodging-house people around him got along. They didn't seem to do anything. Perhaps they begged—unquestionably they did. Many was the dime he had given to such as they in his day. He had seen other men asking for money on the streets. Maybe he could get some that way. There was horror in this thought.

Sitting in the lodging-house room, he came to his last fifty cents. He had saved and counted until his health was affected. His stoutness had gone. With it, even the semblance of a fit in his clothes. Now he decided he must do something, and,

1. **codger.** Good-natured term for an elderly man

Words For Everyday Use

stout • ness (stout´nes) *adj.,* fleshiness and sturdiness of body

walking about, saw another day go by, bringing him down to his last twenty cents—not enough to eat for the morrow.

Summoning all his courage, he crossed to Broadway and up to the Broadway Central hotel. Within a block he halted, undecided. A big, heavy-faced porter was standing at one of the side entrances, looking out. Hurstwood purposed to appeal to him. Walking straight up, he was upon him before he could turn away.

"My friend," he said, recognizing even in his plight the man's inferiority, "is there anything about this hotel that I could get to do?"

The porter stared at him the while he continued to talk.

"I'm out of work and out of money and I've got to get something—it doesn't matter what. I don't care to talk about what I've been, but if you'd tell me how to get something to do, I'd be much obliged to you. It wouldn't matter if it only lasted a few days just now. I've got to have something."

The porter still gazed, trying to look indifferent. Then, seeing that Hurstwood was about to go on, he said:

"I've nothing to do with it. You'll have to ask inside."

Curiously, this stirred Hurstwood to further effort.

"I thought you might tell me."

The fellow shook his head irritably.

Inside went the ex-manager and straight to an office off the clerk's desk. One of the managers of the hotel happened to be there. Hurstwood looked him straight in the eye.

"Could you give me something to do for a few days?" he said. "I'm in a position where I have to get something at once."

The comfortable manager looked at him, as much as to say: "Well, I should judge so."

"I came here," explained Hurstwood, nervously, "because I've been a manager myself in my day. I've had bad luck in a way, but I'm not here to tell you that. I want something to do, if only for a week."

The man imagined he saw a feverish gleam in the applicant's eye.

"What hotel did you manage?" he inquired.

"It wasn't a hotel," said Hurstwood. "I was manager of Fitzgerald and Moy's place in Chicago for fifteen years."

"Is that so?" said the hotel man. "How did you come to get out of that?"

◄ *What does Hurstwood finally do when he has only twenty cents left?*

◄ *What does the manager want to know when Hurstwood tells him that he was once a success? What does Hurstwood admit is the root of his difficulties?*

Words For Everyday Use

plight (plīt) *n.,* unfortunate condition

The figure of Hurstwood was rather surprising in contrast to the fact.

"Well, by foolishness of my own. It isn't anything to talk about now. You could find out if you wanted to. I'm 'broke' now and, if you will believe me, I haven't eaten anything today."

► *Why does the manager decide to do something for Hurstwood?*

The hotel man was slightly interested in this story. He could hardly tell what to do with such a figure, and yet Hurstwood's earnestness made him wish to do something.

"Call Olsen," he said, turning to the clerk.

In reply to a bell and a disappearing hall-boy, Olsen, the head porter, appeared.

"Olsen," said the manager, "is there anything downstairs you could find for this man to do? I'd like to give him something."

"I don't know, sir," said Olsen. "We have about all the help we need. I think I could find something, sir, though, if you like."

"Do. Take him to the kitchen and tell Wilson to give him something to eat."

"All right, sir," said Olsen.

Hurstwood followed. Out of the manager's sight, the head porter's manner changed.

"I don't know what the devil there is to do," he observed.

Hurstwood said nothing. To him the big trunk hustler was a subject for private contempt.

"You're to give this man something to eat," he observed to the cook.

The latter looked Hurstwood over, and seeing something keen and intellectual in his eyes, said:

"Well, sit down over there."

Thus was Hurstwood installed in the Broadway Central, but not for long. He was in no shape or mood to do the scrub work that exists about the foundation of every hotel. Nothing better offering, he was set to aid the fireman, to work about the basement, to do anything and everything that might offer. Porters, cooks, firemen, clerks—all were over him. Moreover his appearance did not please these individuals—his temper was too lonely—and they made it disagreeable for him.

With the stolidity and indifference of despair, however, he endured it all, sleeping in an attic at the roof of the house, eating what the cook gave him, accepting a few dollars a week, which he tried to save. His constitution was in no shape to endure.

► *How does Hurstwood lose his job in the hotel? Where is he sent?*

One day the following February he was sent on an errand to a large coal company's office. It had been snowing and thawing and the streets were sloppy. He soaked his shoes in his progress and came back feeling dull and weary. All the next day he felt unusually depressed and sat about as much as possible, to the irritation of those who admired energy in others.

In the afternoon some boxes were to be moved to make room for new culinary supplies. He was ordered to handle a truck. Encountering a big box, he could not lift it.

"What's the matter there?" said the head porter. "Can't you handle it?"

He was straining hard to lift it, but now he quit.

"No," he said, weakly.

The man looked at him and saw that he was deathly pale.

"Not sick, are you?" he asked.

"I think I am," returned Hurstwood.

"Well, you'd better go sit down, then."

This he did, but soon grew rapidly worse. It seemed all he could do to crawl to his room, where he remained for a day.

"That man Wheeler's sick," reported one of the lackeys to the night clerk.

"What's the matter with him?"

"I don't know. He's got a high fever."

The hotel physician looked at him.

"Better send him to Bellevue,"[2] he recommended. "He's got pneumonia."

Accordingly, he was carted away.

In three weeks the worst was over, but it was nearly the first of May before his strength permitted him to be turned out. Then he was discharged.

No more weakly looking object ever strolled out into the spring sunshine than the once hale, lusty manager. All his corpulency had fled. His face was thin and pale, his hands white, his body flabby. Clothes and all, he weighed but one hundred and thirty-five pounds. Some old garments had been given him—a cheap brown coat and misfit pair of trousers. Also some change and advice. He was told to apply to the charities.

◄ *In what way has Hurstwood changed physically during his illness? What "advice" is he given?*

Again he resorted to the Bowery lodging-house, brooding over where to look. From this it was but a step to beggary.

◄ *What must Hurstwood do to live?*

"What can a man do?" he said. "I can't starve."

His first application was in sunny Second Avenue. A well-dressed man came leisurely strolling toward him out of Stuyvesant Park. Hurstwood nerved himself and sidled near.

2. **Bellevue.** Largest charity hospital in New York

Words For Everyday Use

hale (hāl) *adj.,* healthy
lust • y (lus´tē) *adj.,* full of vigor
cor • pu • len • cy (kôr´pyo͞o lən sē) *n.,* fatness

"Would you mind giving me ten cents?" he said, directly. "I'm in a position where I must ask someone."

The man scarcely looked at him, but fished in his vest pocket and took out a dime.

"There you are," he said.

"Much obliged," said Hurstwood, softly, but the other paid no more attention to him.

Satisfied with his success and yet ashamed of his situation, he decided that he would only ask for twenty-five cents more, since that would be sufficient. He strolled about sizing up people, but it was long before just the right face and situation arrived. When he asked, he was refused. Shocked by this result, he took an hour to recover and then asked again. This time a nickel was given him. By the most watchful effort he did get twenty cents more, but it was painful.

► *What does his experience in begging teach Hurstwood?*

The next day he resorted to the same effort, experiencing a variety of rebuffs and one or two generous receptions. At last it crossed his mind that there was a science of faces, and that a man could pick the liberal countenance if he tried.

It was no pleasure to him, however, this stopping of passersby. He saw one man taken up for it and now troubled lest he should be arrested. Nevertheless, he went on, vaguely anticipating that indefinite something which is always better.

► *From whom does Hurstwood decide to beg?*

It was with a sense of satisfaction, then, that he saw announced one morning the return of the Casino Company, "with Miss Carrie Madenda." He had thought of her often enough in days past. How successful she was—how much money she must have! Even now, however, it took a severe run of ill-luck to decide him to appeal to her. He was truly hungry before he said:

"I'll ask her. She won't refuse me a few dollars."

Accordingly, he headed for the Casino one afternoon, passing it several times in an effort to locate the stage entrance. Then he sat in Bryant Park, a block away, waiting. "She can't refuse to help me a little," he kept saying to himself.

Beginning with half-past six, he hovered like a shadow about the Thirty-ninth Street entrance, pretending always to be a hurrying pedestrian and yet fearful lest he should miss his object. He was slightly nervous, too, now that the eventful hour had arrived; but being weak and hungry, his ability to suffer was modified. At last he saw that the actors were

Words For Everyday Use

li • ber • al (li´bə rəl) *adj.*, generous

beginning to arrive, and his nervous tension increased, until it seemed as if he could not stand much more.

Once he thought he saw Carrie coming and moved forward, only to see that he was mistaken.

"She can't be long, now," he said to himself, half fearing to encounter her and equally depressed at the thought that she might have gone in by another way. His stomach was so empty that it ached.

Individual after individual passed him, nearly all well-dressed, almost all indifferent. He saw coaches rolling by, gentlemen passing with ladies—the evening's merriment was beginning in this region of theaters and hotels.

Suddenly a coach rolled up and the driver jumped down to open the door. Before Hurstwood could act, two ladies flounced across the broad walk and disappeared in the stage door. He thought he saw Carrie, but it was so unexpected, so elegant and far away, he could hardly tell. He waited a while longer, growing feverish with want, and then seeing that the stage door no longer opened, and that a merry audience was arriving, he concluded it must have been Carrie and turned away.

◄ *Why doesn't Hurstwood approach Carrie?*

"Lord," he said, hastening out of the street into which the more fortunate were pouring, "I've got to get something."

At that hour, when Broadway is wont to assume its most interesting aspect, a peculiar individual invariably took his stand at the corner of Twenty-sixth Street and Broadway—a spot which is also intersected by Fifth Avenue. This was the hour when the theaters were just beginning to receive their patrons. Fire signs announcing the night's amusements blazed on every hand. Cabs and carriages, their lamps gleaming like yellow eyes, pattered by. Couples and parties of three and four freely mingled in the common crowd, which poured by in a thick stream, laughing and jesting. On Fifth Avenue were loungers—a few wealthy strollers, a gentleman in evening dress with his lady on his arm, some clubmen passing from one smoking room to another. Across the way the great hotels showed a hundred gleaming windows, their cafes and billiard rooms filled with a comfortable, well-dressed, and pleasure-loving throng. All about was the night, pulsating with the thoughts of pleasure and exhilaration—the city bent upon finding joy in a thousand different ways.

Words For Everyday Use

flounce (flouns) *vi.,* move quickly, swishing one's clothing

► *What unusual person stands on the corner of Broadway and Twenty-sixth Street? What is this person's mission?*

This unique individual was no less than an ex-soldier turned religionist, who, having suffered the whips and privations of our peculiar social system, had concluded that his duty to the God which he conceived lay in aiding his fellow man. The form of aid which he chose to administer was entirely original with himself. It consisted of securing a bed for all such homeless wayfarers as should apply to him at this particular spot, though he had scarcely the wherewithal to provide a comfortable habitation for himself.

Taking his place amid this lightsome[3] atmosphere, he would stand, his stocky figure cloaked in a great cape overcoat, his head protected by a broad slouch hat, awaiting the applicants who had in various ways learned the nature of his charity. For a while he would stand alone, gazing like any idler upon an ever-fascinating scene. On the evening in question, a policeman passing saluted him as "captain," in a friendly way. An urchin who had frequently seen him before, stopped to gaze. All others took him for nothing out of the ordinary, save in the matter of dress, and conceived of him as a stranger whistling and idling for his own amusement.

As the first half-hour waned, certain characters appeared. Here and there in the passing crowds one might see, now and then, a loiterer edging interestedly near. A slouchy figure crossed the opposite corner and glanced furtively in his direction. Another came down Fifth Avenue to the corner of Twenty-sixth Street, took a general survey, and bobbled off again. Two or three noticeable Bowery types edged along the Fifth Avenue side of Madison Square, but did not venture over. The soldier, in his cape overcoat, walked a short line of ten feet at his corner, to and fro, indifferently whistling.

As nine o'clock approached, some of the hubbub[4] of the earlier hour passed. The atmosphere of the hotels was not so youthful. The air, too, was colder. On every hand curious figures were moving—watchers and peepers, without an imaginary circle, which they seemed afraid to enter—a dozen in all. Presently, with the arrival of a keener sense of cold, one figure came forward. It crossed Broadway from out the shadow of Twenty-sixth Street, and, in a halting, circuitous way, arrived close to the waiting figure. There was something

3. **lightsome.** Full of light; cheerful, free of care
4. **hubbub.** Commotion

Words For Everyday Use

cir • cu • i • tous (sər kyo͞o´ət əs) *adj.*, indirect, roundabout

shamefaced or diffident about the movement, as if the intention were to conceal any idea of stopping until the very last moment. Then suddenly, close to the soldier, came the halt.

The captain looked in recognition, but there was no especial greeting. The newcomer nodded slightly and murmured something like one who waits for gifts. The other simply motioned toward the edge of the walk.

"Stand over there," he said.

By this the spell was broken. Even while the soldier resumed his short, solemn walk, other figures shuffled forward. They did not so much as greet the leader, but joined the one, sniffling and hitching and scraping their feet.

"Cold, ain't it?"

"I'm glad winter's over."

"Looks as though it might rain."

The motley company had increased to ten. One or two knew each other and conversed. Others stood off a few feet, not wishing to be in the crowd and yet not counted out. They were peevish, crusty, silent, eying nothing in particular and moving their feet.

There would have been talking soon, but the soldier gave them no chance. Counting sufficient to begin, he came forward.

"Beds, eh, all of you?"

There was a general shuffle and murmur of approval.

"Well, line up here. I'll see what I can do. I haven't a cent myself."

They fell into a sort of broken, ragged line. One might see, now, some of the chief characteristics by contrast. There was a wooden leg in the line. Hats were all drooping, a group that would ill become a secondhand Hester Street basement collection. Trousers were all warped and frayed at the bottom and coats worn and faded. In the glare of the store lights, some of the faces looked dry and chalky; others were red with blotches and puffed in the cheeks and under the eyes; one or two were rawboned and reminded one of railroad hands. A few spectators came near, drawn by the seemingly conferring group, then more and more, and quickly there was a pushing, gaping crowd. Someone in the line began to talk.

◄ *In what physical condition are the men who seek help from the captain?*

"Silence!" exclaimed the captain. "Now, then, gentlemen, these men are without beds. They have to have someplace to sleep tonight. They can't lie out in the streets. I need twelve cents to put one of them to bed. Who will give it to me?"

No reply.

"Well, we'll have to wait here, boys, until someone does. Twelve cents isn't so very much for one man."

◄ *How does the captain acquire the money to find beds for the night for the homeless men?*

"Here's fifteen," exclaimed a young man, peering forward with strained eyes. "It's all I can afford."

"All right. Now I have fifteen. Step out of the line," and seizing one by the shoulder, the captain marched him off a little way and stood him up alone.

Coming back, he resumed his place and began again.

"I have three cents left. These men must be put to bed somehow. There are"—counting—"one, two, three, four, five, six, seven, eight, nine, ten, eleven, twelve men. Nine cents more will put the next man to bed; give him a good, comfortable bed for the night. I go right along and look after that myself. Who will give me nine cents?"

One of the watchers, this time a middle-aged man, handed him a five-cent piece.

"Now, I have eight cents. Four more will give this man a bed. Come, gentlemen. We are going very slow this evening. You all have good beds. How about these?"

"Here you are," remarked a bystander, putting a coin into his hand.

"That," said the, captain, looking at the coin, "pays for two beds for two men and gives me five on the next one. Who will give me seven cents more?"

"I will," said a voice.

Coming down Sixth Avenue this evening, Hurstwood chanced to cross east through Twenty-sixth Street toward Third Avenue. He was wholly disconsolate in spirit, hungry to what he deemed an almost mortal extent, weary, and defeated. How should he get at Carrie now? It would be eleven before the show was over. If she came in a coach, she would go away in one. He would need to interrupt under most trying circumstances. Worst of all, he was hungry and weary, and at best a whole day must intervene, for he had not heart to try again tonight. He had no food and no bed.

When he neared Broadway, he noticed the captain's gathering of wanderers, but thinking it to be the result of a street preacher or some patent medicine fakir,[5] was about to pass on. However, in crossing the street toward Madison Square Park, he noticed the line of men whose beds were already secured, stretching out from the main body of the crowd. In the glare of the neighboring electric light he recognized a type of his own kind—the figures whom he saw about the streets and in the lodging-houses, drifting in mind and body like himself. He wondered what it could be and turned back.

► *What does Hurstwood have in common with the men he recognizes as being of "his own kind"?*

There was the captain curtly pleading as before. He heard with astonishment and a sense of relief the oft-repeated

5. **fakir.** Traveling beggar who is reputed to perform miracles

words: "These men must have a bed." Before him was the line of unfortunates whose beds were yet to be had, and seeing a newcomer quietly edge up and take a position at the end of the line, he decided to do likewise. What use to contend? He was weary tonight. It was a simple way out of one difficulty, at least. Tomorrow, maybe, he would do better.

◀ *What does Hurstwood decide to do?*

Back of him, where some of those were whose beds were safe, a relaxed air was apparent. The strain of uncertainty being removed, he heard them talking with moderate freedom and some leaning toward sociability. Politics, religion, the state of the government, some newspaper sensations, and the more notorious facts the world over, found mouthpieces and auditors there. Cracked and husky voices pronounced forcibly upon odd matters. Vague and rambling observations were made in reply.

There were squints, and leers, and some dull, ox-like stares from those who were too dull or too weary to converse.

Standing tells. Hurstwood became more weary waiting. He thought he should drop soon and shifted restlessly from one foot to the other. At last his turn came. The man ahead had been paid for and gone to the blessed line of success. He was now first, and already the captain was talking for him.

"Twelve cents, gentlemen—twelve cents puts this man to bed. He wouldn't stand here in the cold if he had any place to go." Hurstwood swallowed something that rose to his throat. Hunger and weakness had made a coward of him.

"Here you are," said a stranger, handing money to the captain.

Now the latter put a kindly hand on the ex-manager's shoulder.

"Line up over there," he said.

Once there, Hurstwood breathed easier. He felt as if the world were not quite so bad with such a good man in it. Others seemed to feel like himself about this.

◀ *What causes Hurstwood to breathe easier?*

"Captain's a great feller, ain't he?" said the man ahead—a little, woebegone, helpless-looking sort of individual, who looked as though he had ever been the sport and care of fortune.

"Yes," said Hurstwood, indifferently.

"Hub! there's a lot back there yet," said a man farther up, leaning out and looking back at the applicants for whom the captain was pleading.

Words For Everyday Use

con • tend (kən tend´) *vi.,* strive in combat; fight

"Yes. Must be over a hundred tonight," said another.

"Look at the guy in the cab," observed a third.

A cab had stopped. Some gentleman in evening dress reached out a bill to the captain, who took it with simple thanks and turned away to his line. There was a general craning of necks as the jewel in the white shirt front sparkled and the cab moved off. Even the crowd gaped in awe.

"That fixes up nine men for the night," said the captain, counting out as many of the line near him. "Line up over there. Now, then, there are only seven. I need twelve cents."

Money came slowly. In the course of time the crowd thinned out to a meager handful. Fifth Avenue, save for an occasional cab or foot passenger, was bare. Broadway was thinly peopled with pedestrians. Only now and then a stranger passing noticed the small group, handed out a coin, and went away, unheeding.

The captain remained stolid and determined. He talked on, very slowly, uttering the fewest words and with a certain assurance, as though he could not fail.

"Come; I can't stay out here all night. These men are getting tired and cold. Someone give me four cents."

There came a time when he said nothing at all. Money was handed him, and for each twelve cents he singled out a man and put him in the other line. Then he walked up and down as before, looking at the ground.

The theaters let out. Fire signs disappeared. A clock struck eleven. Another half-hour and he was down to the last two men.

"Come, now," he exclaimed to several curious observers; "eighteen cents will fix us all up for the night. Eighteen cents. I have six. Somebody give me the money. Remember, I have to go over to Brooklyn yet tonight. Before that I have to take these men down and put them to bed. Eighteen cents."

No one responded. He walked to and fro, looking down for several minutes, occasionally saying softly: "Eighteen cents." It seemed as if this paltry sum would delay the desired culmination longer than all the rest had. Hurstwood, buoyed up slightly by the long line of which he was a part, refrained with an effort from groaning, he was so weak.

At last a lady in opera cape and rustling skirts came down Fifth Avenue, accompanied by her escort. Hurstwood gazed

Words For Everyday Use	
	mea • ger (mē´gər) *adj.,* of poor quality or small amount
	pal • try (pôl´trē) *adj.,* small
	cul • mi • na • tion (kul´mə nā´shən) *n.,* highest point; climax
	buoyed (boid) *adj.,* lifted or raised emotionally

wearily, reminded by her both of Carrie in her new world and of the time when he had escorted his own wife in like manner.

While he was gazing, she turned and, looking at the remarkable company, sent her escort over. He came, holding a bill in his fingers, all elegant and graceful.

"Here you are," he said.

"Thanks," said the captain, turning to the two remaining applicants. "Now we have some for tomorrow night," he added.

Therewith he lined up the last two and proceeded to the head, counting as he went.

"One hundred and thirty-seven," he announced. "Now, boys, line up. Right dress there. We won't be much longer about this. Steady, now."

◄ *How many people have come to the captain for help?*

He placed himself at the head and called out "Forward." Hurstwood moved with the line. Across Fifth Avenue, through Madison Square by the winding paths, east on Twenty-third Street, and down Third Avenue wound the long, serpentine company. Midnight pedestrians and loiterers stopped and stared as the company passed. Chatting policemen, at various corners, stared indifferently or nodded to the leader, whom they had seen before. On Third Avenue they marched, a seemingly weary way, to Eighth Street, where there was a lodging-house, closed, apparently, for the night. They were expected, however.

Outside in the gloom they stood, while the leader parleyed within. Then doors swung open and they were invited in with a "Steady, now."

Someone was at the head showing rooms, so that there was no delay for keys. Toiling up the creaky stairs, Hurstwood looked back and saw the captain, watching; the last one of the line being included in his broad solicitude. Then he gathered his cloak about him and strolled out into the night.

"I can't stand much of this," said Hurstwood, whose legs ached him painfully, as he sat down upon the miserable bunk in the small, lightless chamber allotted to him. "I've got to eat, or I'll die."

Words For Everyday Use

ser • pen • tine (sur´pən tēn´) *adj.,* winding like a snake

par • ley (pär´lē) *vi.,* discuss

CHAPTER 46

Stirring Troubled Waters

Playing in New York one evening on this her return, Carrie was putting the finishing touches to her toilet[1] before leaving for the night, when a commotion near the stage door caught her ear. It included a familiar voice.

"Never mind, now. I want to see Miss Madenda."

"You'll have to send in your card."

"Oh, come off! Here."

A half-dollar was passed over, and now a knock came at her dressing room door.

Carrie opened it.

► *Who visits Carrie? How does she feel about this visitor?*

"Well, well!" said Drouet. "I do swear! Why, how are you? I knew that was you the moment I saw you."

Carrie fell back a pace, expecting a most embarrassing conversation.

"Aren't you going to shake hands with me? Well, you're a dandy! That's all right, shake hands."

Carrie put out her hand, smiling, if for nothing more than the man's exuberant good nature. Though older, he was but slightly changed. The same fine clothes, the same stocky body, the same rosy countenance.

"That fellow at the door there didn't want to let me in, until I paid him. I knew it was you, all right. Say, you've got a great show. You do your part fine. I knew you would. I just happened to be passing tonight and thought I'd drop in for a few minutes. I saw your name on the program, but I didn't remember it until you came on the stage. Then it struck me all at once. Say, you could have knocked me down with a feather. That's the same name you used out there in Chicago, isn't it?"

"Yes," answered Carrie, mildly, overwhelmed by the man's assurance.

"I knew it was, the moment I saw you. Well, how have you been, anyhow?"

"Oh, very well," said Carrie, lingering in her dressing room. She was rather dazed by the assault. "How have you been?"

"Me? Oh, fine. I'm here now."

"Is that so?" said Carrie.

"Yes. I've been here for six months. I've got charge of a branch here."

"How nice!"

"Well, when did you go on the stage, anyhow?" inquired Drouet.

1. **toilet.** Dressing table; also, act or process of dressing or grooming oneself

"About three years ago," said Carrie.

"You don't say so! Well, sir, this is the first I've heard of it. I knew you would, though. I always said you could act—didn't I?"

Carrie smiled.

"Yes, you did," she said.

"Well, you do look great," he said. "I never saw anybody improve so. You're taller, aren't you?"

"Me? Oh, a little, maybe."

He gazed at her dress, then at her hair, where a becoming hat was set jauntily, then into her eyes, which she took all occasion to avert. Evidently he expected to restore their old friendship at once and without modification.

"Well," he said, seeing her gather up her purse, handkerchief, and the like, preparatory to departing, "I want you to come out to dinner with me; won't you? I've got a friend out here."

"Oh, I can't," said Carrie. "Not tonight. I have an early engagement tomorrow."

"Aw, let the engagement go. Come on. I can get rid of him. I want to have a good talk with you."

"No, no," said Carrie; "I can't. You mustn't ask me anymore. I don't care for a late dinner."

"Well, come on and have a talk, then, anyhow."

"Not tonight," she said, shaking her head. "We'll have a talk some other time."

As a result of this, she noticed a shade of thought pass over his face, as if he were beginning to realize that things were changed. Good nature dictated something better than this for one who had always liked her.

"You come around to the hotel tomorrow," she said, as sort of penance for error. "You can take dinner with me."

"All right," said Drouet, brightening. "Where are you stopping?"

"At the Waldorf," she answered, mentioning the fashionable hostelry then but newly erected.

"What time?"

"Well, come at three," said Carrie, pleasantly.

The next day Drouet called, but it was with no especial delight that Carrie remembered her appointment. However, seeing him, handsome as ever, after his kind, and most

◄ *For how long has Carrie been on stage?*

◄ *What does Drouet expect of Carrie?*

Words For Everyday Use

jaunt • i • ly (jaunt´ə lē) *adv.,* in a carefree, stylish manner

genially disposed, her doubts as to whether the dinner would be disagreeable were swept away. He talked as volubly as ever.

"They put on a lot of lugs[2] here, don't they?" was his first remark.

"Yes; they do," said Carrie.

Genial egotist that he was, he went at once into a detailed account of his own career.

"I'm going to have a business of my own pretty soon," he observed in one place. "I can get backing for two hundred thousand dollars."

Carrie listened most good-naturedly.

► *What news pleases Drouet?*

"Say," he said, suddenly; "where is Hurstwood now?"

Carrie flushed a little.

"He's here in New York, I guess," she said. "I haven't seen him for some time."

Drouet mused for a moment. He had not been sure until now that the ex-manager was not an influential figure in the background. He imagined not; but this assurance relieved him. It must be that Carrie had got rid of him—as well she ought, he thought.

► *What does Drouet reveal to Carrie? Why might Drouet expect that Carrie would have been aware of this?*

"A man always makes a mistake when he does anything like that," he observed.

"Like what?" said Carrie, unwitting of what was coming.

"Oh, you know," and Drouet waved her intelligence, as it were, with his hand.

"No, I don't," she answered. "What do you mean?"

"Why that affair in Chicago—the time he left."

"I don't know what you are talking about," said Carrie. Could it be he would refer so rudely to Hurstwood's flight with her?

"Oho!" said Drouet, incredulously. "You knew he took ten thousand dollars with him when he left, didn't you?"

"What!" said Carrie. "You don't mean to say he stole money, do you?"

"Why," said Drouet, puzzled at her tone, "you knew that, didn't you?"

"Why, no," said Carrie. "Of course I didn't."

"Well, that's funny," said Drouet. "He did, you know. It was in all the papers."

"How much did you say he took?" said Carrie.

"Ten thousand dollars. I heard he sent most of it back afterward, though."

2. **put on a lot of lugs.** Charge a lot

Carrie looked vacantly at the richly carpeted floor. A new light was shining upon all the years since her enforced flight. She remembered now a hundred things that indicated as much. She also imagined that he took it on her account. Instead of hatred springing up there was a kind of sorrow generated. Poor fellow! What a thing to have had hanging over his head all the time.

◄ *What emotion does this news evoke in Carrie?*

At dinner Drouet, warmed up by eating and drinking and softened in mood, fancied he was winning Carrie to her old-time good-natured regard for him. He began to imagine it would not be so difficult to enter into her life again, high as she was. Ah, what a prize! he thought. How beautiful, how elegant, how famous! In her theatrical and Waldorf setting, Carrie was to him the all-desirable.

◄ *How does Drouet feel about Carrie? Why does he feel this way?*

"Do you remember how nervous you were that night at the Avery?" he asked.

Carrie smiled to think of it.

"I never saw anybody do better than you did then, Cad," he added ruefully, as he leaned an elbow on the table; "I thought you and I were going to get along fine those days."

"You mustn't talk that way," said Carrie, bringing in the least touch of coldness.

"Won't you let me tell you—"

"No," she answered, rising. "Besides, it's time I was getting ready for the theater. I'll have to leave you. Come, now."

"Oh, stay a minute," pleaded Drouet. "You've got plenty of time."

"No," said Carrie, gently.

Reluctantly Drouet gave up the bright table and followed. He saw her to the elevator and, standing there, said:

"When do I see you again?"

"Oh, some time, possibly," said Carrie. "I'll be here all summer. Goodnight!"

The elevator door was open.

"Goodnight!" said Drouet, as she rustled in.

Then he strolled sadly down the hall, all his old longing revived, because she was now so far off. He thought himself hardly dealt with. Carrie, however, had other thoughts.

That night it was that she passed Hurstwood, waiting at the Casino, without observing him.

Words For Everyday Use

va • cant • ly (vā kənt lē) *adv.,* in an absent, empty way

► *Whom does Carrie encounter on her way to the theater? Why does this person frighten her?*

The next night, walking to the theater, she encountered him face to face. He was waiting, more gaunt than ever, determined to see her, if he had to send in word. At first she did not recognize the shabby, baggy figure. He frightened her, edging so close, a seemingly hungry stranger.

"Carrie," he half whispered, "can I have a few words with you?"

She turned and recognized him on the instant. If there ever had lurked any feeling in her heart against him, it deserted her now. Still, she remembered what Drouet said about his having stolen the money.

"Why, George," she said; "what's the matter with you?"

► *What does Hurstwood ask of Carrie? What does she give him?*

"I've been sick," he answered. "I've just got out of the hospital. For God's sake, let me have a little money, will you?"

"Of course," said Carrie, her lip trembling in a strong effort to maintain her composure. "But what's the matter with you, anyhow?"

She was opening her purse, and now pulled out all the bills in it—a five and two twos.

"I've been sick, I told you," he said, peevishly, almost resenting her excessive pity. It came hard to him to receive it from such a source.

"Here," she said. "It's all I have with me."

► *What does Hurstwood promise?*

"All right," he answered, softly. "I'll give it back to you some day."

Carrie looked at him, while pedestrians stared at her. She felt the strain of publicity. So did Hurstwood.

"Why don't you tell me what's the matter with you?" she asked, hardly knowing what to do. "Where are you living?"

"Oh, I've got a room down in the Bowery," he answered. "There's no use trying to tell you here. I'm all right now."

► *Why does Hurstwood resent Carrie's concern?*

He seemed in a way to resent her kindly inquiries—so much better had fate dealt with her.

"Better go on in," he said. "I'm much obliged, but I won't bother you anymore."

She tried to answer, but he turned away and shuffled off toward the east.

For days this apparition was a drag on her soul before it began to wear partially away. Drouet called again, but now he was not even seen by her. His attentions seemed out of place.

"I'm out," was her reply to the boy.

Words For Everyday Use

gaunt (gônt) *adj.,* thin and bony

ap • par • i • tion (a pər iˊshən) *n.,* thing which appears; ghost

So peculiar, indeed, was her lonely, self-withdrawing temper, that she was becoming an interesting figure in the public eye—she was so quiet and reserved.

◄ What does the public think of Carrie's manner?

Not long after the management decided to transfer the show to London. A second summer season did not seem to promise well here.

"How would you like to try subduing London?" asked her manager, one afternoon.

◄ Where is Carrie going?

"It might be just the other way," said Carrie.

"I think we'll go in June," he answered.

In the hurry of departure, Hurstwood was forgotten. Both he and Drouet were left to discover that she was gone. The latter called once, and exclaimed at the news. Then he stood in the lobby, chewing the ends of his moustache. At last he reached a conclusion—the old days had gone for good.

◄ How does Drouet feel when he realizes that Carrie is gone?

"She isn't so much," he said; but in his heart of hearts he did not believe this.

Hurstwood shifted by curious means through a long summer and fall. A small job as janitor of a dance hall helped him for a month. Begging, sometimes going hungry, sometimes sleeping in the park, carried him over more days. Resorting to those peculiar charities, several of which, in the press of hungry search, he accidentally stumbled upon, did the rest. Toward the dead of winter, Carrie came back, appearing on Broadway in a new play; but he was not aware of it. For weeks he wandered about the city, begging, while the fire sign, announcing her engagement, blazed nightly upon the crowded street of amusements. Drouet saw it, but did not venture in.

About this time Ames returned to New York. He had made a little success in the West, and now opened a laboratory in Wooster Street. Of course, he encountered Carrie through Mrs. Vance; but there was nothing responsive between them. He thought she was still united to Hurstwood, until otherwise informed. Not knowing the facts then, he did not profess to understand, and refrained from comment.

◄ Who returns to New York? What relationship exists between him and Carrie?

With Mrs. Vance, he saw the new play, and expressed himself accordingly.

"She ought not to be in comedy," he said. "I think she could do better than that."

◄ What is Ames's opinion of Carrie's play?

One afternoon they met at the Vances' accidentally, and began a very friendly conversation. She could hardly tell why the one-time keen interest in him was no longer with her. Unquestionably, it was because at that time he had represented something which she did not have; but this she did not understand. Success had given her the momentary feeling

► *How does Carrie feel that Ames should view her? How does he actually view her?*

► *What kind of acting does Ames think Carrie should be doing? Why?*

that she was now blessed with much of which he would approve. As a matter of fact, her little newspaper fame was nothing at all to him. He thought she could have done better, by far.

"You didn't go into comedy-drama, after all?" he said, remembering her interest in that form of art.

"No," she answered; "I haven't, so far."

He looked at her in such a peculiar way that she realized she had failed. It moved her to add: "I want to, though."

"I should think you would," he said. "You have the sort of disposition that would do well in comedy-drama."

It surprised her that he should speak of disposition. Was she, then, so clearly in his mind?

"Why?" she asked.

"Well," he said, "I should judge you were rather sympathetic in your nature."

Carrie smiled and colored slightly. He was so innocently frank with her that she drew nearer in friendship. The old call of the ideal was sounding.

"I don't know," she answered, pleased, nevertheless, beyond all concealment.

"I saw your play," he remarked. "It's very good."

"I'm glad you liked it."

"Very good, indeed," he said, "for a comedy."

This is all that was said at the time, owing to an interruption, but later they met again. He was sitting in a corner after dinner, staring at the floor, when Carrie came up with another of the guests. Hard work had given his face the look of one who is weary. It was not for Carrie to know the thing in it which appealed to her.

"All alone?" she said.

"I was listening to the music."

"I'll be back in a moment," said her companion, who saw nothing in the inventor.

Now he looked up in her face, for she was standing a moment, while he sat.

"Isn't that a pathetic strain?"[3] he inquired, listening.

"Oh, very," she returned, also catching it, now that her attention was called.

---

3. **strain.** Passage of musical expression; tune or air

Words For Everyday Use

dis • po • si • tion (dis´pō si shən) *n.*, nature
sym • pa • the • tic (sim pä thə´tək) *adj.*, sensitive to emotion
frank (fraŋk) *adj.*, open, honest
pa • the • tic (pə thet´ik) *adj.*, encouraging feelings of sadness

"Sit down," he added, offering her the chair beside him.

They listened a few moments in silence, touched by the same feeling, only hers reached her through the heart. Music still charmed her as in the old days.

"I don't know what it is about music," she started to say, moved by the inexplicable longings which surged within her; "but it always makes me feel as if I wanted something—I—"

◄ What do Ames and Carrie do together? What does Carrie say about music?

"Yes," he replied; "I know how you feel."

Suddenly he turned to considering the peculiarity of her disposition, expressing her feelings so frankly.

"You ought not to be melancholy," he said.

◄ What advice does Ames give Carrie?

He thought a while, and then went off into a seemingly alien observation which, however, accorded with their feelings.

"The world is full of desirable situations, but, unfortunately, we can occupy but one at a time. It doesn't do us any good to wring our hands over the far-off things."

The music ceased and he arose, taking a standing position before her, as if to rest himself.

"Why don't you get into some good, strong comedy-drama?" he said. He was looking directly at her now, studying her face. Her large, sympathetic eyes and pain-touched mouth appealed to him as proofs of his judgment.

"Perhaps I shall," she returned.

"That's your field," he added.

"Do you think so?"

"Yes," he said; "I do. I don't suppose you're aware of it, but there is something about your eyes and mouth which fits you for that sort of work."

Carrie thrilled to be taken so seriously. For the moment, loneliness deserted her. Here was praise which was keen and analytical.

"It's in your eyes and mouth," he went on abstractedly. "I remember thinking, the first time I saw you, that there was something peculiar about your mouth. I thought you were about to cry."

"How odd," said Carrie, warm with delight. This was what her heart craved.

"Then I noticed that that was your natural look, and tonight I saw it again. There's a shadow about your eyes, too, which gives your face much this same character. It's in the depth of them, I think."

Words For Everyday Use

pe • cu • li • a • ri • ty (pə kyo͞o´lē ar´ə tē) *n.*, individuality; unusualness

a • li • en (el´ē ən) *adj.*, not belonging to; inconsistent

crave (krāv) *vt.*, need and want

Carrie looked straight into his face, wholly aroused.

"You probably are not aware of it," he added.

She looked away, pleased that he should speak thus, longing to be equal to this feeling written upon her countenance. It unlocked the door to a new desire.

She had cause to ponder over this until they met again—several weeks or more. It showed her she was drifting away from the old ideal which had filled her in the dressing rooms of the Avery stage and thereafter, for a long time. Why had she lost it?

"I know why you should be a success," he said, another time, "if you had a more dramatic part. I've studied it out—"

"What is it?" said Carrie.

► *In what way does Ames analyze Carrie's facial expression?*

"Well," he said, as one pleased with a puzzle, "the expression in your face is one that comes out in different things. You get the same thing in a pathetic song, or any picture which moves you deeply. It's a thing the world likes to see, because it's a natural expression of its longing."

Carrie gazed without exactly getting the import of what he meant.

► *According to Ames, what are most people unable to do? What has nature done for Carrie?*

"The world is always struggling to express itself," he went on. "Most people are not capable of voicing their feelings. They depend upon others. That is what genius is for. One man expresses their desires for them in music; another one in poetry; another one in a play. Sometimes nature does it in a face—it makes the face representative of all desire. That's what has happened in your case."

He looked at her with so much of the import of the thing in his eyes that she caught it. At least, she got the idea that her look was something which represented the world's longing. She took it to heart as a creditable thing, until he added:

► *In what way is Carrie's gift "no credit" to her?*

"That puts a burden of duty on you. It so happens that you have this thing. It is no credit to you—that is, I mean, you might not have had it. You paid nothing to get it. But now that you have it, you must do something with it."

"What?" asked Carrie.

► *What does Ames say Carrie should do with her asset?*

"I should say, turn to the dramatic field. You have so much sympathy and such a melodious voice. Make them valuable to others. It will make your powers endure."

Carrie did not understand this last. All her comedy success was little or nothing.

Words For Everyday Use

cred • it • a • ble (kred´ə tə bəl) *adj.,* praiseworthy

"What do you mean?" she asked.

"Why, just this. You have this quality in your eyes and mouth and in your nature. You can lose it, you know. If you turn away from it and live to satisfy yourself alone, it will go fast enough. The look will leave your eyes. Your mouth will change. Your power to act will disappear. You may think they won't, but they will. Nature takes care of that."

◄ *About what does Ames warn Carrie?*

He was so interested in forwarding all good causes that he sometimes became enthusiastic, giving vent to these preachments.[4] Something in Carrie appealed to him. He wanted to stir her up.

"I know," she said, absently, feeling slightly guilty of neglect.

"If I were you," he said, "I'd change."

The effect of this was like roiling helpless waters. Carrie troubled over it in her rocking-chair for days.

"I don't believe I'll stay in comedy so very much longer," she eventually remarked to Lola.

"Oh, why not?" said the latter.

"I think," she said, "I can do better in a serious play."

"What put that idea in your head?"

"Oh, nothing," she answered; "I've always thought so."

Still, she did nothing—grieving. It was a long way to this better thing—or seemed so—and comfort was about her; hence the inactivity and longing.

◄ *What does Carrie do with Ames's advice?*

4. **preachments.** Preachings

Words For Everyday Use

vent (vent) *n.,* outlet

roil (roil) *vi.,* stir up; agitate

CHAPTER 47

The Way of the Beaten: A Harp in the Wind

In the city, at that time, there were a number of charities similar in nature to that of the captain's, which Hurstwood now patronized in a like unfortunate way. One was a convent mission-house of the Sisters of Mercy in Fifteenth Street—a row of red brick family dwellings, before the door of which hung a plain wooden contribution box, on which was painted the statement that every noon a meal was given free to all those who might apply and ask for aid. This simple announcement was modest in the extreme, covering, as it did, charity so broad. Institutions and charities are so large and so numerous in New York that such things as this are not often noticed by the more comfortably situated. But to one whose mind is upon the matter, they grow exceedingly under inspection. Unless one were looking up this matter in particular, he could have stood at Sixth Avenue and Fifteenth Street for days around the noon hour and never have noticed that out of the vast crowd that surged along that busy thoroughfare there turned out, every few seconds, some weather-beaten, heavy-footed specimen of humanity, gaunt in countenance and dilapidated in the matter of clothes. The fact is none the less true, however, and the colder the day the more apparent it became. Space and a lack of culinary room in the mission-house compelled an arrangement which permitted of only twenty-five or thirty eating at one time, so that a line had to be formed outside and an orderly entrance effected. This caused a daily spectacle which, however, had become so common by repetition during a number of years that now nothing was thought of it. The men waited patiently, like cattle, in the coldest weather—waited for several hours before they could be admitted. No questions were asked and no service rendered. They ate and went away again, some of them returning regularly day after day the winter through.

▶ Why do most people never notice charitable institutions? Who does notice them?

▶ To what are the men waiting for meals compared?

A big, motherly looking woman invariably stood guard at the door during the entire operation and counted the admissible number. The men moved up in solemn order. There was no haste and no eagerness displayed. It was almost a dumb procession. In the bitterest weather this line was to be found here. Under an icy wind there was a prodigious slapping of hands and a dancing of feet. Fingers and the features of the face looked as if severely nipped by the cold. A study of these men in broad light proved them to be nearly all of a type. They belonged to the class that sit on the park benches during the endurable days and sleep upon them during the summer nights. They frequent the Bowery and those down-at-the-heels East Side streets where poor clothes and shrunken features are not singled out as curious. They are the men who are in the lodging-house sitting rooms during bleak and bitter weather and who swarm about the cheaper shelters which only open at six in a number of the lower East Side streets. Miserable food, ill-timed and greedily eaten, had played havoc with bone and muscle. They were all pale, flabby, sunken-eyed, hollow-chested, with eyes that glinted and shone and lips that were a sickly red by contrast. Their hair was but half-attended to, their ears anemic in hue, and their shoes broken in leather and run down at heel and toe. They were of the class which simply floats and drifts, every wave of people washing up one, as breakers do driftwood upon a stormy shore.

For nearly a quarter of a century, in another section of the city, Fleischmann, the baker, had given a loaf of bread to anyone who would come for it to the side door of his restaurant at the corner of Broadway and Tenth Street, at midnight. Every night during twenty years about three hundred men had formed in line and at the appointed time marched past the doorway, picked their loaf from a great box placed just outside, and vanished again into the night. From the beginning to the present time there had been little change in the character or number of these men. There were two or three figures that had grown familiar to those who had seen this little procession pass year after year. Two of them had missed scarcely a night in fifteen years. There were about forty, more or less, regular callers. The remainder of the line was formed of strangers. In times of panic and unusual hardships there were seldom more than three hundred. In times of prosperity, when little is heard of the unemployed, there were seldom less. The same number, winter and summer, in storm or calm, in good times and bad, held this melancholy midnight rendezvous at Fleischmann's bread box.

◄ *What does one baker do to help the poor?*

◄ *What doesn't affect the number of the hungry who depend upon this baker?*

Words For Everyday Use

pro • di • gious (prō dij´əs) *adj.,* amazing, great

a • ne • mic (ə nē´mik) *adj.,* lacking hemoglobin in the bloodstream, therefore pale

At both of these two charities, during the severe winter which was now on, Hurstwood was a frequent visitor. On one occasion it was peculiarly cold, and finding no comfort in begging about the streets, he waited until noon before seeking this free offering to the poor. Already, at eleven o'clock of this morning, several such as he had shambled forward out of Sixth Avenue, their thin clothes flapping and fluttering in the wind. They leaned against the iron railing which protects the walls of the Ninth Regiment Armory, which fronts upon that section of Fifteenth Street, having come early in order to be first in. Having an hour to wait, they at first lingered at a respectful distance; but others coming up, they moved closer in order to protect their right of precedence. To this collection Hurstwood came up from the west out of Seventh Avenue and stopped close to the door, nearer than all the others. Those who had been waiting before him, but farther away, now drew near, and by a certain stolidity of demeanor, no words being spoken, indicated that they were first.

► *What action of Hurstwood's do the other men resent?*

Seeing the opposition to his action, he looked sullenly along the line, then moved out, taking his place at the foot. When order had been restored, the animal feeling of opposition relaxed.

"Must be pretty near noon," ventured one.

"It is," said another. "I've been waiting nearly an hour."

"Gee, but it's cold!"

They peered eagerly at the door, where all must enter. A grocery man drove up and carried in several baskets of eatables. This started some words upon grocery men and the cost of food in general.

"I see meat's gone up," said one.

"If there wuz war, it would help this country a lot."

The line was growing rapidly. Already there were fifty or more, and those at the head, by their demeanor, evidently congratulated themselves upon not having so long to wait as those at the foot. There was much jerking of heads, and looking down the line.

"It don't matter how near you get to the front, so long as you're in the first twenty-five," commented one of the first twenty-five. "You all go in together."

"Humph!" ejaculated Hurstwood, who had been so sturdily displaced.

Words For Everyday Use

sham • ble (sham´bəl) *vi.,* walk in a lazy or clumsy manner

"This here Single Tax is the thing," said another. "There ain't going to be no order till it comes."

For the most part there was silence; gaunt men shuffling, glancing, and beating their arms.

At last the door opened and the motherly looking sister appeared. She only looked an order. Slowly the line moved up and, one by one, passed in, until twenty-five were counted. Then she interposed a stout arm, and the line halted, with six men on the steps. Of these the ex-manager was one. Waiting thus, some talked, some ejaculated concerning the misery of it; some brooded, as did Hurstwood. At last he was admitted, and, having eaten, came away, almost angered because of his pains in getting it.

At eleven o'clock of another evening, perhaps two weeks later, he was at the midnight offering of a loaf—waiting patiently. It had been an unfortunate day with him, but now he took his fate with a touch of philosophy. If he could secure no supper, or was hungry late in the evening, here was a place he could come. A few minutes before twelve, a great box of bread was pushed out, and exactly on the hour a portly, round-faced German took position by it, calling "Ready." The whole line at once moved forward, each taking his loaf in turn and going his separate way. On this occasion, the ex-manager ate his as he went, plodding the dark streets in silence to his bed.

By January he had about concluded that the game was up with him. Life had always seemed a precious thing, but now constant want and weakened vitality had made the charms of earth rather dull and inconspicuous. Several times, when fortune pressed most harshly, he thought he would end his troubles; but with a change of weather, or the arrival of a quarter or a dime, his mood would change, and he would wait. Each day he would find some old paper lying about and look into it, to see if there was any trace of Carrie, but all summer and fall he had looked in vain. Then he noticed that his eyes were beginning to hurt him, and this ailment rapidly increased until, in the dark chambers of the lodgings he frequented, he did not attempt to read. Bad and irregular eating was weakening every function of his body. The one recourse left him was to doze when a place offered and he could get the money to occupy it.

◄ *What has Hurstwood decided by January?*

◄ *What does Hurstwood consider doing? What changes his mind?*

◄ *What is happening to Hurstwood physically?*

Words For Everyday Use

plod (pläd´) *vi.,* walk or move heavily; trudge

► *How are other people reacting to Hurstwood's appearance?*

He was beginning to find, in his wretched clothing and meager state of body, that people took him for a chronic type of bum and beggar. Police bustled him along, restaurant and lodging-house keepers turned him out promptly the moment he had his due; pedestrians waved him off. He found it more and more difficult to get anything from anybody.

At last he admitted to himself that the game was up. It was after a long series of appeals to pedestrians, in which he had been refused and refused—every one hastening from contact.

"Give me a little something, will you, mister?" he said to the last one. "For God's sake, do; I'm starving."

"Aw, get out," said the man, who happened to be a common type himself. "You're no good. I'll give you nawthin'."

Hurstwood put his hands, red from cold, down in his pockets. Tears came into his eyes.

► *What does Hurstwood plan to do after the passerby insults him?*

"That's right," he said; "I'm no good now. I was all right. I had money. I'm going to quit this," and, with death in his heart, he started down toward the Bowery. People had turned on the gas before and died; why shouldn't he? He remembered a lodging-house where there were little, close rooms, with gas jets in them, almost prearranged, he thought, for what he wanted to do, which rented for fifteen cents. Then he remembered that he had no fifteen cents.

On the way he met a comfortable-looking gentleman, coming, cleanshaven, out of a fine barber shop.

"Would you mind giving me a little something?" he asked this man boldly.

The gentleman looked him over and fished for a dime. Nothing but quarters were in his pocket.

"Here," he said, handing him one, to be rid of him. "Be off, now."

Hurstwood moved on, wondering. The sight of the large, bright coin pleased him a little. He remembered that he was hungry and that he could get a bed for ten cents. With this, the idea of death passed, for the time being, out of his mind. It was only when he could get nothing but insults that death seemed worthwhile.

One day, in the middle of the winter, the sharpest spell of the season set in. It broke gray and cold in the first day, and on the second snowed. Poor luck pursuing him, he had secured but ten cents by nightfall, and this he had spent for

Words For Everyday Use

chron • ic (krän´ik) *adj.,* continuing indefinitely; habitual

food. At evening he found himself at the Boulevard and Sixty-seventh Street, where he finally turned his face Bowery-ward. Especially fatigued because of the wandering propensity which had seized him in the morning, he now half-dragged his wet feet, shuffling the soles upon the sidewalk. An old, thin coat was turned up about his red ears—his cracked derby hat was pulled down until it turned them outward. His hands were in his pockets.

◄ *Why does Hurstwood regret having come here? In what way does his situation contrast with what he sees?*

"I'll just go down Broadway," he said to himself.

When he reached Forty-second Street, the fire signs were already blazing brightly. Crowds were hastening to dine. Through bright windows, at every corner, might be seen gay companies in luxuriant restaurants. There were coaches and crowded cable cars.

In his weary and hungry state, he should never have come here. The contrast was too sharp. Even he was recalled keenly to better things.

"What's the use?" he thought. "It's all up with me. I'll quit this."

People turned to look after him, so uncouth was his shambling figure. Several officers followed him with their eyes, to see that he did not beg of anybody.

Once he paused in an aimless, incoherent sort of way and looked through the windows of an imposing restaurant, before which blazed a fire sign, and through the large, plate windows of which could be seen the red and gold decorations, the palms, the white napery,[1] and shining glassware, and, above all, the comfortable crowd. Weak as his mind had become, his hunger was sharp enough to show the importance of this. He stopped stock still, his frayed trousers soaking in the slush, and peered foolishly in.

◄ *How does Hurstwood feel as he gazes in at the restaurant?*

"Eat," he mumbled. "That's right, eat. Nobody else wants any."

Then his voice dropped even lower, and his mind half lost the fancy it had.

"It's mighty cold," he said. "Awful cold."

At Broadway and Thirty-ninth Street was blazing, in incandescent fire, Carrie's name. "Carrie Madenda," it read, "and the Casino Company." All the wet, snowy sidewalk was

1. **napery.** Table linens

Words For Everyday Use

pro • pen • si • ty (prə pen´sə tē) *n.,* natural inclination
un • couth (un ko͞oth´) *adj.,* awkward; clumsy; crude
in • co • her • ent (in´kō hir´ənt) *adj.,* not logically connected; unclear

► *What does Hurstwood do when he sees Carrie's lithograph?*

► *What does Hurstwood decide to do once again?*

► *Why might Hurstwood's sense of shame return to him? Do you agree with Hurstwood? Why, or why not?*

► *What does Hurstwood feel that Carrie owes him? Do you agree with Hurstwood? Why, or why not?*

bright with this radiated fire. It was so bright that it attracted Hurstwood's gaze. He looked up, and then at a large, gilt-framed poster-board, on which was a fine lithograph of Carrie, life-size.

Hurstwood gazed at it a moment, snuffling and hunching one shoulder, as if something were scratching him. He was so run down, however, that his mind was not exactly clear.

"That's you," he said at last, addressing her. "Wasn't good enough for you, was I? Huh!"

He lingered, trying to think logically. This was no longer possible with him.

"She's got it," he said, incoherently, thinking of money. "Let her give me some."

He started around to the side door. Then he forgot what he was going for and paused, pushing his hands deeper to warm the wrists. Suddenly it returned. The stage door! That was it.

He approached that entrance and went in.

"Well?" said the attendant, staring at him. Seeing him pause, he went over and shoved him. "Get out of here," he said.

"I want to see Miss Madenda," he said.

"You do, eh?" the other said, almost tickled at the spectacle. "Get out of here," and he shoved him again. Hurstwood had no strength to resist.

"I want to see Miss Madenda," he tried to explain, even as he was being hustled away. "I'm all right. I—"

The man gave him a last push and closed the door. As he did so, Hurstwood slipped and fell in the snow. It hurt him, and some vague sense of shame returned. He began to cry and swear foolishly.

"God damned dog!" he said. "Damned old cur," wiping the slush from his worthless coat. "I—I hired such people as you once."

Now a fierce feeling against Carrie welled up—just one fierce, angry thought before the whole thing slipped out of his mind.

"She owes me something to eat," he said. "She owes it to me."

Hopelessly he turned back into Broadway again and slopped onward and away, begging, crying, losing track of his thoughts, one after another, as a mind decayed and disjointed is wont to do.

It was truly a wintry evening, a few days later, when his one distinct mental decision was reached. Already, at four o'clock, the somber hue of night was thickening the air. A heavy snow was falling—a fine picking, whipping snow, borne forward by a swift wind in long, thin lines. The streets were bedded with it—six inches of cold, soft carpet, churned to a dirty brown by the crush of teams and the feet of men. Along Broadway men picked their way in ulsters[2] and umbrellas. Along the Bowery, men slouched through it with collars and hats pulled over their ears. In the former thoroughfare businessmen and travelers were making for comfortable hotels. In the latter, crowds on cold errands shifted past dingy stores, in the deep recesses of which lights were already gleaming. There were early lights in the cable cars, whose usual clatter was reduced by the mantle about the wheels. The whole city was muffled by this fast-thickening mantle.

In her comfortable chambers at the Waldorf, Carrie was reading at this time *Père Goriot,* which Ames had recommended to her. It was so strong, and Ames's mere recommendation had so aroused her interest, that she caught nearly the full sympathetic significance of it. For the first time, it was being borne in upon her how silly and worthless had been her earlier reading, as a whole. Becoming wearied, however, she yawned and came to the window, looking out upon the old winding procession of carriages rolling up Fifth Avenue.

"Isn't it bad?" she observed to Lola.

"Terrible!" said that little lady, joining her. "I hope it snows enough to go sleigh riding."

"Oh, dear," said Carrie, with whom the sufferings of Father Goriot were still keen. "That's all you think of. Aren't you sorry for the people who haven't anything tonight?"

◄ *Of what does Carrie accuse Lola? What is Lola's excuse?*

"Of course I am," said Lola; "but what can I do? I haven't anything."

Carrie smiled.

"You wouldn't care, if you had," she returned.

"I would, too," said Lola. "But people never gave me anything when I was hard up."

"Isn't it just awful?" said Carrie, studying the winter's storm.

"Look at that man over there," laughed Lola, who had caught sight of someone falling down. "How sheepish men look when they fall, don't they?"

"We'll have to take a coach tonight," answered Carrie, absently.

In the lobby of the Imperial, Mr. Charles Drouet was just arriving, shaking the snow from a very handsome ulster. Bad weather had driven him home early and stirred his desire for those pleasures which shut out the snow and gloom of life. A good dinner, the company of a young woman, and an evening at the theater were the chief things for him.

"Why, hello, Harry!" he said, addressing a lounger in one of the comfortable lobby chairs. "How are you?"

2. **ulsters.** Long, loose, heavy overcoats

"Oh, about six and six," said the other.

"Rotten weather, isn't it?"

"Well, I should say," said the other. "I've been just sitting here thinking where I'd go tonight."

"Come along with me," said Drouet. "I can introduce you to something dead swell."

"Who is it?" said the other.

"Oh, a couple of girls over here in Fortieth Street. We could have a dandy time. I was just looking for you."

"Supposing we get 'em and take 'em out to dinner?"

"Sure," said Drouet. "Wait'll I go upstairs and change my clothes."

"Well, I'll be in the barber shop," said the other. "I want to get a shave."

"All right," said Drouet, creaking off in his good shoes toward the elevator. The old butterfly was as light on the wing as ever.

► *To what does the narrator compare Drouet?*

On an incoming vestibuled Pullman,[3] speeding at forty miles an hour through the snow of the evening, were three others, all related.

► *Who are the three people on the train? In what way have the fortunes of Mrs. Hurstwood and her daughter been altered?*

"First call for dinner in the dining car," a Pullman servitor was announcing, as he hastened through the aisle in snow-white apron and jacket.

"I don't believe I want to play any more," said the youngest, a black-haired beauty, turned supercilious by fortune, as she pushed a euchre hand away from her.

"Shall we go into dinner?" inquired her husband, who was all that fine raiment can make.

"Oh, not yet," she answered. "I don't want to play any more, though."

"Jessica," said her mother, who was also a study in what good clothing can do for age, "push that pin down in your tie—it's coming up."

Jessica obeyed, incidentally touching at her lovely hair and looking at a little jewel-faced watch. Her husband studied her, for beauty, even cold, is fascinating from one point of view.

"Well, we won't have much more of this weather," he said. "It only takes two weeks to get to Rome."

3. **Pullman.** Railroad passenger car with convertible berths for sleeping

Words For Everyday Use

su • per • cil • i • ous (so͞o´pər sil´ē əs) *adj.*, proud, scornful

Mrs. Hurstwood nestled comfortably in her corner and smiled. It was so nice to be the mother-in-law of a rich young man—one whose financial state had borne her personal inspection.

"Do you suppose the boat will sail promptly?" asked Jessica, "if it keeps up like this?"

"Oh, yes," answered her husband. "This won't make any difference."

Passing down the aisle came a very fair-haired banker's son, also of Chicago, who had long eyed this supercilious beauty. Even now he did not hesitate to glance at her, and she was conscious of it. With a specially conjured show of indifference, she turned her pretty face wholly away. It was not wifely modesty at all. By so much was her pride satisfied.

At this moment Hurstwood stood before a dirty four-story building in a side street quite near the Bowery, whose one-time coat of buff[4] had been changed by soot and rain. He mingled with a crowd of men—a crowd which had been, and was still, gathering by degrees.

It began with the approach of two or three, who hung about the closed wooden doors and beat their feet to keep them warm. They had on faded derby hats with dents in them. Their misfit coats were heavy with melted snow and turned up at the collars. Their trousers were mere bags, frayed at the bottom and wobbling over big, soppy shoes, torn at the sides and worn almost to shreds. They made no effort to go in, but shifted ruefully about, digging their hands deep in their pockets and leering at the crowd and the increasing lamps. With the minutes, increased the number. Three were old men with grizzled beards and sunken eyes, men who were comparatively young but shrunken by diseases, men who were middle-aged. None were fat. There was a face in the thick of the collection which was as white as drained veal. There was another red as brick. Some came with thin, rounded shoulders, others with wooden legs, still others with frames so lean that clothes only flapped about them. There were great ears, swollen noses, thick lips, and, above all, red, blood-shot eyes. Not a normal, healthy face in the whole mass; not a straight figure; not a straightforward, steady glance.

---

4. **buff.** Light tan

Words For Everyday Use

con • jure (kän´jur) *vi.,* make appear as if by magic

In the drive of the wind and sleet they pushed in on one another. There were wrists, unprotected by coat or pocket, which were red with cold. There were ears, half-covered by every conceivable semblance of a hat, which still looked stiff and bitten. In the snow they shifted, now one foot, now another, almost rocking in unison.

With the growth of the crowd about the door came a murmur. It was not conversation, but a running comment directed at anyone in general. It contained oaths and slang phrases.

"By damn, I wish they'd hurry up."

"Look at the copper watchin'."

"Maybe it ain't winter, nuther!"

"I wisht I was in Sing Sing."[5]

Now a sharper lash of wind cut down and they huddled closer. It was an edging, shifting, pushing throng. There was no anger, no pleading, no threatening words. It was all sullen endurance, unlightened by either wit or good fellowship.

A carriage went jingling by with some reclining figure in it. One of the men nearest the door saw it.

"Look at the bloke[6] ridin'."

"He ain't so cold."

"Eh, eh, eh!" yelled another, the carriage having long since passed out of hearing.

Little by little the night crept on. Along the walk a crowd turned out on its way home. Men and shop-girls went by with quick steps. The cross-town cars began to be crowded. The gas lamps were blazing, and every window bloomed ruddy with a steady flame. Still the crowd hung about the door, unwavering.

"Ain't they ever goin' to open up?" queried a hoarse voice, suggestively.

► *To what does the narrator compare the men who wait to be allowed inside the cheap lodging house?*

This seemed to renew the general interest in the closed door, and many gazed in that direction. They looked at it as dumb brutes look, as dogs paw and whine and study the knob. They shifted and blinked and muttered, now a curse, now a comment. Still they waited and still the snow whirled and cut them with biting flakes. On the old hats and peaked shoulders it was piling. It gathered in little heaps and curves and no one brushed it off. In the center of the crowd the

5. **Sing Sing.** New York state prison
6. **bloke.** Man, fellow

Words For Everyday Use

un • wa • ver • ing (un wā´vər iŋ) *vi.,* not changing in intent

warmth and steam melted it, and water trickled off hat rims and down noses, which the owners could not reach to scratch. On the outer rim the piles remained unmelted. Hurstwood, who could not get in the center, stood with head lowered to the weather and bent his form.

A light appeared through the transom overhead. It sent a thrill of possibility through the watchers. There was a murmur of recognition. At last the bars grated inside and the crowd pricked up its ears. Footsteps shuffled within and it murmured again. Someone called: "Slow up there, now," and then the door opened. It was push and jam for a minute, with grim, beast silence to prove its quality, and then it melted inward, like logs floating, and disappeared. There were wet hats and wet shoulders, a cold, shrunken, disgruntled mass, pouring in between bleak walls. It was just six o'clock and there was supper in every hurrying pedestrian's face. And yet no supper was provided here—nothing but beds.

Hurstwood laid down his fifteen cents and crept off with weary steps to his allotted room. It was a dingy affair—wooden, dusty, hard. A small gas jet furnished sufficient light for so rueful a corner.

"Hm!" he said, clearing his throat and locking the door.

Now he began leisurely to take off his clothes, but stopped first with his coat, and tucked it along the crack under the door. His vest he arranged in the same place. His old wet, cracked hat he laid softly upon the table. Then he pulled off his shoes and lay down.

It seemed as if he thought a while, for now he arose and turned the gas out, standing calmly in the blackness, hidden from view. After a few moments, in which he reviewed nothing, but merely hesitated, he turned the gas on again, but applied no match. Even then he stood there, hidden wholly in that kindness which is night, while the uprising fumes filled the room. When the odor reached his nostrils, he quit his attitude and fumbled for the bed.

◀ *What does Hurstwood do? What are his final words?*

"What's the use?" he said weakly, as he stretched himself to rest.

And now Carrie had attained that which in the beginning seemed life's object, or at least, such fraction of it as human beings ever attain of their original desires. She could look about on her gowns and carriage, her furniture and bank

Words For Everyday Use

at • tain (ə tān´) *vt.,* gain through effort

► What type of friends does Carrie have?

► How does Carrie feel about her situation? What does she again spend her time doing?

► According to the narrator, in what way do intellectual and emotional natures differ? What different careers do these two types end up following? To what does the narrator com-pare those of an emotional nature?

► What has played no role in Carrie's actions? For what has she longed? What has been proven false?

account. Friends there were, as the world takes it—those who would bow and smile in acknowledgment of her success. For these she had once craved. Applause there was, and publicity—once far-off, essential things, but now grown trivial and indifferent. Beauty also—her type of loveliness—and yet she was lonely. In her rocking-chair she sat, when not otherwise engaged—singing and dreaming.

Thus in life there is ever the intellectual and the emotional nature—the mind that reasons, and the mind that feels. Of one come the men of action—generals and statesmen; of the other, the poets and dreamers—artists all.

As harps in the wind, the latter respond to every breath of fancy, voicing in their moods all the ebb and flow of the ideal.

Man has not yet comprehended the dreamer any more than he has the ideal. For him the laws and morals of the world are unduly severe. Ever hearkening to the sound of beauty, straining for the flash of its distant wings, he watches to follow, wearying his feet in traveling. So watched Carrie, so followed, rocking and singing.

And it must be remembered that reason had little part in this. Chicago dawning, she saw the city offering more of loveliness than she had ever known, and instinctively, by force of her moods alone, clung to it. In fine raiment and elegant surroundings, men seemed to be contented. Hence, she drew near these things. Chicago, New York; Drouet, Hurstwood; the world of fashion and the world of stage—these were but incidents. Not them, but that which they represented, she longed for. Time proved the representation false.

Oh, the tangle of human life! How dimly as yet we see. Here was Carrie, in the beginning poor, unsophisticated, emotional; responding with desire to everything most lovely in life, yet finding herself turned as by a wall. Laws to say: "Be allured, if you will, by everything lovely, but draw not nigh unless by righteousness." Convention to say: "You shall not better your situation save by honest labor." If honest labor be unremunerative and difficult to endure; if it be the long, long road which never reaches beauty, but wearies the feet and the heart; if the drag to follow beauty be such that one abandons the admired way, taking rather the despised path leading to her dreams quickly, who shall cast the first stone? Not evil, but longing for that which is better, more

Words For Everyday Use

heark • en (härk´ən) *vt.*, listen
al • lure (ə loor´) *vt.*, tempt or entice
nigh (nī) *adv.*, near
un • re • mu • ner • a • tive (un rē myo͞o´ nər ə tiv) *adj.*, not profitable

often directs the steps of the erring. Not evil, but goodness more often allures the feeling mind unused to reason.

Amid the tinsel and shine of her state walked Carrie, unhappy. As when Drouet took her, she had thought: "Now am I lifted into that which is best"; as when Hurstwood seemingly offered her the better way: "Now am I happy." But since the world goes its way past all who will not partake of its folly, she now found herself alone. Her purse was open to him whose need was greatest. In her walks on Broadway, she no longer thought of the elegance of the creatures who passed her. Had they more of that peace and beauty which glimmered afar off, then were they to be envied.

◄ *Why does Carrie find herself alone?*

Drouet abandoned his claim and was seen no more. Of Hurstwood's death she was not even aware. A slow, black boat setting out from the pier at Twenty-seventh Street upon its weekly errand bore, with many others, his nameless body to the Potter's Field.[7]

◄ *Of what is Carrie unaware? Where and how is Hurstwood buried?*

Thus passed all that was of interest concerning these twain in their relation to her. Their influence upon her life is explicable alone by the nature of her longings. Time was when both represented for her all that was most potent in earthly success. They were the personal representatives of a state most blessed to attain—the titled ambassadors of comfort and peace, aglow with their credentials. It is but natural that when the world which they represented no longer allured her, its ambassadors should be discredited. Even had Hurstwood returned in his original beauty and glory, he could not now have allured her. She had learned that in his world, as in her own present state, was not happiness.

◄ *What did Drouet and Hurstwood once represent to Carrie? Why would she never be impressed with such men again?*

Sitting alone, she was now an illustration of the devious ways by which one who feels, rather than reasons, may be led in the pursuit of beauty. Though often disillusioned, she was still waiting for that halcyon day when she should be led forth among dreams become real. Ames had pointed out a farther step, but on and on beyond that, if accomplished, would lie others for her. It was forever to be the pursuit of that radiance of delight which tints the distant hilltops of the world.

◄ *What will Carrie always be doing?*

7. **Potter's Field.** Burial place for paupers or unknown persons

Words For Everyday Use

po • tent (pō´tənt) *adj.,* powerful

dis • cred • it (dis kred´ət) *vt.,* reject

de • vi • ous (dē´vē us) *adj.,* not in a straight path

ra • di • ance (rā´dē əns) *n.,* shining rays of light

▶ *What prediction does the narrator make for Carrie's future?*

Oh, Carrie, Carrie! Oh, blind strivings of the human heart! Onward, onward, it saith,[8] and where beauty leads, there it follows. Whether it be the tinkle of a lone sheep bell o'er[9] some quiet landscape, or the glimmer of beauty in sylvan places, or the show of soul in some passing eye, the heart knows and makes answer, following. It is when the feet weary and hope seems vain that the heartaches and the longings arise. Know, then, that for you is neither surfeit nor content. In your rocking-chair, by your window dreaming, shall you long, alone. In your rocking-chair, by your window, shall you dream such happiness as you may never feel.

THE END

8. **saith.** Archaic form of "says"
9. **o'er.** Over

Words For Everyday Use

striv • ing (striv iŋ) *n.,* struggle
syl • van (sil´vən) *adj.,* forested
sur • feit (sʉr´fit) *n.,* satisfaction

Responding to the Selection

Discuss whether a moral or a lesson can be drawn from this story. If so, what might this lesson be? Has this story changed in any way your thoughts about fame? about poverty?

Reviewing the Selection

Recalling and Interpreting

1. **R:** In chapter 43, what does Carrie realize after her picture appears in the papers? What role does Carrie receive in a new play? Why does Carrie frown initially when playing this role? What is the crowd's reaction to her frown? In what way does the frown help Carrie's career? In chapter 44, what offer does Mr. Withers make to Carrie, and why? What does Carrie note about Mrs. Vance's manner when she calls upon her again? What type of letter does Carrie constantly receive?

2. **I:** In what way has Carrie's attitude toward the social world changed due to the "lessons of Hurstwood and Drouet"? What role do "the vagaries of fortune" play in Carrie's becoming a success? What is significant about the way in which Carrie attains success? In what way does success change people's attitudes toward Carrie? Why does Mrs. Vance call upon Carrie again? Explain whether she is truly Carrie's friend. Why isn't Carrie interested in such letters? What is the significance of chapter 44's title, "And This Is Not Elf Land: What Gold Will Not Buy"?

3. **R:** At the beginning of chapter 45, how much money does Hurstwood have, and where is he living? What does he spend his time doing? What does Hurstwood finally do when he has only twenty cents left? What happens to worsen his condition? What does Hurstwood do to survive? To whom does he resolve to turn for help? What prevents him from seeing this person? What does the captain do to help the poor?

4. **I:** In what way does Hurstwood's situation contrast with Carrie's? Explain how Hurstwood views this contrast. How would you characterize Hurstwood's mental condition? Why does he wait so long to take any action to save himself? How must Hurstwood view his situation in order to turn to this person for help? What has he lost? What type of person does the captain seem to be?

5. **R:** In chapter 46, what does Drouet expect Carrie will do when he visits her once again? What does he reveal about Hurstwood? What is Carrie's reaction when she sees Hurstwood again? What advice about melancholy and longing does Ames give Carrie? According to Ames, what is the key to Carrie's success? What does Ames say will happen if she does not make use of her gift correctly and "change"?

6. **I:** Why does Drouet expect Carrie to act as he wishes? Why doesn't Carrie consider this a possibility? What does Carrie's reaction to this news about Hurstwood reveal about her character? Why does Hurstwood resent her reaction? Why, given Carrie's character, is the "gift" Ames discovers in her not surprising? In what way does Carrie's manifestation of this gift make her different from the musicians, poets, and dramatists to whom Ames compares her? Why is Carrie unable to follow Ames's advice?

7. **R:** In chapter 47, at what two charities is Hurstwood a frequent visitor? Why is Hurstwood finding begging more difficult? What does he consider doing? What does Hurstwood say as he looks in the restaurant window on Broadway? After looking in the window, to whom does he decide to turn for help once again? What prevents him from receiving this help? What are the other major characters doing as Hurstwood plans his death? What are Hurstwood's final words? What is Carrie doing immediately after the scene in which Hurstwood dies? What does the narrator say Carrie will do forever?

8. **I:** What does the scene in which Hurstwood gazes through the window reveal about his relationship to the "walled city" which he occasionally mentions? How do you think he feels as he gazes in the window? Why do you think Hurstwood's last failure is the one that makes him determined to die? How do the situations of the other characters contrast with Hurstwood's? To which character at this point in time does Hurstwood seem most similar? What do Hurstwood's final words reveal about his state of mind? What does the narrator indicate lies in store for Carrie in the future?

Synthesizing

9. According to Ames, and to the view of the world in this novel, most people spend their lives longing for things just out of reach. In what way is Carrie the perfect example of this phenomenon? Explain whether you agree with this view of human nature. What is Dreiser's opinion of this human tendency? Explain whether he sees it as leading to positive action or happiness. What are the negative effects of this tendency in human beings to long for things just out of reach?

10. At the end of this novel, the narrator reveals that Carrie will be "alone." Explain how Carrie's attitude toward men has changed over the course of the novel. Is it possible for Carrie to experience true love for a man? Would it be possible for Carrie to love Ames? Would it be possible for Ames to love her? Explain whether Carrie's solitude is the result of fate or of her own free will. Earlier in the novel, Carrie accused Drouet of trying to make her into a "toy" and a "plaything." How might a feminist critic view Carrie's attitude toward men? (See the Handbook of Literary Terms for a definition of feminist criticism.) How do you think Dreiser regards her attitude?

Understanding Literature (QUESTIONS FOR DISCUSSION)

1. **Naturalism, Image, and Marxist Criticism. Naturalism** was a literary movement of the late nineteenth and early twentieth centuries that saw actions and events as resulting inevitably from biological or natural forces in the environment. As you read at the end of chapter 36, Naturalist writers extensively researched their subjects to portray them as realistically as possible. An **image** is a word or phrase that names something that can be seen, heard, touched, tasted, or smelled. **Marxist criticism**, based upon the work of the German-born political philosopher Karl Marx, evaluates and interprets works of art with regard to the material, economic forces that shape them or with regard to their origins in or depictions of struggle between the social classes. Explain why a Marxist critic would find a wealth of material to analyze in this novel. Find some vivid images Dreiser uses to depict the life of the poor. Explain whether it seems that Dreiser extensively researched this subject. What forces do you believe Dreiser saw as leading to the disparity between the lives of the wealthy and the lives of the poor? What do you think the author is trying to point out about social classes? about poverty?

2. Character and Didacticism. A character is a person who figures in the action of a literary work. **Didacticism** is the use of works of art to convey moral, social, educational, or political messages. How would you describe Ames's interactions with Carrie? What do you think of Ames as a character? Why might he be described as "superior" to the other characters in the novel? Why does he so freely share his own opinions? In what way does the author wish the reader to view Ames? Explain how the use of Ames as a character is didactic.

3. Scene and Parallelism. A **scene** is a short section of a literary work that presents action that occurs in a single place at a single time. **Parallelism** is a rhetorical technique in which a writer emphasizes the equal value or weight of two or more ideas by expressing them in the same grammatical form. Parallelism may also be used as an organizational technique in longer works. Just before Hurstwood's death scene, Dreiser juxtaposes a number of brief scenes, each featuring one or more of the significant characters in the novel. Why do you think he used this technique to lead into Hurstwood's death scene? In what way does one of the scenes parallel the novel's beginning? Why do you think Dreiser chose to include these parallel scenes at the beginning and end of the novel?

Plot Analysis of *Sister Carrie*

The Parts of a Plot

A **plot** is a series of events related to a **central conflict**, or struggle. The following diagram, known as Freytag's Pyramid, illustrates the main parts of a plot.

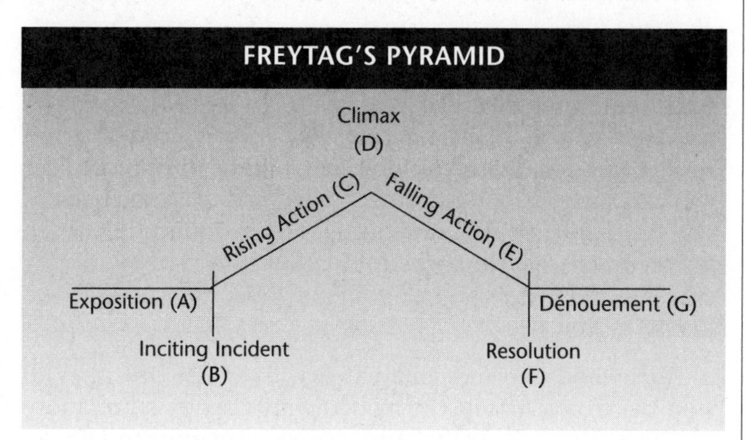

The parts of a plot are as follows:

The **exposition** is the part of a plot that provides background information, often about the characters, setting, or conflict.

The **inciting incident** is the event that introduces the central conflict.

The **rising action**, or **complication**, develops the conflict to a high point of intensity.

The **climax** is the high point of interest or suspense in the plot.

The **falling action** is all the events that follow the climax.

The **resolution** is the point at which the central conflict is ended, or resolved.

The **dénouement** is any material that follows the resolution and that ties up loose ends.

Exposition (A)

The reader is introduced to Carrie as she leaves her family in Columbia City behind and departs by train to seek her fortune in Chicago. Carrie meets a flirtatious young man named Drouet on the train. Carrie moves into the apartment where her sister Minnie and brother-in-law Hanson live, and realizes that they live a very economical and bleak life. Carrie looks for work and after much difficulty finds a job in a shoe factory. Due to illness, Carrie loses her job and must search for another. If she is unsuccessful in her search, she knows that her sister and brother-in-law will send her back to her family in Columbia City.

Inciting Incident (B)

Carrie meets Drouet again while she is looking for a job. Drouet sympathizes with Carrie, takes her out to a fine restaurant, and offers her twenty dollars so that she might buy new clothes. Carrie accepts the money, and she and Drouet find an apartment for Carrie, where, presumably she will continue to look for work. Carrie, however, soon trades her virtue for Drouet's support. Drouet introduces Carrie to his friend George Hurstwood.

Rising Action (C)

Hurstwood becomes infatuated with Carrie and tries to woo her from Drouet. Hurstwood wins Carrie's admiration; she increasingly feels that Hurstwood is superior to Drouet. Hurstwood's infatuation with Carrie leads him to neglect his wife and family. Drouet gives Carrie a part in the play his lodge is putting on to raise money. Carrie's performance in the play further inflames the affection of both Drouet and Hurstwood. Hurstwood determines to get Carrie away from Drouet. Drouet discovers that, in his absence, Carrie has been spending time with Hurstwood. Hurstwood promises to marry Carrie. Certain friends and acquaintances reveal information that leads Mrs. Hurstwood to suspect her husband of having an affair; she confronts him and threatens legal action. Drouet reveals to Carrie that Hurstwood is already married and leaves Carrie, angered by her lack of loyalty and gratitude. Carrie resolves never to see Hurstwood again, and Hurstwood is surprised when she doesn't show up at their appointed meeting. Hurstwood tries to return to his home only to find that his wife and family have locked him out.

Climax (D)

Hurstwood receives letters from his wife's lawyers, threatening that they will initiate proceedings for a divorce and alimony if he does not come to some financial agreement with her. Hurstwood does not respond to these letters, being more concerned with Carrie's silence—he assumes that she has discovered he is married. Feeling that she has lost Drouet's support and worried about her financial future, Carrie unsuccessfully tries to find a job in department stores and theaters. Alone one night at Fitzgerald and Moy's, his place of employment, Hurstwood steals thousands of dollars from an unlocked safe. He goes to Carrie and tells her that Drouet is hurt and asking to see her in order to lure her away to a train headed for Montreal.

Falling Action (E)

Although she discovers Hurstwood's ruse (but not his thievery), Carrie stays with Hurstwood and they are "married" in Montreal. A detective finds Hurstwood in Montreal, and Hurstwood sends back most of the money to his former employers before leaving for New York with Carrie. Hurstwood finds a less prestigious saloon to manage in New York, and for a time all is tranquil, although his finances are somewhat straitened, and Carrie increasingly longs for the glamour and excitement that Hurstwood can no longer provide. During this time, Carrie meets Mr. Ames, a young man who impresses her with his intelligence and strong values. After Carrie and Hurstwood move to a smaller, cheaper apartment, Hurstwood's saloon closes and he becomes unemployed. Although his savings dwindle, Hurstwood's attempts to look for work are only halfhearted. Angered by Carrie's alarm about the situation, Hurstwood reveals that their marriage is not legal or binding. With Hurstwood's encouragement, Carrie goes out to find a job in the theater, and soon gets a job in a chorus line at the Casino theater. Hurstwood spends his time reading the papers in his rocking-chair and running errands while Carrie works to support them.

Resolution (F)

Carrie feels increasingly resentful about being forced to support Hurstwood. Hurstwood works briefly on a trolley line while the trolley workers are striking, but the violence of the strike frightens Hurstwood away. Carrie receives several promotions and raises at work, first to leader of the chorus and then, after she gets a line in a play, to a small acting role. Carrie does not tell Hurstwood about her pay raises, planning to keep the extra money for herself. When Hurstwood suggests that they move to a cheap two-room apartment, Carrie decides to move out and rent a room with her friend and coworker Lola Osborne. Carrie leaves Hurstwood twenty dollars and a note explaining that she is leaving.

Dénouement (G)

Carrie frowns on stage when she does not like her role as a Quaker, and this frown makes her an instant sensation in the theater. As Carrie's fortunes rise, Hurstwood's remaining funds decrease until he is forced to beg for money for food and a bed in a cheap lodging house. When Hurstwood again encounters Carrie, he is so altered that she does not recognize him and he begs money from her. Carrie meets Drouet again, but she is now too experienced in the ways of the world to fall for him again. Hurstwood's condition becomes more and more desperate, and he finally kills himself in a lodging house one night. His body is buried in an unmarked grave in Potter's Field. Carrie has achieved financial success, but she remains lonely and unhappy, longing for things just out of her reach.

Creative Writing Activities

Creative Writing Activity A: An Apostrophe and a Continuation

An apostrophe is a rhetorical technique in which an object or person is directly addressed. Dreiser uses this technique at the end of *Sister Carrie*; the narrator addresses Carrie directly to say that she will experience "neither surfeit nor content," and that she will spend her time alone in her rocking-chair, dreaming of happiness that she will never feel. Spend five minutes freewriting your thoughts about the ending of *Sister Carrie*. Now imagine that you are the author of this work and are planning to write an apostrophe directly addressing Carrie. What would you have to say to her? Would you view Carrie's future as bleakly as the author does? Would you give her advice or encouragement? Would you comment on her past actions? Write your own apostrophe to Carrie. Then, in three or four paragraphs, begin an additional chapter (chapter 48) for the novel, describing what you believe will happen in Carrie's future. Try not to be overly influenced by Dreiser's vision of Carrie's future; rely on your own imagination. You might try to mimic Dreiser's writing style by giving your chapter a title similar to the others in the novel and by imitating his language and sentence structure. Your apostrophe and continuation can be as straightforward or humorous as you wish.

Creative Writing Activity B: Modernizing *Sister Carrie*

Sister Carrie is set in the 1890s, and obviously that time period was much different from ours. Among many other differences, people relied on horses and trains for transportation rather than on cars and airplanes, salaries and the cost of living were much lower, and there was a much stricter standard for proper behavior. What would happen to Carrie in modern Chicago or New York? Choose a brief scene from *Sister Carrie* and "modernize" it by setting it in the late twentieth (or even early twenty-first) century. You may choose to "modernize" Carrie, or you might imagine that Carrie is a late-nineteenth-century person transported suddenly a hundred years into the future. For example, you might choose to rewrite the opening train scene and describe Carrie as a confident, modern young woman on a plane trip to Chicago, openly chatting with Drouet with no sense of impropriety and maybe even asking him for his phone number. You might imagine Carrie as Dreiser created her seeking a job in the modern world, never having seen or imagined such things as computers or fax machines. Imagine what would happen if she got an entry-level job in data entry. What would she think of a modern salary? modern prices? You might begin by choosing a scene you enjoyed and then freewriting your thoughts about possible ways to update that scene.

Creative Writing Activity C: Realistic Description

Dreiser strove to portray people, places, and events as realistically as possible. He portrayed New York and Chicago as they were at the end of the nineteenth century so realistically that his editors felt readers would be shocked and urged him to change some names of people and places to avoid offending anyone described in the novel's pages. Choose a part of your town or city that you know well and write a two- or three-page description of the place and the people who live or work there, portraying the scene as accurately and vividly as you can. You might want to visit the area you have chosen to take notes to aid you in your description.

Creative Writing Activity D: Wish List and Plan

Most of the characters in this novel spend their time longing for things, but they seldom know how to go about attaining these things. Write a wish list in which you describe some of your hopes and dreams for the future. You might list career or educational goals and plans for self-improvement, as well as material things you hope to attain. Then, for each wish you list, come up with a plan to attain this thing. For example, if you hope to buy a new mountain bike, you might decide that you should start baby-sitting to save money, and cut back on spending money for clothes and movies.

Critical Writing Activities

The following topics are suitable for short critical essays on *Sister Carrie.* An essay written on one of these topics should begin with an introductory paragraph that states the thesis, or main idea, of the essay. The introductory paragraph should be followed by several paragraphs that support the thesis using evidence from the novel. The essay should conclude with a paragraph that summarizes the points made in the body of the essay and resolves the thesis.

Critical Writing Activity A: Analyzing Dreiser's Depiction of a "Fallen Woman"

One of the reasons that *Sister Carrie* was considered so shocking when it was released is because readers felt that Dreiser did not punish his heroine for her immorality. In most novels before *Sister Carrie,* women who fell from virtue were punished by the author—they received some hard blow of fate and ended up repenting their actions. American novelist E. L. Doctorow has noted that "Carrie hardly suffers any of the standard fates the convention requires. Dreiser saw to it that she would not end up happy, but neither is she punished or repentant. What is more important, the author never suggests that her alternatives, had she been capable of choosing them, would have given her a finer life or made her a better person." What is your view of this statement? Write an essay in which you explain whether Dreiser punishes Carrie for her fall from virtue and whether the author passes judgment on Carrie's actions. Before you begin, you might freewrite your responses to the following questions: Would you describe the author as judgmental or nonjudgmental? Why? How does the author view Carrie's fall from virtue? Is denying Carrie happiness a form of punishment? Why does Dreiser deny Carrie happiness? What is Dreiser's view of morals in an industrial, economically driven society?

Critical Writing Activity B: Analyzing Foils and Plot Structure

A foil is a character whose attributes, or characteristics, contrast with, and therefore throw into relief, the attributes of another character. The plot of this novel centers on Carrie's rise and Hurstwood's fall through society's levels.

Write an essay explaining the way Dreiser uses Carrie and Hurstwood as foils to describe different stages of a person's position in an economically driven society. Explain what Dreiser sees as the path through society that most people take. What are the possible fates he sees for most people? Finally, indicate whether you think Dreiser believed that Carrie would retain her current position in society or whether she, like Hurstwood, would experience a fall.

Critical Writing Activity C: Biographical and Feminist Criticism

Biographical criticism attempts to account for elements of a literary work by relating them to events in the life of its author. Feminist criticism evaluates and interprets a work of art with regard to its portrayal of or influence upon gender roles. As you read in Dreiser's biography on page v, Dreiser's own sister became the mistress of an architect and later ran off with a married man named L. A. Hopkins. Like Hurstwood, Hopkins worked for a high-class saloon and stole money from this firm to run away with Dreiser's sister. Write an essay in which you explore the way women, in particular Carrie, are portrayed in this literary work. How might events in Dreiser's life have affected his portrayal of Carrie as a character? of women in general?

Critical Writing Activity D: Exploring Hurstwood as a Tragic Hero

The best definition we have of tragedy was written by the philosopher and critic Aristotle in a work called the *Poetics.* Tragedy depicts the downfall of a character of high status who is neither completely good nor completely evil. The hero's fall is brought about by some flaw in his or her character, known as a tragic flaw. Aristotle's term for the tragic flaw, *hamartia,* has also been translated as "an error in judgment." One of the most commonly presented tragic flaws is that of *hubris,* or excessive pride. Aristotle believed that witnessing the downfall of a basically good but flawed individual not unlike the audience would evoke the emotions of pity and fear in that audience (pity for the suffering the hero experiences and fear for the audience that they could be in the hero's situation). Aristotle stated that the emotions of pity and fear bring about the "catharsis of such emotions," meaning that in watching or reading a tragedy the viewer or reader experiences a sort of emotional cleansing or release.

One of the marks of the tragic hero is that he or she remains great enough, strong enough, to bear his or her fate. Even after his downfall, Oedipus, one of literature's great tragic heroes, takes responsibility for his fate, "the hand that struck me was none but my own," and boldly claims, "no man but I can bear my evil doom." Based on this description of tragedy and tragic heroes, explain whether Hurstwood is a tragic hero. To support your position, refer both to this definition of tragedy and to events in the novel.

Projects

Project A: Preparing to Enter the World of Work

Much of this novel centers on its characters' struggles to find work. Dreiser portrays the process of looking for work as arduous and intimidating, and while such a search can certainly seem to be so at times, proper preparation can make looking for a job less stressful and more rewarding. Work with your classmates to hold a Career Fair. Invite family, friends, and other members of your community to share information about their professions. After your fair, create a resume that highlights your career objectives, skills, experiences, and interests. Share your resume with a group of peers for comments and suggestions. Finally, work in pairs to hold mock interviews. Prepare interview questions for your partner as well as responses to questions that you believe that you might be asked. Remember that your responses should sound natural and not rehearsed. You might get ideas for interview questions from books and manuals about the job search. Each interviewer should prepare a written evaluation of the person he or she interviewed.

Project B: Helping the Poor

In *Sister Carrie,* Dreiser realistically and sympathetically portrays the lives of the homeless and of the desperately poor. He also describes many charities, carried out by both organizations and individuals, that help the poor and the homeless to survive. Working in small groups, use your library's resources and the Internet to research poverty and homelessness in your city, town, or state. Is poverty and homelessness on the rise or on the decline? What charitable services and organizations exist in your community to help the poor and the homeless? Each group should brainstorm a way for the group to help the poor and the homeless. Your group might organize a food or clothing drive, or donate time to an organization that feeds, clothes, or provides housing for the homeless. Your group should keep a journal in which you describe members' experiences. Then, each group should report on their activities, progress, and experiences to the class.

Project C: Holding an Amateur Production

Carrie's interest in the theater is sparked when she takes a role in an amateur theater production. Work in large groups to produce your own amateur performances. The first task of each group will be to find a play to stage. You may wish to explore plays that were popular during the end of the nineteenth century, such as melodramas or comedies of manners. You may even wish to stage a production of the very first play Carrie worked in, Augustin Daly's melodrama *Under the Gaslight.* Next, your group should assign tasks. In addition to actors, you will need a director, a stage manager, and people to design, build, or find the necessary scenery, props, and costumes. Plan rehearsal times so that you will get enough practice before performing for the rest of your class or for other classes.

Project D: Representing *Sister Carrie* through Art

Choose an interesting person, place, or scene in *Sister Carrie* to represent artistically. You may draw or paint a picture, make a sculpture, make a collage, construct a model, or put together an appropriate costume. For example, if you wish to represent Carrie on stage as the frowning Quaker, you might paint a picture of her on stage in the theater, create a scale model of a typical theater and clay models of Carrie, the other actors, and some of the theatergoers, or create a costume for a Quaker worker and present yourself as Carrie would have appeared. Do not worry if you feel that you are not a skilled artist; simply use your imagination to make some person, place, or scene from *Sister Carrie* come alive visually for your classmates.

Glossary

a • bash • ing (ə bash´iŋ) *adj.*, embarrassing; humbling
a • bate (ə bāt´) *vi.*, lessen
a • bode (ə bōd´) *n.*, residence; home
ac • cli • ma • ti • za • tion (ə klī´mə tə zā´shen) *n.*, process of growing used to different circumstances
ac • cord (ə kôrd´) *vt.*, grant
ac • cost (ə kôst´) *vt.*, approach in an intrusive way
ac • cre • tion (ə krē´shən) *n.*, accumulation
ac • qui • esce (ak´wē es´) *vi.*, consent without protest but without enthusiasm
ac • tu • a • ted (ak´choo ā təd) *adj.*, motivated
a • cute • ness (ə kyoot´nəs) *adj.*, extreme sensitivity
ad • junct (a´juŋkt´) *n.*, addition
a • dorn (ə dôrn´) *vt.*, ornament
a • dorn • ment (ə dôrn´mənt) *n.*, dress
a • droit • ness (ə droit´nəs) *n.*, cleverness
ad • u • la • tion (ad´joo lā´shən) *n.*, intense admiration
ad • vo • cate (ad´və kāt´) *vt.*, speak or write in support of
af • fa • bly (af´ə blē) *adv.*, in a friendly manner
af • fec • ta • tion (af´ek tā´shən) *n.*, artificial behavior meant to impress others
af • flict • ed (ə flikt´əd) *adj.*, affected, as by a disorder
af • flu • ent (af´loo ənt) *adj.*, wealthy
af • fray (ə frā´) *n.*, noisy brawl
a • gate (ag´it) *n.*, hard, semiprecious stone
a • gil • i • ty (ə jil´ə tē) *n.*, quick and easy movement
ail (āl) *vt.*, trouble
air • i • ly (er´ ə lē) *adv.*, in an airy or light manner
a • lac • ri • ty (ə lak´rə tē) *n.*, speed
al • cove (al´kōv´) *n.*, recessed section of a room
a • li • en (el´ē ən) *adj.*, not belonging to
a • light (ə līt´) *vi.*, get down from
al • lied (a līd´) *adj.*, united
al • lure (ə loor´) *vt.*, tempt with something desirable
a • loof (ə loof´) *adj.*, emotionally distant
al • ter • ca • tion (ôl´tər kā´shən) *n.*, heated argument
a • mass (ə mas´) *vt.*, pile up; accumulate
a • mend • ed (ə mend´'d) *adj.*, corrected
am • nes • ty (am´nəs tē) *n.*, pardon
am • ple (amp´əl) *adj.*, abundant; adequate
a • ne • mic (ə nē´mik) *adj.*, lacking hemoglobin in the bloodstream, therefore pale
an • guish (aŋ´gwish) *n.*, great suffering
a • nom • a • ly (ə näm´ə lē) *n.*, oddity; peculiarity
an • tag • o • nism (an tag´ə niz'əm) *n.*, hostility
an • tip • a • thy (an tip´ə thē) *n.*, strong dislike
ap • a • thy (ap´ə thē) *n.*, lack of emotion
ap • par • i • tion (a pər i´shən) *n.*, thing which appears; ghost
ap • prise (ə prīz´) *vt.*, inform
ar • bi • trar • y (är´bə trer´ē) *adj.*, based on whims, not rules
ar • dent (ärd´'nt) *adj.*, passionate

ar • dor (är´dər) *n.*, emotional warmth

ar • rayed (ə rād´) *adj.*, dressed

ar • ro • gate (ar´ə gāt) *vt.*, claim or seize without right

arch • ly (ärch´ lē) *adv.*, mischievously

as • cend (ə send´) *vi.*, go up

a • skance (ə skans´) *adv.*, with a sideways glance

as • per • sion (ə spʉr´zhən) *n.*, damaging or disparaging remark

as • sent (ə sent´) *vi.*, accept

as • sid • u • ous • ly (ə sij´o͞o əs lē) *adv.*, diligently

a • tone (ə tōn´) *vt.*, make amends for

at • tain (ə tān´) *vt.*, gain through effort

au • dac • i • ty (ô das´ ə tē) *n.*, shameless boldness

au • di • ble (ô´də bəl) *adj.*, able to be heard

aug • ment (ôg ment´) *vt.*, add to

au • gur (ô´gər) *n.*, omen

aus • pi • cious (ôs spish´əs) *adj.*, promising

au • tom • a • ton (ô täm´ə tän´) *n.*, robot

a • veng • er (ə venj´ ər) *n.*, returns injury for injury

bad • i • nage (bad´'n äzh´) *n.*, playful, teasing talk

balm • y (bäm´ē) *adj.*, warm, mild, pleasant

ban • dy (ban´dē) *vt.*, exchange words carelessly back and forth

bar • ren (bar´ ən) *adj.*, having little or no vegetation

bask (bask) *vi.*, warm oneself pleasantly

bau • ble (bô´ bəl´) *n.*, showy but worthless thing

bawl (bôl) *vi.*, shout out noisily

be • drag • gled (bē drag´əld) *adj.*, wet, limp, and muddied

be • fit • ting (bē fit´ iŋ) *n.*, suitable to

be • lie (bē lī´) *vt.*, disguise or misrepresent

be • moan (bē mōn´) *vt.*, mourn, complain of

be • nef • i • cent (bə nef´ə sənt) *adj.*, good, favorable

be • reaved (bē rēvd´) *adj.*, grieving

be • stir (bē stʉr) *vt.*, busy

be • stow (be stó) *adj.*, mournful

big • a • my (big´ ə mē) *n.*, criminal act of marrying while a previous marriage is still in effect

blanch (blanch) *vt.*, whiten

bland • ly (bland´ lē) *adv.*, smoothly

blight (blīt) *n.*, thing that destroys or devastates

bound • en (boun´dən) *adj.*, necessary

brawn • y (brôn´ ē) *adj.*, strong and muscular

bra • zen • ly (brā´zən lē) *adv.*, boldly

broach (brōch) *vt.*, bring up an issue for discussion

buoy (boi) *vt.*, lift up in spirits

buoy • ant (boi´ənt) *adj.*, high-spirited

buoyed (boid) *adj.*, lifted or raised emotionally

ca • la • mi • ty (kə lam´ə tē) *n.*, disaster

cal • i • ber (kal´ə bər) *n.*, degree of worth or value

cant • ing (kant´iŋ) *adj.*, meaningless, conventional

cav • a • lier (kav´ə lir´) *n.*, gallant or courteous gentleman

ce • ler • i • ty (sə ler´ i tē) *n.*, swiftness

ces • sa • tion (se sā´shən) *n.*, stopping; end

chafe (chāf) *vt.*, annoy; irritate
cha • grined (shə grind´) *adj.*, shamed and annoyed
chan • nel (chan´əl) *n.*, course; route
chasm (kaz'əm) *n.*, deep crack in the earth's surface
chron • ic (krän´ik) *adj.*, continuing indefinitely; habitual
cir • cu • i • tous (sər kyo͞o´ət əs) *adj.*, indirect, roundabout
cir • cum • scribed (sʉr´ kəm skrībd´) *adj.*, limited
cir • cum • spect (sʉr´ kəm spekt´) *adj.*, well-behaved and proper
cir • cum • spect • ness (sʉr´ kəm spekt´nəs) *n.*, proper behavior
clad (klad) *adj.*, clothed; dressed
clam • or (klam´ər) *n.*, loud complaint
cler • ic (kler´ik) *adj.*, having to do with business writing
clod (kläd) *n.*, lump
cock • sure • ness (käk´sho͞or´nəs) *n.*, overconfidence
com • mend (kə mend´) *vt.*, praise
com • men • da • tion (kam´ən dā´shən) *n.*, act of praise
com • men • su • rate (kə men´sho͞or it) *adj.*, equal to
com • mo • di • ous (kə mō´dē əs) *adj.*, spacious
com • pla • cen • cy (kəm plā´sən sē) *n.*, quiet satisfaction; contentment
com • pla • cent • ly (kəm plā´sənt lē) *adv.*, in an unconcerned, self-satisfied manner
com • plai • sance (kəm plā´zəns) *n.*, willingness to please
com • pli • ance (kəm plī´əns) *n.*, submission
com • ply (kəm plī´) *vt.*, act in accordance with
con • ceive (kən sēv´) *vt.*, form in one's mind
con • cep • tion (kən sep´shən) *n.*, notion; idea; understanding
con • ces • sion (kən sesh´ ən) *n.*, act of yielding or granting
con • cil • i • ate (kän sil´ē āt) *vt.*, soothe; placate
con • cil • i • a • to • ry (kən sil´ē ə tôr´ē) *adj.*, intended to make up with another
con • coc • tion (kən käkt´shun) *n.*, combination of ingredients
con • de • scen • sion (kän´di sen´shən) *n.*, manner of a superior to an inferior
con • fer (kən fʉr´) *vi.*, meet for discussion
con • form • i • ty (kən fôrm´ə tē) *n.*, harmony
con • glom • er • a • tion (kən gläm´ər ā´shən) *n.*, mixture or collection of miscellaneous things
con • jec • ture (kən jek´chər) *n.*, theory or prediction based on guesswork
con • jec • ture (kən jek´chər) *vt.*, guess
con • jure (kän´jʉr) *vi.*, make appear by magic
con • ser • va • tism (kən sʉr´və tiz´əm) *n.*, traditional principles and practices
con • so • la • tion (kän´sə lā´shən) *n.*, comfort
con • sti • tute (kän´stə to͞ot) *vt.*, make up
con • ta • gion (kən tā´jən) *n.*, spread of something from one thing to another
con • tempt (kən tempt´) *n.*, scorn
con • tend (kən tend´) *vi.*, strive in combat; fight
con • tra • dic • to • ry (kän´trə dik´tə rē) *adj.*, opposing
con • ven • tion • al (kən ven´shə nel) *adj.*, conforming to formal or accepted standards
co • quet • ry (kō´kə trē) *n.*, flirtation
co • quet • tish • ly (kō ket´ tish lē) *adv.*, flirtatiously
cor • pu • len • cy (kôr´pyo͞o lən sē) *n.*, fatness
cor • pu • lent (kôr´pyo͞o lənt) *adj.*, overweight
coun • te • nance (koun´tə nəns) *n.*, facial expression

coun • ter • bal • ance (kount´ər bal´əns) *vt.*, offset
coy (koi) *adj.*, not serious
crave (krāv) *vt.*, need and want
cred • it • a • ble (kred´ə tə bəl) *adj.*, praiseworthy
crest • fal • len (krest´fôl ən) *adj.*, disheartened
crys • tal • lize (kris´təl īz´) *vt.*, take on a definite form
cul • mi • nate (kul´ mə nāt) *vi.*, result
cul • mi • na • tion (kul´mə nā´shən) *n.*, highest point; climax
cu • mu • la • tive (kyo͞o´myo͞o lāt´ iv) *adj.*, growing as time progresses
curt (kʉrt) *adj.*, brief to the point of rudeness
cur • tailed (kər tāld´) *adj.*, cut unnaturally short
cyn • i • cal (sin´i kəl) *adj.*, believing that people are motivated only by selfishness
cyn • i • ci • sm (sin´i si´ zəm) *adj.*, scornfulness toward the motives, virtues, or integrity of others
de • ci • sive (dē sī´siv) *adj.*, determining what comes next
de • fault • er (dē fôlt´ ər) *n.*, one who fails to pay money where due
de • fer (dē fʉr´) *vt.*, postpone
def • er • en • ti • al • ly (def´ər en´shə lē) *adv.*, respectfully
def • er • ence (def´ər əns) *n.*, courteous respect
deft (deft) *adj.*, skillful
deg • ra • da • tion (deg´rə dā´shən) *n.*, that which brings one to a lower position
deign (dān) *vt.*, condescend to something beneath one's dignity
de • lib • er • a • tion (di lib´ər ā´shən) *n.*, design, forethought
de • lude (di lo͞od´) *vt.*, fool, as by false promises
de • lud • ed (di lo͞od´ed) *adj.*, deceived
de • mean • or (di mēn´ ər) *n.*, outward behavior; conduct; manner
de • mure (də myo͞or´) *adj.*, affectedly modest or shy
dep • re • cate (dep´rə kāt´) *vt.*, express disapproval of
de • signs (de zīnz´) *pl.n.*, plans
de • spoil (dē spoil´) *vt.*, rob; deprive
des • o • late (des´ə lit) *adj.*, lonely; solitary
de • spond • ent (di spän´dənt) *adj.*, dejected; discouraged
des • ul • to • ry (des´əl tôr´ē) *adj.*, disconnected; not methodical
de • tain (dē tān´) *vt.*, keep late
de • terred (dē tʉrd´) *adj.*, held back
de • vi • ous (dē´vē us) *adj.*, not in a straight path
de • volve (di välv´) *vt.*, fall
dex • ter • ous (deks´tər əs) *adj.*, skillful
dif • fi • dence (dif´ə dəns) *n.*, lack of confidence; shyness
di • gres • sion (di gresh´ən) *n.*, movement away from the true path
di • late (di´ lāt) *vt.*, speak or write in detail
dim • i • nu • tion (dim´ə no͞o´shən) *n.*, lessening
dip • lo • mat (dip´ lə mat´) *n.*, person skilled in dealing with others
dire (dīr) *adj.*, urgent
dis • clo • sure (dis klōz´zher) *n.*, revelation
dis • con • so • late (dis kän´sə lit) *adj.*, unhappy
dis • cord • ant • ly (dis kôrd´´nt lē) *adv.*, not harmoniously
dis • course (dis´kôrs´) *vi.*, give a long, formal talk
dis • cred • it (dis kred´ət) *vt.*, reject as untrue
dis • cre • tion (di skresh´ən) *n.*, authority to make decisions
dis • en • tan • gle (dis´ in taŋ´gəl) *vt.*, free from bonds

dis • mount (dis mount´) *vi.*, get off or down
dis • pose (di spōz´) *vt.*, incline
dis • po • si • tion (dis´pō si´shən) *n.*, nature
dis • sen • sion (di sen´shən) *n.*, conflict
dis • so • lu • tion (dis´ə lo͞o´shən) *n.*, disintegration
dis • tend (di stend´) *vi.*, stand out
di • vert (də vʉrt´) *vt.*, distract the attention
di • vest (də vest´) *vt.*, strip of clothing or equipment
doff (däf) *vt.*, put aside or discard
dog • ged • ly (dôg´id lē) *adv.*, persistently; stubbornly
dog • ma • tist (dôg´mə tist) *n.*, one who arrogantly asserts an opinion without evidence
dole (dōl) *vt.*, give
drawl (drôl) *vt.*, speak slowly, prolonging the vowels
dray (drā) *adj.*, used to haul loads
droll (drōl) *adj.*, humorous
du • ly (do͞o´lē) *adv.*, in the right time and manner
ear • nest • ness (ʉr´ nist nes) *n.*, sincerity; seriousness
ebb • ing (eb iŋ) *adj.*, weakening
e • go • tist (ē´gō tist) *n.*, self-absorbed person
e • la • ted (ē lāt´ ed) *adj.*, happy or joyful
e • la • tion (ē lā´shən) *n.*, joy or high spirits
em • a • nate (em´ə nāt´) *vi.*, come out of
e • man • ci • pa • tion (ē man´sə pā´shən) *n.*, freedom from restraint
em • ber (em´bər) *n.*, smoldering remains of a fire
em • bold • ened (em bōl´dənd) *adj.*, made braver or bolder
em • i • nent (em´ ə nənt) *adj.*, high in rank or achievement
em • phat • ic (em fat´ik) *adj.*, strong and definite
em • u • late (em´yo͞o lāt´) *vt.*, imitate
en • act (en akt´) *vt.*, perform
en • croach • ing (en krōch´ iŋ) *adj.*, advancing beyond former limits
en • deav • or (en dev´ər) *vi.*, try
en • fold (en fōld´) *vt.*, embrace
en • gross (en grōs´) *vt.*, occupy
en • light • en • ment (en līt´'n mənt) *n.*, understanding; clarification
en • list (en list´) *vt.*, engage
en • meshed (en mesh'd´) *adj.*, tangled
en • sue (en so͞o´) *vi.*, happen as a result
en • ti • ty (en´tə tē) *n.*, any thing which exists
en • vi • rons (ən vī´rənz) *n.*, districts surrounding a town or city
ep • i • thet (ep´ə thet´) *n.*, adjective, noun, or phrase used to characterize a person or thing, often disparaging
e • qua • nim • i • ty (ek´ wə nim´ə tē) *n.*, evenness of temper
e • quiv • o • cal (ē kwiv´ə kəl) *adj.*, hard to interpret as good or bad
e • quiv • o • ca • tion (ē kwiv´ə kā´shən) *n.*, deceitful, ambiguous expression
er • rant (er´ənt) *adj.*, straying from the right course
err • ing (ʉr´iŋ) *n.*, falling into error
er • ro • ne • ous (ər rō´ nē əs) *adj.*, mistaken; wrong
es • ca • pade (es´kə pād) *n.*, reckless adventure
eu • pho • ni • ous (yo͞o fō´nē əs) *adj.*, pleasing to the ear
ex • or • bi • tant (eg zor´bi tənt) *adj.*, very expensive

ex • pi • a • tion (eks´ pē ā´shən) *n.,* atonement for wrongdoing

ex • pos • tu • late (eks päs´chə lāt´) *vi.,* reason with and object to another

ex • tri • cate (eks´tri kāt) *vt.,* disentangle

ex • u • ber • ant (eg zo͞o´ bər ənt) *adj.,* full of life; uninhibited

ex • ult (eg sult´) *vi.,* rejoice greatly

fa • ce • tious (fə sē´shəs) *adj.,* inappropriately humorous

fas • tid • i • ous (fas tid´ē əs) *adj.,* immaculate

fee • bly (fē´blē) *adv.,* weakly

feign (fān) *vt.,* pretend

fe • lic • i • tate (fə lis´i tāt´) *vt.,* congratulate

fe • lic • i • ty (fə liś i tē) *n.,* happiness

fer • vid (fʉr´vid) *adj.,* impassioned; fervent; intensely devoted

fla • grant (flā´ grənt) *adj.,* glaring; brazen

fleec • y (flēs´ ē) *adj.,* soft, light, and woolly

flounce (flouns) *vi.,* move quickly, swishing one's clothing

floun • der • ing (floun´dər iŋ) *adj.,* moving in a lost and awkward way

flour • ish • ing (flʉr´ish iŋ) *adj.,* thriving; succeeding

flur • ried (flʉr´ ēd) *adj.,* agitated

flushed (flush'd) *adj.,* pink in the cheeks

fol • ly (fäl´ē) *n.,* foolishness

fore • bod • ing (fôr bōd´ iŋ) *n.,* feeling of coming evil

fore • fen • da • tion (fôr´ fen dā´shən) *n.,* warning

fore • stall (fôr stôl´) *vt.,* prevent

for • lorn (fôr lôrn´) *adj.,* without hope; desperate

for • sak • en (fôr sāk´ən) *adj.,* abandoned

for • ti • tude (fôrt´ə to͞od´) *n.,* strength to calmly bear misfortune

frail • ty (frāl´tē) *n.,* weakness

frank (fraŋk) *adj.,* open, honest

fro • lic (fräl´ik) *vi.,* play

fur • nish (fʉr´nish) *vt.,* supply; provide

fuse (fyo͞oz) *vt.,* unite or blend

fu • tile (fyo͞ot´'l) *adj.,* worthless; useless

gab • bling (gab´bliŋ) *n.,* chatter

gain • say (gān sā´) *vt.,* speak out against, contradict; deny, oppose

gait (gāt) *n.,* manner of walking

gall • ing (gôl´iŋ) *adj.,* bitterly irritating

gam • bol (gam´bəl) *vi.,* move playfully

garb (gärb) *n.,* clothing

gar • ru • lous (gar´ə ləs) *adj.,* characterized by much talk

gas • tron • o • my (gas trän´ə mē) *n.,* art of fine dining

gaud • y (gôd´ ē) *adj.,* bright and showy

gaunt (gônt) *adj.,* thin and bony

ge • ni • al • i • ty (jē´nē al´ə tē) *n.,* kind, cheerful sympathy

gen • i • al • ly (jēn´yə lē) *adv.,* in a friendly manner

gen • u • flec • tion (jen´yo͞o flekt´shən) *n.,* bow; servile action

gild • ed (gild´əd) *adj.,* coated with gold

goad (gōd) *n.,* sharp prodding

gos • sa • mer (gäs´ə mər) *adj.,* light, thin, and filmy

gran • deur (gran jər´) *n.,* greatness

grate (grāt) *vt.,* irritate

grat • i • fied (grat´ i fīd) *adj.*, pleased
grave (grāv) *adj.*, serious; important
grim • mest (grim´ mest) *adj.*, most stern and unyielding
grop • ing (grōp´iŋ) *n.*, feeling about for blindly
grudge (gruj) *vt.*, envy and resent
guile (gīl) *n.*, slyness and cunning
guise (gīz) *n.*, deceptive appearance
gump • tion (gump´shən) *n.*, courage and initiative
ha • rangue (hə raŋ´) *n.*, long, noisy, or scolding speech
hag • gard (hag´ərd) *adj.*, having a wild, worn look
hal • cy • on (hal´sē ən) *adj.*, tranquil
hale (hāl) *adj.*, healthy
har • row (har´ō) *vt.*, distress
has • ten (hās´ən) *vi.*, move swiftly; hurry
heark • en (härk´ən) *vi.*, give careful attention to; listen carefully
his • tri • on • ic (his trē än´ik) *adj.*, theatrical
hive (hīv) *n.*, place where many are busy
hue (hyo͞o) *n.*, general appearance; color
ig • no • min • i • ous • ly (ig´nə min´ ē es lē) *adv.*, shamefully; dishonorably
im • bib • ing (im bīb´iŋ) *n.*, drinking, especially of alcohol
im • part (im pärt´) *vt.*, give
im • pend • ing (im pend´ iŋ) *adj.*, threatening to occur
im • per • a • tive (im per´ə tiv) *adj.*, absolutely necessary
im • port (im´pôrt) *vi.*, mean, signify
im • pu • ta • tion (im pyo͞o tā´ shən) *n.*, charge
in • au • gu • ra • tion (in ô´gyo͞o rā´shən) *n.*, formal beginning
in • can • des • cent (in´kən des´ənt) *adj.*, glowing
in • censed (in sensd') *adj.*, enraged
in • ces • sant • ly (in ses´ənt lē) *adv.*, without stopping
in • cip • i •ent (in sip´ē ənt) *adj.*, beginning to emerge
in • ci • sive (in si´siv) *adj.*, keen; sharp
in • cite (in sīt´) *vt.*, rouse
in • cli • na • tion (in´klə nā´shən) *n.*, tendency; urge
in • co • her • ent (in´kō hir´ənt) *adj.*, not logically connected; unclear
in • con • gru • ous (in käŋ´gro͞o əs) *adj.*, ridiculously unsuitable
in • con • spic • u • ous (in´kən spik´yo͞o əs) *adj.*, hard to see or perceive; attracting little attention
in • dic • a • tive • ly (in dik´ə tiv lē) *adv.*, with suggestion and authority
in • dig • na • tion (in´dig nā´shən) *n.*, anger in reaction to injustice
in • duce (in do͞os´) *vt.*, cause
in • ex • press • i • bly (in´eks pres´ə blē) *adj.*, in a manner that is impossible to describe
in • fan • tile (in´fən tīl) *adj.*, childlike
in • fat • u • a • tion (in fach´o͞o ā´shən) *n.*, foolish or shallow love or affection
in • fer • ence (in´fər əns) *n.*, implication
in • flec • tion (in flek´ shən) *n.*, change in tone or pitch
in • fu • ri • at • ed (in fyo͞or´ē āt´əd) *adj.*, enraged
in • fused (in fyo͞ozd´) *adj.*, filled
in • gra • ti • ate (in grā´shē āt´) *vt.*, bring oneself into another's favor or good graces
in • gra • ti • at • ing (in grā´shē āt´iŋ) *adj.*, able to insert oneself into another's good graces

ink • ling (iŋk´liŋ) *n.*, small notion
in • nate (in nāt´) *adj.*, inborn
in • sa • ti • a • ble (in sā´shə bəl) *adj.*, constantly wanting more
in • scru • ta • ble (in skro͞ot´ə bəl) *adj.*, not easily understood
in • sin • u • a • tion (in sin´yo͞o ā´shən) *n.*, intent to win favor
in • so • lence (in´sə ləns) *n.*, disrespect
in • ter • po • late (in tʉr´pə lāt´) *vt.*, insert an interruption
in • ter • ro • ga • tion (in ter´ə gā´shən) *n.*, questioning
in • ter • stice (in tʉr´ stis) *n.*, narrow opening
in • tro • spect (in´trō spekt´) *vt.*, look into one's own feelings or mind
in • veigh (in vā´) *vi.*, make a violent attack
in • vig • or • at • ing (in vig´ər āt iŋ) *adj.*, lively; energetic
in • vin • ci • ble (in vin´ sə bəl) *adj.*, unbeatable
i • ras • ci • bil • i • ty (i ras´ə bil´ə tē) *n.*, irritability
ire (īr) *n.*, anger; wrath
irk • some (ʉrk´səm) *adj.*, tiresome or annoying
ir • rep • ar • a • bly (ər rəp´ə rə blē) *adv.*, beyond repair
ir • re • press • i • ble (ir´ri pres´ə bəl) *adj.*, that cannot be repressed or restrained
jan • gle (jaŋ´gəl) *n.*, harsh sound; discordant
jaunt • i • ly (jaunt´ə lē) *adv.*, in a carefree, stylish manner
jest (jest) *vt.*, joke
jo • cose • ly (jō cōs´lē) *adv.*, playfully; jokingly
jos • tle (jäs´əl) *vt.*, bump against
jot (jät) *n.*, smallest bit
jo • vi • al • ly (jō´vē ə lē) *adv.*, with good humor
ju • di • cious (jo͞o dish´əs) *adj.*, wise and careful
knav • ish (nāv´ ish) *adj.*, mischievous
lab • y • rinth (lab´ə rinth) *adj.*, maze
lad • en (lād´'n) *adj.*, burdened
lan • guor (laŋ´gər) *n.*, pleasant stillness
las • si • tude (las´i to͞od) *n.*, lack of energy
la • tent (lāt´ 'nt) *adj.*, present but inactive
laud • a • to • ry (lôd´ə tôr´ē) *adj.*, expressing praise
leer (lir´) *vi.*, look at with evil appetite or malicious triumph
le • ni • en • cy (lēn´ yən sē) *n.*, easiness
li • ber • al (li´bə rəl) *adj.*, generous
li • on • ize (lī´ən īz´) *vt.*, treat as a celebrity
lis • some (liś əm) *adj.*, graceful, easy, and light
list • less • ly (list´ lis lē) *adv.*, without spirit or vitality
loaf • ing (lōf´iŋ) *adj.*, idling, dawdling
loft • y (lôf´tē) *adj.*, high in status
lore (lôr) *n.*, specialized knowledge
lorn (lôrn) *adj.*, empty, abandoned
lu • mi • nar • y (lo͞o´mə ner´ē) *n.*, body which gives off light, such as the sun or moon
lur • ing (lo͞or´iŋ) *n.*, attempt to attract
lust • y (lus´tē) *adj.*, full of vigor
lux • u • ri •ant •ly (lug zhoor´ ē ənt lē) *adv.*, characterized by richness and extravagance
mag • nate (mag´nāt) *n.*, important, influential person
ma • jes • ty (maj´ is tē) *n.*, grandeur or statliness

man • i • fest (man´ ə fest´) *v.i.*, reveal; show plainly
maun • der • ing (môń dər iŋ) *n.*, rambling
mea • ger (mē´gər) *adj.*, of poor quality or small amount
me • chan • i • cal • ly (mə kan´ə klē) *adv.*, without thought; in a machinelike way
mel • an • cho • li • a (mel´ən kō´ lē ə) *n.*, extreme depression of spirits
mel • an • chol • y (mel´ən käl´ē) *n.*, sadness and depression of spirits
mel • o • dra • mat • ic (mel´ ō drə mat´ ik) *adj.*, having sensational conflicts and song
mer • can • tile (mʉr´ kən tīl) *adj.*, commercial; characteristic of a trader
me • trop • o • lis (mə träp´əl is) *n.*, large city or center of population
mis • con • strued (mis ´kən strōōd´) *adj.*, misinterpreted
mis • giv • ing (mis´giv´iŋ) *n.*, disturbed feeling of fear, doubt, apprehension
mock • er • y (mäk´ ər ē) *n.*, ridicule
mod • i • fy (mäd´ə fī´) *vt.*, alter
mod • i • fy • ing (mäd´ə fī´iŋ) *adj.*, changing
mod • ish (mōd´ish) *adj.*, fashionable
mod • u • late (mäj´ə lāt´) *vt.*, regulate; adjust
moil (moil) *n.*, confusion; turmoil
mol • li • fy • ing (mäl´ə fī iŋ) *adj.*, soothing the temper
moor • ing (moor iŋ) *n.*, hold
mor • al • ize (môr´əl īz) *vi.*, state the terms of right
mor • sel (môr´səl) *n.*, dainty tidbit
mot • tled (mät´'l'd) *adj.*, of different colors
muse (myōōz) *vi.*, meditate; think deeply
mus • ing (myōō´ziŋ) *n.*, meditation; reflection
nigh (ni) *adv.*, near
non • plussed (nän plüs'd´) *adj.*, perplexed
nov • el (näv´əl) *adj.*, new and unusual
no • vi • ti • ate (nō vish´ē it) *n.*, one new to something
ob • lit • er • ate (ə blit´ər āt´) *vt.*, do away with
ob • scure (əb skyōōr´) *vt.*, cover with darkness
ob • scur • ing (əb skyōōr´iŋ) *adj.*, making less visible
o • gle (ō´gəl) *vt.*, look over boldly
o • gre (ō´gər) *n.*, hideous tyrant
om • i • nous • ly (äm´ə nəs lē) *adv.*, in a threatening manner
o • pine (ō pīn´) *vt.*, express opinions
op • u • lent (äp´yōō lənt) *adj.*, very wealthy
out • crop • ping (out´kräp iŋ) *n.*, emerged top of mostly underground rock
o • ver • awe (ō´vər ô´) *vt.*, overcome or subdue by inspiring awe
o • vert (ō vʉrt´) *adj.*, open, apparent
o • ver • ture (ō´vər chər) *n.*, opening moves
pal • at • a • ble (pal´ə tə bəl) *adj.*, fit to be eaten
pa • la • tial (pə lā´shəl) *adj.*, large and magnificent like a palace
pa • lav • er (pə lav´ər) *n.*, idle chatter
pal • pa • ble (pal´pə bəl) *adj.*, obvious
pal • pa • bly (pal´ pə blē) *adv.*, evidently
pal • pi • ta • tion (pal´pə tā´shən) *n.*, fluttering or tremble
pal • try (pôl´trē) *adj.*, small; practically worthless
pang (paŋ) *n.*, sudden sharp physical or emotional pain
par • a • pher • na • li • a (par´ə fər nāl´yə) *n.pl.*, collection of articles, belongings, or tools

par • ley (pär´lē) *vi.*, conference or discussion

par • tak • ing (pär tāk´iŋ) *adj.*, sharing

par • ti • tion (pär tish´ən) *n.*, wall

pa • the • tic (pə thet´ik) *adj.*, encouraging feelings of sadness

pa • thos (pā´thôs) *n.*, feelings of sorrow, pity, or compassion; drama intended to excite those feelings

pa • tri • cian (pə trish´ən) *n.*, person of high social rank

pa • tron • age (pā´trən ij) *n.*, behavior that shows awareness of another's lower standing or ability

pa • tron • age (pā´trən ij) *n.*, clientele

pe • cu • li • a • ri • ty (pə kyo͞o´lē ar´ə tē) *n.*, individuality

pend • ing (pen´diŋ) *adj.*, awaiting decision

pen • i • tent (pen´i tənt) *n.*, one who seeks mercy

pen • sive (pen´siv) *adj.*, deep in thought

per • ad • ven • ture (pʉr´əd ven´chər) *n.*, doubt

per • cep • ti • ble (pər sep´tə bəl) *adj.*, easily noticed

per • e • gri • na • tion (per´ə gri nā´shen) *n.*, travel

per • fi • dy (pʉr´fə dē) *n.*, betrayal of faith

per • force (pər fôrs´) *adv.*, by or through necessity

per • func • to • ry (pər fuŋk´tə rē) *adj.*, without care or interest; superficial

per • me • at • ing (pʉr´mē āt´iŋ) *adj.*, able to spread

per • tur • ba • tion (pʉr´tər bā´shən) *n.*, disturbance; agitation

per • ver • si • ty (pər vʉr´sə tē) *n.*, deviation from the norm

pet (pet) *vt.*, pamper

pet • tish • ly (pet´ish lē) *adv.*, in a sulky manner

pil • grim • age (pil´grim ij) *n.*, long journey

pi • quan • cy (pē´kən sē) *n.*, flavor

pla • ca • ted (plā´kā təd) *adj.*, appeased

plac • id (plas´id) *adj.*, calm

plain • tive (plān´tiv) *adj.*, mournful

plau • si • ble (plô´zə bəl) *adj.*, acceptable; believable

plight (plīt) *n.*, unfortunate condition

plod • ding (pläd´iŋ) *adj.*, walking or moving heavily; trudging

pon • der (pän´dər) *vt.*, think deeply about

pon • der • ous (pän´dər əs) *adj.*, heavy

pop • u • lous (päp´yo͞o les) *adj.*, full of people

port • ly (pôrt´lē) *adj.*, fat

po • tent (pō´tənt) *adj.*, powerful

prec • e • dence (pres´ə dəns) *n.*, priority

pre • cip • i • tate (prē sip´ə tāt´) *vt.*, cause to happen before needed or desired

pre • dic • a • ment (pre dic´ə ment) *n.*, difficult situation

preen • ing (prēn´iŋ) *vt.*, showing off; primping

pre • fig • ured (prē fig´yərd) *adj.*, imagined beforehand

pre • mon • i • tor • y (prē män´i tôr´ē) *adj.*, warning

pre • ten • sion (prē ten´shən) *n.*, claim to distinction

pre • var • i • cate (pri var´i kāt´) *vi.*, evade the truth

pris • tine (pris´tēn´) *adj.*, characteristic of an earlier period or condition; unspoiled; clean

pri • va • tion (pri vā´shən) *n.*, quality of lacking the necessities of life

pro • cliv • i • ty (prō kliv´ə tē) *n.*, taste

pro • cure (prō kyo͞or´) *vt.*, obtain

pro • di • gious (prō dij´əs) *adj.*, amazing, great
prof • fered (präf´ərd) *adj.*, offered
pro • fu • sion (prō fyo͞o´zhən) *n.*, rich or lavish supply
pro • pen • si • ty (prə pen´sə tē) *n.*, natural inclination
prop • o • si • tion (präp´ə zish´ən) *n.*, something set forth for consideration
pro • pri • e • tor (prō prī´ə tər) *n.*, owner
pros • e • cute (präs´ i kyo͞ot´) *vt.*, put forward
pros • per • ous (präs´pər əs) *adj.*, well-to-do
pro • tes • ta • tion (prōt´es tā´shən) *n.*, strong declaration
pro • tract • ed (prō trakt´'d) *adj.*, prolonged; drawn out
prov • erb (präv´ʉrb´) *n.*, traditional saying that expresses some obvious truth
prov • ince (präv´ins) *n.*, territory
pro • vi • sion (prō vizh´ ən) *n.*, condition
prov • o • ca • tion (präv´ə kā´shən) *n.*, irritation
prox • i • mi • ty (präks im´ə tē) *n.*, nearness
pug • na • cious (pug nā´shəs) *adj.*, eager and ready to fight
punc • til • i • ous • ly (puŋk til´ē əs lē) *adv.*, very carefully
quaint • ly (kwānt´lē) *adv.*, in an unusual and pleasing manner
quan • da • ry (kwän´də rē) *n.*, state of uncertainty; dilemma
qua • ver (kwā´vər) *n.*, shiver
que • ry (kwir´ē) *vt.*, ask about
quip (kwip) *n.*, joking remark
rab • id (rab´id) *adj.*, violent
ra • di • ance (rā´dē əns) *n.*, shining rays of light; glow
ra • di • ant (rā´dē ənt) *adj.*, shining
ran • cor • ous (raŋ´kər us) *adj.*, characterized by continuous ill will
ran • kle (raŋ´ kəl) *v.t.*, cause lingering irritation
ra • pac • i • ty (rə pas´ ə tē) *n.*, greed; plundering
rasp • ing • ly (rasp´iŋ lē) *adv.*, harshly
realm (relm) *n.*, region; kingdom
re • buff (ri buf´) *n.*, refusal; rejection
re • buke (ri byo͞ok´) *vt.*, scold; blame
reck (rek) *vt.*, have concern for
rec • on • noi • ter (rek´ə noit´ər) *vt.*, explore
re • cede (ri sēd´) *vi.*, slip away
re • coil (ri koil´) *n.*, drawing back
rec • ti • tude (rek´tə to͞od´) *n.*, conduct based on high moral principles
red • o • lent (red´'l ənt) *adj.*, smelling of; fragrant
re • fined (ri fīnd´) *adj.*, elegant; cultivated
re • frac • tor • y (ri frak´tər ē) *adj.*, hard to manage
ref • uge (ref´ yo͞oj) *n.*, shelter
re • it • er • ate (rē it´ə rāt´) *vt.*, repeat
re • kin • dle (rē kin´ del) *vi.*, become lit again, like a candle
rem • nant (rem´ nənt) *n.*, remainder
re • mon • strance (ri män´strəns) *n.*, protest, warning
re • mote • ness (ri mōt´nəs) *n.*, distance from another
ren • di • tion (ren dish´ən) *n.*, performance; version
re • past (ri past´) *n.*, meal
re • pent • ant (ri pen´tənt) *n.*, one who feels sorry for having wronged
re • pine (rē pīn´) *vi.*, express unhappiness

re • plete (rē plēt´) *adj.,* well-supplied; full

re • pose (ri pōz´) *n.,* rest

re • press (ri pres´) *vt.,* restrain; hold back

re • pres • sion (ri presh´ ən) *n.,* state of being subdued or restained

re • proof (ri pro͞of´) *n.,* correction, scolding

re • pu • di • ate (ri pyo͞o´dē āt) *vt.,* disown

re • pulse (rē puls´) *vt.,* push away

re • pute (ri pyo͞ot´) *n.,* reputation

req • ui • site (rek´wə zit) *adj.,* required

re • sound (ri zound´) *vi.,* echo, reverberate

re • tort (ri tôrt´) *n.,* sharp reply

rev • er • ent (rev´ ər ənt) *adj.,* with deeply respectful feeling

rev • er • ie (rev´ər ē) *n.,* daydream

re • ver • sion (ri vʉr´zhən) *n.,* return

re • vert (ri vʉrt´) *vi.,* go back in action, thought, or speech

re • vul • sion (ri vul´shən) *n.,* drawing back in disgust

right • eous • ness (rī´chəs nəs) *n.,* virtue, right action

roil (roil) *vi.,* stir up; agitate

ro • se • ate (rō´zē it) *adj.,* rosy

ro • tund (rō tund´) *adj.,* round and plump

rous • ing (rou´ziŋ) *n.,* violent stir

rous • ing (rou´ ziŋ) *adj.,* provocative

rout (rout) *n.,* disastrous defeat; mob

rove (rōv) *vi.,* wander

rud • dy (rud´ē) *adj.,* healthy; red

ru • di • men • ta • ry (ro͞o´də men´ tər ē) *adj.,* not fully developed

rue • ful (ro͞o´ fəl) *adj.,* moved by regret

rue • ful • ly (ro͞o´ fəl lē) *adv.,* regretfully

ruf • fled (ruf´əld) *adj.,* disturbed

rug • ged (rug´id) *adj.,* harsh

ru • mi • na • tion (ro͞o´mə nā´shen) *n.,* thoughts

ruse (ro͞oz) *n.,* trick; deception

sa • lac • i • ty (sə las´ə tē) *n.,* lecherousness

sal • low (sal´ō) *adj.,* sickly in complexion

sal • ly forth (sal´ē fôrth) *vi.,* go out, as to battle

salve (sav) *n.,* anything that soothes or heals

sa • pi • ent (sā´pē ənt) *adj.,* wise

sar • don • i • cal • ly (sär dän´ ik lē) *adv.,* bitterly; sarcastically

sav • age • ly (sav´ij lē) *adv.,* fiercely

scorn • ful • ly (skôrn´fəl lē) *adv.,* in a manner that is filled with or shows contempt

scout (skout) *vt.,* reject as absurd

scru • ple (skro͞o´ pəl) *n.,* consideration based on ethical or moral principles

scru • pu • lous (skro͞o´pyə ləs) *adj.,* extremely careful

scud (skud) *vt.,* blow swiftly before the wind

sear (sēr) *adj.,* withered

se • date (si dāt´) *adj.,* calm, composed, serious

self- • ab • sorp • tion (self´-ab sôrp´shən) *n.,* preoccupation with one's own affairs or interests

self- • com • mis • er • a • tion (self´-kə miz´ ər ā´shən) *adj.,* self-pity

sem • blance (sem´ bləns) *n.,* outward form or appearance

sen • ti • nel (sen´ti nəl) *vt.,* guard

se • ques • tered (si kwes´tərd) *adj.,* secluded
ser • pen • tine (sʉr´pən tēn´) *adj.,* winding like a snake
ser • vile (sʉr´vəl) *adj.,* humble; servantlike
sev • er (sev´ər) *vt.,* separate
sham (sham) *vt.,* pretend
sham • ble (sham´bəl) *vi.,* walk in a lazy or clumsy manner
shan • ty (shan´tē) *n.,* small, shabby dwelling
sheaf (shēf) *n.,* harvested bundle, like a bundle of hay
shift • less (shift´lis) *adj.,* lazy
shirk (shʉrk) *vt.,* neglect
shoul • der • ing (shōl´dər iŋ) *n.,* nudging
shrewd (shro͞od) *adj.,* having keen intelligence; cunning
si • dle (sīd´'l) *vi.,* more sideways in a shy or stealthy manner
sift (sift) *vt.,* pass through, as if through a sieve
sim • u • late (sim´yo͞o lāt´) *vt.,* pretend
sin • u • os • i • ty (sin´o͞o äs´ə tē) *n.,* quality of having supple movements
slay (slā) *vt.,* kill
slov • en (sluv´ən) *adj.,* sloppy
so • lic • i • ta • tion (sə lis´i tā´shən) *n.,* care
so • lic • i • tous (sə lis´ə təs) *adj.,* attentive; affectionate
sor • did (sôr´did) *adj.,* dirty; filthy
spec • u • la • tion (spek´yo͞o lā´shən) *n.,* process of thinking over the various aspects of a subject
spright • ly (sprīt´lē) *adj.,* full of energy and spirit; lively
staid (stād) *vi.,* resisting change; fixed
stal • wart (stôl´wərt) *adj.,* strong and well-built
stat • ure (stach´ər) *n.,* height of a person
stig • ma (stig´mə) *n.,* something that detracts from the character or reputation of a person
stilt • ed (stil´tid) *adj.,* stiff, not natural
stol • id (stäl´id) *adj.,* having or showing little or no emotion
stout (stout) *adj.,* strong, sturdy; fat
stout • ness (stout´nes) *adj.,* fleshiness and sturdiness of body
stra • tum (strāt´əm) *n.,* level
striv • ing (strīv´iŋ) *n.,* struggle
stul • ti • fied (stul´tə fīd) *adj.,* worthless
suave (swäv) *adj.,* smooth
sub • dued (sub do͞od´) *adj.,* low, diminished
sub • se • quent (sub´si kwənt) *adj.,* following
sub • sid • ence (sub sī´dəns) *n.,* lessening
suc • cumb (sə kum´) *vi.,* yield; submit
suf • fi • cient (sə fish´ənt) *adj.,* enough
suf • fuse (sə fyo͞oz´) *vt.,* overspread and fill
sul • len (sul´ ən) *adj.,* resentful; sulky
sump • tu • ous (sump´cho͞o əs) *adj.,* richly splendid
su • per • cil • i • ous (so͞o´pər sil´ē əs) *adj.,* proud, scornful
su • per • cil • i • ous • ness (so͞o´pər sil´ ē əs nəs) *n.,* prideful manner
su • per • fi • ci • al • i • ty (so͞o´pər fish´ē al´ ə tē) *adj.,* proud, scornful
su • per • flu • ous (sə pʉr´flo͞o əs) *adj.,* unnecessary
su • per • in • duced (so͞o´pər in do͞osd´) *adj.,* added as a complicating condition
su • per • scrip • tion (so͞o´pər skrip´shən) *n.,* written heading

su • pine • ly (so͞o´pīn´ lē) *adv.,* inactively, passively, listlessly; lying down

sup • pli • ant (sup´lē ənt) *n.,* one who asks humbly or petitions earnestly

sur • feit (sʉr´fit) *n.,* satisfaction; enough

sur • feit • ed (sʉr´fit əd) *adj.,* more than satisfied

surg • ing (sʉrj iŋ) *adj.,* heaving

sur • ly (sʉr´lē) *adj.,* bad-tempered

sur • mise (sər miz´) *vt.,* guess or figure

sus • te • nance (sus´tə nəns) *n.,* means of support

sus • te • nance (sus´tə nəns) *n.,* support

swag • ger (swa´gər) *vi.,* move with exaggerated arrogance

swash (swä´sh) *vi.,* swagger

syl • van (sil´vən) *adj.,* forested

sym • pa • the • tic (sim pä thə´tək) *adj.,* sensitive to emotion

tac • it • ly (tas´it lē) *adv.,* not openly, but by implication

tac • i • turn (tas´ə tʉrn) *adj.,* uncommunicative

tack (tak) *n.,* course of action

tap • es • try (tap´əs trē) *n.,* heavy woven cloth, decorated with pictures, used as a wall hanging

ten • or (ten´ər) *n.,* tone

ter • mi • nate (tʉr´mə nāte) *vt.,* end

thor • ough • fare (thʉr´ ō fer´) *n.,* public street

throng (thrôŋ) *n.,* great crowd

toil • er (toil´ər) *n.,* one who works hard with tiring effort

tract (trakt) *n.,* large area

trac • ta • ble (trak´ tə b'l) *adj.,* easily managed

trans • pierced (trans pirsd´) *adj.,* pierced through

trans • plan • ta • tion (trans´plan tā´shen) *n.,* resettlement from one place to another

trem • u • lous (trem´yo͞o ləs) *adj.,* trembling

trep • i • da • tion (trep´ə dā´shən) *n.,* fear

tri • fle (tri´ fəl) *vt.,* dally; *vi.,* fuss

trite (trīt) *adj.,* stale through overuse

trounce (trouns) *vt.,* defeat thoroughly

trudge (truj) *vi.,* walk wearily or laboriously

trun • dling (trun´dliŋ) *adj.,* moving on wheels

un • a • vail • ing (un´ə vāl´iŋ) *adj.,* producing nothing

un • bound • ed (un bound´əd) *adj.,* unconfined

un • couth (un ko͞oth´) *adj.,* awkward; clumsy; crude

un • du • lat • ing (un´dyo͞o lāt iŋ) *adj.,* wavy

un • du • ly (un do͞o´ lē) *adv.,* unjustly

un • her • ald • ed (un her´əld əd) *adj.,* unannounced

un • re • mu • ner • a • tive (un rē myo͞o´nər ə tiv) *adj.,* giving no payment or reward

un • toward (un tō´ərd) *adj.,* inappropriate

un • tram • meled (un tram´əld) *adj.,* unconfined

un • war • rant • a • ble (un wôr´ənt ə bəl) *adj.,* unreasonable

un • war • rant • ed (un wôr´ənt əd) *adj.,* unjustified

un • wa • ver • ing (un wā´vər iŋ) *adj.,* not changing in intent

up • hol • stered (up hōl´stərd) *adj.,* fitted and covered with material

up • well • ing (up´wel´iŋ) *n.,* rising flow

u • surped (yo͞o zʉrp´d) *adj.,* taken by force or without right

va • cant • ly (vā kənt lē) *adv.*, in an absent, empty way
va • ga • ry (vā gər´ē) *n.*, odd turn of fortune
vain (vān) *adj.*, proud; conceited
ve • he • ment (vē´ə mənt) *adj.*, forceful
vent (vent) *n.*, outlet
ven • ture (ven´chər) *vi.*, go at some risk
ver • i • ta • ble (ver´i tə bəl) *adj.*, real; true
ves • sel (ves´əl) *n.*, ship
ves • tige (ves´tij) *n.*, trace of something that once existed
vice (vīs) *n.*, evil or wicked conduct or behavior
vig • or • ous (vig´ ə rəs) *adj.*, strong and active
vir • tu • ous (vʉr´cho͞o əs) *adj.*, moral; chaste
viv • i • fy (viv´ə fī´) *vt.*, give life to
vol • u • ble (väl´yo͞o bəl) *adj.*, characterized by much talk
vol • u • bly (väl´yo͞o blē) *adv.*, by means of words; fluently
vul • ner • a • ble (vul´nər ə bəl) *adj.*, open to attack
wade (wād) *vi.*, go forward with effort or difficulty
wane (wān) *n.*, gradual end
wane (wān) *vi.*, lessen
wa • ver (wā´vər) *vi.*, teeter between choices
wax (waks) *vi.*, grow
wax • en (wak´ sən) *adj.*, waxlike
wend (wend) *vt.*, proceed
wile (wīl) *n.*, sly trick; deceitful artifice
winc • ing (wins´iŋ) *adj.*, grimacing
win • some (win´ səm) *adj.*, delightful
wisp (wisp) *n.*, something delicate or frail
wist • ful (wist´fəl) *adj.*, showing or expressing vague yearnings
wrath (rath) *n.*, intense anger, fury
wreak (rēk) *vt.*, give free play to
wrest (rest) *vt.*, take by force
wretch • ed (rech´id) *adj.*, miserable; despicable
yield (yēld) *vt.*, surrender

Handbook of Literary Terms

Allusion. An **allusion** is a rhetorical technique in which reference is made to a person, event, object, or work from history or literature.

Archetype. An **archetype** is an inherited, often unconscious, ancestral memory or motif that recurs throughout history and literature. The notion of the archetype derives from the psychology of Carl Jung, who described archetypes as symbols from humanity's "collective unconscious." The term is often used, more generally, to refer to any element that recurs throughout the literature of the world.

Character. A **character** is a person (or sometimes an animal) who figures in the action of a literary work. A *protagonist,* or *main character,* is the central figure in a literary work. An *antagonist* is a character who is pitted against a protagonist. *Major characters* are those who play significant roles in a work. *Minor characters* are those who play lesser roles. A *one-dimensional character, flat character,* or *caricature* is one who exhibits a single dominant quality, or *character trait.* A *three-dimensional, full,* or *rounded character* is one who exhibits the complexity of traits associated with actual human beings. A *static character* is one who does not change during the course of the action. A *dynamic character* is one who does change. A *stock character* is one found again and again in different literary works. An example of a stock character is the mad scientist of nineteenth- and twentieth-century science fiction.

Characterization. Characterization is the use of literary techniques to create a character. Writers use three major techniques to create characters: direct description, portrayal of characters' behavior, and representations of characters' internal states. When using direct description, the writer, through a speaker, a narrator, or another character, simply comments on the character, telling the reader about such matters as the character's appearance, habits, dress, background, personality, motivations, and so on. In portrayal of a character's behavior, the writer presents the actions and speech of the character, allowing the reader to draw his or her own conclusions from what the character says or does. When using representations of internal states, the writer reveals directly the character's private thoughts and emotions, often by means of what is known as the *internal monologue.* See *character.*

Conflict. A **conflict** is a struggle between two forces in a literary work. A *plot* involves the introduction, development, and eventual resolution of a conflict. One side of the *central conflict* in a story or drama is usually taken by the *main character.* That character may struggle against another character, against the forces of nature, against society or social norms, against fate, or against some element within himself or herself. A struggle that takes place between a character and some outside force is called an *external conflict.* A struggle that takes place within a character is called an *internal conflict.*

Crisis. In the plot of a story or a drama, the **crisis** is that point in the development of the conflict at which a decisive event occurs that causes the main character's situation to become better or worse.

Didacticism. Didacticism is the use of works of art to convey moral, social, educational, or political messages. A didactic work is one in which the artistic values of the work are subordinated to the message or meaning. Didacticism was a common element of literature in the Middle Ages and of the proletarian art and literature produced in Communist countries in the twentieth century.

Dynamic Character. See *character.*

Feminist Criticism. Feminist criticism evaluates and interprets works of art with regard to their portrayal of or influence upon gender roles. Many feminist critics and scholars have been particularly concerned to rescue women writers from the obscurity that male critics, editors, scholars, and teachers may have forced upon them. Other feminist critics point out gender bias in literary works by analyzing variations in literary depictions of males and females, and by analyzing the effects of literary works, activities, and movements on cultural norms related to gender.

Foil. A **foil** is a character whose attributes, or characteristics, contrast with, and therefore throw into relief, the attributes of another character.

Foreshadowing. Foreshadowing is the act of presenting materials that hint at events to occur later in a story.

Image. An **image** is a word or phrase that names something that can be seen, heard, touched, tasted, or smelled. The images in a literary work are referred to, collectively, as the work's imagery.

Irony. **Irony** is a difference between appearance and reality. Types of irony include the following: *dramatic irony,* in which something is known by the reader or audience but unknown to the characters; *verbal irony,* in which a statement is made that implies its opposite; and *irony of situation,* in which an event occurs that violates the expectations of the characters, the reader, or the audience.

Marxist Criticism. **Marxist criticism,** based upon the work of the German-born political philosopher Karl Marx, evaluates and interprets works of art with regard to the material, economic forces that shape them or with regard to their origins in or depictions of struggle between the social classes.

Melodrama. A **melodrama** is a play with unrealistic, or exaggerated, characters and plots. The characters are mostly one-dimensional stock characters—completely good heroes and heroines and entirely wicked villains. Melodramas were extremely popular, dominating the stage in the late nineteenth and early twentieth centuries.

Metaphor. A **metaphor** is a figure of speech in which one thing is spoken or written about as if it were another. This figure of speech invites the reader to make a comparison between the two things. The two "things" involved are the writer's actual subject, the tenor of the metaphor, and another thing to which the subject is likened, the vehicle of the metaphor. When the narrator says, "words are the vague shadows of the volumes we mean," he is using a metaphor:

TENOR	VEHICLE
words	vague shadows

Personification and similes are types of metaphor. See *personification.*

Narrator. A **narrator** is one who tells a story. In a drama, the narrator may be a character who introduces, concludes, or comments upon the action of the play. However, dramas typically do not have narrators. Works of fiction, on the other hand, always do, unless they consist entirely of dialogue without tag lines, in which case they cease to be fictions and become closet dramas, drama meant to be read but not performed. The narrator in a work of fiction may be a central or minor character or simply someone who witnessed or heard about the events being related. Writers achieve a wide variety of ends by varying the characteristics of the narrator chosen for a particular work. Of primary importance is the choice of the narrator's point of view. Will the narrator be omniscient, knowing all things, including the internal workings of the minds of the characters in the story, or will the narrator be limited in his or her knowledge? Will the narrator participate in the action of the story or stand outside that action and comment on it? Will the narrator be reliable or unreliable? That is, will the reader be able to trust the narrator's statements? These are all questions that a writer must answer when developing a narrator.

Naturalism. Naturalism was a literary movement of the late nineteenth and early twentieth centuries that saw actions and events as resulting inevitably from biological or natural forces or from forces in the environment. Often these forces were beyond the comprehension or control of the characters subjected to them. Taken to its extreme, Naturalism views all events as mechanically determined by external forces, including the decisions made by people. Much of modern fiction, with its emphasis on social conditions leading to particular consequences for characters, is naturalistic in this sense. Great writers of fiction informed by the philosophy of Naturalism include Émile Zola, Stephen Crane, Jack London, and Theodore Dreiser.

Parallelism. Parallelism is a rhetorical technique in which a writer emphasizes the equal value or weight of two or more ideas by expressing them in the same grammatical form.

Personification. Personification is a figure of speech in which an idea, animal, or thing is described as if it were a person.

Plot. A **plot** is a series of events related to a central *conflict*, or struggle. A typical plot involves the introduction of a conflict, its development, and its eventual resolution. Terms used to describe elements of plot include the following:

- The **exposition**, or **introduction**, sets the tone or mood, introduces the characters and the setting, and provides necessary background information.
- The **inciting incident** is the event that introduces the central conflict.
- The **rising action**, or **complication**, develops the conflict to a high point of intensity.
- The **climax** is the high point of interest or suspense in the plot.

- The **crisis**, or **turning point**, often the same event as the climax, is the point in the plot where something decisive happens to determine the future course of events and the eventual working out of the conflict.
- The **falling action** is all of the events that follow the climax.
- The **resolution** is the point at which the central conflict is ended, or resolved.
- The **dénouement** is any material that follows the resolution and that ties up loose ends.
- The **catastrophe**, in tragedy, is the event that marks the ultimate tragic fall of the central character. Often this event is the character's death.

Plots rarely contain all these elements in precisely this order. Elements of exposition may be introduced at any time in the course of a work. A work may begin with a catastrophe and then use flashback to explain it. The exposition or dénouement or even the resolution may be missing. The inciting incident may occur before the beginning of the action actually described in the work. These are but a few of the many possible variations that plots can exhibit. See *conflict*.

Realism. **Realism** is the attempt to render in art an accurate portrayal of reality. The theory that the purpose of art is to imitate life is at least as old as Aristotle. The eighteenth-century development of the novel, with its attention to details of character, setting, and social life, can be thought of as a step toward increased Realism in writing. However, the term *Realism* is generally applied to literature of the late nineteenth century, written in reaction to Romanticism and emphasizing details of ordinary life.

Rising Action. See *plot*. (The **rising action**, or **complication**, develops the conflict to a high point of intensity.)

Scene. A **scene** is a short section of a literary work that presents action that occurs in a single place or at a single time.

Sentimentality. **Sentimentality** is an excessive expression of emotion. Much popular literature of the nineteenth and twentieth centuries is characterized by sentimentality.

Static Character. See *character*.

Symbol. A **symbol** is a thing that stands for or represents both itself and something else. Writers use two types of symbols—conventional, and personal or idiosyncratic. A *conventional symbol* is one with traditional, widely recognized associations. Such symbols include doves for peace; laurel wreaths for heroism or poetic excellence; the color green for jealousy; the color purple for royalty; the color red for anger; morning or spring for youth; winter, evening, or night for old age; wind for change or inspiration; rainbows for hope; roses for beauty; the moon for fickleness or inconstancy; roads or paths for the journey through life; woods or darkness for moral or spiritual confusion; thorns for troubles or pain; stars for unchangeableness or constancy; mirrors for vanity or introspection; snakes for evil or duplicity; and owls for wisdom. A *personal* or *idiosyncratic symbol* is one that assumes its secondary meaning because of the special use to which it is put by a writer.

Theme. A **theme** is a central idea in a literary work.